# NOVEL
# EXPLOSIVES

# NOVEL EXPLOSIVES

*A NOVEL IN 3 PARTS*

# JIM GAUER

ZEROGRAM
PRESS

ZEROGRAM PRESS
An imprint of GREEN INTEGER
København / Los Angeles
6022 Wilshire Boulevard, Suite 202C
Los Angeles, California 90036, USA
www.zerogrampress.com
www.greeninteger.com

Distributed in the United States by
Consortium Book Sales and Distribution/Perseus
www.cbsd.com
Distributed in England and throughout Europe by
Turnaround Publisher Services
www.turnaround-uk.com

First Edition 2016

Cover design: Miladinka Milic
Book design: Pablo Capra

LIBRARY OF CONGRESS CATALOGING-IN-PUBLICATION DATA

Names: Gauer, Jim, 1960- author.
Title: Novel explosives : a novel in 3 parts / by Jim Gauer.
Description: First edition. | Los Angeles : Zerogram Press, 2016. | "The
    events in the novel take place over the course of a single week,
    April 13 through April 20, 2009."
Identifiers: LCCN 2016011346
Subjects: LCSH: Identity (Psychology)–Fiction. | Experimental fiction.
Classification: LCC PS3607.A9645 N68 2016 | DDC 813/.6–dc23
LC record available at https://lccn.loc.gov/2016011346

ISBN: 978-1-55713-436-3 (hardcover)
ISBN: 978-1-55713-433-2 (paperback)

Printed in the United States of America on acid-free paper.

The events in the novel take place over the course of
a single week, April 13 through April 20, 2009.

The characters in the novel are fictitious, and any
resemblance to individuals, real or fictitious, is deliberate.

*To Meredith*

"To imagine a language means to imagine a form of life."

LUDWIG WITTGENSTEIN
*Philosophical Investigations*

# PART I

# 1

The story of how I came to live in Guanajuato, Guanajuato, is a fascinating one, fascinating. It is not, however, it should be noted, right up front, a story that I am in any way well-equipped to tell, in the sense, in the very real sense, in the *I'm sorry to be the one to break this to you* sense, that I myself have no idea how I came to live in Guanajuato. In some such sense of the word, I found myself one day, living in Guanajuato, as though I'd picked up a curious object while walking a mountain trail, with no conception whatsoever of how I'd come to be living here, apparently some time ago, no recollection of whatever chain of events I was myself at the end of, and no sense at all of having led a prior life. I certainly had a prior life; I am, after all, in all probability, somewhere in my mid-fifties, and no one comes to be living somewhere in his mid-fifties without having had a prior life; it takes time in any case to become of a certain age, time in which events would no doubt have taken place, even if one can't recall them, and these events would have made up what amounts to my prior life, so I had no doubt that I had one, whatever it had amounted to. The fine lines and wrinkles that appear on one's face, with the passage of time and exposure to sunlight and the gradual accumulation of certain habitual facial expressions, don't just appear out of nowhere one day, and assume their positions around the downturned mouth, or the worry-furrowed eyebrow, or the scrutinizing eyes; I had no doubt that time, and the pressure of events, and the long narrative chain of time-sensitive circumstance, had produced these lines and wrinkles I could read on my own face, even if I myself was unable to recreate them. Somewhere along the way, however, the narrative chain had come unlinked, the chain of cause and effect by which one set of circumstances gives rise to the next set of circumstances. I myself was a link that was both the end of one chain, one I had no recollection of, and the beginning of another chain, of whatever would happen next. While I don't doubt for a moment that my story must be a fascinating one, I, to put it bluntly, do not know a word of it; I *found* myself one day, like finding a link of anchor chain in the mountains of central Mexico, and not only was this chain link *me*, but I had no way on earth of explaining how I'd come to be here; as far as I could tell, as I stood there trailside, I might as well have appeared out of thin mountain air.

I woke up one morning in a room, as it would soon turn out, in a small hotel, with no clue at all as to my identity or whereabouts. I showered, shaved, dressed, using clothing I found lying in a comfortable-looking chair, went down to what was recognizably a hotel lobby, and was told by the desk clerk, a man almost certainly of Indian and perhaps Spanish descent, that the town I was in was called Guanajuato. I looked around the room, at its warm terracotta flooring tiles, covered with blue, yellow, magenta, purple, and white woven rugs, at its rough-hewn wooden seating, its paintings, of wildly colored mythic birds, hung somewhat erratically on whitewashed plaster walls, its glassed-in display cases of hand-painted ceramic plates, its front door facing a narrow cobblestone street, a street I almost certainly must have walked upon previously, and found nothing at all that I recognized, nothing that served to trigger even the faintest of memories, of drinking too late, say, at a local bar, of a wild night of revelry, of buying one too many rounds for newfound companions who were enjoying my company, of discovering to my amazement the lateness of the hour, my state of inebriation, my need for a good night's sleep, and having to seek therefore shelter from the cool air of the night. Nothing, as they say, came back to me. There was nothing whatsoever here in this room, however warm and authentic it appeared to be when I looked around at the room's belongings, which reminded me of anything of a personal nature; as far as personal reminders go, the room might as well have been empty. The room itself, however, far from being empty, held beautiful weavings and hand-painted ceramics and rough-hewn wooden furniture and wild mythic birds, things that I could see with my own two eyes, or perhaps I should say the eyes that, for the sake of simplicity, would need be thought of as my very own two eyes.

To be clear, it's not that these objects lacked associations; they were not in any way cut off from the rest of history and somehow stranded here. I knew, for example, that one of the painted mythic birds was Quetzalcoatl, sacred god of the Aztecs, god of sky and creation, patron of the priesthood, of learning and knowledge, this bird had lost nothing of its history and associations, but this had nothing to do with me, there was nothing about the bird that I could associate with personally, it was the same bird to me that it would have been to any other man, any man with a knowledge of Quetzalcoatl, except that any other man would find, in addition to his knowledge, a connection to himself, a set of associations he took personally and therefore regarded as properly his. These associations did not, in any sense, belong to me; they belonged, properly, to the bird. I don't want to convey the impression that I was uninformed or ignorant. To the contrary, I seemed to know quite a lot of things, it's just that none of the things I knew belonged to me; my own knowledge was not in any way a personal possession, it could just as well have belonged to anyone. I knew, to give another example, simply by looking at them, that the colorful rugs on the square-tiled floor were hand-woven on a loom, as was indicated by the manner in which they lay on the floor, not quite flat, with small bubbles and waves caused by the uneven weaving, an effect that is not normally produced by a machine. I also knew that they were, in all likelihood, colored with natural dyes, indigo from the Anil plant, deep magenta from the cochineal insect, the yellow of rock moss, the sea snail purple, the very sea snail, *purpura pansa*, from the Pacific Coast of Oaxaca that was so prized by the Europeans after their invasion of the New World, these were all things I knew, I just didn't know them personally, they could just as well have been known by someone else. I had knowledge, in other words, I was clearly the sort of man in possession of a set of facts, but there are, after all, all sorts of men in possession of facts, so what sort of man was I? I had no idea.

I left the front desk, climbed the stairs back up to my room on the third floor, used the key that I had somehow acquired to enter the room, and made a conscious decision to take a good look around. The room itself was spacious and light-filled, once I'd opened the shutters, situated as it was at the front of the building, with two tall windows sunk deep into thick whitewashed walls, over-looking what appeared to be a large town or small city, set between steep hillsides in an undulating ravine, filled with church spires topped with crosses and weathervanes, and the basilica domes of nearby cathedrals, and closer to the earth, a winding maze of nar-row streets. From my perspective, on first sight, I mean really and truly on first sight, since I had no impressions at all that would have preceded these first impressions, I appeared to be situated on a hill-side just above the center of the city, a conclusion I drew no doubt tentatively from the evidence gathered by my eyes, evidence that the buildings grew more dense and somewhat taller around a plaza just below me and perhaps twenty degrees to my left. The hillside opposite was jammed with box-shaped houses in every imaginable hue, forest green and royal purple and orange and pink flamingo, stacked up the slope above the city center, with a large stone statue at the hill's highest point. The heart of the city, I concluded, lay at the bottom of a valley between these two hillsides, the one I re-sided on, and the one rising opposite me, with a statue at its peak. The city center itself struck me as genuinely beautiful, though in fact I had nothing other than impersonal images, like pictures in books, to compare it to, deep yellow and pale green and dusty-rose-colored buildings, interspersed with townhouses with wrought-iron balconies and window boxes filled with red and yellow flowers, and here and there, laundry hung out on a balcony railing to dry; the sun was out, as might be expected, on the sort of day when people put out laundry on a railing, at least assuming they were expecting their laundry to dry. The narrow streets were filled with scores of people, walking from one place to another, on their own two feet, the way people could be expected to walk, on a day when the sun is out, in order to get from here to there, from one point to another point, from where, in some sense, they *are* already, to somewhere, altogether, *elsewhere* instead.

The first order of business, now that I had my physical bearings, though to tell the truth, I had been uncomfortable with the idea, when speaking with the desk clerk, of asking him directly "What is Guanajuato?" as it seemed to me that such a question might have struck him as somewhat odd, as odd perhaps as asking him a question like "Who am I?" and I was not as yet convinced that it was a good idea to begin striking people as odd; I mean, let's face it, at this point, while I had my physical bearings, I had no idea where I was, since it was apparent, if the clerk could be believed, that I was in Guanajuato, but the truth is I had no idea where or what Guanajuato was, it was almost certainly in Mexico, if Quetzalcoatl could be relied upon, but otherwise, what and where was it?...in any case, to get to the point, the first order of business was to examine my belongings, or at least to look at the things in my room, assuming that they belonged to me, assuming that I was the one to whom they could best be said to belong. In the closet of the room, I found several linen shirts hung neatly on hangers, two pairs of well-pressed slacks, a pair of dark loafers, and a large green duffel bag that I could only assume was mine. In a chest of drawers along one wall, I found boxer shorts, pairs of black dress socks and clean white athletic socks, two pairs of folded jeans, and a stack of short-sleeved knit shirts, clothing that I would, from this point forward, unless and until someone else came forward to claim them, regard as belonging to me, and therefore among my belongings. The bathroom proved to be a far easier undertaking: it contained a hairbrush, toothbrush, razor, and toothpaste, things that could have belonged to anyone; frankly, if someone had come forward to claim them, I would have simply handed them over, I really didn't care to whom they in fact belonged; if someone had identified them as theirs, I was prepared to identify them as theirs. With the possible exception, then, of the items in the bathroom, I now had a set of personal belongings, whether borrowed or owned, I had certain things to begin with, it was a good place to start, and I clearly needed to start somewhere, so I began right here, by assuming that I was the sort of man who would be in possession of just these items. At least for now, these things were mine, they were already taking on this association, and if turned out later I had borrowed them, I would have to deal with that when the time came.

I sat down on the edge of the bed, taking stock of my situation. I had, on the one hand, a roof over my head, clothing to wear, toiletry

items, at least for the time being, and the name of a location. I had a
native tongue, American-accented English; when speaking with the
desk clerk, it had quickly become apparent that I possessed only the
most rudimentary knowledge of Spanish, the sort of Spanish one
might acquire from a few carelessly attended courses in secondary
school, words of basic courtesy to be used in initiating and concluding a brief conversation conducted primarily in English, words for
where and why, words for how much, the ability to conjugate the
verb "to be" in the present tense, and a miscellaneous collection
of curse words like "puta" and "swate" and "ojete" and "pendejo,"
words that would indicate some previous association with native
language speakers under circumstances outside the boundaries of
basic human courtesy. A brief review of my facial features while
shaving had revealed that I was deeply tanned and therefore dark-
skinned from sun exposure, my face was in fact as dark as the desk
clerk's, and judged by color alone, I could have passed for a Native
American, I was in fact so deeply tanned that it was something to be
accounted for, I looked like a man who might have washed ashore
on a beach and found no place to take shelter from the sun for
quite some time, perhaps the victim of a shipwreck, or some foul
play at sea, it was apparent that left unchecked my mind was prone
to wandering off into romantic and adventuresome fantasies, I took
note of this propensity, and brought these speculations to a halt. I
was an American with little Spanish and a deep, inexplicable, tan. I
was slightly taller than medium height for an American. I was lean,
whether from some hardship or natural body-type. I wore wire-
rimmed eyeglasses. My hair, bleached from the sun, had not been
recently cut. And I had a large painful knot, the size of a baseball
cut in half, on the back right center of the top of my head.

   And on the other hand, I seemed to be in possession of a large
collection of facts, none of them personal, and I seemed to be capable of producing, as I sat there taking inventory, a great many
thoughts on a variety of subjects, but had no personal context for
any of these thoughts. Other than their variety, there was nothing
to distinguish them from the thoughts of any number of reasonably
well-educated men. I could, for example, explain to myself how
Riemannian geometry laid the foundations for General Relativity, I could briefly describe Green's Theorem, and place it as the

two-dimensional limited case of Stokes' Theorem, but I couldn't tell myself if any of this mattered to me, and it was apparent that beyond a certain point, my knowledge of Riemannian geometry became vague and unstable. I could recite quite a number of poems, the way a man might do when attempting to distract himself from some uncomfortable dental procedure, but I identified more with the man seeking distraction from the drilling of teeth than with anything to do with the poetry itself. If I'd been told that I was the sort of man who had memorized poetry as a means of distracting himself from some sort of unpleasantness, I couldn't have disputed this. I seemed to know the names and models of a great many automobiles. Did this mean I'd been an auto salesman? And so on. Without any organizing principle, my thoughts were just thoughts. When I searched around in my thinking for something I took pride in, for example, as a means of providing context, and organizing my thoughts, I could find nothing at all that gave me a sense of pride. I went category by category among a large number of subjects, looking for something that might signal a growing sense of self-esteem, and nothing I could think of gave rise to a sense of esteem, all of my thoughts seemed more or less equivalent, they didn't seem to be organized around the rising and falling of some sense of myself as someone to be esteemed. Perhaps I'd done nothing in my prior life that I was proud of, perhaps I was the sort of person for whom knowledge itself was a form of distraction from unpleasantness, but one might think, under the circumstances, that I'd at least feel some sense of pride regarding the depth and variety of the knowledge I could make use of in order to distract myself. I was like a man sitting in the attic of another man's home, finding objects that have been stored away, as having value for another day, and feeling only a mild sense of amusement over what the other finds valuable. It was with some difficulty, I must admit, that I came to recognize that I was, evidently, precisely that *other*, and that while I might find him amusing, he was, after all, evidently *me*.

So much, I decided, for taking an inventory of my thoughts. Clearly I'd simply forgotten my organizing principles, and I was not, let's face it, being particularly inventive in my search for principles around which I myself might be organized. Pride, self-esteem, aversion to unpleasantness, certainly there were more possibilities than these. I tried out the idea of functional cunning, my knowledge as a means of gaining some personal advantage, something of utility in possessing an edge in a situation, for monetary gain, or in the exercise of power, or simply as a weapon in the normal human arsenal for asserting oneself and putting the other in his place. There even seemed to be some support for this, as I sat on the edge of a bed in a place I now called Guanajuato, not knowing how I'd come to be here, not even knowing why I didn't know, and yet apparently knowing a great many things that seemed to apply to the accumulation of power and money, concepts like Warrants for Common Stock on short-term bridge loans, broad-based weighted-average anti-dilution formulas, rights of co-sale and first refusal, super-majority voting on Preferred Shareholder protective provisions, S-3 registration demands, piggybacks and lock-ups, clawbacks and ratchets, cramdowns and pay-to-plays and washouts, all apparently concepts for taking advantage of a situation, and putting those around me in their place. And to be honest, as I sat there in the metaphorical attic of the other man's home, pulling large piles of document-stuffed envelopes out of a steamer trunk labeled Power and Money, this was only one among many envelopes, there were a great many others, envelopes stuffed with marketable derivatives, envelopes full of put and call options, envelopes stuffed with envelopes stuffed with currency arbitrage and Conduits and Structured Investment Vehicles and Collateralized Mortgage Obligations. It would have been a great relief to find even one sack filled with potatoes, and what I found instead was another envelope containing corn, wheat, coffee, oil, and pork belly commodity options, not the products of the earth, but the means of applying leverage to the monetization of their concept, their idea not their existence, as things of the earth. No wonder I'd felt the need for memorizing poetry, to drown out the drilling noises of the machinery of the market, and distract myself from unpleasantness, and let my mind drift off to an altogether different place.

And now I was in an altogether different place, on a bedside in Guanajuato, staring out a window at people going from here to there. There didn't seem to be much point, at least for the moment, in looking backward in order to determine who I was. First of all, nothing in either my inventory of knowledge, or my catalog of organizing principles that might lend a context to my knowledge, struck me as in any way personal and self-determining; nothing seemed to resonate. And secondly, it wasn't at all clear, given this lack of real resonance, that I really wanted to know the man that I'd been. If the apparently vast accumulation of methods and means for taking advantage of others were any indication, I might not like the man. Would I be better off knowing, and through this knowledge, enable myself to change the things about myself that I didn't like? This wasn't clear. At the moment, knowing nothing about myself, I seemed perfectly comfortable with myself as I was; why would I want to change this? Something, something perhaps related to the baseball-sized knot on my head, had changed everything, and it wasn't altogether clear that I had any reason to change it back. If I somehow knew what I was, that would clearly have been what I was, which might prove to be unfortunate. I might feel pride or a sense of shame at whatever it was I'd made of myself, but why be burdened with either one of these? The narratives that we tell ourselves are our own, and thus something we are bound to abide by, in order to keep ourselves going, and lend some coherence to our activities, struck me at the moment as unnecessary. Was I improving or growing steadily worse, was the narrative arc of my life headed toward comedy or inevitable tragedy? Since I had no narrative to begin with, it seemed to me that the choice was mine to make, and if I felt like feeling gradually better and expanding and growing, that might as well be my choice. If someone had handed me my biography, I might have tossed it out the window. My biography would no doubt be filled with character flaws and limitations, I'd have to take a long hard look at whatever it was I'd become, and all things considered, I preferred the view out the window, the beauty of the landscape, with its houses traversing the hillsides, the intricacies of the pastel streets, with their cobblestones and cast iron lanterns, the window boxes filled with flowers, the church spires and basilica domes, the immediacy of existence set free from my limitations, more than willing to overlook me, and allow me to simply look. A woman stepped out onto her iron-railed balcony with a small tin watering can, tipped the can dispensing water onto her yellow and red geraniums, looked up at the deep blue sky, down on the rooftops and small back gardens of her neighbors, and then disappeared back inside, going about her life.

Having abandoned my past for the moment, and left my own personal narrative to fend for itself, it was time to go about living my life, a process I began by examining the contents of the nightstand next to the bed. First of all, on the top of the nightstand, I found a copy of a book, José Saramago's *The Year of the Death of Ricardo Reis*, a book that I was apparently rereading, since I had folded the corner of the page where I'd left off, nearly halfway in, while at the same time recalling the book's basic narrative. Fernando Pessoa, the great hero of 20th-century Portuguese poetry, has recently passed away, although he continues to walk among the living, while Ricardo Reis, one of Pessoa's heteronyms, those various characters named as authors of Pessoa's poetry, has returned from exile in Brazil to Lisbon, to go about his life for a number of months, stopping occasionally in the course of the narrative for a conversation with his author, the great dead Portuguese poet, Fernando Pessoa. An interesting book, curiously conceived and masterfully executed by Saramago, who was himself an interesting creation, a dyed-in-the-wool Marxist, even Stalinist, long past the time when Marxism was fashionable, much less Stalinism, who, following a period of over fifty years of self-inflicted tedium, re-created himself as an author, and became world-renowned. Saramago's books all follow the same pattern, beginning from some improbable founding principle, let's say a plague of white blindness gradually infecting an entire city, and letting the principle play itself out, in intricate detail, toward whatever conclusions it permitted itself to draw. Having no founding principles of my own to speak of, other than the single improbable principle of having no founding principles, other than the intent to live my life, from this point forward, as though I'd taken out a fresh sheet of paper and begun to author myself for myself, Saramago's example struck me as useful, its validity underwritten by vitality rather than probability, by its simply being the case, without having to prove that the case was probable. We are all, no matter what our founding principles, improbable, existence itself is improbable, whatever its founding principles, and nevertheless the case, however improbable and utterly unlikely. Next to the book, I found a harbor map of the Port of Los Angeles; a wallet containing a single banknote, an ATM card, and a piece of personal identification; and a small scrap of neon-orange plastic, an unlikely detail, part no doubt of something larger, within which it might be contextualized. I had opened the wallet with a certain amount of trepidation; I had no real desire at the moment to discover my identity, to find that I in fact had a narrative to which I'd be forced to adhere. It was with some relief, then, that in staring at my identity card, I found that it was utterly improbable, and nevertheless, in and of itself, precisely the case.

I looked out the window again, and the woman had returned to her iron-railed balcony, with a small armful of wet laundry, to be hung in the sun to dry. The sun had begun the final hour of its climb toward noon, the clock in the room said an improbable 11:11, and a mild breeze was blowing, up the hillsides of the ravine, as piece by piece she attached the family clothing, colorful yet no doubt functional, to an improvised clothesline strung across her porch. She seemed utterly absorbed in what she was doing, item by item, taking a yellow blouse in her hand, draping it across the clothesline, and attaching it with two clothespins that she removed from a blue plastic bucket, item by item draping and attaching, holding things in place. I looked down again at the identity card, a United Kingdom driver's license, with an address in Scotland, and a photo and a name. The photo and name, which lent the card its air of the unlikely, of having no doubt been produced by someone with a peculiar sense of humor, and a sense of narrative logic within which the unlikely had its place, were the photo, no doubt clipped with scissors from an old book of the author's, of Fernando Pessoa wearing a hat, in particular a fedora, looking like a detective from a 1940s noir film, and the name Alvaro de Campos, another of Pessoa's numerous heteronyms. For those unfamiliar with Pessoa, and thus unlikely to recognize the eccentricities of this identity card, Campos is quite a character, an oversized Whitmanesque version of Pessoa himself, filled on the one hand with Futurist triumphalism regarding the Age of the Machine, and on the other with a deep sense of anguish and existential unreality, due no doubt in large measure to Pessoa's own peculiarities, in particular the lack of any sense of foundation for himself as an actual self. Being everyone and no one, feeling everything in every way, Campos has no idea who he is. I looked out my window again, at this point almost expecting an unlikely detail, and there it was now, a man coming out of a tobacco shop wearing a grey fedora, reminding me of the words of Campos in his poem "The Tobacco Shop": "How should I know what I'll be, I who don't know what I am?" Campos, for all his anguish, lived a practical life, whether in Glasgow, Scotland, or in Barrow-in-Furness, Cumbria, in the United Kingdom, at the extreme southwest corner of the Cumbria region, just on the edge of the Irish Sea, where he studied naval engineering, read widely and felt deeply, and went about his improbable existence as one of the authors of Pessoa's poems. One of the problems of leading such an improbable existence is that Pessoa seemed to believe that Campos lived in Scotland, while Campos is convinced, perhaps as a result of some lie that Pessoa had told him, that he was actually in Cumbria, near the edge of the Irish Sea; my own improbable identity card apparently sided with Fernando Pessoa, the author of Alvaro, rather than take the word of Alvaro himself, who had, after all, likely been lied to, because my driver's license address was somewhere in Glasgow, which is far from the seaside and the edge of the Irish Sea. To complete this brief overview of the peculiar sense of humor of whomever it was that had landed me here, with Alvaro de Campos' driver's license, bearing an old photo of Fernando Pessoa in a detective's grey fedora, it might be worth pointing out that, from the face I'd seen in the mirror, I am myself Pessoa's double, if one took away his pallor and the anguished look of unreality, and substituted my smile, my apparent sense of immediate reality, and added, for good measure, a deep, shipwrecked, tan.

Would this identity do? On the one hand…and here we go again with this "on the one hand" formulation, I seemed to be intent on proving that I had, in fact, two hands…no one could be expected to look at this old photo of Pessoa without doing a double take. There could be no question that this was *me*, the resemblance was uncanny, and at the same time, the photo was maybe eighty years old, from an age when men wore hats, even detective grey fedoras, without anyone giving it a second thought. People are generally willing to concede that photos become outdated, particularly on a driver's license, but eighty years out of date? This might require a rather broad suspension of disbelief and straining of credulity, I might need to come up with some sort of story, perhaps a story about being photographed after a costume party, where I'd dressed up as a noir private eye, maybe Robert Mitchum as Jeff Bailey in *Out of the Past*, from 1947, you wouldn't remember the story, where a small town gas-pumper has his past come roaring back at him, in the form of a big-city gambler, Whit Sterling, and a femme-fatale and stolen money and who knows what else, everything else, the whole thing a suspension of disbelief in a solution of oneiric eroticism and Jane Greer and Acapulcan tax evasion. Let me see if I've got this straight: I'm coming out of a costume party, and it suddenly occurs to me that I need to renew my driver's license at maybe 2 am, and thus and therefore and such as and so on; not only was this improbable, it couldn't possibly be the case. All of that was on the one hand. On the other hand, it was all I had, it would have to do, and there was the added benefit that the wallet contained an ATM card in the same name, Alvaro de Campos, and thus access to cash, which would soon prove to be a necessity, as the only remaining item in the wallet was a pale purple and cyan banknote, in the amount of 1,000 pesos, with a picture of a balding priest on one side, and a fountain and large stone building, maybe a museum or a library, on the back. The banknote wouldn't last long, who knows how big a tab I'd already run up at the hotel, and I didn't have a credit card, in anybody's name.

It was immediately apparent, from this catalog of my resources, that what I needed most was an ATM PIN. At some point, in the hours up ahead, I would begin receiving change from a purple and cyan banknote, and my 1,000-peso status would begin to be reduced, transaction by transaction, toward next to, or even less than, nothing whatsoever; I would need to seek a source of fiscal renewal, since filing for bankruptcy, in another man's name, would almost certainly strain the credulity of the Guanajuato legal system. I returned to the trunk labeled Power and Money, assuming this to be the most likely place that one would file away the numbers that give access to currency, and found, to my amusement and then mounting dismay, a nearly overwhelming array of integer strings, nearly as many short blocks of digits as I'd found when I'd searched for memorized poetry. What was I doing with all these numbers? What mode of life or method of making a living required one to memorize so many sequential integers? A man living under assumed identities might be required to know a variety of Social Security numbers, but what sort of man would assume the identities of what appeared to be, at a minimum, several hundred separate persons? Perhaps, on the other hand, I was selling myself short; a man who specialized in identity theft, and had looted the accounts of hundreds of people, might take some pride in memorizing his victims, including the Social Security numbers that were the keys to their identity. Upon closer examination, however, it was apparent that most of these numbers I'd memorized were organized in blocks of ten or eleven digits, while the Social Security system used blocks of nine; if it turned out in the end I was an identity-theft artist, I was, almost certainly, painfully inept, and pride over my skillset would be entirely inappropriate. One would have to assume that, in addition to memorizing their numerical identities, my imaginary identity artist would have retained at least a handful of credit card numbers, and the fifteen or sixteen digit-blocks of credit cards were not to be found among my nearly endless hoard. Bank accounts, however, were an excellent possibility, ranging as they typically do from eight to twelve integers. Was I the sort of man who held quantities of money in several hundred bank accounts or with securities brokers? Perhaps numbered Swiss accounts with their identities redacted, in order to facilitate the accumulation of money without attracting the attention of the income tax authorities? While I was certainly the sort of man whose identity had been redacted, a numbered Swiss account was generally twenty-one digits, so it struck me that methods of tax evasion were not to be found among my personal preoccupations. I had, in any case, wandered off course here, looking for clues to my own identity, when what I needed most, right at the moment, was to locate a Personal Identification Number, an ATM PIN, from four to twelve digits, which would identity me to a machine, rather than to myself. Was it possible that one of these hundreds of strings could be safely relied upon to comfort a machine, and reassure its admittedly anonymous façade that I was, in all likelihood, precisely who I claimed to be? I had no idea. On top of everything, examined in isolation, these numbers looked suspiciously like telephone numbers, with many of them clustered around what might well be area codes, 212 and 301 and 213 and 202, New York, Maryland, Los Angeles, and Washington, while others appeared to have been initiated by country codes, the 33 of France, the 32 of Belgium, and the 351 of, let's see here, Portugal. I couldn't help noting that the 44 country code of Scotland, or for that matter, Cumbria, on the edge of the Irish Sea, was not among the numbers around which these strings were clustered, so whether Pessoa or de Campos had in fact got it right, I had nothing to unite me with the United Kingdom. Perhaps I could phone Pessoa and ask him to explain this. To make a long story short, before once again beginning the process of making a short story longer, I had far too many numbers, and no personal history to contextualize any of them. I suppose I had the option of phoning a friend, by randomly dialing any one of these integer strings, and asking whomever answered if he happened to have a friend who was prone to wandering around Mexico as a character out of Pessoa. And oh, by the way, do you happen to know his ATM PIN? Even to me, with my disbelief suspended, if only because I had no personal beliefs to begin with, beyond the simple belief that these were mine to choose, this sounded to me beyond improbable, and I was not as yet prepared to choose to believe in the absurd.

My resources, in short, while apparently vast, also appeared to be for the most part useless, beyond a handful of items that I knew I could count on, though whatever it was they counted toward, or how to go about even accounting for their existence, was not, at the moment, in any way clear: a book, a map, some neon-orange plastic; an ATM card with no obvious PIN; a belief-suspending, credulity-straining, identity card with a Glasgow address; a 1,000 banknote in pale purple and cyan; some personal items, borrowed or owned; and a temporary willingness to let the past go, though I had, admittedly, little choice in the matter, and no idea at all where it ends up going, when we, for whatever reason, "just let it go." These were all that I had, at least for the moment, though if I encountered any unpleasantness, I had an ample supply of memorized poetry, and a suspicion that no one has ever been harmed by the reciting of a pleasant and memorable poem.

The woman of the iron-railed balcony came back out to collect her laundry, apparently I'd spent quite a lot of time straining my own credulity, it was well past noon, the clothing was dry, and ready to be removed from the improvised line. Item by item, she gathered the garments, precisely in reverse of the order in which she'd hung them, removing the clothespins from the last item she'd hung, and then the clothespins she'd used for the next to last item, reversing the normal temporal order, where the first to be hung would be the first to become dry, removing the clothespins from last used to first, tossing them backwards into the blue plastic bucket, pausing only briefly to look up at a bird as it landed on her rooftop, a pale grey dove, una paloma blanca, maybe my Spanish was coming back to me, or maybe, in reverse, I was coming back to it, though whichever it was, the bird's existence seemed to resonate, I felt closer in fact to the pale grey bird, with its beakful of something that a bird would find useful, some piece of old newsprint or the remains of a ball of twine, than I did to my own headful of another man's material, which looked about as useful as a patch of empty sky. The bird paused only a moment and then took off flying, making its usual flight to elsewhere, *elsewhere* altogether, wherever birds disappear to when they suddenly up and disappear. I watched the woman watch it go, and then followed its flight over the red-tiled rooftops, over the church spires and dusty-rose basilica domes, gathering speed, gathering distance, riding the updrafts, gathering absence, until all that seemed to remain was a kind of homesick sense of longing, a bird-flight silhouette against a timeless patch of sky. As if reading my thoughts and disapproving, there was a heavy knock at the door, Buenos días Señor, Buenos días Señora I replied, then a blur of literal Spanish having to do no doubt with servicing the room, she was pushing a large metal cart full of cleaning supplies and towels and soap bars and trash bags, and it was evident that the time had come, that I, Alvaro de Campos, a well-trained ship's engineer, educated in the workings of things at Barrow-in-Furness, in the region of Cumbria, on the edge of the Irish Sea, must now go forth into the world and its workings, on the one hand and on the other of my impersonal two hands, with a deep sense of utterly improbable reality, in search of my own personal ATM PIN.

# 2

*I* exited the room to make way for the cleaning woman, climbed
down the stairs to the hotel lobby, and walked through the
front door, and out into the street. My first thought was that
I'd been able to carry this out, this exit from my hotel room, without betraying any sense of uncertainty whatsoever. My second
thought was that I'd need to find a process by which to reverse this,
to walk through the city streets and return to this same door, passing through the doorway and the hotel lobby, climbing the stairs
and returning to my room, all the while giving the impression that
this procedure was a familiar one, a process with which I was thoroughly acquainted. There are few easier ways of drawing unwanted
attention to oneself than to become lost in an unfamiliar city, and
when asked to state the location you are looking for, to respond
to your inquirer "I have no idea." It was with this in mind that I
had asked the desk clerk for a map, and then crossed the street to
the opposite sidewalk, looking up at my hotel window, studying the
building façade and surrounding buildings, trying to memorize the
scene for future reference. My hotel was called El Mesón de los Poetas, The Inn of the Poets, a fact whose significance I might need to
ponder later, but whose lack of probability struck me immediately
as all but inevitable; a plaque on the building displayed the number
35; and the name of the street was Calle Positivo, all things that
could prove useful in returning to this location, while at the same
time providing me with a Positive point of reference, an attitude, if
you will, with which to begin. To the left of my hotel, which was the

color of saffron rice, was a hot-chocolate-colored four-story building, also a hotel, named after Don Quixote, or Quijote in Spanish,
a difference without a difference, I decided on the spot, and then
almost as quickly began to regret, as I savored the syllables of the
English word "quixotic"; the Quixote had a semi-circular tunnel of
some kind running improbably through the lobby of its own ground
floor, passing right through the heart of it and deep into the hillside,
forcing the street-level lobby-desk nearly out of the building. As I
watched, several automobiles and pedestrians entered the tunnel,
leading me to conclude that this was in fact a passageway, not the
entrance to a cave or some sort of mineshaft, not simply a way into,
but also a way out of, the hill rising abruptly behind my small hotel.
Houses were stacked like children's blocks up the hillside as far as
the eye could see, in every color imaginable, and a few colors that
were not. Honeydew melon, red bell pepper, the orange of tanger-
ines, eggplant purple, cotton candy pink, cantaloupe, watermelon,
sweet pea, mango, the deep red-orange flesh of papaya mixed with
guava paste, banana skin, celery, lemon custard, honey, perhaps I
was simply hungry, and it would soon be time to eat. And then colors out of a dream, when we dream that we are deeply hungry, and
find that what we're about to swallow is something only a skeleton
could eat. I turned away from the hillside and back toward the city
center, looking for something tangible to help me get centered;
this fruit-cube-pyramid spun-sugar concoction was the last thing I
needed on an empty stomach. As for whatever that skeleton were
eating, I, Alvaro de Campos, a man made of books, with my quixoti-
cally concocted heteronymic-identity problems, was in no position
to criticize anyone's diet, as I had already proved prepared to swallow almost anything.

My next step, if you could call it that, was to stand there on
the sidewalk, facing a T-bone intersection maybe forty feet ahead
of me, and study the desk clerk's map of Guanajuato. It was, unfortunately, one of those crude tourist-map abstractions that bear
very little relation to the fine-grained reality of an actual city. I pictured myself wandering from place to place, searching for, what,
a bank branch I supposed, an imaginary bank branch where the
teller-window clerks were a little off the grid in terms of temporal
reality, at least as it applied to photo IDs; once I'd finally aban-

doned my search for the imaginary bank branch, and found that
the time had come to retrace my steps, I would look up at a street
sign, and down at my feet, and discover that I myself had strayed
from reality, and was now precisely *here*, in the middle of a cobbled
lane, which according to my map, didn't exist in the first place.
This map, clearly, was more trouble than it was worth; it was far too
similar to the map of my own interior, where I'd apparently turned
up missing without leaving my own hotel room. So what did I have
to work with here? Did I, perhaps, have an innate sense of direction? Some built-in mental compass that would guide me back to a
thoroughfare? Was I capable of building a sort of internal map, by
memorizing landmarks I'd observed along the way, putting them
in sequence according to the order in which I'd observed them,
such that when the time came to retrace my convoluted steps, I'd
be able, with some precision, to reverse my way back through this
landmark-sequenced narrative, and arrive at the beginning of my
Guanajuato journey? As I searched through my files for anything
resembling a map, something I might have built in the course of
a journey, I found, to my amazement, and then gradual dismay,
that I possessed a kind of mental image of the entire Pan American
Highway, from a stretch of gravel road in Deadhorse, Alaska, to a
glacial-mountain-waterfall forest in Tierra del Fuego, 30,000 miles
away, at the tip of Argentina, although as far as I could tell, I hadn't
travelled a single inch of it, and my map was not a map, it was the
image of a mapping, of a road that was not a road, it was the idea
of a roadway, which might as well have been a drainage basin or a
vascular system, not a way from *here* to *there* in the physical world,
but the rebus-strip pictogram for *elsewhere* in a dream; *elsewhere* in
a dream wasn't exactly what I was looking for, I was already *elsewhere* enough as it was, and if I wound up *elsewhere* in a dream of
Guanajuato, I'd face 30,000 miles' worth of dream drive ahead of
me. I snapped out of this maybe two-minutes' worth of reverie still
standing on the sidewalk in front of my hotel, and began searching
for a map of even a moderate-sized city, something that would indicate an innate capability to find my way around, both forwards and
backwards, in a manifest city, situated squarely in the readily apparent, without falling into semblances, and drainage-basin ditches,
and finding that I faced a dream-slog ahead of me. While I came up

with several fairly lucid-looking city maps, particularly of New York, or Manhattan at least, and the downtown area of what I recognized immediately as Washington D.C., these were cities whose order had been thoroughly pre-planned, and from my bird's-eye window view of the winding Guanajuato streets, it didn't possess the order of even a lucidly planned maze. Now what? I would need, at a minimum, a good place to start, and from there, who knows, we would, as they say, just have to *see*, though I couldn't help wishing that my own interior weren't an ill-conceived maze of random assorted facts and roadway reveries that hadn't to all appearances been either travelled or pre-planned. I would start at the city center, in the Plaza de la Paz, just in front of the Basilica of Our Lady of Guanajuato, marked on my map with a small red star; it probably goes without saying that I wished my own interior were similarly star-marked and in possession of some semblance of a manifest center, from which to embark and then find my way back.

I walked the forty feet from the front of my hotel, turned left at the first intersection, where Calle Cantaritos T-boned orthogonally into Calle Positivo, descended the cobbled hill another twenty or thirty feet or so, and halted abruptly beneath the blue Guanajuato sky, just below the apartment of the laundry-hanging woman, Our Lady of the Balcony, with her blue plastic clothespin bucket, and her red and yellow geranium boxes. While this was a location I couldn't possibly forget, as I already knew by heart her clothes-pinning methods, holding things in place by attaching them to a line, and then detaching them one by one by working backwards, with the first clothes hung the last to be detached, and folded away and restored to her apartment, a method that struck me as temporally unsound, as the first to be hung would be the first to become dry, and she had reversed the natural temporal order; while I couldn't, as I was saying, forget her sense of order, as it was the same sense of order that I was trying to acquire for myself, the memory of this method struck me as troubling. This was, in a sense, a physical manifestation of the method I would need to return to my lodgings, detaching my memories precisely in reverse, beginning with my standing in an unmarked lane, and working my way back toward my first memories last, memories which, if I didn't carefully attach them to myself somehow, and add them to my list of personal pos-

sessions, would blow away or dry up or evaporate completely. The
natural order, in the temporal sense, where the oldest of my memories would be the first I'd forget, would not work at all in reversing
my journey; somewhere along the way, as I worked my way backwards, I'd be standing there alone at a blank-slate intersection, in
the twilight gloom, with the evening growing dim and then dimmer
and dimmer, and the lamp-post lanterns as yet to be lit, and have
no memory at all of where I was, or how I'd come to be standing on
The Street That's Nowhere Near Here, and worst of all, as I imagined this moment, or more precisely the moment of this morning's
dim awakenings, no conceivable way of beginning to remember
just who it was who'd forgotten his own beginnings. That man you
find wandering lost and alone, searching, or so he says, for a "star-
marked center," isn't so much lost in the physical city, as he's utterly lost in his featureless interior, because the things he held dear,
that kept his memories pinned down, and preserved them intact as
his personal possessions, have vanished completely into narrative
thin air; he no longer has his own personal possessions, because he
knows, deep down, there is no such person.

I came out of this admittedly convoluted reverie still standing in front of the Cantaritos balcony. Several things were clear: I
needed to stay away from convoluted reveries, where a man can get
lost without even moving; I'd do well to avoid poetry altogether, as
my skeleton-eating-the-inedible fruitstand-display had nearly swallowed me whole in front of my own building; and I would need to
just move forward, with my own eyes open, and maybe *see* what we
would *see* as far as star-marked centers, a sort of stopgap measure
for my gap-filled interior, a provisional self until I found something
better. As if reading my thoughts, and this time approving, the pale
grey dove, una paloma blanca, returned to its home on the red-tiled
rooftop, a nest made of twigs and kite twine and refuse, anything
and everything that the bird had found useful; a provisional self,
the bird seemed to say, would make a far better home than would a
featureless interior.

I waved an imaginary goodbye to the lady of the balcony, made
a mental note to keep an eye out for kite twine, and walked down
the cobbled street toward the Guanajuato city center, marked on
my map with a small red star, to get myself centered in the physical

city. While there was nothing that struck me as even vaguely familiar, it was apparent that Guanajuato was a city of churches, I could see three or four in the first few blocks, and by the time I reached the city center in the Plaza de la Paz, I had the feeling that I knew the sort of place I was in, a Spanish colonial city that, despite my own forgetfulness, took a good deal of pride in preserving its own history. From the churches I could see, with the baroque ornamentation of the late 17th and 18th centuries, Guanajuato must have passed through a period of great wealth, and displayed its wealth in the construction of churches. I ducked inside the cathedral that faced the Plaza, the Basilica of Our Lady of Guanajuato, a rich custard yellow topped by dusty-rose domes and wedding-cake belfries and balustraded clock towers (the poetry of its look required only that I look), and the interior was a wellspring of beautiful beginnings, sparkling with thousands of shades of immaculate green, everything seeming to glow with its own green lamplight, lit up from within by the radiance of its being, though it was no doubt dependent on ordinary sunlight for this being-at-its-most-becoming springtime effect. A Mass was being conducted as I watched, and though utterly incomprehensible, whether in Latin or Spanish, I had the feeling of being in the presence of something holy, though it seemed to be the presence of holiness itself, not something specifically Catholic, which struck me as holy. I stood a few feet inside the church, to observe the observants, and didn't feel the need to in any way participate; the church pews were full, the congregation alternately sitting and kneeling, and the liturgy of the Eucharistic service was being mumbled by a priest in a language I could not make out, neither Spanish nor Latin, but the ritualistic language of Religion itself. The side walls of the Cathedral were lined with the statues of saints, with names like Santa Ana and San Joaquin and San Diego, saints that reminded me more of places on a map than of anything saintly that I associated with the names. If I had once been a Catholic, it was clear that it no longer mattered, and if I felt a sudden hunger, it was simply time to eat.

Returning to the Cathedral steps, I took a seat on the smooth pink quarry stones facing the Zócalo, and pulled out the crude tourist-map abstraction that the desk clerk at the Inn had donated to my improbable cause. While the map was rather vague about the rest of Guanajuato, here in the city center it was surprisingly concrete, with a level of detail bordering on the obsequious. At the center of the Plaza, roughly triangular in shape, stood the Monument to Peace, a classical bronze statue of an apparently unmentionable goddess, possibly Eirene, the Greek goddess of Peace and Spring-time, with her Green Shoots epithet in Hesiod's *Theogony*, looking slightly out of place, and uncomfortable with the disarray of her unfortunate clothing, her garment having fallen from a rounded left shoulder to reveal, here in public, a bare left breast. The Plaza was faced with the former homes and local residences of various counts and marquesos, of San Clemente, Valenciana, Conde de Rul, Perez Galvez, the Alaman and Chico families, evidently the sources of the wealth that had built the churches. As the center of the city, the Plaza was the destination of an array of narrow lanes and winding cobbled streets, Calle San Diego, Cruz Verde, Pasaje de los Arcos, La Tenaza, Zapateros, La Condeza, Cuesta de Marques, La Estrella, and so on, the streets having made their way here by twisted irregular routes, as though they could have been going anywhere, but having found themselves unexpectedly and suddenly *here*, at the center of the city, and overwhelmed by the display of wealth in the Cathedral and aristocratic houses, had abandoned their twisted journeys, and stopped at the Plaza to have a long look around. This was not, in other words, the normal layout of a Spanish Colonial city, with its square Zócalo at its center, and its orderly grid of streets. Something twisted and irregular had evidently overcome the city planners, and they'd surrendered to disorder, and simply left it where they'd found it, right here at the heart of things, enjoying its own wealth. The wealthy had no doubt found ways of deploying a sense of order behind the facades of these beautiful four-story houses, with their wrought-iron balconies and richly planted flower boxes, leaving the twisted streets and winding lanes to fend for themselves. An irregular triangular-shaped city-center Zócalo; crooked streets and meandering cobblestoned lanes; irregularities built into the cobbled-together heart of things; these were minor inconveniences one could no doubt put up with, as long as servants were present in opulent abundance. If the streets hadn't had a clue where they were headed when they started, they knew where they were when they arrived here at the Plaza, their twisted zigzag journeys had all made perfect sense in the end, as journeys to sudden wealth, and the order of abundance. Of course the streets could simply turn around and go back the way they came, they maintained a physical memory of the path by which they'd arrived here, whereas I had no memory at all of the journey to Guana-juato, irregular or otherwise; if I had decided to simply head back, to retrace the steps that had brought me here, I might just as well have spun a de-magnetized compass needle, and called wherever it pointed "my only way back."

Instead, I spun my internal compass, saw that it pointed imme-diately forward, and crossed the Plaza de le Paz to find my lunch at an outdoor café. I ordered a mineral water, picked something at random off the lunchtime menu, and sat there in the sunlight, tak-ing it all in, enjoying the pure poetry of the day being the day. My meditation on wealth and irregularity, while seated on the Cathe-dral steps, personifying the streets, viewing them as sentient beings, reminded me once again that I still had a tendency toward poet-izing reality. Perhaps I was simply distracting myself from the un-pleasantness of my situation, perhaps the experience of the church, and the sense of something holy, had caused me to locate a depth in things, a depth they had no need to possess. These streets, after all, were just streets, there was no "as if" and "as though" about them; there was no reason to treat them as similes, this was not at all how they were constructed. I wondered what it was that caused me to think in terms of *as if* and *as though*, when clearly *as is* was already more than enough, and would more than suffice without adding any poetry. I was myself already *as if*, a man whose identity was improbably constructed, and what I needed now was clarity, not po-etry, a clear sense of things as they are, beginning with my existence *as is*. The distance between *as if* and *as is*, between the world as we might imagine it, and the world as it actually is, was a problem for a philosopher, not a well-trained ship's engineer, and in any case, my food had arrived, though even this, apropos of nothing, seemed to be food for thought. Carne tampiquena, enchiladas rojas, refried beans and guacamole, I wondered if I had a taste for any of these things. Did I eat meat? Did spicy food disagree with my stomach? I was drinking plain mineral water, would I have preferred to drink beer or wine? I ate for a while without thinking, and the food didn't remind me of anything, these things that I was chewing on were simply being chewed. The food was good, I ate what I wanted, and when the time came to stop eating, I put down my silverware, and came to a stop.

Directly across the Plaza from my seat in the café was an HSBC bank branch, the issuer of my ATM money card, useless without its PIN. I wondered about the wisdom of presenting myself at the bank branch, telling them that I'd lost my PIN number, and showing them my improbable photo ID. I had the feeling that they might nod sympathetically, say soothing things in Spanish, gently remove the cash card from my hand, along with my phony driver's license, and send me on my way. No one with any sense of judgment would accept the fact that I was Alvaro de Campos, no matter how uncanny the resemblance to Pessoa; I simply had no way of explaining a photo that was 80 years out of date. I could hear the branch manager now, unfortunately a reader of Pessoa, chuckling over the resemblance, sure that this was some kind of joke. The heteronym of a long-dead poet is not the norm among their valued customers; they would have to assume that I myself wasn't normal, and perhaps posed something of a threat to their everyday sense of normality. They would view me as the sort of person better viewed from the other side of the window, passing through the street, mumbling to himself in the throes of delusion, it would be best if I just left quietly, without making any sort of fuss. People who keep their money in banks tend to be fairly lucid, they know pretty much who they are and where they stand in the world of the everyday, and my presence, there among them, would not be taken lightly. There are places in the world set aside for the delusional; they don't belong, for the most part, in the waiting rooms of banks. The manager would nod imperceptibly to one of the well-armed private guards, who would casually saunter over, without alarming the normal customers, who need to know that their money is safe, entrusted with those whose judgment can safely be trusted, "Is there a problem here?" the guard would ask, and the manager would offer him a brief explanation, "This gentleman was just leaving, perhaps you could escort him to the door," while I, understanding nothing of what they were saying, in quiet rapid Spanish that was no cause for alarm, would look from one to the other, with no sense of comprehension, reinforcing their belief that the man before them would be better off in the street. And out I would go, with the guard gripping firmly the upper half of my arm, just above the elbow, quietly showing me out of the place, anything and everything under firm control. Perhaps a customer would steal a glance as I passed, wondering if there were something wrong with me, careful to avoid staring, doing nothing out of the or- dinary, by all means avoiding the unpleasantness of a scene. There I would stand in the sun-drenched street, now stripped of my bank card and driver's license, with my dignity still intact, and everything else in a shambles. You've seen this sort of person yourself, lost and alone, sick and delusional, believing they are some long-dead poet perhaps, mumbling scraps of his poetry, and we both know how we treat them, we give them a good wide berth. That man there lost in the world of *as if*, stay away from him if possible, and continue to walk away without pausing or even looking, on into the world of the everyday *as is*.

I set my single 1,000 note, with the obverse side up, on top of the check that the waiter had presented, and waited for the man to collect it. As I sat there staring at the peso note, contemplating the likely behavior of an HSBC bank manager, a man of sound judg- ment, and a taste for Portuguese poetry, surrounded by well-armed guards, men of brute force and the means to employ it, my reverie was brought to an abruptly commanded halt, Parese! in Spanish, and I picked up the note to study it more closely. The building pictured, on the obverse side of the 1,000 note, was a building I could see with my own two eyes, just behind and to the right of the bank branch office, and my tourist map made clear what exactly the building was, the University of Guanajuato, the resemblance was uncanny. I set the peso note back on top of the restaurant check, and both were swept away by the waiter in passing, who returned a moment later with the appropriate change, apparently in Guana- juato the uncanny was legal tender, and I was now free to go, my lunch had been paid for, the transaction was complete. I looked again at my improbable ID, with a newfound respect for the power of the uncanny, I mean, really, who was to say, this might as well be me, since I in fact wasn't anyone. I might have felt better in an eighty-year-old suit, and a detective's grey fedora, but as I studied the photo of Pessoa, his nose was clearly my nose, and the glasses

he wore were virtually identical to my own. Whoever came up with
the expression "as clear as the nose on your face" knew what he
was saying, though to be honest, the more I thought about this expression, the less I understood it; evidently, I was not the original
source of this bit of wisdom. For all practical purposes, if something
is self-evident, a fact in and of itself, the expression is applicable,
we would no more question such a fact than we would question
whether or not the nose on our face is our own, but in what sense
did I think of my own nose as mine? From a certain perspective, my
nose was in fact Fernando Pessoa's, and thus the self-evident was not
properly a realm that belonged to me, it belonged more properly to
Pessoa. If my next actions, including the pressing question of how
to obtain more money, were to be guided by the self-evident, by
that which could be said to be true "on its face," and thus taken at
face-value, without further need for probing and questioning, could
anything be said to be self-evident to me? I needed money. I now
had banknotes and coins of various denominations that totaled 880
pesos, an amount that would be successively reduced with each
transaction that I conducted, until, at some point, I would attempt
to conclude a transaction, and find that the funds that I had in my
possession were in no way sufficient to fully conclude it, and at this
point, everyone, including yours truly, would know within a peso or
two exactly who I was, the sort of man who goes about entering into
transactions with no way of completing them, a man, in short, of insufficient funds. Working backward from this point, from the point
at which I had eaten a meal that I was unable to pay for, the point at
which it was as clear as the nose on Pessoa's face that I was the sort
of man who could no longer pay for his own meals, a man caught
in the embarrassing position of having to explain his situation to a
waiter or small tavern owner in a language he could barely speak,
a man in fact with no real grasp of the language needed to explain
himself, a man who in fact needed money, not language, to clear up
the situation and allow things once again to speak for themselves,
working backward, therefore, from this point, it was easy to see who
I was, this was a monetary not a linguistic or ontological question, I
was a man with precisely 880 pesos. I was a man who had started out
with 1,000 pesos, in the form of a single banknote, in pale purple
and cyan, a banknote that seemed to have been uniquely chosen to

reflect a sense of place, the 1,000 note and the city of Guanajuato were in some sense of the word *meant* for each other, but I was no longer that man, and with each transaction, the memory of myself as the 1,000 man would recede, transaction by transaction, until I found myself to be the sort of man who would consume an entire meal with no means of paying for it, with no way of giving the meal back and rescinding the entire transaction, and with no language at all that would be in any way sufficient to explain himself to anyone, even to himself. In short, the one self-evident fact that I possessed, clear on its face and thus able to be taken at face value, as clear as the nose on the face of a long-dead poet, a nose that was in fact my nose, the resemblance was uncanny, was that I was no longer the 1,000 man, I was the man now reduced to 880 pesos, and that if I didn't do something about it, I would soon be down to nothing. And no amount of memorized poetry, or some strange inner tendency toward poeticizing reality, or some memory of a dove building a home out of refuse, would prove sufficient to distract me from such unpleasantness, the unpleasantness of finding that I had just eaten a wonderful, satisfying meal, and being myself next to nothing, would have some serious explaining to do, and no language at all that would clearly suffice.

I noticed at some point that the waiter had been staring at me, evidently I had been occupying one of his tables for quite some time now without ordering anything, and that if I wanted to continue to occupy my seat, I would need to order something, so I ordered a coffee, with a mumbled apology in my miserable Spanish. As I turned away from the waiter and back toward the HSBC bank branch, knowing that my place in the world, and my ability to continue to occupy even a single outdoor café seat, was going to depend on dealing with the bank branch, obtaining an ATM PIN number, and then going about my business, without running the continual risk of reducing myself to nothing, I discovered that the woman from the balcony across from my hotel was standing over my table, with a smile of recognition on her already-memorable face. I pulled out one of the café table chairs, offering her a seat with a silent wave of my arm, that universal language of welcome that begins by placing one's right hand next to one's heart and motioning with open palm toward the seat that is being offered, and

she took the seat that was silently offered up, sparing me the in-
dignity of once again exposing my execrable Spanish. I take it you
don't speak our language, she said, where are you from? Without
really thinking about the consequences, the result no doubt of my
sense of relief at being able to make myself understood, in simple
declarative sentences, I began to speak, without any real regard for
the truth, since it was, after all, as clear as the nose on Pessoa's face
that I was not in possession of any sort of truth, other than a transac-
tional truth, the truth that would result from my buying her a drink,
and thereby slightly reducing my slowly diminishing sense of myself
as the 880 Peso Bona Fide Man. Well, it's something of a long story,
my parents were Portuguese, and I was raised in the U.S., but I'm
living now in Scotland, inland from the Irish Sea, what about you,
are you originally from Guanajuato? Yes, let me see, how can I best
explain this, I am living now in an apartment, as you could plainly
see from your hotel window, and prior to that, I was sharing a room
in the housing provided for students, and before I came to study
English as a student at the University, I lived for many years just outside Irapuato, a city to the west of here, perhaps 45 minutes away,
an agricultural city at the foot of the Arandas mountains, famous
for its strawberries, much in the way that Guanajuato is famous for
its silver mines, although my parents brought me to Irapuato from
Guadalajara when I was a child, and I have no memory at all of
living in Guadalajara, so I suppose you could say I am originally
from elsewhere. I understand; it's difficult to place your origins in
a place you do not recall; I have a somewhat similar problem in
placing my own origins. Your English, in any case, is excellent; you
must have studied long and hard and been well-instructed. Can I
get you something to drink? I'll have a glass of red wine, thank you.
I couldn't help noticing you staring at me out of your window, you
looked a little lost, perhaps in need of some guidance, and I myself
am a guide here, I know the city well. Perhaps I can be of some assistance?

On the one hand...no, delete that, I had only one hand, I was
using the other hand to signal to the waiter to ask for a red wine...
on the only hand I had, then, I needed some assistance, and the fact
that my stature would be further diminished by having to pay for a
guide would soon prove to be irrelevant, a few simple transactions

from now I would be down to nothing anyway. I would love your help, I don't know my way around here at all, but perhaps we could begin at the bank across the street, I have an account at the bank, but I find myself short of cash at the moment, and I seem to have forgotten my ATM PIN. Oh I understand, of course, I myself have a terrible time remembering numbers. I'll tell you a little secret, I've been forced to write my PIN number down on a business card I keep in my wallet. I know this isn't safe, if someone were to steal my purse, they would not only find my ATM card, but they would soon find themselves in possession of my PIN, though I've taken the precaution of writing it down backwards, such that the thief would need to be clever enough to read the number from back to front, you might want to think about doing something similar, write down the last number first, the next to last number next, and so on, until you have the last number first, everything in reverse, if you see what I mean. Then, of course, as you stand at the ATM machine, ready to enter your PIN number on the keypad of the machine, remember to begin at the end and proceed forward by moving backward, one number at a time, number by number, until you reach the end, ending at the beginning. If you're anything like me, I'm sure you'll find this to be helpful, it's easy enough to remember. I tried many other ways, and none of them seemed to work for me, I tried using the date of my birth, for example, as my PIN number, but when it came time to remember the number, I would remember the fact that the number was something significant to me, something that I associated with myself, but I couldn't remember what the significance was, all sorts of numbers occurred to me as significant, my driver's license number, the number on my passport, the zip code of my home address, the final six digits of my telephone number, and by the time I'd tried each of these in turn, the machine would simply return my card, and I was forced to begin all over. The advantage of my little trick is that there is very little to remember, I just have to remember to start at the end and work back toward the beginning, which is very much the way my memory works in the first place, so that the simple act of trying to remember the PIN's beginning reminds me to start at the end. I'm sorry to go on and on about this, but I suppose that memory is a tricky thing for some of us, I'm the sort of person who will tie a string around my finger to remind myself of something, and find that, when I look at it, it reminds me of the time, the time that is fast approaching when I will begin to untie the string, since having a string around your finger can quickly become annoying.

The waiter had returned with the glass of wine, greeted the woman as Gabriella, apparently they were acquaintances, and left me with another check to be paid, and yet another reminder of my diminishing sense of worth, itself a kind of string that was quickly becoming annoying. I take it you are Gabriella, my name is Alvaro; I'm pleased to make your acquaintance, I like your system very much, though at the moment I must admit I have no number at all to write down, even backwards, to begin with, I don't seem to recall what sort of system I myself might have used, though I'm sure that I must have had one. Alvaro, my new friend, don't worry yourself, I know very much how you feel, it's very much a helpless feeling, having a system you can't recall, let me just finish my wine, and we'll go across the street to the bank branch. As it happens, my uncle is the manager there, I'm certain that he can help. Is your uncle by any chance a reader of the Portuguese poet, Fernando Pessoa? My uncle may be any number of things, he's a bit of a character, my uncle is, but one thing I can assure you of is that he is not a reader of poetry. Why do you ask? Is your system of memory somehow tied by a string to Pessoa? It's possible, Señorita, it wouldn't surprise me in the least, but how I might have gone about tying my memories of Pessoa to my ATM PIN is completely beyond me. In any case, how much do you charge for your services? I seem to be running low on pesos, and I may not be able to pay you until I relocate my PIN. Please, Señor Alvaro, I can see by your face that you are one to be trusted, you can pay me when the time comes, assuming of course that one of us can remember, perhaps I should tie a string around my finger. That won't be necessary, Gabriella, I will make a mental note of any debt that I incur, if you like I can write it down backwards, and if you wouldn't mind helping me with this business at the bank, and then showing me around Guanajuato for an hour or so, shall we say 300 pesos? You are far too generous, permit me to help you out of friendship, we will consider this glass of wine to be more than sufficient payment. Well, in that case, let me at least buy you another glass of wine. That would be lovely, I would enjoy that, but why don't we go across the street to the bank, before we both forget that we have business to attend to, and then we'll make our way to the Jardín, and have a glass of wine in front of the Teatro and the Templo de San Diego. Let us say that you will owe me a glass of wine, once this business has been concluded, for even I can remember a debt of wine, you can tell me all about yourself, and we will drink to your memorable poet friend, Fernando Pessoa.

Gabriella pushed her seat back from the table, standing up to leave, brushing imaginary breadcrumbs away from the front of a sky-blue blouse, having forgotten perhaps that she hadn't in fact eaten, that she'd only had a single glass of wine. She had a lovely face, warm and open, an angel's face, like the face in a story, in the sense that when we are being told a story, we ask ourselves to imagine a face that properly belongs there, and we can't help imagining the face of an angel, she had just that face, the one that we imagine. Perhaps I had long ago forgotten the story itself, the way we forget our own dreams within the first few moments of the time when we awaken, but the dream had left behind it a long trail of breadcrumbs, and I followed them back and recognized her instantly, she had the face of the angel in the dream. From this point forward, when I found a thing to be self-evident, it would be as clear as the nose on Gabriella's face; I was already a little tired of this nose of Pessoa's.

# 3

*T*he story of how I came to be holed up in my office, at 2:00 am on a Monday morning, the morning after Easter as a matter of fact, drinking mugs of cold coffee to wash down the Dexedrine, and making one final push on completing my memoirs, whose working title for the moment, *Tales from the Crypt: Memoirs of the World's Only Marxist Venture Capitalist*, should give you some idea of the problems I'm up against, is a story that, unfortunately, will just have to wait, until I come to write the chapter on Dacha Wireless. This, I can tell you, is not what I had in mind, back when I was presented with the Lifetime Achievement Award, and promised my publishers, in exchange for a miniscule advance, something along the lines of *Venture Capital: The Inside Story*. What I actually had in mind, some ghostwritten piece of fluff, modestly self-deprecating yet ultimately self-glorifying, came apart in my head somewhere along the way, as I sat with this title, on an otherwise blank white page, and started pondering the question: *inside of what?* No one in his right mind, if he wanted to stay in the venture business, would consider telling the story of how the business actually functions, any more than a guy marketing Healthy Heart Power Bars would tell you what that shit you're eating actually does to your heart. And then the ghostwriter shows up, inside my head, with the scruples of a supermarket tabloid journalist, and the disciplined work habits of Hunter S. Thompson, asking all kinds of questions, like someone had clued him in, about where all the money came from, and where it all went, until he finally got

around to his actual question, the one I should have answered with
a crisp No Comment: What do you suppose is *inside of you*? So
here I am sitting at my Parnian Custom Power Desk, several chap-
ters short of completing my chronicle, and two days away from my
April 15 deadline, knowing that I will have to go back to the beginning, and fill in some blanks that don't appear on my resume, but
paralyzed completely by the power of my desk, with its exotic wood
inlays from dying tropical rainforests, Zebrawood, Iroko, Cordia,
Purpleheart, and some burled piece of something that's probably
long extinct, and while it's altogether possible that I'm bothered by
the trees, or the fact that my desk cost as much as a Lamborghini,
the deep inner reality that I'm actually trying to face is how to live
up to the Parnian motto: *Live Like You Mean It*, like how in God's
name am I supposed to do *that*?

By the time I got started in the venture capital business, back
in what must have been the late-1980s, I was already, give or take,
two distinct people, one a practiced businessman with a creative
flair for mendacity, and the other a published poet, slowly dying of
the usual self-inflicted truth. We were living together, though not
exactly under the same roof, in a house in the Hollywood Hills that
was rented from a real character, a dyed-in-the-wool Stalinist and
dysphasic entertainment lawyer who was trying to write a history of
the Communist 1950s in Hollywood; Fred, let's call him, since that
was his name, was somewhere in his 80s, and twenty years in to his
history lesson, which had netted him twenty-five pages or so, due
to a stroke-induced language problem that had emptied his mind
of linguistic content, a problem so eerily similar to mine that his
attempts at speech were like a mocking of the afflicted. The house
itself was high on a ridge, up Beachwood Canyon, near the Hollywood sign, with an enormous picture window overlooking the toxic
haze, open beam cathedral ceilings in a flagstone-fireplace living
room, and a study the size of a walk-in closet, where my language,
unbeknownst to me, had apparently come to die. Actually, that's a
bald-faced lie; by the time I arrived at the walk-in closet, my poetry
was down to skin and bones already, the result of a malignancy that
was rapidly taking over any sense I tried to make of poetry as meaningful, a cancer I proposed to cure with a two-pronged attack, by

putting my language on a starvation diet, and my mind on a radical chemo program. The details of this care path are probably not relevant, since nearly every dying poet has tried something like it, although to the usual antimetabolites and alkylating agents, mostly vodka in my case, heavily supplemented with Halcion and Xanax, I'd added something experimental that I can't really recommend, immense quantities of Post-Structuralist philosophy and Frankfurt School Marxism. So, you're wondering, how does this work? Guy's got some weird sort of oncogenic neoplasm, which he's basically trying to starve to death, by grinding up his poetry's cancer-ridden skeleton, and feeding it nothing but semiotic bonemeal; he's hooked himself up to an IV drip of ethanol and benzodiazepine, which may not cure cancer, but likely renders it irrelevant; he's up somewhere on the 500th or 600th Plateau of Deleuze and Guattari's *Capitalism and Schizophrenia*, with altitude sickness, and night setting in, and the only way down, the sickening plunge, leaving what Deleuze and Guattari call the Body without Organs; and yet he's still suiting up for work, headed off in the general direction of the Venture Capital Walk of Fame? What are we missing here? Guy sounds like a train wreck. You want our advice? Take another Dexie, and lose this whole poetry character; no one gives a shit about poetry in the first place, much less some guy who can barely speak, holed up in a broom closet, trying to *Die Like He Means It*.

So picture it this way: I'm working out of my rented house, with the Hollywood sign looming in the background, at an eight-foot folding buffet table, equipped with a three-line phone, that I've set up in a corner of the Meaningless Living room, under the open beam cathedral ceiling, where some foul bag of bones is now swinging from the rafters; I have an enormous picture window overlooking the Hollywood Bowl, to remind me occasionally that the world is still out there, not that it looks quite real after a half-quart of vodka; the dress code is a loosely enforced Hospital Casual, consisting of bathrobe, boxer shorts, and Decaying Grey T-shirt, although my phone voice is strictly Brooks Brother's flannel, with a half-Windsor knot in my imaginary rep stripe; and no matter how strange this sounds, the reality is even stranger, because not only am I good at the work, I'm earning the firm a stone cold fortune. Firm? What firm? Someone was actually employing you? Yeah, maybe I skipped

that part; I'm working for a venture fund called let's call it TechA-
non, set up by the Belgian Government's Ministry of Technology,
cold-calling in to the Chief Financial Officers of info-tech companies that were already successful, and mostly getting the brush-off
before my training kicked in, like most of these guys not only didn't
need our money, they didn't actually believe that Belgium had a
government. I had, however, mastered the art, essential in telesales,
of speaking Pure Bullshit, and of never asking a question to which
No might be an answer. I started doing phone work when I was
barely sixteen, as a bill collector on fiscal degenerates, the sort of
morons who bought things like massive TVs, and kitchen appliances, and stereo systems, on department store credit, back in the
days before Visa and MasterCard turned every last American into
a true fiscal moron; as a result of this training, by which I'd honed
my technique, I had heard the word No more times in a week than
a normal venture capitalist will hear in a lifetime, such that No
was not a word by which I was easily discouraged, and became in
fact a word that I eliminated from the vocabulary. Even when I was
sixteen, working in a squat, derelict office complex a short drive
from my high school, in a boiler-room office with maybe eighty
desks, manned by veteran collectors with a deep knowledge of scare
tactics, I had a voice that conveyed authority, an "I'm on your side,
I can help you, I know what you're up against" authenticity, despite
the fact that at the age of sixteen, I had very little authority in relation to anything. As the new kid in a room full of hardboiled veterans, I was given the worst accounts; not only had the department
stores stopped holding their breath, and sold the accounts off for
five cents on the dollar, but the accounts had already been worked
by the pros, you could see this on the faces of the three-by-five account cards, the coffee stains and cigarette burns, the ink smudges
and donut grease and grime of the things, the notations of collection attempts sometimes a year or two out of date, these accounts
had been thoroughly worked by the strong-arm guys already, and
somewhere along the way, all hope had been abandoned. I'd get
a three inch stack of the blood-from-a-stone index cards, hear the
Brylcreem-coiffed cynics chuckling behind me, pick up the phone
and start in dialing; I could just as well have been calling from an
insane asylum, dressed up in a clown suit, with a rubber ball for a

nose, if someone answered, they heard a pin-striped voice, the voice of authority, a man who was all business.

At the bottom of the food chain of the ecosystem of capitalism, which is itself rapidly cannibalizing our living and breathing eco-system, by converting our desire for meaning into the meaningful objects of desire, stands a welfare mother with three screaming chil-dren and an oversized TV/Stereo console that she bought on credit and still owes every nickel on, with interest still accruing on years of accrued interest. Miss O'Neal? Speaking. My name is Mr. Bullshit, I'm calling about the outstanding payment due on your television. I told that last motherfucker who called to leave me the fuck alone, I got no money, I sure as shit don't, what the fuck is wrong with you people, you must be hard of hearing or something. I understand Miss O'Neal, that's why I'm calling, I'm sure it must be difficult with the kids and all, all these bills your ex left you with, what was his name again...? William. Right, William left you with the kids and this debt you owe to Robinsons and you've barely got money to pay the rent, am I right? You got that right, I never wanted no big-ass TV in the first place, and the piece of shit ain't paid me a dime of child support in goin' on two years now, I'm four months behind on the gas as it is, how the hell someone expect me to pay for that asshole's TV? I hear you, Miss O'Neal, that's what I'm here for, let's try to find a way to clean this thing up, you don't want this on your credit report, someday you're going to want to buy a home for those beautiful kids, and no one will loan you a penny with your credit all messed up, you know William's not going to be there for you, isn't that so? Sure as shit won't, he be down at the Tap Room with that whore he's got, he don't give a damn about these kids. But you sure do, don't you ma'am, and that's why we've got to clean this up for you, make sure those kids have got a yard to play in, if William's not going to care for them, we have to put our heads together, figure out a way to take care of this Robinson's debt, what time of month does your next welfare check come in, next week sometime, am I right? That's right, next Tuesday, $431.80. What you need to do today is send me $20, right now, I'll take your name off of this bad debt list first thing, first things first, and then when you cash your check, you send me $20 more, I'll send you some envelopes, every time you cash that check, first thing you do is mail that $20, first thing, right away, and before you know it, this whole thing will be long forgotten, you make yourself a fresh start on things, set things right with the finance company, you do that for me now, right now, and I'll get your name off of this list. What you say your name was? John Q. Bullshit, Miss O'Neal, you just call me John, you send that $20 right away and we'll straighten this out together, no reason for William to be ruining your whole life. You tell those other assholes to stop calling me during dinner? I got to feed my kids, they can't be calling no more at suppertime. You have my word, Miss O'Neal, you keep your word to me, and I'll take care of that for you, no one will be bothering you while you're trying to put supper on the table, but I need you to put that $20 in the mail this afternoon, do it right now, the minute you put the phone down so you don't forget, you're going to do that for me, I can count on you, first things first, am I right?

How was I supposed to know the job would leave permanent scar tissue, an absolute must for a decent VC? It was a huge, I thought, improvement on my previous work, washing dishes eight hours straight, with one short Pepsi break, from 4 pm to Midnight at a Ponderosa Steakhouse for $1 an hour, I was underage and illegal at the time, the guy could pay me whatever he felt like, busing tables, spraying the plates, trays, and bowls and loading the machine, stacking the clean stuff back out front to get dirty again, the place had amazing turnover, it was a dirty-dish machine. Fifty hours of dishes, at age 15, paid for my first real car, a 1959 Hillman Minx, a somewhat eccentric vehicle, with oxidizing blue paint that wore thinner the more I scrubbed it, leaking brake lines, a severe shimmy at anything over 50, and an automatic window opener on the passenger-side door, if you slammed the door too hard, down crashed the window. One time when I'd let the brake fluid get a little too low, I pulled into a service station, barely got it stopped, was told to pull around back, where I found myself on an incline, with no brakes to speak of, and had to drive it, carefully, into a red brick wall. I narrowly missed two startled auto mechanics who were bent over the engine block of a gold Chrysler New Yorker, exited the car, told them I needed brake fluid, and stood there maintaining a kind of quiet dignity, while they wiped the grease from their hands, contemplated the damage, and absorbed this, in retrospect, rather obvious fact. One of the mechanics, evidently convinced that I was unsafe at any speed, made the slight miscalculation that he'd be able to drive my car backwards maybe eight or ten feet, getting in behind the wheel, trying to throw the on-the-column gear shift into reverse, not realizing that the steering column had been moved, from British right-hand to American left-hand drive, without reorienting the gearshift pattern, leading to six or eight futile attempts at finding reverse, each time driving deeper into the unyielding brick wall, then throwing up his hands and stalking off in silence. The other mechanic handed me a can of brake fluid, shrugged, turned around, and walked back to the service office. Between the time I crashed into the red brick wall, and my exit, in reverse, from the service bay area, beyond my bare statement of the facts of the case, not a single word was uttered, as an uncanny silence enveloped the place, as though speech itself had been rendered speechless, and if you ever find a company that behaves this way, respecting the silence as the business plan crashes, I'd be happy to put in a dollar or two, since the normal process of the brakeless crash, at 90 MPH into red brick nothingness, is always accompanied by a lot of BS, and delusions of teleportation psychokinesis, with the car-through-the-wall trick considered a kind of given.

Before the Ponderosa job, I'd worked at a neighborhood 7-11, one particularly famous for its frequent holdups, by lying about my age, and fudging a few details about the direction of my career path. I worked the armed-robbery shift from 10 pm to 6 am, then off to a groggy day of maybe it was high school, a little physics and calculus to prepare me for the nights, I could have given you the parabolic equations for the effect of gravity on a bullet fired at my head from two or three feet, a very minor effect unless you shot it straight up. During the time that I was there, the hold-up action had shifted to a 7-11 one mile over, so I never really got a chance to point to the sign that said "Cash Register Contains $50, Safe Cannot Be Opened By Store Employee," a sign that apparently had had little or no effect on the drug addicts with guns who had been frequent-shopper customers in the six months prior, but I gained a good deal of experience with cleaning the Slurpee machine and restocking the beer shelves and making change from a $10 bill for a $1.09 six-pack of Bud or Miller High Life. I don't want to make it sound like all we sold was beer and Slurpees, this was back in the days when marijuana was becoming popular, so I also became adept at ringing up junk food, mostly packs of powdered Doughnut Gems and Twinkies and Devil's Food Zingers, and then counting up the piles of change dumped by the handfuls on the cash register counter, and pointing out that the customer would need to put one item back or else come up with an actual quarter or fifty-cent piece to supplement all the pennies and nickels. I worked alone into the wee hours in the supernaturally bright lighting, and became quite well-adjusted to feeling like a space alien, that sense of unreality and disconnection from my individuality that continues to haunt my nights in Holiday Inn Express hotel rooms, there's just no way to escape it, any sense you may have had of possessing some personal uniqueness is immediately dispensed with by the unwrapping of plastic cups. We live in an age of anonymous replication, with one Taco Bell pretty much like the next one, and the illusion we have, of being the proud possessors of an individual identity, is difficult to maintain, there's just not that much authenticity left, though you always have the option of walking in to a Taco Bell, muttering sick demented gibberish, and waving a handgun.

In any case, the bill collection agency was a big step up for me, and I was good at the job, I treated the deadbeats as individuals. Then one day, after maybe my thirtieth phone call of the afternoon, and tenth or twelfth success with my manipulation routine, playing on people's hopes and dreams to elicit the behavior I sought, an approach, as it would turn out, that became the basis for my venture capital career, although we like to call it "persuasion," and think of it as serving the common good, in any case, a call came in, a call for me, from one of my collection accounts, a woman named Sandra. Mr. John, Mr. John, is that you? Thank the Lord, my baby's sick, you got to help me, my baby's sick. Just calm down Sandra, tell me about the problem, we'll see what we can do. My baby, my three-year-old, she real sick, the doctor told me. There's something wrong with her heart, the doctor said to tell you, let me see, I wrote this down, Kawasaki disease, he said to tell you she got an aneurism, he said something about maybe drinking cleaning solvent and doing something to her ventricle, he said to tell you she got rickets from no milk, that's why her legs look kind of bowed and funny, I got to feed her real milk he said, he told me to tell you, he think my baby goin blind, she need to eat more green vegetable and get some sunlight, she got what he call it Bitot spots, she got, I think he said, V-A-D, she got something called e-n-c-e-p-h-a-l-o-p-a-t-h-y, I had him write it down for me, he told me to tell you she need to eat better, stop eating those paint chips, that paint be bad for her, what should we do Mr. John, what should we do, we got to put our heads together. I have, in short, no idea what she's talking about, I'm sixteen years old but I sound like I'm thirty, and she believes in me because I told her to, I told her I'd take care of things, as long as she sent me that monthly check. Now no one can expect me to take the blame for any of this, a sixteen-year-old kid cleaning Slurpee machines and busing dirty tables and driving his Hillman Minx into red brick walls, I was just a kid with a job to do, I mean give me a break, the job needed doing, and we all know the meaning of doing our jobs. Where would the world be if we started abandoning our posts? I mean, you know what I'm talking about, am I right? That said, Sandra, let me tell you something, I'm sorry I told you to trust me, I don't trust myself, so please don't believe in me, first thing you do is feed your sick baby, the world can get by without its $20, first things first, do it right away, as soon as you put the phone down, so you don't forget, let me just tell you, Sandra, I'm sorry about your baby, I'm sorry about everything, right now I'm sorry, first things first, I'm sorry, I'm sorry, we got to feed our children, am I right, Sandra, am I right?

Of course, being the VC-in-training that I was, what I actually said to Sandra was something slightly different. I tell you what I'll do, Sandra, I'll talk to your doctor, but first thing you do, when you put down the phone, is send me that $20, just like you promised.

# 4

*I* finally moved on to a real Venture Capital firm, Avis Partners, in 1992. After years of working in my underwear, selling money by phone and pretending I was a professional, the move came as quite a shock, dressing up in handmade bespoke suits, going daily to my office as though my profession were thoroughly respectable, and attending the weekly Partner meetings, those exercises in organized antipathy and interpersonal animosity that are one of the keys to an understanding of the praxis of the Venture business. I was brought in to run the firm's Information Technology (IT) practice on the strength of a fictional resume that I was naturally proud of, a resume so full of half-truths and quarter-truths and creative prevarications that any twelve-year would have seen right through it, but these weren't any twelve-year-olds, they were seasoned professionals, men with a deep and abiding appreciation for imaginative distortion and creative untruth, particularly when it came to lying to themselves. I had not, for example, to pick a detail at random, had a single full-time job in my entire career, which is not the sort of detail that a well-crafted resume dwells on, particularly when the open position pays millions of dollars in annual compensation. After ten months of interviewing with the Partners themselves, dinners with the spouses, a background check so thorough I might as well have been joining the intelligence community, and yet another round of interviews once I'd finally made the short list, and a whole separate set of interviews with a sister fund in Silicon Valley, it never occurred to anyone, out of maybe thirty rounds of questioning, to probe a little deeper into my rich and varied background, like oh say, by the way, just as a for instance, have you ever actually held down a fulltime job? Of course I have, remember the 7-11? Remember the Ponderosa, at a dollar per hour? What we're looking for here is something a little more recent. Well...let's see now...I've been a fulltime poet for nearly 20 years, works out to around a third-of-a-cent an hour, and I did have one year, in the early '80s, when I pulled down nearly $600, though I'll readily admit that, if you actually hire me, I'll make more than that in the first full hour. We see; let us talk this over; you're resume is impressive; too bad it's not real.

Not that anyone in the venture industry would be there in the first place if it required some sort of commitment to the 40-hour workweek; one well-known VC, asked to comment on the fact that, in the twelve months prior, he'd apparently managed to squeeze in over a hundred rounds of golf, while making a base salary of call it $6 or $7 million, sniffed at the question, wasn't fond of its bouquet, and said something about the golf course being an excellent place to network. One of my own new partners, in fact, one of the firm's two founders, a man of such pure and unalloyed greed that wealth and possessions had long ago lost all meaning, leaving him with a vicious streak, common among the greedy, for whom success means nothing unless those around them fail, this partner, as I was saying, whose greed was so voracious that it was devouring its own entrails, still found time, one beautiful Aspen winter, to put in nearly 70 full days on the slopes. The other founder, a vacation connoisseur, and a man for whom wealth was the bedrock of his vanity, that sense of himself, common among the wealthy, of being a man of true discernment and inexhaustible sagacity, this other partner, as I was saying, whose vanity was so thorough that it had swallowed him whole, could always be found, in the midst of a crisis, missing in action on a sun-drenched private yacht. And my third and final partner, the junior of the three, a delusional apopheniac whose specialty was conspiracy theories, who was constantly finding proof, in meaningless random data, of vile acts of perfidy that he himself had initiated, this final partner, in short, whom I'm hesitant to speak of, as it might tend to confirm his suspicion that it is he of whom I speak, scarcely worked at all, other than on his conspiracy theories, knowing that none of us was truly above suspicion, unless we'd only recently joined his latest plot. So my failure to commit to the 40-hour workweek was not the real problem here, as I went through the interview process; a man who punches a time clock, logging 80-hour weeks, has no place in the venture business, he belongs in some sort of service industry, red-lining our deal docs, or auditing our companies, or maybe washing dishes at a Ponderosa Steakhouse, or working the eerie-lighting shift at a neighborhood 7-11, while being held at gunpoint by Twinkie-eating spacemen. Even the fact that my resume was slightly embellished, an exercise in verisimilitude with a propulsive narrative thrust, would not, in and of itself, have given my interrogators pause; the character I'd invented was obviously ambitious, with a bootstrap mentality, and a quiet sense of confidence, and would, as such, have been expected to embroider, we're talking about a resume here, a creative collaboration between the literal and the imaginary, not some sort of GAO report, with an overly prosaic sense of reality. The nerve-wracking problem that I actually faced, over the course of perhaps 100 hours with these men, including dinner conversations of a more casual nature, designed to reveal any cracks in my façade, boiled down to this: how does one stay in pitch-perfect character, as a quietly confident but supremely competent man, a man whose very body language, and mode of articulation, conveys a sense of character strength, whose success is predetermined, a man not subject to the whimsical laws of chance, combined with a mastery of situational ethics, the sort of man who can get the job done when it comes to dealing with the so-called truth, when what I was, at bottom, the embodiment of failure, a man whose inner life had completely given up on him, threatened at any moment to shatter the whole illusion, by giving voice to one or two more intimate impressions, like Jesus you guys are morons, what a gullible bunch of windbags, get a fucking grip, what the hell is wrong with you people, don't tell me you're actually buying this line of utter bullshit, most of my bill-collection deadbeats were savvier than you three.

I don't mean to pick on these particular individuals; most wealthy VCs share a similar ethos, with an asset-backed ontology, and a money-means-wisdom accrual-based epistemology, and also share the problem, common among the merely moneyed, of never having enough of it to constitute true wealth. Picture it this way:

if your standing in the world is measured in dollars, and your net worth is a VC-like $75 million, you can't even look around the table at a dinner party, where no one is worth less than a quarter billion, without feeling tiny, nearly invisible, so lacking in tangible assets that speech would seem presumptuous; the guy with the quarter billion, who must feel truly wise, looks around the table, sees three billionaires, and knows deep down, given his current liquidity, that he has no chance at all of ever attaining such stature, and he too falls silent, he's been living a lie; the three billionaires, absolute Titans, so stooped under the weight of all their recent account statements that they can barely keep their chins from dipping into their bowls of soup, having recently seen the list of the Forbes 400, know they're several billion short of even breaking the top 100, meaning that, in essence, in terms of true net worth, their existence is negligible, you'd have to use a magnifying glass to even find them on the list. One of the reasons that such men often seem to despise the impoverished is the deep fear they have that, despite their poverty, the poor may be leading meaningful lives, which almost seems cruel, given the foregoing, when despite all their money, they barely feel viable. So how was it possible that men such as these, who would never truly feel happy until the masses were starving, wound up selecting, out of hundreds of candidates, a fulltime poet and Frankfurt School Marxist who had never, in his business career, worked a single 8-hour day? I haven't got the foggiest, though if I had to guess, when my inner life died, it left an enormous gaping hole in what was left of my identity, and it was just this very hole inside me that they hired, as it so nearly resembled the architectonics of their spirits, that they thought of me as one of them, which through an obvious bit of irony, given my presence on their payroll, it turns out almost immediately that's exactly what I am.

So where are we now? We're inside my first Partner meeting, one of those vain sadistic exercises in structured paranoia by which we somehow manage to arrive at decisions within our partnership, as to how to invest the money with which we've been entrusted. Say what? People trusted you with their money? What in heaven's name would possess them to do that? Don't ask me; remember I'm the new guy. We're seated at an enormous, forty-foot-long conference table, occupying maybe the first six feet, and my first impression, as I stare out the glass walls toward Newport Beach, and the Pacific Ocean, off in the hazy distance, is that the vast expanse of utterly empty table surface bears an eerie resemblance to my own interior. We've structured the deal as a Redeemable Preferred, with a 40% slug of cheap Common, with $4 million going in at $2 million pre; assuming the company cashflows on plan, we'll get our Redeemable bait back in 36 months, and own 40% of the company with nothing at risk. If the company sells before the redemption, we'll be holding a standard Participating Preferred, with a 4X liquidation preference, so even a real fire sale, at $20 million, leaves us with just under $18.7 million of the proceeds. Let's see; what am I leaving out here? We set the Protective Provisions at a two-thirds supermajority, and have dragalong rights on the 28% of common held by the Founders, so we can block a sale even if we're holding common, or force a sale under either scenario. Think that pretty much covers it; any questions? I'm sorry; I'm a little lost here; what exactly are we investing in? Nanotube Transistors. Nanotube Transistors? I thought you guys covered the healthcare sector; isn't this more of an IT product? You're missing the point here. Their initial design wins are with the HP division that produces Life Science devices like Mass Spectrometers and Gas Chromatographs. They're also in testing with Teledyne, for example, for the Tekmar HT3 Dynamic Headspace Autosampler, and with Shimadzu for their MALDI TOF AXIMA series. We see a huge future in the use of Mass Spectrometers for protein analysis of the human genome. Yeah, but…No, go ahead, you have some sort of problem here? Don't like the deal structure? What exactly is your problem? This is Mr. Vicious Streak, the deal's sponsor, who cares more about the potential for a head-on confrontation than he does about the potential of the deal itself. Well, I was just thinking. A Mass Spectrometer is like a $200,000 product, and a three-wire transistor is like a $2 part; how many of these things they planning on selling HP? Jesus, what a question; what the fuck's the difference? Sequencing the genome is the opportunity of a lifetime, the entire practice of medicine will be changed forever, and you've got some sort of problem with the price of the part? You have to be fucking kidding me. What the hell is wrong with you? Excellent question; if you're at all interested in poetry, I can try to explain it. What I set out to do was to strip the language bare of poetry's conventional resources, figurative language, metaphor and simile, ornamental elements that produce the "poetic effect," and try to find the nexus between the self and language, that ontological moment where the self both forms and is formed by its language, in order to reposition the self in the discourse, and free it from its entrapment within the discourse of consumerism. This proved, in the end, to be somewhat difficult, particularly given the fact that, other than one guy who called me from a mental facility, no one on Earth seems to have read my published poetry; on top of everything else, the things were hard to write, like a single thirty-line poem might take a hundred pages of drafts, and my immortal final masterpiece, setting man free, was a four-inch stack of blue-lined yellow paper, with maybe, if I'm generous, twelve decent lines, not that any two of them belonged in the same poem. It occurred to me, somewhere along the way, maybe three inches in to my four inch final masterpiece, that I needed to start thinking about getting a real job, which may be how I ended up here, though to tell you the truth, that part's a little fuzzy, possibly due to the fact that I was heavily sedated, and was having some trouble adjusting to my chemo meds.

As my silence mounts up, in the face of Mr. Vicious Streak's full-frontal bullying, I begin to pick up a weird sort of vibe, like Mr. Apopheniac and Mr. Vanity aren't saying anything, they're staring at the tabletop, staying out of bully range, and not only do they not have an opinion on the deal, they wouldn't express it even if they did. This, as I'll soon learn, is the essence of our decision process, particularly when it comes to dealing with Mr. Vicious; once he finally gets up a full head of steam, he's already invested so much ego in the deal that the money itself becomes a minor consideration. I'm also beginning to get a sense, perhaps peculiar to the venture industry, that the enormity of our conference table, with maybe thirty empty chairs, is itself somehow contributing to the deal's inevitability, as the table is so large and out of proportion to our scale, that it can only be an expression of the Partnership's grandiosity, and that if it came down to a vote, the opinionless would abstain, but the vast expanse of conference table would side with Mr. Vicious. If we're not in the business of funding Big Ideas, the sequencing of the genome and the future of human medicine, why do we need nearly thirty empty chairs, we might as well be sitting around a cozy little dinette set. I also have the problem, perhaps peculiar to me, that my own inner life is full of useless vacant surface area, exactly like our conference table, with its empty leather chairs, leaving me to occupy a tiny corner of my interior, while a vast expanse of emptiness prepares to vote against me. There is, however, despite the foregoing, one peculiar feature of the venture capital decision process that needs to be accounted for before we count the votes: when it comes to making investment decisions, the affirmative vote must be conclusively unanimous, an approach so counter to basic human nature, and the rudimentary structures of human ambivalence, particularly among VCs, most of whom can barely cope with ordering off of a breakfast menu, that one begins to suspect that most of our deals can only be attributed to decisions made by the furniture. As Mr. Vanity begins tapping his Meeting Agenda on the conference table, preparing to move on to the next item on the agenda, I mumble something noncommittal like I guess maybe I'm OK with this, which in the parlance of the venture business is the essence of the Yes vote. You're OK with this? You're *OK* with this? What the fuck does that mean? I've been working on this goddamn deal for it must be going on three or four weeks now, and you *guess* you're *OK* with it? Did you actually *read* their business plan, or are you just *guessing* that *maybe* you read it? Where I come from, son, guessing is horseshit, come time to plant the corn, we plant the fucking corn, we don't stand around with our thumbs up our assholes *guessing* we should plant it, we load it all up in the John Deere seed box, and *get it in the goddamn ground.* Vanity and Apopheniac seem mildly amused, knowing that the decision is a foregone conclusion, having already heard this *get it in the ground* speech on numerous occasions, as I'll soon learn, to justify everything from medical devices to motorized surfboards and self-cleaning bathrooms; debating the merits isn't part of our process, there's far too much money that needs to be planted, though from what I've seen of our current portfolio, we could have planted most of it in one big hole. I then make the obvious rookie mistake of getting up from the table without saying anything, not so much to organize my thoughts, or attempt to break the tension, which is more or less bulletproof, as to get a cup of coffee, with a slice of dry toast, which sets Vicious off on another venomous tangent. What the *fuck* are you *thinking* about? Anything *maybe* you'd like to share with the group? You *guess maybe* you might be OK with getting your thumb out of your asshole and getting on with this meeting? Personally, I've got better things to do than sit around all morning watching you eating breakfast. You *guess maybe* you're OK with this. Jesus. Is there anything else you feel like *guessing*? We're in the *venture* business, son, we're not in the business of sitting around *guessing*. You don't know the first damn thing about the future of medicine, is there some particular reason you want to *venture* an *opinion*?

Yes, as a matter of fact there is, there's a reason I want to venture an opinion, if for no other reason than that I'm pretty much dead inside, and while I no longer give a shit what anyone thinks of me, including myself, I might as well act like I think I'm still alive. I don't like the idea of empty chairs getting a vote, as they remind me too much of my own inner life, and while I may well be down to a tiny corner of the table surface, I guess maybe I plan to own it until someone takes it away. I *have* read their Business Plan; it reads like a piece of Magical Realist fiction, maybe the diary of Clara del Valle Trueba, from Isabel Allende's *The House of The Spirits*, with her paranormal psychic powers and preoccupation with three-legged tables and whose only real operational experience was running a small clairvoyance center; their VP of Marketing must have been recruited out of something of Gunter Grass', like maybe *The Tin Drum*, as he seems to be some sort of auditory clairvoyant baby, apparently working remotely from inside an insane asylum, with his mind fixed permanently at the level of a three-year-old, constantly drumming on the same stupid message, which admittedly isn't far from the VP Marketing norm; and I'm pretty sure the CEO, and in fact the whole narrative arc here, was lifted from Garcia Marquez' *100 Years of Solitude*, where the Founder and Senior Patriarch, José Arcadia Buendía, ran the Arcane Mysteries Lab, and reported his findings in medieval Latin, and wound up with his subordinates tying him to a chestnut tree. I sit back down at my corner of the conference table, and the nine square feet of surface area that seems to be all that's left of me, and decide to make a stand with what remains of my identity, like I'm pretty much down to next to nothing already, so I might as well own it, before the morons take it away. Okay, look. If these guys are going to produce nanotubes in

volume, they're going to need to build a carbon structures fabrication plant, which is nowhere to be found in their current capex
spending plan, so they're $5 million short, just to begin with; if they
think they can build a million transistors, as they seem to be claiming for right around Q3, using the Arcane Mysteries Lab at UC
Irvine, they're smoking something funny that we should maybe try
to get a piece of. You'll be $8 million in before the first dime of
revenue, which means that your redemption feature is essentially
worthless; it'll take you twelve years just to get half your bait back.
The second little problem, which you've no doubt analyzed, is that
no one's going to risk a $200K piece of gear on a $2 part with maybe
a 3X improvement in signal-to-noise ratio, and no real testing on
Mean Time to Failure, which means your little part will end up on
a future daughter card, like you'll maybe sell $6 worth of three-wire
transistors for every $200,000 worth of Mass Spectrometers, most
likely some new models they've got scheduled for 2008. If you want
my *opinion*, you'd be better off investing in three-legged tables; by
the time they get any MTF data, you'll be $14 million in out of our
$60 million fund, and the entire human genome will already be se-
quenced. You can put in all the dragalongs you want, you still won't
find anyone to buy a nanotube R&D facility, with maybe $500K
in revenue, and like 2 or 3 customers. You've been spending too
much time talking to engineers; try calling one of the HP product
management guys, ask him if he's planning on putting nanotubes
on the motherboard, or risking his job over a $2 part, check and see
how long he laughs before he hangs up the phone.

Mr. Vicious falls silent; he's willing to reconsider. The other
two partners, who have no idea what I'm talking about, are nodding and smiling, if only to themselves, with what I'll eventually
learn to recognize as smug self-satisfaction. I'll also learn eventually
that Mr. Vicious' silence, which I think of as a reasoned response
to my critique of his deal, is not actually a sign of his adapting to
my perspective, and rethinking one or two of his baseline assumptions; Vicious, in reality, is not reconsidering, he's so radically angry
that he's lost most of his faculties, and is no longer able to either
reason or speak. The deal, in short, has been summarily executed,
and buried in a hole, never again to be spoken of, a hole that will
eventually become a mass grave, as over the next three years, at the

request of his partners, I kill maybe fifteen of Vicious' deals, like load them all up in the John Deere seed box, and when no one is looking, *get them in the goddamn ground*. This idea of making me the designated assassin, and burying Vicious' deals long before they reach the conference table, comes from Apophenia, with the support of Mr. Vanity; Vanity likes the idea of avoiding confrontation, which he considers unseemly, out of keeping with his fantasy that our process is one of consensus building, a minor bit of narcissism that proves to be somewhat ironic, given the fact that his two partners are so sick of his preening that they've already reached agreement that the man has to go, and will come to me as one, maybe three weeks later, trying to build a consensus to remove him from the Partnership; and Apophenia, our conspiracy theorist, has seized on the opportunity to set a plot in motion, a plot so convoluted, and full of meaningless random stimuli, that only the delusional would find patterns in the data, although those who are true believers in pareidoliac phenomena, like finding the face of Jesus on a slice of cinnamon toast, may find it interesting that, five years later, what appears to be my signature, in an eerie ghostly scrawl, can be found at the bottom of a four inch stack of severance documents, as I exit the partnership and disappear without a trace, after five long years spent blocking the conspiracy to remove Mr. Vanity, and bury him in a hole. Vanity himself, our consensus builder, was an obvious supporter of this plan to do away with me, as this was, after all, the essence of consensus building, and with me out of the way, and the vote now unanimous, his own eerie scrawl appears out of nowhere, at the bottom of his own set of severance documents, a satisfying conclusion for believers in the paranormal, those delusional apopheniacs who struggle so with breakfast menus, only to find meaning, and something to order, in pareidoliac dishes of cinnamon-dusted exit agreements.

By the end of my first partner meeting, I'm essentially dry toast, and though I will go on to produce nearly a billion dollars in profits, $200 million of which will be distributed to the Partnership, this only serves to accelerate my eventual downfall, since men such as these can only feel successful if they alone succeed, while those around them fail. If none of this makes sense, don't look at me; remember I'm the new guy; and while this may well be what my publishers were seeking when they asked me to provide some sort of *inside story*, I can't help asking questions like *inside of what*, and what in God's name is *inside of me*? I'll remind you that I'm still sitting at my Parnian Rainforest Power Desk, powering down Dexies with cold cups of coffee, knowing that my working title, *Tales from the Crypt: Memoirs of the World's Only Marxist Venture Capitalist*, won't make much sense, even to me, until I come to write the chapter on Dacha Wireless, a deal that, unfortunately, I'm still in the midst of, involving power amplification systems for cell phone towers, and the bauxite industry in Paramaribo, Suriname, and dogs disappearing from the top of my nightstand, which has to make you wonder what I've gotten myself into, like the dog was in a photograph, just to give you some idea. *Live like you mean it?* You've got to be fucking kidding me, I mean I guess maybe I'm OK with this, at least until I come up with a better idea, but when dogs start disappearing from inside a photograph, it has to make you wonder *what the fuck does that mean?*

Before we move on to the inside stories of some of my successes, and how I ended up here, with my own venture capital firm, and my own enormous conference table, and my April 15 deadline at my Lamborghini desk, let me go back to my beginnings at Avis Partners, and fill in some details that I think I may have skipped.. I told you that I was a fulltime poet, and you no doubt concluded that I don't know what I'm doing, which is probably correct, but maybe not the full story. The truth is I'd been working on computers for years, building real-time operating systems when I was still in high school, learning to program hardcore computing devices in machine language and assemblers from my bipolar-lunatic genius of a mother, running "real" companies, while working part-time, since the age of 25, including doing a turnaround on a maniacally mismanaged $50M software company in the Magical Realist town of Everberg, Belgium. The fact that my whole career was something of an inside joke, levitating through the ranks just for the hell of it, while constructing an inner life out of 20,000 hours of reading nearly everything I could get my hands on, from mathematics to philosophy to poetry itself, which is an awful lot of furniture for such a vacant interior, was a joke all right, and I was the punch line. My own mother, in fact, off on yet another of her cosmic manic binges, where she could see the whole Universe written out in code, and compile it all down to some evil lines of machine language, which landed her in a lockdown facility for maybe the eighteenth time, my mother, as I was saying, whose disease was so maniacal that it could decompile her whole mind, taught me the punch line one vibrant April morning, when I asked her in purity if something was bothering her, and she fired right back, *Your existence bothers me.*

If you want the whole truth, the real inside story, my life is a cosmic joke, and my existence is the punch line.

Knock Knock.
Who's there?
Your existence.
Your-existence who?
Knock Knock.
Who's there?
No one, stop bothering me.
No-one-stop-bothering-me who?
Knock Knock.
Who's there?
Look, how the hell should I know, you're the one who's knocking, if you don't know the goddamn punch line, get off of my fucking porch.

# 5

G abriella, my angel, and I entered the glassed-in customer area of the HSBC bank branch, located in one of the honeydew-colored colonial buildings facing the Plaza de la Paz. Just inside the door, we paused for a moment, or perhaps it would be more accurate to say that Gabriella paused, in search of something stashed in a voluminous handbag, while I had a bout of claustrophobic panic, and froze up completely, unable to take a step. Just moments before, as we'd crossed the Plaza, I'd been free to look around me, whoever I was, admiring the view up the long curving street that led to the Jardín and the Templo de San Diego, the wrought-iron balconies, the display windows of shops, the pale pastel shades of the townhome facades, more than willing to overlook me and allow me to simply look, and now my eyes were locked on a teller-window clerk, time-stamping deposit slips, swiping magstripe cards, counting out currency stacks with no wasted motion. It was immediately clear that my sudden fear of confinement had nothing to do with confinement in space, as the customer area of the bank branch itself was an open and airy high-ceilinged place; it was, however, also apparent that I was about to become enmeshed within the tight narrow confines of established procedure and institutional rigidity and the mechanized processing of a time-stamped routine; the teller-window functionaries, behind their bulletproof anonymity, appeared more than willing to stuff me inside a tiny pine box. The teller I'd been staring at looked up and stared back, fixing an eye on me; I would need to be watched. Mother's maiden name? Father's date of birth? Last four digits of a social security number? Date of last deposit? Name of a favorite pet? We see here that your account has been flagged by our security people. Please follow us; we don't like the looks of this. I felt, I supposed, the way a man might feel when, after several hours of ignoring an odd pain in his chest, he passes at last through the automatic doors of an emergency hospital's antiseptic waiting room, knowing full well that if he continues on this path, and registers as a patient with an "odd pain in his chest," he will soon be confined within a regimented order, trapped within administrative procedures he can't begin to comprehend, and with no hope of leaving without his discharge papers, which don't in fact exist for heteronymic anonyms. What, in other words, was I getting myself into? Who was Gustavo, and what did he know, and how would I get out of whatever I was in? Can you do me one favor, before you call the guards? Remind me who it is I am claiming to be? Just *who* did I think I *was* when I originally came in here?

In any case, I was going to have to face my money problems eventually, and it might as well be now, with a friend by my side, and with pesos in my pocket, in case I had to make a run for it. As I slowly came out of my claustrophobic reverie, with Gabriella continuing her mysterious search, it was apparent that I'd been listening, in background mode, to a tour guide monologue, a sort of odd running commentary on her thoughts parading by, more often than not in a reversed chronology, having something to do with the honeydew bank building, and its place in the history of Guanajuato wealth. I had already reassembled some of this narrative into something resembling a temporal order, one in which cause still preceded effect, and time marched forward without turning back, and a baseball-shaped knot on the top of one's head wasn't a kind of portent, a premonitory sign, that someone was about to hit you over the head with a bat. Apparently the bank branch had been a *finca urbana*, one of those glorious residences of the fabulously wealthy, the Houses of Rul or Valenciana or Perez Galvez, the Guanajuato mine barons who to Gabriella's way of thinking must have discovered that they were fabulously wealthy, and needed to go back, in the 1550s, to dig up the sources of this vast silver wealth: Peregrina, Villalpando, Penafiel, San Nicholas, Sirena, La Garrapata, Rayas-

Mellado, La Cata, Tepeyac, Valenciana, Santa Ana, La Luz, El Cedro, El Cubo, Calderones, and so on, an awful lot of holes to be dug, and silver itself to be reverse engineered, just to prove that your wealth in fact had its sources. Picture poor Juan Rayas, surveying his vast holdings, out riding the fences of his immense hacienda, slowly dismounting from his magnificent stallion, and trading it in on a broken down mule, in order to go back and discover the first silver mine, the origin in fact of dozens and dozens, mines that by the 18th century, with the price of the metal soaring, were shipping over a third of the world's entire silver supply, as a result no doubt of the city's monumental wealth. Then, in 1810, the real troubles started, not just in Mexico but in my narrative reassembly problem, when Generalissimo Hidalgo, leader of an army nearly 100,000 strong, started rampaging through the towns of north central Mexico, robbing, looting, ransacking, pillaging, killing on a whim, shooting prisoners at random, and thus forever becoming known as Father of the Nation, a curious designation for such a violence-prone predator. Somewhere along the way, however, between the time when the General was put to death for his depredations, and the time, some months earlier, when he was demoted to a parish priest, with a tiny congregation and a few impoverished followers, it became clear that the General was in fact Father Hidalgo, the bald-headed Jesuit on my 1,000 note, and that the army he headed was mostly unarmed peasants, who objected to the methods by which the Spanish distributed silver, picking out a handful of the enormously wealthy, and requiring them to go back and discover their wealth's origins. This at least explained what had happened to the fincas: in order for the wealthy to have a place to put their money, the peasants had been forced to seize the homes of the needy mine barons, and turn them into honeydew-melon-colored banks. Fortunately for me, right about here, when emergency heart surgery, and a lengthy hospitalization, seemed preferable to another word of Gabriella's twisted chronology, she suddenly discovered, at the very top of her bag, the cell phone she'd been attempting to exhume from the depths, and she telephoned her uncle to come to my rescue, though given the logic of her narrative of history, it's a wonder she even bothered with placing the call, as she must have been expecting him to phone her that very instant, and apologize profusely for making her wait.

Thirty seconds later, we were ushered past the customer area, which could have been a morgue for all the functionaries seemed to care, and into the private, ornamental recesses of the officers of the institution. Apparently, Gabriella was well known here, as the niece of the senior officer, and she was greeted with waves and copious salutations, as we made our way deep into the inner sanctums, through a labyrinthine maze of walnut-panelled walls. An administrative assistant showed us into a plush antique conference room, offered us coffee or water in return for enduring our nearly two-minute wait, and returned with Señor Hernandez, who greeted his niece with a smile and a laugh and a kiss on both of her angelic cheeks. He turned to me with the same pleased smile, and opened his arms as if to hug me, a gesture so unexpected and obviously inappropriate that I found myself nearly hugging him back.

"Señor Alvaro, you no longer love me?"

"Excuse me, Sir?"

"I see that you have made the acquaintance of my beautiful niece. Esta muy linda, verdad?"

"Oh yes, of course. She's offered to guide me around Guanajuato."

"This is most fortuitous for you, Señor Alvaro, a more beautiful guide there is not, truly. You find you are in need of a deeper understanding of our marvelous city, after all these times, this is wonderful to hear, perhaps you will make Guanajuato your home after all, you will permit me to welcome you with open arms."

He made as if to hug me again, a gesture that threw me into deeper confusion. He was a short, ample-bellied oval of a man, with an enormous drooping mustache and sweat stains on his shirt, and a wide pale forehead covered in perspiration, like a man who's already had two or three of something or other, in anticipation of the coming sweetness of the twilight, and ultimate savor of the cool evening air.

"I'm sorry Sir, do we know each other?"

"Ah, my friend Alvaro, you are as always, como se dice, what a kidder."

"You know my new friend, Alvaro, Tío Gustavo?"

"Si, claro. As a banker knows his client, of all relationships, the most
intimate. How may I be of service, Señor Alvaro, of all my many
customers, most to be honored?"

While this at least solved the problem of the credulity-straining
identity card, this apparent familiarity introduced a new dimension
to my situation, one for which I was not as yet prepared. I had no
idea who this man was, which wasn't unusual, since I had no idea
who anyone was, including me, but he seemed to know me well,
there was a personal association, and he might have some insight
into my own personal history. To him, I was someone, whereas to
me, I could be anyone. What did he think about when he thought
about me?

"Permit me to inquire, Señor Hernandez, how long have I been
banking here?"

"Please, my friend, speak of me as Gustavo, of intimate relationships, those of money matters being the most."

"Yes, of course, Gustavo, but how long has it been since the beginning of our relationship?"

"What, in Guanajuato, is time? One day giving way to the next?
You are speaking of the day of the large green duffel bag, a day I
will treasure, a day that my superiors in Ciudad de México will
long honor as ours, the day you honored me with your trust,
and your large green duffel bag. We must drink a toast to this
day most honorable, you will join me of course, in honor of this
memory, and in honor of your family, may they rest in peace."

He opened the low doors to an immensely well-stocked liquor cabinet in an antique sideboard, extracted a bottle of 1956 Armagnac,
three hand-blown snifter glasses, and holding them together in a
single meaty hand, poured them all half full of the smoky brown
liquid. The fragrance of it drifted around the room as he uncorked
it, like the smell of a distant era whose essence we remember, and
whose details we have long forgotten, in the evaporation of the days.

"You remember that day, of all our days making way for each other, day upon day, when you brought me this lovely bottle, from the year of my birth, and we toasted with a smile and a wink to your large green duffel. I propose a toast to that day, and to most intimate and profitable relationships."

I took the glass, raised it to my lips after the kiss of hand-blown glasses, inhaled deeply from the smoldering liquid, hesitated, hesitated, and pictured myself downing half the snifter in honor of my hosts. The Armagnac would go down my throat with barely a whisper, and then settle deep inside me with a breathless and silent scream. I was half-intoxicated already just from the alcoholic scent of it, and now it would begin its twisted, and highly irregular, journey through the cobblestone alleys of my bloodstream, looking, in my imagination, for the Plaza de la Paz. There would be a long silent moment of reverence for the essence of things, and distant eras of history whose details need not be recalled. Instead, I mimicked drinking the toast, and set the glass aside. Having no idea who I was when sober, it didn't seem quite the time to discover I was a vicious drunk.

"Now what were we saying, my friend Señor Alvaro?"
"The date of my initial deposit. Perhaps we can look this up later. In the meantime, possibly you could update me on the balance in my account."
"Just as I thought, Señor Alvaro, I was preparing for this precisely from the moment of your arrival. Perhaps you would prefer if my niece would be so kind as to wait outside."

Gabriella looked at each of us in turn, as though posing some sort of question, then set her glass down on the table, retreated back through the doorway, and silently shut the door. I thought I saw a look of mutual comprehension pass between her and her uncle, though it might have been a mutual appreciation for the subtleties of the Armagnac. Was there perhaps some bad news to be conveyed, news that had already been shared among the Hernandez family, news regarding the gentleman who had arrived here from Scotland, with no identity whatsoever, and a strange, no doubt foreign, and possibly Portuguese, name? I prepared myself for the worst, though since I knew nothing to begin with, it would have been difficult to calculate if things were going from bad to worse, and I had, in any case, almost 840 pesos, so the worst was a case for which I was temporarily prepared.

"Including the Geneva and Shanghai accounts, held, as you well know, in Swiss francs and Chinese yuan, your account in American dollars holds $19,736,431.80."

I staggered forward slightly, whether from the dollars or the imaginary Armagnac, and placed a hand on the conference table, holding myself steady. I pictured myself downing the remainder of the Armagnac, and setting my empty glass on the table next to my steadying hand. Swiss francs? Chinese yuan? Ten green jiao to the lilac yuan, ten gold fen, called "sin" in Cantonese, to the jiao, a currency kept artificially low in value by The People's Republic of China, to aid them in their relentless quest for world economic dominance, and build on their massive trade surplus and staggering capital reserves. Reinvested in U.S. Treasuries, the yuan, known technically as the renminbi, propped up the U.S. economy, allowing Americans to go on spending like there truly was no tomorrow, buying thousands of times their weight in imported Chinese goods. And the Swiss franc, one of the world's most stable currencies, with the ISO Code CHF, for Confoederatio Helvetica Franc, with Le Corbusier on the yellow 10 franc note, Giacometti on the blue 100, and Jacob Burckhardt, great historian of the Renaissance, on the beautiful lavender 1,000 franc note, it was apparent that whatever else I was, I was a connoisseur of currency. I flashed back to the morning's search for the organizing principles of my being, on the principle of functional cunning, on the trunk labeled Power and Money, crammed full to the lid with knowledge of financial instruments, and their utility in gaining a personal advantage. And now, on top of everything, I possessed a deep knowledge of the aesthetics of banknotes, in their variety of colorful and oneiric manifestations.

"And of course, Señor Alvaro, we have your gold bullion in our vault, the safest vault north of Mexico City, encased in four inches of solid steel, modeled on the vault of the German Federal Reserve."

Of course. I pictured uncle Gustavo adding another inch of smoke to my glass, and me polishing it off without even thinking. Gabriella reappeared in the room; perhaps she had never left it. She had a strange cold gleam in her eye, the color of smoke and bullion; possibly it had always been there. I could hear the imaginary Armagnac-tainted blood pounding inside my eardrums. I was no longer the 1,000 man, I was the man of the twenty millions, in Swiss francs and yuan, and who knew how much more, in bars of gold bullion, safely locked in a bank vault, encased in solid steel. The baseball-shaped knot on the back of my head started pounding, and not in my imagination, as though trying to send me a message in telegraphic Morse code, dots and dashes, dits and dahs, and while I had no idea what it was saying, thinking about it hurt. There were little semaphore lights going off in my eyes, and my heart seemed to have skipped the last six or eight beats, like it was trying to spell out a warning in Baudot or ASCII code. Gustavo and Gabriella said nothing; I must have looked like a man who had just seen a ghost.

"Alvaro, my friend, you are pale as the moonlight. You are finding this insufficient? You are not well pleased with our performance to date?"

"No, no, Gustavo, I have a bit of a headache. Do you perhaps have some aspirin?"

"But of course. It is all this talk of money, for all men a headache. To look upon our money is to gaze too long among the stars for signs of our fate. I will find for you a pill."

He evaporated from the room, though still perspiring heavily, leaving me alone with Gabriella, and her eyes the color of smoke. She stood across from me at some carefully calibrated distance, holding herself at an oblique angle, looking neither at me nor away. She turned as if to say something, thought better of it, stayed silent, and then fished around in her purse as though searching for something tangible. She came up with a lipstick and a compact case, whose mirror she used to apply a little face powder, and a touch-up to her lips, in small precise gestures whose meaning I couldn't guess. Her silence and obliqueness began to strike me as deliberately unnerving; she seemed to be feigning ignorance, although I wasn't sure of what. I thought about her working on her iron-railed balcony, hanging out the laundry on an improvised line, picking out clothes-pins from a blue plastic bucket, holding things in place, item by item, and then gathering the garments precisely in reverse, working her way back toward her work's beginnings. What had seemed to me so appealing, her utter sense of self-absorption, her lack of any self-consciousness, her sense of ease with herself, struck me now as a pose, as though she'd known that I was watching her, and had taken each action for calculated effect. She'd admitted as much, that she'd seen me watching from my window. Had she already known back then whatever she was pretending not to know now? If she worked her way backwards toward *me* in her workings, where was the end of her work's beginnings?

"What are you thinking about, Gabriella? Did you know about the money?"

"I knew there was money, this is all my uncle talks about. I had no idea that the money perhaps was belonging to you."

"So our meeting at the café was completely accidental?"

"I don't know. Who can say what I was thinking? You seemed a little lost, in need perhaps of some guidance."

"So you decided to guide me here, without thinking about the money."

"A wealthy foreigner, here in Guanajuato, my uncle is telling me this. You are sitting alone, looking lost in the café. I thought you were looking lost. Maybe this was in my mind. My own memories work themselves backwards from the present. I am remembering you now only from now."

"And what are you remembering right now?"

"That you are having a headache, and that my uncle will find a pill."

"And then what will happen?"

"You will no longer have a headache, and you will buy me a glass of wine."

"And then buy you something else?"

"I am sorry if my uncle has been upsetting you. Perhaps we will go to the Jardín, and forget about my uncle. We will have some

wine, watch the sunset, take a walk in the cobbled streets. By
the time it is evening, you will have many things to remember, starting with the evening, when the shadows are among
the buildings and the sun high on the hillsides, you will not be
remembering this time of your upsetting. The time of evening
will be now, we will remember it together."
"Last things first. You will teach me to remember backwards."
"And this time now will be the last that you will think of. I will teach
you to remember the ways to forget."

She smiled a memorable smile, and made me remember her way of
forgetting everything, including the everything I'd already forgotten,
like my own identity, which was impossible not to forget. Twenty
million dollars was a lot of money, and who knew how much more,
stacked up in bars of gold bullion, apparently transported here in
a large green duffel bag, likely the same bag that I'd found in my
hotel room, enough money to constitute an entire identity. Does
a man with $20 million, and then some, need to know anything
more? He might be curious to know how he'd come to possess it,
but once a man has $20 million in his possession, what value does
he place on his own curiosity? Does the man who holds the winning lottery ticket question his own identity? He presents himself to
the authorities, whose duty it is to redeem the ticket, tells them he
has no idea who he is, and hands them the ticket. They look at the
ticket, double-check it against the winning numbers, and noting
that it's signed by Alvaro de Campos, they ask him if this is his signature. Yes, it appears to be mine, but I seriously doubt that I am Alvaro de Campos, he is in fact one of Fernando Pessoa's heteronyms,
he isn't a real person, he has no actual identity. We understand your
desire for anonymity; please sign this blank sheet with the name Alvaro de Campos. The signatures are checked, one against the other,
there can be no question that the man before them is the owner of
the ticket, even if he chooses to remain completely anonymous; he
could be Alexander the Great for all they care. It is not their duty to
locate his identity; their duty is to redeem the ticket, and the signatures are identical. But you don't understand, I cannot possibly be
Alvaro de Campos, even he himself had grave doubts about his own
existence, he might have had a passing feeling or two that he had

an identity, but he was in fact an atheist regarding his own feelings, and beyond all that, even if he existed, by now he would be long dead, and therefore long past the point where one has either doubts or certainties, much less winning lottery tickets. Excuse me? Sir, is this your signature? Of course it's my signature, it just isn't me. You clearly don't understand at all how Campos looked at the world, he himself was simply a set of impressions he received from the world around him, among which were impressions of himself, but under no circumstances did he allow himself to believe that these impressions of himself were his identity. He felt things, just like the rest of us; he just didn't necessarily conclude that he was the one who felt them. This whole idea of him winning the lottery is therefore, on the face of it, preposterous. If you like, I'll get you a copy of his poems, you can see for yourself. We understand, Sir, that this has come as something of a shock, you're not the first to feel the shock of being the lottery winner, this reaction of disbelief is entirely natural, we've seen this many times, and while you may be feeling like a long-dead poet, we can assure you that you'll soon get over it. You've no doubt regarded yourself for some time as the sort of man who does not have money, perhaps you have formed a deep connection with just that sort of person, one who has to scrimp and save to get by from day to day; you naturally feel a deep bond with that man, a bond with his identity, no one can really blame you, you've almost come to believe that this is in fact who you are. We can assure you you're mistaken. Just try to relax and forget about who you think you are, the feeling will soon pass, the money will soon take care of all that. You are the lottery winner, and the one who had to scrimp and save will soon be a distant memory. No one expects you to live as a distant memory. We ourselves were once anxious children, but now we are adults, and we think of ourselves as adults; we may recall our childhood anxieties from time to time, but none of us takes these seriously, we may have felt these things at the time, but only in the distant past. I really must protest, this man Alvaro de Campos is someone else, surely you must believe that, even if he didn't in fact believe it himself, he was after all a heteronym, not a real person, I can't say I blame him. Of course, Sir, and we're not blaming you either, you won the lottery fair and square, and we, the administrators, can't be passing judgment on

the winners for doing the winning. There would be no such thing
as a winning lottery ticket if the winner didn't win, no matter what
their actual identity. Some must win the lottery so that those who
do not can continue to believe in the justice of the lottery. You can't
very well expect people to play the lottery if there are no winning
tickets; we'd all be out of jobs. Our job, as the administrators of the
lottery, is to award the money to the winner. Your job, whoever you
are, is to be the winner of the lottery. This is how the system works;
each of us has our duties. I just want to go on record as saying that
I am not Alvaro de Campos. Of course, of course, we understand,
no one ever heard of him anyway. You are The Lottery Winner, not
the long-buried remains of some imaginary poet.

My conversation with the Lottery administrators was interrupted by Gustavo, who reentered the room holding a large talking
bird, a tangerine orange, lime green, and turquoise Macaw, with
delicate black and white feathers around the eyes, like an India-ink
sketch of a hawk in flight. The bird let out a scream, really more
the statement of a scream than an actual expression of feeling, and
began speaking gibberish. For all I knew, the Macaw was speaking
Serbo-Croatian; the syntax was obviously elaborate, but I couldn't
make out a single word. Gustavo fed the bird, perhaps ironically
named Palabra, some cashews, and handed me a pill that looked
like a horse tranquilizer. I pictured myself washing the thing down
with the last of the Armagnac, straight from the bottle, and waiting
in a chair for whatever the thing was to begin to take effect. In other
words, I stuck it in my pocket; reality was already badly estranged
from itself, and did not seem to need any chemical assistance.

"Gustavo, my friend, where did all of this money come from?"
"You are, como se dice, waxing philosophical, is it not so? This is
    the Armagnac speaking. If it were not yours it would be an-
    other's. Some must have money so that others may have dreams
    of money. You would prefer perhaps the dream?"
"No, I mean literally, where did the money come from?"
"It came from a large green duffel bag, with which it was my honor
    to be entrusted."
"And before that?"
"From your hard work, as with all such money. From whatever it

was you were working."

"And what is it that I was working?"

"This is a question we do not ask among men. Your business is your business."

"And what exactly was my business?"

"One supposes it was making money. Without this, there would be no green duffle."

"So you don't know the actual source of this money."

"Who can know the sources of money? The man drinking water from the mountain stream does not ask where the melting snow is coming from, he drinks the water to quench his thirst, and is grateful to the Heavens."

Gabriella left the room for a moment; perhaps she'd forgotten she needed to use the restroom. The Macaw muttered something as she left, and pulled at it its feathers from a turquoise wing, fluttered up for a moment, settled once again on Gustavo's hand, and started up with more elaborate gibberish. All this babbling from the Macaw, on top of all of the silence that seemed to surround my sudden wealth, sent me off on another tangent about the nature of bird talk, African Grey Parrots with 800-word vocabularies, Hill Mynas, Crows, green and yellow Budgerigars, Lyrebirds and Starlings, Rose-ringed Parakeets, Moluccan Cockatoos and Australian Cockatiels, experimental parrots that had apparently mastered the concept of zero; I had no more idea what bird talk meant than I did who I was or where the money had come from. If you show a Grey Parrot three red blocks, he answers three when prompted; if you take the blocks away, one by one, and he says "none" at the end of the sequence, what does this tell us? There seems to be something missing here, there seems to be more to "nothing" than what a bird means by "none." What part of nothing does a bird not understand? This was the sort of question that Wittgenstein would have had a field day with, out in a sunny wheat field full of brightly colored birds, all of them talking Wittgenstein's language, precise, functional, and slightly inhuman. What makes us think that the bird is missing something? In Wittgenstein's world, other than useless poetic concepts, the 2,500-year-old tradition of philosophy's misunderstandings regarding the nature of language, there isn't much more to nothing than what a bird means by "none." I could hear myself now, Alvaro de Campos, whispering "I'm nothing" to myself, the opening line to "The Tobacco Shop," and meaning neither more nor less than what the parrot intended, when prompted by the missing red blocks. Suppose we cover the birdcage, and teach the bird to say "darkness." I was truly in the dark, about the nature of my identity, about the sources of my fortune, stowed in offshore accounts, in colorful Swiss francs and beautiful Chinese yuan, and if the bird started squawking "in the dark, in the dark," maybe that said it all, and there was nothing for me to add. In my case, however, I wasn't sitting in a covered birdcage, the darkness seemed to be there inside me, as though something were truly missing, my identity for example, though maybe this was just a case of making something out of nothing, and twenty million dollars left nothing to be said. I started counting backwards from three red blocks, and finally arrived at what appeared to be left of me, zero, meaning none, meaning absolutely nothing, meaning neither more nor less than not a single one. And then I started counting forward, in bird talk, toward twenty million, give or take, toward some identity, in dollars, that even a bird could understand. "I'm rich," says the bird, "I'm rich." Palabra dismissed the whole exercise with more squawking and muttering, or maybe translating twenty million into Serbo-Croatian.

"Gustavo, as long as I'm here, I need my ATM PIN number. It seems I have forgotten."

"Ah, yes, but no, you have not forgotten, we have spoken about this often."

"Perhaps you could refresh my memory. What was the nature of our discussion?"

"You are not, for the moment, to be using the ATM devices."

"And the reason for this would be…"

"We have been all over this. Transactions on the machines may be traced. You will not be like the man drinking water from the mountain stream, you will be like the man beside the stream wearing a GPS tracking device. Those who may be looking for you will be like the gods looking down from the Heavens, knowing the stream you drink from, knowing the very water you hold, in the hand you shape like a cup."

"Very colorful, Gustavo, you should have been a poet. And why am I afraid that others may be looking for me?"

"Señor Alvaro, we are men here, we have no secrets besides our secrets, and yours will be respected, wherever your secrets are being kept. You who have crossed the border at Ciudad Juárez, with a large green duffel, to me so honorably entrusted, and so reliably transferred offshore, these are things we do not need to speak of among men. As to these others wishing to look down from the Heavens, let us not afford them an unfortunate opportunity. We will not kneel by the stream with our ATM PIN."

With that, he handed me a 1,000 note, with the courageous, balding head of Father Hidalgo, Father of the Nation, and violence-prone predator. Gabriella returned, having managed to remember the location of the conference room, at the end of a short, backwards, or was it upside down, list of her memories. And I, Alvaro de Campos, once again the 1,000 Peso Man, and then some, and then some, with $20 million plus from somewhere or other, now stashed, PIN-less, utterly *elsewhere*, felt like a bird trying to tell the difference between something and nothing, and hearing more than a little gibberish in my lime green head. Around my eyes, if you didn't look too closely at what turned out to be crow's feet, you would have noticed the black feathers of an immaculate drawing, an India-ink sketch of a hawk in flight, emblematic of time, and man's place in the tattooed scheme of things, a hawk flying gracefully away above a streambed, practicing the word for nothing, nothing whatsoever, by gradually disappearing somewhere high above the treeline, leaving the silence, rather pointedly, to speak for itself.

# 6

G abriella and I left the HSBC bank branch, crossed diagonally in front of the greying stone steps and candlelit interior of the Basilica of Our Lady, walked down to Calle
Luis Gonzalez, and turned left toward a glass of wine in the Jardín
de la Union. It was shadowy dusk in the cobbled streets, though
still afternoon high up on the hillsides, and high on the tops of the
domes of the churches, as though time were split in two, one half
still day on the straw-colored hills, and the other already moving
on toward evening. The four-story buildings of the Calle Luis, with
their pastel facades and tall narrow windows, were on the evening
side of time, still glowing as they cooled, turning resinous shades
of honey-smoked amber, not yet ready to call it a day, not yet ready
for the lighting of the lanterns. School children in blue and white
uniforms passed in intimate groups, animated, confident, while
older men who were not so sure smoked slim panatellas in the doorways of their tiendas. A woman up ahead in the long curving street
stepped out on the ledge of her third floor balcony, looked up at the
afternoon blue of the sky, down on the shadows that were gathering in the Calle, and stepped back inside, drawing the curtains.
Gabriella asked me to wait outside, while she stopped for a minute at a One Hour Photo shop, and I stood there in the last of the
honey-tinted twilight, having one of those timeless moments when
it's easy to doubt that we still exist, or have any real reason to have
ever existed. Everything was doing just fine as it was, quietly radiant
and luminous and lovely, nothing seemed to require or in any way

involve me, as though the street itself had already left, and sent me back this beautiful postcard, and while the card wasn't addressed to anyone in particular, it seemed to be trying to tell me "Wish you were here."

Gabriella returned with three envelopes full of photos, and we continued on our way down Missing-Me Street, past a retail arcade full of window displays, and the doors of a lechería closing shop for the evening, past the Templo de San Diego, a confused-looking place, with its ornament-encrusted Churrigueresque façade masking a barefooted Franciscan mendicant simplicity, and finally entered the neighborhood of the Jardín itself, a spacious tranquil garden filled with flowerbeds and fountains, with seating on cast-iron benches along meandering stone walkways, but boxed-in and trapped by an unfortunate mistake, an enormous trapezoidal or perhaps triangular box hedge, made of tightly planted clusters of foot-thick trueno trees, that might have been entitled "Revenge of the Gardeners." First of all, as a hedge, it didn't really work; between the rose-tile floor and the bottom of the hedge was a five-foot-high gap, which meant that people could come and go more or less as they pleased, by stooping over slightly, and however undignified, squeezing between the white-limed bases of the trees. And then once it started in on the actual business of hedging, separating and enclosing and walling off and excluding, it did so with a vengeance, in a soaring forty feet or so of six-foot-thick impenetrability, all of it perfectly squared-off and clipped, as though the hedge had forgotten it was a little late for all that, now that the unwelcome had already gained entrance. Someone had apparently left instructions with the gardeners to surround the garden with a tall, thick hedge, allowing for some means of ingress and egress, and when they'd come back several hundred years later to check on the results, they'd found a garden that was about as welcoming as a vegetable fortress. We crawled in around the painted bases of the trees, took our seats at opposite ends of one the ornate iron benches, and were now, at least visually, enclosed and imprisoned, surrounded by solid walls of inscrutable greenery. I could hear some wealthy hacendado, returning to his enormous ranch after hundreds of missing years, calling over the jefe of his jardineros, asking "Diego, what the hell were you thinking?" But Señor, you asked for a hedge, is this not a hedge to be marveled at? Not a twig out of place, we trim it day after day for the endless decades of your absence, and now it has grown to be tall and thick, it is, is it not, formidable? Yes, yes, Diego, it is truly formidable, but I've been sitting here for twenty minutes, waiting for a glass of wine, where are all the servants? Ah, for that Don Hernando, you must go into the house, the servants they do not much come in here anymore, if the trees grew any thicker, they would never get out. I left Gabriella looking through her photos, slipped back through a gap in the manicured walls, and ordered our refreshments at a nearby café. When I returned, she had assembled a small stack of photos, maybe eight or ten deep, which she apparently thought would bring me some amusement.

The amusing thing, if you could call it that, was that the photos were all of *me*, surrounded by a group of unsmiling companions, men apparently posing with a certain amount of reluctance, at a restaurant or party or celebration of some kind, and not only did I not recall this particular occasion, I had no recollection whatsoever of ever having met even one of these individuals, including the individual apparently posing as *me*. I, Alvaro de Campos, whose existence I didn't doubt, but whose existence, to be honest, was beginning to have doubts about me, obviously enjoyed a good party or celebration now and then, and the photos showed an instance of just such a celebration. I appeared to be seated at the head of the table, smiling broadly at something that the cameraman might have said, with my arms thrown around men who didn't smile in the least. I was wearing a thin white linen shirt, like the one I was wearing now, entirely inappropriate for the evening's occasion, and the men around me were dressed in suits and ties, as though teaching me a lesson in proper decorum. The seriousness of their demeanor bordered on the grim; it made me feel like apologizing for my unseemly behavior. All of the men, maybe five or six in total, were staring straight ahead at the camera lens, with thin tight lips, and unblinking eyes, radiating authority and utter indifference, while I, in each photo, seemed to be clowning around, and laughing at something odd that none of the others found funny. Gabriella, who are these men, they don't seem to find me the least bit amusing. From the look of things, Alvaro, you seem to be inebriated, I think it is safe to say you are muy muy borracho, en un sopor etílico, a drunken stupor, it is altogether possible that you have had too much to drink. It is also possible that you are de pocas luces, one of little light, lerdo, idiota, a man who as you say is slow and dimwitted. I do not recall the nature of the occasion, but permit me to offer, you are not giving the appearance of an understanding of its nature. No kidding; these guys look like they're ready to kill me. Oh, no, my friend Alvaro, of this I would have my doubts, you are lacking understanding but not yet a sense of life, it is some public place, where dimwitted men are free to come and go. But who are these men? When were these photos taken? From the evidence of my eyes, I would say that these are men who knew the gravity of the occasion, and as to when, who can say, sometime previously. Gabriella, really, this habit you have of lacking normal memory is beginning to get on my nerves. But Alvaro, you are being silly, I do not lack my memories, I remember these photos were in an envelope, I selected them for you personally, and before this I recall having stopped at the photo shop and paying the young man there 96 pesos, and before this we made our visit to my uncle Gustavo at the bank, for reasons that for me were not altogether memorable; of other things that were previous to this, I recall them as being previous. I am not to blame if this occasion wasn't memorable. If these men wanted to kill you, it may be you who should recall. Gabriella, please, do you have any idea where these photos came from? They came from the photo shop, and before this, their existence was in a camera, and before this, there were certain instances of a camera's presence at an occasion, and a photo came into existence in each of these instances. Do you not see how a camera works? It captures the instant in which the photo comes to exist. In just this way I remember these photos, each of them has come from just such an instant; I am sure if you look closely, you can see these things for yourself. But who are these men, why do they look like they want to kill me? Ah, with men, who can say, they are all a bunch of dimwits.

Gabriella sipped her wine, thoroughly at ease with her idiosyncratic memory procedures, while the hills turned toward evening, and the streets of Guanajuato, the paseos and avenidas and calles and callejóns and bulevars and caminos and cobbled callejuelas, had turned on their lanterns, if they had them, awaiting the coming of the Guanajuato night. The time of the present moment and the time of the grim-faced photos existed on different planes, floating off in parallel toward two altogether different futures, whereas the hour of the streets and the hour of the hillsides would soon merge together in darkness at nightfall. I picked up each of the photographs in turn, and studied it closely, looking for something, anything at all, which might help illuminate my current situation. In the first of the photos, I am seated directly behind a seven-glass wall of nearly empty wine balloons and cut-crystal whiskey tumblers, and holding, in one hand, a liter of tequila, or perhaps I should say a one-liter tequila bottle, since the contents themselves were one-third liquid, and two-thirds gases from a drunkard's exhalations; several photos deeper in the ten-photo stack was a portrait of *me* drinking straight from the bottle, which offered a likely explanation for the liquid/gas content ratio, and at least three possible sources for my *de pocas luces* grin, but left me a little puzzled as to why this man were still upright, rather than lying comatose in a pool of his own vomit. In the other hand, I am holding up a long-stemmed white bouquet, lilies of some kind, with the trumpet shaped, outward facing, six-inch-wide blossoms of what appeared at first glance to be overblown Easter lilies, with the yellow-orange stamens and yard-long stems that would tend to confirm this initial impression; they also appeared to have been ripped up abruptly straight from the ground out of a carelessly tended garden, as they still have their root systems attached to the stems, basal roots, stem roots, lily bulbs and all, and the lily stems themselves are an unsightly mess, covered from top to bottom with parasite-riddled foliage. The man sitting next to me, closest to the bouquet, is leaning away at perhaps a 30 degree angle, which led me to conclude that I'd been waving the things around, causing the man to assume this uncomfortable position, in hopes of avoiding the root-ball soiling and insect-infestation of a beautifully tailored jacket, apparently unaware that it is a little late for all that, as I've already deposited a dark mound of topsoil, mottled with something pinkish and oblong and larval, on the proximate left shoulder of his handcrafted suit. On first sight, I mean really and truly on first sight, since this was a person, no matter how close the resemblance, that I had never to my knowledge even once laid eyes on, this man would make a thoroughly inconsiderate companion, with an apparently inexhaustible tolerance for alcohol, but he couldn't possibly illuminate my understanding of myself, or the organizing principles of my random body of knowledge. I turned to the possibility that the presence of Easter lilies, caught in the act of being present to just this instant, before vanishing forever into the Garden of Fleeting Moments, a garden from which, apparently, I'd been boxed out and excluded, might, in spite of everything, help establish a date, or a time frame at least for this particular occasion that would give me some sense of this man's temporal bearings. My Easter-blossoms timing-device might well have worked, had the lilies themselves been supplied by a florist, or even stolen from a church before an Easter sunrise service; this yanked-from-the-garden, root-ball-and-all, nature of the lilies portrayed in the photos, did not, however, establish much of anything, since garden-variety Easter lilies, where nature has run its course, and where the Easter-blossoming timeline has not been imposed via lily-bulb case-cooling by a commercial greenhouse lily grower, are prone to throwing shoots up in the middle of whenever, mid-summer perhaps, or the third week in October, leaving me in Guanajuato, sipping a glass of mineral water, and the *me* in this photo in temporal nowhere. Of deeper concern was the next photo down, where I appear to be pointing an improbable-looking weapon directly at the camera lens, though my aim is a little low, and off to one side, as though trying to shoot a highball glass off the cameraman's shoulder, which should have been easy enough from six feet away, if it weren't for the fact that the weapon itself is a matte-black up-and-under sawed-off shotgun. What on earth am I doing with such a weapon? As Gabriella might have answered, I am pointing it somewhere, in just that very instant when this photo came to exist, and not giving the appearance of an understanding of its nature, waving it in one hand as if I think it's a kind of pistol, when it is altogether possible that I have had too much to drink, and am grinning like a dimwit who is just clowning around, while the grim men grow grim and then grimmer and grimmer. And then four photos down I finally got spooked, and gave up my search for bearings altogether: I look like a man who's just returned from a long vacation, with a deep shipwrecked tan, in need of a haircut, still wearing the sort of clothing that would be appropriate to the islands, only in place of the usual Hawaiian lei, made of lime leaves, perhaps, and tuberose and plumeria and star jasmine petals, I am wearing what appears to be a funeral wreath or casket spray, made of carnivorous-looking orchids and evergreen conifer branches. A funeral wreath? At a party? What precisely is the nature of this particular occasion? As the deep-blue sky grew deeper and deeper, as though time were getting ready to move on without me, I held up my photos to the light of the lanterns, and assembled a brief list of the things that might have spooked me: one-third of a bottle of superfluous tequila, like a man adding dimmer switches to a room with no light bulbs; a bouquet of Easter lilies, straight from the ground, that seem to be crying out for immediate re-burial; a matte-black shotgun, extended from one hand, playing William Tell playing William S. Burroughs; and a man, perfectly centered, in the photographer's flashbulb glare, who doesn't, to be honest, look altogether human, with laser-red pupils at the center of his eyeballs, a shotgun-extension like a robotic prosthesis, and carnivorous-looking orchids that may be part of some sort of wreath, but that seem to be feeding directly on the man's own interior, as he sits at a funeral wake that he himself may have occasioned. And the half-baseball knot, beginning to throb, at the back right center of the top of my head? Here's hoping, for everyone's sake, that the blow was self-inflicted. I wish I could say that I suddenly snapped out of it, knowing that what had spooked me, those glowing red eyeballs, was a flashbulb effect, not something intrinsic, but the more closely I looked at this alienated semblance, radiating otherness, luminescing indifference, the more certain I became that these red-laser eyes could see through the photos, and were staring *straight at me*. I took a deep breath of the slowly cooling air, looked up at a hawk in the last rays of daylight, and handed the photos back to Gabriella without comment; it was time to move on, into the Guanajuato evening, while attempting to forget what I'd long ago forgotten.

I slipped out through the hedges, paid our bill at the restaurant, and we walked arm in arm up the Calle Luis toward the Plaza de la Paz, turning right under the lanterns on a street beside the Basilica, and entering the Café Del Truco in search of dinner. What month is this? Was this the time of year when it would be appropriate to be seeking dinner at an hour such as this, when the lanterns have just been lit? Apparently so, the restaurant was crowded with what appeared to be locals, who would know what was appropriate; I didn't see anyone with a camera or a map, or wearing Bermuda shorts or a Red Sox baseball cap, and if English were being spoken, it wasn't being spoken here. The locals were sitting at rustic wooden tables, eating from plates full of *enchiladas mineras* and drinking wine from pitchers or bottles of beer. We took a table in the front room, near the bar facing the street, ordered something or other, and acted, to all appearances, like an old married couple, a thought so odd, under the circumstances, that it must have sent me off on yet another of my flights of fancy, like a man out flying a kite that isn't tethered to much of anything; apparently a man untethered to his past is prone to flights of fancy and imaginary discourse, in the same way that a child, with his limited personal history, conducts experiments on reality, and the nature of the self, using his own private language with imaginary friends; Wittgenstein, needless to say, would not have approved, though perhaps he'd long forgotten the imaginary friend that accompanied him as a child to relieve his sense of solitude. The congruence between us that would have been the source of this impression, of agreement and harmony, along with a certain amount of mutual indifference, was a matter of memory, as with all old couples. Juanita and Ramon, after all these years together, have come to an understanding. The battles they have fought, in the early years together, over Ramon's lack of ambition or Juanita's constant flirtations, have long ago passed, neither can summon the energy that would be required to resume them, or even to recall what it was that was at stake, in their arguments and constant bickering, in their terrible verbal brawls. They both had high hopes for what married love would bring them, and what arrived instead is something that they can live with, as we all learn to live with our disappointed hopes. What they share, in fact, is the same disappointment, it is the common bond between them, they are truly in harmony, and now is not the time, nor can either find the energy, to upset the sense of harmony and disturb the common bond. The memory that they share is the memory of so much forgetting, of what life was supposed to be, of what beauty, of what elegance, of whatever it was that life was to have been and failed to become, and they've forgotten even the reasons they had hopes in the first place. They eat their meal, sip their wine, share an occasional observation, and the young couple in the corner, bristling with so much passion, look at Ramon and Juana as a couple to be envied, grown gracefully as one together, and carefully, harmoniously, painstakingly, old. In time, children, in time. The tone of this last thought must have struck me as slightly windy, because my kite-flight reverie crash-landed in a restaurant; I was, after all, maybe 12 hours old, and the voice of experience didn't strike me as quite appropriate; I ate another bite of my cheese enchilada, made another mental note to keep an eye out for kite twine, and noted that the young couple that I'd been presuming to advise were ignoring me completely and gazing at each other, with a look of pure wonder in their candlelit eyes. Nevermind, children, nevermind. Gabriella and I resembled an old married couple by being precisely the opposite, a couple with little or nothing to remember, and no memory at all of what we needed to forget. I was already getting used to her annoying habits, of remembering only Now and the few things that preceded it, and she didn't seem to mind that I had no identity whatsoever; in her mind I was as present as people ever get. Was there still some possibility of passion between us? I had no more idea of the answer to such a question than I did to the question of beer or wine with my dinner. And in any case, since I had neither, such a question was probably moot, though I certainly didn't intend to start drinking tequila.

For all that Gabriella lacked in terms of the depth of her personal memories, she had an encyclopedic knowledge of the history of the town. It was a history, however, without any timeline; she skipped around from Nuño de Guzman's slaughter of the Chichimecs in the 1540s, to Chupicuaro ceramic figurines, of dogs and bats and hummingbirds, from 400 B.C., to the countless wars of conquest against Americans, Aztecs, French, and Spaniards, to Revolution after Revolution and several more Revolutions that occurred before that and before that, to Father Hidalgo's stoic bravery, giving thanks to his executioners for their humane hospitality, to the Valenciana silver mine, producing, in the 18th century, nearly one-third of the world's entire silver supply, to the inevitable discovery, in the 1550s, of an enormous vein of silver in the Guanajuato hills, permitting the Counts of the Valencianas, when asked to explain the Churrigueresque-mess that they'd made of the simple

façade of the Templo de San Diego, to point toward the hills that
surround Guanajuato, where they'd apparently struck a vein of ornamental statuary; all in all, a history so convoluted and warlike
and nonlinear that I gave up any attempt at putting things in order,
and abandoned all notions of cause and effect. In place of History
as such, as one thing following logically from another, I came away
with some random details that were picturesque and arresting, how
Nahuatl words for "rope" and "dog" had turned into a general term
for the indigenous peoples, the Chichimecs; how the Guachich-
iles got their name from painting their warrior's heads blood red,
and the Zacatecas from painting their own death black; how the
Guamares were so well regarded for their wisdom and bravery and
treacherous astuteness, that they came to be known as "chupadores
de sagre," suckers of blood, now wasn't that astute; and how El Pípila, whose monumental statue I had seen on the opposite hilltop,
had become a local hero by strapping a rock to his back to deflect
a rain of Spanish rifle fire, and setting the Granary ablaze, trapping
the Spaniards, who had mistaken the concept of a place for storing
grain for a concept that, in their minds, resembled a kind of fortress.
In the end, Guanajuato made no more sense to me than I did to
myself, but if you said the word Chichimeca, I would know what to
make of it, a Spanish term of derision for the indigenous peoples of
Mexico, and an image of a dog, or "Chichi," being led on a "me-
catl," a Nahuatl word for rope. Gabriella ate her food by dividing
the plate into quadrants, and eating them counterclockwise while
talking nonstop, each speech a piece of history arrived at randomly,
by hopping around froglike, the whole Quanax-juato history, the
Land of the Hopping Frogs.

When we left the Café, it was utterly night, and the twin streams
of time had been ultimately unified. The city streets were jammed,
teeming with locals who seemed uniformly celebratory, rancheros
in white straw hats and tendoras in their day clothes and young
women in beautiful gowns and dangerous high heels, chaperoned
by their mothers, and musicians in black costumes with silver-
studded pant legs, gathered under the lanterns with accordions and
bass fiddles, singing harmonies genetic to the constellated heavens.
Gabriella, what day is this? It is Friday, Alvaro, and before today
would come Thursday, and tomorrow, who can say, for this will

always be Friday night. We strolled back toward the Jardín, and took a seat on the steps of the Teatro Juárez, named, as I now knew, for Benito Juárez, the first indigenous state governor, whose ancestors had painted their faces matte black, during the never-ending search for peace during wartime, and who, despite their nobility, would be regarded by the Spaniards as just the sort of people you could lead around like dogs, though you might want to keep them at the end of a long rope. The Teatro was ablaze with special lights for the occasion; it was roped off and red-carpeted, with official-looking men, in the swallow-tailed coats of wealth, or the silk-striped tuxedos of local government officials, arriving with beautiful women for a special evening at the Opera. The Teatro itself was another obvious mistake, a Temple to the Greek Gods, pedimented and porticoed and elaborately columned, in a land of barefoot Franciscans and magical hopping frogs. Overlooking the street from our place on the marble steps, we watched the crowds flow and swirl, like a river whose banks were overhung with pushcarts, selling candy and nuts and jugos and fruit cups, where the river would whirlpool, and eddy, and backtrack, and then again resume its flow toward the Friday of the night. This was, admittedly, a two-way river, with one half headed off toward the brightly lit Basilica, and the other headed precisely in the opposite direction, toward a darker part of town I had not as yet visited, but it didn't seem to matter which path you took, because that feeling of a Friday, of relief from our burdens, of something bright and effervescent after the staleness of the workweek, that sense of something glittering and dazzling and brilliant, on a jewel of an evening, an absolute jewel, was everywhere I looked, and nowhere in particular, like the beauty of a face, or the fulfillment of a promise. Next to us on the steps, still wearing the plaid skirts of their Catholic school uniforms, was a group of young women listening to music on a laptop, Olivia Newton-John and the Bee Gees and Queen and Pink Floyd and Billy Joel, while the silver-studded-pant-leg bass-fiddle quartet sang Cielito Lindo, los corazones, accompanied by an accordion with three missing keys, which itself posed a few musical tune-hopping difficulties. If the bird leaves his nest, and returns to find it occupied by another bird from elsewhere, he gets what he deserves, their song made this clear. And me with my lime green head, and frog-hopping histories, and an India-ink sketch of a hawk around my eyes, where was my own nest, and what would I find if I ever returned there, this much wasn't clear, what did I deserve? I had an image of the grim-faced men from Gabriella's photos, arriving at my nest, tearing it twig from twig, and tossing into the river that flowed by on the street.

Gabriella, what is going to happen to me, I don't know who I am, I don't know where I've come from, and I don't know what I've done to disturb the grim-faced men. I didn't say this aloud, the streets were far too noisy, and I didn't, to be honest, quite like the sound of it; it sounded like a man slowly filling with self-pity, bemoaning his fate using the language of the lament, perhaps this was a character that I'd borrowed from a book, the sort of charac-ter who would be invented to employ this sort of language, itself also borrowed from yet another book, by an author who no doubt loved the sound of a good lament. Life swirled by on the Calle Luis, commemorating the evening and the end of the workweek, women freed at last from their mind-numbing cubicles, men unchained from the legs of their desks, ranch hands in work jeans and lizard-skin boots, with bone leather inlays like the sound holes on cellos, even the men of the dubious day's-end panatelas, freshly showered and shaved, regaining their confidence, everyone smiling and out for an evening, an evening in Guanajuato, where this would always be Friday night. The woman of the third-floor balcony ledge, who'd given up on day by drawing her curtains, stepped back outside to observe the celebrations, and stood there for moment, silhouetted in the floodlights, staring off into space, as though remembering something, perhaps remembering the evenings of her own beauti-ful gowns, and dangerous high heels, and chaperoning mother, and made the sign of the cross, counting her blessings. Given all this, this gift of the evening, what possible use did I have for self-pity, and characters in books lamenting their fates, fates that they were chained to and would never escape from, not even for an evening at the end of a long workweek? Even characters in books deserve an evening now and then, to stroll up the Calle Luis Gonzalez, and laugh at the creations they'd somehow been ensnared in, and the mind-numbing narratives they'd been forced to adhere to, as they made their way forward through the inevitable chain of events that would lead to their doom in the pages up ahead, a fate that even now, given the status of their author, long since famous for his dark view of the cosmos, could only be avoided if their author put his pen down, and went for a stroll under the Guanajuato heavens. My fate? What fate? As far as I could tell, I was fated to sit here, on the brightly lit steps leading up to the Teatro, looking up at a woman silhouetted in the floodlights, as she studied the chaos of the celebratory streets, and struck, no doubt, by the utter randomness of existence, made the sign of the cross, and counted her blessings.

Having already decided to author myself for myself, beginning again with a fresh sheet of paper, and proceeding on the basis of the improbable premise that my existence itself was an improbable premise, I had settled on the fundamental narrative principle of living my life without narrative principles, of letting life as I found it be my one and only guide toward a life of better feelings and growth and expansion, in the hope, I suppose, of meeting my doom with an ample supply of improbable blessings. And now I had found an improbable blessing: everywhere I looked, among the tendoras in their day clothes and women in organdy gowns and silver-studded pantleg all-black musicians, among the street-vendor pushcarts with jugos and fruitcups, among the whirlpooling back-tracking eddying throng, I found an ample supply of life as I'd found it, in the beauty of a Friday on the streets of Guanajuato, but I found no trace at all of that alien semblance, that dimwitted *me* with the luminescing eyeballs, either out on the streets or anywhere inside me. What possible use did I have for such a man? He not only looked to be a thoroughly inconsiderate companion, with an apparently inexhaustible tolerance for alcohol, but he would probably infest anyone who got near him. Now was not the time, nor did I have any inclination, to begin filling pages with the language of the lament, borrowed from some author with a dark view of the cosmos, much less view myself, or the self that I'd discover, through the blazing red eyes of some alienated *other*. I looked up again at the balcony ledge, and in honor of everyone who keeps a count of their blessings, I made my own sign of the cross by crossing my heart, the sign of a man both counting and pledging, thanking his lucky stars that those red-laser eyes had nothing to do with this beautiful evening, and pledging himself to stay true to his stars, his own lucky stars in the improbable heavens.

I came out of this heart-crossing blessing-count reverie with Gabriella herself still seated beside me. It was as clear as the nose on
Gabriella's face that the man in the photos couldn't possibly be me.
Why would I be sitting with a bunch of grim-faced friends, wearing
some sort of funeral wreath, and waving a sawed-off shotgun? If you
want my honest opinion, that man looks dead already, I think we
should burn his photos and forget we ever met him. Before we both
forget him, however, let me ask you, Angel: have you ever met him?
What did you say, Alvaro? Nothing, Gabriella, nothing, I was talking to myself, I'm just double-checking that I know to whom I'm
talking. I didn't say this aloud, my thoughts were far too noisy, and
I already knew her answer, having already absorbed, from a full day
of listening, that idiosyncratic, reverse-existential, logic-free logic at
the heart of her ontology. Which of us knows who we are, what is to
be made of ourselves aside from the sequence of our actions? And
you, Alvaro, who don't know the sequence, and thus can't be expected to enter it in backwards, have nothing to worry about, nothing at all, not even an ATM machine would know you from Adam.
This man who was previous, remember him as being previous. If
some men wanted to kill him, it may be he who should recall. Gabriella, were you at the party? Excuse me? Were you at the party
where the photos were taken? Was that your camera? Did you take
the pictures? Were you there at the instant when the photos came
to exist, holding the camera, clicking the shutter button at just that
instant? Honestly, Alvaro, you are asking silly questions. Can you
imagine how many instants have passed between now and then?
How many instants do you expect me to remember? You act like a
man who thinks the birds should sing backwards. Why should the
birds sing backwards? It would spoil the whole song. But you are the
one who likes to remember things in reverse. I'm only asking you to
think back to the beginning, and remember what you were doing
when the camera shutter clicked. Of course, Alvaro, I understand
what you ask, and I can see by your face that my words are distressing you. I am sorry I called you silly, such words are distressing; perhaps your face made me say this, you look a little silly with distress
on your face. You will always be wonderful just as you are, but let's
not spoil our evening together by living it all backwards. This song
of the past is causing you bad feelings, let us find another song, and

we will sing it together, from this point forward, in the manner of the birds, beginning at the beginning where all songs begin, no one has bad feelings once the birds begin their singing, and the time of our distressing in the long night is over, and the morning sun is rising just to hear the birds sing.

I couldn't argue with that, even if I'd wanted to; if I knew nothing at all about the grim night occasion, and the song of bad feelings that must have caused the whole thing, at least I now knew the history of a Friday night in Guanajuato, the way a frog knows a river, by hopping from place to place. We stood up, entered the river, and flowed back toward my hotel room; there wasn't much point, on this particular occasion, in waiting around forever for grim men to sing. We followed a young woman, in a beautiful burgundy gown and high black stilettos, flowing over the cobbles like a leaf over a streambed, apparently unaware of the hard stones beneath her, and the dark-eyed men, waiting for her to stumble, as she floated past the lanterns, her mother by her side. The Calle Luis was brilliantly lit, the Basilica of Our Lady was flooded with lighting, and the path to my home at the Inn of the Poets made a map of itself and pointed the way homeward. We traversed the Plaza de la Paz, found the star-marked center where I'd centered my journey what felt like several years ago, turned up Calle Cantaritos, toward Gabriella's apartment, rediscovering in the process my bird's-nest reminder to keep an eye out for kite twine and anything useful, and climbed the brief cobbled slope to the street of my hotel, a hotel, as I would soon discover, that I'd carelessly misplaced, though I did manage to find it, strangely enough, right back in the place where I'd carelessly misplaced it.

This very day, when I was leaving the hotel, I had been certain that my street was called Calle Positivo, Positive Street; of this, at least, I'd felt certain. I had no idea who I was to begin with, and had doubts about my ability to make a mental map of my journey, but I did, at a minimum, know the street of my hotel, such that if anyone had asked whether I knew where I was going, I could have answered with some conviction, Calle Positivo. Positive Street had made a good place to start; an uncertain journey had at least begun with a positive attitude and certain beginnings. Beneath the bright lanterns at the top of Cantaritos, beside the dark tunnel that bore into the hillside, with the semicircular shape of an upside-down smile, like the grimace of a man infested with insects, and now far too angry to produce human speech, I found a small rectangular tile with the name Calle Pocitos, meaning that the street of my hotel was not Positivo, it was Calle Pocitos, Cups of Coffee Street. Having only that morning abandoned my own biography, and left my own personal narrative to fend for itself, I had departed my hotel as Alvaro de Campos, a man with no identity but with a positive attitude, setting off on an impossibly quixotic journey in search of the identity of an ATM PIN. And now my own street was telling me to wake up and smell the coffee, I was a man with a full bank account and a bunch of grim-faced friends.

We arrived at the doors of the Mesón de los Poetas, I said my goodbyes to my inimitable companion, and I began to repeat, precisely in reverse, the sequence that had led me from the room of my belongings. On a stool at the small reception desk just inside the doors, reading the back of a local newspaper, the *Correo de Guanajuato*, sat a man I didn't recognize, with a nametag that called him Pablo, who greeted me like a long-lost cousin whose cards and letters have gone unanswered. Buenas noches, Señor Alvaro, como esta usted, you have had perhaps a wonderful evening with our good friend Gabriella, the madrina to my wife's nephew's mischievous children; it is good to see you are returning again; after all these times, we were beginning to have our worries. I have a package for you that has been arriving today; perhaps you would do me the honor of signing for this package, and placing today's date beside your signature. Certainly, Pablo, and buenas noches to you as well, but perhaps you could remind me of the date today; it seems I have forgotten. Ah, sin duda, April 17, the same as the date on the front of my *Correo*; it is not so much the date of a day that is important; I think it is the day of a date we should recall, the day of your evening with our friend Gabriella. While I hadn't quite absorbed Pablo's wisdom, I signed and dated Pablo's register, and then tore open the 8-by-11 FedEx envelope, which contained a pile of newspaper clippings from the El Paso Times, reporting on the recent discoveries of a number of mass grave sites, in vacant lots near the assembly plants, in the sand dunes of a mesa, in the backyards of residences in a Ciudad Juárez subdivision. Along with the articles,

which I had only scanned quickly, as their subject was a little gruesome for reading around bedtime, was a handwritten note on unlined paper in an idiosyncratic but legible backward-slanting hand.
The note was unsigned, and left deliberately somewhat cryptic, and
though the message it contained was certainly enigmatic, it was far
from lacking eloquence, it conveyed an entire precept in a single
four-word sentence. "We have not forgotten," was all that it said, a
memorable message if there ever was one, in a backward-slanting
longhand that was flowing and neat and effortless, like a bird flying
backward, reversing the flow of thought.

# 7

*E*xcuse me for a moment while I refill my coffee, and take another couple of Dexies to top off the tank; I never should have agreed to this April 15 deadline, or my ghostwriter's proposal to *fill in the blanks*, as I'm beginning to get the feeling that there's more blank space than substance, as though the substance itself were somehow slowly going blank. I'm sitting in my office, 17 floors up, staring at an award that says *Lifetime Achievement*, so this whole going blank thing must be some sort of lighting problem, like it's so pitch-black out and so bright in my office that I can't see anything but my reflection in the window glass, which makes me look a little like a night-shift mortician, trying to pump embalming fluid into a twenty-year-old corpse, by which I mean not some sort of physical cadaver, but the inner life I buried because it wasn't achieving anything, much less the sort of thing that constitutes a *Lifetime*. This, let me tell you, doesn't seem fair, like I didn't kill it, the thing just died, and here I have this desk screaming *Live Like You Mean It*, and I feel like screaming back at it, *as if*, motherfucker, *as if*, and on top of everything else, it's going on 3:00 am, and tomorrow, unfortunately, is a brand-new day, when I'm going to have to face some unusual problems that have come to my attention regarding Dacha Wireless. This fucking company…no, delete that…Dacha Wireless is something of a long story, involving Other People's Money, some unorthodox accounting, and some guy driving around on the outskirts of Tongatapu, using WiMAX overlays and Software-Defined Radios and 12-by-12 MIMO schemes on his

4G cell phone, when all he's trying to do is watch a little television. Not that this makes any more sense to me than it does to you, but the guy's driving an oxcart, just to give you some idea. So what happens next? I haven't got the foggiest, but I need to get this story down before I can file my taxes, and it feels like I'm shipwrecked in Fantasyland, run aground on Skull Rock in the middle of Never Never, still searching for my copy of *The Annotated Alice*, while trying to figure out the banking laws on the island in *The Tempest*. And as long as we're on the topic of cryptic allusions, remember my inner life? It's a little late now to be attempting to embalm it; I buried it in a box at the end of the *Book of Genesis*.

Of course there wouldn't have been a Dacha Wireless in the first place if I hadn't had the bright idea of starting my own venture fund, call it Blanco Ventures, back in April of '99, on the strength of all the profits I'd piled up at Avis, like close to a billion dollars off of $50 million invested, on top of the hundreds of millions I'd already made for the Technology Ministry, by bullshitting people about Belgium having a government. My track record was so solid and optically transparent that it might as well have been made out of bulletproof glass, like Armormax or Makroclear polycarbonate thermoplastics, the sort of stuff that holds up under a lot of small arms weapons fire from institutional investors, as they examine your prior investments, or let's face it, in this case, I'm way underselling it, the stuff I was made of was way beyond bulletproof, it was a whole new class of transparent armor, with a strike-plate layer made of aluminum oxynitride, like it would have held up under .50 caliber machine gun fire, using armor-piercing shells for the due-diligence scrutiny rounds, I mean I could have taken rocket fire from a ballistics accountant, you would have needed some sort of tactical-nuke artillery shell, like...wait, wait, we thought you said you got booted out of Avis in 1997, and yet you didn't raise Blanco I until April of '99; we're having a few problems with this whole bulletproofing timeline, like why would it take you nearly two full years to raise an $80 million fund with such an armor-plated track record? $80 million barely qualifies as a fund; most of your peer group were raising ten times that; maybe you'd better tell us, just for the record, how much profit you'd banked by '97, like how much of the billion was actually in the bank? Well, to be honest, right around zero. Zero? What do you mean zero? You're five years in, with $50 million invested, and you haven't made your investors a single dime of profit? So how much of the $50 million had you actually returned to them, were they at least getting close to getting their initial investment back? Well, no, not really, they weren't all that close; I'd have to say at this point, in 1997, they were right around $50 million in the hole, not counting management fees of, I don't know, millions, it takes a lot of time and effort to dig that deep a hole. They pay you to dig the hole? That seems peculiar. What if they took a look at how deep the hole was getting, and said something along the lines of That's deep enough, just please stop digging, and send us back whatever you haven't dumped down the hole? That, to be honest, just isn't feasible. There seems to be some confusion here. If you ask us to dig you, say, a $500 million hole, and pay us maybe ten million annually for the privilege, we can pretty much guarantee you'll get a $500 million hole; no one in the venture business would ever stop digging until the hole is completed, and every last nickel is buried in the hole. So you guys are running some sort of cemetery for money; can't imagine there's much of a market for your services, but if our money turns up dead, we'll know who to call. I'm not really sure you're getting the full picture here; first off, we go back, maybe five or ten years later, and try to dig up the money, and sometimes, it's amazing, there's billions more than we buried, and everyone is smiling, and thinking about how smart they are, and sometimes, to be honest, we sort of forget where we buried it, and somewhat mysteriously, the money's all gone. Jesus; that sounds crazy; you guys are like grave robbers, looting your own cemetery; your investors must be morons; what on earth do you do if the graves are all empty? Sometimes we send out an apology letter, but normally we're too busy, digging them another hole. Look, let me be frank. Most of our time is spent digging up corpses, searching through the bone piles in the burial vaults and catacombs for something we can salvage, a half-decent hip-socket, a fully formed femur bone; the work is pretty gruesome, you wouldn't even want to look at most of the stuff we dig up. But let me ask you something: do you believe in miracles? Have you ever been involved in founding a new religion? Can you imagine being present at an actual Resurrection, like a true Easter sunrise, when the Savior has arisen? You have to be joking; what's that have to do with our asset allocation? So you're up on Golgotha, it's probably long past Easter, seeing nothing but fractured jaw bones, and skulls bashed in by two-by-fours, and abandoned skeletons everywhere, after pointless crucifixions, and just as you're getting ready to write the whole thing off, wishing you'd never mentioned the Savior in your last Quarterly, you look up at the sky, in the direction of Mount Olivet, and suddenly there it is, the deal of the millennium, emblazoned across the Heavens at the moment of its Ascension, the Word made flesh, the Creator Spiritus, the Logos of logos, through which all is made divine, and light shines in the darkness, and you know in your heart the ultimate redemption, for the Spirit searcheth all things, yea, the deep things of God, even if the search results are occasionally inscrutable: *Google*. Let's face it, at this point, it's not about the money, the questions you're asking yourself are like Where do I land my jet? and Which should I cure first, cancer or malaria? Not only are you part of the founding of a new religion, but you actually own a piece of it, or you will own a piece, just as soon as the 6-month lock-up comes off. Wow. You were in on that? Not exactly, but I know some guys who know the guys; we're all in the same network; could have easily been us. Wow. How much did you say your minimum was? Normally, $20 million, but for you, since I like you guys, we could probably make it ten.

Not that I had anything quite like Google buried in my own $50 million pit; Google, at its peak, hit a quarter of a trillion dollars in market capitalization, and at the time of this writing, mid-April of 2009, its enterprise value is around $150 billion. I did, however, have several minor miracles that eventually topped out above $10 billion each, as the NASDAQ climbed from 650 when I started, somewhere in the back half of 1992, to above 5,000, like 5,132, not that anyone was counting, before the market bubble imploded, on March 10 of 2000. The particular years between '95 and 2000 were the Golden Age of Venture Capitalism: men lived like gods, without sorrow of heart, remote from toil and grief, made merry with feasting, while not only was there no such thing as the past or the future, but the Cosmos itself, that Spindle of Necessity, spun in reverse, and Man aged backwards; one guy I knew, whose net worth in '95 was right around $2 million, and who was, to be honest, more

of a feaster than a venture capitalist, spent nearly a year, near the
end of the Golden Age, earning $2 million a day via direct deposit;
while you may well be skeptical about the Cosmos reversing, by the
time he was finished making his $700 million haul, his marriage of
thirty years had gone backwards to zero, and he was living in Bel
Air with a twenty-year-old starlet. The five guys who backed eBay,
which started off as an auction site for PEZ dispensers, put in $6.7
million of their investors' money, including $67,000 out of their
very own pockets, and made $2.5 billion as their share of the prof-
its, or nearly 40,000 times their actual investment, which is a pretty
good indicator of how well our model works; the VCs themselves
contribute 1% of the cash, and receive in return at least a 20% "carried interest," meaning the money gets buried 99:1, and dug up
later 80:20, or in the case of Kleiner Perkins, the Walt Disney of the
venture business, 65:35, which only seems fair, since you can't get
into Kleiner without agreeing that this seems fair. Just to give you
some idea how all this feasting pays off, and how remote from grief
were the Kleiner partners, by the end of the Golden Age, when the
mood began to darken, as the great Pan died and the Oracles fell silent, and we headed into the Iron Age of weeping and lamentation,
every senior Kleiner partner could be comforted by the knowledge
that he, at a minimum, was a billionaire, if not a billionaire many
times over. In order to match the wealth accumulated by a VC,
at least the real Titans who rule over Sand Hill, the Magic Kingdom Tomorrowland of the venture industry, you would have had
to have been the tyrant of a mineral-rich African nation, looting
your nation's treasury of every last nickel, or maybe running a hedge
fund or one of our banks, whose Treasury-looting business model
would humble a tyrant. At the height of the Golden Age, before the
bubble imploded, and the looting started up in the mortgage industry, men dwelt in peace and ease upon their lands, rich in flocks,
beyond the reach of their investors, for the fruitful earth bore them
fruit abundantly, as they were blessed by the gods that live inside a
market bubble. The fact that we were all about to get chained to a
rock, with some ominous-looking turkey buzzards chewing on our
livers, was the furthest thing from our minds, living as we were with
Nature and Reason in perfect harmony, with the Earth spinning in
reverse, and all of our clocks running backwards.

So what about me, how am I doing? To tell you the truth, I wish I could skip directly from mid-'97, when I parted company with Avis, to late '99, my *annus mirabilis*, when I cashed out of everything, and finally banked that billion in profits I promised. If there's one thing I've learned from this whole *inside story*, and how to *fill in the blanks* with a shitpile of money, it's never to hire a ghostwriter that's inside your own head, and thinks of you as a Missing Person disguised as a man of substance. I mean I know that whole poetry character vanished without a trace, wandering off into the silence, never again to be heard from, but the self that both forms and is formed by its language, intertwining its inner being with the world that surrounds it, and thereby becoming, beyond the discourse that owns us, the being who thus has spoken, in the act of *being present*, has no real place in the venture business, like why even bother having a self to begin with, when a billion dollar profit sort of speaks for itself? You think you get extra credit for actually *being present*? You think your inner being matters to anyone? Try having a meltdown in front of your investors, see if they think you have *any* intrinsic value; you are either an instrument for the creation of wealth, with a face value attributable to the minting authorities, or your investors, frankly, will skin you alive, since your melt value in manganese and copper and zinc amounts to less than a dollar, while your fourteen to eighteen square feet of skin is worth about $3.50, or nearly 80% of your intrinsic value. So what's my point? This ghostwriter has to go; first he tells me to lose this whole poetry character, whose worth netted out to like a third of a cent an hour, and now he seems to be trying to hold me accountable for the fact that he's vanished; I mean, what am I missing here? Why should a man who returns a 20X on his investors' money have to answer to anyone, much less himself? Who the hell cares what's *inside of you* when your investors are cashing checks in $100 million increments? If you'll just let me skip to the autumn of '99, when I at long last became the Billion Dollar Man, I'll be happy to answer any remaining questions regarding the stuff that I am made of, beyond manganese and skin.

Unfortunately, at this point, in mid-'97, my investors aren't actually cashing my checks, they're listening to the music of my Empty Promise Variations, my melodically ornamented Quarterly Reports, full of everything from sarabandes to quodlibets and can-

ons, plausibly concocted as if to convey information, as to the progress of my companies in the fund's portfolio, but in reality designed
to keep my investors sedated, since *progress* is one of those things
that most of these companies don't do. The Quarterly Report, like
the resume discussed previously, is a poorly understood art form in
the venture business. An individual fund, let's say Blanco Ventures
III, the fund that's invested in Dacha Wireless, is made up of let's
say $250 million in commitments from pension funds and Univer-
sity endowments; the fund in turn invests in 20 to 30 companies
that make up the "portfolio" of that particular fund, and our investors seem to think, for whatever reason, that it would help them
to know how their companies are "progressing." Since the normal
progression of two-thirds of our companies is from high hopes to
mild concern to bitter recriminations, we bury the grim details of
the financial results in the back of the report, where hopefully no
one can find them, and put right up front, where no one could miss
them, the melodious narratives, artfully contrived, of each of our
companies that remains among the living, though a company, in
reality, could be right at death's door, on the brink of insolvency,
preparing to sell the plumbing fixtures, and all you would hear from
us is a vague but soothing melody, as the music must play on until
the money at last runs out, and the creditors shoot the orchestra
for stealing the sinks and toilets. If your company, for example, has
begun with the premise of building ATM NIC cards for desktop
computers, and several years later, it's building ATM SARS for DSL
routers, your investors will hear this as a simple theme-and-varia-
tion, a normal melodic variant, coherently composed. If one of your
investors, most likely some rookie who still does his homework, and
thinks it's his job to understand what you're up to, doesn't like the
sound of this, and asks a stupid question, like "Are you saying that
the company has had to do a total restart?", and then follows this
up with an even more stupid question, like "Aren't both of these
products addressing nonexistent markets?", then you'll have to dig
deeper into your musical repertoire, and come up with something
that's a little more ornamental, something that makes it sound like
they've invested with the *maestros*, men of deep insight into motivic
development, those recurring motifs and melodic ideas that create
the illusion, vital to the process, that the progress of technology

is any way coherent. Simply take a moment, in the midst of your executive summary, to explain, in plain English, without all the acronyms, why the future of humanity depends on your new product, since the 53-byte cells of Asynchronous Transfer Mode require link layer controllers at the network nodes, to do the Segmentation and Reassembly of variable length packets from the Internet Protocol over Ethernet frames, and your investors will not only feel that they've gained a deeper understanding, the way a man feels he "understands" the Goldberg Variations, but even your rookie will stop asking questions, since he knows, deep down that, despite all his reading, he doesn't know the difference between a quodlibet and a sarabande, and is beginning to get the feeling that he's in over his head, particularly given the fact that the sarabande in question, Variation 26 of the Goldberg Variations, is a two part toccata, with one part in 3/4, but with the remainder in a deeply confusing 18/16 time signature. I know what you're thinking: I spent seven years at Intel, working on the Itanium's VLIW, learning modulo scheduling on overlapped loop bodies, and pipelining techniques for the reduction of tail code; I have a Stanford double E, a Wharton MBA, and know more about PowerPoint than any man living; and now you're trying to tell me, on top of predicate registers, and hidden 65th bits to support data speculation, I should have been listening to Bach in my spare fucking time? Yes, that's exactly what I'm telling you; your investors know nothing about overlapped loop bodies, in fact they don't know the difference between a byte and a bit, so you'd better start playing them something that sounds melodious, or they're going to start worrying about why you're hiding bits, and building some sort of pipeline while your company's code base is vanishing, and doing data speculation, which is a whole separate asset class, like are you really a VC, or have you totally lost focus, and are now running some sort of quantitative hedge fund?

So wait, wait, we're getting a little lost here. We appreciate your insights into how you produce your Quarterly Reports, it will save us the trouble of ever bothering to read them, but we're trying to understand this two-year gap in your employment history, which doesn't seem consistent with *Lifetime Achievement* plaques, and Parnian Power Desks, and *living like you mean it*. Can we return to the topic of how far you'd progressed by the time you left Avis in 1997? You're five years in, you have zero liquidity, and you appear to be trying to sedate your investors with two-part toccatas on link layer controllers, which strikes as more than a little cavalier given the $50 million hole you'd put them in. How were your actual companies doing? Not well. Not well? Not well. You sure we need to go through all this? Why don't we just skip to the autumn of '99, when I banked the billion, and everyone was smiling, and the investments themselves were converted into their legal tender equivalents, which I'll readily admit, at this point, have no intrinsic value, aside from the fact that fiat currencies purport to be, what's the word, self-explanatory. This could be something of a slippery slope. Do you not understand the true nature of money? Do you think a guy holding a 9-figure check really cares about 5-byte routing headers? If a windfall of cash drops out of the trees, are you really asking questions about hybrid-echo on playback buffers? If I offered you the option of your share of the billion, or a detailed explanation of queuing delays and data jitter, which of the two do you suppose you'd choose? We understand your perspective, and you can rest assured that we know all about money; we hope you understand that, from our perspective, the billion dollar profit could have been some sort of fluke. A fluke? Yes, a fluke, an accident, a matter of, shall we say, *just plain luck*. Of course it was *luck*; how else would you explain it? We were hoping for something a little more replicable, something to do with your investment methodology, and the procedures you follow for selecting your investments. My investment methodology? Certainly; there must be a process by which you analyze the market size, determine who the competitors are, gain a detailed understanding of their relative strengths and weaknesses, ensure that your potential investment has sufficient differentiation; we'd have to assume that the Business Plan must be carefully examined, that you'll need to be sure that their 5-year projections are truly realistic, that the executives understand their capital requirements and their time to profitability and their run-rate required to reach positive cash flow and their actual net margins once they've finally reached scale, such that you then have a basis for placing a value on the business, using some sort of discounted cash flow analysis; and then of course there's the technology itself, this will need to be reviewed for architectural soundness, measured against certain benchmarking criteria to prove that its performance meets or exceeds expectations, supplemented, naturally, by reference checks with the initial customers, regarding their real-world experience with utilizing the product, the quality of documentation, customer support, difficulties encountered in actual deployment; by the time you've finished checking all of the executives' personal references, you must have built up quite a sizable file, along with a written summary of the investment thesis, the deal's pros and cons, the risk-adjusted alpha, the downside protection on low-value exits, discounted cash-flows through which your pricing has been derived, a list of the company's potential acquirers, exit values on comparable companies that have already been acquired, the market capitalization, with P/E ratios, of all known competitors that are publicly traded, an estimate of cash-on-cash investment returns, and capital multiples, and the ROR on an annualized basis; perhaps it would be useful for us, to gain a deeper understanding of your approach to the business, to examine one of your deal files, perhaps one of those $10 billion monsters you mentioned. Do you understand what we're asking for here, in terms of getting a look at your actual methodology? Oh sure; I get it; though to be perfectly honest, I don't actually have one, a methodology that is; sounds like a lot of work. Did I mention to you guys that I'm actually a poet? Or at least I used to be a poet, until suddenly I wasn't. Talk about flukes; you should try writing poetry. One day you're staring at a blank sheet of paper, thinking about your unpaid water bill, the next thing you know, you have a whole fucking poem, with no idea at all where the damn thing came from. You think there's any sort of *methodology* involved? Do you suppose I'm doing reference checks on blank sheets of paper? Try to take a guess what sort of Rate of Return you get on 30 lines you spent 80 pages drafting. Of course, of course, we completely understand, we know that you have something of an unusual background, but can we at least take a look at your investment files? I don't see why not; there's nothing in them.

To give you some idea how my *method* actually works, and how I go about thoroughly analyzing my investments, my $10 billion monsters, none of which, by the way, you could possibly have heard of, all started out on a blank sheet of paper, with the simple idea to come up with an idea, the sort of plan that's so pure it couldn't possibly go wrong, like how can you fault a plan if you don't even have one, and two entrepreneurs at the meta-planning stage who are fundamentally committed to staying open for business. So how do you place a value on a meta-business? A business whose plan is to come up with a plan? A company whose focus on its target market is nearly maniacal, like totally zeroed-in, meaning that they don't, as yet, have many distractions, since it's hard to take your mind off of a thought you don't have? What they do in fact have is a weird gleam in their eyes, the sort of gleam I'd learned to recognize from my lunatic mother, herself one of the founders of a monster back in the '60s, eventually sold to Xerox for a billion real dollars, back in the days when NASDAQ was at right around zero, when NASDAQ itself was a meta-market, suitable only for imaginary companies, and this gleam in their eyes is worth around $2 million, or $2 million "pre" as it's known in our parlance. If you take this $2 million gleam in their eyes, and add, say, $3 million of actual money, you end up, in our jargon, at $5 million "post," meaning the investors own 60% of the lunacy, and will likely require heavy dosing with Thorazine, and whole classes of meta-meds as yet to be invented, to shield us from the knowledge that we're totally psychotic, and are likely to remain this way for the next three to seven years. Market sizing, competitive analysis, double-checking the technology, talking to customers? Frankly, why bother? If the market already exists, it's too late now; some guys with a business plan already own it. Five Year Plan? You have to be fucking kidding me; my guys barely know where they'll be in five weeks. Humor me for a moment; pretend we're in the autumn of 1999, and it's apparent to everyone that I know what I'm doing, which admittedly isn't possible, since my fundamental precept is to proceed without knowing, and then call me, for example, a *Real VC*, which if you look at my files, isn't all that credible, it's like saying that Don Quixote was a *Real Knight-Errant*, who knew exactly what he was doing when he invented the word *quixotic*. So. What *Real VCs*, entrepreneurs, and lunatics have in common, aside from the fact that they all require medication, is the radical intent, or at least meta-intention, to commit themselves totally to an absolute fiction, and attempt, over time, to make this fiction factual, through what I personally like to think of as "the poet's incursions on reality"; if you think that my background in software engineering, building real-time operating systems for computing devices, had anything to do with my becoming a *Real VC*, you're missing the whole point here about the nature of startups; the real strength of startups is blank sheets of paper, along with a tolerance for heavy doses of unreality, starting out with nothing but radical intent, getting the first line down and making sure that it's adequate, before adding the next line, and then the line after that, and conducting the whole dialogue, the Hegelian dialectic, between that which *isn't* as yet much of anything, and that which *is*, like some pre-existing reality, and bringing into being the inevitable surprise, which somehow, out of nowhere, you can take to the bank, for a third of a cent an hour if it turns out you're a poet, and for hundreds of millions if it turns out you're not. If it turns out you're Don Quixote, the quintessential VC, this process is already second nature; you may be a lunatic, heavily invested in windmills and solar, with no sense of reality whatsoever, but when the last drop of oil has been drained from the earth, we'll still see the Don, silhouetted on a hilltop, moving off toward his next incursion on the real.

So, let's see now, where were we? By mid-'97, after five years of listening to my Empty Promise Variations, my investors were a little tired of my whole song and dance routine, and beginning to wonder, and I can't say I blame them, how they ended up in a $50 million pit, with a man playing the harpsichord beside a smoldering pile of money. I am not, to be honest, a *Real VC*, I'm a *Long-Dead Poet* with a very short obituary. My existence at this point is so optically opaque that it might as well have been constructed in neo-Hegelian, following Hegel's obiter dictum that *a man's Being is his Act* to its logical conclusion that I haven't amounted to anything, or let's face it, at this point, I'm way overselling it, I'm out in Hegel's pasture, where all cows are black, and not only is it dark out, but someone stole the cattle, and while Sartre may be right, that *existence precedes essence*, and that a man's real meaning is determined by his actions, you won't need to dig too deep to see what I am made of, unless you're having trouble making sense of my financial statements, like what do you suppose is *inside of you* when everything you stand for has a minus sign in front of it, and I can't help thinking that Heidegger's seen my deals, because *being-unto-death* is right where they're headed, with an *angst-is-the-only-authentic-*

*sensibility* overall assessment of *the being who thus invested,* which I'll readily admit I stole from Lacan, but when you're $50 million down, you'll steal from almost anyone, and now I've got Kierkegaard, which is like the last thing I need, trying to tell me how *life can only be understood backwards,* I mean what part of *zero* does he not understand, or maybe he's expecting me, like right on the spot, to draw him some sort of picture of a *negative ontology,* like…OK, OK, we get the point; you're something of a loser, but then what did you expect? You maybe should have considered doing some work in the first place.

So where are we really? We're in 1997, in venture capital oblivion, three floors up above the San Vicente sidewalk, in my one-man office in Brentwood, California, which is functioning perfectly, but probably overstaffed. Avis has been kind enough to leave me with a desk, a black lacquer monstrosity from the age of Louis Quinze, with cabriole legs and ormolu hardware and false drawers on the reverse, where my inner being has been stashed, and whose motto isn't so much "Après Moi, le Deluge" as something along the lines of *This Is Not a Desk.* I still have my Board seats, and attendant duties, and some stories to tell that we'll eventually get around to, but at this point, let's face it, I'm the minus $50 million man, and very few people would even want to talk to me, much less invest in the Amazing Minus Man, meaning that I am not, in short, much of a force to be reckoned with, since nothing on earth is as dead as a venture capitalist without a single nickel of capital to invest. So what's my problem? Without much to do, and too much time to do it in, my 20,000 hours spent reading philosophy, building an inner life for my so-called poetry, have come back to haunt me, with something of a vengeance, and I don't, to be honest, have a clue who I am, as I seem to be some sort of Heideggerian-Existentialist Neo-Hegelian, which makes about as much sense as my *This Is Not a Desk* having a full set of keys for its imaginary pigeonholes. You want to know something funny? The keys actually work: you turn the key, the lock clicks open, but whatever you try to do, the drawers won't budge, which has to be paradigmatic of something or other, but whatever it is, the drawers still won't budge.

There is only so long you can live like this, with a full set of keys to drawers that won't open, a $50 million hole in the center of your being, and something trying to tell you *This Is Not a Desk*, before you take action, just as Hegel would suggest, to fill in that hole with some sort of substance. In my case it was vodka, but it could have been pills, or charity work, or twenty-year-old starlets. I go down to the sidewalk, on my way to the Vicente market, to pick up another quart of 100 Proof Smirnoff, and who do I see but Wendell the Poet, a post-traumatic stress disorder Vietnam vet, living under a freeway bridge somewhere in Compton, and while Wendell himself is something of a mess, mildly schizophrenic and occasionally incoherent, he writes poetry for a living, like $1 a page, in rhyming tetrameter bouncy-bounce quatrains, and I love him like a brother, he's like exactly who he is, and he's maybe the last man on earth who thinks I'm still worth talking to. JB, my man, how you been hittin' 'em, I got some new stuff for you, let me just see here, did I give you a copy of "Stop and Smell the Roses"? I don't know, Wendell, let me have a look. Or how 'bout "Sweet Lorraine" or "Night Train to Nowhere" or where is that new one, let me just see, must be in here somewhere, "My Morning Bowl of Cherries," or here, take this, "The Screaming Meemies," and this one here, "How the Stars Keep Count." Wendell has a briefcase full of hundreds of poems, he writes them by flashlight in his cardboard Compton study, and no matter what the titles say, Cherries or Screaming Meemies, every last poem is an expression of gratitude, since Wendell, no matter what, is grateful to be alive, clean and sober like 15 years, a little short of breath at times, from some misguided Napalm, but every breath as deep as Wendell can make it. JB, my man, you don't smell so good, what I tell you about that, that shit'll kill you, you need another meeting, straighten you out? What Wendell's referring to is a 12-step meeting he took me to one time, down on Skid Row. Let me just see, must be in here somewhere: "No Running in the Trudging Lane." My name is Robert, I'm an alcoholic and an addict, Good morning Robert, I want to tell you all how grateful I'm am to be here today, it's a wonder I'm still alive. I lost my wife and family to drugs, I lost my house and my business, I sold my car and my watch, I stole cash and jewelry from my neighbors, I borrowed money from my mother, then started cashing her social security checks, I pawned her stereo and her wedding ring, I pried the thing off her finger while she was sleeping, she didn't want to let me in the house, so I crawled in through the doggy door, I panhandled when everything else had been sold off, I stole bottles of Boone's Farm from the neighborhood liquor store, back in the days when I still had a neighborhood, I live in a cardboard box right now, it's just around the corner. I've been clean almost three weeks so far, this is my eighth time trying to get sober, but I'm serious this time, I think I've finally hit bottom after fourteen years of using, but you know? It's hard sometimes, it's really really hard. Sometimes I just can't seem to control my mind, I'll be trying as hard as I can to surrender to my Higher Power, and my thoughts just won't hold still, I think about how good it would feel to have just one more hit off the crack pipe, how much easier my life would be, I get a little lonely at night, and I remember how just having a dime bag of scag in my pocket used to keep me company, maybe a few bluebirds or some fiorinal or butisol, things would be so much easier some nights if I had a pocketful of 714s or a little ro-shay or some cat valium, it gets so cold and lonely in the dark sometimes that I just know I'd feel better huffing a can of room deodorizer or some cleaning solvent or transmission lubricant, maybe sniff a little of that typewriter correction fluid, have you ever tried that? God, I'd give anything for a little Ruff-up, you know, some Rope or R-2, just get roached for a while, forget all my memories. I remember how my little girl used to look up at me when I was high, and her mother was screaming at me to get out of the house, What's wrong, Daddy, don't you feel good? and I just can't stand the memories, anything would be better than remembering how much my little girl loved me, how she used to look up at me with those wide blue eyes with all the love in the world, all the love in the Universe, I was her Daddy, she used to put her hand on my arm and say Just lie down, Daddy, I'll make it better, I'll make it stop hurting, you just lie down, wherever it hurts, I'll kiss it and make it better, I love you, Daddy, please don't go, just lie down on the couch here, show me where it hurts.

# 8

The gunmen arrived at the motel just before dawn, driving a heavily customized Dodge Ram pickup whose false-bottomed flatbed held several hundred pounds of high-grade product. That the morning star had arisen, and that the first few flashes of a deeply refracted long-wavelength red light had begun to reflect rosily off the low clouds along the horizon, was irrelevant to them, it was beneath their professional dignity to take notice; in their experience, the sort of amateur they were dealing with would not be an early riser. They were still slightly irritated that Gomez had sent them out here in the first place, it was twenty miles out of their way, and they had business to conduct with professionals. Any one of a number of low-level mozo's could have handled this sort of mop-up work; the level of challenge it presented was unworthy of their talents, and they sat in the truck for a moment or two puzzling over the message this sent. It was true that there had been a slight miscalculation at their last exchange; there had been a good deal of glare coming off of the gravel roadbed, and what turned out to be a silver cigarette case, drawn from the inside breast pocket of the jacket of a three-piece suit, had appeared to them both to be a chrome-plated mini-revolver, causing a few inadvertent shots to be fired. They had been told to expect two men at the site, and the presence of a third, in inappropriate apparel, had caused them some distinct unease, which might have accounted for their nonproportional response. This had all been explained to Gomez by now; surely he understood the nature of their decision-making process. That the man had expired instantly from the first of the TEC-9 rounds, absorbed by the middle of his forehead, had not been apparent in the cataract glare; they'd explained all this, it had not seemed irrelevant at the time to fire off a few long bursts into the redundantly lifeless corpse. Gomez had simply shaken his head, looked down at his desk, muttered "brevity is the soul of wit; this business is not well-ended," leaving them to wonder if it was the killing itself, or the needless expenditure of FMJ ammunition rounds, that had led to this cryptic rebuke. They had already reasoned with Gomez on multiple occasions about replacing the evil-looking TEC-9 autos with something that could shoot straight, without constantly jamming and going off cockeyed, maybe the Cobray M11/9 or Glock 18, but Gomez seemed to prefer the intimidation factor of the TEC-9's association with lunatics and mass murderers. How were they to know, under the ambient circumstances, that they'd actually hit something in particular? What was the guy doing out there in the first place, particularly dressed in a 3-piece suit? Given the facts on the ground, who could really blame them, if the result involved a certain amount of overkill? Pleonastic, Gomez called it, whatever the fuck that meant; they'd had to go home and look it up in the dictionary.

They sat in the warmth of the truck cab, still absorbing Gomez' message, both of them blaming the TEC-9s for their apparently tarnished reputations. There was something inherently contradictory in combining the appearance of lunacy with the wit of brevity; there was, to their considerable knowledge, no such gun. And now, as a result, they had been sent on an assignment that was distinctly below their skill level, and evidently left to calibrate the duration and severity of this diminishment in their well-established stature. They looked up at the unlighted window of Room 219, three doors down from the visible internal stairway, and at the unlighted windows on either side, both of them knowing implicitly that decoding Gomez' message was not a question of vanity; if there had been some sort of permanent regauging of their assessed capabilities, it was a practical matter to be dealt with practically. A permanent loss of stature, to the point of outright expendability, could have broad ramifications; neither of them, under the circumstances, could afford another cryptic rebuke. As such, the combination of the pistol-grip Mossberg 12-gauge, loaded with triple-decker lead-ball shells, and the thin minimalist walls of the hot-pillow motel rooms, was cause for a certain amount of concern. Ideally, the adjoining rooms would be empty, and the occupant of 219 recumbent, in order to avoid collateral damage and minimize any possibility of a recurrence of the superfluous. They sipped their doughnut shop coffee, wondering about the wisdom of the rifled and choked 12-gauge, with the triple-decker load insisted upon by Gomez, for reasons the gunmen could not begin to fathom, knowing that any misstep, given the de minimus scatter-pattern of the unfathomable ammo, could lead to an enormous and poorly vectored hole into the adjoining motel room, leaving them with unintended consequences to explain, and perhaps another trip to the cryptic-rebuke dictionary. A closer look at the grey pooling of light, now massing on the horizon, or even a simple study of the vehicles parked in the motel lot, a collection of battered pickups and heavily damaged sedans with exposed urethane undercoats, would have revealed a separate problem, one of a temporal nature whose consequences they had not as yet anticipated. They exited the gleaming black Dodge Ram Magnum, latching the doors without boasting about it, climbed the stairs to the external second floor walkway, with the Mossberg tucked under a nondescript trenchcoat, jimmied the flimsy lock on the door, and entered the room, room 219, pistol-grip shotgun first. The room was not only empty, it appeared not to have been slept in; it was in fact an open question whether or not the room had even been occupied. The bedspread was smooth, the sheets still tucked in hospital corners, the disposable cups in a tray on the bathroom counter were still shrink-wrapped in their plastic, and most disturbing of all was the toilet seat, with its paper-strip rebus of sanitization. They exited the room, had a look through the gaps in the adjoining room curtains; both were unmistakably vacant. Reentering 219, they could find nothing even vaguely recrement, a stray pillow hair or fluff from a sock or dirt tracked in from the external environment. As they were ready to leave, one of them paused to take a leak in the sanitized toilet, and found that the fixture wouldn't flush, the water in fact backed up in the bowl to the point of overflowing, and an uncoiled coat hanger divulged the cause of the clog, a baggage claim ticket labeled ELP, the airport code for El Paso, from a Delta flight, #1128, with baggage checked through from Los Angeles.

They made their way to the motel lobby, and spoke to the clerk at the desk, a young man with a moderate speech impediment who had started his shift at 5 am. What time did 219 check out? Not s-sure, never s-s-saw him. Auto make and model, color? N-not s-s-sure, never s-s-s-saw it. Check the registration card. A b-b-blue Chevy Cobalt, with Texas tags, DMZ 911. Very precise, our early riser, or more likely precisely deceptive. Not many men would recognize a Chevy Cobalt even if they looked straight at one, and the odds of a man being so precise, in the context of perhaps feeling hunted, were minimal at best, and the information adduced, to a man like Gomez, was likely to be heavily discounted. In place of their previous exorbitance, in the TEC-9 discharge incident, they were faced with a serious dearth, and some highly minimalistic adductions. This left them with the baggage claim ticket to work with, and an empty feeling in the pit of their stomachs. It was now 7:40, an awkward hour, and one that would need to be darkly redacted, in the event of a debriefing with Gomez. What was the name he was registered under? The non-adducible name of Jonathan Q. Bullprick. Credit card receipt? M-must have p-p-p-paid c-cash. More and more dearth. The coffee shop across the street, what time does it open? It's open all n-n-n-n-night, followed by a long and unimpeded sigh as the calibrated men swung through the office doors to the praise-the-Lord otherness of the sidewalk. They crossed the street in a brake-screeching slant to the all-night diner and another dearthful exchange with a woman who had been on duty since give or take midnight. No Sir, I'd a seen him if he come in, had two drunk whores and a hobo stealing crackers, then the breakfast folks since 6 or 6:30, mostly I know 'em by heart. Your guy have a name? Back on the street, glancing urgently north and south at the featureless strip-malled indeterminacy of the environment, they got a grip on the LAX-ELP baggage claim ticket, thank God for the singularity of that, and goddamn the pleonastic superfluous redundancies of those motherfucking Intratec TEC-9 full-autos.

They still had hours to kill before disposing of their cargo, and the wisdom of greeting Gomez at this time of day, with very little to tell him and a deficient vocabulary, was briefly debated, with the affirmative case coming out more or less decisively ahead, on the basis of an *argumentum ad hominem*, and an effective, if fallacious, *argument from adverse consequences*. The negative case, based as it was on a popular fallacy, *post hoc ergo proptor hoc*, that their having slept in late had caused them to miss their target, would likely be taken up by Gomez himself, and would need to be rebutted by fudging the chronologies. They roared out under full power from the V10 Magnum, gleaming with darkness and loaded down with product, and not without noting the unfortunate angle of the full morning sun, it was nearly 8:30, what the fuck had they been thinking? They found Gomez alone in his office on the 17th floor, and discovered a few flaws in the argument they'd prepared, flaws not likely to be overlooked by the judges, of whom Gomez at his desk was the sole representative. You missed him? How the fuck could you miss him? What time did you get there? I don't know, Sir, it was well before sunup. Exactly how well before sunup would you say it was then, Gentlemen? Not really sure, it was dark out, I didn't check the clock. So what time did he leave? The desk clerk said sometime around must have been 4:40. So would you say you just missed him? That's right, Sir, we must have just barely missed him. So let me see if I've got this straight. It's 9:20 now, you just barely missed him, and he's been gone almost a full five hours. What the fuck have you been doing in the meantime? Well, we did a little investigating of the immediate area, tried to see if we could pick up the track. And? Not much to report, Sir, we seem to have lost him. You seem to have lost him. You seem to have lost him. Perhaps we should try going back through this again, beginning at the beginning, at whatever time of day you'd care to designate as the beginning. The beginning, Mr. Gomez? That's right, the beginning, the precise time of day when your little adventure was initiated. What would be the reading on the alarm on your clock? I don't know, Sir, somewhere before sunup. The sun wasn't even up by the time we got there. Perhaps you fail to understand the nature of temporal coordinates. Your alarm clock time is not set at a place somewhere, and your arrival time at the site is not best determined by longitude and latitude. I will grant you that longitude itself can be calculated by comparing the time at Greenwich, England, with local solar noon by using a particular instrument that is known as a chronometer. It is, however, the original reading of the chronometer itself that interests me. What the fuck time did you two pendejos get up?

They had, in the end, been forced to concede the point, that they had badly overslept, and that, given that the time of sunup was 6:37, they had arrived nearly must have been two hours late, and botched the entire assignment. Gomez called in one of his numerous functionaries, handed him the luggage tag, asked him to track down the passenger name, and see if he could find the source of the automobile rental. The gunmen sat mute in their chairs, hoping to be dismissed from any additional interrogatives, and any further recourse to the cryptic rebuke. As Gomez studied a series of what appeared to be financial reports, official-looking things full of upside-down numbers, occasionally applying a calculator that he kept close at hand to double-underlined numbers that seemed to be of particular interest, the silence began to feed on itself, growing larger and still larger the longer they sat. Adding to their discomfort was the fact that Gomez kept a large collection of clocks, rotated through his office from his hacienda in the country, on a timetable known only to him and some minion, banjo clocks and scroll clocks; Westminster mantel and pillar clocks; bronze doré, porcelain, boulle, and marquetry clocks; Vienna and German and Dutch regulators with their deadbeat escapements; marine chronometers salvaged from long-sunken ships; and unfortunately for the gunmen on this particular occasion, two clocks that seemed to particularly weigh on them, as they watched them and waited and waited out their wait. One was a seven-foot tall Grandfather clock, designed by Joseph Knibb at his Suffolk Street workshop in the 17th century, that was nicknamed a "coffin clock" and not without reason. The other, on a bookcase behind Gomez' desk, was a clock that did nothing to hide the workings of its movement; the gears, wheels, springs, and mysterious sprockets, were all on display as if to deliberately taunt them, and that this type of timepiece is appropriately known as a "skeleton clock" would not have given them any comfort. They were mesmerized by the outward display of the inner workings of the thing, the strange synchronicity of purely mechanical movement with the actual time of the sunlit day, the skeletal dance of wheels and cogs and time in itself somehow darkly coincident. On the top of the elaborate marquetry and marble of its case, there were two gold birds that stood facing each other: one headed forward in the direction of all time, and the other pointing backwards, as though hoping, like the gunmen, to go back and start over, beginning once again from an earlier hour in the darkly recriminant day. The two birds were gazing at the exact same moment, the moment called *now*, from the opposite directions, with one peering through it toward a golden-hued future, and one gazing backwards, with the vacant look of nostalgia. And the fact was that the birds were not going anywhere; they were locked in the present moment's own timeless coordinates, staring blankly like cadavers that met an untimely end. The gunmen, in other words, were feeling highly expendable; so soon the time arrives when there is nothing left to wait for, and coffins and chronometers and skeleton clocks start sounding the true alarm for superfluous men.

Gomez looked up from his stack of red herrings, those official-looking announcements of impending IPOs, as his man came in bearing a short slip of paper, with fresh data on the early-riser the men needed another crack at. He's traveling under his own name; flight 1128 arrived an hour and forty late, at 9:03 pm via Salt Lake City; he picked up a Hertz rental, a grey Ford Fusion, license SXS 537, at 9:21; if he crossed over here, he must have done it on foot, our guy on the border says there's no sign of a Fusion going into Juárez yet, he may just be stalling. Gomez took the slip, handed it to the gunmen, and said "The time is out of joint; you two ojetes better take care of this immediately, or you'll wind up like Hamlet, wishing you weren't born." Fucking Gomez and his Shakespeare. "And I'll remind you, gentlemen, that it's the package we're after. Even if he's carrying it in 500-euro notes, that luggage has to weigh a good hundred pounds. He's not going to cross on foot without a luggage cart or a pack mule; I'd suggest you two locate that rental car pronto, and bring me my money, and a few pounds of his flesh." The Mossberg alone would account for the flesh weight, though they'd have to pick it off of a sidewalk with tweezers; it might just be better to take a hacksaw to his arm. How they were supposed to find a single Ford Fusion in the great city of El Paso was a weightier question, a question they thought it best not to pose. Gomez dismissed them by ignoring them completely, turning back to the functionary with a question about the Hong Kong Stock Exchange, followed by detailed instructions regarding unloading some stock. "The lockup comes off on 02565 tomorrow morning. I want it divided up into million-share blocks among our traders on the ground there. Tell them to dribble it out five or ten thousand shares at a time. I don't care if it takes three months to unwind this; tell them to dump it all but take their fucking time. We're going to hold onto the ADRs until we see some volume-buying to trade in to. If we start to see weakness, tell them to sit tight. And tell our in-house guys to stay out of the stock; remind them we're insiders here, and I don't need any short-swing problems." This all made about as much sense to the gunmen as the deadbeat escapement on a Vienna regulator, and by the time they'd made it out into the 17th floor hallway, they felt about as useful as a pair of TEC-9s at the Fort Bliss rifle range. It was time to do some damage to the fuckhead in the Fusion, with the Mossberg and a hacksaw and maybe tweeze out his brains.

But first they had a little business to attend to, involving co-caine and crystal meth and armed men with money. They roared up the exit to the underground parking booth, snapping off the exit guard of the Scranton SB-25 ArmBarrier, just at the base of the arm shaft, it's half-sinusoidal acceleration action proving a beat or two slow to match the heavily customized rhythm of the Magnum, an otherwise-ordinary Dodge Ram truck that looked like a pickup, and drove like a Lamborghini, and then careened off up Stanton Street and down the entrance ramp onto Interstate 10, in the general di-rection of Las Cruces and Mesquite, toward their meet to the east of Vado. The sky above White Sands missile range was a spiderweb of contrails from several batteries of THAAD launchers, with rockets firing everywhere, and hitting nothing in particular; the Hera target missile was gliding gracefully across the sky maybe eighty miles up, in the direction of the Organ or San Andres Mountains, apparently untroubled by the reputation of the THAAD defense system, the word "Terminal" in its acronym somewhat overstating the case. A strong wind out of the south was blowing up vast clouds of gypsum dust, playing havoc with the effectiveness of the X-band radar and sensor interface guidance systems, and the next-generation Scud-busters were proving terminal only to themselves. With a decent amount of data in the onboard computer, and a twenty kiloton warhead like the one used on Hiroshima, the Tochka SS-21 that the Hera might be emulating could have taken out Las Cruces, or

Jerusalem, if the wind were right. Boys and their toys, boys and their fucking toys. If you knew where to look in White Sands, even in the mysterious Trinity sector, site of the first A-bomb test, you'd find an impossible collection of flora and fauna living out there in the vast gypsum wasteland, Silky-pocket mice and Bleached Earless lizards and White-throated wood rats and Red-spotted toads, and claret cups and chollas and yucca plants growing up out of nothing, like how in the hell does a Barred Tiger Salamander survive in a place that's like a giant sandtrap? The men roared on toward the meet off Vado Road, they'd only know a fauna from a flora if it bit them, though they were enjoying the rocket-missing-the-target practice and contrail display, it reminded them of trying to hit a single green Heineken bottle with their cockeyed-firing but evil-looking Intratec sidearms; what the Army might want to consider, in terms of their proof-of-accuracy test, was starting all over on a bright clear morning, and placing the target about five feet away.

As they veered off of the hardtop on to a rutted track in the middle of nowhere, one of their deeply encrypted cell phones rang, and presented the men with a temporal dilemma. Gomez told me you were looking for a guy trying to cross the border in a grey Ford Fusion, license SXS 537; he's sitting parked on Stanton Street, fifty feet from where I'm standing. Can you keep him there? We have a business meeting. I'm a customs official, not a babysitter, and in any case, I'm on the wrong side of the fence for that, and it's not my mode of interdiction. Jesus, now what the fuck do we do. At a minimum, the exchange of drugs for money would involve a lot of time and waving of weapons. If the fuckhead crossed into Ciudad Juárez, and they had to chase him down with a Dodge Ram Falsebed full of dubious substances, they'd have more problems than they could count; they'd have to offload the drugs ASAP, or face a lot of good hard questions from customs officials, or yet another reversion to the cryptic rebuke. Can you keep an eye on him while we take care of business? Sure, sure, no problem. At the end of a long mile of bumping and rocking, they came to a barbed-wire fence, and a gate that needed opening, and went on over a rise headed into a deep depression, at the bottom of which four guys in grey coveralls stood next to a plumber's van, Ron's Root and Drain. They pulled the Ram Magnum off at an angle in the dry desert scrub, mesquite, acacia, saltbush, and rabbit brush, and ended up parked on a cock-eyed incline. The meeting got off to a good clean start, with the buyers jabbering away in rapid Cyrillic, Russians or Georgians or Ukrainians, apparently, and apparently without a word of God-given English. Our men asked them politely to shut the fuck up, which transliterates into Cyrillic letter for letter, and started taking apart the flatbed truck, working on the body bolts with metric hex wrenches. The Russians, or Montenegrins, or Bulgarians, or what-ever, were waving around oh shit not-this-again Micro Uzis, appar-ently intent on speeding up the process, a use for which the Uzi is an excellent selection: not only does it fire at 1,200 rounds per minute, but its grip-mounted 50-shot sheet-metal magazine gives it a highly distinctive and memorable profile, while the telescoping overhung bolt, wrapping as it does around the breech end of the barrel, makes for a nice clean compact well-balanced weapon, ideal for clearing bunkers in a timely fashion; the only real drawback, out here in the open desert, was that the Uzi has the exact same open-bolt blowback-operated who-gives-a-shit design that made the TEC-9s prone to firing parabellum rounds almost anywhere in the world but where they were intended. This wasn't a good time, at 4,800 rounds per minute, to get into a serious disagreement with their clients, but the plumbers seemed more than a little impatient, and somewhat nescient in their understanding of the nature of the auto bolts holding the false flatbed in place above the product. As they continued to offer gibberish in their incomprehensible al-phabet, one of the gunmen held up an arm counseling forbear-ance, and worked away feverishly at freeing the magic bolts. One of the bolts, conveniently enough, was unnaturally threaded and refusing to budge, an opportunity for our men to demonstrate their improvisational skills, by taking a hammer and chisel to the bolt head and breaking the fucker off, while the Macedonians showed their patience, and an understanding of due process, by firing a twenty-round burst of hollow-point Uzi-ness off into the middle of the nowhere desert, toward the cane-like branches of an Ocotillo cactus, filling the dry desert air with 9.53-gram projectiles, and the subtle smell of nitrates from smokeless propellants, and flying brass cartridge-cases, in a pinkish-shade of taupe, now emptied of their Hydra-Shok jacketed contents. If the gunmen knew a little less about 9-gram projectiles, and a little more about almost anything else whatsoever, this might have been the time to think things over, maybe consider reconsidering their whole line of work.

And then, as so often happens, in the course of this sort of unmediated interchange, something else went wrong, and one of our gunmen had had enough. The men had parked the Dodge on the slope of the hill headed into the depression, maybe 50 yards off from the restless Dagestanis, far enough away not to worry too much, unless it turned into an all-out firefight, but as the Albanian moron firing the Uzi in the air turned back around from the empty desert, he neglected to set the safety, so conveniently located on the pistol grip itself, and the twenty-first shot in a twenty-shot burst went off of its own volition toward nowhere in particular, and into the left rear radial tire of their shiny black Magnum V-10 pickup. As the tire began to whistle and ooze, and settle toward the roadbed, Raymond, one of the gunmen, Raymond Carlisle Edmunds III, we think we can call him Ray by now, we are all, so to speak, in this together, picked up the 12-gauge Mossberg shotgun from behind the seats where he'd left it in the just-missed-him morning, and started walking slowly toward the crazy Chechen plumbers. Ray had grown up near Alamogordo, he'd lived all his life around weapons and weapon systems, and horses when his dad was still working and could afford them, and he didn't much care for sloppiness with guns, or for changing truck tires on a cockeyed incline. He paced off fifty yards or so, with the Chechens looking baffled, came to a halt maybe five feet away, looked the four of them over slowly and evenly, all four at once, and none in particular, and then leveled his cognate weapon at the sloppiness itself. It had been a long morning: empty motel rooms with backed-up toilets; skeleton clocks impugning his promptness; some dickwad headed into Ciudad Juárez, in a grey Ford Fusion full of a muleload of currency, currency that, for all he knew, belonged to his employer; and now these four Cyrillic types, putting a 9mm slug in his left rear sidewall; Ray for short had had enough; one way or the other, the sloppiness would cease. Now Ray, or Raymond, or Trip as they called him, didn't stand a chance against all these Uzis, but he had the slight advantages, difficult to calculate, of a sense of moral clarity, an apparent indifference to his own mortality, and the complete and utter bewilderment of the miscreant Serbians. Stop it, he said. He reached in the pocket of his Scully plaid shirt, pulled out his cigarettes and an ancient steel Zippo, shook one free from the Pall Mall pack, and lit the thing, eventually, after five or six cracks with his thumb on the flint wheel, with the Mossberg held level by its matte-black pistol grip, leveled at everything, and nothing in particular. The wildly inaccurate rocket trails were still drifting away in the thin blue air, and Raymond himself had time to kill, he was drifting a little further off of dead-level center. Indifference is a weapon in and of itself, particularly when it's backed by an absolute 12-gauge, and everyone in fact just stopped it, and waited in silence while the hex bolts were worked. When his partner signaled that the drugs were loose, Ray motioned for a look at the dusty brown briefcase, doubled-checked that they weren't getting paid in Uzbek cyms or Latvian lats or Kazakh tenges, at .00827 to the dollar, and then he and his partner took the money up a ways, sat on a hill, and waited for a while, as the plumbers loaded up on high-grade contraband.

It had been a long morning, and it was bound to get longer, but it was nice to have a smoke and rest for a while, under the blue Texas sky, out in the White Sands contrailed desert.

# 9

Raymond and Eugene, the gunmen of record, headed back into town in their Dodge Ram pickup, having replaced their Uzi-flattened left rear tire, and re-bolted the false panel, now one hammered-and-chiseled body-bolt short, into place near the bottom of their virtually drug-free flatbed. Gene was working the encrypted phones, trying to get a fix on their grey Fusion target, while Ray drove the 10 and let his mind go adrift, wondering how the hell he ever got into any of this. Something about the whole Cyrillic exchange had left him a bolt or two short himself, and he wasn't feeling all that bolted down to begin with, at least not to Gomez and his increasingly cockeyed schemes; Ray's loyalty was to his sense of the next indicated action, like if a thing needed doing, go and get that thing done, not that thinking things over, and getting crosswise with Gomez, would make for good examples of the indicated act. Ray wasn't much one to pause and reflect; ever since he was twelve, and his folks had died, he'd moved from one thing to the next, from house to house to house in foster care, and then into the Army when he was finally emancipated, into the Blackjack Brigade out of Fort Hood, Texas, and then on to Iraq and Operation Knight Strike and the Highway of Death and other stuff he didn't much think about; whatever it was that was next, that was the thing he did next. He'd seen a lot of men die in the first Gulf War, most of them Iraqis, but Jesus that was years ago, he wasn't exactly lying awake at night, worrying about the health of a bunch of dead belligerents. He hadn't come back as some war-torn type;

he'd spent a few bad hours, up against a battery of Iraqi AT-12s, dug into the side of the Wadi Al Batin, the Blackjacks having been assigned to carry out Schwarzkopf's Desert Storm feinting action, crossing the Iraqi border along the empty Wadi sands from Saudi Arabia in the south, before the main attack began farther north and to the west of them, in a huge and effective Joe Frazier left hook, not that Frazier, come to think of it, would have made too big a deal out of knocking out some half-starved carpet-bombed flyweight. If Ray had to guess, he'd come out of the Army the same way he went in, with nothing much to do, no marketable job skills, and knowing more about weapons, and fighting with his hands, than was absolutely essential for survival in the workplace; two months on the loading docks at the El Paso Convention Center had taught him all he needed to know about dying of utter boredom. His entry into the drug trade had been, in retrospect, moronic, ripping off drug dealers while they were out of the house, playing golf with Ray's partner, a genuine moron. One day he'd found himself in some big shot's rec room, dressed up like a ninja, on a bright sunny day, with an AK-47, a Marine Raider Bowie Knife, and a sports bag crammed full of MAK-90 banana clips, when the guy waltzed in with his golf clubs and kids; Ray'd taken the guy's cash out a window above the toilet, and sworn off rip-offs and dealing with morons. The moron had wound up half dead in a ditch, and Ray had joined Gomez, who was not a moron, and that's about all there was to it. If the next thing was indicated, Ray pretty much took care of it; when Gomez said "Get this done," getting it done was what was indicated, and the next indicated action would be to get that thing done.

So what's my fucking problem? Ray swerved out and around some traffic that had backed up from the exit on to the 85, and continued south and then east on the 10, along the Southern Pacific Railroad lines. "He's traveling under his own name," followed by a short slip of paper with no name on it, preceded as it was by a shotgun-first entry, in the first light of morning, into the vacant motel room of Jonathan Q. Bullprick; his problem was all in a name, and its deliberate withholding. Gene came up for air, put the cell phone down on the seat beside him, and let Ray know that the no-name guy was still sitting in his car, parked on South Stanton, not fifty feet from the southbound bridge, a minute or two away from Ciu-

dad Juárez, and grey-Ford-Fusion untimely disappearance. Why
was the guy just sitting there? And who the hell was he, that his
name required withholding? There was something here that didn't
seem indicated, and while he wasn't in the habit of asking too many
questions, the questions seemed to be posing themselves, as though
the guy with no name were posing for them, by sitting in his car
with the crossing right there, with Ray bearing down in his Dodge
Ram Magnum. Ray took the downtown exit onto North Mesa, and
headed south toward East San Antonio, where he'd make the right
turn on South Stanton in a couple of blocks, and be there at the
bridge before even he knew it. A bolt or two short, that's what he
was feeling, the indicated action not feeling quite indicated. He
could hear Gomez' voice if he called asking questions, with clock
chimes and bells going off in the background, and Gomez shouting trading instructions, around a hand held over the mouthpiece,
and then returning to Ray, Could you please repeat that? Who is
this guy, and why am I supposed to kill him? That dog didn't hunt,
which would normally be one of those pre-fab bits of ballast that
kept Ray's thoughts from getting away from him, but that in this
case had nearly the opposite effect, setting him, if anything, even
further adrift, to the predawn mornings he'd spent with his father,
out hunting birds in the New Mexico desert, scaled quail and bobwhites, mourning doves and white wings, sandhill cranes when the
season was right, and blue grouse that had wandered down out of
the Sangre de Cristo Mountains. Out there in the scrub with a shotgun and a dog, and his father for once not drinking twelve-packs
in the yard, watching the morning star come up and then the first
rays of daylight, it was the only time he'd ever felt a bond with the
man, as though the world had suddenly righted itself, and he and
his father could stand and walk upright. Nature never did betray
the heart that loved her, some line from a poem that his father must
have trusted, and just being a part of the nature his father loved
made the boy feel a sense of belonging somewhere, out there in the
desert, in the mesquite and saltbush, where nature could be trusted,
and never would betray them. And then a drunken skid on an icy
patch of roadway, and off Dad went into altogether elsewhere, without so much as a morning star, or a poem to protect him, or a sense
of belonging to anything ever. Though knowing his dad, he was

probably sitting around in Elsewhere's yard, smoking an unfiltered Pall Mall, and drinking a Pabst Blue Ribbon, and smiling at something odd that struck him as funny; he wasn't a man who sweated the small stuff, and from where he was sitting, drinking and grinning, all of the stuff was small.

Ray came out of his drift crossing Paisano Street on Stanton, with the cell phones ringing and the Fusion in the toll line and the sudden realization that it was April 15, and he'd completely forgotten to file his taxes. Gene was telling one phone Yeah, yeah, we see him, we just crossed East 4th coming south on Stanton, and Ray was letting the other phone ring on and on, muttering O you stupid fuck, don't go into Juárez, I don't want to have to hurt you, I want to know who the hell you are. Ray had another sweating-the-small-stuff moment, remembering all of the powder that had been left in the flatbed dead space, where the Cyrillic guys had left it, after cutting open more than a few bags of the stuff. If dickwad crossed over before they could catch him, and then doubled back to El Paso, over the Santa Fe Bridge, they had an immediate problem, either chance it by recrossing, in the grip of Customs paranoia, or stopping to hose the truck bed out, running the risk of losing track of him. The ringing phone had gone to voicemail and there was a backup at the crossing and Ray was thinking about a last minute call to his accountant, when he noticed that not only had the Fusion reached the tollbooth window, but that the last call in was from Gomez himself, which was rarely, if ever, a good thing to ignore. He swung around the line of cars and juked back in near the head of the line, to the sound of honking horns and fisted threats and a widespread sense of personal aggrievement, as he pounded the wheel with an open palm, come on come on, go back, turn around, whatever you do, don't leave El Paso. Before he even had a chance to try something stupid, like firing the Mossberg through dickwad's rear window, the grey Ford had dealt with and passed through the booth and was nearing the top of the five-lane arch bridge and had now dropped from sight, in no particular hurry, apparently unaware of Raymond's hot pursuit. Ray lurched forward maybe four or five inches, stopping one car back from the toll-payment window, where a woman wearing hair-rollers in an ancient brown Seville, obviously reluctant to part with her currency, scrounged around mindlessly at the bottom of her purse, searching for nickels and dimes and pennies. Christ, Ray, chill out why don't you, that Fusion wasn't going much more than about 20; at the rate he's going, we could catch him with a cutting horse. Having finally, at long last, reached the head of the line, Ray offered payment with a magnanimous twenty, only to watch as the grim-faced tollbooth attendant gave it the patently-counterfeit-currency treatment, holding it up to the ultraviolet scanner, and turning it over at least three or four times, no doubt checking for traces of the one-sided Xerox copy; once he'd finally given in on the twenty itself, he started up a painstaking change-making ritual, counting and recounting a large stack of ones that looked like they'd only this moment been printed, torturing each bill as though it might well be hiding something, and then repeating the entire process into Ray's sweaty palm, ensuring that this breach in toll-paying etiquette had been fully absorbed, and would never, for any reason, be mindlessly repeated. Suppressing the impulse to TEC-9 the tollbooth, Ray pointed the exorbitant fuel-swilling Magnum's 510 horsepower, and all 535 of its foot-pounds of torque, toward the far left lane of four lanes going south, and nearly rear-ended some college kids from UTEP, climbing the hill in a smoke-gasping Datsun. Where in the fuck is the mother-fucking Fusion? He must have turned off somewhere. For Christ sake Gene, keep your eyes open, he couldn't have turned off in the middle of the bridge, and then the Gomez phone started ringing again, and on and on and on it rang, like something had malfunctioned in the voice mail ringer setting, and if it hadn't been for the distraction of a large flock of crows, flying off toward nowhere, in every conceivable direction, the Gomez cell phone would, to this very day, be ringing from the bottom of the murky Río Bravo.

Ray bobbed and weaved the Magnum over the Stanton Street Bridge, crossing the Southern Pacific railway lines and the Rio Grande, out of Texas into Mexico, and continuing south toward the end of the border crossing zone, until he hit the stop sign at Avenida Malecon, with all of Juárez before them, and no sign whatsoever of a grey Ford Fusion. Which way? Sitting there at the Alto sign, faced with Ciudad Juárez mass transit confusion, trying to hazard a guess as to where the no-name man might be headed, among the senseless profusion of Juárez streets, and with Heckler and Koch G3 automatic battle rifles, air-cooled vehicle-mounted M2 Browning .50 caliber machine guns, and a Mauser BK autocannon, courtesy of the Mexican Army's 20th Motorized Cavalry Regiment, all urging him on toward a rapid decision, Ray was struck by the sheer quantity and quality of information that they lacked. What was the man's nationality? What was his purported mission? Did he perhaps know his way around Juárez a little, or would he soon be hopelessly lost? Did he have friends here or an organization of some kind? Was he making progress or fleeing, and did he know the difference between the two? How, in short, were they supposed to know where he was going without knowing why he had come? What was the narrative logic of the story that was guiding him, from LA to El Paso to Ciudad Juárez, toward what or was it where or was it maybe whom? Ray felt like he'd landed in the middle of some man's story, without having heard a word of it, and with a storyteller who'd vanished abruptly, leaving Ray to make sense of the man's story for him. They crossed Malecon, continued south on Calle Lerdo, the obvious choice from a tourist perspective, a wide one-way street through the center of town, and headed toward Avenida 16 de Septiembre, intending to make a left toward the hotels along Paseo Triunfo de la Republica, hotels that a typical American traveler would find vaguely comforting, Hotel Lucerna, the Fiesta Inn, or the Holiday Inn Express, making the assumption that their man was a typical American, in possession of some sort of tourist map, with a more than adequate but foreign supply of currency, lacking friends or an organizational structure, seeking comfort in a strange new place. This not only fit most of the unknown facts of the case, but it also had the advantage of soothing Ray's nerves, by avoiding the side streets of Juárez altogether, where accidents seem to happen with alarming frequency, and tend to get blamed on whomever dies first. Ray kicked back, lit another cigarette, and put on one of the local music stations, featuring the soothing sounds of the narcocorridos, whose accordion-based polka rhythms are easy on the nerves, unless you happen to be driving in Narcoland itself, listening to the lyrics instead of the accordion, and know even a smattering of Narco-Español.

Ray realized his error as they were nearing the Avenida, when he suddenly remembered that it was a one way street, headed away from Paseo Triunfo in the exact wrong direction. The two-way Paseo and the one-way Avenida are in some sense the same long street in Juárez, as long as you are driving from east to west; the attempt to drive the Avenida in the opposite direction, however, runs a 30-block gauntlet of punishing traffic, a solid wall of cars basically headed straight at you. Raymond had a moment of quiet desperation, knowing that he would need some sort of side-street workaround, circumventing the one-way Avenida altogether, re-joining the Paseo farther to the east, and then doubling back to cruise past the Paseo Triunfo tourist hotels, where he was now virtually certain he would find the grey Fusion. The more Ray thought about the difficulties involved in reaching the hotels via the Juárez side streets, and thus correcting this error in judgment he'd made by driving down Calle Lerdo in the first place, the more certain he became that he was on the right track; the Paseo by now was so hard to get to, and this one-way fuck-up so difficult to live with, that the Fusion had no other place that it *could* be, other, of course, than somewhere else, like *wherever it was* would be a place worth checking. As Ray slowed to a crawl to replan his route, he thought he heard gunfire several blocks over, followed by the bird-whistle of an RPG round, and saw a dark cloud of smoke drift over the rooftops; for all Ray knew, the Fusion could be over there, snarled up in traffic on a street full of smoke, though this, by now, would be all but inconceivable, since Raymond could reach there in a three minute walk. Where are we headed, Ray? I'm thinking, Gene, I'm thinking. He has to be over at one of the hotels on the Paseo; where else would you go if you were down here as a tourist? A tourist? What sort of tourist would go into Juárez with a hundred pounds of luggage packed with 500-euro notes? Besides, there's no way to get to the Paseo from here; you need to go back to Malecon and start over. Starting over, of course, is out of the question; Ray got them into this, he can certainly get them out. Juárez itself is a circuitous rat maze of one-way streets and dead-end blind-alleys and detours to nowhere you can get to from here, nearly impossible to navigate without a plat map and a Ranger compass; a man driving the back-streets without some sort of map is like a man telling a story whose ending he's forgotten, spinning out loops of narrative thread that go on and on but don't in fact lead anywhere, at least not in the sense of anywhere in particular; Raymond, however, has a map in his head, and a story he's sticking to, no matter what, and he not only intends to get where he's going, but is thoroughly convinced that somehow this will matter. Ray continued on, with a kind of grim determination, by crossing the Avenida, making a left on De la Pena, left again on Ramon Corona, and then a right on Ignacio Mejia, running parallel to his Avenida Septiembre tale, the tale that ended in hotel-room comfort, and then finally right on Juan de la Barrera and right yet again on Paseo Triunfo, positioning him perfectly for the east to west journey, where he would soon find the inevitable grey Ford Fusion right where it belonged, at a tourist hotel, in a triumph of persistence over rational thinking. It might be worth noting, right up front, that not one of these streets, other than the Paseo, has an actual street sign to guide the poor storyteller; the side streets of Juárez, in the oral tradition, must be memorized first, before the storytelling starts, and a man with no memory of his tale in the first place should keep his mouth shut, and go back to El Paso; his story, in all likelihood, is dead on arrival. Raymond, however, knows exactly what he's doing; Ray knows Juárez like the back of his hand. How well does Ray know the back of his hand? The Holiday Inn Express, the comfortable Fiesta, and the Hotel Lucerna, the very gist of his memorized logical chronicle, should be right up ahead here, and needless to say, given the obstinate nature of concrete and rebar, they were no doubt right where they were supposed to be, these things don't just suddenly up and vanish, but wherever it was that they were supposed to be, they were there all right, but nowhere to be found.

In three short blocks, Ray was right back where he started, headed the exact wrong way, away from the Paseo, down the unidirectional corridor of the Avenida 16 de Septiembre, at a twenty-block remove from the Holiday Inn Express, which can plausibly be reached using Ignacio Mejia, but the route is so ornate that we'd hesitate to describe it, and Ray, right at the moment, was in no mood for the ornate. Now that it was apparent that the path they had taken had been pretty much pointless, Ray pulled in to a parking space at the neon-orange Mercado, turned off the engine, removed his set of keys, and stalked off in silence toward the Apollo Café, in search of a taco or a burger or a schnitzel, as though the point all along had been to get something to eat. He pulled up a plastic chair at an outdoor table in front of the Mercado, took a mind-numbing breath of the tourist-trinket air, declined a vendor's offer of an enormous red sombrero, and ordered himself a beer, as in *muy frío, Señor, gracias, pronto*. Gene, who at this point was just trying to be helpful, had taken a seat just opposite Raymond, holding a Gene-sized handful of overly ornate communication devices, their feature-rich selection of customized cell phones, and was about to make the suggestion that they phone in to Gomez, seeking guidance, perhaps, as to what to do next, when Ray gave him that look that tends to indicate silence, as in *whatever you do, Gene, don't fucking speak*. One of the features of their encrypted phones, a feature with which Gene seemed somewhat unfamiliar, was that they apparently knew the difference between Juárez and El Paso; if the SIM card picked up the Location Area Identity number of a Telcel basestation on the wrong side of the border, it immediately fried its memory logic, meaning basically no more cell phone. As Gomez had explained it: "Don't fucking call me from Juárez you morons; half the people at Telcel work for the Sinaloans." This inability to communicate, up the chain of command, if you got yourself in a tight spot somewhere, like anywhere in Mexico, reminded Ray of a day he'd spent, getting battered by Iraqi anti-tank shells, with the bad guys firing away, and no one firing back. He was forward-spotting on the Iraqi positions, calling in the firing coordinates, ready to carpet the silent AT-12s with a shitpile of DPICM, when the Tactical Operations Center turned hard of hearing and then deaf and mute, the suggestion to issue the Commence Firing! order met with silence and stillness, they might as well have used a megaphone, or formed a line of men back to the brigade artillery, saying Tell them to fire away, pass it on, pass it on, when all at once the Iraqi AT-12s opened fire, right before Raymond's forward-spotting eyes, taking out a Bradley CFV, a Vulcan full-track, and eight or ten good cavalrymen. It was quite a day, February 20, the morning and afternoon after the opening night of Knight Strike, their beautiful battalion wedge formation descending into chaos and complete disorder, with Medevac copters whirling around, bodies flying, blood and stretchers, and then at last the DPICM and HE shells coming in overhead and almost down on top of them, and finally smoke shells exploding to cover their retreat, whatever point they'd been making having apparently been made. The Battle of Ruqi Pocket, a feint, a fake, a diversionary disaster, hailed by the upper echelons as an outright success, having convinced the Iraqi's that Saddam was right, that the main attack would come up the obvious Wadi, keeping four full Iraqi Armored Divisions, and the Republican Guard, otherwise occupied, while the real attack came from out of left field, somewhere else, in the middle of nowhere; the 2nd Blackjack, Raymond's brigade, had been stuck right there at the center of it all, and had an excellent view of what a success might look like. The guys who thought they were in the middle of a mess, with no communications, and shells raining down on them, had been looking at the story from a narrow perspective, they hadn't quite seen the ephemeral beauty and sweep of the whole blood-and-stretchers scenario, while the Generals sat back and watched it all from a decent and no doubt sanitary distance, and the story to them had looked intricate and flawless.

Ray tried to imagine some perspective from which his flailing around Juárez might look flawless to Gomez, and decided there was no such thing; from any perspective, this was still a fucking mess. The assignment had been straightforward and simple: go to the motel, enter the room of an unarmed man, locate the money and the man himself, and remove them both from the immediate picture. It was this certainty that the man lacked arms that had positioned the task as distinctly beneath them; it was also the reason, as he reasoned it through, that the indicated action might not seem quite so indicated. In all the years he'd been working for Gomez, or following orders within a chain of command, he'd never been ordered to remove a known civilian; if the no-name guy were a seasoned professional, part of the army of mercenaries doing battle with the money, why were they so sure that he wasn't armed and dangerous? Why had the name he was traveling under, his actual name, been discretely omitted from a short slip of paper? And why would a mercenary, with a mule-load of currency, sit there for hours at a proximate border crossing? Why in God's name were they chasing after someone whose flight was so slow that they could catch him with a plow horse? Fortunately for Raymond, their waiter appeared, and ran through a list of inedible-sounding specials; this whole line of thinking was getting him nowhere. Unfortunately for Raymond, Apollo's is a tourist trap, and ten seconds after the reading of the specials, both El Paso gunmen had ordered their burgers. While Gene sat puzzling through the problems with their cell phones, knowing not to use them, but not knowing why not, Ray continued on down this unidirectional corridor that was leading him away from his mission's stated objectives, with his mind drifting back to the Highway of Death, Highway 80 from Kuwait to Basra, where a few well-placed bombs had sealed off and trapped an unlikely-looking convoy of slow-moving vehicles. Heavily redundant firepower had been methodically applied, using fighter bombers, gunships, and armored battalions, and then B-52s had carpet-bombed what was left, leaving a many-mile traffic-jam charred to a crisp. Strictly speaking, the war was already over, the Iraqi's had surrendered, and were headed on home to their wives and their children, and the Geneva Convention frowned upon such things, but then what did the Swiss know about actual warfare? It was possible, as the Generals claimed, that the Republican Guard had been simply regrouping, and needed to be dealt with right there and then, and wiped out completely in a miles-long extinction. Raymond had been there after the fact, and knew that what the Generals were selling was a complete crock of shit, that these people were fleeing in buses and pickup trucks, loaded down with loot, but essentially civilians, Iraqi conscripts running for their lives, Kuwaiti's escaping from politics and prisons, some ragged Palestinians who had looted their own households; not a pro there among them. The Republican Guard's 1st Armored Division? APCs with anti-aircraft guns and MT-LBs with rocket-pod launchers and Lion of Babylon Asid Babil tanks, no doubt intent on moving north and then violently regrouping? Try looking over on the coastal road, as the Generals well knew, since they searched and destroyed and then carefully re-destroyed it, in a 60-mile stretch of sitting-duck extermination, turning 50-ton tanks into piles of metal feathers. The Highway of Death was a long line of refugees, conscripted into nothingness, in 1,400 or so secular conveyances, or fleeing into the desert to die of thirst or exposure, it didn't much matter, they were goners, get over it. Seen up close, there was no real depth to the actual big picture, this was basically a crime scene, for which no one, in the end, would even think to be held accountable. Ray had made the mistake of checking out some of the vehicles, their drivers utterly charcoaled in their fire-bombed cars, and couldn't believe how *straight* they were sitting, staring up ahead, into the mangled-miles of desert, with this blanked-out look on their carbonized faces, and their hands welded shut on the steering wheels to nowhere, like death hadn't even bothered to stop and give them a lift, and they were facing a long drive, with no clue how to get there. Jesus, what a mess. Why in the hell would you waste thousands of tons of ordnance on a bunch of dead civilians who were totally clueless? Here's hoping this guy driving the Fusion has a clue, because he sure as shit is headed in the exact same direction.

Who do you think he is, this guy we're chasing?
I don't know, Trip, what the hell's the difference? If he ripped off Gomez, he won't last long anyway, and it won't much matter who the hell he isn't.
I'd feel better knowing he had it comin'.
Trust me, Raymond, you rip off Gomez, you're too stupid to live.
Why do you think they didn't tell us his name?
Don't think he needs one at the rate he's going.
Doesn't seem a little strange to you, them knowing his name, not telling us what it is?
Why's need a name? He'll still be just as dead.
Sits in his car for three fucking hours, like he doesn't know we're after him. I'm missing somethin' here. How long would you sit around with a bag of Gomez' money?
Not very smart, I'll grant you that. Dumb as hell, if you're asking me.
Just supposing you ripped off Gomez. Why would you come to El Paso, in the guy's backyard?
Dumber than dumb. Too stupid to go on living. You want I should give him an IQ test, just to make sure?
I don't know, Gene, there's somethin' don't seem quite right about this whole damn set-up.
Since when you start worrying about what's right and wrong? Right's where you do your job, Gomez don't start thinking you're too dumb to live.
Yeah, there's that. Still like to know what the fuck the guy is up to.

I tell you what, Trip, we find him and point that Mossberg at his
    head, I bet you can get him to tell you his whole life story.
Probably right. We'll track him down and ask him. Then we'll have
    to kill him for being stupid enough to tell us.
Don't much matter either way.
Don't much at that. Still like to know who the hell the guy is.

As if the next indicated action depended on some dickwad's identity. Sitting there in a tourist trap in Ciudad Juárez, with a truck full
of leftovers, and a guy lost in the confusion, Ray had enough things
to think about as it was, like how to tell Gomez that they'd lost the
guy, without having to consult with a foot-thick thesaurus. Why was
he even thinking about ancient history in the first place, about his
drunk of a father and crock-of-shit senior officers and a bunch of
dead civilians going nowhere in a hurry, stuff he hadn't thought
about in at least fifteen years? As if any of that mattered, as if getting
some douchebag's story straight involved making some sort of sense
out of his own what's-next story; this was just the sort of thinking
that it made sense to start avoiding, unless the indicated action was
to get them all killed. Ray didn't have a story; he had a job to do, a
job that could get him to feeling expendable if he didn't start taking
care of business fairly soon. He wasn't going to track this Fusion guy
down by sitting around watching a bunch of grainy home movies.
Ray finished up his coffee, left a twenty and a handful of the newly
printed ones on top of the check in its brown plastic tray, and headed for the truck; time to stop thinking and just get fucking moving.
    They continued on down the Avenida Septiembre to Avenida
Juárez, and then headed north through the heart of the garbage-
littered tourist zone, back toward the Santa Fe and Stanton Street
bridges, with a clean view of the skyline of El Paso straight ahead
of them, including a tall cell tower to which Raymond needed access, backlit by all of that blue Texas sky. Ray, at this point, wasn't
listening to music; he was checking the side streets for a grey Ford
Fusion, while organizing his thoughts on what to tell Gomez, and
trying not to think too much about the profusion of Juárez lamp
posts. Every last lamp post on Avenida Juárez was littered with pink-
and-black memorial crosses, markers for the hundreds if not thousands of young women who'd been "disappeared" forever from the

streets of the Ciudad, as though the dead were intent on continuing to multiply, despite Sally Field and Jane Fonda protests, despite 60 Minutes and 20/20 exposés, despite Amnesty International official condemnations, and all the Ni Una Mas spare-the-innocent earnestness; it was possible, Ray thought, that they didn't quite have a handle on how Juárez actually worked. They parked near the head of one of the side streets off of Malecon, a block or two east of the Stanton Street Bridge, just under one of the brown and white Bienvenidos Welcome signs, and maybe eighty feet away from their immediate destination, a nondescript establishment known as Roberto's Bar and Cambio.

Ray cut the engine and just sat there in the truck, smoking a cigarette, not doing much of anything, with his thoughts turning opaque, even to us, an unusual and possibly unhealthy development. Perhaps he was thinking about Roberto's encrypted phone, with its ability to function from the wrong side of the river, without running the risk of a SIM-card nervous breakdown, while placing a call to Señor Telcel Paranoia; perhaps he was picking up a bit of the local street vibe, as a pure black Escalade, with dark tinted windows and gleaming chrome spinners, drifted past the Ram, up the pink and green side street, in a frictionless display of chromium indifference; for all we know, Ray could have been staring at a lamp post, since like every last human who's spent time in Juárez, he knew three or four young women who'd ended up on a light fixture, or a telephone or utility pole, after climbing into the back seat of the exact wrong auto. You all right Ray? Ray didn't answer; he stubbed out his cigarette, exited the truck, and locked up the doors to the tune of a tiny siren. The emptied-out street was lined with peddler's carts and carne grills, pastelerias and tortilla shops, lecherías and pharmacias and corner-store tiendas, using burlap potato sacks for makeshift awnings, and purple and pink taco shacks, with chrome stools set out for their now invisible customers. Ray peeled a green five off of a large roll of bills and gave it to one of the ever-present corner boys, a razor-thin kid in a sky-blue Adidas, made-in-Hangzhou, polyester running suit, and asked him to keep an eye on the motion-sensitive vehicle. The Money Exchange half of Roberto's establishment had its sulfur-yellow rolling-steel theft-proof security grill pulled down and padlocked, and Roberto's Bar itself was bolted shut and windowless. The four-story turquoise-stucco bullet-riddled tenement that housed Roberto's, freshly painted maybe forty or fifty years ago, and in an advanced stage of business-as-usual deterioration, stood next to a smoked-glass and reinforced-concrete 12-story office tower that would have looked right at home in Portland or Atlanta, and housed American business representatives for DuPont and Alcoa. Ciudad Juárez is full of these odd juxtapositions, third-world poverty and local-color whimsy meeting first-world blandness and purchasing power; if you're commuting in from El Paso, overseeing electrical-harness systems for Alcoa Fujikura, the local-color poverty doesn't look all that bad, particularly if you're looking at it through a bulletproof window. If you're down here on a business trip, however, feeling a little queasy about leaving your own hotel room, you may want to pay slightly closer attention to the local-color color-coding of the Juárez transportation system: that green and white bus that goes smoking right past you at 5:30 am is not, in fact, intended for you, waiting out front of your pale-pink hotel for your sleek black sedan and uniformed driver; it's picking up 16-year-old girls on their way to the maquiladoras, where they will turn your new silicon chips, fresh off the plane from a fab in Taiwan, into fully assembled circuit boards, ready to go to market. If you work in Santa Clara for a venture-backed startup, for $220,000 a year plus stock options and healthcare, wait under the lamp post for your glossy-black auto; if you're a 16- or 15- or 14-year-old girl, making $16 a week in one of the maquilas, wait for the green and white bus to arrive, and never, meaning never, meaning absolutely never, get into the back of a stranger's black sedan.

Ray rattled the double doors, managed to make enough noise to arouse an indifferent suspicion, and was greeted by one of Roberto's obreros, sporting a Roberto's-branded apron and a wood-handled broom. Roberto was in his office at the back behind the bar, dwarfed by an enormous brown sheet-metal desk, piled high with faxes and wrinkled American currency. This immense pile of small bills off the El Paso streets was being sorted into stacks and run through a bill counter, a Ribao BC900, with UV, magnetic, and infrared counterfeit protection, a nice, tight, compact, high-tech-looking thing, about the size of a fax machine, a device to be proud of, and yet the bane, if you asked him, of Roberto's existence.

Roberto's existence, positioned as it was at the bottom of some pre-Columbian, maybe Toltec, pyramid, at the top of which was Gomez' state-of-the-art trading floor, depended on sorting and counting bills, and wrapping them up in plain brown bank wrappers, and depositing them at the bank, where a Cambio's currency deposits would rarely, meaning never, arouse the slightest suspicion. There were hundreds of Robertos in Gomez' world, in Cambios from Tijuana to Matamoras, and hundreds more of deposit smurfs, stuffing currency into banks in thousand dollar increments, in the "placement" phase of the laundering process, before layering or agitation or "commingling" as it's called, followed by "integration" into nice clean funds, where the money was free to travel the planet by electronic transfer, in hundred-million-dollar increments, wherever it was needed in the trillion-dollar drug world. Roberto stared at the four-digit display on the LED control panel of the repulsive Ribao BC900 bill counter, hating the thing for being what it was, a machine that required manual sorting before counting, instead of being the thing that he longed for it to be, maybe a Billcon D-551, with automatic bill sorting, and 1,200-bill-per-minute blazing performance. Roberto looked up from his mind-numbing task, and his hatred for manual currency sorting, and glared at Ray like it was all his fault, this difference between a $600 piece-of-shit bill-counter and a $4,000 automatic sorting machine, an impeccable instrument, of which a man could be proud. We need to use the Gomez phone. Go ahead, maricon, and tell Gomez to feel free to go ahead and fuck himself.

Ray picked up the encrypted cell phone, glanced around at the why-the-fuck-bother office disarray, as though maybe Roberto kept a dictionary handy, or the Complete Works of Shakespeare in case of an emergency, and slowly dialed home, dreading yet another allusive encounter with Gomez' limitless Elizabethan condescension, and the porcelain marquetry of his elaborate lexicon. We lost him. You lost him. The meeting took a little longer than we expected, and by the time we got down here, he was over the bridge. You lost him. He's here in Juárez somewhere, we saw him cross the border, but we may need some help in tracking him down. You lost him. "How poor are they that have not patience! What wound did ever heal but by degrees," did not seem, at the moment, to be part of the boss' repertoire. Ray felt a bit unnerved by the simplicity of Gomez' diction, as though he and Gene were no longer worth the bother of supercilious castigation, and in the next step down from here, Gomez would cease to speak altogether. And then, as if reading Ray's mind, Gomez disconnected them, leaving behind him not so much as a good-old-fashioned dial tone, and in the absence of a directive, a subtle unraveling of some intrinsic and ancient weave. What's he say? Says we fucked up, more or less. Yeah, no kidding, driving all over Juárez looking for a fucking taco shop that happens to serve burgers. What the fuck, Ray, you think this guy come down here hunting for a hamburger? Gentlemen, Gentlemen, you are searching for someone in Ciudad Juárez, permit me to make a brief call to the Municipal Police; he'll be dead in five minutes. Appreciate the thought, Roberto, but I'm guessing Gomez wants us to handle this. The guy has something that belongs to Gomez, something that had best not fall into the hands of the police. Ray didn't want to imagine Gomez' reaction to the news that his money was now in police custody; his reaction would not be altogether good. The very thing that made the no-name man so sought after, and that put him in some jeopardy, was likely the one thing protecting him now, from Gomez making a phone call, and bringing in the absolute impunity authorities. Money, Señor Gomez? We have not noticed such money, we have taken care of the problem; we are pleased to have been of service. The no-name man wandering around Juárez in a grey Ford Fusion, SXS 537, had no idea how lucky he was; in all probability, he had no more idea of the power structure of Juárez than did Sally Field or Amnesty International, with their moronic appeals for spare-the-innocent justice. Justice was what was found, among the scorched and blistered bodies, carved into their living flesh, before dumping the things at dawn in a lumpy-looking cotton field. Justice was what prevailed, for some baffled maquila bus driver, when you electrocuted his genitals, and offered him a chance for a much better life, in exchange for a signed confession, and a quick trip to oblivion. Justice was what was carried out, on a stretcher whisked away to the city's morticians, with a single gunshot to the back of the head, of some lawyer who was asking far too many questions. Justice, simple justice, was continually being upheld for the destitute and impoverished, in the form of six-day torture trials, involving satanic rites and anal gang-rapes and part-by-part brute-force dismemberments, to remind the poor of their powerlessness, and teach them to be more what's-the-word judicious.

Chopped in quarters and disemboweled; dissolved into goo in alkaline vats; gouged-out heads spiked with three inch nails, absent their requisite mutilated corpses; justice. The do-gooders and Amnesty-types come to Juárez seeking justice. They should be careful what they wish for. Justice, in Juárez, is not for the faint of heart.

# 10

*J* esus, I'm tired. Why am I still sitting here, at this ridiculous
Parnian Power Desk, trying to make a *whole book* out of my life's
cryptic fragments, when in maybe three hours the sun will be
coming up, and the office will begin filling with Blanco employees, going about their normal Monday start-up routines, brewing
fresh coffee, turning on the phones, and filing this whole Dacha
mess under *Parasomniac Accounting Problems.* I should probably
be home in bed, trying to *Sleep Like I Mean It*, but I've been getting
some crank phone calls, the last four or five nights, someone calling
me up to tell me that I'm dreaming, which is not only annoying,
but doesn't help at all in terms of meaningful sleep, and I still have
this book to write, and Dacha to deal with, and just to give you
some idea of the sort of problems I'm up against, I feel like I'm living under twilight anesthesia, somewhere along the borderland between waking and sleep, where the hypnagogic and hypnopompic
unite in the anomalous, which is particularly annoying, in terms of
Dacha Wireless, where I'm asking myself all sorts of incongruous
questions that no one who's been sleeping well would ever have
to ask, like *What is Prospero really trying to tell me?* and *Where did
the dog go?* and *How do you drown a book?* Just in case you're not a
student of parasomnial anomalies, these questions may be instances
of motor-breakthrough dream speech, also referred to as audible
somniloquies, so if you have no fucking clue what the hell I'm talking about, don't worry about it, neither do I. And not that this will
help if I'm talking in my sleep, but I'll give you a few hints that are

somewhat less anomalous: Prospero's set up shop somewhere in the Caymans; the dog was in an open field on the top of my nightstand; and the books I'd like to drown have already passed an audit, as if no one from our accounting firm had ever read *The Tempest*, or even J. B. Bobo's *Modern Coin Magic*. If this still doesn't ring a bell, let me just add this: Prospero isn't real, he's a character in a fiction, though he's one of my Dacha co-investors, which may be part of my accounting problems; those books that I referred to aren't real either, Prospero actually drowned them, at the end of that whole *Tempest* business; and the dog in the empty field, running toward me in a photograph, must be around here somewhere, he got out through an open gate. A dog in a black-and-white photograph can't just disappear, unless he somehow stumbled upon a quantum-field Euclidean wormhole, and wound up out in a grassy pasture, chasing a redbird around in the deep green clover, back in the days when still photography had yet to be discovered. And while this is only a small sample of what happens to reality when you get fact and fiction commingled in your accounts, I've got a plan to solve this by paying a visit to a sleep clinic, although by the time I get around to the Dacha chapter, I may need a clinic in Paramaribo, Suriname.

So I guess you'd have to say, if you want my opinion, that this whole *fill in the blanks* thing seems to be getting worse, like I started out with a book deal for some sort of *inside story*, and now I can't help wondering, given all these anomalies, *How far in am I?* and *What is a book?* I've got the signed contract sitting here in front of me, so the book deal must be real enough, but what if I'm sound asleep, and am only dreaming the deal is signed? I wake up in the morning, facedown on my desk, and the book deal is there all right, but someone forged my signature. I'd have to say, at this point, I'm like thirty pages in, but maybe they'd let me out of this if I handed in a *pamphlet*. *What is a book?* Did you know that, strictly speaking, at least according to the U.S. Copyright Office, a book could be a single page, and it would still be called a *book*? As Karl Kraus put it, the closer the look one takes at a word, the greater the distance from which it looks back, which reminds me of one of those anxiety dreams, where you're chasing after something, and the faster you run, the farther away you get. So what is a *book*? According to my *Dream Dictionary*, it's an expression of *me*, which in my case is clearly next to impossible, since the faster I run, the farther away I get, and now on top of everything, there's this whole meta-problem of what to make of a *Dream Dictionary* showing up in a dream; no wonder I'm tired, and forging my own signature, and wandering around my office in a non-volitional twilight state, like I should be taking sleeping aids, and home in bed with the phone unplugged, but I'm afraid of waking up in front of my own refrigerator, and finding out I'm gorging on Ambien poultry, like how the hell else am I supposed to explain a *pamphlet* called *Oneiric Confessions of a Hypnophobic Somnambulist*? You want to know something funny? The *Dream Dictionary* in the dream has an entry for itself, a nearly two inch space of page left blank, as though I've not only become trapped in a twilight-state recursive function, but the meaning of *me* is a two inch blank.

So let me get your opinion on something. Do you think that a reader who skips a few random pages can still be considered to have read the whole book? How many pages do you think you could skip, before having to admit that you haven't actually read it? Maybe you see where I'm headed with this. Suppose the author skipped just the right random pages, could he still be considered to have authored a *whole book*? Or let me put it another way: how many memories are you allowed to forget if you're legally obligated to produce some sort of *Memoir*? Why do I ask? It's 4 in the morning, I've run out of pills, and this coffee I'm swilling is getting a little stale; I'm about to tell the *inside story* of how I got rich, and became a *Man of Substance* and *Lifetime Achievement*, a story that even to *me* sounds like a dream, flying around on private jets, chartering yachts, chasing after starlets, becoming *a man to reckon with*; there are, however, some random pages I'll need to skip, since it isn't really a matter of *filling in the blanks*, it's like how the hell did *blanks* show up here in the first place? What exactly am I talking about? Remember my inner life? The one that just died of natural causes? The Long-Dead Poet with a very short obit? I have, I suppose, a confession to make: the guy didn't in fact just suddenly up and die, it turns out in the end I actually killed him. As the money at long last started rolling in, and I started getting the feeling that I was turning into *someone*, my skeletal inner life crawled out of the crypt, and started asking questions like *who the hell are you*? So how did I kill him? It doesn't really matter; it could have been the vodka and starlets and jets, or maybe it was all that money, which will certainly do the trick, but the point is, by now, I've completely forgotten, and the whole sordid story is a complete and utter blank.

So where are we now? We're deep underground, in the Wine Cellar at Del Frisco's, a legendary steakhouse with an epic-length wine list, somewhere in North Dallas, wherever the hell that is, it must be near the office tower that houses Elicit Networks. We're just about to start our IPO celebration party; you should probably pull up a chair, have a glass of vintage Krug, though if you have the slightest shred of moral decency, some sense of a physical world where there are those who go hungry, a world where several billion live and die on a dollar, and a fifteen cent school day is a fiscal impossibility, you may want to wait outside, because this, almost certainly, is going to get ugly. If you know that a mosquito net costs about a Double Latte, and that 700,000 children, in Africa alone, will die as a result of our drinking too much coffee, you should wait at the bar, give me maybe four hours, we have an awful lot of wine to drink, and only one corkscrew. If you're even vaguely aware that 10 million kids could be saved from starvation for what we pay for basic cable, you should wait in the parking lot, near my chauffeured black sedan, and my driver will drop you at your four-star hotel when the feasting is finished and the starving is over. If you're easily nauseated by conspicuous consumption, and somehow think that well water for a Zambian village is worth more than a bottle of '82 Lafite, the toilets at Del Frisco's are quite a ways away, and the carpet in the Wine Cellar, if you begin to get my drift, is Persian and precious, so let's not cause an incident. So you're staying? I completely understand; the famine in Bahr El Ghazal, for which the people of the region have only themselves to blame, for living in such a fucked-up region in the first place, thus leaving themselves open to human rights abuses, by the Baggara and the Nuer and the SPLA, and the Dinka Warlords, and the Khartoum Government, not to mention the Russians and the Chinese People's Republic and the U.S. and France and Great Britain and so on, anyone, basically, with arms to sell, and an interest in oil, meaning basically everyone, this famine, as I was saying, will just have to wait, until it mutates into Darfur, and gets a lot more famous. The bubbly, by the way, is something I've provided; everything to follow will be paid for by our investment bankers, who unfortunately for them are unable to join us, as they're far too busy, on another IPO roadshow, unfortunate in the sense that they'll miss a great meal, and also in the sense that they'll be picking up the tab, and once we get started with the corkscrewing process, nothing can stop us until the last cork has been pulled, and the evening's expenses have been tallied up and tidied, as we savor that last snifter of '17 Armagnac, and then stagger our way out into the crisp October night, or maybe stop at the bar for a few final boilermakers. The evening will end up in a two foot stack of expense reports from similar occasions, sitting atop the Lucite desk of some low level accountant at let's say Goldman Sachs or Credit Suisse, whose job it is to make the evening itself disappear, write it off to T&E, as if it never happened, as it is, after all, in relation to their profits, vanishingly trivial, a rounding error.

Shall we get started, then? The rectangular table has been set for ten, with crisp white linens, a simple white rose centerpiece, silverware, steak knives, butter dishes, bread plates, tall tapered candles flickering with flame, tulip-folded napkins centered on the dinner plates; other than the fact that the table has been set with at least 50 wine glasses, there is nothing out of the ordinary here, though you might want to take note of the fact that you're completely surrounded on all four sides by floor-to-ceiling wine bottles, to the height of fourteen feet, all of which are what's known as "library wines," which has nothing to do with *books*, thank God, it has to do with quality and proper aging, and while more than a few of these library wines are truly extraordinary, and priced as such, some of them are something altogether Other, and might best be thought of as hideously expensive liquefied heirlooms, monstrously costly antique inebriants, barbarously exorbitant fermented objets, easy enough to look at, frightening to corkscrew. We, it should be clear, are in possession of the corkscrew, so if you spot something interesting among the liquiform artifacts, don't hesitate to ask; while that '82 Petrus you're currently eyeing costs more than the two-bedroom house I grew up in, you might want to consider the '45 Mouton, which you could easily trade in for a late-model Mercedes, though the Philippe Jullian wine-label art, if we're honest with ourselves, is more of an illustration than an actual art work; when it comes to Mouton's justly famous wine labels, you'd be far better off with the '73 Picasso, just as long as you flush the decrepit-tasting and dilapidated contents down the upstairs toilet right after we've pulled the cork, and keep in mind that your new Picasso, one of his series of Bacchanales, which showed up on the bottle shortly after his demise, has apparently been emptied of substance altogether, and is worth on the order of a 3-mile cab fare; we're here, after all, to celebrate a *liquidity event*, so let's try to stay focused on liquefied significance. Before we sit down, while the big wines breathe, and while Renoir finishes up with his painting for the occasion, we're tasting the bubbly, a magnificent '88 Krug Vintage Brut Champagne: just a hint of orangey fruit and bruised pear on the nose, tiny streaming bubbles rising up through the golden and emerald-tinged liquid, releasing a bisquity doughiness, with a touch of buttery fat, something lean and mineral on the palate at first, rounded with crisp mousse and, yes, I think, truffle, with a briskly precise presence and poise throughout, followed by a grapefruit and lemon pithy dryness, with scintillating balance, beautiful finesse, and a huge, huge finish as the wine begins to open, all in all, a gorgeous champagne, perhaps a somewhat more *intellectual* Krug than one might have hoped, but since we have several magnums of this magnificent stuff, maybe instead of talking to it, we should *just fucking drink it*. Our companions this evening are members of the Board of Elicit Networks, along with one or two soldiers from the management team, and this is an occasion, so richly deserved, for which we've been in training for six brutal years. Since it's highly unlikely that you survived the Siege of Leningrad, by drinking jammy Cabs, and mundane Chardonnays, you have no real idea how we made it here alive, or developed such a tolerance for high-grade alcohol, so perhaps I'd better tell you before it's too late, and the evening disappears into misty legend, and Lucite accounting, and alcoholic blackout.

We did not, I can assure you, begin in the Wine Cellar; in fact, we started out on a cocktail napkin, at my offices in Brentwood, three stories up from the San Vicente sidewalk. Wendell the Poet is right out front, hawking his dollar poems to the neighborhood pedestrians; Robert the Roofie guy, the man from the "Trudging Lane" 12-step meeting, with the wide-blue-eyes memory problems, hasn't yet started his sobriety program, and is probably on the nod somewhere, after two or three yellow and pink balloons full of black tar heroin, also known as *pigment*, or maybe thinning the deep blue memories out, with a Starbucks cup full of vaporous paint thinner; and I'm in my office, three floors up, completely unaware that my desk is not a desk, or that there's nothing of substance in my imaginary pigeonholes. This would make the year around 1994, several years prior to my Smirnoff vacations, those 100 Proof Vodka strategic retreats from confronting the fact that I've come up empty, and have buried my investors in a $50 million pit. At this point I'm maybe $10 million down, and seriously doubt the hole will get any deeper; in fact, right at this moment, I have a deal on my desk to sell one of my companies, of which I own 50%, for $80 million and a $38 million profit; what I don't, to be honest, actually know is that the founder of this company, crucial to the deal's impending consummation, has a $100-a-day diamorphine problem. So all in all, given my level of ignorance, I'm feeling pretty good about the world today: the Coral trees planted in the San Vicente median are in full orange bloom, and actually look like trees, as opposed to the naked and writhing monstrosities they turn out to be after too much vodka; I have imaginary profits about to start rolling in, "putting numbers on the Board" as we say in the business; and the guy I'm about to meet appears to be a winner, at least on paper, a computer I/O wizard, with a mastery of protocol stacks, and one of the authors of a monster success story called Silicon Graphics, or SGI; SGI, which long ago went bankrupt, is best known for its Onyx graphics rendering machines, powerful mini-supercomputers that are used for constructing 3-D illusions, those Computer Generated Imagery special effects that James Cameron will use to sink the *Titanic*, in a masterful display of machine-generated disaster, like sinking a real ship into virtual waters. Coincidentally, my soon-to-be winner, a computer game company that builds First-Person Shooter games, like id Software's *Doom* and the sequel to *Castle Wolfenstein*, uses the Onyx Reality Engine to produce its 3-D illusions, splattering blood, flaming explosions, and $38 million in illusory profits. So how many illusions are you allowed to buy into if you have a fiduciary duty to stay attached to reality? Right at this moment, I would appear to be on a roll, maybe two weeks away from reaching the docks with a boatload of money to refill my coffers, and if you want

my opinion on buying into illusions, and living in a reality that's
been generated by machines, I'd have to say, at this point, my ship
is unsinkable, I mean who ever heard of a ship going down after ripping its hull on a heroin iceberg, and I'm pretty much running on
cruise control, with *Reality Engines all ahead full.*

So in walks Chase Dailey, our virtual cocktail napkin, soon to
be the founder of Elicit Networks. Before Chase sits down, and the
PowerPoint slides come out, perhaps we need a word or two on
naming conventions. Chase Dailey? Yeah, I agree; not very likely;
would it help if I told you his real name was Bailey? I can tell you
for a fact that Chase couldn't give a shit what the hell we call him;
at this very moment, he's living on the Ile Saint-Louis, in a $12 mil-
lion apartment overlooking the Seine, and we could call him Fred
Mertz for all he cares. Did you know that Fred Mertz' actual full
name was Frederick Hobart Edie Mertz the Third? That he wasn't
actually born in that *I Love Lucy* apartment, but rather in India-
napolis, and had already fought in World War I, long before he met
Ethel and moved to New York? You need to keep in mind that this
man, Chase Dailey, made nearly $300 million when he cashed out
of Elicit Networks, a name that even to me sounds suspiciously fictitious, evocative of a world, which some of us have problems learning to inhabit, where reality and unreality have completely different
engines. I know what you're thinking: $300 million sounds pretty
real; guy must have earned it; built one hell of a machine. What if
I told you that maybe $280 million of Chase's massive profit was a
direct result of the fact that I fired him? That our actual CEO, who
may or may not have been named Mark Lloyd, was unable to cash
out while the NASDAQ was soaring, due to SEC regulations that
govern the sale of stock, and wound up making maybe a paltry $25
million? That Chase got rich because he was gathering unemploy-
ment checks, and SEC stock-sale restrictions don't apply to the unemployed? So was the $300 million that Mr. Mertz cashed-out with
real or unreal? Despite the fact that money is the ultimate signifier,
unless we're in the middle of a *Dynasty* episode, I'll be damned if
I know what sort of machine generated the reality of Chase's monster profit. As far as I'm concerned, that $300 million is a complete
misrepresentation of reality as I know it. Of course, as Wittgenstein
put it, "One of the most misleading representational techniques in

our language is the use of the word 'I'," so I already have a problem right in the middle of this sentence, where my use of the word 'I' already sounds suspicious, a kind of Ouroboros serpent swallowing its own tail. What sort of Reality Engine is an Ouroboros serpent? What if I told you that my real full name is Frederick Hobart Edie Mertz the First? And what about *you*, what do they call you? How much reality do you actually represent?

Chase has been introduced to me by a dear old friend; we'll call him Larry Black, though his name was Larry Green. Larry and I had been involved together in a deal that sank to the bottom, I can't remember the name of it, but suffice it to say, it was a complete disaster; let's call it Protocol Engines, since that was its name, though the engine that drove it was an absurd fabrication. The idea of Protocol Engines, to rearrange the building blocks that underlie the Internet, was so completely wrongheaded and demented from the beginning that it would be senselessly cruel to force us to recall it, but the idea in essence was to levitate the Internet, slip TCP and IP out from under it, and replace them with something called a Transfer Protocol; there's a reason you've never heard of a Transfer Protocol, since the Internet Protocol underlies reality, and reality, in the end, proved difficult to levitate. This, to be clear, was not our fault; when the Internet started in 1969, it had exactly two nodes connected together, and had a whole different name, let's call it the Arpanet, after Jean Arp of Alsace, one of the founders of the Dadaists, whose *tabula rasa* attitude was to demolish rationality, and replace it with something a bit more deviant, sort of the Anarchist's equivalent of a Transfer Protocol; when we started Protocol Engines, in April of '89, no one in the real world was actually attached to it, and though it *was* called the Internet, which should maybe, in retrospect, have been some sort of clue, it had like 10,000 nodes in its entire worldwide network, so our levitation project still sounded reasonable; today, of course, it's the Beast of a Billion nodes, all of them connected by the Internet Protocol, and the Beast isn't fond of people trying to mess with it, much less a bunch of Anarcho-Dadaist semioticians trying to get it to fucking levitate in order to rename it, maybe something like the TransferNet, in honor of the absurdity of our imaginary protocol. If you don't have a clue what the hell we were thinking, don't worry about it, neither did we. You might as well be asking a schizotypic mental patient to describe the foundations of some extended bout of delusional thinking, I mean really, what was he thinking, how could reality have gone so horribly awry? He'll shake his head in wonder, trying to re-engender his mental state, he remembers feeling amazing, with no foundation at all, floating through space in the Tadpole Galaxy, firmly convinced he's about to turn into a butterfly, and by the time he's placed his face in his hands, perhaps recalling an initial impulse, from which others seemed to follow in an anomalous progression, you're inclined to put your arm around the man, to offer solace for the pain he'd no doubt be facing, if you insisted on pursuing the toad-like truth. So let's not pursue it, suffice it to say we were all delusional, and that Larry was a dear old friend, and return to the present, and traditional reality, where nothing, as yet, could possibly go wrong.

Chase himself, it might be worth noting, is completely surrounded by an enormous unreality zone, more than enough to fill my tiny Avis conference room, in fact more than enough to fill the colossal upstairs dining room at Del Frisco's Steakhouse, where we used to hold our Board dinners, even back in the early days, surviving the Siege of Leningrad, or at least its first few months, on mediocre Cabs, and Chardonnays so wooden they might have made a decent tool shed; even six-bottles-in on a wine-soaked evening, with his own personal ice bucket at the ready by his side, he'll still make perfect sense speaking schizo-packet gibberish, with his zone of unreality expanding to enshroud us. Chase's founding assumption, and the basis for our new company, is the belief that in the future the Earth's desktop computers will be linked together by something you've likely never heard of, so-called Asynchronous Transfer Mode, or ATM, instead of Ethernet, of which you've no doubt heard. There is a reason you've never heard of ATM, other than as a technology you extract your ready cash from, a reason that when you buy a computer for your desktop, you make sure it's equipped with Ethernet, and not with ATM, since "ATM to the Desktop" is an example of an idea, like the Transfer Protocol replacing TCP/IP, whose time was fast approaching, as innovation hurtled toward us from out of the future, but whose time, in reality, never in fact arrived. Every great idea you've never even heard of had a similar history in technochronic time, a time when in the moment your technology seems inevitable, when you peer into the future and see nothing but brilliant butterflies, only to find out later, through the dead eyes of reality, that toads are now so prevalent that they've eaten all your butterfly larvae, and your beautiful fluttering concept has had no chance to fly. When a VC places a bet on some larval technology, believing that *metamorphosis* is a year or two away, you'll often hear him speak of a "paradigm shift," some all-but-inevitable transformation in the underpinnings of reality, and 9 times out of 9.01, he needs to get a grip, he's wandering around somewhere in the Tadpole Galaxy, caught up in the *Outer Limits* of the Zone of Unreality, and having totally lost touch with the power of inertia, he's about to lose his shirt, so exquisitely monogrammed, by betting against *stasis* as the dominant paradigm. "ATM to the Desktop" is a paradigmatic example of what happens when we have a "paradigm shift" and the paradigm, for whatever reason, declines to be shifted, a perfect instance of inertia, and the dominance of stasis, and what becomes of an idea, so beautiful on paper, when it has a brilliant fluttering future only in the past. We are, in short, completely deluded; whatever it is that we are currently thinking is not about to happen in the real world ever, even in the future of the now distant past.

All that aside, we have a brilliant future, this was long ago, you get the idea. It's time to start the meeting, time flies in the technology world, if we want to be the dominant player in ATM to the Desktop, we need to get fucking moving, before we're too late, it's been nearly three weeks since the cover article of *Business Week* announced the New Paradigm, and it's ubiquitous ATM. The time has come at last to hear from our proverbial cocktail napkin, and make with the fucking PowerPoint, and formulate a plan. Now to be fair to Chase, he isn't actually a cocktail napkin, he's more of a kind of suction device for truly expensive wines; by the time we came to realize that the Germans were serious, and weren't about to leave the Leningrad countryside when the air turned chilly, and the snow began to fall, we totally abandoned our siege mentality, and started drinking wines that were fit for a Czar, so forget I ever mentioned Chase in the context of cocktail napkins; as far as Chase was concerned, we might be nearly bankrupt, but we fully deserved to drink with the gods. Some years later, after we'd all cashed out, Chase

spent $2 million on wine at the Napa Valley Wine Auction, includ-
ing $500,000 on a single bottle of Screaming Eagle, Heidi Peterson
Barrett's renowned cult wine, the '92 in particular, given a perfect
100 score by the wine critic Robert Parker. As an aside, it would be
nearly impossible to understand the culture of the Silicon Valley
Technology Bubble, that Prelapsarian Eden for Brilliant Fluttering
Butterflies, without understanding California cult wines and Robert Parker's scoring system, based as it is on power and elegance,
since power and elegance are the technocentric essence of Silicon
Valley's own scoring system for itself. And to be fair to Chase, the
bottle he paid half a million dollars for was a very large container,
known as a Methuselah, the same Methuselah who, as you may
recall from the Bible, Genesis 5:27, lived to be 969 years old, a
very long lifespan, even back in the old days. So here sits Chase,
looking like Methuselah, with flowing white hair and unlined skin,
of indeterminate age, somewhere between adolescence and four
or five hundred, with an armful of PowerPoint slides, redolent of
charisma, Essence of Unreality, and an elusive scent of danger that
would prove hard to pin down. The actual sources of this sense of
something dangerous about Chase would become clear only later;
for now, he has a strange blue gleam in his eye, the baritone voice
of an opera villain, and the sort of gleeful air of a teenager who's just
gotten away with something, sneaking a steer into the Headmas-
ter's office, or maybe defiling the altar of his stepfather's church.
The slides themselves are completely incomprehensible, filled with
slide after slide of block diagrams on computer I/O and bypassing
the operating system and the Segmentation and Reassembly of
Asynchronous Transfer Mode packets, fine, fine, whatever, power
and elegance in its purest form. I nod along the way VCs tend to
do, when they understand nothing and want to pretend that they
get it, give him a perfect score based on power and elegance, tell
him to get rid of Larry, he's a dear old friend but not a CEO, commit my firm to the deal, and go looking for co-investors, both of
whom surface quickly, pooling $3.5 million, cutting the deal, at
$2M pre, with Chase and the new CEO, Mark Lloyd, at Chase's
dining room table in a tract house outside Dallas, and thus having it
come to pass that Elicit Networks is born, in the strip-mall Paradise
of suburban Wherever, and the days of Elicit were nine hundred

and sixty-nine years, give or take nine hundred and sixty or so, and the containers of wine, the Jeroboams and Nebuchadnezzars, that would naturally be consumed in such a Biblical lifespan, at least back in the days of our Elicit Genesis, is a topic we will get to, before we reach the Book of Exodus, where we exited Elicit by selling it to the Germans, Siemens to be specific, for $2.4 billion. In order to tell you the end of this tale, before returning again to tell you its beginnings, perhaps you'll excuse us if we conflate separate myths. If you try to imagine a company, worth $14 billion at its peak, back in the Golden Age of NASDAQ 5000, unable to attract a single offer, when the Germans tried to sell it for $100 million, you'll get a pretty good picture of how the Iron Age worked, and why all of Silicon Valley was filled with weeping and lamentation, as the turkey buzzards arrived to gnaw on our livers, and the Valley was invaded by the inevitable plague of toads.

So at this point we have more investors, three, than we do employees, two, and we are well on our way to everlasting greatness. The rest of the Book of Genesis, detailing the actual buildup of the company, the hiring of twenty or thirty software and silicon engineers, the circuit designs and Verilog testing and ASIC tape-outs and wafer lot shipments, and launch of the product, and failure of the market, we can let these run, in computer jargon, in background mode, while we run in main memory. VCs have nothing much to do with building companies; we have everything to do with Board Meetings, and most of all, Board Dinners. The Board Dinners at Elicit were strictly regimented, drinks first upon arrival while the five of us gathered, standing room only, at the marble-topped bar, then on to our upstairs table where the first wines would be ordered, two or three bottles of Cabernet to get us started, while we contemplated the menu, though we knew it by heart, and a bottle of Chardonnay, in a silver ice bucket, standing next to Chase, to supplement the reds. The reds would start out at moderate levels, maybe a Mondavi Reserve or Phelps Insignia or Silver Oak Cabernet, before progressing to the true cult wines, the signature wines of the great 1990s technology bubble, wines like Araujo and Bryant and Dalla Valle "Maya", Harlan, Screaming Eagle, Grace Family Vineyards, and maybe Colgin or Dunn's Howell Mountain or Sine Qua Non, with its magnificent Rhone-style "Red Handed" Syrah,

each of them ten times what I'd paid for my first car. If we were
feeling particularly optimistic about the coming quarter, we might
follow our sixth or eighth or twelfth bottle of Araujo with something
more lavish from the Bordeaux region, a Chateau Lafite or Mouton or Margaux, particularly the 1982s that made Robert Parker famous, when he showed more than a few of these indelible creations
a grave and sententious 100-point enthusiasm. For the moment,
however, while the quarter looks adequate, we're going to have to
order another bottle of the Araujo, a wine that combines extraordinary power and richness with remarkable complexity and considerable finesse, a saturated purple/black color in the glass, followed
by aromas of sweet vanilla and crème de cassis, intermixed with
riveting scents of black currents and exotic spices, with overtones
of minerals, coffee, and buttered toast, a subtle yet powerful giant
of a wine, a wine that should age effortlessly for 30 or more years,
though in this case we're drinking it at the tender age of four, and
while it is, undoubtedly, an alcoholic beverage, it's so fucking tan-
nic that you can't feel your teeth, which seem to be cracking under
the wine's brute ferocity. Parker's rating? Precisely a 98. In spite
of our stomatological problems, we're seriously discussing business,
how the whole thing has stalled, how ATM to the Desktop doesn't
seem to be happening, how we've just had our eighth or twelfth
or sixteenth quarter in a row of the exact same revenue, the company is going nowhere, while we sip another glass of an exquisitely
fragrant but pugilistic beverage with a vicious left hook and anger-
management issues. One night in particular stands out from the
rest, the memory is a little hazy, when one of my firm's investors
had come to check on his investment; at this point we're the market
leaders in a $0 billion market, with our losses slightly bloated by
Board Dinner expenses, when we're joined by Dan Leary, from the
self-proclaimed legendary firm of Hartley, Budge, et al., systematic
and analytical and precise investors, with riveting scents of Pynchon
intermixed with a pithy skepticism, and just a hint of the paranoiac
when it came to their money, which was gradually being converted
into ethanol molecules, in order to pass cleanly through the blood-
brain barrier, and Dan wasn't much of a wine connoisseur, no matter what sort of analytics were precisely applied, although he was,
apparently, capable of counting, and the wine-bottle body count

was shall we say staggering. Dan was…I think appalled would be the word…I'm not sure he understood the nature of true power and elegance, and everlasting innovation in the ATM field, and may well have regarded our drunken Bacchanalia as somehow inappropriate with the company under siege, and a liquidity crisis rapidly approaching, as we appended a couple of snifters of Delamain Très Vénérable, and savored its lingering fade from Russian leather to Eastern spice, and steeled ourselves at last to face the dark winter evening, knowing that while the real work had finally been completed, we still had to undertake some vital unfinished business: to stand up, in a stupor, and negotiate the stairs.

Somewhere along the way, after yet another Quarter of $1.5M in revenue, it began to occur to us that the company was dying. Ethernet was still there, in the same way that the rail gauge on English railroads was determined long ago by the ruts left behind by Roman chariots, whose design specifications not even a Caesar could alter, since the entire Roman Empire was already deeply rutted by Neolithic oxcarts designed in the Stone Age, and just in case you're thinking some prehistoric VC, with a 20% stake in Invention of the Wheel, came up with something new for standard-gauge oxcarts, you need to get a grip, remember what we taught you about the power of stasis, because that oxcart layout was already predetermined by the time some hunter-gatherer clan, deep in the Paleolithic, huddling by the fire after a long day of hunting, decided they needed a meat sled to haul back the kill, and set their new sled-rails at about 4'8", to permit them to slide more easily over the deeply rutted fields. This isn't precisely accurate, but you get the idea; standard-gauge thinking is as old as the species. To make a long story short, the Ethernet standard was pretty thoroughly dug in, and ATM to the Desktop was not going to happen, just as the British were not about to rip up all the train tracks in England and put in monorails, no matter how elegant and powerful the solution looked on paper. My own contribution, beyond picking up my share of the tabs at Del Frisco's, comes here, a contribution that to this day is disputed by all, it just didn't happen, that at least is irrefutable. I'd been to visit another apparent wreck of a company that was working on something called Digital Subscriber Line, or DSL, technology for carrying video signals over normal twisted-pair telephone lines, to allow the phone companies to compete with the cable systems by wiring up your television with a normal twisted-pair, something that, as yet, has never actually happened. It occurred to me that it was vaguely possible that ATM "cells" might be carried over DSL to speed up Internet connections; I suggested to someone, maybe one of the janitors, that they might check and see if the phone companies were planning to carry ATM cells, which were already sledding around their network backbones, all the way out, beyond the telephone exchange local access switches, to the customer premises, the home or small office. As it turned out, accidentally, I happened to be right, and our CEO marched in, maybe six months later, to announce that we were now in a whole new business, we would make "DSL modems," which today are ubiquitous. Let's say I was wrong, it was not my idea; however it happened, it was still accidental, and the result is still ubiquitous. In any case, we scraped together the last few millions of dollars we could find, from "strategic investors" like ADC, Siemens, and Texas Instruments, and relaunched the company in DSL. When the technology bubble started to expand, two or three years later, and anything "Internet" was wildly overvalued, we would become among the best positioned of the wildly overvalued. Three or four Christmases in a row, in the meantime, we nearly went bankrupt, we were huddled in the rubble while the Nazis shelled North Dallas, before a last minute bailout by one of the "dumb money" guys that invest for corporations. We were still doing the same $1.5M per quarter in revenue, and technically insolvent again, when the last $10M came in, from the original investors, the last $10M on God's green earth, which would be gone in an instant if sales didn't accelerate, the phone companies are notoriously slow at launching new technologies, if it didn't happen now, the company would be history, and then, mysteriously at first, and in retrospect, inevitably, sales began to levitate, to $5M and then $10M and then $50M per quarter, the company went public, became wildly overvalued, with the stock price rising from $13 when we opened, to $65 in the first three hours, which has at last brought us here, to the wine cellar at Del Frisco's, for our Vintage Krug toast to life's indelible effervescence, and the power of liquidity to convey our true substance, since without it we'd all be a bunch of lavish drunks, trapped underground, feeling distinctly taphephobic, and preparing ourselves to participate in a premature burial service, like getting buried alive by our stone-sober investors.

We should, at this point, probably take our seats; the salads have arrived, and the wine is being poured, and with our market cap now hovering above $10 billion, and plenty of oxygen trapped in the ever-expanding market bubble, death by live burial would seem to be out of order. We're starting with an ethereal Corton-Charlemagne, a $500 white from the Burgundy region, which is about as far from Bahr al Ghazal as you can possibly get, a wine that in my understated Elicit Networks tasting notes is "all but inevitable" and "brilliantly executed" and "seemingly accidental but so richly deserved," though to be perfectly honest, let's not kid ourselves, no one in Silicon Valley, much less North Dallas, really gives a shit about ethereal Burgundies, since they're more about earthy poetry, and epiphanic moments, than power and elegance, measured in fruit-pounds of torque, and Parker, rather famously, no longer bothers to even taste them. White wines are tolerated, to wash down a first course, but it isn't clear that "ethereal" is precisely what we're looking for, to power through an iceberg wedge with an enormous mound of Roquefort dressing. Perhaps we should focus on the first of the reds, an '82 Lafite, from the chateau-laden Pauillac, a wine that I know well, on an intimate basis, since I have several cases of it stored in a bedroom broom-closet: a knockout nose of lead pencil, minerals, and Provencal flowers, with blackberry liqueur, kirsch, truffles, currant, and incense overtones, a fat mid-palate, with explosive fruit and richness, and a sweet yet impeccably balanced fifty-second finish, a wine of such nobility, so impressively endowed, that it must be considered among the wine world's true aristocrats, a wine so expansive and yet supple and lithe that...no, wait...our apologies...that's an entirely different wine...the '82's perfume is the stuff of which legends are made, cedar, spicy oak, currants, herbs, and minerals, a dazzlingly powerful wine of monumental proportions, impeccably poised and balanced as it lingers on the tongue, with all of the elegance one expects but so seldom encounters, perhaps a somewhat more *rich* Lafite than one might have guessed, but then again, aren't we all, so *for Christ's sake let's just swallow.* That gentleman sitting across from you, swirling his second or third glass, is a man you should probably recognize from a previous encounter; notice how his minute hand is beginning to turn backwards; he's only just started his nearly yearlong run of $2 million a day in capital-gains-taxed income, and won't be living with starlets in the hills for another year or two, as it takes time to unwind a 30-year marriage, but just give him on the order of four or five hours, and he'll be undressing our waitress in his suite at the Ritz Carlton, because *Live Like You Mean It*, which he fully intends to do, does not appear to him to be utterly baffling nonsense. So why do I have Lafite stashed in a bedroom closet? Isn't proper cellar-aging vital to the maturation process? Doesn't this magnificent '82 Lafite, as compellingly profound as any wine in Bordeaux, not due to reach maturity for 30 years or more, deserve better treatment than broom-closet aging? I suppose; the way Parker describes it, with all its elegance and poise, it probably deserves a marriage proposal and a six-carat ring, over a candlelit dinner at a villa on Cap Ferrat, where you profess that, at long last, you've finally found your soulmate, and can't bear the thought of ever living a day without her. So let me ask you something. Have you ever awakened in the dead of night, after four or five months on a quart-a-day vodka regimen, and discovered, to your horror, that the vodka has run out, and you're about to undergo some rather unpleasant perceptual disturbances, giant spiders on the ceiling, rats on the bathroom floor, or the curious sensation that bugs are crawling on your skin, a tactile hallucination known as *formication?* Let's just say that your tasting notes on the '82 Lafite, after guzzling 20 ounces or so of its impeccably balanced poise, wouldn't have much to do with spicy oak perfume, they'd be more like *O my God, get these fucking insects off of me.* This isn't, to be clear, precisely applicable to me, as I managed to taper off while I was still at the pupal stage, and came up well short of delusional parasitosis, with its chitinous-mandibulate hexapodal motorcades; besides, the 3:00 am chugging of Chateau Lafite, in order to get some sleep when my neurons were hacksawed, and my ethanol-starved mind was writhing and seething, hasn't even happened yet, it's still a few years off, so let's return to dinner, and flickering tapered flames, and tulip-folded dinner napkins, once a lovely ivory white, now heavily smeared with dead-steer grease and burnt bits of T-bone.

So, you must be thinking, where the hell is Chase? What was the *inside story* on how you happened to fire him? Wasn't there something about *danger* you mentioned, something that was maybe a little off-kilter, an elusive charisma that proved hard to pin down? You can't just leave us with a gleaming blue strangeness, and flickering tapered candles, and burnt bits of bone. What exactly was *inside of Chase*? This, to be honest, is one of those pages I'd like to skip, or cover up completely with a thick layer of Wite-Out, leaving a note at the bottom, like a Top Secret document, This Page Left Intentionally Slightly Tacky and Blank. Let's just say that Chase went a little off the rails, and had to be removed, and leave it at that. Besides, I'm not altogether sure I was actually present; the year that I fired him was 1997, and I may have been away on one of my Smirnoff vacations; after 22 years in the venture business, and a billion or two in profits returned on investments, why should the sort of man who's become *a man to reckon with* have to account for much of anything, much less his own *presence*? *Absent-mindedness*, let's face it, is one of the prerogatives of the powerful. Are you somehow under the illusion that the people who run our country actually hold themselves accountable for knowing their own *whereabouts*? Does the phrase *I don't recall* begin to ring a bell? It's apparent that more than a few of our moronic foreign adventures were launched by the sort of men who were acting *in absentia*, and were nowhere near the neighborhood of *themselves* when the shit went down. Do you suffer from the delusion that the men who rewrote our banking laws, and made perfectly respectable businessmen out of a bunch of fucking gangsters, had *minds of their own*? What's this got to do with Chase? I have no idea; I'm afraid, ladies and gentlemen, that *I simply don't recall*. If you want my opinion, Chase went a little crazy; guy had to go, simple as that. I'm sitting at a desk that certainly speaks for itself, with a *Lifetime Achievement* plaque, and a boatload of money, and the sunrise is coming in maybe 20 or 30 minutes, though I can't help noting, just for the record, that the sky seems to be turning a weird shade of grey, and doesn't look at all like the beginnings of a morning, it looks like yet another of those twilight-state anomalies, where you're chasing after something, and the farther away it gets, the more you come to realize that it's been sneaking up behind you. According to my *Dream Dictionary*, a sunrise in a dream is a sign of new beginnings and personal renewal, so why do I get the feeling that the new day's dawn has snuck up from behind me in a malignant shade of grey, and that the sunrise itself, that illusory bent-light instant, when the sun's upper edge appears to cross the eastern horizon line, will not come to signify my personal renewal, but will spread across the sky in the colorectal crimson of an oncogenic neoplasm slowly beginning to metastasize. Jesus, I *am* tired; this, even to me, sounds slightly fucked-up; like what in God's name is *colorectal crimson*, and since when did a Monday morning, the morning after Easter as a matter of fact, start feeling like it needed chemo treatment? I haven't had a drink in fourteen months, and I have to get my taxes filed, and I'm nowhere near the bottom of this whole Dacha Wireless mess, though I've got a pretty good handle on how Prospero's magic bookkeeping worked, via a spiderweb of companies, woven inside a willow hoop, like a Chippewa Dreamcatcher, known as Third World Partners; Chase, come to think of it, originally introduced them to us. Not that this makes any more sense to me than it does to you, but I'm going to need a tax accountant who's fluent in Ojibwa, understands the bauxite industry, and can help me cross the Black Sand Desert, searching for WiMAX cell phone towers. You want to know something funny? This *Dream Dictionary* I'm using has an entry under taxes, something about a price to be paid for living the way I'm living, which may explain the sneaking suspicion that my past is catching up with me, with a strange blue gleam in its eye, and like a half-gallon of vodka.

So where are we now? We're deep in my bedroom, in *the dead of night*, a genitive-link metaphor which I sometimes wish were literal, shortly before the 3:00 am chugging of five-sixths of a bottle of Chateau Lafite, an impeccably balanced, and aristocratically poised, ethanol-based pesticide and insect repellent. I'm not trying to tell you that the bugs have arrived, but with my neurons hacksawed and my mind now seething, I certainly don't intend to take any chances. In the absolute blackness of one of my walk-in closets, I'm searching for a Reality Engine that doesn't in fact exist, a half-quart of vodka that I'm fully convinced must lie at the bottom of a pile of old clothing, made up, for the most part, of $3,000 suits, the pinstriped-camouflage of a full-fledged alcoholic. The darkness itself is like a physical substance, far more real than my long-gone vodka bottle, that seems to have altered its matter-phase state from some sort of gas into liquefied agony, a punitive substance which is preparing, even now, to begin its final passage through the blood-brain barrier, and enter my central nervous system in the next 18 seconds, if I don't find my bottle of liquid irreality. And then. Nothing. No vodka bottle, no solid substance, nothing to get a grip on, nothing at all. And then. A moment of panic. I can make it to the broom closet, but how will I find my corkscrew? And then. Dear God, what was that noise? Someone, or some *thing*, is inside my bedroom, itself a dank container of cerebrospinal subarachnoid fluid, the stuff the human brain finds itself floating around in, where some sort of crudely cerebral neuro-necrotic *pulsing* is slowly floating toward me with a mind of its own. *Chase.* I perform a rapid calculation, as my neurons demyelinate, and corrode down to dendrites with sawed-off axons: if I do find my vodka bottle, in the next few seconds, can I drink the half-quart, and retain enough mass to use it as a weapon? Chase will have a knife, a MACV-SOG, left over from his days as a Phoenix Program assassin, a Vietnam-era counter-insurgency monstrosity that liquidated humans while they slept in their hootches. How many men and women has Chase butchered already, of the 25,000-plus that Phoenix eradicated? I have no idea. I try not to picture the knife itself, a thin two-edged dagger with a foil-ring grip, modeled on the gleaming Fairbairn-Sykes trench knife, with its seven-inch penetrant rib-cage blade, but with a non-reflective luminosity-absorbent *dead-of-night* finish on the carbon steel alloy, the SOG-assassin's equivalent of a dark-body window, or the one-way mirror of death-glazed eyes. I try not to picture the iceberg-blue brilliance of Chase staring into me, the final time I saw him, finding nothing even vaguely worthy of his reflection. I grope around mindlessly in the liquid-agony gruel, but it's too late now, it's already inside me, and at this point I don't care at all if I die, just as long as Chase will help me find my vodka bottle; I don't want to die in liquefactive agony, I just want to die, in peaceful irreality. And then. Nothing. And then. More and more nothing, slowly drifting toward me, dripping cerebrospinal drool. And then. A miracle, Spiritus Sancti, an unheard-of stroke of luck, a solid mass of something that has to be a bottle. Somehow, in a blackout, several hours ago, I must have had a brilliant flash of radiant illumination, because what I now hold in my quivering right hand, a bottle of '82 Chateau Lafite, has not only been moved from the bedroom broom-closet, don't ask me why I have a bedroom broom-closet, maybe the drunken architect thought it up during a blackout, but the cork has been pulled, and placed back in the bottle for ease of access, and I am, even now, not thinking of death at all, I'm halfway though swallowing five-sixths of its substance. And Chase? What do you mean Chase? Why would you bring up Chase at a moment like this? Chase is nowhere near here, he's on the Ile Saint-Louis, I thought I told you that whole story already, and I, Frederick Hobart Edie Mertz the First, you can call me Edie, or First for short, am having a little nightcap, right around bedtime, so let me ask you something, as long as you're here, who do you think you are floating around in my bedroom, and how in God's name did you get in here in the first place?

# 11

*I* awoke the next day to the cacophonous sounds of starlings and swallows, or maybe it was mockingbirds, thrashers, and warblers, or Calliope Hummingbirds, or Rose-throated Tanagers, and the warm morning sun seeping in through the shutters, and a curious assortment of personal memories now a full one day old. Among the clearest of my memories, of course, and the first to come back to me in the dimly lit room, was the memory of having awakened on a similar occasion in a dimly lit room, exactly like this one, with no sense at all as to where on earth I was; I couldn't help wondering, in an idle sort of way, in the manner of a man who is not really wondering, but toying with the idea of beginning to wonder, where I was now, and what I would find if I reopened the shutters, and whether or not, given my odd prior history, I might have fled in the night, in some borderland dream state, to start my life over in a whole new locale. Having only, in some sense, reawakened once, or really, come to think of it, this was something of an overstatement, as I had only actually *awakened* on a single prior occasion, and found myself in that case in a strange new city, could I really be confident that I hadn't moved on, to Tangiers or Istanbul or Paramaribo, Suriname? How long had I been asleep? Had I slept my way through an entire three-day journey, and found myself once again in a dimly lit room, a room whose only distinguishing feature was the absence of any sort of distinguishing features, other than shutters whose plantation-style louvers leaked only enough light to define them as louvers? There are all sorts of rooms that come equipped with plantation shutters, and beds like the one I was idling in now, where a man could lie back on very similar pillows, toying with ideas, enjoying the songbirds, and beginning to wonder, in an idle sort of way, why he knows that Suriname is on the north coast of South America, with Paramaribo as its prime port and capital, and with an economy dominated by the bauxite industry. What sort of man knows the capital of Suriname? Why would this man, this apparently prior *me*, be the least bit interested in the future of the bauxite industry? Was I the sort of man, perhaps a speculator in aluminum futures, who might have stopped off in Guanajuato to see the Mummy Museum, on his way farther south to his true destination, some vast strip-mined wasteland full of reddish-orange alumina pits and turquoise-tinted tailing ponds and lavender-yellow-copperish piles of bauxite agglomerate? Other than the fact that Rose-throated Tanagers prefer overgrowth and scrubwoods to dense tropical rainforests, was there any real reason that I couldn't be in Suriname? Was my Rose-throated Tanager, with its pale violet plumage and rich Cardinal warbling, really a Blue-black Grosbeak, with its harsh monotonous tweeting, and its glossy-black beak, droning from the top of a Paramaribo Sandbox tree? And the deeper I dug here, the worse I began to feel: since I seemed to know nothing about aluminum itself, other than the fact that nanometric aluminum powder was used in the construction of new classes of explosives, was I really some sort of weapons dealer, down here on a buying spree, seeking hundreds of tons of aluminum oxide? As I thought this matter through, without really thinking much of anything about it, it occurred to me that I seemed to know all sorts of places that might have an interest in metal-enhanced explosives, from Abuja, Nigeria to Kampala, Uganda to the Black Sands Desert in the middle of Turkmenistan. Before I was fully aware of the change taking place, or even for that matter being fully wide-awake, these thoughts that I'd only been toying around with had started up a cacophonous and reason-defying process that had apparently decided to start *toying around with me*: this planet is overflowing with nearly limitless possibilities for blowing things all to hell and gone, just who do I think I am, where on Earth am I?

I got up out of bed, groped my way forward in the direction of the seepage, took hold of the frames beside the horizontal louvers, and bracing myself for anything from tailing ponds and smelter stacks to Caterpillar roads through agglomerate mountains, threw open the shutters on a blue-sky day and a warm morning sunshine cascading deluge and the bright-noted warbling and trilling cacophony of a large flock of sparrows that whirled and circled and came in for a perfect landing, in the acacia-tree-silence of a Guanajuato Saturday. I opened the bolt on the double-leaf casement window; pulled the windows inward to let in some air; and took a deep breath of the early morning silence; I wasn't in a suite at the Paramaribo Hilton, I was back in my room at the Inn of the Poets. The Basilica clock tower read 7:20; the cobblestone streets were swept-clean and empty; the tourist-goods shops and retail arcades, as might be expected at this hour of the morning, had their rolling-steel shutters pulled down and padlocked, and were no doubt hours from opening for business. In the early-morning silence and stillness of the city, downtown Guanajuato seemed completely self-contained, a rose-domed and custard-walled and church-spired display of beauty for its own sake, with no need whatsoever for human activity; as I stood there in the window, idling away the moments, existing as an instance of being for its own sake, with no sense at all of being anyone in particular, I couldn't help wishing that I were similarly self-contained, because while downtown Guanajuato would still have its beauty once business resumed, and the city filled with activity, I had no way of knowing just who would show up, at my face-to-face meeting with my new day's identity. Having already awakened on a prior occasion with no sense at all as to who on earth I was, could I really be certain that I hadn't moved on, not to Tangiers or Istanbul or Suriname, but to a whole new *me* that I'd have to learn to live with, the way a man who wakes up on his 40th day of sobriety, feeling once again like a new-found man, discovers that the man that he'll be meeting at lunchtime is the dead-drunk self he thought he'd left for dead.

Just who do I think I am? Where on Earth am I? These, in essence, were the exact same question; Guanajuato and I were ontologically intertwined; Guanajuato, in some sense, was only what I'd made of it, and I, of course, was what Guanajuato had made of me. Having let the past go and pointed myself forward and determined to make myself out of all new materials, it was time for me to see if we'd survived through the night, or if it was time to start over after a long night's absence, brick by ontological brick by brick. I felt more than a little like Alvaro de Campos, looking out his window in his poem The Tobacco Shop, waiting for Esteves to acknowledge his existence, and affirm Alvaro's own improbable reality, by spotting him in the window, and waving his goodbyes, knowing that in my case, equally improbable, my own Tobacco Shop was padlocked and shuttered, and the people who knew me, at least well enough to wave, were probably sound asleep, at just past 7:20 on a Guanajuato Saturday. In the quiet and calm of a picture-perfect morning, with even the songbirds, after calling me from sleep, off reinventing silence among the branches of an acacia tree, I found myself, in some sense, in a *whole new world*, a world that I for one had never once laid eyes on, full of church spires and cathedral domes that were right back where they started, with every last lamppost present and accounted for, along narrow cobbled streets that had managed to lay their stones down precisely along the routes that they'd stubbornly adhered to, and while this new world, admittedly, was identical to the old one, it was just this very identity that brought the *new world* home to me, with a *welcome back* greeting, and a banner-day homecoming, to this high mountain valley of my first *welcome home*. The dusty-rose basilica dome of the Cathedral of our Lady, with its wedding-cake bell tower above custard-yellow walls, and its clock face overlooking the city-center Zócalo, hadn't moved an inch in the hours that I'd slept through; the royal-purple, orange-green, and pink-flamingo houses still climbed the slope of the exact same hillside, on the far side of the ravine, with El Pípila at its peak; and the winding cobbled streets, with their pastel-colored townhomes, and red geranium flowerboxes, and black wrought-iron balcony railings, continued to make their way to the Plaza de la Paz. Here I was again, right back where I'd started, with the bright-noted birdsong cardinal cacophony having perfected its new invention among the branches of an acacia tree, and the warm morning sun pouring in through my windows, and all of Guanajuato silently acknowledging me, on the first second morning of my improbable reality.

And then, of course, I found the FedEx package, right where I'd left it, beside me on the window ledge, reminding me that I had not been forgotten, though whatever it was that I might best be remembered for, I could not in the least recall. One of the sparrows from the acacia flock landed on the window ledge, eyed me suspiciously as I picked up the package, and then vanished abruptly, as though it had come to the wrong window. While I seriously doubt that sparrows actually harbor suspicions, I don't doubt for a moment that sparrows are psychic, as I was beginning to wonder if I should find a whole new window, something high above the tailing ponds at the Paramaribo Hilton. There was no getting around the feeling that Gabriella's photos of the grim-faced men, taken upon some occasion where the appropriateness of my attire and personal demeanor might well be called into question, and the FedEx message from out of the blue, backward slanting and cryptically ominous, were trying to tell me something, some story about myself that I didn't like the sounds of, a story that included my HSBC bank balance, apparently deposited in hand-carried currency. I couldn't account for any of this, much less recount it; I had ominous acquaintances, an oversized bank balance, and nothing resembling a personal account. What could possibly possess a man to carry $20 million across the Mexican border? This in itself was both dangerous and illegal; what could I possibly have been thinking? Excuse me, sir, where do you think you're going with all this money? I'm not sure, Officer, I suppose I must be going into Mexico. Are you aware of the fact that it is illegal to carry more than $10,000 in unreported hard currency into or out of the country? Of course, of course, but I seriously doubt that breaking the law was among my intentions. So this wasn't what you intended, then. No, no, I wouldn't think so; it appears to me to have been completely inadvertent. Maybe you'd better come with me; I'm guessing my supervisor may have one or two questions. I'm sure he does, I myself have any number of questions, but you must understand that I personally know little or nothing about this. Is this your bag, sir? I suppose it is, I seem to be carrying it, but as for the bag's contents, it strikes me as slightly odd that a large pile of money would be found there among them. So this is not your money? Ah, as for that, I have yet to form a personal opinion, it seems to me highly unlikely, I mean how many men do you know that have 20 million dollars in ready cash? And yet the money is in your possession. I'll grant you that it appears to be among my possessions, but as for actually possessing it, I'm really

not sure that I would go that far. Do I look like the sort of man who
would have 20 million dollars? Not really, now that you mention it.
Well, there you go, this whole thing strikes me as highly unlikely, it
seems to be one of those inexplicable incidents, not really the sort of
thing for which anyone could be held accountable. So it's just one
of those things. Precisely, precisely, it's just one of those things; life
seems to be full of such things, these inexplicable incidents, these
improbable occurrences for which we just can't account. Take that
bird there, for instance, I think that it may be a Red-Breasted Nut-
hatch; how could anyone possibly account for an occurrence such
as that? I would hate to be held accountable for life's improbable
occurrences, life itself is an improbable occurrence; you couldn't
very well hold me accountable for that. I see; I suppose not; so it's
just one of those things for which no one could possibly account.
Yes, yes, exactly. Very well then, carry on, but try not to let it happen again. And be careful in Juárez, almost anything can happen,
anything. Certainly sir, I appreciate your understanding. Perhaps I
should skip Juárez altogether, and go directly to Guanajuato, where
apparently the improbable is considered legal tender.

   I threw the FedEx on the bed, threw open the other shutters,
and acknowledged the morning, itself unaccountable. The cobblestone streets, the wrought-iron balconies, the houses climbing the
hills in improbable colors; how does one account for the existence
of any of this? I couldn't, I didn't; I showered and shaved and went
down to breakfast, in a small outdoor garden, where I sat in the
shade, beside a musical stone fountain. Water flowed from a hidden
source at the top of the fountain, collected in a high basin that filled
to the brim, and then overflowed on down over a carved granite column, where it pooled and waited and then returned to its source.
Time passed and yet it didn't, there were moments of waiting, but
they were all the same moment, as though history, to the fountain,
had already happened, and time moved forward by flowing back
toward its source. The music of the fountain was faintly nostalgic,
a nostalgia for the present, the very moment that never came. I can
see you shaking your head over my drifting off and meandering;
believe me, when I think about it, I too shake my head. A man re-
ceives an ominous message, via FedEx, from someone actually out
there with a time-stamped reality, and immediately drifts away into

timelessness and poetry; such a man, whoever he thinks he is, probably can't be helped. Do you see this hole, sir? Why yes, it reminds me of the sort of hole used to bury a person's body. Precisely; what we have in mind is putting a bullet in your head, pushing you in the hole, and covering you up with dirt. But wait, before you do, I have a poem that I think might be suitable for the occasion, I'm sure that by the time you've heard it, putting a bullet in someone's head will be the last thing on your mind. Well, let's hear it then, but you might want to be aware of the fact that we don't have much use for poetry in our line of work. And keep it short, it's getting late, and we still have a lot of dirt to shovel. On the other hand, I was still alive, eating breakfast all alone in my musical garden, and few men wind up with bullets in their head while filled with poetic thoughts. The trees were full of songbirds, tuning out the threat of violence, maybe Beethoven's Nightingale, quail calls, and cuckoos, from the serene second movement of the composer's 6th Symphony, or the Chopin sounds of a Canyon Wren, or Mozart's pet Starling, singing two songs at once, one on each vocal cord, Mozart's own Piano Concerto in G major, together with Vivaldi's Goldfinch, a flute concerto in D, one song flowing off over the sunlit rooftops, and one hiding in the shadows, reminding me of me. Where exactly did I plan to hide, what bush was I expecting myself to crawl down under, if time started up again for the men who had not forgotten, and some bird started singing, reminding them of me? What was I, Alvaro de Campos, who could never be said to have planned his existence, or to remind himself of anyone, least of all himself, supposed to do about a future that had already happened, as it flowed steadily backwards toward an unremembered source? The musical fountain played on while I sat and ate my breakfast, and wondered about the future, toward which I was slowly headed, evidently in reverse. Be careful in Juárez, almost anything can happen, and who knows what can happen, particularly when, as in my case, it apparently already has.

   When I'd finished my breakfast, I returned to my room, to take a closer look at the FedEx package, and the newspaper clippings that alluded to violence, and the cryptic note in a backward-slanting hand. First of all, the time-stamped packing slip showed a Juárez address, and a Sender identified as Third World Partners.

The newspaper clippings were full of gruesome news, with bodies buried everywhere, in empty lots across the street from circuit board assembly plants, in the backyards of houses in residential neighborhoods, in official mass gravesites that anxious parents hadn't known about, for reasons of State Security, and protection of the dubious. Thirty-six skeletons in sixteen graves, at a house on Pedregal street, and nine more at 1847 Cocoyoc, all properly buried in holes five feet deep; ten bodies found elsewhere in four backyard pits, five left whole but apparently tortured, three found missing the operative appendages, and two lacking all but their actual heads; thirty-three "corpses" in a weedy vacant lot, behind a cinderblock wall in a low income subdivision, and even with the help of dozens of pickaxes and shovels, a fleet of backhoes, and a large pack of sniffer dogs, it had taken a good two weeks to find all the pieces, given the general and widespread state of dismemberment, and disorganization of the integral body parts; the House of Death at 3633 Calle Parsonieros, where a DEA informant supplied the quicklime and duct-tape, and kept the U.S. apprised of the exigent processes; an officially sanctioned mass hole-in-the-ground, containing 4,000 loved ones, many of them women, who had made the grave error, in the eyes of officials, of leaving their bodies lying around far too long uncollected; after a good 90 days, what were they expecting? And so on. The body-count alone was enough to unsettle any sense of the proportionate, much less the poetic; there seemed to be more violent death in the local War on Drugs than in the War on Terror in the entire nation of Afghanistan. The backward slant of the handwritten note, which had looked to me like a bird flying backward, now resembled the subtle tilt of a hand-wielded butcher's knife, readying a young woman to be disassembled into piece parts. Beyond this, the whole business displayed a number of familiar themes: the early dominance of the market by a visionary enterprise, the Juárez Cartel, founded by the brothers Carrillo Fuentes; the ongoing struggle for market share in Juárez, between the Sinaloa, Gulf, and Carrillo Fuentes cartels; and the vital role played by Government, Local, State, and Federal, in encouraging free enterprise, and ensuring an uneven playing-field. The rewards for success were readily apparent: the Juárez Cartel earned $200 million a week in top-line revenues, less, no doubt, certain officially sanctioned business expenses;

if one assumed that they had even decent net margins, a business like this, with zero discernible debt, and no readily auditable income taxes, would have had a $50 billion market capitalization, or a little less than Walt Disney Corp., and three times the value of Alcoa Aluminum.

And somewhere among them were men who had not forgotten. I sat back on the bed and stared out the window, thinking about my large green duffel, my bars of gold bullion, and my HSBC bank balance, rendered inaccessible via ATM. What sort of business had I gotten myself into? Was I in this thing alone, as an owner and sole proprietor, or was it structured as a Partnership, with management fees and carried interest? As I thought about the nature of clawbacks and lock-ups, Gabriella came out the door onto her intricate iron balcony, with her blue plastic bucket and an armful of laundry, and began to pin her clothes up to dry, in the mid-morning sun of this improbable valley. The colors of the day were all I-Surrender White, sheets and pillow cases, bras and panties, and I pictured a man climbing the steps to a plane, turning to wave to his friends with a clean white hankie, and boarding a flight to a faraway place, Bolivia perhaps, no wait, make it Senegal, or Bangladesh or Tibet, or Mozambique or Sri Lanka, somewhere on Earth far away from the drug lords, a place with no fixed address, off the grid, unreachable, where they'd never heard of FedEx, or Vicente Carrillo Fuentes. There was something about watching Gabriella and the domesticity of her laundry that made me begin to think that I was about to feel lonely, and I wondered if that was the sort of man I was, the kind who feels lonely when confronting aloneness. From the evidence at hand, the answer was not apparent; I was a man who admired the works of José Saramago, at peace all these years alone with his library, his Soviet of books, and living in an utter wasteland of a Paradise of remoteness, in exile on the Canary Islands, far from his homeland, and creating the sort of unreachable characters that seldom seem to depend on a shared sense of community, or any of the usual connections to the workings of the heart. And then I remembered that Saramago himself had a wife, Pilar del Río, who had come to love him through his writing and keep him company in his aloneness. The Doctor's Wife in *Blindness* was the only one who could see; perhaps this implied that in my blindness to myself and my own personality, I might be in need of a companion, one perhaps with a sharp pair of scissors, to look into my nature, and do my seeing for me. Gabriella looked up from her armful of clean white laundry, caught me staring at her uncertainly, and graciously shared a smile that was a beautiful thing to see. On the other hand, we had Alvaro de Campos himself, a man who had lived a full life, in Burrow-in-Furness, Cumbria, apparently unimpeded by the burdens of companionship, without a single friend, except perhaps his author, a man, meaning Pessoa, whose constant companion was loneliness, a feeling he held up to the light, and ever so carefully examined, the way a skeptical mineralogist might go about the study of a taken-for-granted and common and widely familiar rock. How was I to know if I were similarly hard-hearted, or was about to succumb to loneliness, on a long flight to elsewhere, Flight 000, if I didn't reach out to someone who would make me feel like me?

In any case, the thought, that I was about to feel lonely, and in need of some companionship, gave way to a far more practical thought, which was Now what exactly do I propose to do next? I needed to see Gustavo, and confront him with the photos of my unpleasant-looking companions, and ask for an explanation as to what makes grim men grim. And by the way, Gustavo, I know it's none of your business, but what on earth is the meaning of my possessing so much money? I pocketed the leftovers from the previous night's spending, having once again reduced myself, my 1,000-peso stature, to something in the 700s, and a pile of indecipherable coins. I exited the hotel, walked past the tunnel leading to elsewhere, whose semicircular open mouth was still swallowing autos and men, and called up to Gabriella to come down and take a walk with me, and bring along her photographs, as if she still had any memory of them, on her short, backward, upside-down, or maybe inside-out, list, her bear-with-me-for-a-moment-I-have-it-here-somewhere listing of her memories of where she'd put her list. What photos do you mean, Alvaro? Check again, Gabriella, they must be there somewhere, down near the bottom of your memorable list, where maybe the last thing you did before going to bed last evening was to hide them in your Bible. Ah, but of course, Alvaro, though I would never hide them in my Bible, perhaps in my copy of Cervantes, to remind me of how I'm reminded of you by the journeys of Don Quixote. Remind me to show you our museum full of art works inspired by the Don; you might be able to learn something useful to your own situation. I remind you of whom? She didn't answer, she returned through the balcony doorway, and joined me in the street a moment or two later, with the photographs of the grim-faced men tilting from her purse. We began walking away from La Casa Del Quijote, the hotel next to mine, with a tunnel through its lobby, and I asked her again, I remind you of whom? Don Quixote, Alonso Quixano, he too was a fiction of a fiction, his history so thoughtfully ascribed by Cervantes to the work of a fictional Moorish historian, Cide Hamete Benengeli, and Quixano too came from somewhere or other, a place whose name he refused to remember, de cuyo nombre no quiero, "whose name I do not wish to recall." So I remind you of Don Quixote? No, no, not really, it's more a kind of mnemonic device, to help me to remember the name of you. I don't understand. Alonso is a name that means "ready for battle," a posture that the Don so humorously adopted, and your name, Alvaro, if I remember it correctly, comes from the Visigothic Alewar, one who is ready for anything, constantly on his guard. Honestly, Gabriella, you can barely remember ten minutes ago, where did you ever come up with this? It is the string around my finger, reminding me to tie a string. A string tied to a string? A fiction of a fiction, don't think for a moment I'm unaware of the fact that your assumed name, Alvaro de Campos, is a fiction of Fernando Pessoa's, who himself seems far from real. So you know my real name is not Alvaro de Campos? But of course it is, Alvaro, you yourself gave me the name, what could be more real than the name that you've assumed? Well, maybe my actual name, the name that's tied to my history. I don't see how you can expect me to remember you by a name that you yourself refuse to recall. Does Don Quixote have a name more real than Don Quixote? If Cervantes wanted him to have another name, he would have given him another name, and this would be the name we would remember him by, but what could be more memorable than the name Don Quixote? If he had a different name, not even Cervantes could remember it, or perhaps, much like you, he simply refused to recall.

Each of us finds intelligence only in those whose thoughts are in the same state of disorder as our own. In any case, unlike Proust, hovering over his correlative madeleine, writing it all out in long-hand, and bringing so much memorable order to his dilettantish life that he would one day become Marcel Proust, my problem had nothing to do with disorder; my thoughts about myself were all perfectly orderly, but it was difficult to take them seriously, since they were, after all, only one day old. We continued down Calle Cantaritos toward the Plaza de la Paz and the HSBC bank branch on Calle Benito Juárez. An impromptu restaurant had been set up in the cobbled street, with red and white checkered tablecloths on white plastic tables, where people were beginning to gather for lunch, carnitas and tamales and carne asada, served from a street vendor's stainless steel pushcart. The air was filled with the aroma of steaming masa and roasted pork shoulder, and tortillas toasting on a hot comal, and dozens of beer cans popping open, scents that took me back, as though jolted by a sudden whiff of something, all the way back to this exact present moment, and the primitive and everlasting smell of right now. We passed by a building that housed the Legislature of the State of Guanajuato, which might explain the attire of many of the restaurant's customers, men in dark suits and white shirts and responsible neckties, rep stripes and paisleys and polka dots and the occasional solid yellow or powder blue power tie, tied in four-in-hands and Pratt's and half-Windsor-with-a-dimple knots, and here and there a full Windsor, denoting power and privilege and a certain amount of manual dexterity. Of the eighty-five possible knots that can be made from an ordinary necktie, using a limit of nine moves, beyond which the knots be-come unsuitably unwieldy, the Legislature exhibited a fairly lim-ited range and repertoire; these were men who knew their place in the world, and tied their knots accordingly. On an impulse, or more precisely, as though imitating the actions of a man who acts on impulse, a man who knows the difference between an impulse and a whim, I removed the photos from Gabriella's purse, and looked at the neckties of the grim-faced men. They were all wearing the same tie, like members of a secret society, navy blue or forest green or mud-hut brown or whatever, all with a single ornament, drawn in bright gold thread in the bottom third of the Windsor-knotted tie, a draftsman's compass and right-angled straightedge framing a sin-gle gold letter, a letter that, unfortunately, from the photographer's careful distance, I could see quite clearly, but couldn't begin to make out. The precision with which these knots had been tied was blatant and measured and somewhat unnerving. The seven-move knot of the aristocratic Windsor requires a good deal of practice and an innate sense of length, without which the result can look clownish and sloppy. These were evidently practiced and calibrated men; there was nothing even remotely sloppy about them. My casual attire and jovial demeanor looked increasingly out of place among the brazenly secretive and aristocratic men; they didn't appear to be finding much history of intelligence in my crooked and clueless and dimwitted grin.

I returned the photos to Gabriella's purse and we continued on toward the watermelon Basilica dome, and the custard-yellow exterior of the nearby Cathedral, and the honeydew flesh of the HSBC bank branch, to see if Gustavo would see us; perhaps he could teach me how to mind my own business. The sky was an uncanny blue, the indelible blue of a timeless moment, with a few thin clouds sketched out across the sky, like a drawing of clouds entitled *Nothing Lasts Forever*. You are not so much speaking, Alvaro. It is something that is bothering you? My existence is bothering me, Gabriella, I don't know who I am, or how I ended up here, I'm a mystery to myself, an absolute mystery. How am I ever going to know what I am doing, when I don't know what it is I've done? I kept this to myself, this was really not her problem, and instead said aloud It's a beautiful morning, isn't it? I love your improbable city, I wish I could go on living here, just living in the present moment, and let the future take care of itself. You are worrying the future may not care for itself? I had a package waiting for me last night at the hotel, I'm afraid that my past may be finally catching up with me; someone knows who I am, and knows where to find me, and I'm afraid of what may happen if my past is catching up. But you are not hard to find, are you, Alvaro, you are here in Guanajuato, even I remember that. As for your past catching up with you, this seems odd for you to be saying, with each day that passes, the past becomes more distant; if it is trying to reach Guanajuato, your past is going the wrong way. We entered the bank branch, probably walking backwards, asked to see Señor Hernandez, and were told that he was out, having lunch at his usual café. His administrator

pointed out the window to where Gustavo was seated, at an outdoor table at the Tasca de le Paz, eating with a friend or business
acquaintance, an elegant-looking man in a chalk-striped suit. We
crossed the cobbled street to the Plaza's miniature garden, home to
the bronze statue of the unmentionables goddess, overlooking her
modest flowerbeds with foot-high box hedges and low wrought-iron
railings, and the gravestone of someone who was buried beside a
sprinkler head; we took a seat on a park bench, to wait for Gustavo.
The goddess still seemed to struggle with her place in the general
scheme of things, just across the street from the Basilica de Nuestra
Señora de Guanajuato, home to Catholic Saints and the Virgin
of Guadalupe; while the traffic swirled around her, full of buses,
bikes, and pedestrians, the goddess stood stock-still, ill at ease in
the midst of everything, publicly exposing her immortal left breast.
And then Gustavo must have spotted us, he rose from the table
and waved to us to come and join them, and the gentleman he was
seated with stood up as we approached. The men greeted Gabriella with familiar smiles and phantom cheek kisses, my hand was
shaken firmly by the chalk-striped man, and then we all sat down
together at Gustavo's usual table, observing a curious moment of
disproportionate silence, like the white space in a novel used to
punctuate a discourse shift, where they've been talking about the
weather or local gossip at a dinner party, and a friend is about to
announce he has an inoperable disease.

"Alvaro de Campos, permit me to introduce Señor Raúl Antonio Ramírez Tabares, a friend of ours." This was Gustavo speaking,
in a tone denoting deference, bordering on subservience.

"Please call me Raúl. Perhaps you don't recall our having have
met on another occasion. That is a most interesting name you have,
a name of high honor in Portuguese poetry. I must admit to a preference for the work of Mário de Sá-Carneiro, among the generation
of Pessoa, but it is no doubt an idiosyncratic preference. His suicide
was a great loss to 20th-century letters, and perhaps a useful lesson
in the dangers of sentimentalizing prostitutes. You are familiar with
his work?"

"A few of his poems in *Dispersão*. I don't speak much Portuguese."

"Most unfortunate. This must pose something of a difficulty given your name."

"I suppose. Perhaps there are those who would assume from the name that I must understand Portuguese. I doubt there are many who expect me to understand Alvaro de Campos himself."

"Of course not. He didn't really expect to be understood by anyone, least of all himself. And yet you share his name, though I might point out that you're mispronouncing it; in Portuguese, it's Álvaro, with the stress on the antepenúltima sílaba. It must be difficult to have such a namesake, an entire identity that exists only in a language that you yourself don't speak. A bit like Don Quixote, whose own identity existed only in translation from the Arabic, a language the Don himself no doubt didn't speak."

"It's funny you should mention that. Gabriella said only this morning that I remind her of Don Quixote, though I doubt that Cervantes was serious about the strange story of his character's origins."

"No less serious than Pessoa himself regarding the origins of Álvaro de Campos. Pessoa claims that de Campos was a bisexual dandy who traveled widely in the Orient and lived an outrageous life in London; nothing could be further from Pessoa's own truth. If Cervantes and Pessoa choose to tell us outlandish lies about their characters, we have no choice but to take them at their word, a word that admittedly may have been "destruído na traducão," destroyed in translation. Pessoa's own native language was literary English, the English of Shakespeare and Wordsworth and Milton, from his childhood days in South Africa; his first books of poems were both written in English. Perhaps this was part of Álvaro's problem, feeling that he was himself already a translation."

"And thus doubting the authenticity of his own voice. I suppose it would be difficult to feel authoritative about yourself when someone else had actually authored you, and then compounded the alienation by losing you in translation. Curious riddles inscribed in riddles; they certainly make my own problems seem relatively straightforward."

"You're referring to your memory problems?"

"We've spoken of this? Yes. Yes, of course. I'm referring to my memory problems. I seem to remember everything that I've learned, but I have no memory at all regarding my personal identity."

"I believe the clinical term for this is 'dissociative fugue' amnesia. This would also be the clinical diagnosis, coincidentally, for Alonso Quijano. Assuming a new identity, embarking on sudden journeys, an inability or refusal to recall his own origins, Don Quixote had all of the classical symptoms of a man in a fugue state. The term "fugue" itself comes from the Latin for "flight"; the Don's adventures as a knight-errant are not acts of lunacy, they are the characteristic response of a man suffering from dissociative fugue. He recalls his original identity only on his deathbed, surrounded by the priest, Samson Carrasco, Master Nicholas, his niece Antonia, and so on; the deathbed scene is not a renunciation of lunacy, but a resumption of his original identity. It is one of the beauties of Cervantes, to grant the Don his dignity; he may have suffered from a fugue state, but his character has an essential integrity."

"A fugue state; I've heard of this condition, though I've always associated the term with a man wandering around in a sort of daze. I'm not in a daze; I'm perfectly lucid; I just don't know who I am. I suppose it's a comfort to know that I'm not alone in this, and that others may have suffered from a similar condition."

"Other than in literature, and as a premise for the sort of idiocy shown on television, the condition is extremely rare, though there can be little doubt as to your diagnosis. The Merck Manual precisely describes your loss of identity, your sudden, unexpected, and purposeful travel, from wherever you make your home, to Juárez, apparently, and then on to Guanajuato, and then who knows where next, this could be almost anywhere, a man in a fugue state knows nothing whatsoever about the future; you are suffering from dissociative fugue, it's as simple as that. One could certainly imagine that Pessoa, occupying the identities of his many heteronyms, was a victim of the periodic recurrence of fugue states; even when he writes as 'Fernando Pessoa,' he has very little memory of just who Fernando Pessoa is. Pessoa, however, was not prone to travel; the fugue-like flight of his heteronym Ricardo Reis, to Brazil in 1919, was entirely imaginary. The proper clinical term for Pessoa's condition, characterized as it is by the loss of a sense of authentic self, and the split into multiple, fully formed identities, all of them interacting with one another in an elaborate inner world, is "dissociative identity disorder."

"I would hardly think that Pessoa's genius, and his profound examination of the manifold nature of identity, was due to some clinical mental disorder. Pessoa's work is not intended for the diagnostician, it's intended for the sympathetic reader of poetry; I would assume from your detailed knowledge of Pessoa's intricate world that you yourself must be such a reader. Your interest in the great loss to 20th-century letters due to Sá-Carneiro's suicide does not strike me as clinical; it would seem to me that you yourself must be a sympathetic reader of the great Portuguese Modernists."

"Oh certainly, I can assure you that they have my sympathy, and my deep admiration and gratitude. It has always seemed to me to have been to their great credit that there were so very few of them. Pessoa, Sá-Carneiro, Almada Negreiros, and perhaps a handful of others in their short-lived Modernist movement; there is a certain dignity in an entire generation having recognized its own futility, don't you think? All Modernism was futile, of course, the extraordinary pretense of believing artistic production could influence the outcome of a century dedicated to the exercise of unfettered power. At least with the Portuguese this futility was made explicit, and for this I feel nothing but the deepest sympathy and admiration. What was it, perhaps two volumes of their little magazine *Orpheu* that they put out before retreating into silence? Even Pessoa published next to nothing in his lifetime, publication must have seemed pointless under the circumstances, and then sank into alcoholism and death of the liver. Sá-Carneiro publishes his little book and a few bits and pieces, and then becomes a rather explicit and sentimental suicide at the age of 26, hanging himself in a Montmartre garret, over a woman of low station, and considerable ill-repute. Their great precursor, Pessanha, disappeared into Macao and opium addiction. Ferro, de Lima, Mário Saa, they barely exist; these men were all their own personal-history erasers. Negreiros I suppose was something of an exception, he at least managed to stay alive until 1970, but then he wasn't really much of a poet, was he, and he doesn't seem to have been under any illusions regarding the power of art in the face of the Salazar regime. He makes that most Modernist of gestures, announcing his intention "to give public taste a slap in the face," and then begins feeding at the public trough under Salazar, so he must be considered at best a disingenuous figure, a critic of a regime whose funding he was pragmatic enough to seek out. There is something very refreshing and profoundly admirable in seeing an entire nation's Modernist movement sinking into oblivion in the face of absolute power."

Ramírez rattled off this speech with a kind of mechanical precision, as though he'd made it many times before, or practiced it perhaps, in front of a full-length mirror, while tying his impeccably Windsor-knotted tie.

"An interesting perspective. You would have to admit that Pessoa, at least, despite the decades of oppression of the Portuguese under Salazar, has become something of a national hero in Portugal."

"Oh, undoubtedly, it is the same impulse that led Sá-Carneiro to find something ennobling in the profession of the prostitute. Sentimentalizing the pathos of the poet is a common enough human trait; I'm sure it does no real harm, other than to the poets themselves. The true artist is always a pathetic figure in relation to the actual, and the tendency of society to find this somehow ennobling is for me a source of considerable amusement. I would only observe that it is far easier for society to elevate the artist to heroic status than to modify its own relationship to that which renders the poet pathetic and powerless. It is a most human trait to allow someone else to die for our sins, don't you think, and then offer as recompense a retrospective heroism. You might say I find the Portuguese Modernists to be among the most truly noble of poets, in that they at least had the grace to recognize how pathetically powerless they were in relation to pure ruthlessness."

"Pessoa, it seems to me, is in no way a political poet. His work seems to stand comfortably outside and beyond the superficial world of politics and its exercise of power. I doubt that power interested him in the least; perhaps he considered politics to be beneath the dignity of the poet."

"Of course, precisely, this is one of the beauties of Pessoa. Nothing could be more political than believing that poetry is above all politics; this is a position I wholeheartedly support. You may recall one of your fellow heteronyms, Alberto Caeiro, saying 'I myself

would never take a step to change what is called the suffering of
the world; a thousand steps taken for that would just be a thousand
steps.' This is not exactly a call to action on behalf of the underprivileged. Caeiro's was a world of rocks and flowers and sheep,
not secret police and political detentions; even Salazar must have
recognized that there was little to be gained from the torturing of
sheep. Ricardo Reis reminds us to 'see life from a distance, never
question it,' and for those who may have had one or two questions,
they could always pay a visit to the Cape Verde prison of Tarra-
fal, the 'Campo da Morte Lenta' or 'Camp of the Slow Death,' a
wonderful place from which to see life from a distance. Your own
namesake, Álvaro de Campos, begins as a fanatical Futurist, joins
the Modernists in announcing and embracing a brave new world
full of masterful machinery, and then withdraws from the world
into an existential nothingness, and a rather thorough embrace of
his own lack of self. What could possibly be more politically correct
than believing that your own self does not in any way exist? It seems
to me that Salazar would have liked nothing better than to have a
whole nation of those who doubted their own existence. This would
be, you must admit, a rather pliable populace."

"And yet Pessoa was widely admired among the opposition to
Salazar; even Saramago, that diehard Communist, venerated Pessoa. There seems to be something missing here; perhaps there is
more to the politics of poetry than its literal relationship to politics
itself."

"Of course, of course, 'the miracles of the spirit,' 'the spontaneous overflow of powerful feelings,' 'the healing of the wounds
inflicted by reason,' and all of that. I couldn't agree more, though
when it comes to Saramago, I doubt that being a Stalinist was what
Vallejo had in mind when he spoke of performing the miracles of
the spirit. I find nothing at all objectionable in letting poets be the
unacknowledged legislators of the world of poetry, while others go
about the business of running the actual world. As to poets somehow believing that they are acting on behalf of the impoverished
and disenfranchised, I myself have found a good deal of pleasure in
observing such exercises in utter futility."

There was probably some argument to be made against

Ramírez, I in fact thought of several arguments that could plausibly be made, but while I seemed to know a great deal about the poetry in question, I knew nothing at all about what I myself believed in regard to its significance. It is difficult to argue with a man of apparently absolute conviction when you yourself have no beliefs to speak of, other than one or two objections that struck me as purely theoretical. Wasn't there something to be said for the survival of the poetic impulse after a century of brutality and annihilation of the spirit? My theoretical objections didn't seem to be able to withstand even an internal investigation, on the basis of what must have been my own readings on the topic. I tried out several arguments, but each of them seemed to be overwhelmed by Adorno's observation that "to write poetry after Auschwitz is barbaric." It wasn't clear that I myself had any answer to Adorno, much less Ramírez. As far as I knew, poetry might be something I'd memorized to distract myself during a visit to the dentist, and now Ramírez seemed to be using it to drill holes in my impersonal teeth.

"But certainly, in spite of everything, the spirit of poetry and dissent lived on somehow in Portugal. There were many outstanding poets in the next generation, many of them more politically engaged than Fernando Pessoa."

"You are thinking perhaps of the generation of the magazine *Presenca*, José Régio, Edmundo Bettencourt, da Fonseca, Miguel Torga, or Adolpho Rocha, or whatever it was he called himself. "Presence," what an absurd and utterly typical name for a little magazine. The Fascists are in the midst of demonstrating the nature of absolute presence, and these poets are trying to pretend that their existence somehow matters. They were barely present to themselves, much less the 20th century."

"Certainly Torga, at a minimum, was both an outstanding poet, nearly a Nobel Prize winner, and a socialist who was arrested many times for his beliefs."

While Gustavo seemed to be following the back and forth of the conversation, his eyes darting left and right like a man trying to develop a rooting interest in the outcome of a tennis match, Gabriella had passed beyond boredom to some higher state of active disinterest, and signaled to our waiter to bring her a glass of wine. I had the vague feeling that something must be at stake in the outcome of this discussion, that something needed to be done to dull Ramírez' sense of self-certainty, that his dismissiveness toward poetry, his coldly dismissive intensity, was a hazard to others, to the weak and dispossessed perhaps, whoever they were, that his attitude was somehow toxic, and that he himself posed something of a threat. It occurred to me, however, that I might simply be borrowing my beliefs from those of others, perhaps a poet like Yeats, let's say his line from The Second Coming, that "the best lack all conviction, while the worst are filled with a passionate intensity," and that for all I knew, I was on Ramírez' side, and was equally dismissive of poetry and its ridiculous pretensions. It was clear at least that my own lack of conviction did not accrue to my benefit, that I couldn't assume the best about myself, simply out of ignorance regarding my own beliefs. Ramírez lit a small cigar and leaned back from the table; whatever procedure he'd been performing was apparently all but complete.

"You would suggest Adolpho Correia de Rocha, then, a man who chose to call himself Miguel Torga, claiming for himself a certain hardiness I suppose, Torga being the Portuguese word for 'heather,' among the hardiest of plants. It is true that he managed to get arrested once or twice along the way; nearly anyone could get arrested by Salazar's police, though I suspect the only way for Pessoa to get arrested would have been to get wildly drunk in a public place. I hardly think this makes Torga a model for the poet of political engagement. As he himself put it, 'I was born a subversive, starting with subversive feelings about myself.' This is not really the sort of attitude that would have attracted much attention from Salazar's secret police. Why bother with secret detentions and public show trials and beatings and torture? Leave the man alone, he'll soon be torturing himself. Of course this in fact was something that Torga himself complained about: 'unfortunately, people won't let me alone, to think alone, to feel alone.' If you wanted to torture a man like this, sit down at his table and buy him a drink, he'd be tortured by a modest amount of spurious companionship. The PVDE of Salazar had better things to do than to worry about a man who felt that 'the humiliating fruits of failure have a bitter taste that excites me.' A man with an exquisite taste for failure does not pose much of a threat to the workings of a police state. 'We are born alone, we live alone, we die alone' is not exactly the code of conduct for the model socialist citizen. If the PVDE arrested him, and read a few lines of his self-lacerating poetry, for signs of opposition to the Salazar Regime, some call for a utopian end to totalitarian oppression, my guess is they must have had a good laugh among themselves, and then released him out of indifference, and a sense of sheer boredom."

By now it was clear that Gabriella had had enough, and that Gustavo had selected a winner in his lopsided tennis match, and that whatever I felt was at stake in this hypothetical discussion was an attitude I must have lifted from some long-dead poet.

"Most impressive, Señor Ramírez; you certainly seem to have marshaled a good many facts, though perhaps there is something to poetry that transcends such facts. I'm curious as to why, in any case, if you find poetry to be something so easily dismissed from a political perspective, you've paid it so much attention? Perhaps you are not immune to poetry's spiritual consolations."

"I will grant you that poetry does have its transcendent moments; I wonder if this is of any consolation to those who have had their spirits crushed. As Shelley put it, "Poetry is the mirror that makes beautiful that which is distorted"; it would have been interesting to know what Shelley would have seen in such a mirror held up to a man with a cattle prod applied to his genitals. As for me, during my days with the Federal Police, back in the Mexico City of the late 1960s, I was paid to keep an eye on the poets and agitators. It is obvious in retrospect that this was a waste of official energy; the poets were mostly children, fighting among themselves. By now I suppose my reading is a matter of habit, just as the poets themselves continue writing out of habit. It passes the time, for me, as for them."

"And what is it you do now, if I may ask."

"Certainly, certainly, we are all friends here. These days I'm involved in private security."

"I can't help noticing that necktie you're wearing. I've seen photos of an occasion where many men were wearing similar ties. What is the significance of the small gold symbol?"

"Ah yes, our little monogram, it is something of an inside joke among the members of our group, using the symbols and metaphors of our poetic brothers, the Freemasons. Gustavo, perhaps you'd like to explain to our friend Alvaro something of the nature of our modest organization."

Gustavo had long ago finished the last of the wine from the bottle they were sharing, and called to the waiter to replace the bottle, apparently buying time in a careful search for phrasing. He shifted once or twice in his seat, picked up a fork and appeared to study it for hints of something, then let out a sigh of relief when the waiter appeared and poured the red wine for Gustavo's tasting, a process that involved more sniffing and swirling and holding up to the light than actual ingesting, he was testing for something more ethereal than real, he was sloshing and gurgling and inhaling and oxygenating, through his O-shaped lips; he was evidently stalling. He nodded his assent, allowing the waiter to fill the glasses from the cloth-wrapped vessel, and then looked up at the group from the depths of his concentration, saying Lovely to us all, and meaning Now, where was I, what were we saying?

"I'm afraid Gustavo is more at home with index funds and bond ratings than with the nature of our enterprise; perhaps you'll permit me. We are, like the Freemasons, less a secret society than a society of secrets, a system of morality veiled in allegory and illustrated by signs and symbols, such as those of our necktie emblem, the right-angled square, the compass for inscribing circles, and a T where the Masonic G would be, at the center of our symbols. We too, like the Masons, have our "blood penalties" and Third Degrees, though in our case the Third Degree has less to do with instruction and a mastering of principles than it does with certain modes of in-depth interrogation; we are involved, shall we say, in spiritual law enforcement. The G at the center of the Masonic Lodge is the central point of spiritual focus, where Divine Energy is concentrated, and man is called to stand in direct alignment with the descending ray of the Supernal Light, the Light of the moment of Creation. There is an interesting Gnostic and Kabbalist history here, though I suspect Gabriella's patience may be wearing thin, and this may not be the time and place to discuss it. Suffice it to say that the mystic tradition calls for a Supernal Light that is linear and direct, unfaltering and unwavering, unaffected by external forces. We take a somewhat different allegorical view, that the Supernal Light, shall we say, can be bent and redirected as needed to suit our duties and our own particular purposes. We are, one might say, those for whom the bending of the Supernal Light is a matter of some pride, through techniques we have mastered in the course of our training as former members of the Army and Federal Police Special Forces."

Now it was my turn to study my fork. These were the grim-faced men who were my friends in Guanajuato? This speech had been recited with a sense of ironic precision, like a door-to-door salesman selling vinyl siding for slowly disintegrating houses. There was a kind of tongue-in-cheek quality to Ramírez' whole demeanor; the only problem was, when I stuck my tongue in my own cheek, I seemed to find some gaping holes in several of my molars.

"To be honest, Señor Ramírez, I'm afraid you may have lost me. I take it from your alluding to private security and a background in Special Forces that the group is some kind of club for retired policemen?"

"Oh certainly we are a club. I'm not sure we consider ourselves to be particularly retired."

"I'm not sure I quite followed your analogy with the bending of light. If you'll pardon my saying so, it isn't clear to me that you yourself believe a word of this."

"Belief is a rather complex topic. I can assure you that I mean exactly what I say. As to my own beliefs, I believe you will find it useful to take me at my word, however veiled in allegory and illustrated by signs and symbols."

"I didn't mean to imply that I doubted your word. You just don't strike me as the sort of man who would have a penchant for mysticism."

"On the contrary. I believe there are many things that transcend ordinary human understanding. As I recall, you yourself have a background in mathematics, a field that is full of things that surpass understanding. That fork you keep staring at is itself a kind of allegory, a tale of empty space portraying itself as substantial. This in no way prevents you from picking up a fork and using it to eat your meal."

I put down my fork and looked up at Ramírez, who seemed to be smiling at me sardonically, like a man who has offered a bite of something that he himself has already fully consumed. The plate sitting in front of me was, perhaps allegorically, empty.

"I'm almost afraid to ask. What does the 'T' stand for?"

"I understand your reluctance; we seem to have grown somewhat cryptic with advancing age, the price one pays for living too long, surrounded by ignorance and intellectual indolence. As for the 'T,' there are perhaps, as with the Masonic 'G,' both exoteric and esoteric interpretations. The Masonic initiate might say the G stands for God, or perhaps later in his initiation, Geometry; still later he may find its connection with the Hebrew letter Yod, the image of the phallus in Kabbalistic teachings. Our T at the exoteric level could be said to stand for Truth, or perhaps more precisely, Theta, the Federal Police radio code-name used by our founder for encrypted communications with other members of Special Forces. Perhaps a slightly more esoteric interpretation, on analogy with Masonic Geometry, would hold that the "T" stands for Tensors, meaning something that stretches or causes tension or exerts its own special force; tensors play an interesting role in Non-Euclidean Geometry. There is no doubt also a parallel to the Mason's own phallic interpretation, based on the orthogonal nature of the symbol itself, a certain sense of being phallically perpendicular to the sentimental norm. We have, in any case, been over all of this once or twice already, but it seems to have fallen victim to the peculiarities of your memory. My suggestion at the time was that you, as an initiate to our society, focus on Truth, while contemplating the uses to which a Tensor might be put; in your own particular situation, it is also safe to assume that the T might stand for Terror, as in Pascal's observation that 'the eternal silence of these infinite spaces terrifies me'."

I rummaged around in my attic of I'm-not-sure-what-these-mean-to-me facts, and found the Pendaflex file containing everything I knew about Mathematics, setting Pascal aside and looking specifically for the folder on Einstein's General Theory of Relativity, painstakingly written out in the language of Tensor Calculus. It seems a tensor is an object in and of itself, independent of any chosen frame of reference, and invariant under changes in spatial coordinates, a kind of universal fork or drill bit; the geometry of gravity's spacetime curvature was determined, for example, by a stress-energy tensor; the effect known as gravitational time dilation, by which a clock runs more slowly near a massive body, could be described by the fundamental metric tensor. I was about to fly off into an infinite series of pure-spin spherical harmonic tensors, with simple eigenvalue connections for deriving the spherical harmonic expansion of gravity potential, when it occurred to me that I'd be better off just staring at my fork, and trying to figure out whether or not there was a meal that I'd forgotten to eat; perhaps I wasn't ready yet, after my dental procedure. These were certainly men, my grim-faced friends, of an independent cast of mind, no doubt capable men with dental tools, and adept at bending light, Supernal or otherwise, like gravitational lenses in the General Theory of Relativity. Special Forces. Ramírez was beginning to remind me of that recurring dream people have, of facing an examination for a course they haven't taken, where you find out in the dream that you have a single day left, to learn an entire subject, or face an agony of humiliation. It might be interesting to know whether or not I'd had this dream myself, but then maybe it didn't matter; I was certainly having it now.

"My apologies if my memory lapses have caused you any difficulties. I seem to have taken some sort of blow to the back of the head."

"Don't give it a second thought, Alvaro; perhaps you are not well-suited to the requirements of our society. It is easy to see you are capable of keeping secrets; it is not altogether clear where your secrets are being kept."

"An interesting formulation, though I'm not entirely sure that I find it comforting or reassuring. I seem to have found myself in the uncomfortable position of having no insight at all into my personal situation."

"Most uncomfortable, yes; I can understand your lack of comfort. You have, how should I put this, come to be regarded as unamiable by certain people, men with whom we ourselves don't share a sense of amity, an enemy of our enemy, so to speak. It is altogether possible that you have performed certain services for these men, services they regard as not yet satisfactorily completed."

"It is these services that worry me; it seems they have not been forgotten. Perhaps you could refresh my memory by describing them to me."

"Allegorically, perhaps. You have inscribed let us say a circle. It is the completion of this inscription that would seem to be of interest to our unamiable friends."

"You'll have to excuse me Señor Ramírez, but this entire conversation is beginning to give me a headache. What exactly do these men expect me to do for them? What is it that they want from me?"

"This is difficult to say. The circle, as you know, is always complete in and of itself. Perhaps they have an interest in the safekeeping of your secrets, even though, in your case, they are being kept from yourself. Perhaps they too have certain oaths and blood penalties, and tasks to be completed before administering the Third Degree. If you are looking for reassurance, I think you can rest assured that these are men of high principle, however veiled in allegory and illustrated by signs and symbols. I believe they have in mind the symbolic task of disgorging certain benefits, and completing your mastery of alignment with the Supernal rays of light of the Divine Energy, by squaring, shall we say, the circle, and burying yourself alive."

Just then a pigeon, who must have been eating breadcrumbs from the ground beside our table, took off in a burst of flight that seemed to startle poor Gustavo, who nearly spilled his wine, before catching the glass in mid-descent, and setting it upright before him as though nothing had happened. I followed the pigeon's course, in a curving ascent like the path of a boomerang, as it made its way up toward the right-hand spire of the twin-spired Basilica, the spire containing the clock, and topped by what appeared to be a radio transmitter. The clock tower reminded me of something: Einstein on his Kramgasse tram, moving steadily away from the Zytglogge clock tower, with its glockenspiel figurines of animals and humans, imagining the tram moving faster and faster, at let's say the speed of light, with the hands of the clock thereby frozen forever, and time standing still for the lightspeed traveler. I would need to proceed slightly faster than that, at a rate just beyond the lightspeed limit, to catch up to the light that had already departed, and make the clock hands run backward, overtaking my missing past. As I watched the pigeon glide through the midpoint of its flight, apparently losing lift, and gradually drifting lower, before hurling itself upward, in a fresh burst of wings, making a tensor-defying climb through the spacetime curvature, it occurred to me that I knew a far more elegant solution, from an article that I must have read on the behavior of light, in which light had not only exceeded its own limits, but had managed to divide into two separate identities: an experiment in a lab at a U.S. university had shown that a burst of light, inserted in a loop of Corning glass fiber, had returned to its source slightly before it was emitted, arriving improbably before it had even left, and reaching its destination on the eve of its own departure, to a general scratching of heads, and a revisiting of a host of Einstein's equations, until it must have dawned on someone that the speed of *information* must be preserved, such that with the light in the loop on its improbable journey so greatly exceeding the speed of itself, the light would require two separate itineraries, one headed forward toward the light-loop exit, and one headed off in the opposite direction, traveling backwards in the loop to greet itself, at the moment of arrival at their joint destination; if my own identity were similarly constructed, part of me, evidently, must have taken the wrong exit. As the pigeon seemed almost to stop in mid-flight, slowing so rapidly that it appeared to be hovering, backpedaling forward, in a rising descent, pulling a hurling-itself-nowhere tensor-inverting stall above the dusty-rose rock of the ledge atop the clock-face, and preparing to come in for a feet-first landing in an implausibly colored purple-orange-green pile of sticks, and bits of stray yarn, and discarded shreds of fabric, as though the bird had built its nest out of dragon-kite debris, I pictured myself standing at a freshly scrubbed whiteboard, beginning once again with my

own new equations, restarting the whole narrative of how I came to
live in Guanajuato, perhaps boiling it all down to a Feynman diagram, proving conclusively that my own identity had so greatly exceeded the speed of itself that it managed to overshoot Guanajuato
altogether, and wound up at a gravesite near a Juárez death house,
while I, evidently, must have arrived traveling backwards, and come
to live at the Inn, just slightly before my time, and could hardly be
expected to recount my whole journey, much less uncover where
all the money had come from, as I was only just now departing
my own house, and then pausing dramatically to allow a few strag-
glers to catch up with the fact that they were hopelessly lost, and
that their only way home was to be there already, by lighting my
straight-grained briar pipe, with the flare of an old Diamond Strike
Anywhere kitchen match, a match whose light was headed extem-
poraneously backward, toward the origin, let's face it, of the improbable Universe, the it's-just-another-one-of-those-inexplicable-things
Big-Bang Event at the start of everything, an event that, inevitably,
must have been there all along, awaiting the moment of its imminent arrival, but unable to remember, or perhaps refusing to recall,
that singular *information* it contained at its origin, until suddenly,
who knows, maybe the whole thing just exploded, as the beauty
of it all must have all hit home, in a blinding flash of insight into
its own singularity, and the beauty of its containing such *explosive
information* somewhere deep in the opaque heart of so radiant an
*origin*, toward which I myself appeared to be meandering, pipe-
puffing and head-scratching and seriously *misinformed*, and about
to arrive on the eve of my own departure, no doubt landing, with a
thud, *headfirst*.

# 12

Raymond and Gene were getting mentally prepared to head out of Roberto's and back to the Magnum, a Viper-powered variant of the Dodge Ram flatbed that sits parked at the head of an unmarked side street, directly across from the double-door entrance to a reinforced-concrete smoked-glass office tower, a building that even now was slowly refilling with the hard-working minions of Pennies Shaved, S.A., and Pauper Labor, Inc., and Remorseless Flows of Bottom Feeder Capital, Unlimited, most of whom, in turn, were getting mentally prepared to head out of Juárez and on to Guangxi, where a vast pool of illegals out of Vietnam and Cambodia have long ago hit bottom, and are prepared to work for nothing, and live on thin air. The accountants and number-crunchers for the local maquiladoras were returning from a good long lunch in Juárez, looking a little buzzed on margaritas and camarones, from Mariscos d'Mazatlan, or maybe bourbon and T-Bones from El Herradero, or Tsingtao's and sweet and sour from Restaurant Shangri-la, with their suit coats over their shoulders and collars subtly unbuttoned, and their half-Windsored neckties ever-so-slightly askew. The next indicated action for the inventory masters was to kill an hour or two in their spreadsheet cubicles, digesting these massive meals that had cost as much in two hours as the girls on the maquila lines made in a month, before heading on home to their subdivision Colonials in friendly old El Paso, and their well-groomed wives and 1.8 children, and their smiles-all-around "Honey, how was your day?" Meanwhile, some 14 year-old kid, in a tin-roofed shack in Colonia de Anapra, with six brothers and sisters and an absence of any sort of semblance of plumbing, was preparing for her shift from 4 pm to midnight, inserting Schottky rectifiers into PCBs for power supplies that would wind up, eventually, an hour or two later, in a host of enormous plasma TV screens, ideal for the recreation room of your 5-bedroom duplicate of a replicant Colonial. At this very minute, having swept the dirt floor and washed the dishes in a drainage ditch and hung out the laundry, she is putting on her uniform and 8-straight-hour shoes, getting ready for the dusty walk from her home made of packing crates and garbage dump salvage to her bus stop in the colonia, an easy though frequently deadly twenty-minute walk, where the bus will pick her up and drop her in the city center, perhaps an hour or so later, where maybe she'll find her rickety-white ride to the maquila, or maybe she'll find three strangers and an ominous black Suburban. If she somehow makes it home alive, long past midnight, smelling her way along, under the garbage-light stars of the barrio cosmos, past the angel-dusted street thugs and K-holed narco-niños and buzz-bombed orphans sniffing turpentine cans, waving Armalite-analog Rock River carbines, she'll have earned enough rapidly shrinking Mexican currency for almost a gallon of real whole milk, or maybe a down payment on a burlap sack of pinto beans, or nearly two cans of stewed tomatoes, unless, of course, she's saving up her pay, for tomorrow's 70-cent round-trip to the maquila. Two of her sisters will have already left for their midnight shift at the Sylvania plant, located on Calle Fulton, in the immaculate Parque Industrial A. J. Bermudez assembly plant, where they too will work their way through the mind-deadening night of what-the-fuck-is-this electronic componentry, having something to do with silicon-controlled rectifiers having something to do with dimmers for lighting fixtures having something to do, eventually, with something to do with light bulbs, which while well out of reach and abundantly scarce for a family of 9 in packing-crate housing, are powered by the modern miracle of pure electricity, something Colonia de Anapra has an amazing overabundance of, as long as you're adept at stealing it, while avoiding electrocution, and setting fire to your family, by tapping into the power lines that sizzle high overhead. Our 14-year-old comes home in the zombie-eyed wee hours, to a loneliness so acute that she no longer even feels it, and a dream-free piece of rug on a dirt-cheap patch of flooring, and no one, meaning no one, meaning not a soul on Earth, to greet her arrival, and kiss her on the cheek, and ask her "Honey, thank God, how was your night?" The reality of globalization, like the praxis of justice, is not for the faint-hearted or do-gooder types, or even for someone who could give half a shit, so permit us to suggest a cool drink and a comfy chair in the downstairs bar and wood-panelled rec room, and maybe a little CNN or CNBC, or a ball game or a porn channel if we think we can find one, just kick back in our recliners with our shoes off and our feet up, and remote-control the channel-surf stupefaction tsunami, washing out of our enormous Schottky-rectified televisions.

What Raymond had in mind did not involve reclining and a putting up of feet. The reduction of Gomez' lexicon, to the three simple words "you lost him," followed by the abrupt termination of their cell phone call, without so much as a simple "go find him," or the traditional courtesy of a call-tear-down dial tone, was more than a little worrisome, and called for something other than a state of relaxation. Gomez wielded and displayed his perlocutionary powers through one of two modes: either precise verbal flourishes and Shakespearean wit, which reminded his men of their innate inferiority; or a vast reduction in the need for locution, through basal elimination of the colligated interlocutor. The illocutionary force of Gomez going silent wasn't the sort of thing that Ray would normally tend to dwell on; Ray got paid for his expertise with weapons, not for his understanding of how to do things with words, though the gist of Ray's problem, as far as Gomez going silent, was losing the ability to tell the two fields apart. Think of it this way: weapons themselves are difficult to silence; even a Beretta M-70, with .22 Long Rifle subsonic jacketed hollow-point ammunition and integral silencer, a popular choice among professional assassins, while capable of diminishing the auditory component of a muzzle blast's rapidly expanding propellant gases, cannot eliminate the whoosh-whishing sonance of a bullet in flight through the requisite air, and thus the best one can hope for is sound suppression, a subtle but often important distinction; the man being silenced, on the other hand, the man whose voice Gomez has tired of hearing, will find that his silence is absolute, since a bullet passing through the parietal lobe, in the brain's left hemisphere, where speech is centered, not only does away with the capacity for speech, but also with the capacity for making subtle distinctions. What Raymond had in mind, while he still had cognition, was to find the stupid fuck in the grey Ford Fusion, and silence him himself, with a resonant blast from the 12-gauge Mossberg, equipped with its integral stupid-fuck silencer; with Ray at some risk of losing locution, he was in no mood at all for subtle distinctions. What Ray had in mind was to stop listening to dead civilians; whatever voices he was hearing from the charcoaled men, with their hands welded shut on the wheel to oblivion, would have to be silenced by other means, though maybe the best he could hope for was sound suppression. He handed the silent cell phone back to Roberto without comment; double-timed a marching cadence out past the push-broomed bar; punched the double doors wide open with his fists; and headed for the Magnum, as in no time like the present. What Raymond had in mind was to get his ass in moving gear, before whatever was on his mind became unutterably irrelevant.

What Ray did not have in mind, at this particular juncture, was the need to downshift rapidly into Mexican time, and deal with the subtle vagaries of Juárez jurisprudence. By the time Ray's feet hit the Juárez pavement, he was double-clutching and heel-and-toeing and then just flat-out locking the brakes, and skidding to a halt, and abandoning this whole metaphor. A quiet little side street just off the Malecon, full of local color tiendas and purple and pink taco shacks but emptied of human beings by a slow-moving Escalade's chrome-wheel display of frictionless indifference, had been transformed into a crowd scene, with a whole different vibe, by the razor-thin tracksuited sky-blue-tailored corner boy, originally assigned to keep an eye on the truck, who had apparently decided that the safe-keeping of the Magnum might best be ensured by recruiting a few more guards; he'd managed to assemble quite an impressive array of his corner-boy amigos and Tsingtao-ed accountants and bourbon-buzzed number-crunchers and body-armored members of the local constabulary, and was amply rewarding their safeguarding efforts with a display of armed force and lunatic behavior, standing on the truck hood, with head and arms held high, shouting "Tierra y Libertad" and "No Pasaran" and "Para todos todo, para nosotros nada" and "Patria o muerte, venceremos," and waving a pair of compact submachine guns, like a manic Che Guevara in a Hangzhou-blue running suit. What the fuck, Ray, are those our TEC-9s? You forget to lock the truck? Ray didn't answer; Ray didn't have to; the answer to the former could be immediately inferred from the fact that the truck doors were now conspicuously wide open; and any questions Gene might have had as to how the security had been breached were answered simultaneously with his posing of the question, as one of the local corner boys, holding a chisel and a coat hanger as though he'd forgotten what they signify, dropped them in a trash pile, and buried them in garbage. Now what? This was the sort of question that was rapidly growing complicated. In addition to the crowd that was gathering in the street, the windows of the office tower were filling with spectators, half of them calculating bullet trajectories, and the other half wondering, now that the Revolution had arrived, whether they could still make it home to watch the whole thing on television. Ray, despite himself, couldn't help but smile; while he knew for a fact that Hernando's theatrics, Hernando being the name of the sky-blue-suited corner boy, a kid Ray'd known since he was maybe like 6, and whose father, Baudilio, killed eight or nine months ago in the usual drive-by, had been some sort of foot soldier in the Chiapas Rebellion, and had no doubt taught the kid his antiquated slogans; while Ray, as we were saying, knew with some certainty that Hernando's Rebellion had been pharmacologically incited, he couldn't help smiling at the balls of the kid, and his fuck-with-the-anglos rebellious sort of attitude. The kid was putting on a pretty good show; too bad the city cops were getting ready to steal it; Raymond, for one, could use a good laugh. Raymond, however, is not about to laugh; what Raymond's about to do is get sick to his stomach.

As Ray studied the scene, at the head of the street, where his Viper-powered Magnum sat trapped between squad cars, maybe eighty feet away from his current position, his mind, which in some sense has been idling in neutral, amused by Hernando's whole wild-eyed exhibition of lunatic weaponry and antique sloganeering, and content to let the cops, the Policía Municipal, put down the Rebellion without outside interference, suddenly, without warning, lurched into reverse, and began drifting backwards, over the day's prior events, as though searching for something lost in the pit of Raymond's stomach: back through the deadpan phone call with Gomez, with its miniaturized lexis, and its toneless termination, regarding this meaningless chase after a no-name man wandering unmarked streets for no known reason they had bothered to clue him in on, like OK, OK, Ray can take a hint, the silence was closing in, but something else was missing here; back through Roberto's manual-sorting revulsion, and the loathsome Ribao, and the blazing auto-Billcon, and that immense pile of bills off the streets of El Paso being sorted and counted and wrapped up with bank straps and fed by the tellers of Deutsche Bank Juárez into Gomez' enormous Toltec machinery, all of which, to Ray, was ringing a kind of bell, but the bell sounded muffled, off in the distance; back locking his truck to the tune of a tiny siren, while thinking of a child who went missing in Juárez, only to show up later on a pink-and-black lamp post, now what was the meaning of that siren serenade, something to do with things that go missing in Juárez having something to do with poster pictures having something to do with lighting fixtures having something to do with something that was probably *staring him right in the face*, but Ray, for the life of him, couldn't find a light switch; back through the streets of Ciudad Juárez, and the 20-blocks-short side-street workaround, and the disappearing rebar of the Triunfo hotels, and the black Ram Magnum, parked in front of the orange Mercado, so close that Ray could almost reach out and touch it, and the firebombed cars on the obliterated Highway, like sit up straight, just keep driving, whatever it is you're looking for is many miles ahead of you; back through his session with the tollbooth attendant, where his counterfeit twenty had been tested and retested, and the exact-change lesson had been mindlessly repeated, and 17 singles had been tortured for concealing something, exactly the way Ray was torturing them now, but all he could find was 17 singles, no matter how many times he tormented the bills; drifting back down the 10, dodging traffic and clock chimes, and drifting on out to the predawn mornings, hunting scaled quail and bobwhite in the saltbush and acacia, and finding his father, not sweating the small stuff, drinking 12-packs of Pabst in Elsewhere's yard, which was right where Ray was headed at this very moment, if he couldn't find the source of this queasy sort of feeling; and then back to the meet on a slope outside Vado, and the bullet through his sidewall, and the steel-Zippo lesson on the power of indifference, and the blue-sky smoke out in the contrailed desert, and the…wait, what's this here, on a knoll in West Texas, about to go up in smoke under the blue Juárez sky? Ray looked up at last, up the taco-shack side street, toward the Stanton Street Bridge across the bone-dry Río Bravo, with downtown El Paso silhouetted against the sky, like something brooded up out of the scrub-brush Texas desert, including a tall office tower with a state-of-the-art trading floor, where Gomez was probably sitting, 17 floors up, past the point of brooding over Raymond's incompetence, and got a terrible sinking feeling in the pit of his stomach, like a man walking into court on a parking ticket, the Juárez equivalent of his TEC-9 problem, suddenly remembering that those bodies in the garden, the Juárez equivalent of what's stashed in Ray's truck, are bound to get dug up and entered into evidence, stuffed inside a million-dollar dusty-brown briefcase.

Shit, Gene, I forgot about the money. What money? Gomez' money. How could you forget Gomez' money? We been chasing it all morning. Not that money, the money from the drug deal. Oh that; it's underneath my seat. Why? You think someone took it? I don't know, Gene, if they haven't taken it already, they're just about to. If they search the truck now, or impound it and search it later, we're going to end up high on Gomez' shitlist.

The last thing Ray needed, right at the moment, was to get any higher on Gomez' shitlist; the time had come at last to deal with the judiciary, before he and Gene got impounded in a hole, out beyond Juárez, in the empty Chihuahuan desert, where any final appeals would be quickly exhausted. Ray surveyed the crowd that was gathering for the trial, did a rapid assessment of the immediate legal issues, and offered to serve as counsel, *pro bono publico*; Ray got them into this, he can certainly get them out. One of the convenient features of Juárez jurisprudence is the latitude granted to the municipal police to dole out justice, or dispense with it altogether, at the local level, just as long as any fines are dealt with promptly, and the legal questions involved are kept fairly simple, and the matter of court costs is dealt with in chambers. By the time they arrived at the head of the street, bypassing Hernando's gunwaving act, from high atop the vast expanse of the Dodge Ram Magnum's enormous truck hood, Ray was beginning to sweat the small stuff, like he was down to the count of three in his Pall Mall pack, and running low on fuel in his ancient steel Zippo. His first thought was of the Mossberg, under the driver's side seat; his second was of the truck bed, full of coke and meth residue; and his third was with regard to that well-accoutred briefcase, apparently overlooked in all the excitement over the weapons, containing well in excess of a million U.S. dollars in spanking new cash in neatly stacked packets, with each of the packets professionally wrapped with brown Kraft ABA-color-coded currency straps, suitable for direct deposit into the United States Federal Reserve, assuming one were able to certify its provenance. Weapons and drugs, in Ciudad Juárez, would be about as serious as breaking the leash laws; a million dollar briefcase in unmarked bills, left unattended while placing a phone call, and about to disappear into the Juárez judicial system, would earn Ray a place, however, in the Moron Hall of Fame; as he prepared to approach the bench, he took a long last look around, and said a quick final prayer to Our Lady of La Mordida. The panel of judges, three local police, headed by what appeared to be a district Captain, showed unholstered sidearms, body-armor vests with thin SAPI inserts, and a single tight smile being shared among the three. The vehicle just behind them, a Ford F-150 flatbed labeled Policía Municipal, with its driver's side door swung casually open, had ample room inside for transporting a briefcase; it was also emitting an intermittent radio squawk that served as a warning regarding failures in communication; a single wrong word, and the local Policía would phone this whole thing in to the nearby Attorney General's office, the Juárez franchise of the Federal PGR, conveniently located in an upscale modern office complex, where Gomez' money would soon come to rest behind a large steel door, on its way to oblivion. Just above the truck was yet another warning, a poster on a light pole announcing VENIMOS A AYUDARTE! WE HAVE COME HERE TO HELP YOU! with the picture of a no doubt helpful sort of man, wearing desert-camouflage tan to distinguish him from the crowd, and a don't-even-look-at-much-less-fuck-with-me expression, perhaps to distinguish him from anything even remotely human; replicas of this man, in a steel-plated Gun Truck Improvised Fighting Vehicle, wearing a shrapnel-proof K-pot helmet, and manning a .50 caliber machine gun with what looked to be confidence, were at this very moment maybe 300 yards away, right where Ray had left them, on the Stanton Street Bridge, and would be here in 40 seconds at the first sign of gunfire. And then on top of everything, spectators were gathering rapidly on both sides of the street, and overflowing and spilling out onto Avenida Malecon, and searching for higher ground on the grassy knolls of the median, all disinterested parties who had taken an interest in the case, and were now jostling for position and craning their necks, wishing they'd planned ahead and brought those platinum-finish opera glasses, half of them mentally preparing a statement for the press, and the other half ready to duck, in a hail of stray bullets. They all had that this-ought-to-get-interesting air, and the sense of morose delectation of bystanders everywhere; it may not be true, as Nietzsche once said, that "humor is just Schadenfreude with a clear conscience," but everyone loves a calamity, truer words are seldom spoken, in Finnish or Dutch or Thai, or Malay, or Romanian, "the misfortune of others is the only true joy," and the spectators, if necessary, looked ready to fire the first shot.

¿Hay un problema, el Capitán?
This boy waving weapons, he is guarding your vehicle?
I don't know if it's being guarded, but the truck is certainly ours.
Perhaps you'd care to explain his possession of such weapons.
He had permission to guard the truck, not permission to carry fire-
    arms.
So these TEC-9s he is brandishing without your permission.
Strictly prohibited. Highly irregular.
Such weapons in Juárez can have unfortunate consequences.
I agree. This young man does not appear to have been properly
    trained.
And with such a crowd looking on. It creates a poor impression.
A breakdown in discipline. A clear lack of professionalism. A most
    unfortunate exhibition in the presence of civilians.
I'm glad we understand each other. We have your permission there-
    fore to make a search of the vehicle?
Of course, of course, but you will find nothing missing.
Perhaps, for your peace of mind, you will want us to just make sure.

Just to be safe.

One can never be too careful. If you will permit me a suggestion, I would personally recommend a complete inventory of the vehicle.

Make certain it's all there.

Or if you prefer, we can offer you the services of our nearby facilities to disassemble the truck, and conduct a more thorough search for any missing items.

Set our minds at rest.

I believe we would both sleep more easily.

We would hate to take up any more of your valuable time.

It is our pleasure to serve. Shall we get started then? Or you would prefer perhaps the disassembly service?

Whatever you recommend, Capitán. In either case, I'm certain that Señor Gomez would be most grateful for your assistance.

Ah, Señor Gomez, and how is his health?

He is well. I will pass on your regards. He will be most appreciative of your concern for our vehicle.

Toward Señor Gomez we have nothing but the highest regard.

I feel certain he would want me to give you his compliments. Your attention to detail is worthy of tribute.

It is an honor to be of service to so estimable a gentleman.

Your assistance in this matter will not go unnoted. I have all of the necessary documents in the glove box of the truck. Shall I retrieve them for you?

That won't be necessary. Señor Gomez is understood to be most meticulous.

I'm glad we understand each other. You'll accompany me then to examine our documentation, and secure these unfortunate weapons?

Yes, I will personally attend to the examination of the documents. With such a crowd looking on, we would not want to create any poor impressions.

You are a true professional. I will personally commend you, Captain, to Señor Gomez at the earliest possible convenience. And as for this young man who is guarding our vehicle, he is perhaps overzealous, but a friend of the family. Señor Gomez would be grateful if you would treat him accordingly.

Certainly, certainly. It is always a pleasure to be of such service. He
    will be treated as I would my own son. He would seem to be
    something of a dreamer, this boy, full of lofty ideals, you would
    say?
He is certainly a boy who is full of something lofty, though I doubt
    that it's ideals. I suspect that this dream of his will pass fairly
    quickly.
I completely understand. To such things our nation's youth would
    seem to be susceptible. With maturity will come a more
    grounded perspective. But perhaps we should proceed. This
    crowd appears to be growing increasingly impatient.
I'm not certain they have an understanding of the demands of your
    profession.
Sadly, we are often misunderstood. Why only last week…
As you say, Capitán, we should probably proceed. This crowd is
    getting restless, and were shots to be fired, we would soon have
    the demands of the 20th Cavalry to deal with.
Bien dicho, mi amigo, vamos rápidamente.

While one of the Captain's men took possession of the Intratec
firearms, and placed them in his trunk, where they came to a comfortable rest in a FedEx package that had been prepared for such
occasions, Raymond and the Captain paid a visit to the truck, from
which an envelope was produced for the officer's close inspection.
The Captain made an elaborate show of selecting certain documents, from among the ten one-hundred-dollar notes that were not
subjected to open scrutiny, and carefully unfolding and displaying
and examining them, while the crowd looking on became increasingly disillusioned. As the envelope was whisked away, and the
overnight delivery package gently placed on the floor of the Viper-
powered truck bed, the formal ceremonies were concluded, and
court was dismissed, with a shaking of hands and a nodding of heads
and some gratuitous grace notes and diplomatic embellishments,
and people just generally were sent on their way, among them more
than a few, holding American passports and FM3 visas, who were
still too full from lunch to even think about spreadsheets. The general air of dissatisfaction will later be dispersed, and the patience
of the people most memorably rewarded, when a gunfight erupts,

predictably enough, just a few short blocks southeast of this locale, permitting things to return to normal, in the Ciudad Juárez sense, leaving sixteen people supine and permanently immobilized, and hundreds of random bullet holes to pockmark the occasion, and 1,400 spent and empty parabellum cartridge casings, rendered temporarily useless and scattered about the street. If you're a visitor to Juárez, when a lull has broken out, and you're finding it not much different from your own hometown, maybe a little poorer in certain respects, a little more ragged around the edges, out among the burst-fire Armalite crowd, on the toluene backstreets of the neurotoxic suburbs, just give it a moment or two, you shouldn't have long to wait. In the few short years since the national crackdown began, deploying 40,000 troops, 5,000 Federal officers, and maybe 2 billion something of your hard-earned tax dollars, over 40,000 and counting hardworking citizens have simply ceased to exist, among them more than a few who waited patiently in Juárez to lie down and be counted among the 7,000 supine; patience, in Juárez, is always richly rewarded.

As for Raymond Edmunds, now back behind the wheel, his patience with himself was running a quart or two low, not that you'd really notice, to look at the man: staring straight ahead, watching the crowd thin out, with an unlit cigarette dangling from his lips, and an ancient steel Zippo being twirled between two fingers, he appeared to be the picture of near-perfect self-containment, though what Ray had in mind, in terms of completing his inner peace, was to fire the black 12-gauge through all four sidewalls, and then kick back in the truck cab, blowing smoke rings out the roof, after lighting his cigarette off the muzzle-flash of the Mossberg; this memory lapse over the briefcase, the latest in a series of Gomez-related mental blunders, was, to put it bluntly, about the final fucking straw. Any moment now, news of this whole debacle would begin filtering back to Gomez Central, where word would make its way up the chain of command that Raymond and Gene had suffered yet another setback, and made yet another in a long line of procedural errors; Ray stared out the windshield, twirling the Army-issue Zippo, reviewing this latest in a sequence of fuck-ups, and knew deep down that, as sure as he was sitting there, one way or the other, these fuck-ups would cease. Ray put the Pall Mall back in the pack;

returned both pack and Zippo to a Scully-plaid shirt pocket; left the Mossberg where it was, under the driver's side seat; and cleared his mind of everything but the next indicated action. While Gene retrieved the sidearms from the false-bottom truck bed, and placed them at his feet on the floorboard just in front of him, Ray fired up and redlined the Viper V-10, gently eased out the clutch pedal to the tune of shrieking truck tires, pointed the Ram south, down the chrome-spinner side street, and then headed west toward the Mariscal Tolerance Zone, and an out-of-the-way dive-bar called El Arbolito, soon to be known to all of us as The Bar of the Wounded Tree.

An out-of-the-way dive-bar? In the middle of the afternoon? Where are we headed, Ray? Tell you the truth, Gene, I'm not all that sure. You know if the Arbolito's still open for business? What the hell, Trip, we're going to a bar? We don't find that guy in the Fusion pretty soon, Gomez will hang us both from an árbol by the balls. Ray didn't answer; Ray didn't want to; to Ray's way of thinking, it was likely Gene was right, and they needed to find the Fusion pretty damn soon, but it was also equally likely that they were dead men already, as soon as Gomez found someone to break the bad news. Either way you looked at it, Ray didn't like their odds. The chances of finding an unnamed man by wandering around Juárez, a city of God knows what, maybe 2 million people, without any help from Gomez Central, were incalculably small, particularly given the nature of the one-way street problem, where the signs all point in the exact wrong direction; the odds were about even on Ray and Gene getting lost, while sitting stock-still at an ordinary traffic signal, when the most famous men in Mexico, the Unknown Assailants, pulled in behind them, and rolled to a halt. When it comes to mysterious violence in Ciudad Juárez, if there's one thing Ray knows like the back of his head, it's the extraordinary variety of Unknown Assailants: from the local street gangs, 400 strong, with names like the Aztecas and Artistic Assassins; to the outsourced enforcers and designated decapitators, with names like La Linea, Los Zetas, and Los Negros; to the Policía Municipal and Chihuahua State Police; to the Military Police of the Tercera Brigada; to the Policía de Caminos, in their shiny Dodge Chargers; to the Policía Fiscal and the IM investigators and the SSP men from the National Security Center; to the 40,000-man Federal Policía; to anyone, frankly, with a ski mask and a weapon, meaning half of Juárez would look pretty suspicious, and the Mexican Armed Forces would be well worth avoiding. The indicated action was to stop wandering around Juárez, running red lights in case someone was trying to kill them. The indicated action was to clean up the truck, and get out of Juárez as soon as practicable. In the meantime, of course, to Ray's way of thinking, the indicated action was for Ray and Gene to lie low, and you can't lie any lower than El Arbolito.

Ray made a right at the end of Chrome-Spinner Side Street onto Calle Tlaxcala, back-tracked down Lerdo to Avenida 16 de Septiembre, and then headed west toward the Zona de Tolerancia, almost as though he knew where he were going, though since he spent half his time studying his rearview, he might just as well have driven the whole thing backwards. The Mariscal, the city's historic red-light district, an area Raymond remembered well, from the days and nights of his El Paso adolescence, had a number of distinct advantages under the ambient circumstances. First of all, the place was a wreck, in the midst of being demolished to improve Juárez' image, and was lightly patrolled by the local armed forces. Formerly the land of opportunity for Texas teenagers, full of bars and whorehouses that packed the Mariscal streets, The Rainbow Bar and Kentucky Club, The Panama and Dia y Noche, Casa Colorado and the glorious Irma's, the place was being demolished brick by brick, which made it ideal for reconfiguring the truck bed, and placing the Mossberg and TEC-9s and money in the false flatbed dead space for recrossing the U.S. border. Situated at the foot of the Paso del Norte Bridge, the area also had fireproof proximity to a particular Verizon cell phone tower, which meant that their encrypted links to Gomez Central would once again function, on the off chance that the boss regained his sense of humor. And finally, come to think of it, Ray could use a drink, and The Bar of the Wounded Tree served alcoholic beverages. Ray crossed Avenida Juárez, in the direction of Calle Ugarte, searching for the remains of El Arbolito, and entered a zone that looked like Beirut, with every third building now a bombed-out vacant lot, full of gutted piles of cinderblock and rebar and plaster. Dia y Noche, where Ray had spent part of his misspent youth, had been bought out and bulldozed, leaving only a grid of brightly colored plaster on the building next door, squares of poisonous peach, blacklight green, and paranoid turquoise, like a painting by Mondrian, if Mondrian had been a brujo spaced-out on datura. They passed El Choque Gym, where Ray had learned boxing, with its royal blue heavy bag, and its magazine covers and bullfight posters, papering every last inch of the walls and ceiling, and its free weights set off to one side in the rear, seven-foot Olympic bars, with well-knurled handgrips, and weight plates like wheels on a Third World oxcart; he could still feel the rhythm of his Everlast-gloved hands, working the maroon-colored USA Country Pride speed bag, with a blur of hand-speed as precise as a chronometer. Around the corner were the La Chocha and Lucha Libre gyms, full of hungry-looking kids with grimly lit dreams, their gang-battered bodies a roadmap of scars and grotesque tattoos and knife-fight-reminders of the alternatives to boxing, trying to shadow-box their way out of Juárez oblivion.

El Arbolito was still in one piece, its brown stone bar top littered with beers, with a few old regulars nursing a warm one, sitting on a yard-sale assortment of bar stools, on the purple-washed concrete in a blaze of fluorescence. While Gene stayed with the truck to work with the hex wrench, Ray took a seat and ordered a chucho, chucupaste stirred in to something like Tequila Orendain; the drink smelled like celery and tasted of the past, an ancient Shaman remedy for those who feel ancient. Chucupaste comes from the root of the Osha plant, which is difficult to distinguish from poisonous hemlock, and maybe the stuff was better left to the bears, who eat it when they awaken from a long hibernation, but Ray ordered another and a bottle of Superior, poured the beer in a glass that the barkeep provided, and thought about El Conejo, his old boxing mentor, who'd taught him to take a punch and then drink a few chuchos. Ray drifted off again while he waited for Gene, to boxing and gyms, and living on porous borders. He'd been placed with a family in an old Victorian ramshackle mess in the Magoffin dereliction zone, one of the original downtown neighborhoods east of the Stanton Street Bridge, an area full of brothels and machine shops and dive bars; he had a key to the guest house in the back of the place, an easy walk to Juárez and punching and drinking, and was in some sort of holding pattern, on his way to Fort Hood. He

felt more at home at El Choque Gym, circling the ring and duck-
ing and counterpunching, than he did at Magoffin High School,
mangling quadratic equations in algebra class. Boxing was a pure
form of the next indicated action, catching on to the rhythm of an
opponent's left jab, throwing a choppy overhand right to the side of
the headgear, and taking a left hook to the ribs or the liver. There
were guys at El Choque who knew what they were doing, with their
dreams of being the next Julio César Chávez, or Rúben Olivares,
or Morales or Barrera, though most of them ended up like Salva-
dor Sánchez, a great young fighter who beat Danny "Little Red"
Lopez and became a world champion when he was just 19, and
ended up dead at the age of 23. Sánchez was killed by high speed
impact in his brand-new Porsche; the promising kids in Juárez died
by walking the streets, wearing a tough-guy attitude and the exact
wrong tattoos. And then there was Kirino Garcia Vargas, a kid about
Ray's age, a petty thief and street hustler who was good with a knife,
and thought that training was for pussies, and took his beatings in
the ring like a man who can take a beating. The coyotes used to
smuggle him across the border at Rio Bravo, in the sand dunes 100
miles west of his street life in Juárez, and take him to El Paso, or
Phoenix or Tucson, where he'd fight without much sleep, or much
of anything resembling foodstuffs, and take his losings to a steakhouse, and keep on eating until he recovered. After 18 or 19 straight
poundings-for-a-living, and sometime after Raymond returned from
Iraq, Kirino started training, if only just a little, won a fight or was it
two, decided he liked winning, and started training like a maniac,
running the dusty roads out beyond Lomas de Poleo, working in
the gym until they had to throw him out, and turned into the sort of
bull that you didn't want to fool with, and then a World Champion
prizewinning bull, a Mexican Jake LaMotta, with Juárez street-scar
gangland tattoos.

Raymond came out of his drift with Gene on a stool beside him,
their cargo safely stored and the flatbed re-bolted, and Gene mumbling under his breath about some guys over there, at a table in the
corner, under the mural of a bent and twisted tree, the árbol of El
Arbolito. The tree itself, rooted in turquoise soil, grew straight up
for a ways, then doubled-back toward the ground as though second
thoughts were in order, and then once again started to climb and

drift off and curve away in a sea-green arc toward, oh, who knows what, eternity maybe, the sort of tree that grows only around the edges of a dream, and makes you think twice about the benevolence of nature, unless, admittedly, you're a guy like Raymond, who's had maybe twenty years to study the árbol, watching as the tree completed its twisting climb up the pockmarked stucco sky of the Arbolito side wall, with its cankerous upper branches growing stunted and deformed, and that beautiful sea-green arc of its drifting-away foliage turning a strange shade of let's call it chemical-toilet blue, in which case you'd wonder, if you're at all like Raymond, whether the tree were truly twisted and bent by nature; not that Trip's ever heard of a phocomeliac tree, but that turquoise shit it's planted in looks particularly fucking toxic. At the base of the tree sat five dark men wearing wraparound shades, radiating don't-even-think-about-it-once malevolence, and maybe studying Gene and Ray, with the body language of cops and the paramilitary smiles of Soldier of Fortune mercenaries. This was neither the time nor place, not with the weapons bolted away, and Gomez not on speaking terms; Gene and Ray stared at the bar top and did their best to look inconspicuous, until the second or third Hey, Gringo forced Raymond to come up out of his hunch-backed stance. Ray signaled the bartender to buy the shaded men a round, pointing at their table and twirling his X-crossed fingers in a rapid double circle, and then swiveled on around on his yard-sale stool, as if confessing in fact to his gringo existence. Yes? The bartender scurried back and forth behind the bar, uncapping five dark bottles of Dos Equis Vienna-style amber-brown lager, and then carried them out and set them down, on the árbol-shaded table in a nice tight group, ten red X's in the center of the circle. While Gene confided Sit tight, Sit tight, Ray picked up his chucho and his glass of Superior, and sloshed them on over toward the base of the wounded tree, dragging your basic chair with one hand behind him, and then inserting himself, or more properly, his chair, between two men who could not have been more different: a man to Ray's right, wearing an elegant grey suit, and an equally elegant blank expression; and a man to Ray's left, in an impressive shade of black, and an equally impressive role as the group's sole spokesman. You drinking chuchos, hombre? Something wrong with you? Eso huele a mierda. Ray sat forward in his backward-facing chair, holding the chucho in one hand, the Superior in the other, and smiling as if he shared their morbid sense of bemusement, and agreed with their olfactory assessment of the hibernation chucho. He downed the ancient remedy in memory of the past, and set the glass before him on the table's rough edge, where it rested for a moment, or maybe it was two, before being casually swept aside like an annoying insect, and shattering in a burst of glittering fragments. Something wrong with you, pendejo? Ray could see Gene coming out of his stool, but waved him off, and instead placed his beer in the exact same spot, the one recently vacated by the empty flying chucho, and leaned in a little with the ghost of a smile, toward the center of the circle with its ten red X's. ¿Es sordo, culero? Ray nodded once or twice, agreeing that he was deaf, if not necessarily an asshole, while four dark sets of wraparound clichés, and one still blank but eloquent expression, studied his pale beer for any sudden movement. After a beat or was it two, when the beer hadn't moved, Ray drained it in a gulp, placed it back precisely in its own condensation ring, and started counting out in somber tones, uno…dos…tres…quatro…like a referee counting when a fighter goes down, holding up fingers as the knockdown count progresses, then waving his arms when the count reaches ten, and the fighter hasn't moved, he's been counted down and out. Ray shook a cigarette loose from his pack, offered it all around to the handlers of the downed and counted-out fighter, then returned to his yard-sale stool with a shrug, leaving five men staring at an all-but-empty beer glass, and ten red X's in the center of the ring.

And Gene, poor Eugene, how does he ever get into this shit? Gene, in spite of his imposing stature, was not a large man, and he'd prefer it if he were smaller. Gene never much liked thinking for himself, and he'd be thinking a lot less if it weren't for Raymond's fuck-ups. As long as he could remember, since they'd met at Fort Hood, he'd been following Ray around, and getting himself in deeper. Gene liked to keep things simple and true, a straight line in the sand should more than suffice, this side is mine, it's just that simple, but whenever Ray started in on being Raymond once again, or Trip if you like, it's all the same to Raymond, the lines kept getting crossed, and X'ed out, and squiggled over, there were lines from here to there that were drawn all over everywhere, lines from here to hell and gone, Gene just couldn't see it, but when Ray drew a line, Gene considered that line as drawn. Which it helps then, if you can picture this, that Gene was as big as a good-sized house, if maybe not as nimble; that one time at The Hood, when Ray and Gene put the gloves on, and climbed into the ring, Eugene could not believe the shit that he wasn't seeing, meaning mostly Raymond's hands, as fast as Kansas lightning, though since he outweighed Ray by maybe eighty pounds, and managed to get a punch in, out of dozens and dozens and dozens, there was a weird kind of whooshing sound that came out of Ray's insides, and he nearly dropped to a knee, before stepping back and circling. Where Gene grew up, near Grainfield, home to a once-famous opera house, and maybe 300 people, every line was straight and true, and boundaries were never subtle; if you walked straight out in your Red Wing boots, from the porch of their Kansas house to the property line, where the Booker family farm just called it a day, and all of their days had hard-earned endings, you came to a nice straight edge of barbed-wire fence, or a stretch of gravel roadway, and beyond it was everything that belonged to the neighbors. When Gene harvested wheat, at the wheel of their green John Deere 9650 Combine, everything was straightened up and trued and aligned: the concave and cylinder on the Combine thresher running parallel from side to side; the cylinder good to go, no faster or tighter than absolutely necessary to thresh the grains undamaged from the wheat; and the Combine itself running in long slow lines, knowing the only way to reduce the harm from straw-walker overloads was to just SLOW DOWN, and do things right. When Gene baled hay, in ninety-pound bricks wrapped with good Bridon baling twine, he stacked it up neatly so the edges were aligned, and things had a tendency to stay where Gene had stacked them; when Raymond got involved, the lines got a little crooked, and the bales tumbled over, and someone could get hurt, as far as Raymond's involvement. Gene was a large, trued-up kind of guy, and Raymond really wasn't; Ray was a misaligner.

Says Gene in a whisper: What the fuck, Ray, you playing some kind of game here? Relax, Gene, what's wrong with a little Tic-Tac-Toe, or maybe it was Hangman, I forget how that one goes. You ever see those Tic-Tac guys at English horse tracks? They wear these white gloves and stand on a wooden box and signal out the track odds like guys using semaphore. Say the odds are 5 to 2, they point a glove at their face; horse goes off at 33 to 1, you call that a double carpet, the semaphore guys cross their arms against their chest, may not be a horse you wanna bet the whole ranch on. Jesus, Ray, what the fuck you talkin' about, how many them chuchos you drink fore I come in? Just figuring the odds, Gene, just figuring the odds, figure it's about what it looks like, 5 to 2, call it a Face. Hunh? First of all, none of them is armed; one of them got a Glock, you'd call that a Century, odds are 100-1, you go up against them. Second, the one with his back to us, the wiry-looking guy in the sweet grey chalk-stripe, type who barely moves, acts like he isn't here, I've seen a picture of him before, up in Gomez' office, back when he wore a uniform and worked for the Federales, with one of those red-marker crosshair circles drawn around his face; probably means these guys are whatchoucallem, Thetas. Fuck sake, Ray, the Sinaloa Cartel's assassins? Don't get all dramatic, Gene, these guys are just enforcers, same as you and me. Bullshit, Trip, there's hundreds of these guys, and they're all stone killers. That's about the way I figure it too, 'bout 5 on 2, long as we're not playing basketball, or 5-man team squash, we just need to stick a hand in somebody's face, and get the fuck out of here, and fire up the Magnum. Just about then, in the middle of this disquisition on the English and their betting habits, the chalk-stripe-suited gentleman decided to issue a statement, without so much as turning around, addressing himself to the wounded tree, and talking like he was talking about nothing in particular.

"Permit me to pose a question that has plagued the philosophers: what is left over if I subtract the fact that my arm went up from the fact that I raised my arm? Can we deduce some sort of cognitive process or human intention or freedom of the will from the difference between these two statements of fact? The question is really one of action minus movement: what remains if I subtract the fact that the tree was uprooted from the fact that the wind uprooted the tree? What remains seems to be the causal process by which the uprooting comes about; we certainly wouldn't say that the wind has cognition, or attempt to infer that the wind acts with intent. Now suppose, hypothetically, we knew that a man was driving around

Juárez in a grey Ford Fusion, and instead asked the question: what remains if we simply subtract him?"

Now Raymond didn't quite follow this, or know the first fucking thing about the plaguing of philosophers; as a man who was bent on the next indicated action, Ray was not a big believer in cognitive processes; if you subtracted the fact that a punch to the head had been thrown from the fact that you threw a punch to the head, there was nothing much left over for anyone to think about, you just kept your hands up, in case the punch was ineffective. And if the punch started the other guy in to thinking and cogitating, so much the better, you just hit him again, or, if you prefer, the guy just gets hit. On the other hand, and maybe more to the point, if the mule-loaded dickwad ended up subtracted, and removed, give or take, from the oh shit sum of things, that would certainly give Raymond some pause for thought, like how to get away how far from El Paso, and what sort of flights could you get to Tanzania. If the Theta's had some sort of bead on the grey Fusion guy, Raymond was fucked, and even Gene could do the math.

"No idea at all what you're talking about."

"Of course not, how could you, I'm not posing these questions to anyone. This is simply a case of certain questions being posed."

"What is it you want us to do?"

"We couldn't help marveling at the vehicle you arrived in. As you know, in Juárez, there are only three sorts of people who might arrive in such a vehicle. First we have the Juniors, the sons of the wealthy families that control the maquiladoras. Next we have law enforcement officials, many of whom have not been discrete in manifesting signs of their purchasing power. And finally we have those whose sources of income may be such that our officials would be wise to show more discretion. We'll set aside the possibility that you two could be tourists. The Mariscal, sadly, can no longer be commended to the casual visitor. Beyond this, one doesn't encounter many tourists who are capable of the sort of demonstration you performed with the beer glass. Since you are working neither with us nor with our various friends in the Alliance, we are forced to conclude that you are otherwise employed, possibly by Señor Gomez, perhaps by Señor Carrillo Fuentes himself."

"I'm still not hearing what you want us to do."

"We intend to send a message to our Juárez friends regarding limiting the scope and scale of their local operations. We have tried repeatedly, and have repeatedly failed. Now whether one delivers the message or the message is simply delivered, this is a question for the philosophers. Either way, a message will be sent."

"So you're just fucking with us."

"Or one might just as well say: you are being fucked with."

Now this Ray could follow, particularly given the fact that the exits were being barred, with one man posted at the yellow paneled door in the rear of the lounge, and another at the rustic mesquite entrance facing the street, where egress had been blocked, and casually bolted. At some signal that passed unseen between the backward-facing man and the rest of his companions, four Fairbairn-Sykes fighting knives were mysteriously introduced, their vase-handled grips and double-edged blades ominously optimized for close quarters combat, which presented Gene and Ray with certain tactical difficulties, and evidence that the odds had been badly miscalculated. The bar's other customers, all veterans of Juárez, appeared ready to fall asleep, their heads drooping down over the brown stone bar top, staring heavy-lidded into their glasses of warm beer, preparing to tell the cops that their thoughts had been elsewhere, and that they hadn't noticed the corpse until rigor had set in, when they'd found it hard to move to get into the bathroom; the bartender, if anything, seemed over-prepared, having vanished completely into the room's murky air; if anyone asked, he'd be more than happy to testify, though at the time of the incident, he hadn't actually existed. Raymond waited a beat, or maybe it was two, apparently lost in thought over the lull in the conversation, and participating fully in the sudden drop in animation, staring at the label of his bottle of Superior, or perhaps trying to face the fact that the bottle itself was empty, and then absentmindedly tossed the empty beer bottle out, in the general direction of the bar's far wall, and the turquoise-rooted shade tree of the bent and drifting mural. As the empty bottle arced through the not-long-to-be-placid air, and time seemed to slow, awaiting the impact, Ray went kinetic, coming up out of his stool, and headed for the ten red X's in a circle, and the dead-level center of the middle of the ring. The shattering of empty bottleware produced an instant of inattention, ample time for Ray to grip two of the full brown lager bottles, and break them over the back-left-center of a chalk-stripe-suited head. A knife passed silently under Ray's chin; a table was overturned, leaving open the possibility that someone had overturned it; a knife passed back in the return direction, opening a gash in his Scully plaid shirt, at a 45-degree angle to the correlate horizontal; two X-less bottle necks were absently dropped, rendered useless by skull-bone impact and excessive fragmentation; a third metallic gleam of miscreant knifeness, having completed its cryptic passage in a looping knife-blade longhand, concluded with a flourish, unseen by the naked eye, the tachygraphic backslash of a message termination symbol, leaving Raymond wearing a large red X across his chest, and an unknown to solve for upon his Scully-clad selfhood. None of the logical positivists or analytic philosophers were available for comment, and even among the more interesting contributors to the literature, including several with a focus on the philosophy of mind, Hilary Putnam, John Searle, David Chalmers, Richard Rorty, even Donald Davidson's Swampman, not one could read a street map of Ciudad Juárez, much less find El Arbolito amid the ruins of the Zona, meaning that questions regarding cognition were held for the moment in abeyance, and the disputants themselves were left to settle the dispute. The point of the chin of a knife-wielding assailant was refuted by a fist; an elegant left hook disarmed another combatant; a chalk-stripe-suited man sat slumped in an armless chair, his apparent lack of clarity causally linked to broken lager bottles; and at the far end of the room, near a rustic mesquite entryway, a weird sort of whooshing sound issued from the depths of a hollow man's insides, while a man the size of a house, not known for his mobility, stepped to one side and let the hollow man drop, in a blaze of fluorescence, to the purple-washed concrete; as an empty whooshing sonance drifted through the mist, and the last acoustic waveform was damped down by lager vapor, the bar fell silent, and the wounded tree just shrugged, fully cognizant, as it were, of man's inherent uprootedness.

Eugene Patrick Booker and Raymond Carlyle Edmunds III, you can call him Ray, or Trip if you like, Raymond at the moment could give a shit what you call him, came flying out of the árbol bar, trailing blood and broken lager fragments and a variety of encrypted cell phone devices, and ignited the Viper-powered Magnum V-10, having accomplished approximately nothing, and roared off in the direction of Avenida Juárez, and the El Paso Street Bridge alien-interdiction zone. Time to get the fuck out of Ciudad Juárez. Gene was doing the driving, while Raymond did his best to put some pressure on his chest wounds, just doing what he could to keep these nicks he'd picked up from ruining what was left of one of his favorite Scully plaids. This being Juárez, of course, the first thing Gene noticed was the sun in his eyes, now acute-angling down out of the blue Chihuahua sky, but slowly headed lower and maybe two hours away from leaving blazing-red contrails over the western horizon, meaning they'd actually roared off, not toward the Avenida, which would lead them due north onto the Paso del Norte Bridge, and maybe a little downtime at their home in El Paso, but more in the direction of the empty Chihuahuan desert, which unfortunately, in this case, is a complete waste of gas, since it's where they'll wind up anyway if Gene isn't careful, and downtime, in Juárez, is a plentiful commodity. A couple of tire-torquing rights on the Mariscal street-grid got the truck reoriented in the proper direction, and left Gene pointing the Magnum directly due east, picking up speed, adjusting his rearview, and beginning to get slightly ahead of himself, thinking about the problems they'd face at the border crossing, with Ray looking like something a wolverine had dragged in, and the dead space of the flatbed stuffed full of contraband. It's not like Gene wasn't worried about Raymond; Ray seemed a little woozy and was oozing some fluids and there wasn't much left of that hacked-up old shirt; but it certainly felt good to be back behind the wheel, in charge of the route, keeping things simple, not having to worry what the heck Ray was up to with his strange crooked detours through the Juárez backstreets and his refusal to drive in a plain old straight line; as far as Gene's concerned, it's just not that complicated. He would readily admit that he had no real idea what exact street he was on at this instant, but with the Mariscal laid out in a good old-fashioned grid, it was safe to assume you could just head east, make a left on Juárez Avenue going one-way to the bridge, and then deal with the CBP-inspection complications at their proper place and time, meaning basically when you get to them, not that Raymond's current appearance wasn't causing him some concerns, in terms of someone thinking that maybe the truck needed searching. Gene, in other words, with his head-due-east-and-turn-left strategic foresight, and his just-keep-it-simple Grainfield trued-up ethos, was driving like a man who has drifted off to fantasyland, and has completely forgotten, or maybe doesn't know, the first rule of the road in Ciudad Juárez: if something can go wrong, it already has. By the time Gene had covered the first twenty feet of pavement, and torqued around the first of a great many street corners, he was already getting close to hopelessly lost, and was substantially orthogonal to toponymic reality. To reach Juárez Avenue, by heading due east, from deep in the Mariscal Building Demolition Zone, requires a certain amount of stealth, an approach by indirection, and some sense of the furtive and surreptitiously covert, like a squirrel hunting an acorn when predators may be present; what Gene wasn't seeing with his due-east thinking was that the streets of Juárez are a bunch of psychic predators, laid out in the guise of a kind of ground truth phronesis, while *lying in wait to prey* on your delusions of mental health. Every last street headed east in the Mariscal, with two known exceptions, T-bones into an unmarked street that drifts south and curves away from the mysterious Avenida, which for all Gene knows, is in Greenland by now, and won't return to Juárez for another few millennia. In the meantime, of course, Gene was headed east, convinced he was steering them in the exact right direction, just generally driving with no sense of stealth, and thinking about his problems with the border crossing guard station.

By the time Gene discovers his lone way out, down Maria Martinez, and then left on the Avenida, and makes his way up to the CBP inspection area, not only will a good thirty minutes have elapsed, but his current concerns over Raymond's appearance, in terms of putting their truck under general suspicion, and inviting further scrutiny of the flatbed dead space, will be amply justified by conditions on the ground; in fact, by the time Gene reaches the border crossing guard station, Ray will be well past the wolverine stage, and will look like his body had been used to send a message to the living of El Paso to stay out of Juárez. This would not be the best time, for any number of reasons, to get into a long convoluted discussion with U.S. Customs and Border officials, regarding the hypermedia messaging strategies employed by the Mexican Drug Cartels, particularly their use of the ordinary human body in a medium-is-the-message pathomorphic modality, from the sound-suppressed .380 Magnum behind the ear, to the burlap-sacked heads left in quantity by the roadside, to the carbonized corpses in the yard of an airy spec house, after a forty-man hit-squad rocket-propelled-grenade renovation, to some of the more startling innovations in reputational marketing, like a man's face and scalp skinned and stitched to a soccer ball, possibly a message to the dead to just stay dead. Given the bloodless semiosis and allopoiesis of a man's own face flesh appliquéd to a game ball, how could the CBP be expected to understand that an elite team of Thetas, handpicked by Joaquin "El Chapo" Guzman, and trained up in the foothills of Iztaccíhuatl as Airborne Special Forces, with their "even death can't stop us" motto, and their thorough brutality-training-and-testing against the EZLN in the state of Chiapas, had come up with nothing more viscerally compelling than a man with a deep red X across his chest, and blood sloshing around on the floorboards of his truck cab? In the context of the Sinaloan's pathomorphic norms, this red X glyph, in Fairbairn-Sykes longhand, was nearly inexplicable, a failure to leave their mark, on the part of the Theta's, within the necrographesis of the Juárez semiosphere; Gene, in other words, currently headed due east, down a typical one-way in the Juárez semiosphere, should probably consider keeping one eye on the road, and the other on the lookout for a necrographologist, because Raymond, in essence, is a typographical error, and the streets of the Ciudad are jampacked with proofreaders. And then, unfortunately, there's always the possibility that, instead of the CBP, Gene runs into some cryptanalyst type, on loan from the NSA to Homeland Security. If you're the sort of guy who's been buried underground, in a ten-acre bunker under Fort Meade, Maryland, studying the messaging traffic patterns at your mil-spec desk out in the rat-maze cubicles, and you've just seen a handful of the latest Narco-blog videos, say a man hung by his feet against a mountainous-grey background, surrounded by men wearing black balaclavas and the green jungle camouflage of an infantry battalion, before first being doused with anhydrous perchloric, castrated by a switchblade that appears from off camera, having hands and feet removed and placed in a plastic sack, visual acuity reduced, and then permanently impaired, via icepick insertion through the cornea to the retina, and finally disemboweled using a phosphate-coated bolo machete, and carelessly decapitated with an ordinary carving knife, with the intestines left in the road dust in a disorganized state, and the head placed in what appears to be a Styrofoam cooler, you'd really begin to wonder what the hell Ray was up to: this cleartext X on the subject's upper torso appears to be the cryptonym of a Sinaloan messenger; the man must be hiding something; send him back to Juárez, and have the body decrypted. Of course, if Gene manages to find the El Paso Street Bridge, and makes it through the line to the CBP inspection area, Ray's going to have about thirty minutes to live, so this whole cryptoglyphic reputational-marketing topic might better be discussed upon another occasion, perhaps when Raymond's mysterious blood-red inscription has been sutured up with Ethibond, augmented by a couple of dozen 3M surgical crossbar staples, dispensed from a disposable pistol-grip staple-gun, maybe the 3MP-GX-15R1, 15 staples to a pistol load, 6 sterile staples to a box of fresh ones; watching a wide-eyed Anglo getting shot full of crossbar staples, to the tune of one of El Chapo's latest narcocorridos, might make for a lot more compelling communiqué, posted on the net as a YouTube video.

We're joking, of course; if Ray and Gene don't get out of Juárez fast, they're far more likely to wind up in the Pronaf, at one of those velvet-roped, Narcos-only, gangbanger clubs, as a brand-new pair of face-flesh maracas. As Gene finally T-boned into the no-name ending of Calle Due East, and was guided to make a right by the white-on-black one-way, and simply set adrift, like a raft on the currents, free to travel anywhere, just as long as it was south, he thought he caught a glimpse of Avenida Juárez, maybe eighty feet away, in a gap between buildings; a crowd of pedestrians was ambling due north, holding cups of margaritas and shiny new maracas and armloads of cheap but authentic Mexican goods, L'Oreal eye shadow, lip gloss, and blush from Yinchang and Zuzhou, in Jiangsu Province, Air Jordans and Adidas from Nanjing and Qingdao, handbags from Chanel, Coach, Gucci, and Fendi, with that Hecho-in-China label as protection against knockoffs, and with one

man in particular standing out from the crowd, wearing an enormous red sombrero of dubious origins, possibly made somewhere
in Mexico itself, or made, whole cloth, out of a Juárez narrative.
This was no time to panic, of course; the street up ahead looked
thoroughly promising, although the one-way arrow, upon closer inspection, was pointing in the direction of what promises to be, in
under two hours, a spectacular sunset, a thought that consumed a
moment of Gene's homeward-bound attention, a moment during
which he slid straight through and went right on past and altogether
missed that magical-Maria-Martinez lone-way-out intersection; the
next street on was a perfectly acceptable-looking unmarked two-
way, which had unfortunately just concluded its passage through
Juárez, though it did afford Gene another glimpse of the Avenida,
maybe 300 feet off, meaning farther away, as though Gene, on his
raft, were caught in a riptide, being carried far from shore, and the
Pearl River Delta, headed toward Malaysia in the South China Sea;
and then two blocks on, at yet another wrong one-way, Gene hit the
brakes, torqued a hard but silent right, and abandoned both the raft
and the lost-at-sea metaphor by heading straight inland, and seeking Ray's guidance, with one of those Where the fuck are we? basic pleas for help. Unfortunately for Gene, Raymond, at this point,
upon closer inspection, doesn't really look like he's feeling all that
well; in fact he looks like a fucking ghost with a bad case of anemia.
You all right, Ray? Yeah, no problem, just get us the fuck out of
here. Think that guy with the knife must have cut me pretty good.
What Ray was referring to, in his abbreviated fashion, was his recent
discovery that a large patch of flesh, in the shape of two legs of an
equilateral triangle, had come loose from his razored rib cage, and
was no longer providing cover for the pounding of his heart.

From this point on, things just naturally began to deteriorate,
with Ray slumped over in his bloody bucket seat, and the streets of
Juárez finally closing in. Gene headed west, toward the soon-to-be-
setting sun, up yet another signless side street, known by the few who
live on it as Calle Donato Guerra, made a right on a similarly anonymous byway that goes by the pseudonym Calle Mariano Abasolo,
and finally reached a two-way with an actual street sign, and a name
he happened to recognize from another occasion, the exact same
street that Raymond happened to take when they drove what felt

like years ago into the Mariscal, on a street we all know to be Calle Ugarte. Gene just naturally drove right on by; not only does Ugarte run diagonally to the grid, but Ugarte got them into this, it couldn't possibly get them out. At the next street on, Gene turned right, and knew almost immediately precisely where he was, four blocks from his raft in the South China Sea, and the long drift to somewhere to the south of Indonesia. Several things, at this point, happened nearly simultaneously: Gene pulled to the side, and considered the idea of taking Ray to Juárez General; almost immediately dismissed it as next to impossible, remembering that the hospital was on the Paseo de la Republica, within walking distance of the tourist hotels and the rubble-pile remnants of the Holiday Inn Express, which would be easy enough to get to via Medevac chopper; a red-tailed hawk, looking a little out of its element, landed on a warehouse roof four blocks dead ahead, and peered down on the pedestrians headed north on the Avenida, apparently searching for something, among the armloads of cosmetics and handbags and spreadsheets, to carry off to the Mercado and exchange for raw meat; and a shiny black Ford, with high performance radials on maybe twenty-two inch rims, and a tubular steel nudge-bumper wrapped around its head-lamps, and an unlit Whelen light bar stretched across the roof, just your normal everyday Crown Vic P71 Policía Interceptor, pulled in behind them, and rolled to a halt. As two white doors, with orna-mental gold stars, opened in Gene's rearview, he waited just a beat, or maybe it was three, and then eased down the accelerator pedal, halfway through the floor, and roared about four blocks in a fishtail-ing squall, leaving Ray pushed deep into his slippery bucket seat, and a couple of Policía Federal de Caminos standing on the pave-ment, leaning on their two white-and-gold-starred doors, apparently talking to someone on a two-way radio.

After two or three high-speed unguided tours of the exit-proof neighborhood while staring in his rearview, Gene went off the grid, down Calle Ugarte, and hit our old friend, the Avenida de Septiembre, at a weird acute angle, about a half a block short of Avenida Juárez, which as Ray could have told him, is not going to help, since while September Avenue sounds perfectly lovely, the street itself runs in the exact wrong direction, out toward the desert where we'll all die of thirst. Eugene, however, is about to prove us all wrong: he acute-angled back up Avenida de Septiembre; slammed on the brakes and brought the truck to a halt; and then reversed down September going the exact wrong way, half-K-torqued in reverse onto Avenida Juárez, and roared off toward the bridge, dead-straight ahead, leaving both Ray and us swallowing I-told-you-so soliloquies, and proving once and for all that two wrongs make a right, a problem-solving approach that maybe our Government should consider, when it comes to dealing with drug prohibition. By the time Gene reaches the CBP inspection zone, he won't have to listen to a single fucking word about hypermedia messaging and bloodless allopoiesis; the CBP guys know no more than Gene does about the Internet strategies of the drug cartels, or how half of the drug war was being captured on video, and fought online, to the tune of dueling narcocorridos, in a classic insurgency battle for ghost-haunted hearts and terrorized minds and bullet-riddled hacksawed decapitated bodies. The fact that every last drug merchant in the Estados Unidos de Mexicanos, from Juárez to Sinaloa to Tijuana to La Familia Michoacana, not to mention the Zetas or the Gulf or Colima or Sonora or Guadalajara or El Cártel de los Valencia, was involved in an all-out war for control of the Juárez *plaza*, using every last weapon at their disposal, including going viral with Narco-blog videos, seeking an absolute death-grip on the mood-altering substance trade, and that the violence was now being supplemented by 7,000 soldiers, and 3,000 federal cops with fancy Belgian pistols, was not the sort of thing that Eugene was currently brooding over; with Ray bleeding out in the front of the truck cab, and the streets of Juárez beginning to chew on his nerves, Gene's sole focus was to expedite their trip through the eighty feet of pavement dead-straight ahead of him, pavement that would carry them, once the light turned green, out onto the bridge for the long trip to freedom, over the thousand-foot span of the Paso del Norte Bridge, over the bone-dry Rio Grande and the Port of El Paso, over a large flock of pigeons in a pool of Texas wastewater, back into the good old home of the brave, and the yearning-to-breathe-free-and-be-in-a-better-mood God-help-us-all Altered States of America.

At this point, of course, he wouldn't quite be home free, as he'd still have the border patrol and customs to deal with, but at least he'd be off the streets of the Ciudad, and the drug wars of Juárez would be far behind them, unless, for some reason, he felt his neck hair bristle, and just happened to check in his rearview mirror. Horripilation aside, if the CBP needed intel on the war in Juárez, they shouldn't be asking Gene, or staring at Narco YouTubes, they should be reading the fucking papers before the last reporter dies, or trying to find someone, at ICE or the DEA, who wasn't paying his mortgage by consulting for the drug lords; not only does Gene lack the first damn clue, but he's got maybe 30 minutes to get Ray shot full of crossbar staples, and even a partial enumeration of the guys who pay all the consulting fees, including Juan José Esparragoza Moreno, Vicente Carrillo Fuentes, Gregorio Sauceda Gamboa, José de Jesús Méndez Vargas, Sandra Avila Beltrán, Ignacio Coronel Villareal, Armando Valencia Cornelio, Jorge Eduardo Costilla Sánchez, Nazario Moreno González, Sergio Villareal Barragon, Heriberto Lazcano Lazcano, Joaquín Guzmán Loera, Eduardo and Enedina Arellano Félix, Ismael Zambada García, Arturo and Hector Beltrán Leyva, Ezequiel Cárdenas Guillén, Iván Velázquez Cabellero, José Luis Ledezma, Edgar Valdez Villareal, Patricia Amezqua Contreras, Teodoro García Simental, Dionicio Loya Plancarte, Miguel Angel Treviño Morales, and "unknown others," as the saying goes, would take a good twenty minutes even to begin to discuss, and another forty-five just to explain their ominous nicknames. The fact that one of them, Edgar Valdez, was known as La Barbie, due to the Mattel-like stylishness of his molded brown hair, his clean trim athletic build, and the bluish-green color of his Mexican eyes, which made him look a lot like the Ken Doll Barbie, was an interesting fact in and of itself, but wouldn't do much to control Raymond's bleeding, and Gene, to be honest, has never heard of the man. Ray handed Gene one of his phony Texas driver's licenses, pulled a drab woolen Army blanket from behind his bloody seat, and pretended to go to sleep, while trying to hold his chest parts together with his own two hands and a blood-soaked length of an olive-green textile. It might be worth noting that from Ray's point of view, which he's not making it easy for any of us to picture, that drab woolen Army thing has gone totally psychedelic, and looks like one of those Wixáritari-shaman Corn-god-ritual yarn-painting visions you find if you get lost way up in the Sierra Madre. Ray, right at the moment, has drifted just a little off of dead-level center, and thinks he's with a Brujo at a Huichol Peyote sweat lodge ceremony; while Ray knows for certain that he's finally on the mend, it would be difficult to overstate how tiring it all was, all that singing, whistling, rattling, and blowing, essential to Huichol mushroom healing, and Shamanistic-psychoactive-sorcery therapeutics, and Ray is pretty damned tired all right, and slightly to moderately incoherent, so if the CBP guys start asking pointed questions, don't even bother, Raymond isn't in, and if you cell-phone his Brujo, don't leave a message; another fucking message is like the last thing Ray needs.

Eugene rolled away as the light turned green, accelerated gradually up the Paso del Norte incline, and was just cruising over the top of the bridge, and crossing out of Mexico, into the U.S., when he was halted in his tracks by a solid wall of cars that were backed up nearly to an imaginary line, known to cartographers as the International Border, waiting to be questioned by the CBP interrogators. Gene picked a lane from a selection of five, and pulled into maybe a twenty-minute line, a line that even twelve months ago would have lasted for two hours, a convenience that unfortunately was only recently made possible, by six solid months of centavo-a-dozen murders, maybe eight or nine hundred carcasses in all, a rate of violent death that had proved discouraging to tourism, and was only getting started in the discouragement department, as it accelerated rapidly toward 300 per month. As he guided the Magnum forward in six-inch increments, Gene studied the pattern of CBP vehicle diversions, trying to calculate the odds of the truck being searched. Down one path the autos were waved through without suspicion, and cruised on over the eighty feet to freedom; the path slightly to the right led to the deep-doubt inspection zone, where an odd assortment of unassuming vehicles were being sniffed at by canines, and submitted to nonintrusive imaging-systems anomaly scans, including a state-of-the-art SAIC Portal VACIS Fullscan detection system, just the sort of thing likely to recognize a dead space in the Ram Magnum truck bed, and the undeclared TEC-9s, converted to full-auto, a briefcase full of neatly stacked and bank-strapped currency, and a choked and rifled Mossberg, yet to be fired, along with several dozen boxes of assorted parabellum cartridges, and a grey-Ford-Fusion load of triple-decker shotgun ammo. If they were lucky, one of their guys would be working the gate, and wave them through with perfunctory questions; if they were unlucky, a black Chevy Avalanche, with new chrome spinners and opaque tinted windows, full of pissed-off Thetas and Airborne Special Forces and the Sinaloa Cartel's Artistic Assassins, and maybe topped by an M2 Browning machine gun, or a Heckler and Koch GMG automatic grenade launcher, would soon show up in the rearview mirror, prompting a moment or slightly less of intense introspection. And as luck would have it…maybe four cars short of the CBP inspection gate, Gene feels the hair on his neck stand on end, and checks in his rearview, and spots five men, discretely camouflaged in the standard blue uniforms of El Paso policemen, making their way forward between the long lines of vehicles, headed out of Juárez in the direction of El Paso, holding subliminal firearms low to the ground, and olive-green M67 fragmentation grenades, which as far as Gene knows, are not standard issue for the El Paso police force. One car is agonizingly slow at the gate, and then redirected for further interrogation, with the Costumed Grenadiers still 200 feet off, but closing in quickly, while Raymond is snoring; the second car pauses after missing its mark, backs up a few feet, exchanges quite a mouthful of time-consuming pleasantries, and then finally moves along, leaving Gene's heart racing, and the truck at a dead stop, while Ray continues his weird bubbling wheezing; and then the third, by some miracle, is PortPass equipped, such that the driver swipes a card through the mag-stripe identification reader, permitting the SENTRI AVI security system to turn a red light green, raise up an all-but-impenetrable tempered-steel exit barrier, and cause the ominous-looking tire-shredders to magically retract, releasing the last vehicle in maybe 12 seconds. With the navy-blue bombers still 40 feet off, and his heart in his nasal passages, Gene reaches the gate, shows their U.S. IDs, disavows any intention of importing fruits and vegetables, and is waved on through, on the verge of collapsing. As he rolled the Ram off of the DMZ Bridge, and prepared to enter, at long past last, the peaceful city of Old El Paso, Gene said a few Hail Mary's and half-a-dozen Our Fathers, and would have called Ray's Brujo, if he knew the guy's cell phone number. Sometimes it's better to be lucky than good, and if you needed to say a prayer to some demon or gurgling gargoyle, even an ungodly entity was probably better than nothing.

A large black bird, like an evil omen, sat stock-still on a dead-level rail at the exact dead end of the Paso del Norte Bridge, and then took off flying, in a dark burst of birdness, in the general direction of Juárez and Lord-have-mercy Mexico. Gene drew a long deep breath of Texas air; double-checked that Raymond was still in fact breathing; and thinking back on the forces he'd left behind in the Ciudad, wished the dark bird luck, knowing he would sorely need it.

# 13

Ray kicked back in his waiting-to-heal bed, his chest patched up with surgical tape, 3M Steri-Strip antimicrobial skin closures, with pressure-sensitive adhesive containing an iodopher germicide, diatomic iodine complexed with an ordinary amphiphilic surfactant, and a nonwoven backing, reinforced with filaments of polyethylene terephthalate, for tensile strength and energy absorption, and finer wound-edge approximation; the deep wounds over his heart and lungs had been neatly mattress-stitched, though not as we might have hoped, with Ethibond Excel green-braided polyester, but with Ethicon Monocryl monofilament sutures, and covered with a DuoDERM hydrocolloid dressing, an opaque, biodegradable, and nonbreathable admixture of carboxymethylcellulose gelatin, elastomers, and pectin, which turns into a gel when exudate is absorbed, promoting a natural debridement, whatever the hell that is, if you have to look it up, etc., etc., you probably, deep down, just don't want to know, unless of course the wound tissue has already gone wildly necrotic, and they've started suggesting maggot therapy as a logical alternative; and his head was resting comfortably on basically plain old pillows, the sort of thing you rest your head on, when you can barely lift your head. He was back once again in the land of the free, in trademark-registered name-brand-equity Patent-Pending America, no doubt barely viable, and with his X-marks-the-spot X on his chest, probably unaware of some possible copyright infringements, but glad to be resting in a comfortable bed, just happy to be alive and in possession of his selfhood.

As Gene had reached the corner of El Paso Street and Paisano, and been forced to make a choice, under the adversarial circumstances, between a left toward Providence Memorial, on the campus of the University of Texas El Paso, entailing a likely stay for overnight observation, and a right toward the slightly less orthodox, though certainly still educational, approach, which didn't entail much of anything, and was a bit off the beaten path for weapons-grade observers, he'd taken the obvious right, and arrived at the Abrigado Animal Clinic. After overcoming a certain amount of species incredulity, and patching Ray up with animal products, the Clinic had detected an impedance mismatch, between Raymond's homo sapience and the minimal capacitance of the overnight pet care cages, and rather than attempting a complex conjugate, they'd released him to walk rather meekly away, while resisting the urge to loan Gene a leash, and offer Raymond a doggie biscuit.

Ray and Gene had a rented house, a mustard-yellow double-decker wreck of a place, a safe house if you will, in that Gomez didn't know of its Magoffinesque existence, and that's just where they went to get away from it all, stashing the truck in the garage at the back, hauling Ray off to an upstairs bedroom, and loading him up on goldfish antibiotics. Unaware that the Ethicon sutures in his chest were possibly better suited to a schnauzer's bladder, but cognizant of the fact that even the slightest movement caused far more trouble than it was currently worth, Ray wasn't moving around all that much, and had time on his hands to think things over. His first thought, sleep, was apparently not an option: it felt like whoever'd lashed his chest-parts back together must have installed some sort of motion detector, and wired it to a stretch of electrified fencing that was torque-wrenched tight using bolts through his rib cage, and whatever was in these canine pain pills was no match at all for his razor-toothed chest-wound, and taking deep breaths was not real bright, with a roll of concertina wire coiled around his torso, so this seemed like a good time to maybe just sit tight, try to shed a little light on some points of confusion, sort of sort out one or two of his immediate problems, and who knows, why not, just go ahead and solve them. It was, admittedly, pitch-black in the room, with maybe a little moonlight leaking in around the shades, and he didn't have a clue what the hell the time was, somewhere in that dead-of-night gap before morning, and this whole think-things-over approach to solving problems wasn't really part of Ray's normal routine, but here, in a nutshell, was Ray's current thinking: there was a massive fucking drug war going on in Juárez, and he, meaning Raymond, was now caught in the crossfire, and it was high time that someone, meaning Raymond once again, got the whole damn thing straightened out in his head. If you can picture Ray standing at his own mental whiteboard, drawing up org charts, and color-coded merger histories, and dotted-line arrows from cartel to cartel showing the current state of play among the constantly shifting business alliances, and *plaza*-sharing deals that would need to be restructured, and reseller channel-conflicts yet to be resolved, with a little stick-figure portrayal of Raymond himself, showing dotted-line arrows going straight through his head, you've got a pretty good picture of the problems Ray's facing, but no sense at all of Raymond Edmunds; Raymond's a gunman, not a McKinsey consultant, and it is, after all, pitch-black in the room, and even the McKinsey guy hasn't quite got the picture; not only is his drawing several weeks out of date, but with Gomez and Ray no longer speaking, and the Thetas carving cryptonyms deep into his rib cage, we might be better off, org-chart-wise, portraying Dr. Edmunds as a seated-type duck, about to get dry-erased from the whiteboard itself, leaving a ghostly-looking shade of a sort of Moonlight Yellow feather-pile that might once have been a duck on the porcelain-steel surface. Raymond kicked back in his waiting-to-heal bed, with his boots off and his feet up and his chest full of violet-dyed Monocryl sutures, with a half-lit moon still rising in the east and two hours from its zenith in the black El Paso sky, which would make the time, am-wise, around 3:45, on April the 16th, meaning a few days past Easter, and a little late now to be filing his taxes, just staring into the dark there, thinking things over, and growing more and more confused about the war in Juárez. Since the best they could do at the pet care clinic was 100 mg Tramadol tablets, Ray was perhaps a little fuzzy from the pain, and eating domestic-animal opiates by the half-dozen handfuls, although even in a state of McKinsey-like lucidity, the drug war battle lines could still be disorienting, and with Ray basing his dosage levels on toy Yorkshire Terrier multiples, and chasing the pills down with the occasional pull from a liter-style bottle of Old

Grand-Dad Bonded, he'll soon be having trouble making sense of his own wall treatments. Raymond, in short, has certain practical difficulties, and one or two rudimentary epistemological problems that will need to be addressed before he moves on: if he's hoping to make sense of the war in Juárez, Ray's own thoughts will be no help at all; and even if he's only searching for some inside information, the last place he'll find it is inside his own head.

First of all, the man that he works for, Gomez of El Paso, a man of Shakespearean-wit-brevity and marquetry-chronometer-collection fame, was more of a kind of concept to Ray than anything resembling an actual human, and other than posing a threat to his corporeal existence, Ray had no real idea what the man did for a living. To Ray's way of thinking, Gomez laundered money, while running Ray ragged, and frequently *down*, to supplement his apparently limitless ego, though he is in fact the Treasurer and CFO for the massive-cash balance sheet of the Juárez Cartel, under Vicente Carrillo Fuentes, or maybe it was Ricardo Garcia Urquiza, or Vicente Carrillo Leyva, or José Luis Fratello, a man who in fact runs the Cartel's *sicarios*, a word that goes back to the destruction of Jerusalem, and the slitting of Roman throats using *sicae*, meaning daggers, though the Cartel's assassins are known as *La Linea*, a word that goes back to the "firing line" for cannons, or perhaps it was Rafael Munoz Talavera, who unbeknownst to Raymond has been dead for ten years, found time-travelling backwards through the streets of Juárez in the left rear seat of an armored Jeep Cherokee, with his mind fixed firmly on the rearview mirror, and his bullet-riddled head double-doggie-bagged in plastic, or then again it might as well be Juan José Esparragoza Moreno, known by his nickname, "El Azul," a word that goes back, via Arabic and Persian, to all the Throne-of-God sky-shades of lapis lazuli, from powder blue to azure to a deep midnight indigo, though calling a born killer such a celestial shade of something would seem to defy all predicate logic, and most conventional color theories with regard to human flesh tones; the truth is, even if we skipped the etymonics, Raymond wouldn't even know the rudimentary basics here, like who the hell was running his own brigade, or who reported to who with all these psycho Cartel warlords, and as to where the battle lines were drawn, or whose side was whose in War Zone Juárez, he had no better idea than did the DEA or ICE, and they didn't have enough between the two of them to constitute so much as a whisper of a clue. Ray thought this over, searching for clues, among the baffling contradictions he'd read in the papers, and sort of threw up his hands, metaphorically speaking, since strictly speaking, he could barely fucking move: if he wanted to get out of this jam he was in, he was going to have to give this a whole lot more thought. While it might be educational to listen in on Raymond's thoughts, regarding the drug war battle lines in Ciudad Juárez, as a massive dose of a tramadol-hydrochloride opioid analgesic slowly eases its way through the blood-brain barrier, and makes itself at home, meta-euphorically speaking, among the opiate receptors of Ray's human head, we need to keep in mind that Raymond himself barely knows the names of the people in question; just because a man is really and truly high doesn't mean he's some sort of paronomasial clair-cognizant. We'd probably be better off, once the Tramadol takes hold, having a little chat with some of those plump pink cherubs that are about to show up on Raymond's powder-blue walls.

So how do we make sense of this war in Juárez? Do we need another consult with our claircognizant angelologist, one of those storefront exonymic Gypsy-type Romanis who reads greased palms, and does Tarot-divination using bank-strapped currency, and makes crystal-clear forecasts out of 8-balls of meth? To be perfectly honest, we could probably go straight to the Theophanic Angel Himself, with trumpets blaring away up on top of Mount Sinai, and lightning-filled columns of noumenal phenomena, and the whole flaming mountain about to go up in a pyrolytic feeding-frenzy carbonized rush, and we'd likely get one of those *why is there evil* shrugs, like Ciudad Juárez isn't exactly His department. So how do we make sense of this war in Juárez? The same way we'd deal with a Juárez intersection: look both ways and then *hazard a guess.*

Hazard it this way. It had probably started out simply enough, with the Juárez Cartel attempting to defend its own home turf and eponymous *plaza*, the shipping lanes north via the Port of El Paso into the mood-enhanced States of Operation Dime Bag, against an all-out assault from the Gulf Cartel, of Matamoras, Mexico, in the northeastern corner of the state of Tamaulipas, with its mosquito-infested coastal swamps, and its out-of-the-way *plaza*, via Highway 2, into Brownsville, Laredo, and McAllen, Texas, and its death-squad army of merciless mercenaries that didn't much care for the rules of polite society, much less hanging around in a dump like Matamoros, waiting for some sort of calligraphic-invite to the drug-*plaza* party along the whole U.S. border. If we want to get a handle on this war in Juárez, we're going to have to come to grips with these merciless mercenaries, as their anti-anodyne methods became the standard of care for every last patient ever touched by the drug war. Los Zetas, as they were known, after the police-band code name of their original founder, were NATO-armed-and-disciplined paramilitary types, with particular expertise in communications and savagery, that the Gulf had recruited, using U.S. currency, out of the Mexican Army, specifically the elite Airborne Special Forces, following training at Fort Bragg and the School of the Americas at Fort Benning, Georgia; with their terrorize-the-enemy approach to the human body, and their counter-insurgency training in high-tech munitions, and their unfathomable nicknames, like "El Winnie the Pooh," the Zeta's were a little different, that's all there was to it; the Zeta's were innovators, true battlespace visionaries, and the cartels of the '90s were still fighting the last war. If you pictured a man dressed in dead-of-night black, wearing jungle-warfare facepaint, and spit-shined jump boots, making a minor adjustment to the heterodyning generator on a Stinger Surface-to-Air Missile's focal plane array, while testing the utility of a hickory-handled framing hammer for removing the genitalia from some grave disappointment, you'd have a pretty good picture of the paradigmatic Zeta, and all the more reason to stop fighting the last war. Ray's whole approach to dealing with the Zetas was based on a strategy of situational avoidance, like if a situation arose where the Zetas were *present*, Ray double-checked to make sure that he was *absent*. This particular methodology, with its redundancy algorithm, doesn't, admittedly, sound altogether rational: why would a man have to check twice to make a clear determination as to his presence or absence? A man's either there, facing a situation, or he's somewhere else, and a quick visual check of his immediate surroundings should more than suffice to resolve any questions. It's not like a man can be two places at once; we're talking about a human being here, not some sort of introspective quantum automata; the cartels of the '90s were a little low-tech, but the Zeta's were still years from having quantum computers, using Schrodinger superposition in qubit arrays, where a bit may be set at either zero or one, or both zero and one simultaneously; a man, needless to say, is either present or absent, and he can't be both at the exact same instant; this sort of living-dead moment may be fine for Schrodinger's cat, but it's no way to deal with an ordinary human. Since Raymond himself was more or less rational, and this part of the war was supposed to be simple, something's gone wrong here; we must not quite be getting the full picture. Ray had his truck, an aging and rust-eaten K-series long-box, parked on a little knoll, above a streambed ravine, out in the scrub-brush of the empty Chihuahuan desert; three guys in black pulled a fourth from behind the wheel of a green and white taxi that could maybe use a paint job, removed his straw hat, his wallet, and watch, and gave Ray a brief but impressive demonstration of the Zeta's unique approach to the presence-absence paradox, and it had nothing at all to do with quantum automata. By the time his GMC had driven itself home, quite possibly over the bottom of the bone-dry Rio, Ray found himself doing a quick double-check, feeling around for his face-bones, and searching for his watch-face, not altogether sure, right at the moment, that his head, hands, and watch were even in the same time zone. By now, of course, this where-am-I demonstration is a common occurrence in every war zone in Mexico, but it's based on a trademarked Zeta innovation: the severed, but still living, missing human head. For all you know, for a few moments at least, you could be staring straight up at the blue Chihuahua sky, just kicking back, sort of watching the crows fly, at a 40-foot remove from the rest of your body. It's not like Ray started wandering around Juárez, double-checking his math on Schrodinger's equation; when it came to the Zeta's, however, you were far better off being slightly redundant than finding yourself staring straight up at the sky, not so much, at this point, double-checking your watch-face, as doing a slow fade on some serious *second-guessing*. So when word filtered down that peace was at hand, and that the Gulf, Zetas, and Juárez Cartel were now on the same side, joining forces in the battle against the Sinaloa Cartel, supposedly headed by Joaquin "El Chapo" Guzman, Ray basically shrugged, and took a "wait and see" attitude toward his immediate situation, like *wait* in El Paso, at pre-checked coordinates, and *see* if the Zeta's started crossing the border.

Phase II of the war, where the Juárez Cartel joined the Zetas and Gulf to fight off the newly formed Sinaloa Alliance, appeared, on the surface, to be a pitched-battle standoff, having nothing to do with the citizens of Juárez, though with both sides of the conflict composed of irregulars, the designation of combatants entailed a certain amount of *guesswork*, particularly for those who, for one reason or another, preferred to think of themselves as so-called "civilians." Let's hazard a guess that the year was 2004, when an unprovoked attack by the Sinaloans on the Gulf, no doubt eager to get their hands on the Gulf Cartel's Navy, and supplement their Air Force of Boeing 747s with one of the world's finest assortments of cocaine submarines and crystal-meth submersibles and heroin torpedoes, led to a major realignment of forces in Juárez. At this point the battle was certainly body-bag intensive, but the battle lines themselves were neatly drawn, think trench-war fieldworks at the Battle of Verdun, with their battered and empty stretches of utterly barren ground serving as a signpost, and a warning to civilians, to stay out of No-Man's-Land, and mind your own business, just as a barren stretch of suddenly empty Juárez pavement marks the middle of a side street as a bad place to stand, the sort of place that no civilian would even think to be caught dead in. Not that true civilians were actually dying in Juárez; according to conservative Government estimates, 97% of the Juárez dead were designated combatants, and the remainder were common criminals or complete nonentities, the sort of people who tend to die while being no one in particular. You can't expect much sympathy from the local police if you're the sort of nobody who ignored all the warnings, and the No-Man's-Land signposts of opaque tinted windows in a frictionless display of chrome-spinner indifference to the pointless minutiae of your so-called existence, and having *hazarded a guess* that the street was safe to cross, you stepped off the sidewalk, into minutiae-free oblivion; if you want to be buried with full civilian honors, stop wasting time on your anonymous existence, and don't bother dying as yet another faceless Mexican, because you're not a true civilian in War Zone Juárez, unless your death makes the headlines reserved for the prominent, well-known political figures and red-blooded Americans. As for the rest of you, you know who you are, *questioning authority* with your *hazardous guesses*: don't look at us if you turn out to be criminals. Children caught playing in the middle of the street, and mowed-down by the busloads in the Kalashnikov crossfire, might have fooled some, with their soccer balls and cleats, but the street-savvy agents who patrol the Ciudad know that all dead children are, without exception, either lookouts or runners for the narco brigades; when asked what they were doing in the middle of the street, they all gave the same sort of childish excuses, "I *guess* I thought I was playing soccer." The disappearing women that kept cropping up, and proved so baffling to local authorities, was a problem of a somewhat different nature; perhaps they were streetwalkers posing as civilians. Why hundreds of young women, many of whom were last seen walking the streets, cleverly disguised as ordinary maquila workers, vanished altogether from Ciudad Juárez, only to turn up later as No-Woman's-Land lamp posts, was a mystery the young women must have taken to their graves, as a warning to women everywhere against disguising themselves as women, and wandering around Juárez, *hazarding guesses*, like "I *guess* it would be OK if you drove me home to the barrio," or "I *guess* I blame myself for being gang-raped by the Juniors," or "I *guess* it's only natural that my unemployed husband finally beat me to death when he discovered my paystub." News correspondents, while technically civilians, probably deserved to die for being down there in the first place; the reporters from El Diario or Una Mas Una or even, God knows why, from the El Paso Times, who should have known better than to die by the dozens for continually *hazarding* the exact wrong *guesses*, turned out to be guilty of some serious misdemeanors, rattling the decent citizens of Ciudad Juárez by wandering around at night with their Krylon spray cans, paint-bombing political posters with their nihilistic warnings, vandalizing villa walls, tagging them with bylines, wildstyling LIES on Government property, and just generally intent, for no apparent reason, on posting signed copies of their own personal death warrants; reporters, obviously, were not true civilians. The drug war, as we were saying, had neatly drawn lines, and you can't blame the authorities if people kept crossing them. Rejoining the real battle, already in progress, the Sinaloans were proving to be a formidable foe: El Chapo not only had his own private army, known as Los Negros and led by Edgar Valdez, but the Sinaloans had, in turn, heavily partnered up, first merging operations with the Guadalajara Cartel, headed by Ismael Zambada Garcia, and then loosely aligning themselves with the Tijuana forces of Arellano-Felix, and the meth-masters of Colima, and the Beltran-Leyva Sonora Cartel, though these alliances were prone to breaking down now and then, in a shitstorm of bullets and pedestrian cadavers. Didn't we tell you to mind your own business? No law-abiding citizen would *set foot* in Juárez.

And then, in due course, as the pitched-battle raged, and the dead were discovered to be more and more guilty, guilty of being a lawyer while believing in fair trials, guilty of drinking beer while wearing a blouse with a missing button, guilty of counseling patience in a rehab facility, while a burst-fire cure-all was sprayed all over everything, just generally guilty of being young and alive, while living in Juárez, where youth is wasted on the lifeless; and then, as we were saying, with the death of the innocent at an all time low, and the drug distributors locked in a pitched-battle stalemate, the Mexican Federal Government, finding the national interests to be at risk, and the rule of law threatened by the cycle of violence, decided to intervene, and bring its full might to bear, by marching on Michoacan, and declaring *War on Mexico*. While we'll readily admit that this particular declaration, one of numerous possibilities among the national-security naming-conventions and This-Means-War nomenclature so popular with our leaders, sounds somewhat, shall we say, morphologically ill-conceived, the Mexican Federal Government was in an unusual situation, and may have had very little choice in the matter. Consider the alternatives: a *War on Drugs*, which is by far the most peculiar, a war on a group of inanimate molecular structures that produce, protect, and distribute a sense of fitness and well-being among the psychically impoverished, many of whom, for accounting purposes, just happen to be poor, turns out to be a fight that no sane Government would even begin to consider, particularly if they've been following that exercise in futility known to Rhetorical War historians and sociosemiotic linguistic morticians as the "U.S. War on Drugs," initially declared and launched under the Nixon administration, where after 50-some years in a war of attrition, and a $2.5 trillion treasury-draining ex-

penditure, the Drugs were not only winning, but not a single Drug
had died; a *War on Drugs*, which sounds so simple, as though you've
found yourself at war with an inanimate enemy that couldn't, in
your wildest dreams, possibly be armed, like how the hell would a
drug even learn to drive an automobile, much less tweak the guidance system on a Stinger Surface-to-Air Missile, turns out to be an
expensive lesson in the dangers of mixing discourse worlds, because
you might wind up talking your way into something you can't get
out of, like waking up one morning, somewhere way off the grid, in
a one-man combat tent in Molecular Asia, and finding that what
you're up against is the world's ultimate fighting force, not just the
Viet Cong of Covalent Bonding, but the entire People's Liberation
Army of Entheogenic Chemicals; a *War on Drug Use*, which almost
sounds winnable, waging a simple Just-Say-No public-relations
campaign, or a *War on Drug Users*, which has also been attempted,
filling every last vacancy in our vast U.S. prison system, might well
have worked, under ordinary circumstances, if it weren't for the fact
that both the *drug use* and *users* fell, for the better part, under U.S.
jurisdiction; a *War on Drug Traffickers*, which on the surface sounds
plausible, a war on a group of animate criminal structures that produce, protect, and distribute drug molecules, structures that just
happen to include the entire Mexican Government, from the tiniest town-halls in the poppy fields of Sinaloa, to the Congress de la
Union and the Mexican National Security Service, has the unfortunate connotation that this particular Government, one of the largest of these animate criminal structures, would be willing to declare
a *War on Itself*, which while thoroughly appropriate given conditions on the ground, involves unacceptable levels of collateral damage; and a *War on Drug Violence*, a sort of *War on The Horror*, which
sounds like the kind of war, like the *War on Terror*, that no rational
person could possibly oppose, turns out to be something of a empty
vicious circle, as adding violence to violence, and terror to terror,
has a nasty tendency to exacerbate the problem, like a man trying to
solve his drug use problems by using *a whole lot more* of the drugs
that he's using, as though killing the patient were an acceptable
cure, though we'll readily admit that declaring *War on Mexico*
would appear to represent a very similar solution, destroying the
nation in order to preserve it, which may not reduce the mounting

pile of the cured. All things considered, it would be difficult not to empathize with the Government's position: with the Drugs still controlling the territory to its north, where the world's greediest drug users and world's largest weapons suppliers just happened to reside, in a state of euphoric and blissful ignorance as to what both their drug use and weapons were up to, the Drugs were secretly planning a covert operation to finance and equip, with $50 billion-pallet-loads of hard-currency cash and NATO-grade shitloads of munitions and armaments, the world's most vicious and animate criminal structures, meaning not just the Cartels in their war against the Government, but the Government itself, which will soon find itself in a War against Itself; there was also the problem, easily over-looked, that many of the foot soldiers employed by the Cartels were pulled from the ranks of the nation's treacherous unemployed, in-cluding 20 million half-starved Mexican campesinos, expelled from their lands under the trade rules of NAFTA, and told to move north to work in the maquilas, where their heavily calloused hands and inflexible fingers refused to fit the form-factors of modern electron-ics, and were a far better fit for the steering wheels of trucks; under chemical attack along its entire northern border, and surrounded on all sides by a traitorous peasantry, and unwilling to face that fact that its substance abuse problems, including a $100-billion-a-year drug-exports addiction and a chronic dependence on drug cartel payoffs and a nasty habit, nearly impossible to detect, of hauling drugs north under color of authority, were rapidly escalating and compounding its other problems, it's a wonder that the Govern-ment could even continue to function, much less govern the nation it was chosen to govern, when the Government itself was becoming completely ungovernable, passing rapidly through the stages of pro-dromal paranoia, to a bizarre but still plausible delusional disorder, to a drug-induced psychosis and violent psychotic break and the catastrophic onset of acute schizocaria, before the people of Mexi-co were finally forced to intervene. Unfortunately, in this case, as so often happens, particularly in so-called *democratic societies*, when the Mexican people at long last intervened, and had every last one of its elected officials locked up for their own good in a mental in-stitution, on December 1, 2006, it just so happened that the par-ticular institution in question, jampacked with criminals and senior government officials in an advanced state of pathological cognitive disintegration, turned out to be the recently elected *Mexican Federal Government*, which 10 days later taught the people a lesson about ever again interfering in Government business, by turning on Michoacan, and declaring *War on Mexico*. In reality, of course, as the actual invasion drew near, and any slim possibility for a negotiated settlement with its own belligerence failed to logically cohere, the Government found itself in an intolerable situation: while the declaration itself sounded truly majestic, no one in the Government actually knew what it meant. After severed heads rolled on a dance floor in Morelia, and past the showroom windows of a car dealer in Zitacuaro, and down a dusty road in the Michoacan mountains, you could certainly sell the war, at least to the public, as a *War on the Narcos*, a kind of *War on Weapons of Body-Mass Destruction*, just as long as you steered clear of getting too specific as to how in God's name you thought you could win it; real politicians, however, serious men with a war to be waged, knew with some certainty that this *Narco*-construction was perfectly meaningless, since without the Narcos' campaign contributions, and their willingness to permit duly elected officials to die for their country as a matter of principle, no true politician would be in any position to even climb down off a morgue slab, much less wage a war on his wealthiest constituents. With 40,000 and counting preparing to die as a direct result of the impending invasion, and with only a precious few of the nearly departed prepared to be dead for no particular reason, and yet with Government officials still utterly baffled as to why they were intent on invading their own country, and turning their whole nation into its own worst enemy, the dying, clearly, would need to start soon, or there might be no need for the dying to continue. Seasoned politicians, serious men who know the meaning of a war just as soon as the body-bags begin to pile up on the tarmac, all know the reason that the dying must continue: to ensure that the dead hadn't died without a cause. All wars are just, and inherently self-explanatory, just as long as you can find a way to get the dying to commence, since no one with any true human feeling would ever tell the widower, and his bewildered-looking children, that Mommy just died for absolutely nothing. In the end, as we now know, the *War on Mexico* proved particularly brutal, perhaps the ultimate test, outside Molecular Asia, of a Government's ability to declare and sustain inexplicable wars, a war simultaneously impossible to initiate, since you couldn't expect your people to want to die for their country when theirs was the country hell-bent on destroying them, and yet, tautologically, impossible to terminate, since as with all just wars, it was inherently self-perpetuating, and neither side of the conflict could truly afford to win. With no one about to die fighting a war on themselves, a war only a corpse would ever bother trying to wage, and yet with 40,000 and counting about to die trying, if only to prove the point that any duly elected Government can wage pointless wars whenever the hell it chooses, something's gone wrong here, we've hit yet another of these living-dead ends, and yet another instance of the presence-absence paradox, a nation both at peace and at war with itself, in a war without end that just never got started, and must not, once again, quite be getting the full picture. On December 11, 2006, as the Mexican Federal Government prepared to march on Michoacan, and effectively declare, to all intents and purposes, the *First National War on the Nation of Mexico*, like the first qubit war in the history of modern warfare, a kind of quantum superposition of Mexico with itself, just, as we were saying, as the troops prepared to march, and the *War on Mexico*, which both did and did not really happen in the first place, looked to be inevitable, the Government must have somehow come to terms with the nation, and reached a lasting peace that even the dying could live with, granting 40,000 and counting living-dead bodies the right to quantum-decohere into everlasting peace, because just at the moment when *war was declared*, leaving the streets of Morelia ready to burst with the missing, and the empty desert floors digging holes for the emptied, and the severe-clear azure of the Mexican-blue skies turning a glassy-eyed sky-shade of perfectly ghastly, *every last War Zone*, from the poppy fields of Sinaloa to the swamps of Matamoras to the hallways of Mexico's Supreme Court of Justice to the chrome-spinner side streets of Ciudad Juárez, knowing that only peace could save the Mexican people, made final preparations to *surrender to violence*.

And thus it was that Phase III began, on December 11, 2006, with 7,000 troops preparing to march on Michoacan, and 40,000 waiting for their birth-death certificates, and everything taking a turn for the terminally weird, with everyone involved, including the Government, not only fighting on any and all sides of the battle, but simultaneously at peace and at war with themselves, which didn't make much sense, particularly to Raymond, which in turn led to another of those Raymond-type shrugs, and yet another assumption of the "wait and see" attitude, like *wait* at elevation on a hilltop in El Paso, and *see* if all of Mexico got wiped off the map.

On the glass-half-full side, when the Mexican Army had invaded their land, Zambada Garcia had called for a truce among Cartels, and brokered a simple peace pact between the warring factions, which resulted in a coalition called La Federación, not to be confused with La Federación, also known as La Alianza de Sangre, much less La Nueva Federación, which in turn should not in any way be confused with itself, since La Familia Michoacana both did and did not want anything to do with it; this might be a good time to stop thinking trench warfare, with nice clean battle lines, and barren-stretch No-Man's-Land warnings to civilians, and start thinking back to the Peloponnesian War, and battle lines drawn in the shifting currents of the Aegean, while trying to keep in mind that what Thucydides meant by *stasis* was a steady-state condition of constant civil war, a condition maintained, fortunately for historians, through the ceaseless suppression of any sort of impulse toward decency and moderation and a sense of shared humanity, which even on paper sounds hopelessly bland, in favor of unleashing the far more interesting forces of greed, fanaticism, and human depravity, without which human history would be a far different story; imagine a world without greed and depravity, and the next thing you know, you've never heard of Thucydides, you've just reduced one of the world's great historians to the status, let's face it, of a complete nonentity, just another nameless Greek, really no one in particular, kicking back on his sunlit porch sipping a kylix of Chian wine, staring off at the blue Aegean and the vast Alimos sky, caught up, just for a moment, in one of those out-of-the-blue moments where everything that *is* is just as it should be, and even his own rather ordinary gardens, full of lavender shades of agnos blossoms and crimson anemone and pure white asphodelos, are in harmony with themselves, and momentarily timeless, and then unleashing a sudden impulse to take his kids for a swim. Fortunately for

Thucydides, as far as the drug wars are concerned, he won't have to worry about taking the kids for a swim, because greed and depravity are basically immortal, and any sudden outbreak of a sense of shared humanity won't last long unless it's heavily armed. Zambada Garcia's anti-Army Federation was a kind of Lions Club for Drug Lords, purblind knights in the crusade for utter darkness, or a let-the-free-market-function Chamber of Commerce, with yet another long list of inscrutable nicknames. In harmony at last, in a steady-state of *stasis*, the drug lords were now working together, to fight off the poorly paid and under-equipped Army, and when that didn't work, they recruited their workers, using banners that criss-crossed the Sinaloa and Sonora and Chihuahua state highways, advertising better wages and working conditions: GOOD PAY, FOOD, AND HELP FOR YOUR FAMILIES. It probably goes without saying, just for the record, that senior Mexican Government officials have a whole different deal, based on a formula that goes back to antiquity, and with an entirely different approach to *cost-of-living adjustments*: Dónde están mis dólares putas? which translates loosely to Where's my fucking money? and amounts to a, give or take, *lifetime contract*. On the glass-blown-to-shit side, peace is for lightweights, there's not much point in amassing ungodly firepower and armaments exotica and overwhelming quantities of weaponry paraphernalia, unless it's put to use for the betterment of man, through establishment of more open and democratic societies, and markets free to function without excessive intervention, bringing freedom and prosperity to our brothers in the fight, and raining a fucking shitstorm on the rest of you pussies: Los Zetas found themselves like a landlocked country, a drug cartel without its own *plaza*, and having also discovered that they were deeply tired of swatting at mosquito's in coastal Matamoras, they decided to tackle both problems at once, first filling in the swamps with the cranial debris of Gulf Cartel trade reps in Neuvo Laredo, and then seizing the shipping lanes into Laredo itself, which hadn't looked like much when viewed from the air, but has like 9,000 trucks, and 40% of Mexico's exports, passing through it daily, jampacked with drugs; La Familia Michoacana, an evangelical religious group, whose spiritual leader, Nazario Moreno González, had long been heeding the call to the cloth and divine retribution and eternal salvation, through the beheading of nonbelievers in his family-values cause, became deeply disturbed by Federal Government depravity, having caught them in the act of committing the mortal sin of competing with La Familia in the methamphetamine business, and sent word of their disillusionment back to Mexico City, via twelve Federal agents who were so wracked with guilt that their mutilated bodies had to be shoveled-up and dime-bagged from the dust around a Michoacan roadside shrine, where they had come to do penance and atone for their sins, before traveling home with pieces of La Familia's tortuous message; the Beltran-Leyva Sonora Cartel grew wary of supporting a tyrant named Shorty, perhaps as a result of El Chapo himself dropping a so-called dime on his partner, Alfredo Beltran, leading to a most unfortunate encounter between Edgar Guzman, El Chapo's son, and 15 or 20 of the omnipresent Zetas, apparently still For Hire for special occasions, and by the time the Zeta's had lightened their load of AK-47 8M3 hollow-points, and dropped off their smoking RPG-7s, now rendered grenadeless, in a Guzman-family shopping cart, it turned out that Edgar, El Chapo's heir apparent, was about half the size of his own "Shorty" father; and to add insult and injury to grievous bodily harm, Los Negros abandoned their principles altogether, becoming the drug-war equivalent of Blackwater/Xe, killing Sinaloans, Zetas, Matamorans, Beltran-Leyvians, hanging severed human heads from the bridges of Cuernavaca, providing risk management consulting to every war zone in Mexico, and had to be replaced by the Thetas Ray'd encountered, in an excess of X's and lager-bottle fragments and the plaguing of philosophers with arithmetical esoterics, having something to do with the subtraction of human limbs.

While their aims and ideals were no doubt pure, and both the Drug Lords and Government slept with the clear conscience of all perfectly ordinary socio-psychopaths, from serial murderers to the Joint Chiefs of Staff, the inevitable result of this Reap the Whirlwind Doctrine was a certain amount of confusion among veteran vexillologists and students of emblemology and normative blazonry prescriptive grammarians: the corpse-size Hefty Bag became the state tree of Tamaulipas, planted by the hundreds along the road to Reynosa, while the new state insect, the greenbottle blowfly, waited in San Fernando for the corpses to decompose; per fess azure and

sable, three human heads caboshed, displayed senestré of the sun
in splendor, became the mutilated blazonry of the Sinaloa Coat of
Arms; the Mexican National Flag tore itself in half, right through
the middle of the Eagle gripping the Serpent, and the two halves of
the flag began feeding on each other, which didn't leave much for
the vexillologists to ponder; and a new aerial pennant was designed
for the Airborne, trucking the body-parts to their homes in the
empty Chihuahuan desert, a nasty piece of work, with the Agnus
Dei lamb, no doubt slaughtered for Easter, lying beside a crozier
flying a banner made of paper, the pink-and-black cross of a Juárez
lamp post. If you're hoping to understand the dynamics of the drug
wars, or thinking about becoming a Juárez vexillologist, you might
want to consider spending 8 or 10 years trading counterfeit currency
for mortars in Mogadishu, while leafing through Wittgenstein on
the mythos of volition. If you're thinking that maybe the current
alignment will hold, with Juárez, Zeta, Beltran-Leyva, and Tijuana
Cartels on one side of the produce aisle, and Sinaloa, Gulf, La Familia Michoacana, and the Theta philosophers over there on the
other, remember how well the Athenian Empire held together, and
then loan us a dime, and we'll blow the whole supermarket. If you
believe that a house divided against itself cannot stand, and that a
Government cannot endure, at war with itself, welcome to Mexico,
and God Bless America, who the hell said anything about needing
a fucking Government. If you're deeply troubled by the rate of civilian death, and the destruction of human life in acts of random violence, and the loss of the innocent and wide-eyed and wondrous to
democidal maniacs too hideous to fathom, a bunch of beady-eyed
weapons-crazed indiscriminate killers, you should download some
photos of how we firebombed Japan. If none of this stuff makes any
sense at all, and you're not feeling all that, what's the word, *lucid*,
we could try doing a rewrite, or changing your meds, but as far as
making sense of the war in Juárez, or even beginning to comprehend why it is that human leaders, members of a purportedly sapi-
ent species, tend to act, with some frequency, like messianic robots,
our attitude is: frankly, why bother?

Ray kicked back in his waiting-to-heal bed, with his boots
off and his feet up and his making-sense-of-Juárez mind going in
circles, with a half-lit moon still climbing in the east and maybe

an hour from the summit of the black El Paso sky, meaning we're somewhere along that living-dead rift before morning, where you know where dawn is but not quite how to get there, and sort of threw up his hands, literally speaking, which turned out to be a truly bad idea: Jesus, Ray thought, *what the fuck was that?* Ray, evidently, in all the Juárez confusion, seemed to have forgotten that Juárez itself was not the only problem that needed some attending to; perhaps we need to back up just an instant. As Ray lay in the dark there, thinking things over, growing more and more confused about conditions in Juárez, with his chest full of violet-dyed mattress-stitched sutures, and a Moonlight Yellow feather-pile drifting around beneath the shades, he had, he believed, one fundamental problem: with Gomez gone silent, and unhappy with Raymond, the Juárez Cartel and their army of Zetas would need to be avoided if Ray wanted to stay alive; and with an opposed set of forces from the Sinaloa Cartel, with their Zeta-like equivalent paramilitary unit, known as the Thetas, likely equally unhappy, and also in need of situational avoidance, Ray would have a problem even leaving his own house, much less finding a way of returning to full employment; Ray could picture himself now, taking a walk to the corner store, and buying a quart of milk to put in his morning coffee; what he couldn't quite picture, under the circumstances, was a man lying on the sidewalk in a dark pool of blood, diluted with half a pint of his own cerebrospinal fluid, caring one way or the other about drinking his coffee black. Unfortunately for Raymond, while he's got a pretty good picture of how a man might come to die, by running out of milk and taking the exact wrong bullet wound, he's got no sense at all of how a man in his condition, with an underlying problem he seems to have forgotten, could also wind up dead while reaching for a can of peas, much less throwing his hands up toward the black El Paso sky, in a gesture of surrender to Juárez confusion: *underneath it all*, underneath the DuoDERM hydrocolloid dressing, underneath the Steri-Strip antimicrobial skin closures, underneath the violet-dyed Monocryl sutures, an excellent choice for a two-inch face-gash that in no way belonged in nearly four feet of chest-wound, underneath all of this medicinal paraphernalia that was apparently trying to hold his chest parts together, Raymond, in essence, had the knife-fight equivalent of an *electrical problem*, involving two long stretches of electrified fencing, buried in his rib cage along orthogonally intersecting barbed-steel diagonals, equipped with a sensitive motion detector, and while it wasn't the sort of fence that would hold many cattle, in fact a crossed-X cattle pen, hooked up to the wrong power source, stood a pretty good chance of driving off your whole herd, by the time Ray's arms reached about shoulder-high, he set off the detector, and took a hair-raising jolt of voltage to the torso, which led, instantaneously, to a gut-wrenching exercise in breath exhalation, one of those chest-wracking coughing-fit gut-check outbursts, and the discovery that something blinding, of a laser-red intensity, had taken up a position somewhere deep behind his eyeballs, and the momentary presence of an eerie sort of quiet that Raymond himself seemed completely unaware of, as right on the heels of his hair-raising jolt, like that bolt out of the blue of an oversized dose during a memory-loss experiment in electroconvulsive therapy, he spent a quiet moment alone with a kind of mental-blank clarity, such that by the time Ray noticed that his arms had gone down, and retracted whatever statement they'd been trying to make by throwing themselves upward toward the sky in the first place, you might say that Raymond had already surrendered to Wittgenstein's position on the movement of human limbs, and having subtracted the fact that his arms went down from the fact that he'd spontaneously lowered his arms, found nothing much left but a few stray volts, a brief but thankfully restful period of shallow breathing, and the fleeting-type sensation of an absolute conviction that he had no fucking intention of ever again repeating this particularly hair-raising mind-going-in-circles *what-the-fuck-was-that* arm-movement experiment, much less attempting to make sense of Juárez; *underneath it all*, with the Tramadol, evidently, having not quite taken hold, and with Ray under siege by his own barbed-fencing, he was prepared to surrender, of his own volition, to Wittgenstein and Juárez and gravity in general, just as long as they didn't ask him to stick up his hands.

Jesus, thought Raymond, *what the fuck was that?* Ray took another fistful of his Cocker Spaniel morphine, and another gentle sip of Old Grand-Dad Bonded, and turned his thoughts, deliberately, in a high-speed four-wheel neuron-smoking drift, to the grey Ford Fusion guy, who had to be hauling quite a consequential load, like

Ray seemed to remember something being said about a hundred pounds of currency, even if he was carrying it in 500-euro notes, which was, give or take, about how much money? Ray'd never seen, much less tried to weigh, a 500-euro note, so this particular path to a load-to-value estimation, via euro-notes per pound, didn't lead anywhere that Raymond could get to, a fact that Ray proceeded to prove, through a circuitous process whose details we'll spare you, by taking this particular goes-nowhere path first, and winding up somewhere in the highlands of Burma. It's probably worth noting, right up front, that the man, meaning Gomez, who gave Ray that initial 100-pound quote was maybe 25 pounds off, on the high side, just for starters; the euro-note equivalent of the load in the missing Fusion, which right at this moment, isn't actually missing, it's parked in the lot of a Radisson Hotel, conveniently located on Avenida Tecnologico, would weigh in at right around 72.6 pounds, though since there isn't a single euro note in the entire history of this vehicle, this particular bit of trivia is utterly useless. Misinformation and useless trivia aside, how the hell did Ray wind up in Burma? The path to Burma, from a sickbed in El Paso, wanders back through the bushel-baskets of Ray's Alamogordo childhood, where he didn't need to know that a bushel of oats weighs 14.5 kilos just to feed the horses, and on into the auto shops of Ray's orphaned adolescence, where the 3/8-inch hex-bolts on a old Chevy small-block didn't really tempt him to use a 10mm wrench, and on into the Army, and Operation Knight Strike, where a 155mm artillery shell, which weighed, give or take, around 40-some kilos, and might or might not contain three-quarters of a gallon of colorless and odorless Iraqi Sarin, didn't start him worrying that he might wind up dead, knowing nothing whatsoever about the basics of the metric system. Ray knows weight, of course, but only if you're talking in the tens of kilos, and other than breaking down a pound of cocaine, you could put a sound-suppressed Beretta Bobcat to his head, and he still couldn't tell you what the hell a gram is; if Ray were going to solve his hundred-pound euro problem, he was thinking he'd have to solve it with a pound of cocaine. While Ray, admittedly, had no clue at all that the purple 500-euro note weighs 1.1 grams, and it wouldn't really help much even if he did, he knew with some certainty that a pound of cocaine would break down to right around 453 grams and change; this, at a minimum, would simplify the problem, as all Ray would need was a coke-to-euro converter, and some basic multiplication, to put a price on the euro-stash being hauled by the Fusion. The problem he ran into, down this weight-to-value path, was that right in the middle of trying to put a value on a pound of pure euros, by breaking the problem down into grams of pure cocaine, and applying his simple coke-to-euro converter, an approach to the problem that would be perfectly sound, if Ray actually had a coke-to-euro converter, just, as we were saying, as Ray was right in the middle of going down a path that leads nowhere in particular, that tramadol-hydrochloride opioid analgesic that Raymond's been amassing must have crossed some sort of all-or-none, quantal-type, threshold, as it made its way up the steep dose-response curve, because the more Ray stared at his fluffy mound of flake, from up around Cajamarca in the northern Peruvian highlands, being slowly broken down into 453 grams and change of its Eurozone-currency monetary equivalents, the more he began to worry about his coke getting stepped on, diluted down with mannitol or lactose or procaine, such that by the time his pound of euros eventually hit the streets, it would be worth, who knows, maybe four or five times that, and while five times a pound of complete mental gibberish does not change the value of its monetary equivalents, Ray made an executive decision, right on the spot, to flush the pile of coke down the nearest mental toilet, and begin once again using an entirely different substance: pure Double U-O Globe Laotion Heroin. While Ray knew nothing about U-O Globe heroin other than what he'd heard from some brain-damaged vets, this, indeed, was the genuine article, one of those pure products of America gone massively crazy: General Ouane's No. 4 pure-branded heroin, with its memorable red logo and Cold War Coat of Arms, a terrestrial globe dormant between twin lions combatant, quite possibly lifted from a Pall Mall pack, was not only the product of U.S. Intelligence, in its efforts to protect the Hmong from the evils of Communism, but was certified pure by the CIA itself, prior to sale to our men trying to hold down Khe Sahn, having made it out of Laos, and onto the streets of Saigon, via CIA airmail, without ever once being stepped on by anyone. If you're trying to run a weight-to-value calculation, you need something pure and completely unadulterated, and few things on Earth have ever been so pure as that pure China White we provided for our soldiers; the fact that maybe a quarter of our men came home from the fighting addicted to pure heroin is a testament not only to our fine Laotian chemists, but to the CIA's dedication to ideological purity. If you find yourself wondering what the hell Ray was thinking, trying to value a euro-stash using U-O Globe heroin, try to keep in mind that Raymond's a little drowsy, after a night spent washing his pet pills down with incremental sips of 100-proof bourbon, and has, at a minimum, a decent excuse for this diversion into a somewhat opiated thought process, and then ask yourself this: what in God's name was the CIA thinking? Ray stared into the dark there, thinking things over, with his shoes off and his feet up, just sipping a little bourbon, while rerunning the numbers on his pure foreign currency, and then found himself slipping just slightly off track, into a lovely but passing vision of climbing the Burmese hills, with green terraced lawns and misted-over fields and red and white opium poppies getting ready to blossom and a three-hundred-mule pack-train as far as the eye could see, headed into Laos with burlap sacks of raw currency, ready to be refined into pure 500-euro notes, a vision that gave way, as visions sometimes do, to a somewhat more detailed and empathic version of the exact same vision grown even more vivid, such that by the time a little voice had started up in Ray's head, telling him he was headed in the exact wrong direction, the misted fields were filling with women in violet silk, and men in black pajamas wearing conical straw hats, cutting oats into windrows using hickory-handled scythes, stacking mangos by the bushel into hand-woven willow baskets, and what appeared to be a child, in a crimson slash of red, hauling a cedar bucket up from a stone-surrounded source-of-something that was welling up in Raymond from somewhere deep underground, some sense of fellow-feeling for an ancient and interwoven by-the-handful way of life that needed to be preserved against Ray's Eurozone-incursion, accompanied by a voice, this time slightly more insistent, telling Ray, *Hey Ray, Ray, get a goddamn grip, how the fuck much money is in that moron's trunk?*

Thus passed the late-night/early-morning interval of an El Paso

gunman's initial convalescence, a period that encompassed perhaps 65 minutes, between the dead-of-night gap of 3:45 and the
current 4:50 rift-before-morning; while the gunman, meaning Raymond, barely moved an inch, and managed to get lost while going
nowhere in particular, he would appear to be recuperating, and
well down the path toward making a full recovery, just as long as he
stays in bed for a week, and doesn't go looking for milk for his coffee. Just as long as Ray's not Ray, in short, he should be just fine in a
week to ten days. If only Ray were a dog of some kind, maybe some
sort of Affenpinscher-Cocker hybrid, it wouldn't really matter that
Gene took him to the vets, instead of to the trauma unit of an actual
hospital; unfortunately Ray is a whole different beast, a hybrid between a man and a Mossberg 500 pistol-grip Cruiser, which in turn
leads directly to an entirely different care path, like there's no way in
hell that Ray's lying around in bed, spending a week to ten days going nowhere in particular, because Raymond's not just an ordinary
gunman, a hybrid between a man and a black-on-black shotgun,
Raymond's pure soldier, part man, part weapon, part refusal-to-sur-
render, and as long as he can move, Ray's moving forward. *Underneath it all*, underneath his DuoDERM hydrocolloid dressing, underneath his Steri-Strip wound-support skin-closures, underneath
his violet-dyed monofilament sutures, beautifully mattress-stitched
by a local veterinarian, Ray's all Ray, all no-way-but-forward, and
he has four-feet of chest-flesh, carved down to the bone, that won't
hold together if he winds up on a battlefield, picking yards of loose
threads from the story of Raymond Edmunds. If we began by suggesting maggot therapy as a logical alternative that may need to be
considered, it had nothing to do with the necrosis of wound tissue,
or the failure of his DuoDERM hydrocolloid dressing to promote a
natural debridement, exactly as advertised; it had to do with a man
coming apart at the seams, and headed toward the mango orchards
of imaginary Burma.

# 14

Raymond, evidently, had reached the end of the poppy trail, and come within a mango or two of falling asleep on the job, in the middle of some sort of opiated photo essay for who knows what, maybe *Irrational Geographic*, something along the lines of The Hypnagogic Mango Orchards of Eastern Myanmar, and came to with a start, in a dark El Paso bedroom, knowing that unless he was planning on taking a 10-count, it was maybe about time to sit the hell up. Ray knew the drill, of course, and it certainly wasn't the first time he'd been down on the deck, with no damn clue how the hell he got there, but he had several major muscle groups, at this particular juncture, that weren't real eager to offer their assistance; he managed to recruit a couple of pillows as volunteers, and got himself propped up, to something resembling a seated position, without losing more than two or three rounds, and an inch or so of bourbon, in the sit-the-hell-up process. Ray, in short, had had about enough of all this waiting-to-heal nonsense: from this point forward, whatever shit he had to take, from bourbon and Tramadol to a four-foot chest-wound to some truly twisted shit about Napalm-drool and dragon-clocks that he was currently unaware of the approaching need to deal with, Ray was going to take it, like the good soldier he was, but he wasn't going to take it lying down. *Now how the fuck much money is in that moron's trunk?*

Ray took maybe just the tiniest sip of bourbon, braced himself a little for the road up ahead, and restarted his weight-to-value calculations down a slightly different path; a hundred pounds of euros was almost certainly worth something, but it sure wasn't worth the trouble of getting lost in the Burmese hills. Even a quick and dirty conversion from 500-euro notes to U.S. $100s would weigh in at maybe 800 pounds, like having two massive Sumo wrestlers stuffed inside your trunk, and a grey-Fusion bumper sort of dragging along the pavement, like how in God's name could you manage to lose a car that couldn't climb the hills of a six-inch speed bump? Eight hundred pounds in U.S. hundreds has to be worth what, maybe something in the neighborhood of the tens of millions, since any-thing less than ten or twenty million wouldn't be nearly enough to get Gomez' attention, unless, of course, you worked for the man, in which case you could die making change for a quarter, which wasn't really an answer to the question at hand, but reminded Ray suddenly of his own heavy load, his million dollar and counting, now-what-am-I-forgetting, I-know-I-left-it-somewhere, dusty Uzbek suitcase, a suitcase whose contents belonged precisely elsewhere, in the hands of Gomez, hands that at the moment he was studi-ously avoiding; he could always take the money back to Gomez, of course, just as long as he didn't mind peeling the flesh from his face, after Gomez flame-broiled it with Blazer-grade butane. This, apparently, called for a drink, as Ray threw some neurons into re-verse, and tried to back away from this particular image, in search of a somewhat more nuanced approach, a kind of crème-brûléed face-flesh workaround strategy, though if you could see Ray's eyes in his black El Paso room, you might think he was headed backwards altogether, even if it involved retracing his steps, and crossing the Mekong on his opiated pack-mules; Ray's worked for Gomez for nearly sixteen years, and has maybe seen some shit he wishes he hadn't. Ray closed his eyes, blinked once or twice, and came back with a slightly more palatable image, where Gomez was more of the book-cooker type, and money-into-the-banking-system infusion master, while Ray wasn't much more than a takeout errand boy, like the Taiwanese kid on his forty-year-old Schwinn, delivering Crispy Noodles from Pho Tre Bien; Ray was thinking maybe he should be calling the kid up, and handing him the briefcase, and a $20 tip, take the money to Gomez, in a hurry, chop-chop, though he knew he'd need something a little stronger than Tramadol if the million and counting simply up and disappeared, leaving only a soggy trail of Pho Crispy Noodles. So let's see now, where the hell were we, forget about bone-burns and the million dollar suitcase, the Fusion guy's hauling a couple of Sumos in his trunk, call it ten or twenty million, by Raymond's estimation, and why was a question, and what the hell his name was, and where exactly did the guy fit in, and who the fuck was he in that Raymond wasn't knowing, and the guy was supposed to be DOA already, like give or take *now*, meaning better late than never was not going to cut it. What Ray was trying to picture was how you get from *now* to *already-dead-and-buried* and *long-ago-forgotten*, with the Sumo wrestlers propped-up on Gomez' desk, gift-wrapped in a mile or two of bright-pink ribbon, make for one hell of a pretty fucking picture, if it weren't for the fact that it wasn't really, altogether, what's the word, *real*. Wonder if the Schwinn kid knew any Sumo wrestlers, or had twenty million dollars in change for a quarter, just to tide Ray over until he came up with a plan, maybe something that avoided a lot of Blazer-bubbled face-flesh, or whatever Ray's seen that we're happy to say we haven't.

Face-flesh aside, Raymond wasn't feeling half bad about now, maybe a little thirsty from eating too much salt, tramadol hydrochloride at work on his Mu-opioid receptor sites, and his noradrenergic and serotonin reuptake systems, causing a marked reduction in his perception of things like pain, and a perceptible elevation of his overall mood. Ray's mood, as a matter of fact, was now perfectly sound; whereas Gene, poor Eugene, had a few odds and ends he was worrying over, and several basic concerns that wouldn't keep until morning, although any worries he might have had about Ray losing consciousness, and winding up permanently on the wrong side of the Mekong, and thus leaving Gene in charge of making the funeral arrangements, were cleared up immediately upon reentering Ray's room, and flipping the wall switch on several thousand watts of enough bare-bulb lighting to have awakened the dead. Ray, Ray, you awake? Of course my good man, I am at your service. Perhaps you would do me a favor and bring me the Mossberg so I can dim one or two these unfortunate fucking light bulbs. Sorry, Trip, let me put a lamp on. You feeling all right? Fit as a fiddle, Gene, fit as a goddamn fiddle, happy as a dog with two damn tails, feels like whoever put my chest back together must have rigged me up with a few extra strings, not that I remember specifically asking some numbnuts with maybe eighty feet of trout line and a two-inch suture needle if he could figure out a way to turn me into an autoharp. Now what can I do for you on this glorious morning? I don't know about morning, Trip, it's still pitch-black out, and we're already up to our necks in shit with Gomez. What are we going to do about getting him his money back? Excellent question, Eugene, excellent fucking question, though one wonders in general precisely what money you're referring to, the money we have in our actual possession, or the money on a journey to hell in a handbasket, or maybe it's going to heaven in like a Dandux Loadumper, or then again it might be one of those ballbarrow contraptions with sort of a plastic basketball where the wheel's supposed to go. I don't know about you, Gene, but since when did we start thinking we needed wheelbarrows made of plastic? Saw a guy the other day trying to mix a load of concrete in one of those nylon folding things. You call that a wheelbarrow? Whole world's going down the well in a plastic beach bucket, if you're specifically asking me for my opinion. So what were we talking about? The briefcase, Ray, the money from the drug deal, we need to get that money back to Gomez like yesterday. Yeah, you know what? I was only just now thinking the same damn thing, maybe we go back to around yesterday morning, try to catch that grey-Ford guy before he's way the hell out in the deep blue water. Not what I meant, Trip, not literally yesterday, forget about yesterday, we need to get the money back to Gomez like *now*. Yeah, well, I'll tell you what, I tried that already, and as far as I can figure, you can't get from *now* to anywhere that matters, at least not as far as Gomez is concerned. What do you say we call the Crispy Noodle kid, have him haul the money in that wicker basket on his Schwinn? Start talking to Gomez, we'll spoil the whole morning, I'm thinking we should be out taking the Magnum for a run, maybe headin' up north to that spot up above Cowles or something, park the truck down in the canyon bottom and just head out on foot, take that climb up out of the willows into the cottonwoods and pines, maybe stake out one of those perfect little trout streams that feed into the Pecos up above The Box, be beautiful right now up in the Sangre de Cristos, be like this whole damn world forgot all about us. I'm picturing it's maybe around June sometime, once the Giants start hatching, we could do a little fly-casting with these lines in my chest, catch us a few cutthroats and brookies and rainbows, probably fool 'em with a stonefly in the middle of June, or goldens and red quills, if it turns out it's July, or so maybe we head out in the sagebrush and creosote, I'm thinking we should be out taking the dogs for a run. Which reminds me, come to think of it, do me a favor and see if you can remember to remind me to feed them. Ray, Ray, how about thinking in a straight line for just a minute, and maybe laying off the Grand-Dads and pain pills. So I'm dreaming, is what you're saying. Just not too sure that all the bourbon and pills are doing you much good, at least not as far as helping you think straight. You may be right, Eugene, you may well be right, this may be a good goddamn point that you're making, I've got a feeling this bourbon must be making me thirsty, my mouth is a little dry, I could maybe use a glass of whatyoucallit water. And you should think about eating that sandwich, Trip, you're going to get blasted taking that shit on an empty stomach. I'm fine, just fine, just a little thirsty, my mouth feels a little sort of furry inside, mind like a steel trap, mind like a journey to bed in a pickup. What time is it, anyway? 'Bout 5 am, you get any sleep? Slept like a baby, had the weirdest goddamn dream, dreamt that you took me to an animal clinic. Okay, look, Ray, here's the deal, we're going to need to start thinking about getting our shit back together, try to patch things up with Gomez and his crew, and get with the damn program, before he gets to thinking we pulled a runner with his money. Yes, yes, I believe that Señor Gomez is disappointed in us, if you're asking for my opinion, I'm not altogether certain that we are held any longer in his highest esteem, and if I have the weight-to-value conversion straight in my head, we'd still be short maybe ten or twenty million. What? The guy on the mule, Gene, the guy on the mule, that douchebag on a journey to his funeral in a Fusion, with the hundred pounds of heroin riding around in his trunk, or wait, forget the heroin, that got moderately fucked up, guy's stuck on a speed bump with a couple of Sumos in his trunk, waiting for the CIA airmail plane, probably find him wandering around the streets of Saigon, 'bout to take a quick trip back to reality in a rickshaw, with two or three pistol slugs in the back of his head. Tell you what, Gene, unless you know a way back to yesterday morning, we haven't got a goddamn program to get with, we might as well take a drive out to

Alamogordo, be good to see my dad again, maybe hunt a few quail
or bobwhites or something. Raymond, for fucksake, your father's
been dead for years, wake the fuck up, we need to get moving. Due
respect, Eugene, I don't really feel much like moving this morning,
I think my chest hurts like a son of a bitch, just thank God I can't
fucking feel it. So what are we going to do about Gomez' cash, Ray?
I'm just fucking with you Gene, or like the wiry guy said, you're just
being fucked with, did you see that guy with the English trench
knife, *that* motherfucker was a circus magician, I saw that knife go
past my chin, the next thing I know I'm a letter of the alphabet,
waiting for some trout guide with enough fly-fishing line to convert
me from a fiddle to a violet-string zither. Let me ask you something
Gene. How did I wind up with a chestful of sutures made of two-
pound test, and a hundred-pound fish, way out in the deep water,
that I'm supposed to be trying to get to dry land?

This was a question for which Gene, apparently, was not as yet
prepared to provide an honest answer; Gene, for one thing, has
no clue at all what's underneath all that medicinal paraphernalia,
while Ray, evidently, must have had a quick peek, and not liked
the look of all those violet-dyed mono-sutures, particularly if he's
going fishing in the deep blue waters, and might've preferred something in a green Excel Braid. Raymond shook his head, which was
another bad idea, rubbed his eyes while drinking down a full glass
of water, ate the better part of half of half of a roast beef sandwich,
and was right in the middle of downing a few more Tramadol, and
clearing away the last of the mist-covered mango orchards, when
suddenly, out of nowhere, a path just appeared, perhaps not *the*
path, but a path nevertheless. First thing to do is to get the guy's
name, maybe run some kind of trace on the missing tens of millions. Jenny, what they need now is a little help from Jennifer, Jennifer the Genuine up in Gomez' trading office, who we're guessing
Ray thinks must have access to the money files, and could maybe
get them a name, just for starters, that rings a little truer than John
Q. Bullshit. Jen, needless to say, is a whole different story, and since
there's no way on earth you could possibly have met her, no doubt
deserves a far more proper introduction, but right off the bat here,
there's one small problem, which is that Ray's got the equivalent of
a mild to moderate speech impediment when it comes to dealing

with Jennifer in person. It's not like Ray starts to stutter and stammer, since Ray finds Jen pretty easy to talk to; it's more like Ray's got no language at all that would help him get his bearings in Jen's part of the world. Two or three steps into one of those "what do you do?" discussions, say derivatives trading based on statistical arbitrage using means-reversion and covariance matrices, like the simplest sort of shit that Jen can imagine, and Ray might as well be on the dark side of the moon, assuming one of the moons in the vicinity of Saturn actually has a dark side and one that stays light, which means, as Jen knows, and would be happy to explain, that it's "tidally locked," which would in turn shove Ray out into an entirely different solar system. Raymond, of course, has a word-hoard of his own, drawn from the terra firma of the professional foot soldier; if you needed a tight cluster of M47 Dragons to take out an Iraqi fortified bunker, Ray could get the job done, and tell you how he did it, just as long as you didn't dig too deep on the workings of the rockets; Ray's a *rocket-firer*, as in no more bunker, and Jen's a *rocket-scientist*, with like a fortified-bunkerful of statistical-arbitrage trading profits. Raymond, in other words, is more that just a little *intimidated* by the woman, flying that Mooney Ovation2 GX in a tight yellow skirt and red high heels, with the face of a model from a shampoo commercial, and the IQ of a Carnegie Mellon mathematician, the sort of woman men will stare at until they're blind as bats, and their IQs have dropped into the mid-double-digits; Ray's got no problem seeing through the dazzle, and knows underneath that Jen's the real deal, but Raymond, in essence, has no clue at all as to where in the sentence you'd put the *genuine article*. All that aside, her name is Jen; or maybe it's Jenny or Jennifer or whatever; Ray's pretty sure, whatever she wants to call herself, that he can fit that in a sentence if she'll give him half a chance, and maybe it's just a matter of the narrative of our species, or something to do with this particular species of narrative, but that's a half of Jen she'd be more than happy to give him, because Jen's more than a little *intrigued* by the man.

Gene, I got an idea. 'Bout fuckin' time, you feeling any better? Yeah, I think these pet pills are finally kicking in, see if you can find me a Starbucks or something. That's your idea? Send me to the Starbucks? No, cancel that, Gomez probably got a lynch mob out looking for the Magnum, see if we've got any of that Yuban's left, and see if you can get ahold of Jenny on her cell phone. Jenny? Gomez' Jenny? What do you want with her right now? I don't know, Gene, maybe I can get her to shampoo my hair. Ray, Ray, that's not fucking funny, you need to get serious, you start thinking about women right now, we're both totally fucked, no disrespect to Jennifer. Just call her, Gene, I've got an idea. You said that already. Mind giving me a hint what the hell it is? I'm thinking this dickwad must be in the files, maybe Jen can get us a name, help us figure out what's motivating the guy. Motivating? Motivating? Why's he need any motivating if he's got twenty million of Gomez' money? You want my opinion, sounds to me like he's trying to get himself killed. Driving around Juárez with a shitpile of money, probably got a decent size bounty on his head, maybe he's got it figured he can collect it himself. I'm telling you Gene, none of this adds up, Gomez wanting us to eliminate this guy, gives us a license plate and a description of the vehicle, pretty much specifically won't give us a name. Why would a man come all the way to El Paso, with millions in stolen currency stuffed in a bag, and a whole detailed spec on how to get himself killed? Man wants to die, he don't need to pack a bag, he can crawl into bed, die someplace comfortable. What I want to know is, what's this guy's thinking? I don't know, Ray, what the hell's the difference, maybe the man's insane, we should be checking the local asylums. Not telling us his name, Gene, that tells us something. Tells us what? Tells us what? You back on wondering whether this asshole's got it coming? I told you already, he's too dumb to live, what the fuck's it matter whether or not he's got it coming? Wouldn't be the first man to die of stupidity. You think those Iraqi's digging holes in the open desert, right in the middle of some CINCSAC's CHOPed kill box, had the first damn clue what the hell they were thinking? Heh guys, I got an idea, let's dig a bunch of holes and sit around for a month, let the B-52 Stratos drop 25,000 tons of iron on our heads, see how long it takes 'fore we can't hear ourselves think. Too dumb to live, if you're asking me, dug their own damn graves, just like this moron. Don't seem to remember you complaining too much about the BUFF bombardiers staring down through their Nordens forgetting to get the names of the guys they were laying carpet on. Those guys were soldiers, Gene, just like you and me. That's what I'm trying tell you, Trip,

we don't get that money back to Gomez about now, we'll be two
dumb Iraqi's in a four-foot gopher hole, trying to figure out what
the hell we *thought* we were thinking, wondering why the fuck we
can't hear ourselves think. Something tells me this guy's a civilian.
Okay, okay, so we call up Jennifer, invite her over to shampoo your
hair, next thing you know we got gophers in our lawn, and Zetas in
the parlor, and the two of us drinking Yuban through holes in our
skulls. You're not making any sense Gene. Not making sense? Not
making sense? You're the one wants to send Jen fishing in Gomez'
money files. How deep a hole you think they'll have to dig, 'fore Jen
figures out that there's plenty of cutthroats, but not a single fucking
rainbow in the whole Chihuahuan desert? Very colorful, Eugene.
Just please call her. Use the land line; I'll take the call here. And
make sure our cell phones are all powered off, and then take out the
battery packs and leave them out. And get the TEC-9s and Mossberg out of the truck bed. And make me a cup of Yuban's, whole
milk, no sugar. And for God's sake, Gene, stop repeating yourself;
just do what I'm saying, stop making me fucking nervous.

It would seem that Raymond's mind was beginning to return
to human cogitation mode, not that he's got it right yet about everything he's cogitating; that whole milk in the icebox is easily six
weeks old, so if Ray wants coffee, he should probably drink it black.
He has, however, correctly deduced the need to make a change in
the configuration of their cell phones; given the expertise of the
Zetas, they could not only locate a powered-off handset, but could
download some software that would activate the microphone, and
turn their cell phones into roving bugs and eavesdropping devices,
get a pretty good read on what Ray thought he was up to, right
down to the brand name and color of Jen's shampoo. Just as long
as the phones had their battery packs installed, the Zetas could pin
them down to within 50 meters, and save Ray the bother of having
to wash his own hair, though Ray, to be honest, had no real idea
how the hell you'd locate a powered-off cell phone. When Jen had
offered to explain it, he'd felt like a young Quarter Horse being
sacked-out by a trainer, like she'd maybe waved the equivalent of a
bath towel or saddle blanket somewhere in the vicinity of his too-
old-to-learn head, something to do with roaming signals contacting
nearby antenna towers, and he was already feeling a little wild-eyed

and balky; by the time she'd gotten around to multilateration and hyperbolic positioning and a hand-sketched drawing of a two-sheeted hyperboloid, he was nodding a little vaguely as though pretending to understand, while his mind was making a run for it, out into open pasture. Suffice it to say that Ray knew just enough to call Jen on a land line, and consider dropping those battery packs down the nearest physical toilet.

If Ray, at this point, had stopped for just a moment, and thought things over, and asked Gene to bring him one additional item, say the keys to a large black pickup they've been driving, he might well have put them aside for the time being, in a beautiful little gift that Jennifer had given him, admittedly one of dozens of trinkets she'd brought back from a business trip to the Hong Kong office, one of those Chinese nested boxes he keeps on his nightstand, next to an open book that we'll come to later, and all of what follows would be a far different story; Raymond, however, had other things on his mind, and was far too focused on the Zeta's capabilities. What Ray had in mind, and was now putting into action, via Jenny's brand-new Motorola Rokr E8 Smartphone, new in the sense that it was new to her, though by a few days past Easter, in the middle of the springtime of 2009, most of the E8s were on their way to Guandong Province, and an enormous techno trash-heap that we'll visit in a few hours, just as soon as we take care of a little narrative business; what Ray, as we were saying, thought he had in mind was to send Jen off to Gomez' money files, on a fishing expedition for a hundred-pound trout, while staying well above The Box at the bottom of Pecos canyon, and well away from the *kill box* in the open Chihuahuan desert. By the time Jen's finished with all the strange nested boxes that Ray's well on the way to getting her into, she may wish she'd never unpacked the E8, and just sent it on, packing crate, cell phone, battery pack and all, directly to the trash-heap of Guangdong Province. Springtime in El Paso is a beautiful little gift, but what Ray's getting her into mostly just isn't.

While we're guessing that Jen is happy that Raymond's finally called, though this was, admittedly, an odd time of morning, and she was still in her bathrobe, drinking a cup of tea, with nearly four hours to kill before the CBOT's Open Outcry on Class III Milk Futures, we're also virtually certain that she's bound to have some *qualms*, a disturbing sense of uncertainty regarding the rightness of an action; that's a lovely word, *qualms*, can you imagine a word as lovely as that having origins that seem to be disturbingly uncertain, similar in a way to the feeling itself, which often seems to arise out of uncertain origins. In this case, of course, if Jen has qualms, she won't have far to look to determine their origins; if Gomez finds a spike-print from her red Jimmy Choos, up there in the snow-melt of the money-source files, the result will be something disturbingly certain, similar in a way to the feeling that arises if you try tracing *qualms* back to Old English origins, where some grisly-looking barbarisms like *cwealm* and *utcualm* turn out to mean "death" and "utter destruction." Which would definitely give you the qualms, no doubt about it; probably leave you quaking in your red Jimmy Choos. What is it you're looking for, Ray? There's a guy from LA, recently arrived here, with a shitload of maybe it's Gomez' money; Gomez wants me to find the guy, but no one seems willing to tell me his name. I don't know Ray; I've signed so many confidentiality agreements, I'm not even sure I'm supposed to know my own name. You talking about The Poet? What? The guy's a poet? No, no, like The Poet, like a code name. His code name is The Poet? Yeah, you got it, there's a man in LA with the code name The Poet. Is that the guy I'm talking about? I don't know, Ray, who are you talking about? Beats me, Jen, I have no idea. Some guy gets off a plane from LA through Salt Lake, night before last, at 9:03, a Delta flight, #1128, and I'm supposed to intercept him at some fleabag motel, take back the money, and remove the guy from his immediate surroundings. Remove him? Make him disappear. Just like that? Just like that, and then we miss him at the motel but find his bag ticket, bring it to Gomez, and everyone's talking about him traveling under his own actual name, give me the license tags on a grey Ford Fusion, but won't tell me shit about who he is or what the fuck name he's traveling under, and then I lose him I guess you'd have to say, you'd probably say I basically lost him. You lost him. Yeah, so, he went over the bridge into Ciudad Juárez, and then me and Gene run into some problems. Problems? Seems to me the man's wandering around Juárez with a shitpile of maybe it's Gomez' money, you and Gene aren't the only ones with a few basic problems. Yeah, well, that's probably true, but we've still got to find him, and get back the money. And remove him? I don't know, Jen, that's part of the problem, I don't know who the man is in the first place. This guy The Poet, what's his real name? Doesn't have a real name, only has a code name. Jesus, so even if that's him, you don't know what his actual name is? Sorry Raymond, everything in the office, people, projects, accounts, and so on, well, how do I put this, there's kind of an abstraction layer, it's all done in code; none of it's actual; in computer jargon, it's what they call virtual. So I'm chasing after an abstraction layer. Won't seem too virtual, guy winds up dead. Virtual, eh? Like in virtually dead? Virtual. How do you spell that? V, I, R...Raymond, pardon my saying, this isn't really getting you anywhere. What is it you want me to do? I don't know Jen, I just want to know who the man is before I end up having to hurt him; Gomez isn't saying, but I'm getting the feeling this guy is a civilian. So what if he is? You sound like Gene, that's what he keeps saying, if he's dealing with Gomez, he's too stupid to live, I just don't like the feeling they're not telling me something, there's something going on here don't seem right. And you want to know if you're doing the right thing. I don't know, maybe. It's kind of a long story, but I've seen people dead that should still be living, people wouldn't hurt a flea if it bit them, just trying to get home to their wife and kids, not even armed, calling them combatants. I'll tell you something, Ray, Gomez doesn't deal with many people who are innocent. Shit Jen, maybe the guy is guilty as hell, I do what I have to, feel better about it. Right about now, he's driving around in a rental like he don't know what's coming, got half of Juárez ready to shoot him on sight. And you don't think he deserves it. I guess that's right, I don't think he deserves it. Way I see it, if he's got it coming, they'd a told me his story, and they didn't tell me shit, not even his goddamn name, you'll pardon my French. Listen to me, Raymond, you go poking around in Gomez' business, it'll be you that's got it coming, they won't wait around to hear your whole life story; then someone takes out a file that's code-named Blackjack, and dumps it in the trash, and then the trash gets shredded. That's my name, Blackjack? You're not supposed to know that. So you think this guy The Poet is the one I'm looking for? Yeah, probably him, or maybe any one of fifty-some others, happens to go through LA on his way back from Bangkok, or Kabul or Islamabad, or Colombo, Sri Lanka. Think you can tell me whether this man, The Poet, is a civilian or not? What's your definition of him being a civilian? I don't know, Jen, a guy who's not supposed to die for doing what he's doing. So I pull the file on this guy, The Poet, see what he's been working on, maybe tell you the man's story, but that's not going to help you if Gomez gets wind of this, finds out you're thinking for yourself about his business. I know, I know, I'm already on his shitlist for losing the guy, haven't got a lot left to lose at the moment. You want me to call you back on this same number? Maybe come to your place if I can find the file? Better you don't know where I am, supposing Gomez starts to asking a lot of questions; I'll meet you at Sonny's, over on Myrtle Avenue, you know where that is? Sure, I know the place; I'll call you when I've got something. Thanks Jen, you sure you'll be all right? Oh certainly, what's the worst that can happen, wind up out on the Lomas mesa, someone calling my mom for my dental records. Jesus, you're right; maybe we should rethink this. Knock yourself out, Ray. Meantime, let me go pull this guy's file. This left Ray holding a phone with no dial tone, staring at a box beside a book on his nightstand, picturing Jen winding up on the Lomas mesa, all carved up into meaningless little pieces, all on account of Raymond's having qualms, which seem to have arisen out of uncertain origins.

You ever find yourself living in Raymond's part of the world, don't be having qualms, of any sort of origin. You find yourself thinking about the rightness of an action, you're in the wrong discourse world; better get the hell out of there. Qualms, in the drug world, is not a lovely word.

Jen, or Jenny, or Jennifer if you like, Jennifer, much like Raymond, could care less what you call her, you can even call her Davis, like the junk-mailers do, or the guys who put her name on the Phi Beta Kappa certificate, though there's a beautiful little village in the hills of Mid Wales, with a white, one-room church, beside a wildflower graveyard, where her great-great-uncle the sheepherder, of the flowing white hair and indecipherable speech and telepathic communion with his beloved Welsh Collies, will eventually be buried under a deeply chiselled stone that will read, more properly, Cecille Cadogan Davies, sat back in her disposable Ikea-type chair,

powered-off and disabled her new Rokr Smartphone, and stared
at a favorite painting on the opposite wall, a painting called The
Doctor's Wife, after a character in a novel by José Saramago. In
the book, a contagion of white blindness has inexplicably broken
out, leaving everyone but the Doctor's Wife unable to see, and the
façade of a civilized social order has fallen away, and the inhabitants of an unnamed city, like Lisbon or Porto, have been reduced
to the level of a subhuman horror-show, squatting in abandoned
buildings, scrounging for scraps of food, turning to rotting meat in a
convenience-store cellar, as the city slowly descends into the night-
marish chaos of an every-man-for-himself human-animal existence;
all in all, just not a pretty picture, if you happened to be living in
Lisbon or Porto. If it turns out you're in Juárez, of course, or a favela
run by thugs in Rio or São Paolo, or under a piece of tin that seems
to think it's a kind of house, down around the bottom of a garbage
pit in Lagos, you probably think the world has gone blind already,
just not blind enough to level out the playing field. The Doctor's
Wife, the character in the painting, wears a floral-print dress in
springtime colors, and carbon-black hair flowing down around her
shoulders, and a look that seems to register, on her delicate-featured
face, the terrible turn of events that Saramago has depicted, part
visceral human revulsion, part infinite cosmic pathos, part wide-
eyed shell-shocked horror over the suffering that she's witnessed,
although to be perfectly honest, all things considered, she doesn't
really look like she's been living inside a book, she looks like she's
been living in the world where people suffer; with the air all around
her turned a toxic shade of white, and a mysterious pair of scissors hovering in the background, she may well be reacting, with a
look of some dismay, to the news that the contagion has mysteriously abated, and that the normal civilized social order will soon
be reinstalled, leaving man in his infinite wisdom free to go about
his business, that of healing our dying planet, with its suppurating
head wounds, by stitching it back together using Ultra Sharp Pink-
ing Shears; if there's one thing that's certain about that look in her
eyes, she's not really buying Saramago's whole premise, and can
see right through all that literary-calamity business, and deep into
the garbage pits and shantytown favelas, meaning we're going to
need something more than Saramago's Dog of Tears, we may need

a whole pack of Cecile's telepathic sheepdogs, to absorb such a look of complete non-blindness.

Jennifer, right at the moment, however, wasn't attempting to absorb it, not at 5:30 on a Thursday morning, in fact she wasn't actually looking at the painting itself, she was staring through its eyes into the civilized distance, sipping a small cup of Longjing Dragon Well roasted green tea, and thinking about epicatechins and "dragon well" water. When the cool dense water in a Hangzhou well is covered with something lighter, from a recent spring rain, there is a swirling effect created at the differential interface, a sinuous movement like the tail of a dragon, not the venomous fiery creature of European legend, but the benevolent Chinese symbol of auspicious power; when combined with the polyphenolic antioxidants of the catechins, a preventative for things like stroke and brain aneurisms, the Longjing "dragon well" yellow-green tea gives Jenny the courage for a day at the office, a day of non-blindness without the risk of sudden heart failure. Jenny didn't like the place, is what this is saying, and the green tea helped, and the Doctor's Wife in turn was an ounce of prevention, and maybe in keeping with the Saramago suffering theme, Jenny thought of Senhor José in *All The Names*, fighting the dragon in the Central Registry files where the names of the dead were endlessly housed, not the razor-toothed monster of Old English myth, with furious drooling jaws, snorting smoke and breathing fire through its earthquake nostrils, but the dragon of a dense and stagnant plague of darkness, which was just the sort of shit that seemed to emanate from Gomez, into whose files she was going to have to reach and turn on a let's-cut-the-bullshit light switch. Jenny, in other words, had to go to the office, pull out the file on some code-named moron, and shed a little light on his story for Raymond, and she didn't really want to, is what this is saying, so she poured herself some more of the yellow-green tea, and antioxidized her heart against sudden seizure. Jenny wasn't blind, and Gomez wasn't a moron, and if he caught her snooping around in the exact wrong file, she'd wind up wishing she'd made her tea out of hemlock, a preventive for things like mutilated corpses, and telepathic sheepdogs trying to commune with the headless, and the endless search for housing among the mortified dead. Jesus, what a mess; it's not even 6:00, and I'm already getting ghoulish; this might be a good time to get my shit back together; I need to be at the office in maybe half an hour. Jen took maybe just the tiniest sip of tea, braced herself a little for the day up ahead, and somehow or other, managed to totally lose it, spraying epicatechins all over everywhere, including a few squares of the checkerboard Crêpe de Chine blouse she was wearing, and a drowsy chocolate Lab that was lying at her feet, in one of those gasping-for-air sudden bursts of real laughter; there was something about Gomez that seemed to strike Jen as funny, with his wrath-of-God black-body darkness emanations, and the stagnant sense of humor of an Old Testament prophet, though if Gomez caught her holding The Poet file, laughing in his face was not going to help much. Gomez was something of a strict constructionist, a Biblical literalist, when it came to the Organization and its holy files; he might quote Shakespeare and come off sounding literary, but Gomez was a strictly-by-the-book kind of guy, and Jen really wasn't; Jennifer herself was a bit of a defiler.

Jen ended up here, in a Magoffin apartment and the exact wrong job, by way of El Paso Junior College and two years at UTEP, and most of a Ph.D. in Mathematics and Statistics from Rice University, and a chance to trade derivatives, speaking of abstraction layers, for Real-Time Global, one of the Juárez Cartel's unregistered private hedge funds. By the time she figured out what Real-Time was up to, she was paying off the loan on a Mooney Ovation, and by the time she'd paid off the Mooney Ovation, she was, to put it mildly, completely unemployable, unless she found a quant-type with a fondness for *sicarios*, and a soft spot for traders with holes in their heads. This morning, like always, she leaves her place near Magoffin Park, takes Brown to Texas Avenue, then a left on North Mesa, and left again on San Antonio, to the high rise on Stanton, where she parks on an empty floor maybe three levels down, half-expecting, like always, that an FBI van, full of clean-cut agents and forensic accountants, will pull in beside her, and roll to a halt. The elevator ride was, as usual, uneventful, and while she wasn't necessarily hoping for the cable to snap, she'd have no problem at all taking a twelve-story plunge, and winding up on a feeding tube, in a six- or eight-month coma. The entrance to the office was a single plain door, unnamed, unnumbered, it might as well have been a broom closet; you went through the door and walked down ten or twelve feet of empty carpeted hallway, put your thumb over the optical sensor of an F4 Vista Fingerprint deadbolt system, keyed in your access code, and waited a few milliseconds while the F4 sent a thumbful of TCP/IP communication packets on a roundtrip from the security computer and back to the deadbolt door, then turned the handle and entered the office, almost as though you thought human beings belonged there, and found yourself on the terrace above a massive three-story trading floor, jammed with technology, but very few humans. There were, admittedly, hundreds of desks, crammed with computers and video monitors, tuned to CNBC and Bloomberg and Reuters, but if you're picturing the sort of place where people sat at the desks, and studied the trend lines, and shouted out orders, you've come to the wrong decade, and maybe need an update on high-frequency trading platforms; if some lowlife down on the trading floor started picking stocks, and placing actual bets on the movement of the market, he could easily be wrong, and cost Gomez money, and never make it back through the Vista F4. You think you have a stock that's grossly undervalued, and somehow think the stock is worth buying and holding? No problem at all, just make sure you don't hold it for more that a few hundred milliseconds.

Where the humans used to be there were hundreds of computers, getting in and out of positions before an actual human being would register the fact that a position once existed, all bolted together in an electronic trading platform that was directly connected to the matching-engines of exchanges and ECNs all over the world. Not that all this arcane machinery and high-frequency-trading shit, like computers reading the ticker an instant before it ticks, and front-running the trades by a couple of hundred microseconds, or using ultra-low-latency direct market access to spot pricing deviations between multiple exchanges, or noticing that the price on German bonds is momentarily out of synch with the euro exchange rate, had much of an effect on the overall market; markets are transparent, with a level playing-field for all, and all this sort of techno-shit, which may not be an option in your 401(k), really only accounts for 70% of trading volume, so don't start thinking you're getting a raw deal. Jen looked over the mezzanine rail, and down on a playing field that was nearly deserted, knowing that if some trader was actually at his desk, he was trying to find a flower shop that was open at 6:20, running some sort of arbitrage play that involved trading long-stems, and $200K a week, for acceptance of his occasionally idiosyncratic sleeping habits. Like everyone else, Jenny was a trader who didn't actually trade; she'd designed computer software to do that for her, built in C++ by a squad from their army of distributed-object snipers and let's-game-the-matching-engines low-latency predators, taking advantage of minute discrepancies between the theoretical value of some arcane financial derivative and the price of the underlying asset, like a share of stock or an ear of corn. Over time, if the markets behaved normally, and stayed within historical trading ranges, and her derivatives remained liquid, and no one nuked the New York Stock Exchange or the CBOT trading floor, some trader run amok in the pit after a bad bet on soybeans, say, then Jenny extracted money in nanopenny increments, quadrillions of them a day, maybe eighty million dollars' worth in the last six months alone. Eventually, the hordes of physics quants and rocket scientists at Goldman Sachs and Morgan Stanley and Mitsubishi UFJ would catch on to her arbitrage plays, and force her to switch from equity swaps to back-to-backs and Rainbow options, and recalibrate the algorithms to stay just ahead of the torchlit mob. What Jenny did was watch and wait: watch the bright red ticker lights wheel around the enormous trading floor, and wait for a Kobe earthquake, or 767 crashed into a looming office tower, or some 100-year-flood type of out-of-band market behavior, like Treasury finally deciding to put Lehman out of its misery, and then turn to her basic keyboard and flip her arbitrage apps to Off, until they caught the crazy soybean guy, and things returned to normalcy, and wealth extraction resumed again, at nanopennies per microsecond, and everything worked as it ought to work, here in the normal world, where human beings made tens of billions off of other humans' work. Inverse floaters, barrier options, all-or-nothing binary options, Cliquet ratchets and Iron Condors and path-dependency Lookbacks, with fixed and floating strike variations, Bermuda options, Canaries, Himalaya and Everest and Atlas and Annapurna mountain range and basket options, variance-gamma Asians, and crash-size-to-multiplier CPPIs, and Unit Contingent power-swaps, and plain-vanilla Quantos, and option-on-option Composites, and vega-notional Variance Swaps, if you've never heard of any of this, or somehow think that vega is the name of a goddamn star, you're in the wrong part of our whole hell-bent world, you've been reading too much literature, and placing too much faith in the English Language dictionary, and when the world financial market system finally melts down all around you, and leaves you rooting around for the last ear of corn, in an every-man-and-woman-for-themselves cosmic-horror show, well beneath the level of an animal existence, you can blame it on your vocabulary, you don't have so much as the whisper of a clue.

When people sat around and wondered how some hedge fund guy made a billion or two a year in low-tax compensation, and bought up half of the Hedge Fund Art that had managed to escape the last guy's buying spree, to ensure that others knew he had a sensitive side, and as a hedge against the dollar's impending implosion, Jen just had to laugh, people working as oil-rig mechanics and soy-bean farmers and pork-belly feeders, had no idea at all the part they played in wealth creation, and a billion dollars a year was a little out of their income, much less Art Appreciation, bracket. The fact that a single man, running a fund called Renaissance Partners, "renaissance" being a word that you can actually find in your dictionary, made more in a single year than half of the world's population combined, enough to feed every starving child a hundred times over, or treat half the humans with HIV, or equip every hut with malaria nets, and have enough left over for a good long vacation, was not necessarily wrong, but it sure was odd if you thought about it, though Jenny didn't at the moment have real-time time to think about it, there was something wrong with her currency swaps, and she needed to make a tweak to her arbitrage algorithms. And the fact that underneath it all, where food was grown and water pumped and minerals extracted to feed the beast, the Earth was a blue and gleaming jewel, floating through space in a void of aloneness, that was rapidly eating itself alive, in a consumer-friendly ecocidal biophagic feeding-frenzy, and had a century or two to live at best, before becoming a smoldering garbage-barge and toxic-sludge-effluent containment vessel and rusted-out morning-after party-boat charter, hauling coal-slurry goo-ponds and sulfide slag-heaps and heavy-metal e-waste mutagenic cesspools, and wallowing around forever or so through the whole empty godforsaken vacuum-sealed Universe, was only another fact, and the Universe was full of them, and you can't make sound investment decisions without knowing the facts. And wouldn't you know it, right about now, when she needs to be pulling The Poet's file, something is acting up in the behavior of Jenny's Rainbow options, puts and calls on the best or worst of what the future might hold for N underlying assets, what the traders call *colors*, used for example, by sheer coincidence, to place a value on the future of natural resource deposits, and she'll have to shut her trading down, and make a few minor adjustments; Jen doesn't gamble, of course, she's an arbitrage player, but if she wanted to make a killing on the future of the planet, she'd forget about the nanopennies, try some uncovered calls on our resource deposits, like you can pretty much count on us losing a few colors from this overly sunny Rainbow she's currently using, or maybe just get out of visible light altogether, place some near-term bets some-where deep in the infrared, think long on microbes, short on geese, before eventually switching over to the right of ultraviolet, where you could probably bet the farm on the future of human blindness, and short almost anything keeping the green Earth green, knowing full well that the ultimate pot of gold will be hung at the end of a gamma-ray rainbow. The Rainbow in this case is a literary device, a symbol of God's faithfulness, and his promise to never again destroy the Earth, by flood and trauma, as he did to Noah; and the Rain-bow option is our answer to God, a commitment we've made to traumatize the planet, extracting petapennies along the way, until all of our natural resource deposits are long-gone at last, and the Dragon Wells of Hangzhou are utterly drained, and the life-force that drives fresh colors into the blossoms is into-the-void vanished and completely exhausted.

Not that there's anything wrong with this. Derivatives make the market more whatyoucallit efficient. Figure it out for yourself, my friend; serious people are trying to make a living here. So Jenny sets her Rainbows right, and goes back up to the mezzanine level, where Gomez keeps the hedge fund files, from which The Poet's is soon extracted. She sits down in an empty cubicle, removes the papers from the Pendaflex folder, and sticks the green thing with its Poet label into an absent admin's desk. If Gomez should wander by, and ask her what she's working on, she'll tell him she's hoping to join the naked dead, maybe do a little research on the end of the planet, out in the dust on the Lomas mesa. There are partnership docs and business plans and purchase orders for WiMAX products and Articles of Incorporation for IBCs, located offshore in the Channel Islands, and summaries of the flows of funds and a nice clean copy of a dated GEM Listing Document, maybe ten months old, out from under the trading lock-up, and stock charts from the Hong Kong HKEX Exchange, all scrambled together into who knows what, and since you don't understand a word of this, leave it to us, we'll attempt to explain it. Third World Partners, one of Gomez' smaller, sidecar, hedge funds, has made an equity investment in a startup dealing in cell phone antenna-tower power amplifiers, built it up nicely with actual orders placed by companies with fictional business plans, and cashed in legally when the thing went public, on the Hong Kong GEM Growth Enterprise Market Exchange, and the stock got dumped, and money flowed back, into strictly-speaking-legal Third World Partners. The essence of real-world money laundering, for the profits extracted from mood-enhancement, is a three part process for moving the money, step by step, to the top, as you'll recall, of a Toltec Pyramid: Placement of funds in small amounts, from things like coin-operated laundry shops and money exchanges and pizza parlors, into miniscule-looking bank accounts; Layering of funds from small accounts, into larger bundles, in things like International Business Corps, shrouded in secrecy in the Caymans or Seychelles or Isle of Man, legal in a sense but inherently dubious, and apt to arouse Swiss-banking suspicion; and Integration, the Pyramid's final step, into more or less untraceable and astounding amounts, free to travel the planet by electronic wire, on the speed-of-light S.W.I.F.T. banking-for-only-the-legitimate network. In the old days like the '80s, the heydays of the Medellin and Pablo Escobar and bribing the bankers laundry-methods, the laundering process had a lot of waste, and hot-water worries caused things to shrink, by sometimes as much as 50%, to compensate the private bankers for their collars feeling tight. Jenny is looking at a single instance of money being laundered with less-than-zero shrinkage, turning $180 million in lower Layered funds into $250 million of

Integrated, top-of-the-Pyramid, legitimate substance, completely untraceable unless you knew where to look, like maybe into the eyes of some moron called The Poet. What Jenny in essence is staring at, a variation on Integration using the Stock Laundering process, propelling the value of a small cap stock, through naïve-looking stock purchases from Layered accounts, and then reaping the benefits at the next level up, in a tax-haven hedge fund that sells at the top, was now common practice in the drug-profits world; the stereotype of money laundering, some greasy-looking guy, with a briefcase full of currency heavily dusted with Peruvian flake, and a 5X cut of a mannitol osmotic-style baby laxative, walking into a Florida bank, and depositing the crinkled, coked-up mess, for a 30% fee, through a sniffling and twitchy-looking banker with the runs, was long out of date, and lacking in Toltec Pyramid architectural astuteness. And what Gomez has done is the next logical step up: rather than buying pink-sheet stock, the Layered funds bought amplifier product. The Third World investment in Dacha Wireless, a venture-backed startup building next-generation, WiMAX and LTE, power amplifiers, has done remarkably well, going public on the Hong Kong GEM exchange, on the basis of enormous and actual orders, placed by companies building-out imaginary wireless networks, imaginary networks for real places, places like Suriname and Tonga and Paraguay. The wireless network companies themselves, backed by Third World Layered funds from IBCs in the Channel Islands, have not, alas, fared too well; their plans for delivering WiMAX service to native thatched huts in the savannas of Botswana, have turned out to be a bit ambitious, a bit too imaginative, one might say, and the Layered funds have all sad-to-say vanished, in a shitstorm of orders for WiMAX and LTE power amplifiers, only to have the profits mysteriously reappear, when Third World cashed, in incremental blocks, all of its pumped-up Dacha stock. The essence of money laundering at work at its best: make money disappear from suspicious-looking Layered sources, and magically reappear, at the top of the Pyramid, where Third World Partners sits, well above suspicion.

And The Poet himself, a man whose code name arouses suspicion, of his suffering from some sort of delusional disorder, and not being in possession of a complete set of faculties, what's his story, and now can we hear it? No, of course not, we've never even met the man, although we'll readily admit, now that we've seen the books, that he doesn't look to us like he's been living on Planet Earth, much less in the world where people suffer. He looks like he's been living on borrowed time, in some sort of sugarplum fairy tale.

Ray? Yeah, Raymond, listen, it's Jen. I've got the guy's story. Meet me at Sonny's in let's say 30 minutes.

Gene comes in with the weapons and cell phones, fully powered-off, without so much as a pulse for location, and finds Raymond asleep with the phone lying next to him, puts the handset back in its old-fashioned cradle, and lets it rock itself to sleep, there next to Raymond. Gene has a moment of uncertainty himself, about the rightness of his actions, following Ray around without asking too many questions. He sits down in a chair next to a small dormer window, which reminds him of the bedroom of his home back in Kansas, a room he shared for years with his younger brother, Bobby, it's been how long now since he tried to call him, on his third tour of duty in Liberated Iraq. Bobby probably be ashamed of what it is Gene's doing, questioning orders, what the hell good is that, start to questioning orders, particularly with a guy like Gomez involved, everything you touch turns to complete and total shit. Bobby was a ballplayer, baseball, football, they tell you to run through the 3-hole, you take the handoff and run through the goddamn 3-hole, you start making up plays like your own end-run, you be out there alone without any blockers, what's the fucking sense, pulling guard setting up a nice clean trap block, tackle on the other line comes steaming on through as the left guard pulls, gets leveled by the center, you scoot through the hole, following the fullback nice and close, who takes out the linebacker, next thing you know, Bobby's juking some cornerback, outrunning the safety in the green open field, everything designed to be run the way you draw it up, you run your own play, you be out there on your own. Gene gets the feeling, the way things are going, he's back working on the John Deere Combine, redesigning the thresher to be a strawberry picker, you want to pick strawberries, you do it by hand, you start messing with the cylinder and concave on the thresher, you'll never get things back into proper alignment, find yourself out there trying to bring in the harvest, turn a whole amber wheat field into shitpiles of straw. What Gene is thinking, in his ordinary way, is that Gomez' million belongs with Gomez, and that Raymond's gotten things a little misaligned, maybe ought to take the money back while Ray's still sleeping. Course, on the other hand, depends on how you look at the problem, that'd be like making an end-run around Raymond, but Trip isn't thinking straight, all those damn pills and Old Grand-Dad Bonded, worryin' 'bout some guy maybe bein' a dead civilian. Sort of a quandary, a man might say, think that's what you'd call it, state of perplexity as to what to do next, think that's a quandary, maybe need to look around, find himself a dictionary. But boy, come to look it up, find another one of those words with unknown origins, some more phony Latin down there at the root, how can you be in a quandary if it don't have any origins? First Jen's having qualms, now Gene's in a quandary, and Raymond's still asleep, with an X across his torso. Too many damn unknowns is what this is, no wonder everyone's having qualms and quandaries, and one thing for sure, Gomez don't have quandaries. You think Gomez finds them, he'd be having any qualms?

Gene leans himself back onto two legs of the chair, thinking about Grainfield, Kansas, skies, and wheat field simplicity. Wheat waving away under the blue Kansas sky, mowing long straight lines at the wheel of the combine, no fear at all of straw-walker overloads, got to just SLOW DOWN, do things right. Then sit back on a porch chair as the sun's going down, sipping on a beer, enjoying the sunset, a few wispy clouds blazing trails across the sky, then slowly going grey, burning down to ashes. An honest day's work, when's the last time he felt that? Going in to have supper that it feels like you earned, that too much to ask, considering you earned it? Gene fingers the keys to a large black pickup; sets the chair legs on the floor, trued-up and righted; and sits up straight, ready to get things realigned.

# 15

So where are we now? We haven't actually moved. We're 17 floors up above the Ocean Avenue sidewalk, at maybe 7:00 am on a Monday morning, April the 13th, 2009, where I've just finished watching the colorectal crimson of an oncogenic sunrise go into remission, and clear up completely right before my eyes, and turn to the pale blues of a normal morning sunup, which from where I'm sitting, at my *Live-Like-You-Mean-It* Parnian Custom Power Desk, has to be considered an enormous improvement. Now, unfortunately, I have a full day ahead of me, trying to get to the real bottom of this Dacha Wireless accounting mess, though I have to tell you, at this point, after years on this deal, I'm beginning to wonder if it has a *real bottom*, as it seems to have been constructed more along the lines of Crazy Eddie Antar's infamous luggage, that false-bottom set of faux Louis Vuitton he used for smuggling money past Israeli customs, in laying the foundations for his Panama Pump scheme. If you don't have a clue about Eddie Antar, and don't know the meaning of a Panama Pump scheme, don't worry about it, perhaps we'll get to this latter, because neither does the accounting firm that performed the Dacha audits; if you've never heard of Louis Vuitton false-bottom luggage, and the emptiness created by dimensional discrepancies, you should probably stay away from loading up on Dacha Wireless stock, because the underlying company is riddled with *dead space*. Normally, of course, this would be easy enough to check, by measuring the internal and external dimensions, including the thickness of constituent materials, and accounting for the discrepancy as false-bottom space; the odd thing with Dacha, which I can't quite account for, is that *the interior seems larger by far* than the exterior, meaning that I'm looking at some sort of false-bottom dead space that can't be contained within Dacha itself. This, let me tell you, is about the last thing I need; imagine trying to explain to Israeli customs, or in this case the Hong Kong Securities and Futures Commission, how you crammed a load of money into a space that isn't *in there*. Excuse us, sir, is this your suitcase? Well, no, not really, it's a financial contrivance. Ah, we see, that would explain it. It's not every day that we see nearly a billion dollars smuggled right under our noses in perfectly legitimate luggage. Just for our edification, where did you hide the money? Oh, I don't know, all over the world, places like Uganda and Timor-Leste and Paramaribo, Suriname and the Kingdom of Tonga. What you're looking at here is a false-bottom suitcase, with the dead space itself turned inside out. Have you ever heard the term *spherical eversion*? Do you know anything at all about Smale's Paradox? It may be easier to visualize using a Thurston corrugation, although a minimax eversion preserves far more Willmore energy. Would you like me to explain it? Perhaps you have a differential topologist on staff? No, no, that will do, these financial contraptions are completely beyond us. Please carry on, it looks like a lovely morning, and if you don't mind our saying so, sir: very nicely done. So where did all of this dead space go, and how much of my money did it take along with it? The odd thing with Dacha is that I didn't lose a dime; in fact, come to think of it, I made a stone cold killing, and started thinking deep thoughts about buying a new jet, or a 6-bedroom ski house in Aspen or Deer Valley, meaning a lot of the dead space ended up in my pockets, and then slowly made its way deep inside my head. Perhaps you remember my Louis Quinze desk, with its cabriole legs and ormolu hardware, a black lacquer monstrosity with false drawers on the reverse, where the keys actually worked, but the drawers wouldn't open? The desk whose motto was *This Is Not a Desk*, where I stashed my inner being in imaginary pigeonholes? The desk where I sat in a $50 million pit, which I gradually filled in with 100 Proof Smirnoff? The Dacha deal was that desk in reverse; there was nothing at all in the actual drawers, but the imaginary pigeonholes were stuffed with real profits, though I doubt that the Hong Kong Securities and Futures Commission would marvel over the symmetry of these spatial anomalies, or appreciate the irony of my buying a new yacht, and naming it something like *Setting Sail for the Interior.*

So I guess you'd have to say, if you want my opinion, as far as Dacha Wireless goes, I've been living in something of a wake-initiated dream state, maybe $200 million up above the beach down below me, leaving $20 or $30 million as my carried-interest share of a profitable exercise in Oneiric Ontology, where money comes into Being out of nothing whatsoever, and *nothing* has *everything* to do with what *is*, and imaginary pigeonholes overflow with legal tender, and a lot of mental dead space is stuffed with real cash. Interiors that don't fit in their own interiors? Things that are larger than themselves by far? Vast sums produced out of absolutely nothing? And all of this, somehow, is supposed to fit inside a memoir? I might be better off with a Metro Section news-filler, a single column headline, with maybe an inch or two of greeking-print, and *my pieces* phoned-in, via WiMAX cell phone, from all over *everywhere*, from Abuja, Nigeria to Kampala, Uganda to somewhere deep in the Black Sands Desert: Prominent Local Venture Capital Oneironaut Feared Lost in Spherically Everted Suitcase Disaster. At maybe 7:15 on a Monday morning, with two or three days to give my publishers *something*, I probably need *something* that gets back to basics, like who the hell am I and how did I get here, beginning with some sort of fundamental proposition that everyone from Lucretius to King Lear could agree on: Parmenides' statement that *nothing comes from nothing*, which may just explain how all of this *nothingness* got here. My own particular manifestation of Being, however, as a man of *some substance* and a *Lifetime Achievement* plaque and a rainforest-depleting, Live Like You Mean It, What the Hell Does That Mean, *As If* desk, seems to have been rendered completely irrelevant, like how can I be expected to *share* my identity, even with myself, when this Dacha deal has me stuffed full of dead space, and left me as a man who's so thoroughly made of money that he can't be expected to ever fit inside himself, in a *memoir* whose title, to really capture my true nature, would have to include not only *Nothing Comes from Nothing*, which seems to promise some sort of journalistic account of how I came to be here, as a man of humble origins and very little consequence, but Karl Marx's summary of capitalist estrangement, which doesn't, to be honest, seem to promise much of anything, in the way of an identity I could truly call particular: *Everything is Different from Itself.* Of course, maybe I'm making this way too complicated, since Wittgenstein dismisses this whole problem altogether, as if from Parmenides on, the whole ontology of identity is a bewitchment of the intelligence by means of language: *there is no finer example of a useless proposition* than to state that *a thing is identical with itself*; it's as if we were saying that *a thing fits into itself*, or *fits inside its shape* with a kind of magical precision, as though the thing, when we imagine it, had left itself behind, and returned to fill its emptiness with remarkable fidelity, all of which leaves us feeling slightly bewitched, ready to pick up the pen, before the thing itself returns, and produce some sort of *character sketch* out of *Being and Nothingness*, or a good thousand pages or so of Hegelian dialectics, determined to solve this problem we have with the nature of identity, when in fact, axiomatically, we don't have a problem; well, let me tell you, *I do have a problem*, particularly when it comes to Dacha Wireless, where *"this thing is larger by far than itself,"* because believe me I've tried stuffing Dacha back in there, and there's no fucking way the thing fits inside itself. This reminds me of one of those travel-anxiety dreams, where you're trying to get your belongings back inside your suitcase, and the more you cram it full, the smaller the suitcase gets; dreams, come to think of it, are the paradigmatic example of things that are impossible to fit inside themselves, like saying that "a dream is identical with itself" is not only useless, it's flat out not true, and trying to get a dream to fit inside its shape is a pointless exercise in oneiric futility, like trying to cram some *dead space* into your spherically everted luggage. It may well be true, as Wittgenstein tells us, that when we "call it a dream, it does not change anything," but if my suitcase full of Dacha gets any smaller, I'm going to call it *Wittgenstein's Dream*, and hope it changes everything. My *Dream Dictionary*, of course, has an entry under *suitcase*, a lovely note about *me*, and the stuff of which I'm made, saying that I'm a composed and together sort of person, and not at all Prospero's baseless fabric kind of guy, trying to pack the great globe into his tiny shrinking luggage, which really, if you ask me, from where I'm sitting, means that something's gone wrong here, like I'm working with a Dictionary that's *flat-out fucking dreaming*.

So where does that leave us on this *memoir* business? Unfortunately, at the moment, I don't have much to go on, and don't have a clue what I myself am up to, so I've been pondering the nature of Wittgenstein's methods, and have come up with something that may be better than a narrative, in terms of conveying my sense of my own identity, where the closer the look I take at my life, the greater the distance from which it looks back. What I'm thinking of proposing is to write the thing out in cryptic numbered language puzzles, in the manner of Wittgenstein's *Philosophical Investigations*, like maybe instead of an actual memoir, we'd be far better off with a semiotic-detective fiction, some guy in a noirish-style rakish grey hat, whose card reads something like *Philosophical Investigator*, running a kind of skip trace on what became of himself, like *where the hell is he*, what are his *whereabouts*? What we're looking at here is a cryptic sort of murder memoir, a book full of all kinds of false-bottom dead space: a single blank page, an empty bottle of Wite-Out, and the whole sordid tale of my life in a shrink wrap, the fast-paced and volatile *inside story* of a former Venture Capitalist turned Onco-Ontologist, entitled *Sorry This Happened: I Just Couldn't Contain Myself*. I know what you're thinking: don't try to get cute, just finish up your story, we've already forgotten most of it, and the last thing we need is a self-erasing memoir from some guy sniffing correction fluid and memory-cleaning solvent. And, oh, by the way: how did you see the sunrise, and all those colorectal crimsons, when the office you're sitting in faces due west? I have, I suppose, a confession to make: we *have* actually moved, I wouldn't even have seen that tumerous-looking sunrise if I hadn't suddenly panicked and left my desk in the first place; the malignant-grey beginnings of local civil twilight could have easily been avoided if I'd just drawn my blinds, instead of running sprints down the 50-yard hallways to watch the sun come up through the opposite-corner window office, under the mistaken impression that a cold splash of reality would do me some good against these twilight-state anomalies. None of this, to be clear, is actually my fault; there's a built-in logical fallacy in this *inside story* book deal, something my team of lawyers allowed to slip through the cracks, because in order to tell the tale of my twenty years in the business, and maybe set the record straight as to what I've been up to, I've been forced to reanimate my comatose interior, which is not only going to suffer from some hypnopompic visuals, like *colorectal crimsons* and *oncogenic neoplasms*, as it slowly reawakens from 20 years of catatonia, but is also bound to pose some interesting sorts of questions that no one who's been living well should really have to ask themselves, much less have to answer for in a legal deposition, like *who do you think you are*, and *why did you try to kill me*, and *what in God's name is the deal with this desk?* I know you're probably thinking: *that* can't be right, this whole *inner life* thing is a false-bottom construct, some empty sort of dead space that's not even *in there*; what this guy really needs is to get down to business, stop talking to himself in his own *private language*, which as Wittgenstein could have told him is absurd in the first place, and get back to the story of how he became a *man of substance*, and got some sort of plaque for *Lifetime Achievement*. Let me just say, in my own defense, if you wouldn't mind turning off the tape recorder, I never actually said that *the man I once was* spoke a private language when he came to depose me: he took one look around at the life that I'd made, out of an enormous pile of signifiers with dollar signs in front of them, smiled enigmatically at my *Lifetime Achievement* plaque, and said *Not very imaginative; you call this a Life? You should probably consider installing a giant Wite-Out dispenser, and replacing that old suitcase full of half-empty vodka bottles.*

I know what you're thinking: suitcase full of vodka bottles? That explains a lot of things, like what in the name of God has this man been talking about? While I may have something of a Dexedrine hangover, you can trust me when I tell you that I haven't been drinking. To make a long story short, maybe fourteen months ago, after my sixth or eighth or twelfth time through cold-poultry detox, sweating it out alone in my writhing and seething bedroom, I gave up on vodka, and finally got sober. This is not, to be honest, something I'd recommend; it's like swapping out your flat-panel high-def color television for an old black-and-white with tinfoil rabbit ears. The bright twinkling lights of the City of Angels, full of pink and turquoise neon, and emerald-tinged effervescence, turn a dull malignant grey that you have to learn to live with, and all that you thought angelic turns out to be pedestrian. Thankfully, not a word of this will wind up in my memoirs; few things on earth are more tedious to listen to than a sobriety-redemption tale, the story of some guy using himself as a human pincushion, and eventually figuring out that it's not such a good idea. The only thing more boring I can possible think of is listening to myself on the topic of being sober; it's like picking up the telephone and listening to a dial tone, which may sound interesting enough to an acoustically coupled modem, but it's not the sort of thing that I'm personally attuned to. All I have to say on the topic of being sober is thank God for Dexedrine, which is not as good as vodka, perhaps, but it's better than a dial tone.

So one final time: where the hell are we? I'm staring out to sea at the mighty grey Pacific, though at this hour of the morning, in the low-angle light, it looks like it's made out of corrugated roofing, or something you'd produce using computer simulation; the green hills of Malibu, off to my right, stair-stepping down toward the Colony beach, appear to be painted a phony shade of something, just biding their time until brushfire season; the headlands of Catalina, maybe 20 miles away, only now becoming visible through the marine-layer haze, appear ready at any moment to head straight out to sea, and vanish forever like that island in *The Tempest*; and the empty gold sand beaches of Santa Monica Bay, like a 28-lane highway with a six-foot-wide bike-lane, arc south in the direction of the Palos Verdes cliffs, and crash, without braking, into solid rock oblivion. As I turn in my chair, and face due north, it's a normal Monday morning in the Palisades and Brentwood, gardeners running their mowers over the broad rolling lawns, trimming the roses, refreshing the flowerbeds, as though larkspur and cornflower and baby's breath borders just sprang from the ground in the natural order, though I have to admit, post my dexies all-nighter, this Monday-morning normalcy feels slightly estranged, like a paper-thin façade that's not fooling anyone. The vast LA basin may be covered up with grass, and tall imported shade trees, and gardens full of lilac, but directly underneath it, lying in wait, preparing for the moment when the pipedream evaporates, lurks a scrub-brush desert truth, dry as a bone, millions of years in the making, and infinitely patient. So where are we really? We don't have a clue, but give us a thousand years or so, and we'll maybe get back to you, because LA itself is a false-bottom dead space, and Time's ancient Customs officials have seen it all before, and know what we're concealing, and exactly what we're up to.

With maybe 60 minutes before my Blanco staff arrives, I have just time enough to tell one final tale, before I flee from the building, or leap to my death, in order to avoid the nuisance of running into my employees, who haven't seen my face in maybe three or four months, and think of me now as a disembodied voice, calling in occasionally to check on my Money Pile, now grown so tall you can't see to the top of it, much less actually scale it to leap to your death. The question at this point is what tale to tell: HyperActive Software, a co-investment with Kleiner Perkins in infrastructure software, where I cashed out at right around a 100X return, on $4.5 million invested over the life of the company, a move that in retrospect I deeply regret, since if I'd held to its $9 billion peak in the market, I would, at a minimum, have made four times that; or maybe Rendition, a semiconductor company, which made desktop versions of the SGI Reality Engine, a market that Nvidia eventually won, such that every living human with a personal computer now has a Reality Engine producing 3-D illusions; or maybe given the recent collapse of the housing bubble, I should tell you the story of how I saw this coming, and built a real monster in the mortgage market, a leader, to be specific, in the subprime sector, masters of the art of the no-doc liar loan, and the 125% interest-only ARM, and the pay-whatever-you-feel-like, negative amortization, just-give-us-back-the-house-when-the-idiocy-is-over deal, perfectly suited for the market of its time, a market I bailed out of, in 2004, when the market was only beginning to go truly moronic; or how about my bet on the New Economy, a genetically engineered new species of plant life, designed to permit a plant, no matter how ill-conceived, to Grow to the Sky, with unlimited possibility; or then there's my investment in the...oh, Christ, never mind, who the hell cares how I made all this money, any twelve-year-old analyst with a half-decent track-record, trading Beanie Babies and Barbie Dolls before their markets imploded, could have duplicated my success, and Xeroxed my identity.

I have a better idea: let's call up Sandra. I know what you're thinking: that was 40-some years ago, back when you were a bill-collector, getting dead-beats to send you money instead of feeding their children; how in God's name are you going to find her phone number? To be perfectly honest, there's something I haven't told you, which is that I, to put it modestly, have an amazing memory for telephone numbers. I remember, among other things, the direct-dial numbers, including country codes and area codes, of nearly every last work space and home I ever occupied: my house outside Sintra, in the Colares vineyards of Portugal, where I worked outdoors at a rough wooden picnic table, writing *I don't think I'll work today*, and translating Pessoa; my apartment in the Marais, back when Paris still felt like Paris, a tiny fourth-floor walk-up, too small to be called a garret; my New York studio, on West 68th, where my neighbor the white shutter finally turned into a plant, and the springtime trees were lit up from within, basking alone *in their own quiet lime-light*; the corner on West End Avenue where I lived with my first wife, the mother of my eldest daughter, now a perfectly elegant beauty, who was born at Mount Sinai, in the sweet June of May, on the morning of her own beginnings, *The Morning of a Lifetime*; the Ivarene house, where my poetry finally died, and my second wife survived me, after my drinking got the best of us; the second-chance Cape Cod, off Carmelina in Brentwood, where a blue-eyed second daughter arrived, just like that, as pure radiant proof that Nature still loves us, and has, in spite of everything, managed to forgive us; the houses in Amherst and Hadley and Northampton, and the long summer mornings, at work at the pen-scarred dark-oak desk, where Alma Venus granted peace to *write* and *read* and *think*, and sheer mental windfalls appeared from out of nowhere; the windmill-house in Everberg, Belgium, a village somewhere in maybe it was Flanders, where I went to work each day as a bank-ruptcy alchemist, and lived like a character in a Magical Realist fiction; my homes in D.C., and Baltimore, and Virginia, and the numbers of all the psycho wards my mother laughingly outsmarted; the townhouse on Logan Circle, where my first poems came out to play, because the morning was out there, so really, why wouldn't they, and since the children were wearing *just those very ribbons*, I couldn't help smiling those very ribbons into their hair; the place in Ledroit Park, near Howard University, with its tree-lined red-brick row-house sidewalks, and sweltering-lemonade front-porch stoops, where *dogs bark because the world is singing, and dogs love to sing, but they don't know the words*; the office phones of CSC and Informatics and EDS; the office phones at VSA and SAT and CAP; the number of the Ponderosa and the stickup 7-11 and the mailroom at Fannie Mae and the warehouse on Langford; the house on the double cul-de-sac, Neilwood Drive, where I drove my brakeless car around, and hid from my booze-sick parents; and while this is only a small sample of the structures that I've inhabited, and the places where my dreams lived on until I failed them, every last one of them I hold inside my heart, an act for which, if I were them, I would simply never forgive me.

— — —, — —, —. — —, —. —.

Hello? Excuse me, to whom am I speaking?

I don't know, douchebag. Who the hell are you?

I'm trying to reach a woman named Sandra something. Does she still live at this address?

What address is this?

I'm not really sure. Wherever it is you live.

So you want my address, is what we're really talking about. You one of the collectors from the credit card companies?

Jesus, no, I gave that up years ago.

Because I've told you guys already, that well is dry, blood from a turnip, you hear what I'm saying, you can have the house and furniture if you think you can find them, I'm nowhere near there, you hearing me at all?

Yeah, sure, I hear you loud and clear, but I'm not trying to reach you, I'm trying to reach Sandra. She had a little kid that needed to eat better. I was hoping to hear how the kid made out.

How long ago was this?

Well, let's see now, maybe forty-some years.

You have to be shitting me. Who the hell is this? You sound like a bill collector, what the fuck kind of lame-ass story you trying to sell me, you guys are like roaches, can't stand the light, maybe you can explain to me how my 12% accounts showed up in my mailbox at like 28%.

I guess they must consider you to be a bad credit risk.

So that's why I've got like twelve fucking credit cards, all maxed out, with penalties accumulating, and an equity line where there isn't any equity, and a mortgage in foreclosure with my house underwater, all because I'm such a bad fucking risk. Makes sense to me. Maybe you guys should have thought of that in the first place. How 'bout I send you like $20 now, and the rest over the next seven or eight thousand years?

You out of work?

Fuck no, I've told you guys before, I make the same $40,000 I did twelve years ago, I thought you were the ones supposed to do the math.

So there's no one named Sandra at this address?

I don't know, numbnuts, what address is this? It's the exact same address I wouldn't give you in the first place.

I guess we're kind of going in circles here.

Yeah, like turkey-buzzards circling over what's left of my goddamn corpse, have a real nice day now, wherever the hell you are, hope you're calling from a prison cell in Morgantown or Singapore.

Sorry to have bothered you.

Sorry, my ass.

No seriously, I'm sorry, I'm really and truly sorry.

You got that right, you sure as shit are.

I suppose I was dreaming, trying to call up Sandra; I might have been better off just listening to a dial tone. I'll tell you one thing: I could really use a drink, the morning's turning grey again, a subtle shade of malignant.

So let me get your opinion on something. Does the statement that *a man is identical with himself* strike you as a possibly terrifying proposition?

# 16

abriella and I were eating homemade gorditas, from an odd little shop tucked into an alley off the Calle Luis, down which we'd walked after the Theta encounter, past the One Hour Photo store and centuries-old trueno hedge and the Teatro Juárez, and into the courtyard of the Don Quixote museum, the Museo de Iconografía. The courtyard was in the interior of a beautiful custard-yellow two-story house, with gleaming Tuscan columns and stone-quarried arches and a wood-railed mezzanine that overlooked the sculpture garden. There was a statue in the courtyard, with an inscription written by Eulalio Ferrer, a man who was himself quite a colorful character, not only the collector of much of the Quixote memorabilia on display in various rooms of the museum's second floor, postage stamps and coins and wall clocks and chess sets, but one of the thousands of guests at Generalissimo Franco's far-from-colorful internment camps, in a preview of the blank-shades of Fascist things to come, things like Auschwitz-Birkenau and Chelmno and Treblinka; the inscription advised that we "Read the Quixote, read it at the concentration camp, as a minute hand of human hours, as a place to discover ideals that justify the craziness of genius to get back control of reason," and while this advice seemed peculiarly applicable to me, after my molar-demolishing luncheon with Raúl Ramírez, and his masterful application of the ideals of Nazi dentistry, I was so overwhelmed by the museum itself that I set the inscription aside for the moment, while I tried to absorb both my tour of the place, and a few more inches of my enormous gordita. The surrounding rooms were full of hundreds of paintings, and ceramics and prints, and sculptures of the Don, in various states of haunted lunacy, and flights of the tireless but aging imagination: an old man upright on a broken-down horse; or sitting by a fire with an immense pile of books; or asleep in a bright red sleeping cap, in the midst of a splendid dream of everlasting youth, and gleaming but imaginary poetic armaments; or most haunting of all, the portrayal of Quixote in a lunatic asylum, his pale blue eyes staring off into space, his right hand slowly wearing a hole in the wall, and his left on a splendidly bound brown leather book; nearly 800 images of the artist's search for ideals in an age of unfettered totalitarian power. When I looked at that hand wearing a hole in the wall, I couldn't help picturing Antonio Gramsci, slowly wasting away in one of Mussolini's prisons, writing out the *Prison Notebooks* on toilet paper, three thousand pages' worth of detailed drawings of the Capitalist mental prisons we've built to confine ourselves, thinking "pessimism of the intellect, optimism of the will," with his own right hand clawing absently at the wall, leaving only a patch of darkness from the ink on his fingers, and dreaming of a plate of pasta, maybe, or a gordita he could hold if he put down his pen. "Optimism of the Will": this might have been the title of one of the Quixote paintings, he's 75 or 80 years old at least, he's deeply wrinkled and in need of a haircut, with blood seeping through the bandages on his head, and even his valiant horse collapsing beneath him. The Mental Patient, The Dreamer, The Reader of Too Many Books, or maybe my favorite, a painting called The Menace, Quixote on horseback with his sword held aloft, ready to strike out at anything, real or imaginary, while Sancho scrambles around clearing children out of the way, the last thing we need is real blood right now, particularly in the dust of an imaginary village, just imagine how you yourself would feel, your child struck down by a lunatic in a novel, a picaresque fantasy, of all the crazy things, with the nearest available doctor, some 400-year-old charlatan from Tirteafuera, still many miles away, in a chapter you won't get to without hours and hours of reading. Craziness, indeed; the Don looked like a man who needed to be sedated, and Sancho was probably ready for his anti-anxiety medication; the inscription was still telling me to "Read the Quixote, read it at the concentration camp, as a minute hand of human hours, as a place to discover ideals that justify the craziness of genius to take back control of reason," but I couldn't quite picture my gravedigger friends, having warned me in advance how much dirt they had to shovel, hanging around graveside while I determined the time of death, using the slow-moving minute hand of a 1,000-page timepiece, and it wasn't clear that genius would help much with FedEx, if they suddenly switched over to Counter-clockwise Standard Time, or that craziness would prove to be the trait I most needed if I wore through the patience of my grim-faced companions, and found myself hanging from a Windsor-knotted necktie; for all I knew, I was eating my last sandwich, right in the middle of a war against time, and not even some absolute lunatic of a character, admittedly dead but essentially immortal, appeared to be willing to fight on my side. We finished our gorditas, and a couple of cold bottles of purified water, and abandoning all pre-tence regarding craziness regaining control of reason, set off intent on a whole different course, through a world where books were the sort of things you could audit.

Behind the Museo de Iconografía de Don Quijote, the Quix-ote museum, was a labyrinth of streets that climbed El Pípila's hill, El Pípila of burn-down-the-Granaryful-of-Spaniards fame, though since his real name was Juan José de los Reyes Martínez Amaro, and Pípila, meaning "turkey," with its feminine-sounding ending, could only be the word for the female of the species, it wasn't alto-gether clear that Juan's fame had proved ennobling, though it had earned him a monumental seventy-foot statue, a statue the color of a turkey's pink head, at the top of a tall hill that we decided to climb. We turned off Calle Luis on to one of the narrow callejuelas, a word that means side street or lane or alley, though in this case it might as well have meant stairway, a narrow cobbled staircase with thousands of steps. The callejuela we had chosen was named Calvario, a word, as I might have guessed, that has something to do with Calvary, and the Stations of the Cross, and bearing a burden that is unduly heavy, perhaps in this case the broad flat stone that Pípila had elected to carry on his heavily muscled back, to the top of the fortress-like Granary hill, to ward off the lead balls of Span-ish musketry. Calvario was lined on both steep sides with two-story townhomes, ornamented with flower boxes and green and red bunting, and painted in edible colors, mango and honeydew and lemon and peach, like the rest of the city; in Guanajuato, it was clear, the eye would never go hungry. Near the halfway point of our cobblestone climb, Gabriella came to an awkward halt, as if pretending to catch her breath, and then turned around twice, and backward facing, started de-ascending, claiming that she'd just remembered something, and needed to return to her home at once, encouraging me to continue upward, to the top of the hill, and a view of the city, while she went back in search of something, for whatever it was she'd somehow forgotten, though knowing Gabriella, if it was in fact something that she had suddenly recalled, it could only have been one of her last five steps. I stood for a moment and watched her descending, retracing her actions, step by step, the way a man might do when he's lost his keys, and has no other way of tracking them down than a step-by-step backward retracing. Perhaps she had in fact forgotten her keys; more likely, knowing Gabriella, she'd suddenly remembered the last few moments, when she'd come to the realization that she was tired of climbing, and even more tired of teaching me Spanish. I'd have to continue upward without her now, without her guidance through the maze-like alleys, and without the locution "this word means X or Y in English." If Pípila were in fact the female of the species, and El was a masculine article in Spanish, I'd have to puzzle this out for myself; and if, as I climbed the stair-stepped hill, it became apparent that the statue was a different sort of pink, the pink of a turkey's snood perhaps, snood being an English-language word, more or less, for the flesh on the beak of the male of the species, I'd have to deal with these linguistic discrepancies myself, in relation to how a man, particularly a hardworking miner like Juan José de los Reyes, ended up enshrined as a transgendered turkey.

I came to a simple fork in the staircase steps, with the way to the left named Callejón Desvío, and the way to the right labeled Callejuela Subita, and paused for a moment of linguistic distress, caused by my knowing more French than Spanish, and by my hidden talent, soon to become apparent, for getting thoroughly lost in almost any language. "Mort subite," from the French I remembered, meant "sudden death," which did not make Subita Lane sound particularly inviting. Callejón Desvío felt intuitively right, since Callejón, as I recalled, was the Spanish word for "backstreet," and "vío" was close to "via," from the Latin for "way," which could only mean that Callejón Desvío, in summary, was a kind of alleyway or byway or passage from here to there, and would no doubt lead me to my hilltop destination. Only later, when I was hopelessly lost, would it occur to me that a Callejón could suddenly terminate, and turn a lovely little byway, a cobblestone staircase with walls on both sides, into a "dead end" or "blind alley" or possibly a "cul-de-sac," an odd little hyphenate, meaning "bottom of the sack," that seems both utterly meaningless, even ominous, in French, and perfectly transparent, even comforting, in English; and that Desvío, which had seemed to be instinctively correct, must signify something resembling a "detour." Callejón Desvío: Dead-End Detour or Bypass to Nowhere or Circuitous and Roundabout Way Not to Get There; one has to wonder if some aging city planner had been reading too much Cervantes when he laid out such a street. Only later yet, when I was back in my room, equipped with both a map and a Spanish-English dictionary, would it occur to me that my journey to Nowhere In Particular couldn't all be blamed on that overworked planner; while his layout was sheer lunacy, a quixotic maze of stairways and dead ends and blind alleys that had no apparent intention of leading me anywhere, the Callejón Desvío street-naming problem might well have happened elsewhere, somewhere deeper down in the bowels of the bureaucracy, where some neophyte street-namer, perhaps a native-English speaker with one day on the job, must have been confronted with so overwhelming and insurmountable a challenge that he likely didn't realize that he was about to get me lost. He must have spent hours, perhaps deep into the night, staring at that lunatic's cobbled-together stair-maze, trying to come up with something, anything at all, that would properly describe the mess I was headed into if I somehow turned left at this fork in the road, before finally deciding that the best he could do was to label the left fork Callejón Desvío, knowing deep down that he should never have consented to putting a name on a staircase that required the word "Desvío," when this seemingly simple and straightforward appellation means, quite literally, Deviation. He must have then gone on to compound the whole problem by affixing that Callejón, which by itself means nothing

more ominous than "alley," and has nothing to do with all those
blind dead-ends I eventually ended up getting utterly lost in, when
what he really meant to signify might best be expressed using Callejón Sin Salida: you, my friend, are in an alley without an exit, and
wherever you think you're going, you're headed toward an impasse.
That it might not be useful to have a Deviation to an Impasse, a
Stray-way to a Standstill, a Digressive Divagation Toward the Bottom of a Sack, and that Callejón Sin Salida Desvío, Detour through
an Alley with NO WAY OUT, would never fit on a six-inch street-
plaque, may just be one of those things that seem to happen in the
course of naming things, but to say that I got lost through some
failure on my part is a clear-cut case of blaming the victim. I will,
however, admit to one mistake, a simple typographical error that
I perhaps should have corrected. Had Gabriella stayed, we would
have simply turned right, since the actual street sign does not read
Subita, it reads Callejuela Subida, and Subida, meaning "climb,"
was what I was intending, and has nothing to do with death, either
sudden or lingering, while the path that I took, up the way to the
left, was a staircase detour up a long blind-alley, a dead end, or cul-
de-sac, for those who speak French, or even for those who, sadly,
have been confined to Silence, at the bottom of an empty sack in
their circuitous and roundabout word-proofed heads, since even a
man suddenly struck down by aphasia knows a dead-end blind-alley
when he finds himself in one.

Up the stairs to the left I continued at last, momentarily proud
of my linguistic decoding, a pride that slowly declined as I continued my climb, and my solution to the problem grew more and
more confounding. I had passed from an area of lovely, well-kept
homes, in edible colors and welcoming bunting, into a region of
more or less crumbling wrecks, where every third or fourth house
was a pile of rubble, though rather than simply admitting to my
mistake, and retracing my steps to the source of my confusion, I
pressed on ahead as a man will often do, particularly an American,
who when confronting an inevitable linguistic faux-pas, holds to
the belief that the world should speak English. This area I was in
was neither edible nor welcoming, it was turning a little grim and
abandoned feeling, with busted-out windows and battered-in doors,
most of them hanging uninvitingly open, and the piles of rubble

had no color at all, they were cinderblock signifiers of the English word "ruins." I pressed on ahead, intent on something, though it was no longer apparent just what I was intent on, I was climbing the stairs as if to make a point, the way a man will keeping talking when he's forgotten what he's saying, and believes his own words will somehow remind him of his topic, and bring him around at last to the point that he's been driving at, but we all know how well that tends to work out, as his wife bends near him, whispering "Darling, you're babbling." As the silence sets in, and no one says a word, to the man's vague and increasing and now utter embarrassment, even his own interior monologue begins to strike him as estranged, starting with "now wait, I had a point here somewhere," and moving on to certain questions regarding the nature of himself, we may all be prone to doubts when it comes to our identity, and language being the stuff out of which we are mostly made, his verbiage starts to crumble and fall to ruins all around him, "Am I the sort of man who tends to ramble on toward nothing, boring his friends to tears, isn't that an odd expression, no one in fact is ever bored to real tears, boredom is not a feeling that induces much emotion, I'm virtually certain that I've never seen a man who has broken down crying as an expression of boredom, and here I go again, babbling even to myself, in search of some point that would make me feel coherent, something about tears having nothing to do with boredom, I almost feel like crying myself, I'm feeling a little lost and hopeless and alone, or maybe the phrase I'm searching for is excruciatingly boring." I pressed on again, talking nonsense to myself, getting more and more lost as I zigzagged through the maze of incoherent stairways, until even the cobblestone walks gave out, and became a dirt path, and I too felt like crying. Given the simple task of climbing a standard hill, how could I even conceive of getting lost on a hillside, all that is required is to keep going up, you'll arrive at the top, it's perfectly straightforward, and yet here I was now in a whole different space, where the immutable semiotics of topography had failed me, as though I'd somehow ended up in an M. C. Escher drawing, something along the lines of his *Relativity* staircase. We tend to think of words like "down" and "up" as being permanently affixed to the paths that they signify; you could no more misconstrue walking counter to the force of gravity than you could "sudden death," in almost any language. It began to dawn on me, however, as I continued on the path, noticing here and there what looked like animal droppings, a pack mule or a donkey that had made the same trek, speaking mule to itself to keep from dying of boredom...oh, now wait, where on earth was I, ah yes, right here, at the beginnings of a dawning, it dawned on me now that the "mort subite" I'd been thinking of at the time of my initial Subita Lane-decoding was actually the name of a brand of Belgian beer, a geuze in fact, by which I mean a lambic, though Mort Subite, flavored as it is with sour cherries, is not in fact quite literally a lambic, it is in reality a thing called a kriek, which has something to do with its fruit fermentation, and nothing at all to do with sudden death, unless you drink too many of the weird-tasting things, in the course of a long dull babbling evening, and wind up blind drunk and talking to yourself, lost and alone up a dead-end alley.

And here I was at last, at the end of the path, in a cul-de-sac of sorts, up a linguistic blind alley, and what I found in fact was a large vacant lot, surrounded by wire fencing and a rosebush hedge, a perimeter whose interior contained within it an odd assortment of junk, mostly kitchen appliances and household items: a dinette set with four matching chairs; a battalion of old stoves and cast-off refrigerators; love seats, couches, and vinyl-covered easy chairs; blenders and skillets and toilet tank fixtures; two porcelain tubs with eight claw feet; and a moldering La-Z-Boy Dreamline Recliner. Music blared from an unseen source; there were dogs fast asleep on the love seats and couches; and chickens pecked around in the cinderblock dirt, White Rocks, Shaver Reds, Chanteclers, Cubalayas, I might not know my "up" from my "down," or sudden death from Belgian beer with sour wild cherries, but I apparently knew my chickens, if I do say so myself, though just how or why was completely beyond me. The music that was playing was an album by The Clash, not the most obvious choice in a place like Guanajuato, and the source was a sort of a lean-to thing, a primitive-looking hut, a bricolage of boards and piled rock and tin roofing, out of which a strange man soon elaborately appeared, with wild hair and beard, a cigar between his teeth, and a camouflage-green uniform that seemed to be slowly rotting, to the point that it had turned a shade of jungle-rot black. Craziness controlling reason, indeed; indeed, where on earth was I and how did I get here? Some circuitous inner narrative had brought me to this, and here I was now, at a semantic dead-end. I had gone off on a tangent about fruit-flavored beers, so what did I expect? Not this, exactly. I could have avoided this whole stupid thing, of course, this whole blind-alley hill-climb toward Where On Earth Am I, had I simply turned around and gone back the other way, slowly talking myself backwards toward my misguided beginnings. Language, unfortunately, much like time, gives every appearance of being a one-way street, as though you can't unsay things, once they've been said, even if you didn't have a clue what you were driving at, though I remembered a story about Harold Bloom, the literary critic, as a graduate student at Yale University, reciting Hart Crane's poem *The Bridge*, a long, convoluted, occasionally incomprehensible, magical maze of language, virtually impossible to memorize, word for word, precisely backwards, after drinking a few too many beers one night, or maybe it was krieks, or the cumulative effects of inverted iambics; whatever it was, I had an image of Harold Bloom, the literary critic, and my friend Gabriella, the angel in a fable, sitting by the fire on a cold winter evening, telling old Russian folk tales to each other, all backwards. I also had a far more credible-looking image, an image of myself, in considerable but gradually diminishing discomfort, sitting in a chair, a recliner I'd imagine, at the dentist's office, reciting an endless poem to distract me from the pain, precisely in reverse, while the dentist continued working, doing what he had to in a case such as this, giving my Ramírez-damaged teeth a complete undrilling.

I looked around to get my bearings, and try to shut myself up, and saw Pípila in the distance on a whole different hill, his snood-pink statue striking a Heroic Turkey pose, with a torch held aloft, ready to smoke out the Spaniards. The wild-haired man weaved through the household junk, and opened a gate in the rosebush hedging, and waved me over to come and have a talk, though having talked myself into this dead end in the first place, I hesitated for a moment, not knowing what I was in for, and considered the syntactical difficulties of trying to talk my way back out. There was a huge German Shepherd on the roof of the improvised hut, sitting at attention with his ears pricked up, studying my movements

as though ready to attack, causing me to wonder if I could communicate in Stillness, or knew the words in Dog for "trust me, I'm
harmless." The dog stayed put as I inched my way forward, barked
once or twice, either a greeting or a warning, and was silenced by a
wave of the hermit's hand. The man himself looked like a charcoal
drawing, his face smeared with grime and his hair like a bird's nest,
complete with pieces of twig and rose petals and kite twine, everything black and white except his pale blue eyes; it wouldn't have
surprised me if a bird had appeared, and landed on his head in a
flurry of feathers, even a bird flying backwards, returning to its nest.
The look in his eyes was both vague and piercing; he seemed to
be a man of indeterminate age, maybe thirty or sixty or both at the
same time; and as to his nationality, I didn't have a clue, he looked
like a man who might have eaten his own passport; he was painfully
thin, nearly two-dimensional, a stick-figure drawing that the artist
had abandoned, and tried to erase, line by line, by smearing it away
with a charcoal-dusted thumb. And then he greeted me at the gate
with a nod of his head, and started speaking English in a strange
sort of cadence, not so much the cadence of English as a Second
Language, but more in the rhythm and manner of a man for whom
language itself was not a native tongue.

"Are you lost?"
"I'm not really lost. I meant to be somewhere else, but I wouldn't
say I'm lost."
"So you know where you are."
"Well, no, not really. I have no idea where I am."
"But you wouldn't say you're lost. That's interesting, I find
that interesting, the fact that you wouldn't say that, as far as your
surroundings. When you say the word *lost* and picture your surroundings, this isn't what you picture, what you picture, *what you
picture?*"

Then silence. It was my turn.

"Well, now that you mention it, this place is pretty strange."
"I live here. My surroundings are all here. I have the same surroundings in other places, but not all of them are here. Maybe this

place is a duplicate of something. I have other places where the time work is and where the fields are. Places where growing is and where work is, and the corn is yellow, and sometimes I think they're the same surroundings in other places, like I'm living in a replica. Reduplicative paramnesia it's called. Where are your surroundings?"

"You mean where am I from? To tell you the truth I'm not really sure where I'm from, I'm living here, but I think I'm from somewhere else."

"Where?"

"I'm not sure. It's hard to explain. I woke up, I guess it was yesterday, here in Guanajuato, and I didn't know who I was."

"Like when you've been replaced by an imposter, someone who looks just like you, but you know it isn't you. Sometimes when you look in a mirror, it looks just like you, but you know it isn't you, it's your double, an imposter. Boy, that's murder, that's really something. I've had that, it's called Capgras syndrome, but it's better now, I went out on a beach, I think it was in California, and put bleach in my hair, my hair, *my*...You have to stay away from mirrors. Mirrors are murder."

"Are you all right out here? Do you have enough food and water? If you'll pardon my saying, you look a little thin."

"Well, sometimes when people ask me that, I just tell them it's better now, I went out on a beach and put bleach in my hair. My appearance is thin, but at least I don't have Capgras syndrome like you do."

"Capgras syndrome? I don't know what that is. From the way you describe it, I don't really think I have Capgras syndrome. I woke up yesterday morning, looked in the mirror, and had no idea who I was. But I don't really feel like I've been replaced by someone, I think it's more of a memory problem. I know that it's me, not some imposter, living in Guanajuato, but I have no idea at all who I am or how I got here."

"Like you've just appeared from out of the blue all of a sudden, that's really something, in the book that's called an autochthonous delusion. Wahneinfall, the book calls it, where you think you come from out of the blue. Sometimes that happens to me when the sky is a certain color. I look up at the sky, and I think that's where I come

from, out of the blue, out of the blue, *out of the blue*. In my opinion, don't stare at the sky too long, it makes you feel like an alien,
like you've just appeared all of a sudden from another solar system,
somewhere like Vietnam. Maybe you come from Vietnam, that's
murder. My mother and father didn't come from Vietnam, that's
my problem, I don't think they came from out of the blue, we lived
in a surrounding where the corn is yellow and the trees are green
and the time work is, and I could walk down a path from the little
pink house to the swimming hole swing where the trees turn colors,
but sometimes I think they were a bunch of imposters. If you live in
a pink house with a bunch of imposters, you have to put the scissors
in a small wooden drawer. Would you like some tea?"

"I really should try to get back, but all right, I guess some tea
would be nice. Do you think you could tell me how to get back
to the two streets where I got lost? I came to a fork in the road, at
Callejón Desvío and Callejuela Subita, and I thought Subita might
mean sudden death, so I went the other way."

"That's called dereistic thinking, where you go down a certain
path for illogical reasons. That's not logical, that's my problem. I
know all about these things, I know all the words so things don't
just happen when you're not being logical. Do you sometimes think
your arm is a bird? That's really something, the word for that would
be paraschemazia. That's logical. I have a book in my house, it has
all the words people use for when you're not being logical, so you
don't just go down the wrong path for some reason, maybe the book
would help you, because my mother used to sit around the house
doing nothing but drinking, she'd just sit there and stew, making
stewing noises, chugging her drinks, just getting stewed. She threw
my dad out on his ass. I'll never forget that, the way she did that. So
that's why she was a hostess, so she could help people when it was
time to eat, maybe she could help you, but she was never a book.
Books don't make a lot of noises chugging drinks and stewing. She
used to call him you miserable son of a bitch, why don't you get a
job, making a lot of noises. I'm not trying to make noises, I'm trying
to make sense. If you can't make sense out of nonsense, well, have
fun. In my opinion, I have a book in my house and we'll have tea.
Do you sometimes think your arm is a bird? I can show you the
word so you don't go down the wrong path all of a sudden, or fly off

into space because your arm is a bird. Sudden death, that's murder. I was never a hostess. It's time for tea."

"Are you sure you're all right? I don't want you to take this the wrong way, but I'm having a little trouble following what you're saying, and I have to ask you. Have you ever hurt anyone?"

"Well, it's an even day. I'm fine on even days. On odd days, that's a different story, odd days are murder, because sometimes when people ask me that, I have to think about whether I'll answer because some people think I was born on an odd day and I come from Vietnam even though I don't really think that because my mom was there and the corn was yellow and I think my dad helped out but it's as good a day as any in my opinion, so yes, it's an even day. We can have tea."

I was only able to process about half of this, and I'm not at all sure which half I had processed, but the man seemed harmless enough, meaning that he didn't seem to be physically threatening, he seemed to be suffering from some sort of mental illness, but he didn't seem to pose a physical threat. I had an odd cognitive moment where I realized that I myself possessed an enormous catalog of psychiatric terminology, words that he'd used like paramnesia and paraschemazia and autochthonous delusions, and while I'd never heard of Capgras syndrome, my catalog included things like akataphasia and apophanous perception and asyndesis, along with circumstantiality, which was the term for his last few circumlocutious speeches, as well as perseveration, ataxic dysarthria, clang associations, logoclonia, oneirophrenia, pareidolia, entgleisen and derailment, otherwise known as "knight's move thinking," from the up and over moves of the eponymous chessman, Fregoli's syndrome, alexithymia, schizophasia, sometimes called "word salad," for reasons you could imagine, semantic paraphasia, palilalia, the term for the phrase repetitions of his "what you picture" and "out of the blue" reiterations, tangentiality, Wernicke's aphasia, blocking, würgstimme, meaning the oddly muffled plainstyle voice of a man saying something like "It's not a good omen when goldfish commit suicide," and beyond this a morass of lexical tangentiality and rhetorical schizophasia and logocentric derailment that pointed to psychiatry itself perhaps suffering from some sort of mental disorder, a

case of word salad and akataphasia and logorrhea and anwesenheit
and knight's move thinking, up one over two up two over one, that
was deeply disorienting and made it hard for me to think. I had to
wonder from all of this verbiage whether I myself or someone close
to me, not in the technical sense of Doppelganger syndrome, of
my being followed by my own double, but an actual human being I might have known once and loved, had suffered from mental
illness, and had forced me to learn all of this menacing technical
jargon. Compared to the disordered thinking of psychiatry itself,
whose language struck me as almost comically self-involved, the
man with the wild beard and hair like a bird's nest seemed relatively sane and more or less harmless. It was an even day after all,
the blue of the springtime sky seemed to have appeared from out
nowhere, like a bolt of azure cloth from an imaginary loom, and
who was I to judge the sanity of someone else's thinking, I who had
talked myself up here in the first place, a clear case of akataphasia,
the loss of one's train of thought in the middle of a discourse, and
possibly subsequent derailment, and asyndesis at a minimum. No
one, that's who. I went with him for a cup of tea, cup of tea, *cup of
tea*, and tried to make sure that the NO TRESPASSING sign on
the rosebush hedge didn't lead me off into some sort of apophanous perception, that feeling you have when it's an even day on the
calendar, and you ought to feel safe, but you feel like you're being
watched. It's not a good omen when goldfish commit suicide. This
is not mental illness; it's the God's honest truth.

We went back through his yard to the bricolage hut, where he
turned off the music, lit a Coleman stove, and put on a tea kettle.
The interior of the hut was a facsimile of normalcy, with a mattress on the floor, a weather-beaten coffee table, two Queen Anne
chairs, a desk piled with books and the implements of writing, and
walls papered with posters from old black-and-white films, *Sunset
Boulevard*, *Touch of Evil*, *Sullivan's Travel's*, *Portrait of Jennie*, and
Fritz Lang's *Metropolis*, and posters covered in posters I could barely make out, things like *The Haunting*, and Bergman's *The Seventh
Seal*. There were half-burned candles scattered around the room;
a large vat of what smelled like home-brewed beer that hadn't yet
been bottled; a yellow bucket of water that he had used to fill the tea
kettle; and what appeared to be the barrel of a matte-black shotgun,

three-quarters buried under dirty clothes, useful no doubt against autochthonous aliens, and odd-day-violations of the NO TRES-PASSING code. From the evidence at hand, it was apparent that the bird's-nest man had built himself a home, no matter how out of plumb and misaligned with the vertical. The book he'd been referring to, the *American Psychiatric Glossary*, might have been lying on the packed-earth floor, but it hadn't been ignored, in fact it showed ample evidence of being the subject of regular consultation, having been page-marked in dozens of places with torn-off strips of poster paper. Beside it was a copy of the Third Edition of the *Book of Lists*, perhaps a method he'd devised for keeping his information aligned, things like famous people who had died during sex, or the world's greatest libel suits, or people whose actual speeches had been mangled by Ronald Reagan. On the desk was a copy of John Bickerdyke's 1889 classic, *The Curiosities of Ale and Beer*, which might explain the stout that was fermenting in the brewing crock, and from which one could infer some knowledge of the difference between a lambic and a kriek, fermented with wild cherries. One might infer, by its absence, that he had little or no interest in Bloom's inverted reading of Hart Crane's poem *The Bridge*. I was unable to infer anything at all from the presence of the movie posters; perhaps their shades of grey were soothing by comparison, after too many hours spent staring at the *out of the blue* Guanajuato sky. Once the water had come to a boil, he poured it into a teapot, and we sat in the pair of ancient wingback chairs, like an old English couple having afternoon tea with scones.

"So you feel like you come from somewhere else, like you're an alien, like you appeared here out of the blue, and don't know where you come from. What do the doctors say? Sometimes when they say things, that's murder, and I have to ask myself who hammered this deep hatred in, hatred in, *hatred in*, into my heart. What kind of meds do they make you take? Have you tried Haldol or Proloxin or Trifalon? I hate meds, meds are murder, my mother used to sit around the house chugging her drinks and making a lot of stewing noises and throwing my father out of the house where growing is and the time work is. She used to call him you miserable son of a bitch, bring me another drink. I'll never forget that, the way she did that. She was never a book. She made me take olanzapine because she told me why it was good for me because I gained a lot of weight that's why you lunatic you whackjob you piece of shit nothing and lost my sense of awe. Do you hate meds?"

"I don't know, I doubt that I've ever tried them. You're talking about anti-psychotic drugs, and I don't think I have a psychosis. I woke up yesterday morning, here in Guanajuato, and I didn't know who I was or how I got here. I think I might have something called dissociative fugue. I can remember almost everything, but I can't remember who I am."

"Maybe you're you."

"I suppose that's true, but I don't know who that is because of the dissociative fugue."

"Maybe I should look up dissociative fugue in the book, that's logical. The guys I met at the VA, there were a lot of shells bursting and bullets going past my head and it was wet down in the rice paddies and an explosion would go off when I didn't want to be there, it was a whole different solar system. That's something you never forget, being there in a rice paddy and you can't get out. That's murder. And when people can't remember who they are at the VA, they give them Fluphenazine or Mesoridazine or Levomepromazine or Trifluoperazine, these are what are called phenothiazines, and then you get what's called akathisia or tardive dyskinesia or extrapyramidal symptoms, like you can't sit still or you keep making a grimace or puckering up your lips or blinking your eyes really rapidly like you're trying to see something that's missing or trying to forget something you've seen and really wish you hadn't, and you have to ask yourself who hammered this hatred in and why you can't get out and what about a bullet you miserable schizo. So that's why my name is Tom, Tom Tom, Tahm Tom Tom you conniving little goofball, that's my problem. Vietnam is murder, in my opinion."

"Jesus, Tom, you know a lot about these drugs. How did you ever end up in Vietnam if you were a schizophrenic?"

"I was drafted and then afterward they gave me the books and I have one here that opens up to the right page when you start feeling illogical as far as the rice paddies and you can't get out and another one called the Physician's Desk Reference which is how they get to call them *side effects* of what they hammer in when you hate the meds, that's logical, that's why they tell you say *ah*. Sometimes everything looks smaller than it is, like you see a refrigerator and you think you can drag it up a hill and it turns out later you're really tired, as far as where the time work is and where the hills go up and that's really something, they call those Lilliputian hallucinations, and I'm not a schizophrenic, that's just a word, I'm a man. I'm not trying to make noise here, I'm trying to make sense, and that's why they made me take my meds because they were good for me, and all of the meds have two names so they can hammer them into you twice as hard, like Clorapine is called Clozaril, and Risperidone is called Risperdal, and Quetiapine is called Seroquel, and Ziprasidone is called Geodon, and Thiothexine is called Navane, navigate, nativity, neonatal, fatal nirvana, van a bananas, Anna's sweet, treat me for something, something for nothing, nothing, *nothing*, and that's how they hammer it in twice as hard and then someone has hell to pay, that's murder, *that's murder*, in my opinion. If you don't pick up your clothes you ignorant cretin there'll be hell to pay, I'll throw you out on your ass like your fucking father. And if you can't make sense out of nonsense, well, have fun, that's all I have to say, hell to pay. I wouldn't take my meds either if I were you, you might remember who you are but you lose your sense of awe. So far as you remember, who are you, say *ah*."

"Well, it's a little bit complicated, but let me try to explain it. Like I said, I woke up yesterday morning and I remembered everything I'd ever learned, but I had what the books call an epistemological problem, I knew nothing whatsoever about the one who did all the learning, the one who must have landed me here in Guanajuato. I found a wallet on my nightstand with a driver's license that said my name was Alvaro de Campos, and an ATM card in the exact same name, but I couldn't remember my ATM PIN code, so I set off in search of an HSBC bank branch, and someone to help me remember my PIN. I was sitting at a café table, finishing my lunch, with the bank branch I needed across the street right in front of me, but worrying that the picture on my photo ID would make people think I was a lunatic or something, some phony dressed up in an eighty-year-old suit and a rakish grey fedora like the detective in a movie, the sort of guy who doesn't belong in the waiting rooms of banks, he belongs on the street mumbling Portuguese poetry, when my friend Gabriella just happened to come along, telling me she remembered me from my hotel window, though since she says she only remembers the last four or five things that have happened, it's hard to see how she could have remembered me from my window, that just doesn't make sense, it isn't logically consistent, and while Gabriella herself is the angel in a fairy tale, she may only be pretending to have her memories all backwards. She just happened to know someone who worked at the bank, so she took me across the street to see her Uncle Gustavo, he's another friend who isn't logically consistent, there's something about Gustavo that seems a little bit fishy, because he knew who I was but wouldn't tell me anything, like he was keeping my secret about where the money had come from, and keeping my secret about what I did for a living, which is why the books call it a category error, because these secrets he's keeping aren't my secrets, they aren't actually secrets that I myself am keeping, they're secrets that are actually being kept from my self. And it just so happened I had a lot of money in the bank, and that people I don't know were maybe looking for me and knew who I was, someone sent me a note by FedEx that said they hadn't forgotten, and Gustavo works with these people the Thetas they call themselves, and the Thetas act like they're protecting me from the FedEx men, but I can't help thinking that they're only pretending to protect me and may want the money and are maybe out to get me, and one of them in particular named Raúl Ramírez Tabares seems like the kind of man who would hurt me if he wanted to. And the Thetas all wear the same ties, but that's something of a long story, about tensors and the speed of light and squaring the circle, and if you want my opinion, these people treat me like we're all good friends, but I'm beginning to get the feeling that they're only posing as my friends. I've seen photos of myself, or not really myself but the *self* who must have been planning to meet me in Guanajuato, at a party or a funeral wake, it's hard to tell which, and these necktie men who may be posing as my friends are posing in the photos like they're ready to kill me, or not really me, but the *me* in the photos, the *me* that must have overshot the exit to Guanajuato, and the *me* in the photos was holding up lilies and a sawed-off shotgun and a tequila bottle, and he seemed to be able to stare straight through the photos, and see right through me with his red-laser eyes, and while

I've never even met the man, or ever once laid eyes on him, I'm an exact dead-ringer for this man with blood-red eyeballs. And then everyone keeps saying that my name is Alvaro, but calling me Alvaro just compounds the whole problem, it gives me what the books call an ontological problem, I'm virtually certain that's not my real name because it's the name of a famous poet, or not actually a famous poet, but a famous imaginary poet who didn't think he existed, and Alvaro was invented by a real poet named Fernando Pessoa, and Fernando Pessoa was a man who actually existed, he wasn't at all imaginary, although sometimes he wasn't so sure, sometimes he thought he was Fernando Pessoa's double. Pessoa was really something, he used to sit around a café drinking wine all the time, although he wasn't making stewing noises, he wasn't getting stewed, he was inventing all kinds of replicas of himself, though none of them, to be clear, were replicas of each other, they all had different names and different ways of thinking, and none of them thought like Fernando Pessoa, not even the replica named Fernando Pessoa. So, yeah, that's my name, Alvaro de Campos, but I don't think that's who I really am, Alvaro was the name of one of Fernando Pessoa's replicas, and I think someone gave me the name Alvaro de Campos because I look just like Fernando Pessoa, the resemblance, in my opinion, is really uncanny, I might just as well be Pessoa's double, and when I look in the mirror, I see Fernando Pessoa, but I can't be Pessoa, or even Pessoa's double, that wouldn't be logical, or even ontological, because Pessoa isn't alive, he's been dead for 80 years."

"From my experience, I'd recommend Geodon. It's really good for you is what they try to tell you, as far as this sort of asyndesis you're having, where you keep changing subjects in the middle of a sentence, and the akataphasia they call it, where you're trying to make sense out of the nonsense they tell you and the train gets derailed where the hills go up, and the tachyphemia and tachylogia and cluttering of speech in the way you talk which is why they hammer it in, and this sense you have that your friends are all pretenders, as far as you thinking you're a replica of someone, and your knowing that these posers are all out to get you, which is why they call it Capgras syndrome, or maybe it's because it's Cotard's syndrome, where you don't think you exist but they call you Alvaro. Cotard's syndrome, that's really something, where you look in the mirror and know you're a dead man. Boy, that's murder, being an exact dead-ringer for a man with bloody eyeballs. Of course, from my experience, Geodon won't help at all with the doctors saying you're paranoid, as far as the rice paddies and the shells bursting and you can't get out, but it makes you feel like you don't want to live anyway, even where growing is and where time work is and the corn is yellow, so maybe there's a word called paranoia, that's logical, but you just don't care, and then they hammer it into you twice as hard and you feel like a nothing you fucking psycho and lose your sense of awe."

"I don't know, Tom, I don't think I'm being paranoid, I really think there are people who are out to get me, and it has something to do with the money in the bank and the man in the photos and Ramírez Tabares, and maybe even Gustavo, who acts really friendly, but there's something about him that seems a little fishy. Like they say, it's not a good omen when goldfish commit suicide, and the FedEx guys, whoever they are, I don't know their name but they're the enemy of the Thetas, sent me pictures of a bunch of corpses being dug up from a field, but I don't think it's suicide, I think that somebody killed these people, and they want me to know that things are getting ominous, and while it may well be true that I'm an imaginary poet, I think there are real people who don't want me to exist, and even if they're only looking for the man with the bloody eyeballs, they might wind up putting me in a hole or something, and shoveling a bunch of dirt on top of me instead."

"You could try Chlorpromazine. It's another one of the neuroleptic drugs, neuroleptic from the Greek meaning to get a hold of your nerves and read the book and be logical. What it does is block the receptors in the dopamine pathways to the swimming hole swing, the mesolimbic or mesocorticol or tuberoenfundibular trails through the trees where the hills go up, and then it feels like you've had a chemical lobotomy. We used to walk out the pathway to the swimming hole in the fall when the trees were turning and all the colors of the leaves made the trees feel ecstatic and then we'd swing on the rope and drop into the water and you'd get a sense of awe about nature as a living thing in the out-of-the-blue solar system, and all that goes away, so what I'm saying is when the doctor says say *ah* you ought to take Chlorpromazine and hammer it in where the hatred is, make him take it first, see how he feels swinging on a rope and dropping into a hole and being hit with a hammer, see if he still feels ecstatic about something. You'll definitely get a hold of your nerves, that's logical, it's neuroleptic, but you won't feel like much of anything you miserable prick I can see right through you I know what you're up to I've got my eye on you, that's murder, that's murder, *that's murder*, them calling something a *side effect* when they hammer an ice pick right through your eyeball and expect you to go work at an ice cream parlor. You want some more tea?"

"OK, sure, tea sounds good. All this talk about drugs is making me nervous. So how did you get out of the service? Did you get a psychiatric discharge?"

"No, I got wounded. Everyone in Vietnam is crazy, Vietnam is murder and you're in a rice paddy and the shells are bursting and you can't get out, and if you aren't crazy when you get there, there's hell to pay when you get back home where the time work is and where the fields are growing and the corn is yellow and the hills go up. Post Traumatic Stress Disorder it's called, where you sit around the house surrounded by imposters, and when the corn is yellow or the trees are turning, you go down the path to the swimming hole swing, and you can't even stay in the solar system. That's why they call it Nebraska. I felt like a guest in a little pink house with a bunch of imposters. Why don't you get up off your ass if you can't work the tractor go get a job at the Tastee Freeze or get me a drink you limpdick loser the least you can do is punch a fucking timecard. I'll never forget that, the way she said that, I'll throw you out on your worthless ass how many times do I have to tell you, Dad was here one day gone the next, shape up or ship out, mind your P's and Q's, I'll remind you that you're a guest in this house and you my friend are this close to a goner. That's really something, that's why they call it Post Traumatic Stress Disorder. Here one day gone the next, on a spaceship to Mars with your P's and Q's in the mind of a Martian."

"So is that how you wound up here? Do you still take your meds? I could get them for you in town if you like."

"I hate the meds, because all these anti-psychotic drugs come from another galaxy, from the hatred in my heart, there's like thirty or forty different names they call them, full of P's and Q's, it's out of this world, and in my opinion, it's like ten billion drug money in the P and Q bank, so that's why they have aliens to hammer them in where the hatred is when they make you say *ah*. From my experience, I don't recommend cocaine or Dexedrine or methamphetamine, I tried those meds but it made things worse, dragging things up the hill like you're Alice in Wonderland. Even my mule thought I was crazy. All you need to do is to go to a shrink and talk a little funny and you'll end up on perphenazine or paliperidone or quetiapine or something. Just relax Tom say *ah*. Me, I got away from all the people who like to hammer things in, got back my sense of ecstasy and awe and wonder, except on odd days, and then it's really murder, dragging things up the hill like you're Gulliver's Travels. I tried to live where the time work is and the corn is yellow but I felt like a guest with a bunch of imposters. And then I went to a beach, I think it was in California, and put bleach in my hair so the shrinks at the VA wouldn't think I was my double. If I were you, I wouldn't go to a shrink, even if you feel really large compared to a stove or a refrigerator, or you feel like a guest with a bunch of imposters. Here one day gone the next. Everybody's a guest in this world, everybody's a guest in this world, Simon says, *everybody's a guest in this world*. Might as well enjoy it."

"So you think you'll be all right up here? You sure you have enough food and water? Do you need some money? I don't have very much, because the FedEx men might spot me if I use the ATMs, which really, come to think of it, doesn't make a lot of sense, since they know where I live, and claim they remember all the stuff that I've forgotten, but I could give you some money if you need more food. You look a little thin, like a charcoal drawing."

"I have water where the well is dug, and the water bucket goes and the hills go up, and corn and beans where the time work is, and the fields are growing and the corn is yellow in all my surroundings, as far as I'm concerned. I don't have a swimming hole, but I'm not a drawing, as far as my surroundings, I'm a man named Tom. What are you going to do next as far as your surroundings?"

He had me there. I was wandering around Guanajuato as though time were on my side, and I had no sense at all as to what to do next, while the goldfish, if I had any, were likely contemplating suicide.

"If I were you, I'd go home. What you need now is paraschema-zia, where you know for sure that your arms are birds. When people ask me if my arms are birds, sometimes I have to think whether I'll answer that because some people think you're crazy if your arms are birds but that's as good a way as any in my opinion, as far as the birds knowing how to find their homes even if they're thousands of miles away, a swallow knows how to find Capistrano or where Canada is if you know you're a goose, and home is where the heart is when you need to get away from the noise and the hammers. Nebraska is a place where the time work is and the fields are growing and the corn is yellow and the hills go up but the people in the pink house were a bunch of imposters, they sat around the house chugging drinks and stewing, I'll never forget how they did that, as far as them wanting to hammer things in and block the pathways to the swim-ming hole and take away my awe, and when people ask me if my arms are birds I have to think before I answer because that's how I got here, out of the blue, out of the blue, *out of the blue*. Like some people think their goose is cooked but not if they know how to find their way home and home is where the heart is, in my opinion."

Excellent point. So I finished my tea, said my goodbyes to Bird's-Nest Tom, telling him he didn't need any more household items, if anything looked Lilliputian, he should probably just ignore it, and let gravity guide me back, down the mule-droppings path, until I came once again to the cobblestone steps. I made several up-and-over sideways moves, trying to find my way out of the dead-end alleys, picturing the wild-eyed gaze of the schizoid city planner, huddled over his drawing board, doing knight's move thinking as he laid out this maze, up one over two up two over one, in the dying light at the end of another day. Whatever poem he'd written in the language of the maze, I recited it backwards, step by cobbled step. I came to the fork, where Callejón Desvío met Callejuela Subita, de-cided that sudden death was still not an option, and descended the final stairs back to Calle Luis. It was time to discover ideals to justify all the craziness, and take back control of reason from the men who held the hammers. There were reasons to think my goose might be cooked, but perhaps I'd discover some knight's moves of my own, wearing the bricolage armaments of Don Quixote. Where the time work is and the fields are growing and the corn is yellow and the hills go up, I needed to find some pathway that would lead me to the swimming hole, and a home where the heart is, before I lost the ability to open my mouth and say *ah*. It is not a good omen when the goldfish commit suicide; this isn't insanity, it's plain common sense. As the streets cooled down and the lanterns came on, the edible colors faded while birds sang in the shadows, and I felt like a man in the poster of a film, some old black-and-white like *Touch of Evil* or *The Third Man*, though I wasn't in Vienna at the end of a long war, chasing shadows down a street over fog-slick cobbles, I was in Guanajuato, home of crazy hopping frogs, and the war as far as time goes hadn't even started.

# PART II

# 17

Raymond woke up in a cold sweat from a bad dream. In the dream…wait, strike that, never mind the "in the dream" construction, no one gives a shit about Raymond's dreams, few things are as pointless as listening to human dreams, particularly the bent concoctions of a gunman eating Tramadol. A guy like Raymond, who's in a tight spot, in a bit of a timecrunch, truth be told, is just naturally going to have some pointless sort of dream, about chasing a flying clock that turns out to be a fighter plane that turns out to be three guys in an Ominous Black Suburban, who are now chasing Raymond down a dead-end street, wielding sawed-off lengths of arc-welded SAW pipe that turn out to be Dragon's Breath pyrotechnic shotguns that turn out to be M9A1-7 flamethrowers, three meaningless drooling dragons full of the craziest human shit, pressurized flammable liquid like jellied gasoline, or some sort of high-tech pyromantic super-burn mixture, maybe benzene and polystyrene, or Napalm B, washed over a tiny candle flame that turns out to be a Zippo lighter that turns out to be the sparkwire of an electronic-fuel-ignition system, meaning the shit is set ablaze, and exhaled in an evil rush of inert-nitrogen propellant gases, to a distance of give or take three hundred feet, toward dead-end Raymond dream-incineration. Raymond wakes up in a shivering cold sweat from a badass dream, something about clock towers and dragon's breath and napalm drool, though why the fuck he'd be dreaming about dragons and shit, particularly under the circumstances, must have been something he ate, or maybe it was one of those de-

mented chronometers, that's what it was, just a fucking clock, that
pewter-looking thing that Gomez keeps on his desk, two large dragons with wings and dirty fangs, staring up at a third, sitting smugly
atop the clock dial, the whole thing resting on a coffin-like base,
with the coffin supported by gargoyle appendages, and the dragon
at the top maybe giving you the eye, like you'd better be watching
out if you're delinquent in your duties, he'll napalm your ass until
your face-flesh starts bubbling. Raymond rubs his eyes, checks his
face bones for flesh, and looks out the window where it's evidently
morning, the citizens of Old El Paso probably going about their day,
be nice to be out there with them on a day like today, maybe sweeping off the sidewalk in front of his own bodega, or hosing down the
windows on Raymond's Boxing Gym, or maybe it's one of those
mornings where you call in sick, take the dogs out for a run in the
April gypsum desert, watch them flush a covey of bobwhites out of
the mesquite and acacia brush, birds flying off together in a nice
clean arc, leaving the dogs a little puzzled by the absence of a shotgun blast, letting the bobwhites fly, into the April silence. Be nice.
Probably a lot of things be nice if the truth weren't fucking true,
like him being in a world of hurt if he don't get his ass in moving
gear, needs to meet Jen at Sonny's at like 9:00 am, and it's now past
9:30, which wouldn't in itself be all that bad, if it weren't for the fact
that Raymond is fucking freezing, and has a chestful of pet sutures,
and feels like a dog that picked the wrong damn fight, and wound
up oozy-X-marked with his brain stitched up with Tramadol. What
the fuck? Ray tries rolling over an inch or two on one side, see if he
can move without his stitches exploding, and falls back exhausted
and clammy with sweat, the 3M Steri-Strips losing adhesion, and
the Ethicon Monocryl sutures, like, torqued-up and bursting. Jesus,
feels like shit; now what? More Tramadol; he shakes loose a handful from the half-empty vial and swallows them down with a slug of
Old Grand-Dad. Going to need Gene's help right about here, that
much is apparent, lift him out of bed, get his feet back under him,
and come to think of it, where the fuck is Gene, why didn't Gene
wake him up for his nine o'clock meeting? Gene? Gene? Eugene?
Where the hell are you you miserable shit, I got to get to Sonny's in
like minus thirty minutes.

     Eugene, as we all know, and Raymond clearly doesn't, was last seen fingering a particular set of keys, keys to a Dodge Ram Magnum ignition, and waxing a little nostalgic about an honest day's work, ready to true things up and right some misalignment, it being time to get the money back into the boss' hands, stop worrying about some dickwad maybe being a dead civilian. Eugene, in other words, is off doing the right thing, and he's not coming back in the immediate near-term, at least not near enough to reverse thirty minutes; Gene too has his dreams, full of amber waves and wheat fields, and a few wispy clouds blazing trails on the horizon, and as to what the future may hold for such a man, no one can really say, at least not without our giving him some ominous premonitions, and that, it's safe to say, we don't plan to do; as far as we're concerned, the future can go to hell, and take its premonitions right along with it. So Raymond, in essence, call yell all he wants and it won't change a thing in the premonition department; if Ray needs an inkling that the money's long gone, along with Ray's truck and his friend Eugene Booker, he'll just have to wait for an inkling to come along, and deliver its pointed message on a silver fucking platter. Gene? Goddammit Gene, get your ass in here, I need your fucking help, get me the hell upright and see if I'm still alive, got to get to Sonny's about right this fucking instant, where the hell are you you haymowing son-of-a-bitch, you taking a crap, give a yell if you can hear me, Jesus Christ Gene, I can barely fucking breathe, let's get it the fuck in gear, time's a fuckin' wasting, and so on and so forth, his locutions slowly unspooling, you should probably cover your ears, for the moment at least, maybe Ray will get an inkling that he's filling an empty house with an absolute shitpile of meaningless spewn invective. Ray's obscenity-laced tirade eventually runs its course, and get's him approximately nowhere, meaning right back where he started, in a silent crumbling asylum where he's staring at the walls, in this case the wallpaper, which is never a good thing, some sky blue Jane Churchill decorative shit, covered all to hell and gone with plump pink cherubs, who in God's name would put cherubs on their walls, and what the hell were they thinking is a cherub in the first place, some supernatural entity out of Genesis or the Book of Psalms, or maybe it's the Book of Chronicles is the one that I must be thinking, if they wanted fucking cherubs they should be holding up human skulls, and blowing a golden trumpet, and wandering

around Prague, snarling up Slovak traffic and looking around for a
church or something, for their home in the Sedlec Ossuary, oh shit,
never mind, better cancel that about Sedlec, Sedlec, what's Sedlec,
and what the hell's an ossuary, some chapel with chandeliers made
of Black Death human femur bones, must be around here somewhere, but it's probably not in Prague. Raymond, apparently, has
drifted off just a bit, to the time he spent in Germany, on his way
back home from Basra, at an army base in Schweinfurt, or maybe
it was Mannheim, or Landstuhl, that's what it was, the sort of place
where wounded men tend to wallow around in pain delirium, rolling over and moaning in the ICU dreamland cooker, and dreaming
that even the barracks stink from pipes backed up with Cherub shit,
when all they are really smelling is their own oozing wounds, and
where the hell were we now, got to drop the stupid cherub shit, and
the price we pay for moronic wars, time to get our ass in moving
gear, maybe need a few more Tramadol, and a whole lot fewer of
those Black Death femur bones.

    We, evidently, perhaps following Ray's lead, have veered slight-
ly off our course here, narratage-wise. Perhaps we need a recap.
Raymond has awakened from an abbreviated nap, in a sweet yellow house in the lovely old Magoffin district, and he's somewhat
late for a meeting that was previously arranged. It's something of
a long story, but in essence a friendly co-worker and associate of
Raymond's has been checking around in the company files, looking into the background of one of the company's current clients, a
man known rather loftily as The Poet internally, though Raymond
and his partner, Eugene Patrick Booker, have taken to calling him
dickwad, or fuckhead, upon occasion, or the no-name grey Ford
Fusion guy, which is probably not his name. Raymond would like
to know, not to put too fine a point on it, whether or not this missing man, whose actual name was not supplied to them, deserves to
live or die. The yellow house is on a quiet street, the sky is blue and
the redbirds sing, the oak trees in the yard are an early springtime
limelight green, and maybe it's merely human nature, or maybe
it's something peculiar to Raymond, but he doesn't want to kill this
man unless he deserves to die. Although Raymond is a soldier, and
has certainly killed before, he apparently has qualms about killing
known civilians; this sense of uncertainty regarding the propriety

of an action has left him in a quandary, a perplexing state of uncertainty, as to the appropriate course of action with regard to the
open question of whether or not he should be attempting to put
an end to dickwad's life, and though the redbirds will go on singing no matter what course Raymond takes, he would prefer to base
his actions on solid information, information that his co-worker has
offered to obtain, as opposed to using the facts that are currently
available, and basing his course of action on a bunch of fucking
songbirds. It's probably worth mentioning that Raymond isn't well;
an unfortunate encounter, while having a quiet drink or two at a bar
in the Mariscal known as El Arbolito, has left him with a lengthy,
X-shaped, chest wound, a wound that's been closed, more or less,
using standard U.S. medical products, although the products in
question might be better suited to post-operative care on a Siamese
cat, or for sewing up the mysterious gash some neighbor inflicted
on the family Springer Spaniel. Raymond, as a result, on top of
his having qualms, is bordering on delirium, with a fever of almost
102, and a system full of animal opiates, and he hasn't had much
sleep, other than a dream-plagued nap or two, at least one of which
is known to have been terminated by the distinctive breath of napalm dragons. Now Raymond is not the sort of man who is prone
to complain upon the slightest provocation, but given his delicate
condition, and the fact that the stuff is itself demented, the wallpaper seems to be bothering him, and who among us, whoever we
are, hasn't, upon occasion, wondered about the selection process
involved in various wall treatments; even Oscar Wilde, a tolerant
man, dying beyond his means in a lovely hotel in Paris, is said to
have remarked, toward the end of his hours, "Either the wallpaper
goes or I do." Specifically, it seems that the cute pink cherubim, no
matter how plump and lovely they must have looked on a six-by-six-
inch sample swatch, may be hard on the nerves when fully arrayed,
in an alarming display of pinkly plumpness, and this, along with
his fever, his intake of bourbon and Tramadol, and the fact that he
can't seem to locate his brother in arms, Eugene, has led Ray off on
a bit of a swerve, about which we have very little to add, other than
to say that we too find it odd, and somehow vaguely unsettling, that
a church in the Czech Republic, whatever in God's name that is,
was able to locate an interior designer, with a particular affection

for chandeliers, whose specialty was decorating dark interiors with millions of human bones.

Now that we're all up to speed, and fully apprised of the exigent circumstances, we should quickly move on to the problem at hand, the fact that Raymond, who has things to do, seems to be ever so slightly deranged, and lacking in certain motor skills, such as those required for basal locomotion. Bathed in human sweat, mumbling about benzene dragons, going on and on about bone-pile chandeliers and Slovak traffic and Black Death endoskeletons, and nearing that point at which he'll begin to consider shooting cherubs out of the air of his sky-blue wallpaper, Raymond is in need of a change of scene, like a week or three on a beach in Bermuda. If only Ray were a bird of some kind, and we could just point him east, toward an island in the Atlantic…but no, sadly, no, that just won't fucking cut it, that dog don't hunt, time to stop dreaming and get with the damn program. Ray picks up the scarlet Razr phone, which is all that remains of his so-called partner, and dials the number for Jennifer, who sits alone drinking at Sonny's Bar, wondering about the hedging strategies on her Glory to Man Rainbow Options. Jen, it's me, look, sorry I'm late. I overslept a little, and now I can't find Gene. You can't find Gene? Where have you looked? Nowhere, really. I'm having a little trouble trying to get out of bed. I yelled a few times, but Gene doesn't answer. He could be out in the garage, I guess. I'd invite you to my place but if Gene's out back, he seemed a little jumpy about Gomez coming over, or him maybe having you followed here, and winding up with gopher holes and Zetas in the parlor. No one is following me Ray, unless Gomez has started hiring seventy-year-old drunks. These guys can barely get a shot glass from the bar to their lips; they could maybe fire a handgun if it's mounted on a tripod. What about outside the bar? Anything look suspicious? It looks suspiciously like morning, the time of day when I'm supposed to be at work, and I'm sitting in a bar with a bunch of guys with the shakes. Yeah, I know what you mean, it's beautiful out, been thinking about taking the dogs for a run, doin' a little bird hunting. Quail and pheasant maybe, course the season's not 'til November something, think it's only April now, but sure is a beautiful morning. I don't mean to rush you, Ray, but do you have some sort of plan here? If you're planning on going hunting, I'll

need to change my shoes. Yeah, no, yeah…well, no, listen. Listen.
I'm listening, Trip, but what I'm hearing doesn't sound like much
of a plan, it sounds like one of these drunks with the shakes thinking about asking the bartender for a coaster. Sorry, Jen, my mind's
been wandering, got a little nicked up in a fight last night at a bar
in Juárez. I'm having some trouble breathing. What kind of trouble
breathing? You want me to call 911? You need to be on a ventilator? Been thinking what I need is get out of this whole damn business, maybe buy a little corner store or a place for teaching boxing
lessons. Sounds lovely, Ray, you should get yourself one of those
oxygen tanks you can wheel around behind you, see if anyone pays
much attention to a guy teaching boxing through an oxygen mask.
No, look, I don't need a ventilator, my guess is, if there's a bunch
of guys out looking for me now, the first place they'd look be connected to a ventilator. I need someone to help me get out of bed.
If you want my opinion, you don't really sound like you need to be
out of bed, your voice sounds like maybe you're gargling something.
Yeah, probably blood; like I said I got a little nicked up. So let me
see if I've got this straight, you're gargling blood, you can't really
breathe, you can't stand up to take a piss, and your plan would be
you need a little help, get up out of bed, and then do what, maybe
go to the bathroom? It might be better if I send the drunks; probably
all make a lot of sense to them. You're right, you're right, I'm a little
fucked-up, got a windpipe drip and the walls going crazy, maybe
you should come over and help me out of bed but forget what I
said about taking the dogs hunting. Certainly, whatever you say,
we'll forget about the hunting, all that gurgling you're doing probably scare off the birds. What exactly are you expecting me to do?
Come on over, listen to you gargle, maybe give you CPR if it turns
out you're drowning? You want me to bring you a snorkel while I'm
at it? Sure, why not, a snorkel and some fins, and maybe you can
track down an interior decorator, got to do something about these
fucking pink cherubs. Just double-check you're not being followed,
don't want to deal with gophers in the yard, wind up in the bone
pile at the Sedlec Ossuary. You want my advice, Raymond, first
thing you do is to start making sense. What the fuck is the Sedlec
Ossuary? I hear you, Jen, that's been bothering me too, thought it
was in Prague, I know it's got these cherubs that are blowing on

golden trumpets, but the chandeliers are made of femur bones, that don't sound at all like Prague. I'll make you a deal, Trip, I'll come on over, tell you about The Poet, you hear yourself start thinking something, try not to listen. Probably right, probably can't make a whole chandelier out of something the size of femur bones, makes no sense, come to think about it, must have had something like metacarpals, or maybe it was phalanges, those little bones at the ends of your fingers, where the whatyoucallem finials go. Better pull out the battery pack on your cell phone while we're at it, last thing we need is some ancient Greek like Hippocrates or Polybus, knows nothing at all about the human skeleton, trying to turn us into ossuary bone-chandeliers, after what's his name, Pythagoras, has us whatthefuckyoucallit, triangulated. Tell you what, Ray, do me one favor. If you're worried about Pythagoras maybe tracking our cell phones, don't pull a muscle, let me do the math. Problem you've got has nothing to do with triangles, it's those two-sheeted hyperboloids that'll get you in trouble.

Whatever. A street address is tacked on the end, like the one-bit FIN on a security door TCP packet, with one of Raymond's last few breaths, and then glory be to drugs, a half-vial of Tramadol finally truly kicks in, though not without a few of the perfectly normal side effects, some visual disturbances and vertigo and such, and the distinct sensation that Raymond has of all of a sudden he's truly fucking flying. He levitates off the bed, addresses the need for Steri-Strip adhesion, and first things first, goes to take a leak, with the toilet flushing down all that nonsense about cherub shit, which is probably a good thing, and a great relief to Raymond. After a brief period of mourning for his Scully plaid's squandered life, he finds an old Rockport Shadow Plaid blue-green replacement, scrubs himself off with a wince or two and a piece of white cloth, puts on his shirt, and hides the dead plaid and the bloody washcloth underneath the sink, behind the Ajax and Liquid-Plumr. Jesus, that feels good, just standing up, and knowing that the blood-drip is not in his windpipe, little blood down the esophagus isn't going to kill him, now that he's a bird or a vertebrate at least, can't help but wonder how a windpipe works, or why a grasshopper needs a what's the word trachea. Ray splashes some cold water on his gradually cooling face; one of the side effects of Tramadol must be fever reduction, feels

like a bird flying into the wind, off in the direction of the Sangre de
Cristo Mountains. Raymond makes the mistake, understandable
enough, of attempting to comb his sweat-soaked hair, by lifting his
arms that feel like wings, and notices that much above shoulder-
high, his torqued-up sutures are screech-inducing. Never mind.
Whoever heard of a hawk in flight, or a bobwhite flushed from the
mesquite and acacia, stopping to run a comb through its feathery
hair; the wings of a bird are meant for soaring. Bermuda, Ray; did
we mention Bermuda?

And then even the bird-flight delusion recedes from the occipital region of Raymond's human brain, and leaves him with a quiet
sense of self-determination, the one real delusion he can probably
least afford. He hears a timid knock and then a door swinging open
and bounds down the stairs, though not without pocketing the rest
of the Tramadol, and finding Jennifer alone in the empty hall, and
not some ancient Greek with a chandelier construction manual, he
offers her some instant coffee, and strides into the kitchen, looking
for the Yuban's and some six-week-old milk. We'll have to drink it
black, Jen, this milk smells like cherub piss, no, look, forget that, forget about the cherub piss, this milk's gone sour, we'll have to drink
it black. Black is fine, Ray, you feeling any better? Yeah, little sore
is all, may need a doctor take a look at these sutures. What the hell
happened? Me and Gene were down in Juárez, trying to track down
that douchebag that Gomez sent us looking for, ran into the wrong
crowd at a bar in the Mariscal. They had some sort of message they
were trying to send, wound up writing it down on my chest so I'd
remember. Things got a little hazy, think I must have passed out,
seem to remember coming to in an animal clinic. Gene took you to
the vets? I don't know, probably afraid they'd be out hunting for us,
thinking maybe the emergency room be the first place they'd look.
You want sugar? No, this is fine, so are you fixed up now or what?
You sounded half-crazy when we talked on the phone. You must
have scared off Eugene, I didn't see the truck. Jesus, Gene took
the truck? That stupid fucking farmer. Kept talking about taking
Gomez' money back and getting with the program, like he thought
we had a goddamn program to get with. Gomez probably got a program all right, probably got Gene tied to a chair about now, holding
a Colibri cigar torch up to one of his eyeballs. Better tell me about

the Poet, and drink up on that coffee, won't be long before Gomez knows we're here. Back up just a second Ray, you think Gomez is coming after you? Not too sure I signed up for this. I'm a derivatives analyst, I can tell you all you want to know about stochastic calculus or put-call parity or SABR volatility models or how to use the Greeks in Delta-hedging arbitrage plays, I don't know a fucking thing about driving around El Paso in a Toyota Corolla getaway car. Yeah, you're right, you should maybe just clear out. We'll find a better time to talk about stochastic calculus. And you'll what? Take the bus? I'll be all right, just need to find the Fusion guy and get back Gomez' money before the Zetas find him first. Yeah, well, here's the thing Ray, I'm not really all that sure it's actually Gomez' money. If this guy you're looking for is the guy in the Poet file, he's a venture capitalist from somewhere in Los Angeles. Looks to me like he made an investment in the cell phone business, may not have known it was one of Gomez' laundry schemes. Company he's in, Dacha Wireless, gets a shitload of orders from some of Gomez' laundry shells, goes public on the HKEX, stock runs up before the lock-up comes off, winds up with a couple of billion in market capitalization; that money he's hauling may have looked like his share of the pumped-up stock profits, might not have known he'd invested in the laundry business. That's on the one hand. On the other, the guy would have had to have been either stupid or lazy not to see the whole thing was an outright fraud. Would have taken maybe ten minutes' worth of asking the right questions to figure out the orders were completely bogus. If you ask me, they should send the whole Board into solitary confinement, or some place nice and quiet for the criminally insane, but then that's where I'd have sent the Boards of half of our public companies, starting with Enron and Tyco and WorldCom. You add in the places where the Boards were sound asleep, companies like AOL, Lucent, Sunbeam, Global Crossing, Homestore, maybe throw in Merck, Merrill Lynch, Qwest, Microstrategy, Reliant, Peregrine, Kmart, and then maybe fifty-some others off the top of my head, every bank on earth that was dealing in mortgage bonds, you'd need a lot of new buildings with quiet padded cells just to hold all the dimwits with delusions of competence. Personally, Jen, I'm just a soldier, got no fuckin' idea what the hell you're talking about. Is this guy a civilian? I don't know

Ray, what the hell's the difference? Guy holds up a bank, you'd
have to say he's a criminal. Bank steals from its shareholders while
the Board sits there daydreaming, maybe planning new furniture
for their ranches in Jackson Hole, what do you call it then, maybe
criminal negligence? Guy steals the money or the money just gets
stolen, there's not a lot of difference, as far as I can tell. You sound
like the wiry guy at El Arbolito, guy raises his arm or his arm just
goes up, next thing I know, I'm getting messages written down on
my chest with a trench knife. How the hell'm I supposed to know
whether to kill this guy or not? I'll tell you what, Ray, you start killing all the dimwits, you're going to need a lot more trained morticians and a lot of empty land for cemetery space.

Not that there's anything wrong with that. The motion is therefore tabled, to be resolved at a future Board meeting, and the question of guilt or innocence hereby held in abeyance. In any case, the
grey Ford Fusion guy is not at the top of the list of currently pressing
problems, among which are Gene and the possible application of
a brand name cigar lighter to various parts of his ostensible face.
Raymond repeats his offer to leave Jennifer gracefully out of this,
maybe just drive away in her clean white Corolla, and Jen, for no
real reason, doesn't just drive away, she just sits there sipping her
unadulterated coffee. Possibly Jen's having qualms about leaving
Ray alone, riding a city bus in a deep, deep quandary, but here
we find ourselves wandering around once again in the land of unknown semantic origins, deep in the Broca or Wernicke areas of
the mysterious human brain. Just to remind ourselves, qualms and
quandaries have no known semantic origins, and the region of the
brain involved in semantic processing, Brodmann Area 44, is, cy-
toarchitectonically speaking, bounded caudally and dorsally by the
agranular frontal Area 6, dorsally by frontal Area 9, and rostrally by
the triangular area known as Brodmann 45, and somewhere deep
inside this occasionally empty space is the land of untold quandaries and qualms. If all of this sounds vaguely familiar, like something you've heard from a gullible Uncle, the one who goes on
and on about mental telepathy, and alien spacecraft, and extraterrestrial biological entities, while you're trying to carve the turkey
for a holiday feast, we can assure you it is not, you have simply
fallen victim to the usual confusion between Brodmann Area 44,

an area that fits entirely inside your head, and that unknown land at the edge of the Earth, on the Yucca flats, in the nucular desert, known to us all as Area 51, or in Air Force parlance, Dreamland or The Box. Now Dreamland, as you might have surmised, doesn't exist on Government maps, it's the land of experimental weapons systems, a region well known for the reverse-engineering of a variety of crashed and downed alien spacecraft, a zone dedicated to the research and development of time travel devices and teleportation vehicular contrivances, and the home to an extraterrestrial entity or two, housed at Site 4 in the Papoose Mountains, one of them employed, by the Anomalous Life-Form Linguistics Division, as a telepathic translator of alien communiqués, a being known internally by his nickname, J-Rod, who must be something of a master craftsman of semantic processing in Area 44. On the edge of the zone of the nuclear blast, seven hundred thirty-nine of the magical-mushroom-cloud shaman monsters, where the cobwebs sparkle with a strange empty glimmer and the coyotes walk around with a radiant glow, life is chock-full of difficult semantic problems, like the quandaries and qualms of actual human beings who've been time-traveled and teleported to the land of the living dead. Everyone involved, from the roasted pigs to the radiated spiders to the ill-advised downwinders with little homesteads of their own, lives on in Dreamland, in Area 51, a zone that must be located somewhere deep inside us, in Brodmann Area 44, the mysterious home of telepathic semantic processing, and everything we think we know about origins unknown. Just so you know. Just to keep us all on the same page, semantically speaking; no wonder we're having so many quandaries and qualms. Raymond and Jennifer polish off the last few sips of their coffee; spend just a moment or two searching for Jen's keys; exit the house through a dimly lit doorway; and enter a world filled with the luminescing brilliance and radiant incandescence of a glorious April morning's Manifest of Green, all of which translates to Raymond needing his shades, which are right were he left them, in the glovebox of the truck. Much as Jennifer had surmised, the Ram Magnum's gone missing, though Gene was thoughtful enough to leave the Mossberg behind, so Ray and Jen make a slow but well-equipped curbside departure, with Jen at the wheel of the tragically underpowered, 1.8 liter, Toyota Corolla getaway car, out of the immediate vicinity of Ray's yellow house, out of the familiar Magoffin Historical District, out of the land of the luminescing trees, and deeper into Area 44, deeper into Dreamland, in Air Force parlance, and headed indirectly, not that they know it yet, straight toward spending a little time in The Box.

Jennifer repeated her early morning ritual, down Texas Avenue to a left on North Mesa, and a left again on San Antonio, to Gomez Central in the highrise on Stanton, with Ray shading his eyes against the blazing morning sun, and keeping his head down around dashboard level, just in case aliens had invaded El Paso, and were keeping an eye peeled for Raymond-type specimens. Jen had volunteered to drive, which may or may not have been a good idea, since Raymond was unable to elevate his arms, without running a real risk of suture-torquing screech-inducement, and the correlative risk of him soaring right off, back into one of his bird-flight delusions, or Heaven forbid, back to the land of the plump pink cherubim; where Ray's headed now is deep underground, into the sodium dimness of an excavated reality, where there is no such thing as luminescing trees, or redbirds singing, or sweet yellow houses, and the last thing he needs, if he's going subterranean, is to start hearing cherubs blowing on golden trumpets. Jen steered the Corolla into the entrance to the parking structure, noting that the building maintenance staff had not yet addressed what would appear to be an issue with regard to the operation of the exit controller arm, a Scranton SB-25 ArmBarrier beauty, with half-sinusoidal acceleration action, an arm that at this point was six inches long, having been broken off abruptly only yesterday morning by two seasoned gunmen in a Dodge Ram Magnum. Jen paused at the tollbooth for a moment or two, to say a friendly hello to the blank-faced tolltaker, and ask him to comment on the presence or absence of the missing-in-action Ram-Tough truck. Come in about an hour ago, with a man at the wheel, a good-sized man, the guess would be he's on level four or five, which translates, in this case, to minus four or five. The two of them, then, gunman and analyst, wound their way down the underground incline, to minus five, in the deep-down-under, where they found the empty vehicle and parked nearby. Now what? The question is not a simple one. If Gene has returned the missing money, the million dollars plus in bank-strapped currency, and received a hearty pat on the back, and some where-the-hell-were-you we-were-worried-about-you it's-sure-good-to-see-you smiles all around, then everything is fine and dandy, at least for the moment, and Ray and Jen can enter the Tower. In the strange yellow glow of minus five lighting, powered by 100-watt high-pressure sodium lamps, emptied of any semblance of natural daylight, and thus forming a dense irreality zone, the suspicion formed that this had not been the outcome, and that Gene may in fact sit accused of something, may right at this moment be bound to a chair, and may finally be facing the prisoner's paradox, where the fact that you've forced them to such lengths to get the truth proves that your guilt was a foregone conclusion, a truth that, in time, you will readily admit to; Gene, in particular, may have no way of responding to questions posed repeatedly by a blazing Colibri, as it prepares to show the world that his answers can't be trusted, since his face will not only look deeply suspicious, but won't, at some point, look altogether human. Welcome to the land of subterranean lighting; fortunately for all of us, only the guilty reside here. It's a well known fact, among inner-city law enforcement, that anti-crime lighting causes a lot of crime; if you don't believe this, and believe that it's all a slight misunderstanding, a distortion of notions of cause and effect, a logical fallacy that's quickly corrected, a failure to grasp the scientific method, something easily explained to the next cop you meet, try wandering around alone in the sodium-lit delirium of the urban-mythic shut-the-fuck-up reality-devastation zone, with a cigarette dangling from your miscreant lips, and an open container of Colt 45. Deep deep down in the sulfurous dimness, at precisely minus five in the reality structure, where meaning itself wanders the boneyard, and everything is always already a crime, Raymond came to a dead-level certainty that he and Eugene were fucked already, and headed ever deeper into excavated terrain. And if Gomez were holding a FIREBOY PLUS butane-cartridge Bunsen-burner flame tip, with a Roaring Blue Bunsen Level 4 Flame, up nice and close to Eugene's nostrils, even Jennifer herself might not be safe here, depending on just how far they'd actually progressed, in their tell-us-what-you-know-or-we'll-brûlée-your-pituitary, right-through-your-nostrils, operating procedure. Ray and Jen sat silent and still in the tiny white Corolla, which is Latin for "small crown," as everyone knows, for reasons known only in Japanese by Toyota, and wandered around a little in Area 44, semantically processing the sodium weirdness, and searching for a word that might best express whatever feelings they had about underground terrain, something well beyond qualms and caudally bounded agranular quandaries, and into the glimmering cobwebs and radiated spiders of a cold-blooded psychopathic gaping reality, that region of the human brain that's better left alone. You think I should go in, Ray, see if Gene's up there? No, Jen, I don't, I really really don't.

Just about then, as if J-Rod were listening in, Gene and two henchmen were teleported out, from the 17$^{th}$ floor to the sodium basement, and three large men, two of them wearing trenchcoats, were soon crammed together in the front of Ray's truck cab, with Gene in the middle, pretzelled atop the gearshift, and the Dodge Ram Magnum keyed-up and igniting. The Magnum reversed, scraping a long deep gouge just above its own rocker panel, using the polished chrome bumper of a Chevy Bel Air, maybe parked too close, what the fuck's the difference, and then the Ram shifted forward and roared off up the incline, with a white Toyota Corolla trailing it at a distance, just watching them what-the-fuck hell-bent go, barely grazing, as it were, a wide variety of auto bodies and concrete support columns and load-bearing walls, indicative no doubt of a certain vague indifference toward the nature of gravity in underground parking structures, and a total disregard for the ultimate condition of the wax job on Raymond's once-gleaming truck. There was something a little strange about the handling on the Magnum; with the back end of the truck frame sitting nearly atop the axle, as though the dead space of the cargo bed was loaded down with something heavy, fresh plutonium perhaps for the irradiated desert, the truck weaved around like the rear was on roller skates, in need of something solid to hold itself up. They paused not a moment at the tollbooth attendant and swung south on Stanton in a tire-screeching arc, with the Mopar Hemi revving up around the redline, and the inaccessible gearbox likely stuck in first gear, but nonetheless speeding toward the, oh shit, not this, here the fuck we go again, Stanton Street Bridge, and Ciudad Juárez.

With Jen at the wheel, which both was and was not such a good idea, and the Ram weaving a slalom through the 10:15 traffic, the underpowered Toyota, lagging in pursuit, was forced to run the red light at the Paisano Street intersection, dodging a yellow school bus that went on the green, having apparently overestimated the value of having the right-of-way, and underestimated the impact of a direct hit on its fuel tank. A young man on a messenger bike was swervingly missed, perhaps misinformed as to the import of his message; three men in dark suits were nearly sent to their deaths, with a grave misunderstanding regarding the nature of crosswalks; a Franciscan nun, wearing all seven pieces of her brown and white habit, like something only recently time-traveled here, was seen crossing herself once or twice as they passed, giving thanks to her Savior for His timely intercession, no doubt unaware that her actual Redeemer, a wild-eyed grey squirrel that Jen had nearly crushed, had scurried off down the sidewalk, searching for acorns, and that the Intercessor paradigm, may the Lord save us all, had been time-traveled backwards, via human contrivance, to somewhere in the depths of the dank middle ages; life, in short, went on as before, it was a lovely April morning in Old El Paso, with shoppers bearing gift bags, and mothers pushing strollers, and vultures flying circles high overhead, way up above in the blue Texas April, awaiting the imminent moment of the at-last fatal crash. Raymond closed his eyes, settled back in his bucket seat, and swallowed quite a handful of his bone-dry opiates, without so much as a single drop of water, or stopping off somewhere for a fresh supply of bourbon, or something along the lines of a liter-style Big Gulp; maybe he'd returned to the zone of real pain, or maybe he liked the feeling of soaring above the desert, the fever reduction, the spare gypsum ease; one of the side effects of Tramadol is appetite enhancement, and with Raymond wandering around in the skull-and-crossbones desert, headed dead south in a spotless white Corolla, his only source of sustenance was a bone-pile of pills, not the easiest of meals for any of us to swallow; in Ray's case, of course, the pills slid right down, and wound up in a firepit at the bottom of his stomach, since Raymond, in essence, was nearly in Burma, with its juicy moonlit mango orchards, dripping with dew, and its men in black pajamas, sipping on Shwe le maw, and its stone-surrounded source of something that was welling up inside him, not well water exactly, or even his own saliva, but a small cedar bucket full of his own leaking blood. And those vultures flying circles in the blue Texas April? They *can't* be too concerned about Jen's erratic driving, but they *can* smell blood even a half a world away. As the Dodge Ram Magnum receded into the distance, toward the Stanton Street crossing, and Ciudad Juárez, Ray felt the sutures in his brain stem relaxing, and let his thoughts drift off across the blue Texas sky.

In any case, there wasn't much point in telling Jen to speed up; he was ashamed of himself for having involved her in any of this, no way to treat a lady, as his dad would have said; what his father had to say about women, come to think of it, the sum of his hard-earned scar-tissue wisdom, was "whatever you do, you just have to love them." He remembered one time, in a windowless bar in maybe it must have been Albuquerque, he was 9 or 10 at most at the time, stealing sips from the beer Dad poured from a pitcher, playing 2-man 8-ball, feeding the table with quarters, where the winners play on and the losers drink and wait, and he and his dad had run off 10 or 12 real losers in a hurry, Ray hitting bank shots and corner-to-corner beauties, bit of backspin on the cue ball, setting up his shots, winning a buck or two a game, sipping the glass of beer when his dad wasn't looking, the more beer he drank, the better he played, and a couple of the losers, badass biker guys, had had enough of losing, lost one final time, and decided to change the game, more or less entirely. Two short steel switchblades emerged into view, in the Jim Beam Billiards Lamp bar-room lamplight, some Spanish was murmured of elaborate ill-intent, Ray drinking Dad's Coors and watching him closely, and then his dad set his pool cue on the smooth green felt, walked straight on ahead toward the absolute switchblades, smiling like always, Dad's long-ago always, clapped the two murderous cholos on the shoulders and backs, like they was long-lost Fort Bliss I-missed-you-guys Army buddies, Cervesa mis amigos, necesitas cervesas, ignoring the ill-intent, ignoring the change of game entirely, and buying them a pitcher and a couple of shots, and five minutes later, they're all sitting around drinking, at a beer-soaked pool-hall just-your-basic bar-room table, arguing about the merits of chopped Harley panheads as long-range touring bikes, and the best routes to ride up the Sangre de Cristos, and what to tell the wife when you're three days late, and she's not really buying your complete total bullshit, laughing and drinking and smiling

like always, the bikers buying the next two rounds, as though all of
life's problems and bullshit and headaches could be solved with a
few beers among good companions, and no one on Earth was ever
such a shithead that he couldn't become Dad's true-enough friend.
Jesus, he was a hell of a guy, his dad was, he'd have rather taken a
knife through the ribs, if it came to that, than assume the worst of
anyone; whoever they were, there was good in them somewhere,
and he gave them all whatever he had, his absolute best, when he
had it to give. Which reminded Ray of Jen, his dad did; no doubt
about it, reminded him of Jen.

Of course, that was decades age, long before the drug wars
changed the table stakes entirely; this wasn't a good time to be wandering around Juárez, making goodness assumptions, while they
gouged out your eyeballs and hacksawed your knees. By the time
Ray looked up, wiped the gypsum dust from the corners of his crow's-
feet eyes, they were six cars back in the Stanton Street crossing line.
Fortunately for them, the Dodge Ram Magnum towered over everything, and was so truly black that even a blindman could spot it. If
Ray had to guess, his partner Gene Booker looked ever so slightly,
as it were, ill at ease, even downright uncomfortable, sitting stiffly
in the truck cab between two large henchmen, possibly as a consequence of being positioned atop the gearshift, wedged between
trenchcoats in their wide bucket seats, or more likely the result of
pressure on his rib cage, from a high-caliber handgun, maybe a .48
Ruger or a chromed Smith and Wesson or a massive Desert Eagle
Mark XIX, fifty fucking calibers of gas-actuated blankness, with po-
lygonal rifling and rotating bolt action, reminiscent to any soldier of
his beloved M16, a good solid choice for putting pressure on a rib
cage, if the slug doesn't do it, the dragon's-breath muzzle-flash will
finish up the task. Raymond, it was clear, knew far too much about
absolute weaponry, and far too little about running a corner grocery
store, to be thinking about a job change, some shift in his current
career path; this wasn't a good time to be out sweeping sidewalks,
or looking up his age in the actuarial tables, planning on a life ex-
pectancy of any decent length. Seeing his own partner and long-
standing friend looking so, shall we say, out of place in the truck
cab, squeezed between Grim Reaper heads, clearly not in his element, Ray urged Jen on, toward a breach of common courtesy, one

that Raymond himself had only yesterday been scolded for, looping around the line and cutting in rudely, right behind the Magnum, to a blaring of horns. From this close a distance, even through the gypsum dust, it was apparent that Eugene wasn't feeling at all well; what Raymond had taken for normal uneasiness, a simple case of nerves, which we've all felt under pressure, maybe that meeting in five minutes in front of the Board of Directors, after some accounting irregularities have finally come to light, involving six or was it ten of the top Corporate Officers, and the Board, as always, hasn't the faintest clue, a fraud so pure and timeless you're afraid to show your face in there, these men are going to kill you for telling them the truth, and as you stand there in the hallway with the paper-trail evidence, the indisputable numbers, the smoking-gun proof, you're tempted to dump the whole thing into the nearest trash bin and find a cozy bar and buy yourself a drink or two; so where were we now, before we went off on this paper-trail smoking-gun tangent, ah yes, over here, inside the Ram-Tough Magnum, where what Raymond had mistaken for a brief bout of queasiness now looked a lot like the sudden onset of human mortality, with Gene sitting dead stiff, like a goner already, wandering off alone beyond the usual qualms and quandaries, toward the glowing coyotes and irradiated spiders, out of the known zip codes and into the boneyard stockpile, doing deep semantic processing on the nature of drawing a blank. Gene, to be fair, was certainly under a bit of pressure, and did not look like a man making goodness assumptions, though he certainly looked like a man who could use a stiff drink. As the Ram roared off across the bridge into Dreamland, Raymond handed Jennifer a pile of exact change.

If you ever find yourself headed into Juárez, in a tiny white Corolla, dosed-up on animal opiates, tracking down a brother-in-arms, and in something of a rush, try to remember to keep some coins in your pocket; exact change, at the border crossing, is greatly appreciated, and U.S.-minted coinage, so useful in El Paso, is absolutely worthless inside The Box.

# 18

*I*t's a funny thing about the weather in Juárez. It was a perfectly lovely day, the Corolla was following a banged-up Dodge truck down Panamericana, staying four or five cars back so they wouldn't be spotted, headed south into the suburbs of Ciudad Juárez, toward one of those quiet residential neighborhoods where you'd basically fit right in, picture Albuquerque or Portland, though it's the sort of place, once you've uprooted your whole brood, you can't help but notice certain idiosyncrasies, real head-scratchers in fact, meaning genuine puzzlers, all kinds of Honey-is-that-what-I-think-it-is funny sorts of things; turns out the weather is the least of your worries. The weather outside was blue April spring, cloudless, low-80s, all you could ever ask, while inside Raymond it was not at all spring; his fever was back and his molars were chattering and he'd been tempted to ask Jen to turn on the heat, but instead sat there shivering and staring at nothing and radiating a distinct oh God unease. Had there been a doctor available for a brief consultation, not only would he have reassured us about the weather having a subjective component, but he might have explained the various treatment options for postoperative care on a sternum incision, perhaps the application of dexamethasone or Collatamp G or TELFA AMD Island dressing; in the end, given the likelihood of wound dehiscence and mediastinitis, he might have recommended the use of collagen-gentamicin, and he certainly would have suggested, with a sad subjective shake of his actual head, that the next time Raymond had a trench-war knife-fight, he consider seeing a doctor instead of a veterinarian. Given the strange red flames blazing trails across his chest, the fact that Raymond hasn't got the foggiest, as far as mediastinitis and wound dehiscence, and the general oozing of fluids and shit from his X-marked vet-stitched sutured-up sternum, this was not a good time to be asking about the weather; as far as Raymond's concerned, it's completely fucked up. And as for Jen, she couldn't care less about the goddamned weather. Why are we even talking about the weather in the first place, when Raymond's best friend and longtime partner, Eugene Patrick Booker, is wedged between henchmen, pretzelled atop the gearshift, in an altogether objectively uncomfortable position, and headed straight south into God knows what; she doesn't even want to get out of the fucking car, much less talk about the weather, lovely blue April or not. They'd followed the battered Ram over the Stanton Street Bridge, gone east on Malecon, running parallel to the 375 Border Highway, exited at Abraham Lincoln, made the left on Cuatro Siglos, stayed to the right at the bend onto Rafael Perez Serna, which turns out to be San Lorenzo, which turns out to be Tecnologico, which turns out to be Panamericana, which turns out, for no real reason, to be Highway 45, the Juárez portion of a 30,000-mile network of gravel and dust and bone-jarring pavement, all spliced together like the rebus strips in a dream, that thinks it's a kind of road called the Pan-American Highway, which may mean that the street names are themselves a little off; you find yourself thinking you know pretty much where you are, headed south on a street named Panamericana, well, be careful around here, it may be all in your head. If there's one thing we can all pretty much agree on, it's 11:15 on April 16, and if you haven't paid your taxes yet, they're basically overdue, you start thinking Hell no, it's the dead of winter, that's not their problem, your taxes are overdue, though with Raymond sitting there oozing shit, and red-flame-radiating inexplicable doctor jargon, he's not really thinking about the IRS; the weather around here is getting a little strange, it has in fact turned moderately alien, it may look all lovely and April blue and the-birds-are-singing springtime out, but that sort of weather is a meteorological condition; the weather in Juárez can go absolutely mental.

Which brings us to your new neighborhood. The bashed-in Magnum exited Panamericana onto Ramon Rivera Lara, made the right two blocks later at Calle Canario, and then a final right onto Calle Avanzaro, where it turned into a driveway maybe six houses down, with Jen gliding past to park up the block. Ray adjusted the side mirror and studied the truck, whose occupants didn't move for the longest time; perhaps they were waiting for someone to join them, perhaps they were still adjusting to the new atmospherics. The two men in trenchcoats sat particularly dormant, wearing wraparound shades and meaningless expressions, while Gene hung his head and let it swing side to side, the way a man will do when he's unhappy with himself, while at the same time acknowledging that this is not unexpected. The house itself, a single-story ranch that was painted a pale taupe with off-white trim, fell into that sort of "not quite this, not quite that" in-between category that realtors tend to dread, somewhere in the no-man's-land between "needs a loving touch" and "let's just face it, it's a total teardown." You'd recognize the yard if you saw it, it's that one on your block that's a real eyesore, where the weeds have run amok, and the roses died in the 1950s, and the lawn, if it's under there, has passed well beyond the point of needing a bag or two of Miracle Gro Turf Builder. You and the local Homeowners Association have already left several copies of the rules and regulations for community yard care on the concrete stoop, listing the usual requirements for we're-all-in-this-together maintenance and upkeep: mowing, weeding, edging, fertilization, insect control (the yard in back, in particular, has something of a problem involving swarms of flies), trimming, drainage, removal of dead growth, and so on and so forth, as well as the requirements for seeking Association approval prior to the installation of any item, visible or not, that might have an impact on local property values, all to no avail; not only have your detailed instructions been ignored, but the tenants have taken to carrying pearl-handled revolvers, which needless to say, is both heavily frowned upon and highly ostentatious in a middle-income suburb. What can you do? To make matters worse, this particular neighborhood has developed something of a bad reputation; imagine how you and the Homeowners group would feel about the discovery that, completely contrary to the stated rules, more than a few of the neighborhood homes were being used for the disposal of human bodies. The rules explicitly state, not to be too pedantic about it, "installation of any item, visible or not"; do these people really believe they can flaunt the rules, burying dozens of corpses in the untrimmed shrubbery? Somehow, and this is about the last thing you need, the pleasant 3-bedroom Colonial a half-mile over, at 3633 Calle Parsonieros, was now known widely as "The House of Death," and at the home on Pedregal, a cozy little cottage with an oversized yard, they've recently dug up 36 bodies. What are these people thinking? To top it all off, this eyesore on Avanzaro was only two blocks away from a very similar structure on Calle Cocoyoc, decorated since February with yellow EVIDENT Reflective Barrier Tape, with text reading LA LINEA DE LA POLICÍA NO CRUZA; while no one was complaining about the tape itself, an excellent choice for the securing of crime scenes, even during periods of low visibility, or the unlikely event of inclement weather (and an exceptionally good value, by the way, with a thousand-foot roll of 3" tape available for under $14), it was apparent that this was about the last straw; some heads needed to roll, if you'll pardon the expression. If only to protect local property values, there need to be a few basic policy changes made, effective more or less immediately: any house requiring more than three rolls (3,000') of crime scene tape must have written approval before the killing commences; torture victims, after 10 pm, must be bound and gagged and effectively silenced; severed body parts, including fingers, toes, tongues, and genitalia, must be buried in the holes with their corresponding corpses; headless bodies will no longer be allowed, without burying the remainders at least five feet under; and the explicit display of hacksawed heads, with gouged-out eyes and acid-burned face-flesh, is expressly forbidden, without prior review by the Architectural Committee. Failure to comply with any of the above will subject the homeowner to immediate expulsion, and a corresponding loss of Association privileges. That invitation you received to the Neighborhood Block Party? Consider it cancelled. We apologize for any inconvenience. Just so you know. Honestly, we apologize. We really and truly do. Honey, I'm sorry to keep asking this, but have you seen the kids?

Are you happy now? Of course you are; you would no more move to the suburbs of Juárez than you would to a cellblock in Sing Sing or San Quentin, and we, in any case, have just been killing a little time, in hopes that shivering Raymond's mind would soon clear; if Ray thinks the chattering of his fever-delirium teeth may be a Morse-coded message on how to get Gene out of this, he'll find out soon enough, if he doesn't begin to focus, that he's picking up random chatter and alien communiqués from somewhere in the vicinity of the Cartwheel Galaxy; the time had come for Ray to stop scanning deep space, take a few more Tramadol to cool down his fever, and begin to focus in on springing Gene loose from a deathtrap device that he would appear to have wandered into while Raymond, to put it bluntly, was sleeping on the job, a device that had hauled him from his yellow home in the Magoffin to a pale taupe ranch house in the suburbs of Juárez to his current position, on a mauve-washed driveway, at a 20-foot remove from death's colorless door; as far as Ray's concerned, he got Gene into this, and he fully intends to get Gene out. In order to get Gene out, of course, Raymond would need an exit plan, and Ray, right at the moment, might not make the best of exit planners, in fact he might not know there's a difference between *out* and *in deeper*: he was growing so woozy from loose-suture seepage, had such strange red trails leaking flames across his torso, and was so loaded down with animal opiates, on one of those birder-feeder drip-feed handheld contraptions, that he had no real clue that he was nowhere near the suburbs, he was headed into Dreamland, deep inside The Box, into a zone so jammed with experimental weapons systems and novel-explosives time-bombs and teleportation-transport vehicles and paranormal-warfare spatiotemporal logistical anomalies, that the only way *out* may be to *keep going in*. Ray downed a few pills, studied his side-view, made a brief mental note of Gene's tactical position, trapped behind lines in an enormous black vehicle that appeared to be waiting for the Commence Firing! signal, and was right in the middle of mapping out the battlespace, just trying to get a handle on the lay of the land, when he began to notice one or two little head-scratcher puzzlers that should have served as markers, signposts if you will, of a man wandering off into uncharted territory, and headed ever deeper into unmappable terrain. Why, for example, had maybe 200 crows, who should be flying circles in the blue suburban sky, walked up the block from the corner of Canario and Calle Avanzaro without so much as ruffling a single black feather? It's not like Ray had never seen a crow walk, but 200 crows, marching in formation?

When Ray made the mistake, understandable enough, of turning in his seat to see for himself, trying to figure out what the hell the crows were up to, the entire street was empty of avialan life-forms, an anomaly known locally as the Side-View-Mirror Crow, based on the same principle that states "objects in the mirror are closer than they appear," taken, evidently, to its antithetical extreme. Welcome to Dreamland, folks, enjoy the bumpy ride, but don't even bother with those phony-looking lap belts. Where the hell are we Ray? Not real sure. Somewhere just north of the Parque Hermanos. Beautiful place, lake full of ducks with those little two-man paddleboats, and a miniature electric train you can ride around the park. Sounds nice, Ray; let's get Eugene and maybe go for a picnic. Be a good idea, weren't for the fact that Gene may be a little large, might need the Ram to pull the electric train around, try to put him in one of those paddleboats, thing probably sink. Course that might not be the problem. I'm thinking maybe this shithole must be one of the Zeta safe houses. That dump we passed on Cocoyoc, the one with all the police tape? I'm guessing that's probably the house where they dug up nine or ten bodies. So safe is a somewhat relative term. How many dead would it take before they'd consider a house dangerous? Yeah, well, the place over on Pedregal, the one they found in April, seem to recall the counting stopped when they got to thirty or forty, little hard to count, trying to match up all of the body parts. Excellent, Ray, I've enjoyed our little excursion, now what do you say we go find that lake, paddle around in the boats awhile, maybe feed a few of the ducks. You're probably right, bet those ducks are good and hungry, though I'm not real sure about the lake itself, can't be much more than a couple of hundred yards wide, we wind up catching some RPG rounds, have to throw them in the lake, might not be good for the ducks' digestion. So what are you thinking? Wait for the mailman, pull Gene out of the truck while they're double-checking their water bill? Now you're talking, what we need's some sort of distraction. Maybe I take the Mossberg, shoot out the picture window, and you get Eugene into the Toyota, pick me up one block over, I cut through the yard, meet you out back. That sounds just fine, Ray, except for one or two things. Fuck you. You feel like having yourself a shitstorm firefight, I'm going over to the park and ride around on the little train.

And then, of all things, who should appear, and park out front, in a convenient location, but the no name grey Ford Fusion guy, also known as douchebag, or dickwad upon occasion, which are signifiers of something, possibly a derogatory nickname, though in a world where prominent assassins are known to answer to La Barbie, Douchebag isn't bad, particularly considering the ominous alternatives; Alfredo Beltran, for example, is known as El Mocho-mo, which may be an insect, notorious for its sting, or may be a home-cooked Sinaloan concoction involving boiled and shredded meat, a dish we're hoping, for all our sakes, is not considered appetizing, or in any way edible. Ray's eyes bugged out and zoomed in once or twice, like a character doing a double take in a Daffy Duck cartoon, although mindful of his recent experience with the regimental crows, and unwilling, at this point, to believe his own eyes, much less start believing in optical illusions, he stared into the side-view, in a state of disbelief, half-expecting Douchebag to sprout wings and fly. Douchebag exited the nondescript vehicle, popped open the trunk, and pulled out a large green Army-surplus duffel bag, a bag that was obviously difficult to lift, he nearly toppled sideways trying to come to grips with the weight of it, before staggering a little and righting himself, evidently getting some sort of a grip. We'll see about that. He paused for a moment, holding the bag with both hands, as though allotting a bit of time for a bellman to approach, and assist him with a luggage cart, and finding no one even remotely tied to the local hotel service sector, shuffled up the walk through the waist-high weeds, apparently unmindful of the dented-Magnum henchmen, apparently ignoring a little plaque on the wall, which must have read something like Casa Oblivion. As he wandered into the yard, looking vaguely uncertain, looking, frankly, like a douchebag who's come to the wrong address, maybe something about the yard care, or the condition of the flower-beds, or the faint but persistent odor of boiled and shredded meat, the truck suddenly sprang to life, which all things considered, is an interesting but perhaps inappropriate locution. A trenchcoat appeared from a driver's side door, holding what looked to be a Kalashnikov AK-40-something, and on second thought, given the absence of the distinctive Kalashnikov banana clip, and the ease with which its bearer was waving the thing around, was likely, more precisely, an AR-15, with telescoping stock, aircraft-grade aluminum receiver, and detachable magazine, an object so pure and light and well-adapted to its function, as a high-velocity life-to-death teleportation transport system, that it's Dreamland's correlative to Tinkerbell's magic wand, and while it doesn't use pixie dust as a projectile propellant, it'll get you to Never Never Land in the blink of an eye. If you're beginning to get the feeling that Dreamland sounds familiar, like a place you've been to visit in an animated film, and that the violence in Juárez seems so outlandish that it could only be happening in a 2-D cartoon, it's apparent that you and Douchebag have a lot in common, a topic we'll return to in about two hours; in the meantime, be advised, once our little tour is over, to reposition yourself well north of the border, or get mentally prepared to be thoroughly disabused. Out the passenger door went the other khaki coat, followed by poor Eugene, making a leg-over-the-gearshift awkward sort of exit, with something apparently objectively uncomfortable pressed against the rib bones that surround the thoracic cavity, and something subjective but equally uncomfortable apparently flying around inside him, butterflies maybe, beautiful little creatures that need to stay inside their cage. This sense of discomfort seemed to permeate the group: it wasn't at all clear that these men had things in common; their backgrounds and interests were widely divergent; the language barrier alone was a formidable problem; and they hadn't, in any event, been properly introduced. Douchebag paused on the untrimmed walk, as though contemplating a change to his de minimus nickname, perhaps to something more majestic in Pig Latin; a gunman waved his magic wand, casting a spell in vehement Henchman; and Gene just stood there shaking his head, from side to side, with a sad little smile, expressing himself as best he could, in the eloquent idiom of broken body-language. There was a brief linguistic standoff, inevitable in a sense, a clash of differing discourse worlds, a moment of cultural panic, before everyone suddenly realized that they all spoke perfect Gun, which means what it means wherever you are, even in 7-bit ASCII-code, or X-convention Esperanto. And all the while, Raymond sat in the car, stuck between worlds, between stillness and movement, waiting for the Tramadol to finally take hold, and align him at last with the general misalignment, since while everyone here knows perfectly well what a gun means in Human, it seems to mean something totally different when you're thinking, as Ray is, in Side-View-Mirror Crow.

Ray slouched in his seat, checked over his shoulder, and pulled Jen down, out of Tinkerbell's sightlines. Now what? It was time to get real, that much was apparent; take a fistful of Tramadol, and sit back and wait. No time like the present; Ray finished off his meal, checked his Steri-Strip adhesion and suture coherence, still sweating the small stuff, and started up his wind-in-the-face fever-reduction countdown; given all these opiates, and the need to somehow align himself with the local ballistic weather conditions, Ray was having visions of a rocket sweating LOX on the ultimate going-orbital blastoff launch pad, performing his time-and-temperature routine, counting things down toward absolute zero. The weather outside may be April warm and sunny, with springtime in the air and the bluebirds chirping and the sunlit *prunus avium* trees filling their branches with cherry blossoms, but Ray's mental temperature was growing a little chilly, and was slowly headed down toward morgue-slab cold, the temperature at which pure human-sympathy freezes, the combat-soldier's equivalent to the null point in Kelvin. Raymond, in short, was in no mood to die, without one or two of these bozos dying with him. If you're a paranormalist, of course, one of those reverse-engineering types who's lived on Groom Lake, and landed once or twice on the Cheshire Airstrip, and knows where the grey-alien bodies are buried, deep deep down under the Papoose Mountains, you're thinking there must be an easier way, in fact you're thinking that what Raymond really needs is a late model ceramics-armored Teleportation Transport Vehicle, maybe track down one of the locals who's a qualified operator, get Gene the hell out of there, just teleport him the fuck out; Raymond, you're thinking, should stay in the damn car, his brute-force pistol-grip shotgun solution has so little elegance its liable to get Gene killed. Unfortunately for Gene, the necessary devices, while available in the lab, just aren't ready for widespread use; the Department of Defense research, run at Site 4 under grant out of DARPA, on quantum-mechanics transport systems, has only produced a bench-test model suitable for small white lab mice, weighing up to 90 grams, and not only is Gene Booker, who weighs more in the neighborhood of

120,000, somewhat over the 90-gram weight limit, but the rapturous little mice, which were simultaneously converted to photons of light, and transported through a tube filled with hydrogen gases, were only able to travel 13.7 meters, which is well within range of an AR-15. What Gene really needs is the battlefield version, capable of teleporting full-grown soldiers, with 50-pound packs and assorted gear, using quantum-based interstitial matter-to-photon conversion systems, and one hell of an oversized hydrogen tube, and this one won't be battle-tested and stocked on the shelves of the Dreamland supply room and available at a gun show for a good two thousand years. While it's readily apparent that modern human warfare is, among other things, the Mother of All Inventions, and that Mom is always open to novel methodologies, we would appear to have reached the limits of our current capabilities, and may have to go back to Ray's brute-force approach. So why have we got Raymond, who still hasn't moved, hooked up to some sort of telepathic cyro-cooler, harnessing the energy of the combat-soldier's mind to cool the whole yard, butterflies, cherry blossoms, bird-chirps and all, down to around zero point nothing Kelvin, a temperature at which pure hydrogen freezes, and the crows start throwing off black-body radiation, and threatening us all with an ultraviolet catastrophe? Deep deep down the temperature scale, near minus 273.15 Celsius, where entropy vanishes, and molecular motion ceases, and every crystal lattice structure is infinitely ordered, lies the land of super-conductivity and superfluidity, out in the realm of the Boomerang Nebula, right next door to the zero point of energy, where quantum mechanics physics-mysteries finally rule the firmament, filling the world with boson vortices and wave-duality photon substances and tau-neutrino lepton particles haunted by Popov ghosts, meaning matter has gone completely nonlinear, and quantum effects like zero gravity and spontaneous levitation systems and teleportation photon vehicles are viable at last on a macroscopic scale. If there's one thing we know about Eugene Patrick Booker, we know that he's constructed on a macroscopic scale, and all we need to do is pump him full of rubidium, cool him way down, meaning way the hell down, and sweep him with a readily available Feshbach-resonance energy process, using a spin-flip collision-producing shit-starts-to-happen magnetic field, which will turn him into Super Atoms that implode into nothingness, which as far as Gene's concerned, would make him disappear. Gene, at this point, would be able to stop a light beam; an AR-15, firing macroscopic bullets, would be no match at all for such a Bose-Einstein condensate, though Eugene himself, converted into a series of tricky boson-vortex mathematical equations, and essentially a complete black hole to himself, would probably be having some personal issues, and no hope at all of examining his own feelings. With Gene now a quantum effect, apt to turn up literally anywhere, the trick, in this case, would be the guidance system, which is where the hydrogen tubing comes in, since according to Heisenberg's meticulous calculations, deep deep down in his matrix mechanics, Gene could wind up in the outer reaches of the constellation Virgo, spiraling around the Sombrero Galaxy, or in astronomer's parlance, M104. All things considered, Gene's in fairly good shape here, though by now it must be blindingly obvious that *you*, we're afraid, will have to take it from *here*, as *we*, evidently, are a verbal construct, a kind of cryogenic bird-chirp, a thing made of words: you open up the Yellow Pages, looking for hydrogen tubing, trying to get Gene to stabilize, in the backseat of the car, and it suddenly occurs to you that there are one or two little problems, beginning with the fact that, despite your good intentions, Gene's about to backfire on you, becoming a Supernova, a mass of undetectable but rapidly expanding 2-bonded rubidium atoms, meaning your whole Bose-Einstein condensate, recently known as Eugene Booker, has exploded into nothingness and utterly vanished, taking out the car, this lovely suburban neighborhood, and the whole damn solar system, oh God, I didn't know. We warned you not to fool around with this shit, you and your fucking rubidium, now look what you've gone and done: not only has our own whirling solar system vanished, but this whole verbal construct, butterflies, leptons, bird-chirps and all, has been blown to oblivion, and simply disappeared.

Which brings us back to time machines. Now you might think it best to send Ray off toward the distant future, bring back the quantum-mechanics, battle-hardened, transport system, from somewhere in the fifth millennium, where there are interstitial photon-soldiers flying around battlefields everywhere. You ask Ray, he just wants to turn the clock back a day or two at most, or maybe, come to think of it, make it like 15 years. But time waits for no man, not in a place like Ciudad Juárez, *tempus fugit, momento mori*, Ay fleeth the time, it will no man abyde; time flies like a crow here, out over the Lomas de Poleo wasteland, and you got any particularly bright new ideas, like how to kill time without wasting eternity, better show us the new equations, they'll need to be double-checked. Otherwise, stay out of this, Raymond's head is slowly filling with cryocooler opiates, and his current implementation plan, aside from taking the Mossberg out and shooting the flying bird, is to wait until the drugs have cooled him down to next to nothing, and walk into the Death House, and make the time stand still. In the meantime, Ray is thinking. What are you thinking, Ray? Thinking it might be nice, go back about 15 years, rethink a few decisions, coming out of the goddamn Army, thinking it might be a good idea I maybe try a different life or something. No, I mean about finding a way to get Gene, like, out of this, before it's, you know, too late. Wouldn't be too late I go back about 15 years, stay away from wounded trees, buy my drinks in Phoenix instead of El Arbolito, forget all the shit I learned about following fucking orders, someone hands me a gun, I hand the damn thing back, or take it out in the acacia brush, bring along my bird dog, time starts to fly, I stop it with some buckshot, then maybe find a little shade tree that's not all crooked and demented looking, have a smoke and watch the clouds go by, let my dog go hunting for the wounded bird, maybe bring me some of the good times back, they're probably back there somewhere. Come to think of it, I go back far enough, maybe could throw a little surprise party for my dad's 40th birthday, keep him and Mom off of the icy roads into Albuquerque, for one fucking night, they can drive in when the sun is out and it's nice and warm and the pavement's dry, and it's not too late for a lot of things, once the roads are good and dry. Raymond's misaligned all right, but it's the wrong misalignment. Lovely, Ray, particularly for a guy whose file name is Blackjack. But what about right now, not 25 years ago? Shit, you're right, my dad would be 65 right now, March 19th, he and Mom weren't out driving in the sleet with a six-pack or two under his belt, son of a bitch, you're right, 25 years, March 19th, fucking roads were a mess that night, shouldn't 'a let him drive. You remind me of him, I tell you that? I thought you told me your dad was a drunk. Yeah, he was a drunk all right, sat around the yard drinking beer all day, talking to the dogs, remembering the good old days. Hell of a guy though. Couldn't help but love him, I might have been just a kid and all, I didn't know shit, but I knew what the hell he really was, he was sure as shit a drunk, you got that right, son of a bitch could drink a case of beer, just smokin' a brisket on his homemade smoker, but you ever needed a friend or something, that's what he really was. You remind me of him all right, found some good in everyone, like you helping me out with retrieving Eugene, not asking too many questions. Before it's too late, Ray, what do you say we get Gene back before we're both 65, and it's too damn late. I tell you what, Jen, I live to be 65, I'll buy us both a couple of six-packs, we can sit in the yard and talk to the dogs. Be nice to have a future. Give us both something to look back on, eh Ray? Not a bad idea. What do you say we go get Eugene, maybe talk about the future later?

One turn down, one torque tighter, one last small bundle of Tramadol molecules on the Mu-opioid receptor sites, and an El Paso gunman, even a gunman with qualms, a man who's been off in fantasyland, dreaming of having some sentimental future, finally goes round the last little bend, the orthogonal curve, the squared-off circle, and finds himself at last at absolute zero, in the pluperfect Now, the ultimate *plus quam perfectum*, where everything that's about to happen already has, and it seems a little late to start talking about having a future. Raymond pulled the pistol-grip rifled-and-choked Mossberg from the surprisingly spacious Corolla trunk, wiped down the heat shield and slide-action pump handle with a bit of clean white cloth he kept in his pocket, double-checked that the shell magazine was fully 8-shot loaded, and then stood there for a moment, grinding his teeth, in the manner of a professional whose magazine is loaded with just the sort of garbage only an amateur would use; instead of his preference, a load of Brenneke Gold Magnum pre-rifled slugs, he was stuck with yesterday's shotgun shells, the triple-decker videogame stuff with large lead pellets, insisted upon by Gomez for reasons of his own, leaving Ray holding a weapon, a black-on-black Mossberg pistol-grip Cruiser, full of reasons to think his boss was a load of pure horseshit. If you aimed the customized Mossberg at the side of a barn, and fired one of these pellet-shells through the rifled twenty-inch barrel, the result would be a round, hollow, connect-the-dots O-type of pattern, meaning not the ideal scatter for inflicting maximum carnage, instead of the perfectly solid, Gaussian-distributed, absence created by an un-rifled blast, meaning basically a big ol' hole in the side of the barn. When he'd explained this to Gomez, how the rifling on the Mossberg tended to hollow out the pellet scatter, the banker had just laughed. "If the guy's still alive and complaining about the scatter pattern of lead in his chest, tell him that's his share of the IPO profits, then get up nice and close and blow off his head." It wouldn't have made much sense, under the circumstances, for Raymond to have attempted a detailed explanation as to why the helical-rifling on the militarized Mossberg would produce the letter O, not the number 0, if fired into the center of Douchebag's chest; all things considered, from two feet away, with the Briley conical choke squeezing the shot pattern down, the difference between an O and a zero would be minimal, and easily overlooked in the remains of Douchebag's head. As Ray loaded a round through the Mossberg's ejection port directly into the chamber, he was not, however, unaware of what he had: a 9-shot pump-action Briley-choked-loadful of possibly unfortunate alphanumeric ambiguity; one of the Zeta guys with Gene finds an O on his vest, gets a smile on his face, as opposed to say a plain round nothing in his head, and opens up firing, Ray was going to wish he had the Brenneke slugs, things could stop a bear or put a hole in an engine block, a nice solid hole that didn't take much explaining, and with no need at all for disambiguation. In any case, it was a moot point now; you go with what you got, hope the message is obvious. Ray directed Jen to a corner of the park, told her to wait for him, he was going to get Eugene, and Jen rolled away in her sensible Toyota, pretending she half-believed there was a reason for her to wait. Having no real interest in approaching the house from the front, where a full-grown man was playing with a wand, Ray cut through the yard directly in front of him, needing to find a way to go forward by going sideways, and then going house to house, over chain link and brick, through backyards full of chicken coops, and let's-hope-not guard dogs, and stealthy-looking tomcats, stalking dead squirrels, toward an ultimate destination that was swarming with something, blowflies maybe, hideous little creatures that we wish would go away. Invisible black turkey vultures circled overhead, making O's or maybe zeros in the cloudless Juárez infinite ceiling, and while it may well be true that Ray was late filing his taxes, he'd owe next to nothing if the vultures had it right.

When Raymond reached the edge of the first house in front of him, with the Mossberg at his side and out of Tinkerbell's sight-lines, he encountered an immediate architectural problem. What-ever real authority the local Neighborhood Association thought they wielded, here in the Cuernavaca de Juárez middle-income subdivision, it was apparent that their rules were being flaunted with impunity. The house itself, a two-story assemblage made of stucco and brick, was constructed in three multicolored sections that must have been tacked on indiscriminately over the years, with no rhyme or reason other than adding more space; the mother-in-law moves in, then a grumpy aging uncle, followed by six distant cousins you never knew you knew, there is very little choice but to keep on building, and that they had done, to an alarming degree. The Architectural Committee's explicit specifications, particularly on setbacks from the property line, had been completely ignored; the gap between houses, which should have been ten feet, was more like ten inches. Ray held the shotgun in his left hand by the barrel, and with his arm fully extended, turned sideways in the yard, sucked in his breath, and began to inch his way forward through the ten-inch gap. About fifteen feet in, the pink stucco wall on his immediate left began to lean improbably over toward the brick house on his right, narrowing the passageway at the level of his head to more like two inches, forcing Ray down on his side to wriggle through the opening at the base of the homes, with the shotgun on the ground being pushed along in front of him. The thirty feet of squirming that brought him at last to the backyards of the houses left him gasping for breath, with the Steri-Strips long gone and his X-wounds oozing; he'd also managed to scrape most of the tissue off of the knuckles, without so much as feeling it, on a bleeding left hand. His plan at this point, vaulting over the backyard wall, dash-ing through the stacked-up chicken coops, and continuing forward toward the swarming flies, might well have worked in a suburb of Albuquerque, but here in Juárez he faced a different reality, a verti-cal wall of brick that Raymond might easily have pole-vaulted over, if it weren't for the fact that the thirty-inch Mossberg was about, give or take, fourteen feet too short. Now what? Fortunately for Ray, dead straight ahead of him, up a concrete walk, must lie the rear yards of the next set of houses, the houses facing the street that ran parallel to Avanzaro; unfortunately for Ray, between his yard and the next one, someone must have planted a hedge against intrusion, made of forty-foot tall foot-thick yew trees, that he might need a machete and a chainsaw to get through; fortunately for Ray, the concrete walkway, making a beeline for the trees in a fifty-foot dash, also made a fairly good long-jump runway, such that by the time he hit the hedge in a head-first dive, he was traveling so rapidly that a bullet might have stopped him, but certainly not a bunch of gnarly old trees; unfortunately for Ray, his intrusion upon the hedge had not gone undetected, and his passage through the trees had not gone smoothly, such that by the time he hit the ground in the next yard on, the Rockford Shadow Plaid that covered his damaged torso appeared to have been attacked from the rear by a badger, leaving half-inch claw-marks sunk into his back, making final preparations to initiate bleeding. This next set of houses, also straight ahead of him up a concrete walk, and still facing the street that ran parallel to Avanzaro, had the advantage of being at least four feet apart, but the concrete-block wall that divided the rear yards was maybe twelve feet tall, and the gap between the wall and the house whose rear yard he was currently stranded in was guarded by a gate, made of twelve feet of chain-link, topped off with fresh rolls of glittering concertina wire, musically named but second-thought provoking. Ray tried the padlock with predictable results, and was faced with two choices: either dive back through the trees, and wriggle back the way he came, which had taken a good two or three minutes' worth of wriggling, and had cost him a good deal of back flesh in the process; or scale the chain-link fence, Mossberg and all, and try to exit between houses without his sutures exploding. He stuffed the black shotgun, pistol-grip first, halfway down his jeans in the back, and started in climbing, reaching the level of the concertina problem in two quick moves. It was only at this point, while studying the gleaming razors of the intertwined coils, and with the barrel of the Mossberg pistol-grip Cruiser pointed straight up vertically at the back of his head, that he remembered he'd forgotten to check the status of the safety, so conveniently placed at the top of the receiver tang, so utterly useless if it were set on Fire. Sloppiness with weapons; totally unacceptable. Holding on to the chain link with a stucco-scraped hand, he leaned his badgered back away from the razor wire, shoved a free arm down his pants along the Mossberg heat shield, felt along the receiver at the top of the grip, and found, to his amazement, and then slowly mounting outrage, well…nothing, no safety button, no detent plate, no safety ball or spring, nothing even resembling the most rudimentary safety. The Mossberg had performed its famous "disappearing safety button" trick, caused by a single screw coming loose from its threading through the top of the safety block, no doubt sending the button flying, along with all of its ancillary parts; a $16 replacement assembly, designed by Brownell out of high-grade aluminum, had been scoffed at by Gomez as a frivolous expense. "Cowards die many times before their deaths. The valiant never taste of death but once. Draw thy tool. My naked weapon is out. What possible use would you have for a safety? Your job is to fire weapons, not to prevent them from firing." Ray removed a good foot's worth of arm from the back of his pants, leaving another fifteen inches of exposed Mossberg shotgun barrel, along with its extension tube and gracefully vented heat shield, pointing straight up, completely unsafetied, at the center of the back of his unhelmeted head. "Yes Sir, that's just how we found him, looks like the shotgun blew an O, or perhaps a zero, right in the center of the back of his head." "Good work, Officer; which one of your men planted the weapon?" "No, Sir, the weapon wasn't planted; this gringo must have fired the weapon upon himself." "Permit me to suggest, for recording purposes, that this little incident be reported as a suicide, with a suicide note found upon his person. I will leave it to your discretion whether the note is said to have read zero or O, though I personally prefer the zero as more appropriate for such an incident, and possibly less subject to open interpretation." "Of course, Sir, as you wish. I will see to it right away." "A most succinct note, full of wit and yet brevity; the gentleman has my deepest respect."

Ray regathered himself, pushed Gomez and most of his imaginary police force out of his woozy and opiated head, adjusted his time and temperature settings back to T minus absolute zero and counting, and focused once again on the razor-wire problem, two

closely interwoven helical spirals, maybe three feet thick, like
a DNA molecule that had mutated dangerously. In the end, the
disappearing safety button was completely irrelevant; if Raymond
took a spill from the top of the gate, and landed on the Mossberg,
his Edmunds-family DNA would be scattered all over everything,
safety on or not, and the disappearing safety trick would likely be
overlooked. As he studied the problem from a number of possible
angles, his heavily cooled blood seemed to be pounding down the
seconds, knowing that Eugene was now likely inside the house,
with a gun up nice and close to a Eugene-Patrick-Booker-specific
oversized cranium, though he might soon be identifiable only by
his dental records, or through Polymerase Chain Reaction tests on
a Booker-specific genome fragment. Raymond, in short, was running low on time, and beginning to think things he couldn't possibly think; Ray knows nothing about genome fragments, much less
Polymerase Chain Reaction testing; from this point forward, it's safe
to assume that Raymond is fully capable of thinking almost anything, as Raymond himself is in the same frame of mind as that guy
you saw in a revival tent, speaking in tongues, a paranormal phenomenon known as glossolalia, although in this case Raymond's
actual state produces a phenomenon known as xenoglossia, where
fully formed discourse worlds are apt to spring to mind for no real
reason, other than that we said so. Without much regard for his
corporeal integrity, Ray planted his leg in the tangle of wire, took
hold of a neighboring second-story window ledge, and pulled himself through to hang and then drop, leaving long strips of leg flesh
and denim amid the coils, and landing somewhat awkwardly on a
hominid-specific synovial hinge, or in this case, more specifically,
his own right ankle. As his ankle began to balloon and the razor cuts
to bleed, Ray hobbled shadeless into the blinding Juárez high-noon
day, pulling the Mossberg 500 from the back of his jeans, slouch-
ing up Calle Albatros toward the Calle Canario intersection, and
counting the houses down backwards from eight, hoping to align
himself, at least numerically, with Tinkerbell's small but dangerous safe house. Somewhere along the way, however, maybe three
houses into his backwards countdown, Ray had a brief but complex
encounter with a discourse world he couldn't possibly be aware of,
a preview, if you will, of what lies ahead, as he travels ever deeper

into uncharted territory, and deeper into Dreamland's unmappable terrain. What began as a simple subtraction procedure turned into a moment of mathematical panic, as he noted that the houses on this parallel street did not align at all with the houses on Avanzaro; his plan to rely on a simple isomorphism, by counting down from eight in a one-to-one correspondence, made no sense at all in a polymorphic universe; there might well be some sort of Abelian commutative group, some monoid homomorphic structure-preserving mapping, at work between the houses on the parallel streets, but just as Ray was readying an n-dimensional Hilbert space, whose scalar inner product would be a standard Hermitian form, he discovered that it was simpler just to take a wild guess, and hope that he found a yard that looked strikingly likely, maybe a yard full of recently shoveled piles of bloody dirt. He picked a house at random, or more likely the sort of house that the neighbors kept their distance from, with a well-swept concrete walk, and an absence of concertina wire, and steadied himself at last, as though ready to go to work. Oh, really? And what sort of work do you do, Ray? Fascinating, fascinating. Can someone get this man a chair and a cup of black coffee?

An objective observer, asked to comment on the scene, might have noted that Raymond appeared to be leaking: his stucco-stripped hand was covered with blood; the razor-wired leg-flesh was flayed-off and dripping; his back was a byzantine roadmap of claw-marks; and the Rockport Shadow Plaid, previously blue and green, was no longer plaid, it was an ooze-soaked shade of bloody-brownish. Raymond paused for a moment with his hand on his heart, maybe checking a chest wound for mediastinitis, or maybe saying the Pledge of Allegiance to something, though certainly not to the familiar Stars and Stripes; Trip, to be honest, was not all there, he was somewhere out wandering in the mental Dakotas, perhaps back in the days of the Black Hills War, maybe the Battle of Rosebud or the Little Big Horn, known in the parlance of the relevant Native Americans as the Battle of Greasy Grass. Greasy Grass? Who knows. Maybe the stuff was slippery or something. As far as Juárez was concerned, Raymond had gone native, it's just that the natives were not from around here; with blood-red warpaint streaking his face, and some Sun Dance coyote sutures torqued-up and howling, and maybe one or two sacred eagle feathers flying from his head,

Raymond was out alone in the unincorporated Territories, hunting
vanishing bison down a Juárez street. Doctor, Ray, go find a doctor; you keep this up, you'll be dining with the crows. Raymond, in
short, was losing a lot of blood, objectively speaking, though Ray,
at the moment, pumped-up on adrenaline and animal druggery,
maybe choking down the last of a wolf pituitary, was not thinking objectively, he was probably thinking in something like native
Cheyenne, an Algonquin language related to Arapaho, although
the name Cheyenne, unfortunately for the natives, is not actually a
word in the language of the Cheyenne; the Cheyenne knew themselves by the Cheyenne word Tsitsistas, Cheyenne itself was a Sioux
word for Cree, and if Raymond was feeling maybe twenty pounds
lighter, like a man who hasn't eaten much since the ve'ho'e (think
white man) swarmed his tribal lands, this may, in the end, be an
error on our part, a failure to account for the practical impact of an
exonymic discourse on a xenoglossaic trance; with Ray thinking in
Cheyenne when it turns out he's Cree, rapidly leaking body fluids
through holes in his torso, and in need, not of bison meat, but of an
IV drip and a blood transfusion, he might have been better off, from
a practical perspective, forgetting about Cheyenne and learning the
Cree word for doctor, and getting the hell out of the mental Dakotas, and maybe setting out in search of Juárez General; though,
boy, come to look it up, the Cree word for doctor, maskihkiwiyiniw,
is one hell of a mouthful, not the easiest word to pronounce in a
Juárez taxi, particularly with a mouthful of your own warm blood.
And then Ray, at long last, looked down at the shotgun, took hold
of the pistol grip, put a hand on the heat shield, and finally started
thinking in Professional Soldier, a language that we civilians know
little or nothing of, though the Tsitsistas would have called him a
notaxe, or warrior, meaning a man who is ready for the eve'otse, or
warpath, in perfect alignment with the Great and Ancient Trail,
toward complete and total and absolute mayhem, or in Juárez hack-
sawed-bodies parlance, business as usual. Bleeding and hobbling,
crammed full of Tramadol, with his temperature hovering around
absolute zero, Ray strolled up the walk with a pistol-grip shotgun,
black on the barrel, black on the heat shield, black on the synthetic slide-action pump handle, black all over, absolutely black, and
found what he was looking for, just at this moment, a sweet little

ranch house painted a pale taupe.

Raymond peered over the wall, draped with purple bougainvillea, and found a smallish backyard, with a carelessly tended garden: a number of deep holes, of the usual dimensions; a similar number of dark mounds of topsoil; and a small patch of flowers, near the gate on the far wall, that it's safe to assume have been deliberately planted, one part white jasmine blossoms and two parts Easter lilies, the former a lovely image of peace with oneself, biding their time until the moment comes to pick them, and the latter the perfect picture of a parasite-riddled wreck, slowing losing the battle against aphid infestation. This must be the place all right, not that we'd recommend it, unless of course you're a morpho-dipterologist, with a particular interest in Calliphoridae; just between us, while we're all of course proud of your pioneering work on the role played by blow-flies in human decomposition, it might be best for all concerned if you kept your findings to yourself for the moment. Ray scaled the wall, gripping the tangle of bougainvillea, and landed in a crouch behind a small Apache Pine, a peculiar-looking conifer, native to the area, with nearly foot-long pine needles and spiny purple pine-cones and so few branches that it didn't, on first sight, even appear to be a tree, it looked like a pile of pine needles with phantom-limb syndrome. A small Apache pine? A pale green conifer, named after a tribe of Indians, that appears to be a few limbs short of a tree? On second thought, let's just ignore this. With Ray losing pieces of himself bit by bit, slowly coming apart at the vet-sutured seams, and trying to stay focused on springing Gene loose from a threadbare plot device known as the deathtrap, about the last thing he needs, at this particular juncture, is to follow a little pine tree off across the Pecos, and off the reservation altogether, off on yet another of his xeno-glossaic tangents, and yet another raid into Exonymic Discourse territory: while it's apparent that the Apache tribes are at least in the right neighborhood, it turns out the Apaches called themselves the N'de, and that Apache is a Zuni word for You're Our Mortal Enemy, so wading across the Pecos with some mental Mescaleros wouldn't have helped at all, he'd be right back where he started, trying to think in smoke signals and telling himself wolf-fire stories, and all the while it turns out he's at war with himself, slowly losing the battle against phantom-Raymond syndrome. Trip's begin-

ning to look a little ghostly already, and he doesn't need a pine tree
to tell him where he's headed. Ray gripped the Mossberg, sniffed
once or twice, caught just a whiff of something vaguely familiar,
and studied the rear portion of the taupe-colored house, searching
for the source of this familiar-smelling whiff. A pair of sliding doors
looked out on the patio, a recently poured slab of unwashed concrete, decorated in the manner of a suburban couple who enjoy the
occasional evening of outdoor dining, despite the inconvenience of
blowfly swarms, and the hair-raising odor of decomposing bodies: a
five-piece Alfresco Manchego mosaic-tiled dining set, improbably
adorned with linens and candles; a Weber One Touch Black Globe
Grill, an equally improbable bit of narrative adornment, since the
last thing we need in a Juárez garden is that fishy smell you get
from a literary emblem; a canvas-covered loveseat, with two matching chairs, drenched in something sticky, like barbecue sauce, although given the way the blowflies are behaving, and the fact that
this sticky stuff smells vaguely metallic, we'd be willing to entertain
other possibilities; and a stainless steel box, a commercial Bradley
meat smoker, with its smoke tower loaded, for cold-smoker cooking, with Bradley's famous secret recipe smoke bisquettes. A meat
smoker? Secret recipe smoke bisquettes? Okay, you're right, we've
gone too far, an inexcusable lapse in judgment on our part; let's just
pretend that this isn't here; the last thing we need in a Juárez garden
is a piece of cold-smoked meat that makes your hair stand on end.

What Ray smelled, in any case, wasn't coming from a smoker,
or even from a flowerbed, it was coming from the past: part brick-
laying smell, his father mixing the mortar with pleasant-smelling
quicklime powder; part celery stalks, Dad holstering a shotgun and
drinking spicy Bloody Marys, in the frosty-November bird-dogs-
barking quail-dawn-pinkish extraordinary morning. Ray crawled
along the bougainvillea wall to a small side window, open to let
some Juárez air in, open to let some memories drift out, the crisp
green smell of stalk-snapped celery, and spending first light in the
robin's egg dawn; or maybe it was the root of the osha plant, esto
huele como el pasado, the smell of distant boxing memories, and
drifting through twilight, making the long journey back from a
world-class pounding; the smell that brings the bears around, soaking up sunlight, after spending all winter in a dream-ravaged cav-

ern, maybe searching for roots they can sink their teeth in, maybe searching for proof that the world's still there. He peaked above the window sill, and found seven men seated around a large square coffee table, in a loose-knit circle, a zero or an O, at the center of which was a bottle of something, Osha Extract, chuchupaste, and a squat uncorked bottle of Tequila Orendain. Chuchos, they were getting ready to drink chuchos, the drink his old boxing mentor, El Conejo, had taught him to drink as a cure-all for what ails you, the shaman brew from his X-marks-the-spot, tic-tac-toe, knife-fight encounter, at El Arbolito in the Mariscal, the Bar of the Wounded and Drifting Tree. Whiskey Tango Foxtrot? Ray peaked again, saw Gene on a footstool, seated at 2 o'clock, and Douchebag in an easy chair, at maybe at most 10:30. Tinkerbell was sitting at about high noon, still wearing his trenchcoat but missing his wand, and shaking his head from side to side, a little like Gene while he sat in the Magnum, only this man was having some real doubts about himself, and finding self-doubt to be a foreign concept. Ray bobbed down, resting his chin on the Mossberg, not knowing what to think, not even knowing he didn't know, just drawing a complete and total mental blank, and then started in on doing the math, some simultaneous algebraic equations, trying to solve for something, like what the fuck, why was he doing high school math, with too few equations, and a few too many complete unknowns? Gene; Douchebag; Tinkerbell, wandless; his trench-coated twin on a backward-facing couch, uncomfortably seated at around 4:20; and three strange new variables that couldn't be solved for, at least not with the sound of seven men breathing, and one constant ticking sound, meaning something ticking and driving him crazy, like who the hell are these people, and what the fuck is that ticking sound? Ray quick-peaked over the window ledge, toward the fireplace down at the end of the room, and saw what it was, ticking and constant, one of Gomez' antique ornamental clocks.

Gomez must have had dozens of these things, mantel clocks with animal pairs: golden songbirds on yesterday's skeleton clock, peering through the moment in opposite directions; green-onyx carved dolphins, holding up the clock dial on their twin stone snouts, like they were playing with a beach ball in a porpoise show at Sea World, getting ready to trade what remains of eternity for a couple of mackerel and a handful of squid; and in the current case, of the irritating clock, metallic horses, both of them rearing, and in a hurry to move, like let's get the fuck OUT of here, meaning right fucking NOW, one of them headed, wild-eyed, forward, and the other, equally wild-eyed, apparently going back. Gomez and his clocks; they made Ray's head pound; Trip could maybe use a minute between rounds, sit on his stool, let the cutman work on him, with an adrenaline-soaked Q-tip and a piece of clean white gauze. We're guessing Ray's had to sit through more than one of Gomez' lectures, after some stupid mistake he'd made repeatedly, through lax observation and poor time-management, walking into a room he'd have preferred to be exiting, a lecture not irrelevant to the current situation, on the subject of Janus, the two-headed cliché, of Greek mythology and ancient superstition, the god of gates and doorways and entries, and narrow escapes, when you needed a good out; the god of auspicious beginnings and also of oh shit not this again endings; the god of the progression from the past into the future, if it turns out you're good and somehow your luck holds; the god of the planting and the harvesting also, if it turns out your luck has finally run out. Look both ways before crossing a threshold, watch what you're getting into, like be watching the fuck out, or it's always already the beginning of the ending, and it's too late now to be checking the clock. Ray stayed huddled, having taken a knee, beneath the off-white trim of the window casement, waiting for someone to start in explaining, and all he could hear was the ticking of the clock. The actual timepiece, an antique French Statuary Mantel Clock, cast in rose-gold aluminum, and made by Japy Freres & Cie in Beaucourt, France, showed a young man holding twin horses by the reins, a posture he'd maintained since 1870, despite all the evidence that it was time to move on, as man grew more savage with each chiming hour, and despite his horses' wild-eyed awareness that fleeing ticking time was their only imperative. What Ray was listening to, right at this moment, was coming from the heart of the relentless clock, where a deadbeat escapement movement, with its tick-tock locking faces, was counting down the teeth, severely raked and pointed, on a small round escape wheel, telling the world an age-old story about time itself slowly running out. No one moved or spoke; it was as if they were sitting and waiting for someone, or maybe they were waiting for the clock to run down, and tell them it was time for the endings to commence. As the clock spring uncoiled, it wound Ray tighter, with the hairspring in his chest keyed-up on adrenaline, and torqued-up tight, to the inch-pound threshold, under long-lever loading from an opioid analgesic; he felt like he was waiting for the timekeeper's bell, or maybe for his sutures to finally start popping. This is not to say that Ray's at all misaligned, even if he and the clock were wound backwards; if you got a quick look at that shotgun he's holding, you'd know that he's aligned with the general misalignment, the thing was all black and vicious looking, Briley-choked and gunsmith-rifled and pump-action-tubefeed-triple-decker loaded, its pistol-grip backed by a 9-shot load. Given half a chance, he'd be sighting down the Mossberg barrel, equipped with a Ghost Ring Sight Kit assembly, an O up front, nice and close on the receiver tang, and a square post down at the business end of the weapon, ready to square things up and right some misalignment and zero in on anything, make a ghost out of the first thing that got out of line.

Of course Raymond, at the moment, had nothing at all to shoot at; he didn't need to be told that time's a-fucking wasting, he needed someone to speak up and tell him what to shoot. He stared in over the window ledge, trying to see what all the silence was about, and saw Gene at 2 o'clock, his mouth, hands, and feet wrapped with clear plastic shipping tape; Tinkerbell at noon, similarly prepped, quietly awaiting a pick-up by the parcel post; and Douchebag, at 10:30 or so, apparently unprepared to say or do much of anything, sitting there stupidly with his mouth hanging open, ready to start drooling or trickling warm blood. At 9 and 3 sat men with arms, automatic Beretta 93Rs, their foldable foregrips precisely unfolded, their burst-fire zinc-steel alloy barrels elegantly vented to prevent overheating, the machine-pistol equivalent of a bespoke suit; at 4:20 and 6, Ray had a good clear view of the backs of two men, telling him nothing he didn't already know, that the AR-15 was upright between them, stuck in the couch, between two cushions, and that the man at 4:20, Tinkerbell's twin, had his arms stuffed behind him in an awkward position, and a loose-fitting dry-cleaning garment-bag of plastic, breathing in and out, over the top of his head. Oh, and two final notes: dead center in the middle of the squared-up

coffee table stood a single round glass, one-eighth full of chuchupaste, osha extract, the source of the celery smell, and memories of
wounded trees; and against the far back wall behind the Tinkerbell
parcel sat two open sacks of calcium oxide, CaO, burnt lime or
quicklime, quick in the sense that the stuff's half-alive, and rapidly
absorbing carbon dioxide, a source of pleasant memories of childhood if you're lucky, an aid to irreversible decomposition if you're
not. There was a sense of unreality about the whole ticking scene,
like Ray was watching from the wings for a curtain to go up, and
the play to begin, and the actors to start assuming the lives of their
characters. The notional silence, under the circumstances, was certainly puzzling; it was possible, of course, that the actors were at
odds, with some of them searching for psychological motives, doing some "as if" substitutions and deep emotional recall, following
Strasberg and Stanislavski; and others hunting around within the
current Given Circumstances, in the mode of Stella Adler, searching for tasks, wants, and needs, and silenced by the knowledge that,
after so many years of training, we are what we do, not what we say;
and still others, if this were possible, doing Meisner exercises, seeking truthful spontaneity through immersion in the moment, striving to live truthfully under imaginary circumstances, and unwilling to break the silence until their exercises were complete. Life in
Juárez is hard enough, without having to live it as a method actor;
no wonder these poor people were unable to even speak. Or maybe
they were simply waiting for the houselights to dim, and the stage
manager to come on and make a little welcome speech, reminding
the audience to take a last look around, and locate the nearest fire
exit; to remain in their seats until the curtain comes down, and the
theatre erupts in spontaneous combustion; and to turn off their cell
phones and electronic devices, once and for all, or else.

Imagine our surprise, thinking Ray's in the wings, when one of
the actors on the stage suddenly broke the fourth wall, with the man
at 6 o'clock eyeing him steadily in a mirror, on the wall above the
quicklime sacks, a mirror that, obviously, has been there all along,
and that possibly, in hindsight, should have been reported. Raymond, apparently, was not in the wings, and this wasn't the sort of
theatre that respected the grand traditions; the fourth wall was an illusion that was shattered with impunity, and the audience itself had

nowhere to hide. What are we to make of the nature of Juárez Theatre? While we understand the need for central staging, why set our
stage in the middle of a death house? Is Artaud's notion of a Theater
of Cruelty, with its violent determination to obliterate false reality,
by hurling the spectator into the center of the action, and torturing
the viewer into spiritual submission, and burning the whole theatre
to the ground if necessary, perhaps being taken somewhat too literally? How does one respond, as an audience member, having paid
for a full year's subscription in advance, to a theater whose sense of
cathartic cleansing is based on a purging of the audience itself? Ray
gripped the shotgun by the pistol grip and hoisted it, bringing the
darkness level with the back of a human head, sighting through the
Ghost Ring O, and down along the heat shield of the Mossberg barrel, drawing a bead on the square root of zero, like the Blackjack soldier he always was, an absolute weaponry consummate professional, and the ultimate veteran of the Theater of Juárez; we ourselves,
on the other hand, having gotten the audience into this mess, have
to be a bit concerned about the use of real weapons, particularly
when chambered with live ammunition shells. Is it possible to die
truthfully under imaginary circumstances? It may well be true, to
paraphrase Artaud, that metaphysics enters the mind only though
the human skin, but a point-blank blast from a Briley-choked Mossberg, while a truly effective form of supra-linguistic communication, may be far too much obscure metaphysics for most of us to
absorb all at once. If you're interested in Community Theatre, of
course, the suburbs of Juárez may not be quite right for you; the
place is literally crawling with all sorts of real theatrical types, but
the acting, in Juárez, is absolutely dreadful.

Now if Mr. Edmunds would be good enough to put the gun
down and come and join us, the time has come for us to have a little
talk. My name is Raúl Antonio Ramírez Tabares. Permit me to pose
a question that has plagued the philosophers.

# 19

*B*y the time I reached the last of the staircase steps, of course, it occurred to me that this war against time that I was fighting had not only started, but was well underway. The men who had sent the FedEx package, with its "we have not forgotten" backward-slanted message, likely knew who I was, knew where I came from, and knew where I lived, right down to the street address of the Inn of the Poets; it was something of a puzzle, given all this, that my time war, if you could call it that, hadn't long ago ended. What were they waiting for? If they were hoping to catch me mentally unprepared, without having my own story straight in my head, right about now was a good time to do so; I knew more about the side effects of drugs for schizophrenia than I knew about myself, and my trip to see the Birdman certainly hadn't helped much, at least as far as getting my story straightened out, or getting mentally prepared to fight some sort of time war. It was probably a good time, right about now, to begin getting my thoughts into better mental order, before I wound up in a box on a FedEx truck, without much of anything to get mentally prepared for; if I was hoping to find a home where the heart is to go home to, I'd better do it soon, or I'd be there already, making myself at home in a small but empty hole they'd put through my heart to spare me the bother, a home for the heart, all right, forever untroubled. Of course, by the time I reached the last of the staircase steps, it was already twilight in my home in Guanajuato, and it turns out that twilight, at least in Guanajuato, is a strange time of day to fight a mental time war, particularly with your troops in complete disorder, and your home for the heart in a state of disarray.

At the bottom of Calle Calvario, where it intersected with Calle Luis, I paused for a moment to try to catch my breath, and bring my erratic heart rate down to something closer to chronometrically normal. Given the fact that I'd only been descending the hill, down the cobblestone stairway from Tom's bird-nest perch, it wasn't the breath in my lungs that needed catching; I was mentally winded by all the tachycardiac talk. After chasing Tom's crazy logic around, up and down hills where the time work is and the corn is yellow, I needed to just stand still for a moment, do some deep mental breathing, get my mind to stop skipping and racing and bouncing. I took a few deep breaths of the Guanajuato twilight, hoping to normalize my akataphasic heart, which was doing some up-two-over-one knight's-move pounding, and just not in rhythm with the real-time clock. Before going forward, I was going to need to go backward, back into the attic where that trunk full of learning must be full of clues as to my own prior history; before going either forward or backward, however, I needed to come to a complete mental standstill, right in the middle of the Calle Luis, and right in the center of my own present moment, so I took a little breather and to be honest about it, sort of overshot the mark, as far as time work goes and the spring trees greening and the dopamine pathways to the home is where the heart, and found myself at the bottom of a Guanajuato street maze, feeling a little lost, just slightly off center, and not altogether present to the Guanajuato Now.

The city at this hour seemed to be living in the past; while the bells in the Basilica tower were tolling 6 pm, it might as well have been 6 o'clock in the 17th century, when the Basilica was at long last newly completed, and King Phillip II's magnificent gift, a jewel-encrusted wooden statue of the Virgin Mary, was finally installed beneath the rose-pink dome, after waiting out the better part of nine long centuries, most of it spent hiding in a cave outside Toledo; imagine her relief, after hundreds of years in hiding, and fearing that the Moors, if they found her, would tear her jewel from jewel, at finding herself at last beneath the dusty-rose Basilica, in her home-is-where-the-heart-is home in Guanajuato, where everybody loved her, and made her feel at home. I walked up Calle Luis, past the Teatro Juárez and Don Hernando's time-warped trueno hedge, and past Gabriella's One Hour Photo shop, the source of the photos of my clowning-around-with-grim-faced-men, what-was-I-thinking, special occasion, knowing that I didn't have another nine centuries, or even a cave to hide in, I needed to find a home where I could restart my heart. The street was slowly filling with by-now familiar sights: musicians resplendent in silver and black, tuning and re-tuning their constellate instruments; lawyers and bankers in their pin-stripped suits, drinking pitchers of fruit-filled purple Sangria; and the school girls in blue-and-white Catholic plaid, meandering home, listening to their iPods. At the bottom of the Guanajuato frog-hopping valley, the cobblestone streets were mixing up shades of grey pastels, from the fine-ground pumice of the valley-floor twi-light, while high up above in the surrounding hills, the red-tailed hawks were still circling in daylight, looking down steadily on the sun-struck scrub brush, hunting for rabbits in the mustard hour. And somewhere deep beneath all this, I could feel the rumble of an underground truck, making its way home through the maze of tunnels in the halogen-lit darkness underneath my feet, where the waters used to flow in the silver-mining heydays and flood the city streets every now and then, and where a man could now walk if he knew where he was going, or wander around forever in a halo-gen daze. Daylight, twilight, underground night: the hours were stacked up, one on top of the other, like the books on Quixote's chest when he finally fell asleep, and dreamed through the night of chivalric adventures, while his candles burned down through their youth and adulthood, until they reached old age at the candle bot-tom, where flames licked their pale plates for the last of the light. I followed one of the iPod girls up Calle Luis, dreaming of nothing, and came to the tables of La Tasca de la Paz, where only today I'd been sitting with Gustavo, and Raúl Ramírez, the Theta Special Forces poetry expert, who seemed to know Alvaro de Campos better than I did, better in fact than Alvaro knew himself, Alvaro knowing nothing about himself whatsoever, which was just about as much as I knew about myself. I took a seat at one of the outdoor tables, ordered a basket of tortillas and a glass of red wine, and sat facing the spires of Our Lady of Guanajuato, as the bells tolled 6 in the Templo de San Diego, at maybe ten minutes past the actual hour.

Time, in Guanajuato, was an elastic concept, a matter of emotion without chronometric precision; when the bells begin to sing in the Guanajuato twilight, this isn't the time to be checking your Seiko; the time is in your heart, not on your wrist.

And so what was in my heart, and how did it get there, and at what time had it arrived on my spacetime odometer? I had no idea. How should I know what I'll be, I who don't know what I am? Alvaro's words from The Tobacco Shop, written in fact by Fernando Pessoa, might as well have been my words, although since Alvaro had to know that he was authored by Pessoa, he knew where to look for his own identity, to Pessoa himself, who had written Alvaro's lines. Who was my Pessoa? It was possible, of course, that I was born this way, that nature, essentially, had authored me herself. Gabriella's idiosyncratic memory procedures, her way of remembering things backwards, beginning with last things first and proceeding from there, memory by memory, on a short, last-thing-in-first-thing-out, list, seemed altogether natural to her. Her memories were like miners, trapped in a narrow mineshaft, whose only way out is in reverse chronological order, with the last one to enter the first to escape; a narrative of her day was apt to proceed counterclockwise, with each event followed by the event that preceded it, reversing the normal flow of cause and effect. The waiter came and set my tortillas and wine in front of me, a consequence no doubt of my having ordered tortillas and wine; it wasn't altogether clear that Gabriella had a similar sense of consequence, that it would occur to her that the appearance of certain items from among those on the menu would be a logical consequence of her having ordered just these items. She seemed to live in a present moment, naturally and effortlessly, that was not the result of her previous actions; if the present proved unsatisfactory, if she would have preferred white wine to red, it would be difficult to imagine her blaming herself for having placed the wrong order; rather than sit there and blame herself, she would have been far more likely to simply drink the red wine. Might her life have turned out better had she taken different actions? This didn't seem to be a question that Gabriella would have asked. Should she have married that young man who had so earnestly proposed to her, so many years ago that the man himself was long forgotten, so long forgotten that he might as well not exist?

Would she be happier today with two young children, and a quiet sense of satisfaction at having made the right choice? She seemed to be happy enough with whatever in fact existed, and that fork in the road that might have determined a different outcome, that might have made her far happier, more fulfilled as a woman, was only another fork in the road to Guanajuato, a fork that Gabriella would have long ago forgotten, so long forgotten that there was no such fork. Do you have any regrets, Gabriella? Do you find yourself at night making agonizing reappraisals? You might as well ask a rose in bloom if she regretted being a rose; no one would ask a rose if it is happy with the way that life has turned out. Are you happy, Rose, with what you've made of yourself? Of course I am, what is wrong with you, you ridiculous humans, blaming yourselves for everything, driving yourselves crazy with regrets and reappraisals, having second and third thoughts about your own mistakes, rethinking the long chains of cause and effect, and the outcomes of all your inconsequential decisions; if you keep this up, you'll wind up talking to the roses, and being put in a nice quiet place somewhere, a little home where the delusional and schizoaffective can be cared for, hopefully the sort of place that has some beautiful flowers.

Having been more than willing to discard my own biography, to pitch it out the window of El Mesón de los Poetas, and live my life pointed forward, without regrets, there was no real reason, at least in the abstract, that I needed to answer the question as to whether or not I was born this way, as the sort of man who comes to be in possession of a rather large body of knowledge and no sense at all of how it came to belong to him. Somehow I had twenty million dollars. Did it matter to me whether or not I had earned this, and therefore had a right to a sense of pride regarding my earning prowess? Since I didn't feel any pride, it didn't seem to matter whether or not I had a right to feel self-satisfied; if I had been born with the money, and hadn't in fact earned it, what difference would it make in my assessment of myself? My assessment of myself was that I was worth twenty million, except that none of the twenty million added a dime to my sense of worth. In the same way, if the knowledge that I'd accumulated had been earned through hard work or had simply been accumulated, this made no real difference, at least in the abstract. Had I authored myself, and therefore deserved the credit, or was my current situation something I'd been born to, a product of my nature, in which case nature was my author? Since it was too late now to be other than what I was, why should I care? If I were the sort of person who found himself at regular intervals waking up in a city, with no memory at all of how he'd come to be living there, with a trunk full of knowledge that seemed to belong to someone else, then I was just that sort of person, and there wasn't much point in seeking credit as an author, and I certainly wasn't about to start blaming myself now for the way that I'd been authored; I was more than willing to give nature both the credit and the blame. On the other hand, if I were a self-made man, a product of my own will-power and diligent effort, maybe it was about time I started assuming some responsibility, maybe my own life was quite an achievement, or maybe, when you got right down to it, my life was all my fault. Had I failed my own dreams? Should I consider myself a failure? As far as I could tell, I didn't have any dreams, and if I'd squandered my own hopes, they were only squandered hopes, and it wasn't at all clear that I had any real use for them. Of course, it was certainly possible that I was selling myself short; I had, after all, quite a body of knowledge, even if what I knew didn't seem to belong to me; didn't I at least deserve a little credit? A man who wants to take pride in the knowledge that he's accumulated, through hard work and diligence, through burning the midnight oil, would need to feel sure that he deserved full credit, that he'd given it his all, that his knowledge was the product of a wholehearted effort, and that his pride in himself was thereby justifiable; if you want to take pride in your half-hearted effort, and feel pleased with that half of your all that you gave it, you'll first need to subtract around half of yourself, that half of your all that you just never gave; as for me, I didn't feel any pride, and if it turned out that the midnight oil had simply burned itself, this wouldn't seem to me to be a subtraction of anything; other than oil, nothing was subtracted. In any case, all this deep inner calculus we bring to bear upon ourselves struck me as ridiculous, a complete waste of time. Are we on the rise or in decline? At what rate are we declining? Is our decline rate accelerating? Did we arrive here by force of will or did our natures overwhelm us? Are we pleased with ourselves or filled with bitterness and anguish? Are we happy, after all, to find that we're made of the right stuff, or did it turn out, in the end, that we just couldn't cut it? Apparently, along with my biography, I'd also taken the liberty of throwing my calculator out the window. What difference did it make whether I was happy or unhappy with the way that I'd turned out? I was neither; Guanajuato was beautiful, I didn't need to be happy with the stuff that I was made of, I was perfectly happy with what Guanajuato was made of, cobblestone streets and dusty-rose churches and flowerboxes blooming with azaleas and carnations and red-tailed hawks circling in sunlight, high up above in the blue Guanajuato sky. Would King Phillip's Virgin Mary be less than herself if you stripped away her jewels? Her jewels, in the end, belonged to the King of Spain, and if he wanted them back, he was no doubt welcome to them, she never for a moment asked to be jewel-encrusted, why in God's name do we run around looking for valuables to be encrusted with, money, pride of authorship, knowledge for its own sake? I wasn't running around, I was seated at La Tasca, chewing on a tortilla, and I didn't for a moment ask that the food be jewel-encrusted; I was far better off with a tortilla that could be chewed.

While I certainly would have preferred to have stopped right here, and headed to Gabriella's to take her to dinner, all of this, unfortunately, was in the abstract. In the concrete world, someone, or more likely some group of men, knew who I was, knew my location, was seemingly unhappy with me and one or more of my actions, and would, in all likelihood, be happy to see me dead. I had very little doubt that I hadn't in fact been born this way, with men standing around my cradle, hoping I'd soon be dead. Someone other than me apparently took my history personally, and wasn't likely to be altogether satisfied with my trying to explain that I must have been born this way, and wasn't to be blamed for how my life had turned out. The waiter returned, noticed that I hadn't touched my wine, paused for a moment as though about to ask a question, shrugged, shook his head, and then returned with another basket of warm corn tortillas. If he had been hoping to sell more wine, perhaps he was disappointed, and if I had stopped him and explained that there was no need to worry, that perhaps I was born this way, and didn't drink wine, this would likely have given rise to more questions than answers, and in any case, what's the difference, he would not sell more wine. If he had threatened to kill me, of course, I would have needed a far better answer than that I was abstinent by nature. Gabriella, under the circumstances, would have suddenly remembered that she'd forgotten to drink her wine, and would have slowly begun to drink it, putting the glass to her lips and taking the last sip first. It occurred to me that this Last-In-First-Out approach to her memories was something that I in fact had a good deal of knowledge of; in computer science or queuing theory, this approach is known as LIFO. If I built a computer subroutine in assembly language, placing the results of my calculations into various memory addresses, and then stuffing these addresses into a LIFO stack frame, the last calculation would be the first I'd have access to, a useful approach for certain real-time processes, where the last thing that happens often needs to be dealt with first. Thinking about computers seemed to give me the beginnings of an actual headache, and the bump on my skull began to throb in real time. This knot on my head, throbbing with my blood, couldn't have been more than a few days old; when I touched it gingerly, I felt an unhealed wound, which is not among the features that we tend to be born with. Positioned as it was, at the back right center of the top of my head, it was not the sort of knot that could have been acquired by falling; someone must have struck me, and not long ago. I reached into the LIFO stack, retrieved a particular memory address, where I must have stored the knowledge of having recently been struck, and could make no sense at all of what the address referred to; nothing in my memory seemed to live at that address. Whoever the person was that had burned the midnight oil, learning so much about computers and stack frames and assembly language that it literally made my head hurt, must have been the same person who was struck on the head, and while that person was clearly me, I had an unhealed wound to prove it, it was equally clear that I no longer lived there, and had forgotten to leave myself a forwarding address.

Having apparently wandered off on a bit of a tangent, without much to show for it, aside from having learned that tangents made my head hurt, a no-doubt-valuable lesson that I proceeded to forget, I focused once again on the "birth defect" hypothesis, that all of this was natural, an absence I was born with, and that my lack of identity was something I'd had all my life, but it was difficult to see how a man with no identity could have acquired so much financial acumen and functional cunning; if I knew, for example, how to structure a bridge loan, with 50% warrant coverage, so as to gain some advantage over another human being, I must have had an identity at some point in my life. No one would be willing to grant a financial advantage to a man with no real identity; he'd have to be a fool. I have a deal to propose, given your current financial difficulties; perhaps we should discuss whether or not my terms would be acceptable. And just who are you? No one, really, I seem to have a good deal of money, but no real identity. Do you view this as a problem? Of course it's a problem, I suggest you turn around and take your business elsewhere; I don't make a habit of cutting deals with the sort of people who have no idea at all who the hell they are. Just how did you get in here? Well as to that, I really couldn't say, I seem to have just appeared here, I must have walked in off of the street from somewhere, somewhere down below, how high up are we? Ruth, would you please come in here, and show this gentleman out of my office, I have a business to run, how in God's name did this man get on my calendar, he doesn't even know who he is, what is wrong with you people? Really, sir, there's no reason to get upset, I'm sure you'll find my proposal to be well within the normal parameters. I may not know who I am, but I must know what I'm doing, I certainly have quite an impressive-looking bank balance, it may even be mine, I mean really, who can say? I'm not quite sure how I do it, but the deals apparently get done, though I can't say I blame you for having doubts about my methods; perhaps I can offer a slight reduction in my own personal upside, since I have no idea at all to whom the upside might accrue. Never mind, Ruth, just call Security, and please make sure that they are properly armed, this man seems unstable and may even be dangerous. I'm sure that won't be necessary, sir, I doubt that I'm actually dangerous, I may not be stable in the traditional sense, but I'm only asking for warrant coverage, I wasn't as far as I know planning to hold a gun to your head. Let me just see here, did I even bring a weapon? It was apparent, in summary, that at some point in my life I must have possessed an identity; when I used the term "liquidation preference," meaning my money comes out first, like I'd stuffed it in a LIFO stack, I wasn't referring to anything that involved the use of sidearms, and I likely wasn't expressing a personal preference for anyone's physical liquidation through the use of armed force.

My waiter reappeared, took another dim view of my brimming red wine glass, and gave me something of a withering glance; perhaps my ominous FedEx package had come in fact from a Juárez waiter. I ordered a glass of white to buy a little time, though given the gradual diminishment of my Guanajuato financial standing, through the purchase of gorditas and spring-fed bottled water and now two useless glasses of red and white wine, I would need to move things along here a little, eventually, before I sank below the level of the 500 Peso Man, and lacked sufficient stature to take Gabriella to dinner. As the waiter hurried off, no doubt baffled but satisfied, I returned to the question that was posed by my knowledge of substantial amounts of poetry, specifically as to why a respectable businessman, in the 21$^{st}$ century, would even have bothered to have read the stuff, much less have it committed to memory. If the lines of memorized poetry were meant to distract me from some unpleasantness, such as undergoing a dental procedure, or any of life's many mental equivalents, why wasn't my head full of nursery rhymes or the soothing rhythms of Longfellow? A man who doesn't want to think about the ongoing process of root canal surgery might be better off with something like The Song of Hiawatha, something written in a sing-song trochaic tetrameter, using the meter of some overedited Finnish epic poem, and while I admittedly seemed to know a fragment of Hiawatha, By the shores of Gitche Gumee, By the shining Big-Sea-Water, Stood the wigwam of Nokomis, Daughter of the Moon, Nokomis, this didn't seem to be nearly enough material to get me through a root canal; the lines seemed to be the mental equivalent of endodontic surgery, in and of themselves. What possible use would I have had for learning large portions of Ezra Pound's Pisan Cantos? Perhaps if I'd been caught in some Ponzi-scheme swindle, and been locked up in a cage by my own investors, forced to consider how decades of work had tilted so far from the upright and vertical that it appeared at any moment to be ready to topple, I might have asked for a copy of Canto LXXXI to comfort and distract me, "pull down thy vanity, thou art a beaten dog beneath the hail," "learn of the green world what can be thy place," "what thou lovest well remains, the rest is dross," and so on; while there was more than enough material here to get me though a root canal, it was apparent that memorizing Pound's shattered brilliance and fracturing allusiveness and splintery tangents must have cost me a good deal of torment in the first place, like cracking a tooth in the middle of a procedure in which endondontic surgery is performed upon oneself. The waiter brought my wine, a basket of fresh tortillas, and a small carafe of water, while I counted the silver fillings in my actual teeth, and while admittedly I also found three gold crowns and inlays, ample evidence of dental surgery, well worth being distracted from, no one wants to sit through a root canal procedure, wondering why the hell something smells like it's burning, and thinking about the drill bit boring to the bottom of one of his teeth, I discarded the hypothesis of memorized poetry as a mental distraction from the equivalents of dentistry. Whoever it was that had gone to the trouble of memorizing masses of apparently useless poetry, including, as far as I could tell, the entire 160 lines or so of Wordsworth's Tintern Abbey, and strange large blocks of virtuous Milton, on the glory of Satan in Paradise Lost, tens if not hundreds of sonnets and odes and villanelles and clerihews, Stevens' Sunday Morning, with its casual flocks of pigeons, and countless random others, from Donne and Herbert to Yeats and Auden to Philip Larkin and Gerald Stern, to say nothing of the poems of Fernando Pessoa himself, such a man must have had some sort of identity problem to begin with, if not necessarily from birth, then something he developed along the way; whoever heard of a businessman offering warrant-encrusted bridge loans, while still finding it necessary, or in any way useful, to know hundreds of random poems by heart? If you're not happy with my terms, sir, perhaps I could offer to recite a poem of your choosing. If nothing comes to mind, permit me to suggest a bit of Wallace Stevens, The palm at the end of the mind, beyond the last thought, rises in the bronze distance, a gold feathered bird sings in the palm, without human meaning. Stevens, as you may or may not know, sir, was an insurance executive, perhaps he offered a poetry recitation to compensate the victims of his exorbitant policies; he seems to have been well aware of the fact that it is not human reason that makes us happy or unhappy, the bird sings, its feathers shine, and really, in light of this, I think you'll find that having to pay 50% warrant coverage is no reason at all to feel the least bit unhappy, your company will be saved, the birds will sing, their feathers will shine, and these warrants you'll have to pay are certainly not worth worrying over, they're virtually meaningless, like the palm at the end of your mind. I would suggest you stay focused on the gold feathered bird; these warrants, in the grand scheme of things, are without human meaning.

I had very little doubt that poetry, under the circumstances, would not add much appeal to my onerously structured bridge loans. Perhaps a bit of mathematics would be more to the man's taste. If you don't care for Stevens, sir, perhaps I could be of assistance with the fundamental theorem of Galois Theory, the unsolvability of polynomial equations without knowledge of the normality of field extensions. No? Permit me to point out that without my money, you'll be filing for bankruptcy the day after tomorrow, so why don't you just sit still and be quiet for a moment and let me tell you about the life of Évariste Galois. I may know nothing whatsoever about my own personal history, but I seem to know quite a lot about the biography of Galois: his reading of Lagrange at the age of 15; his father's idiosyncratic suicide as the result of a political dispute with the local village priest; the rejection of his work by Siméon-Denis Poisson himself, the man who became famous for his Poisson Distribution, and who declared Galois' work to be completely incomprehensible. I might point out that Poisson's own work, on the probability of a certain number of events occurring in a fixed period of time, is not likely to help you with your own situation; the probability of your bankruptcy occurring, without my assistance, is really quite high, with or without some appeal to Poisson. If you'll permit me to continue then, imagine Galois, imprisoned for his political convictions, finding that his work has been rejected by the Academy; now I don't know about you, and in fact I don't know about me either, but this must have been infuriating. And then we come to the curious end of our tale, Galois dying in a duel, at the incomprehensibly young age of 20.58 years, over a woman named Stéphanie-Félicie du Motel, after staying up all night to write the letters to Auguste Chevalier that have led him to be regarded as among the immortals. Quite a tragicomic ending, dying over a woman named of all things Motel, which means very much the same in French as it does in English. If I were you, and obviously I'm not, I can't even, strictly speaking, be said to be my-self, I'd sign the deal documents right away, before it occurs to me that I don't know who wrote them, and whatever you do, whether we have a deal or not, stay away from women with the last name Motel.

Would a man who had come to realize that he had no true identity, who was constantly doing business as someone he was not, keep Galois Theory and Laplace transforms and Riemannian Ge-ometry readily available for the opportune moment? I threw anoth-er hypothesis on the "unlikely" pile. If I had built an entire life this way, and cared nothing at all about anything but money, my mind didn't make much sense; if you're looking for 3X Preference rights, there is no need to explain that the spacetime continuum is a 4-di-mensional Lorentzian manifold. A man negotiating a shareholder agreement seldom concludes by reciting a clerihew: The people of Spain think Cervantes/ Equal to a half-dozen Dantes;/ An opinion resented most bitterly/ By the people of Italy; even a businessman-poet like Wallace Stevens would rather go hungry than stoop to this. On the other hand, particularly in view of its randomness, and the execrable quality of some of this poetry, I had no real clue as to the organizing principles that had given rise to my own mode of thought. Had I managed to assemble an entire identity while remaining aloof from the self that I'd constructed? While knowing tensor calculus was not something I took any particular pride in, it's a difficult subject to master if you approach the problem with complete indifference, though suffice it to say you couldn't prove it by me, and perhaps after all there are places in the world, places like Ciudad Juárez for instance, where indifference to what you've made of yourself may have come to be regarded as an actionable offense. This brought me back around to these men standing by, leaning over my cradle, hoping to see me dead; they could safely be assumed to know enough about themselves to know how to act if action were called for, since unlike me, they knew who they were, and as far as I could tell, they weren't born yesterday. Once again, my head began to throb, and my fingers set off on a tentative search of the half-baseball knot on the top of my skull. I knew from reading Hegel the dangers inherent in relying on phrenology, the science of determining one's inner being by searching the bumps on the top of one's head, but if a man's being is his action, as Hegel asserted, and not some sort of mindless head-bump reading, I had at least the being of one who has read Hegel, which may be a headache, but wouldn't have caused this lump. The waiter returned, possibly to ask if I wanted to order dinner, noted that I seemed to be performing some sort of phrenological procedure, reading my inner mental capacities from the bumps on the surface of my skull, and then left me alone to continue my search, for something resembling my own inner being, perhaps assuming the worst, that I'd suddenly discovered, from this baseball-shaped knot on the top of my head, that not only was I the sort of person who has a fondness for pseudo-sciences, but that I wasn't a big tipper, and thus not worth the trouble of being properly served. Hegel, under the circumstances, would have made a far better waiter. The general case of this rejection of physical causality, Sartre's *Being and Nothingness: An Essay on Phenomenological Ontology*, filled with its Dexedrine-fueled gloom regarding man's search for inner completeness, seemed a bit bleak for my current situation, bleaker even than Heidegger's dark *Being and Time*, which unfortunately for me, I also seemed to have read, and it was clear that all of the philosophy I'd managed to stuff somehow inside myself, from Plato to Plotinus to Augustine; Aristotle to Avicenna and Averroes to Aquinas; Descartes to Leibniz, and Hobbes, Locke, and Hume; Kant to Schiller to Hegel; Husserl to Merleau-Ponty; Frege and Russell to Searle and Putnam; Marx to Adorno to Horkheimer and Marcuse; Freud to Lacan to Deleuze and Kristeva; Barthes to Foucault to Derrida and so on; and maybe ultimately to Ludwig Wittgenstein; all of this difficult reading filled in nothing at all inside me, I might not be bleak but I was personally empty, and whatever sort of identity I'd hereby constructed was not much of an edifice, it was like a leaning tower of books. What could be the meaning of this? What sort of businessman would have constructed this tilted tower of learning? What in the world could he possibly have been thinking? What did he have in mind, in short, as the tower began to topple, and his whole inner edifice was in danger of collapsing, while he sat there reading Radishchev, *On Man, His Mortality, His Immortality*, no doubt drinking a toast to some doomed and teetering mental structure, to which, with a certain aloofness, he was slowly adding floors? No wonder my poor waiter couldn't be bothered with bringing me dinner; perhaps I should have mentioned, in addition to all this oblique philosophy, a few decent manuals on the fundamentals of cooking.

In short, then, to net this out, to get to the bottom line, as I, being a businessman, net net and triple net, would have been prone to say, I hadn't been born this way, as a man incapable of assuming an identity; I clearly had an identity, I just didn't have one today. Furthermore, while I had no reason to disagree with Hegel, that a man's being is his act, that our actions, effectively, create our inner being, or with Sartre, that being precedes essence in time's ontology, my being, as constructed, showed no signs of possessing any inner coherence, something that would have allowed me to categorize myself, and narrow down the possibilities as to who in fact I was; from what I could tell, I could be almost anyone, though I couldn't for the life of me imagine reversing this, and finding that anyone could possibly be me. I might have authored myself, but I had no pride of authorship, I was completely incoherent, and simply didn't add up; perhaps I could be said to be my own Pessoa, the sort of author who doesn't bother with making himself cohere, except that Pessoa was famous for his indifference to identity, and I wasn't anyone; as far as I could tell, I was a complete nonentity. And so on. Gabriella, by way of contrast, was, well, simply Gabriella. She couldn't be said to be the artificer of her being; for her, the cause and effect of her actions ran backwards, and her entire inner being was a counterclockwise effect.

As I sat there thinking myself over, like a sketch artist trying to pull together a half-decent composite drawing, from a host of conflicting witnesses' descriptions, of the guy who ran off with an old lady's purse, I saw a woman of indeterminate age, maybe 30 maybe 60, approaching my table from the Calle Luis, wearing absolute rags, dirt-smeared face-flesh, and carrying a sleeping infant on her hunched-over back, held there with a piece of loosely woven sackcloth, possibly the remains of an old burlap sack. She had the features of a Native American, straight black hair, deeply wrinkled skin, and haunted-looking eyes, though they weren't the sort of eyes that seemed haunted by something, they seemed, if anything, to be themselves doing the haunting, which makes no sense at all, but that's how they looked, as though their presence and absence were the exact same thing. She looked straight at me, or maybe it was through me, perhaps seeing something familiar that still eluded me, hopefully something simple, that didn't involve reading Sartre and Hegel; or perhaps seeing nothing at all, which was more or less what I'd seen for myself. When she reached the table, at a distance no more than an arm's length away, she held out a weathered hand toward my tortilla-filled mouth, in the universal language of silent supplication, and it occurred to me that maybe I'd been looking at things the wrong way, looking at the question of my own identity all backwards, because I suddenly saw myself through her own dark eyes, from a distance of three feet that might as well have been infinity, as though the occurrence of my existence, at a table in Guanajuato, in the foothills of the Sierra Gorda, on a twirling blue jewel of a planet among the galaxies, was almost laughably improbable, but here I was anyway, both present and absent at the exact same time. As she continued to stare, I felt a sort of surge of mental intensity, like a jolt of electricity, pass right through me, causing the hair on the back of my neck to stand straight on end, while words from out of nowhere passed through my head and flew off like crows into the darkness and blankness, *this is our body*, now where did that come from? She smelled like the earth, or more precisely like wet soil after a five-minute rainstorm, mixed with the baby-breath sweetness of mother's milk, and then something botanical or medicinal maybe, like she'd been brewing up some sort of a bruja's dream potion, full of animal health and herbal vitality; with her tattered clothing and face streaked with grime, she looked like the bitter end of the human species, and smelled like the earth's nostalgia for something. She had what you'd have to call the ghost of a smile, which all things considered, is an interesting expression; a ghost, being disembodied, can't really be said to be a part of someone's face, it's hard to lend much credence to an absence with presence, but there it was anyway, *this too is our body*. I started to hand her one of my cloth-wrapped tortillas, found that the basket was once again empty, and reached in my wallet for a 100-peso note, though I paused for a moment and held onto the bill, wondering if this might be totally inappropriate, that giving more than a few spare coins to a dirt-smeared street-beggar would be considered grandiose, that she'd take one look at my incongruous currency and laugh in my face for being such a showoff; or maybe she'd long ago been able to size me up, found that I was generous, but only to a point, and would view my donation with a certain suspicion. I could imagine her calling my waiter over, pointing at the money, then at my face, while the waiter himself pointed at my wine glasses, one red, one white, and both of them as full as the moment when he had poured them, there's a pattern here somewhere, something isn't right, this man as a whole isn't altogether plausible. And then I looked at the 100, the red and white wine, my place at the table of all of life's possibilities, and let out a laugh that was itself incongruous, frightening the beggar-woman and causing her to flinch, as though she too had been jolted with electricity. I placed my hand on her weathered arm, murmuring lo siento's, attempting to soothe her, but she must have been wondering what she'd gotten herself into; she was only, after all, begging for a few coins, and now she'd found herself in some existential drama, with a stranger who had appeared to be friendly enough, but who now seemed incapable of the most basic of transactions, like handing a beggar a few peso coins, without laughing out loud about his own improbability. Her place in the scheme of things was to beg for spare change; my place was to supply it or chase her away. The fact that this suddenly seemed utterly ludicrous, that I viewed her as the embodiment of our interwoven lives, of how no man can be rich until the least of us is cared for, did not add a centavo to her own net worth; *this is our body*, we are all in this together, is a lovely sentiment, but is not, in the scheme of things, a good medium of exchange.

If only I'd spoken a bit more Nahuatl, and a lot less Heidegger and Marx and Hegel, I might have explained the sort of problems that I was having, like being worth 20 million in colorful currency, while half of the earth made do with a dollar, the dollar they didn't have and would have to scrounge for tomorrow, to make it through the day and keep their children from starving, while trying to avoid having to hang around cafés, and running into strangers with identity problems. "If you want to know what God thinks of money, just look at the people he gave it to"; if I started trying to translate Dorothy Parker into Nahuatl or Mixtec, it would take forever, and I decided it was easier to just hand her the 100, and stop acting strange and completely implausible, though I hadn't really factored in the currency itself, which as money, per se, had more than a few basic identity problems, and some trouble coming to terms with its own self-worth. In any case, she accepted the red banknote, holding it with both hands and eyeing it suspiciously, with its picture on the front of the poet-prince of the Aztecs, Nezahualcoyotl, 15th century ruler of magnificent Texcoco, the "Athens of the Western World," and author of the poem on the front of the red bill, in microscopic print, in print so small that it had to doubt its own existence: "I love the song of the mockingbird/ Bird of four hundred voices/ I love the color of jade/ And the enervating perfume of flowers/ But most of all I love my brother: man." Nezahualcoyotl, "the fasting coyote," was a poet who would have felt right at home among Fernando Pessoa's heteronyms: "I wish I'd never been born, I truly wish that I'd never come to this earth. That's what I say. But what do I do? Do I really have to live among actual people?" Of course if Pessoa were in charge of putting poetry on currency, the poem on the 100-peso note would have ended with something more like the following: "But most of all I love my brother: man;/ If only, even once, I had actually met him," and the Coyote, for Pessoa's taste, was maybe a little too drunk on quechol flowers and jadestone, while Pessoa preferred cheap wine when he couldn't afford to eat, and needed to achieve a state of sublime inebriation. My new friend, holding her currency, didn't seem the least bit concerned about Aztec poetry or enervating perfume, unless she was thinking about another of the Coyote's poems, "Ye Nonocuiltonohua," meaning basically, "I'm wealthy." She turned the bill over, as if doubting its authenticity, where she found the statue of the god Xochipilli, the deity of summer flowers, good health, and wellbeing, the symbol of the benevolent flowering of the whole Aztec universe, beside an Aztec Sunstone, an ancient, if not precisely accurate, pre-Columbian calendar. She pointed at my carafe, I poured her a glass of water, and I felt for a moment like both of us were time-traveling, maybe back to somewhere in the middle of the 15th century, before King Phillip of Spain could even have been conceived of, before he had taken up Virgin Mary's and wooden-statue jewel-encrustations, back when Aztec time was full of 22-hour days and 5-day weeks and 20-day months and 18-month years and 52-year centuries, and all of us were living in the fifth incarnation of the flower-drunk universe, due to end any day now, in epidemic smallpox and utter starvation; or maybe in fact we had time-shifted forward, to somewhere, give or take, around tomorrow morning, tomorrow being Sunday, when the banks would be closed, and I'd be worth next to nothing without my ATM PIN. "Nitlacoya," I'm sad, the Coyote would have said, tomorrow is *nemontemi*, one of the empty days of abstinence, and it looks like the sort of day when I'll be doing a lot of fasting.

My friend wandered off, murmuring something in Nahuatl, in the general direction of the Mercado Hidalgo. Perhaps she was reciting one of the Coyote's poems from memory, something like Xon Ahuiyacan, meaning basically, "Be Joyful," or something along the lines of Zan Nompehua Noncuica, "I Begin To Sing," a poem addressed, like Lucretius's invocation to Venus in *The Order of Things*, to You By Whom All Things Live, to the power of renewal, and the joy of fresh creation, with the corn flowers blossoming their golden corollas, the quetzal-bird warbling its jingling clamor, and all things made fresh and renewed once again, and even a true poet-prince, who hasn't been well, who's been feeling, for days now, just utterly wretched, anguished and heartsick and desolate and bitter, knowing deep down that, despite his vast wealth, he'll still have to live among actual people, suddenly all at once feeling pleasure again, with the power of fresh creation coursing through his veins and bursting forth all around him and singing of the heavens. As an aside, while it was apparent that I'd committed much of his poetry to memory, and knew far more Nahuatl than I knew what to do with, these joyful poems of the Coyote, for all their sincerity, sounded, at least to my ears, just the slightest bit forced. It was possible, of course, that he was genuinely filled with the spirit of the Life Giver, chanting Ohuaya, Ohuaya, as the corn flowers sing, and the freshness of plant life begins to elevate his spirits; more likely, knowing poets, he'd had a few extra cups of the brutish local pulque, which might make almost anyone feel freshly ennobled. Imagine yourself, a prince among men and a legend among poets, but nevertheless tired of all these empty days of fasting, and gradually growing sick of living with the humans; no one could really blame you for reaching for the maguey-brew, to get the flowers to sing again, and feel joyful and renewed. In any case, the beggar wandered off, and perhaps I was making a little too much out of a single 100-peso note; she'd probably just said thanks, "tlazocamati" in Nahuatl, and moved on toward the market to continue with her begging. I paid my tab, sinking, as predicted, below the stature required for even buying a friendly meal, and instead of going directly to Gabriella suggesting supper, I followed my joyful friend, or maybe my dream of her as joyful, in the direction of the Mercado, thinking about dead poets, and how they had come to be immortal.

It was likely, after all, that Nezahualcoyotl had no more written his own poems than Cide Hamete Benengeli had written *Don Quixote*, or than stoic Epictetus had written his own *Discourses*, or than Alvaro de Campos or Alberto Caeiro had authored even one of their mountains of poems. The Coyote poems were written down, long after the Spanish Conquest, by one of Nezahualcoyotl's many great-grandsons, Juan Bautista de Pomar; the Coyote, as a matter of fact, despite his fondness for fasting, had left behind over 100 children by the time of his death, which is, in and of itself, an interesting path to the realm of the immortals. Imagine poor Juan, passing his days in declining splendor, making his home in one of the poet-prince's magnificently hard to maintain yet unquestionably royal houses, but in reality living more or less as a complete nonentity, one of 5,000 direct descendents of the Life Giving Coyote, sitting down at his ornate desk at last, to put Nezahualcoyotl's pen name to paper. He's no doubt tried his hand at writing his own poems, but poets, after all, are a centavo a dozen; despite all of his admirable efforts, and dozens of cases of noble Spanish wine, or whatever sort of home-brew he could get his shaky hands on, his poetry has disappeared without leaving the slightest trace, it's subtleties apparently lost on a society consumed by greed, by the constant striving for upward social mobility, and finally driven mad by the lust for precious metals, and an absolute indifference to the plight of the average worker. Immortality? Forget about immortality; he's sent out dozens, if not hundreds, of his poems and shorter prose pieces, and now even close friends are ignoring his letters. He's becoming, it is clear, something of an embarrassment. Only yesterday, Don Pedro virtually snubbed him in the street, his butcher is growing insistent about paying some trivial grocery bill, and his in-laws, now that he's well into his 40s, are getting a little anxious about his ability to provide for their admittedly homely but precious young daughter, wasting all of his time on his ridiculous obsession, to say nothing about his drinking, or his psychotropic plant consumption, when there are fortunes to be made in the mining of silver. What in the name of Christ, for Juan is in fact a Christian, is he going to do now? What are things coming to? He takes a deep breath, sets his own failed identity aside, at least for the moment, and begins to write in the voice of Nezahualcoyotl, and suddenly the great poet-prince seems to arise somehow inside him, singing the Xopan Ciucatl, the "Song of Spring," for the Aztec nation. The voice sounds so real that poor Juan half-believes it, and by the time he's done, all of Mexico will believe it, and Juan will be well on his way to becoming Himself, one of Mexico's immortals, forever to be remembered as Juan Bautista de Pomar, the great man of letters, the man who saved the Coyote's poems from their brush with oblivion. Had his in-laws only known that one day he'd have a poem, however microscopic, printed on the front of the 100-peso note, they might well have shown him a little more deference; there may be some doubts about a poem's authenticity, but Government-issued currency is above all reproach. Perhaps in just this way Juan Bautista foretold the lesson of Bertolt Brecht, that "in order to be a poet, it is first necessary to be famous." On the other hand, maybe I was selling both Juan and the Coyote short, and young Juan had sat quietly at the feet of his Aztec mother, and memorized the poems, passed from generation to generation, so that he could write them down later, these magnificent creations of the true poet-prince, poems that had made Juan so happy and bright-eyed as a child, and had so ennobled his diluted sense of selfhood, poems that he loved and couldn't help but recall, since what thou lovest well remains, even if, in the end, you have to cheat just a little.

In some such mood, as though I'd actually consumed my red and white wine, I continued toward the market, remembering Horace on the benefits of tipsiness, after maybe one or two extra glasses of his farm's own product, the cheap Sabine stuff, which couldn't hold a candle to the Falernian of Maecenas: It unlocks secrets, it bids hopes be realized, it impels the coward to the field, it lifts the load from the anxious mind, it teaches new accomplishments, and so on and so forth; maybe I should have raced back before the waiter had cleared the table, and dashed off the glasses of white and then red. The streets around the market weren't nearly as well lit as the area around the Plaza; I could barely make out the hands on the Mercado's grand clock, designed by Gustave Eiffel himself, telling me in sign language that it was well after 7, and that I needed to keep moving if I wanted to take Gabriella to dinner, though if she were hoping for something more extravagant than a simple plate of food, I might have to pay by singing for our supper, or maybe by reciting a poem or two, from the ancient Aztec masters, on the transient nature of life on earth, and the illusory quality of manmade currency. Is there a problem, waiter? As you can see, sir, while your lady friend made a wonderful choice with the wine, we too love the Spanish reds from Ribero del Duero, you seem to be short about 500 pesos; perhaps you'd like to pay with a personal check? While nothing would please me more than to pay you with a check, particularly a check that was truly personal, something perhaps in my actual name, drawn on an account that I could personally account for, I seem to be living somewhat hand to mouth, and have only this cash, and a few spare coins. On the other hand, I think you'll find, if you look more closely at the matter, that the 500-peso note, while undoubtedly impressive, is somewhat depressing in symbolic terms, featuring as it does General Ignacio Zaragoza; while the General's astonishing feat, his victory over the French at the battle of Puebla, is certainly worthy of celebration, and worth every peso of the currency in question, as well as your festivities on the 5th of May, it turns out that the General died a few short months later, on September 8, of typhoid fever, at the tender young age of 33.454 years. It would seem to me that a more appropriate settlement might be reached by my reciting something a bit more inspiring, perhaps a few powerful poems of the great poet-prince, invoking the renewing force and regenerative powers of the Cornflower Life Giver in all of its splendor. I see; well as to that, I can speak with the manager, and while your point is well taken regarding the death of Zaragoza, the next time you are planning red wine with your meal, perhaps you should consider something more modest; we have several perfectly adequate reds from the wine-growing region of central Baja. As I recall, we have one or two examples for less than thirty pesos, though a man with a bank account that he can't quite account for might want to consider switching to bottled water.

As I continued deeper into the region of the Mercado, planning my new career as a quechol-drunk troubadour, the streets, unfortunately, didn't quite fit my mood, and they didn't follow directions quite as well as I might have hoped, given my newfound Horacian powers for bidding hopes be realized, and my wine-tutored sense of getting things accomplished, and I found myself instead suddenly locked inside their secrets, not quite knowing which way to turn to find my way to Gabriella's. The streets, in fact, took a turn for the worse, with the lighting dimming down to a halogen edginess, and beggars covered in blankets every thirty or forty yards, mostly Indians whose corn crops had failed at renewal, or whose Life Giver Corn, under pressure from an influx of industrial mediocrity, from the factories of ADM and Cargill and Conagra, was now of so little value that it was not worth renewing. Nezahualcoyotl could chant all he wanted, singing his heart out to the turquoise bird, but the Aztec corn, so perfectly attuned in its genetic diversity to the harsh conditions of Mexican soil, was now simply useless in a biotech age of transgenic seeds, which had rendered irrelevant something on the order of 15 million Mexican growers; Ohuaya, Ohuaya, I could hear the Coyote chant, but his people have been beggared by the mighty gods of NAFTA. The Coyote's descendants were now the very poorest of the poor, those who in fact had so little money that they couldn't even go north, to be exploited in the borderland maquiladoras. The grinding bad luck, as some poet must have said, of every Guanajuato day was carved into their postures, huddled along old walls, with convenience-store Styrofoam coffee cups in front of them, emptied of everything but a few peso coins. These beggars were mostly women, with their children and belongings gathered around them, and not one of them even looked up as I passed, they were truly feeling desolate and abandoned among humans; Ohuaya, Ohuaya, the Coyote chants again, but bitterness and anguish are the destiny of his people.

No wonder the Coyote wished that he'd never been born, that he didn't have to live among actual humans. Given the fact that I was overdue for dinner, and it was a little late now to start curing world hunger, I tried walking on as the Coyote might have done, inventing a few poems to distract him from the squalor, on the deep love we would feel for our brother, Man, if only, even once, we had actually met him. That boy on the garbage pile, hunting plastics with a stick, earning a few naira in the smoldering dumps of Lagos; the young girl in Guiyu, her blood laced with lead and fouled with dioxin, bathing in the quicksilver-chromium waters, and braving the elements in the heavy-metal e-waste streams; our brother, Man, on the beach at Alang, filling and refilling his lungs with asbestos, and PCBs, and a whole wealth of toxins, while the world's poisonous ships are slowly broken down, and Man, whom we love, is broken down with them: You By Whom All Things Live, we beg you to reconsider the human lives we're laying waste to, and we promise to try to shut up if we can, and spare you any more of our luminous bullshit. I stopped all at once in the Guanajuato street; I was clearly hearing voices, and all of them were mine; maybe the beggar woman's bruja-brew was more powerful than I'd thought, and I'd inhaled too deep a whiff of the earth's nostalgia. By now I'd taken several thousand steps in the dimly lit streets of this halogen maze, and while I'd dropped some spare coins into the Styrofoam cups, I hadn't made a dent in the poverty problem; a thousand steps taken in any direction had just been a thousand steps. Perhaps the Coyote, instead of chanting Ohuaya, might have stopped to have a chat with one his impoverished subjects. I couldn't help noticing, my desolate friend, how wretched your life is; permit me to extend my heartfelt condolences. Well isn't that nice of you, who knows where the poor would be without leaders like you to offer us their pity; I'm sure that the world would be a far poorer place, though as for the poor, I suspect that we'd still live in abject poverty. You don't happen to have a 100-peso note? Perhaps I'd feel better owning some microscopic poetry. Or perhaps Juan Bautista, now a deeply Christian man, and gradually growing wealthy selling phony Aztec poetry, might have paused to say a prayer to the Virgin Mary, to lift the burdens of the poor, and take away the guilt that is the burden of the wealthy. Surely the Weeping Virgin, encrusted with Phillip's jewels, knew the secret to living wealthy amid overwhelming poverty. Are you sad, Holy Mary, that there is poverty among the poor, while you yourself are draped in such finery? Of course not, what is wrong with you, I'm an emblem of pity, a comfort to the poor, I personally had nothing to do with impoverishing them, you seem to have me confused with those bureaucrats at the Vatican; when

I think about the wealth that they've wasted over the centuries, it makes me so angry that I just feel like weeping.

I reached the end of another darkened street, after maybe one too many blocks full of human desolation, and still feeling unfortunately exactly what I felt, that I was lost and alone, and that I still knew next to nothing as to whom I was alone with, and that my feet were beginning to hurt, the feet of a thousand steps that had just been a thousand steps, getting me nowhere but bringing me here, where I found my old friend, the having-seen-right-through-me, grime-smeared, beggar woman. She was staring at her 100-peso note, still looking like she'd only recently emerged from out of the slime and primordial ooze, and could use a good bath, with a decent bar of soap, and a nice warm towel to wrap around herself, with a little left over to cover her sleeping infant, who was still swathed in burlap on the beggar's hunched back, with milk-bubble sweetness on her tiny blue lips, living and reliving one of her microscopic dreams. My friend's shoulders shook; perhaps she was cold, or maybe she was crying or they were tears of laughter; or then again, who was I to say, perhaps her own body language was itself a kind of prayer, a prayer for us all to Ometeotyl, the Aztec essence of the duality of life: Our Lord and Lady of the Far and Near. The Inventor of Itself, The Giver of Life, might have been reminding her that suffering is purely ephemeral, but I myself felt a pain in my feet, and an ache in my heart that was truly a kind of ache. *This is our body*: fire inside and a pot of boiling water on an actual stove, and a warm white towel to wrap around us all, all of us together, with our bodies whole. I stood there looking down, shifting my feet, knowing it was late, and time to get out of there, but reluctant just to leave her to the chilling evening air, with her baby's blue lips bubbling milk and turning bluer. Everything I knew, in my trunk full of knowledge, in my burning-the-midnight-oil learning accomplishments, had taught me next to nothing regarding one essential topic: How does a man learn to live with himself? She looked up at last with the ghost of a smile, into my eyes, acknowledging my emptiness, and then she let me in on a little secret of hers, a secret I would share, but I think I got it backwards; it felt like something inscribed by a flock of birds, crows flying backwards against the grain of time, as though something we all know from the time of our graves would circle back around to our cradles when the time comes. I dropped the next-to-last of my 100-peso notes in her Styrofoam cup and kept on walking, leaning forward like life does, toward a bright new future; maybe I'd return again one day, when I knew who I was, and wasn't wandering around walking the desolate streets in circles, knowing no man is rich until the least of us is cared for; or maybe I'd just walk on the way we all do, and forever forget her, only time would tell.

By sheer blind luck, and maybe some instinct to follow the path back toward the brightness, I came out of the maze onto the street at the bottom of Calle Cantaritos, and suddenly knew where I was, while still not knowing much at all about who knew this, and turned to the left to climb the short cobbled hill of the narrow singing street, toward my own hotel, El Mesón de los Poetas, and Gabriella's apartment, and whatever comes next. *What thou lovest well remains: this too is our body: what thou lovest well is thy true heritage.* An interesting hypothesis, as yet to be tested.

# 20

*B*y the time I took the last of my last thousand steps, and climbed up the stairs to Gabriella's apartment, my twilight skirmish in the war against time had, in due course, long ago ended; I was, to put it bluntly, late for dinner. And my next little battle, The Battle of Starry Night, was likely long-lost long before it had commenced, beginning as it did seeking the first Planck instant, and the sources of Time's own anomalous commencement, not the easiest of battlefields even to locate, much less arrive at in any shape to fight. While underneath the starlit Guanajuato sky is a beautiful place to stand and contemplate the heavens, it's the last place on earth you should stand and fight a time war, particularly with your war chest severely depleted, and an angel cooking stew, maybe thirty feet away, at the red-tiled counter of her wonderfully fragrant kitchen. By the time I took the next of my next thousand steps, defeat, in short, was all but inevitable, though the story of my loss at the Battle of Starry Night had, in time's fullness, quite a lovely sort of ending, and if all of our defeats turned out quite so well, we might well wish that all of our battles ended badly.

I was out on the balcony of Gabriella's two-bedroom flat, amusing myself and just killing time, while Gabriella prepared our home-cooked meal, a meal at home that I'd admittedly necessitated, by giving my immediate fortune away, reducing my 1,000-peso stature to something resembling what you'd find on your nightstand, a single red banknote, worth 100 pesos, and maybe three or four lines of microscopic poetry. It was a cool crisp night in the month of...

in the month of...it was a cool crisp night in the month of something, and the stars were out, the Big Dipper lying nearly straight
overhead, in the northeastern sky, with its tail arcing down toward
ancient Arcturus, from which I could locate Spica, directly to the
south, the brightest star in the constellation Virgo, from which I
could locate, let's see now, something, a lot more stars, a lot more
heavens; this momentarily dazzling mastery of the skies came to an
abrupt and self-deflating halt, right here, when I recognized that
everything I knew, my entire inventory of the names of the stars,
with the exception of Sirius and the polestar Polaris, came from a
bit of memorized doggerel, "follow the arc to Arcturus and speed
on through to Spica." I knew, in other words, virtually nothing at all
about the actual names of the stars in the heavens: out of all the 70
sextillion stars in the observable sky; the 300 billion stellar objects in
the Milky Way alone, among which are maybe two billion objects
with orbiting planets the size of Jupiter; and the 5,000 stars you can
see with your eyes, on a good dark night on a palm-covered atoll,
or lost and alone in the Solomon Islands, searching for a pole star
to guide your way, and forgetting that the South Star is nearly invisible; out of all these stars, I could name exactly four, one of which
was the brightest ball of plasma in the entire night sky, the stargazers
equivalent of a complete no-brainer; another of which was the due
North Star, which apparently even the most hopelessly astray, unless they're in a row boat in the South Pacific, are able somehow to
locate; and the last two of which I knew doggerel-style, for reasons
the Heavens alone would know. Four stars? A man walks through
life for maybe fifty-some years, 17,500 nights, with the stars shining
down from the glittering skies, and manages, somehow, at the end
of the day, to know the names of exactly four stars? How is this possible? To make matters worse, from where I stood on the terrace, I
seemed to possess a somewhat overwhelming variety of theoretical
constructs regarding the cosmos itself. Big Bang, Big Bounce, Big
Rip, Big Crunch, the Big Freeze Heat Death hyperbolic geometry;
oscillating Entropy and the Arrow of Time; Cosmic Inflation, in
a negative-pressure, hot-big-bang, where-the-hell-are-we, energy
vacuum; the Omega Point of Consciousness; the Doomsday Event,
some macroscopic Strange-Matter Quark-Star accident; the Weak
Anthropic Principle; the String Theory Vacua; the Quantum-Foam

Multiverse Bubble scenario; the Cosmological Constant and Dark Energy Density in the Lambda-Cold-Dark-Matter concordance equations: I seemed to know more about the theories of the cosmos than I did about the names of the stars in the sky. What sort of man walks around with his eyes closed and his mind full of hypothetical-conjecture equations, while the night sky twinkles and the North Star blazes and the harvest moon rises on an acknowledged land? Maybe I was myself a theoretical construct, some femtometric strangelet, exhibiting quarky behavior, who'd be far better off as a dark matter candidate than as a lost but still conceivably human sort of specimen. One thing was certain: this might be a good time to stop gazing at conjectures, before I set off some sort of Strange Matter accident, and turned God's Green Earth into a quark-gluon soup. Gabriella stood at her red-tiled counter, chopping green serrano peppers and fragrant cilantro while the chile verde simmered and the pork turned tender, drinking a cold Bohemia beer while she worked at her cutting board, and singing something lovely that might have been a *fado*, those Portuguese folk songs of destiny and fate; while I tried to pry my eyes from the conjectural heavens, she sang and diced away at her earthy condiments, looking like an angel and sounding like Amália. You like it spicy, Alvaro? How should I know what I like, I who don't know what I am to begin with; whatever you like, I said out loud, and what I said to myself was I'd like to kiss her.

I'd like to kiss her? Standing out in the darkness on her starlit terrace, beside a pale green oak tree that was just beginning to blossom, kissing Gabriella seemed next to impossible, like a tune I'd only remember if she hummed the first few bars. She worked in the warmth and light of her kitchen, surrounded by her cooking tools and the remainders of her chile verde raw ingredients, the papery husks of green tomatillos, and the skins of roasted poblano peppers and pink and purple ripe tomatoes, and leftover mounds of garlic and onions, and pork shoulder trimmings of deep bone and fat, and cumin and oregano and dried arbol chilies, ground in a volcanic-stone black molcajete. Her recipe, which I already seemed to know by heart, might have been assembled entirely in reverse, but it wasn't the sort of dish that depended on rigid sequence; it all ended up in one simmering pot, and utilized time, not just-in-time sequence, to fuse the raw ingredients into a savory whole. In a large orange bowl, she'd also combined the elements for making fresh tortillas, masa and water and shortening and salt. An ancient-looking cast-iron use-blackened tortilla press sat beside the bowl on the red-tiled counter, apparently unconcerned about Gabriella's somewhat unorthodox cooking procedures, no doubt gathered, over time, by watching her mother, and then simply reversing things, and performing them backwards: adding a cup of masa to a lumpy gruel of shortening and brackish-looking water, rather than adding the water in last, to a smooth blend of shortening and masa and salt. A fresh ball of dough, pressed between disks of the Iron Age utensil, would produce a tortilla with no memory at all of how it had been formed; made front to back or upside-down and backwards, it would still be a fresh round warm corn tortilla, ready to dip in the simmering stew. Of course if Gabriella had tried serving the meal out of sequence, before she had roasted and seasoned and cooked it, we would likely have gone hungry, standing at the sink with nothing in our stomachs, washing a large pile of dishes that had never been touched. Perhaps she had a list that she'd committed to memory, a list that began at the top, with the last spoonful eaten, followed by testing the pork bites for tenderness, and ending with raw and inedible ingredients, flying backwards toward the cutting board from out of the pot; such a meal would be tough and hard on the stomach, chewing uncooked pork did not sound appealing, but of course Gabriella, knowing herself, would have remembered to work things entirely backwards, reversing her memorized recipe steps, like recalling the sequence of her ATM PIN, and then letting things stew in their own juices for a bit, a procedure that, apparently, I was myself being put through; watching her dance around her red-tiled kitchen, carving and dicing and singing a *fado*, seemed to have brought me, raw and indigestible ingredients and all, to a slow mental simmer, as though my own memory stew were being cooked until tender, and getting ready to be consumed, from last bite to first.

Whatever her methods, they seemed to be working, the stew smelled delicious, and the Portuguese folk song, no doubt memorized note-for-note entirely in reverse, still sounded like a *fado*, no matter how difficult it must have been to produce. Through the cracked-open terrace door, I could hear her joyful singing, and while the song spoke of love that had turned out badly, and ended in bitter sadness and lonely regret, it was as though Gabriella felt only love's promise, that first blush of springtime, when the April birds sing; perhaps the bitterness and longing that love leaves behind it had long ago been forgotten, in her counterclockwise memories of the sequence of her life. As I listened more closely to the joy of her *fado*, it was apparent, however, that I might have been wrong about Gabriella: her joy seemed a joy made of something deeper, as though love's raw ingredients, not just the sweet but the star-crossed and bitter, had all blended together and been cooked until tender, until even the final emptiness was a part of the meal. It was possible, of course, that I was only hungry, and would have made quite a meal out of just about anything, even, if the stew burned, plain corn tortillas, but from the sound of her voice, and the beauty of her singing, it sounded as though love held not only its bright beginnings, but also the ending that had turned out so badly, and had only after all been love's bitter end. I sat beneath the nameless stars, listening to her *fado*, a rich simmering stew made of love and loss and longing, maybe something from Amália, from *Com que Voz* or *Cantigas numa Lingua Antiga*, a song of deep regret that left me happy and humming. Whatever the voice, however ancient and foreign the language, she sang like a bird, from moment to moment, her notes hopping from branch to branch in the conjectural oak of a posited spirit; no wonder I wanted to kiss her, at least hypothetically, and longed for a bite of her upside-down stew.

Apparently Gabriella, about whom I knew virtually nothing, was beginning to have some unfortunate side effects; there were, in all likelihood, certain forces aligned against me, and I might be better off solving a few basic identity problems, instead of standing around under the theoretical heavens, gazing at Gabriella and waxing rhapsodic. If Raúl Ramírez were to be believed, the clock might be ticking, while I wandered around Guanajuato with a pick and shovel, preparing, when the time came, to dig my own grave. Would you like to say a few words, sir, before you're concluded, perhaps something pithy, some memorable tagline or personal motto, which you'd like to have chiseled into your empty little headstone? Apparently not; what I seem to have in mind is kissing this woman. I don't suppose any of you know who she is? Or forget about who or whom, that's far too complicated, I know that you men have dirt to be shoveled, but let me ask you this: just how does she do it? As I stared at Gabriella, who appeared to grow lovelier the longer I watched her, as though her spirit grew more youthful over time as I watched, I seemed to be more interested in learning her secret than in learning my own, which might well prove important but entirely unmemorable. Her secret, however, was a little hard to pin down; she seemed, at times, with her counterclockwise memory, like a recent escapee from a thought experiment, maybe Schrodinger's cat or Maxwell's demon, the sort of being you'd concoct, out of pure conjecture, specifically to violate a primary law of physics, and demonstrate that nature was governed by laws that were only, in a sense, of a statistical nature; Gabriella's violation, if you could call it that, was of the primary laws of human nature, though the statistical probability of my wanting to kiss her seemed, at the moment, to be quite high, and it must have been this purely conjectural kiss that sent me off in search of whatever laws of nature I might need to violate in order to truly kiss her, or at least to increase the statistical probability of my turning my wanting to kiss her into a perfectly lovely and lawless kiss.                                  ·

    If you recited a simple list, of an ATM PIN or a chile verde cooking recipe, Gabriella's method might be mnemonically inverted, putting last things first and retrieving the sequence backwards, but it produced the same result as would an orthodox procedure; when it came time to produce her numerical identity, a PIN was a PIN, and cash would be dispensed. Her own life, on the other hand, was not quite so simple, and it wasn't an experiment, except perhaps on my own humming heart: her memories had accumulated slowly over time, and if you asked Gabriella where all of this was headed, what her story added up to, as an integral arc of life, she would likely just shrug, say what's the difference, adding up my life would not add anything, I would still be Gabriella no matter how you add it up, and as for where I'm headed, I will tell you when I get there, I will know it when I see it with my own two eyes; if you insisted on knowing her personal history, in hopes of discovering what had made her Gabriella, she would, of course, be happy to tell you, in a backwards, reversed, counterclockwise narration that spoke of her becoming, not a product of her past, but a becoming way of being that stands in the world in the ever-present moment of a counter-clockwise becoming, a way of being that I apparently found more attractive by the moment, and couldn't help staring at and longing for and humming over, wondering how the song goes that made me want to hum. Why bother living life, her way of being seemed to say, by extrapolating forward, believing that what we're bound to make of our future, our vision of an expanding or contracting inner universe, is already there in what we've made of our past? We remember those ample hopes of our wide-eyed youth, as we stared off into the distance toward a handsome future, toward the considerable beings we would make of ourselves, the beings in fact that would be so becoming, if life just granted us time enough, for whatever it was we were hoping to become; and then came the days that weren't quite what we'd hoped for, the days that were all just days as such, which wasn't at all what we'd meant by hope; and what came next felt a little empty, the time when we found what we were truly made of, and confronted the limits of our own vitality, and finally had to face the fact of the matter, that it wasn't at all just a matter of time; and maybe in the end we learned to live with our remainders, adjusting ourselves to the law of our nature, that whatever it is we seem intent on becoming grows smaller and smaller the older we grow. Too bad about us, and our extrapolated futures; maybe we all should have hoped a little harder, though having thrown my own hopes out a window in Guanajuato, along with the rest of my missing biography, I was in no position to comment on the value of having hopes; if I'd held out any hope, I must have held it out the window, and dropped it on the cobblestone streets of Guanajuato. As for Gabriella, singing *fado* in the kitchen, her becoming way of being had reversed all this, and moved from regret and sorrow and longing, back in time toward the days of fresh beginnings, as though the fallen leaves were leaping into the limbs of the trees. Reliving her life backwards, memory by memory, precisely in reverse, she passed through each moment of life just beginning, with only the hopes of a fresh new spirit, growing fresher by the moment, which is a beautiful way to grow. The days that are all just days, meaning nothing, were days of new beginnings and promising mornings, as she made her way back toward the bright new mornings and promising beginnings of the morning of her days, until she stood there

at last beside her ever-youthful mother, only now at the beginnings
of her retrospective becoming, in her long-ago hometown of nearby
Irapuato, bursting with vitality, on the threshold of life, watching
as her mother turned the warm corn tortillas back into handfuls of
malleable dough. If this led to a few odd cooking procedures, and
a strange mound of retrograde masa concoctions, the toll on the
stomach was worth every moment, as her spirit continued backward
in time, from dark disappointment toward the dawning of hope.
Though I myself hadn't suffered disappointments, or had tossed
them out the window along with my hopes, I apparently loved the
beauty of her backwards spirit: life might have taken her reasons
for dreaming; it could never take back the stars on which she'd
dreamed. The days that had ended badly, in bitterness and sorrow,
in the dead end of a day that was only another day, seemed to come
back to life, in her way of being, as the first leap of green into the
morning of the trees, singing songs and dancing around and stirring
the chile verde pot, and the more time passed the more it stood still
here; it felt good to be near her, just to be in her presence; she was
alive to the moment, which is a beautiful way to be.

While this hadn't exactly clarified who Gabriella was, one
thing, at this point, was abundantly clear: I needed to pry my eyes
loose from those singing red lips, which were giving me more answers than I could possibly find questions, and find something
simple to rest my two eyes on, before I tumbled backward into the
blossoms of the oak; and while I was at it, I should maybe just sit
down, before my standing in the world became even more precari-
ous. I took a seat on one of the balcony chairs, and looked up again
at the constellated heavens, searching for the Dippers and the belt
of Orion, feeling the sort of hunger that could belong to almost
anyone, only this sort was special, and could only belong to me. I,
Alvaro de Campos, who wasn't really anyone, had the feeling that
what I felt was just what we all feel, the hunger for food and drink,
and maybe some form of human connection, but mine was the sort
of hunger that couldn't belong to just anyone, it could only belong
to me, because I alone wasn't anyone. On the other hand, since I
hadn't followed a word of this whole hunger logic, since it didn't
remind me of me, it reminded me of something that might have belonged to Pessoa, it was probably time to eat, or maybe to steal a kiss

from my homeward-looking Angel, but the meal wasn't ready yet, the stew wasn't tender, and as for actually kissing her, I was afraid this would end up badly, in the first place, before working its way backward toward a truly awkward kiss. This might have been a good time for a memorized poem to enlighten and distract me, a bit of *Drink to me only with thine eyes* and *Leave a kiss but in the cup*, before I made a fool of myself, or started chewing on uncooked pork, but I couldn't for the life of me remember a single whole poem. I found two striking art works on the living room wall, just inside the doors to the starlit and chilly terrace, that would do for the moment of rest I had planned, lithographs by a local painter, Ricardo Curiel, from Gabriella's hometown, nearby Irapuato. Perhaps I should have known, right from the start, that being from Irapuato, these would not prove restful, as it soon became apparent, after a minute or two of study, that as with Gabriella, and that counterclockwise soup she had stewing in her kitchen, I'd bitten off far more than I could possibly chew.

The first was in the language of pictographs, in shades of grey and yellow-orange gold, using a variety of animals and fantastic creatures, some of them partially and whimsically human, drawn as stick figures like a child might do, if the child were an expert on tribal mythology, one who also had a background in electronic circuitry, and circuit-diagram symbols, and mechanical drawing; an interesting child, in other words, maybe a crossbreed of humans with extraterrestrials. The left half of the lithograph was an empty grey box, with an odd gold horizon line laying out a landscape; the sky and the Earth were identically grey, as though the Earth and its atmosphere were in moonwalk shades, and the ashes of Earth had polluted the troposphere. The right half was a grid of funny-looking beasts, part man part animal, set in five rows of four, like a Cornell box entitled Therianthropy, although in this case the metamorphosis that was well underway was headed in the direction of computerized life-forms. The deep inner workings of these otherworldly beasts, with the bodies of quadrupeds and the heads and headdresses of ancient Mayan jungle warriors, were diagrammed within in fine black lines, like the circuit board diagrams for a new line of toys, designed to survive in a difficult environment, or even to outlive their children if necessary, and go right on playing for a good long while, when the last human child would be buried and done with. Part man, part beast, part semiconductor part: they looked pretty hardy, though they'd reverted just a bit, back to a mechanistic hunter-gatherer animal mode, and they were still carrying on some traditions from the past, a few jungle-tribal, digital-human-hybrid, ghost-in-the-machine, ancient superstitions, and they didn't look at all like your upwardly mobile social types, the sort you try to recruit to the Board of Trustees of your local Modern Art Museum. If this is the future, you can close the museum, and put away your pencils, and shut down the toy shop; we've squandered enough wealth to build a trillion museums, but we're all long gone, and we just won't need them. The lithograph presented a truly stark choice: either an empty grey rock with a few strange seed pods on the edge of the horizon; or an empty grey rock with a hybrid-human specimen museum, where the last living things on the boiled-off earth had been preserved for eternity in a Cornell box.

The second lithograph on Gabriella's wall, of an orange moon rising on a dark starlit night, over the same grey rock and same grey Earth, with its empty-of-human-life-forms, what-the-hell-happened, barren-landscape time horizon, sort of, in a sense, explained the first; or if it didn't explain it, it gave us a kind of clue, written as it was in the same cosmic language. Once again the picture was beautifully stark, one-third grey landscape, the bottom one-third, and two-thirds black heavens, with an orange half-moon rising to locate us in time. By now, even the hardiest of the hybrid toys have died, and the Earth is an empty rock whirling through eternity, and the Cosmos is still out there as a matter of fact: 73% theoretical conjecture, something called Dark Energy, also known as the Lambda Constant; 23% Cold Dark Matter, the CDM in the Lambda-CDM end-of-the-Universe, in violence or lassitude, concordance equations; and the last 4% mostly cosmic gases, free hydrogen and helium trailing exhausted neutrinos, with everything stable you can think of in fact, all the spinning galaxies and stars and planets, able to fit forever, or until their time was up, in a nice tight box on a percentage basis, let's say .4% for the sake of convenience. All the heavy elements, as would be needed to support even a miniscule handful of your plain basic life-forms or life-like behavior…if not precisely human life, which was really quite a trick, if you stopped for a moment and thought about it…would fit in a box that is even smaller; the Earth itself is an instance of this, along with 10-million-billion possibly lifeless planets, and the box they all fit in is .03%, meaning the Earth, our living blue-green jewel, is a rounding error, twenty zeros out to the right of the decimal point, in a box so small the human hand couldn't draw it, and can only just barely be said to exist. In Curiel's vision, the moon rises as always, still warm from the sun, which unfortunately for us must be a great Red Giant, somewhere nearby but glowing an ominous orange, and out of the immediate picture frame, with the lithosphere and atmosphere of Venus, for example, which must have boiled-away our oceans and all known life-forms; the moon rises at last on an acknowledged land, whose landscape we destroyed a good billion years ago, and the odd thing you notice about our warm dead moon is that it's filled with the same circuitry of which the toys were made, strangely precise transistors and capacitors and circuit gates, with analog, discrete, and mixed-signal componentry. There is something truly comforting about a rising moon; no matter how difficult your actual day, you watch the moon rise and feel a warm sense of solace, which is just what you'd feel on a day like today, if it weren't for the fact that we've been gone for a billion years, and long ago squandered any semblance of our existence. It's hard to feel solace when you're a lifeless pile of dust, mostly calcium and sodium, with just a small trace of carbon; imagine the Moon, rising as always, in the dark and ancient wonder of the eternal east, looking down on the Earth, and finding nothing left to comfort. What exactly is the Moon supposed to do, still brimming with its wealth of odd cosmic circuitry, now that the toy shop has finally closed down, and the last whirring hybrid is finished and done for? Not that Curiel lacked a sense of humor about all this: if you looked up at the stars in the northeastern sky, after the last human intelligence was long ago abolished, you'd still find a sign of the presence of Man, a connect-the-dots constellation, call it Virgo maybe, whose connections were drawn using dash-marks of white. How can there be constellations in the free-form sky, those astrological signs of ancient prophecy, without our old friend and brother, Man, to connect the dots for all of us, and foretell the cosmic future? There can't be, there won't be, we no longer fit; and so what the artist had in fact left us with here, as we exited the picture of the starlit heavens, was the mark man had left on the cosmic machine, some deeply human laughter over the failure of our schemes.

Too bad about Man. Maybe he deserved it. Or maybe he has simply flown off into Space, searching for the future by slowly flying backwards, through a wormhole warp in the spacetime curvature, singing a song of sadness and longing and regret, and dreaming of chile verde and warm corn tortillas.

My eyes, my own two eyes, which seemed to have a life of their own that I was stuck with, were once again pried loose from an untenable perspective, and phase-shifted back to what was actually at hand, Gabriella cooking at her red-tiled counter, still leaning over her cutting board, wielding a gleaming-steel chef's knife on a red-orange mound of Caribbean Scotch Bonnets, or more likely Habañeros, from the steaming jungle heat of the Yucatan Peninsula, the sort of chilies that should be measured in electron volts, like Type O stars, made of ionized helium; the Scoville scale, of hot pepper magnitude, would not do them justice; they would taste like a fruit, and turn my tongue into an ionized-helium plasma. I might not know who I was, or how spicy I really wanted it, but if this was the sort of thing that Gabriella had in mind, in terms of the heat of her chile verde, I should have told her right there and then, I like it bland, and learned to live with my blandness; she was dicing these searing monsters at a high rate of speed, wearing yellow rubber kitchen gloves to shield her slim hands, and if the whole pile went off into the simmering pot of stew, it would take apart my head, and swallow all the pieces. As I imagined ingesting the first few bites, with the heat building up and my head suddenly throbbing, I realized I was thinking about something else instead, that kiss from Gabriella, which might best be avoided, or at least put off until I knew who I was, and knew what I meant by a kiss in the first place. What I needed from Gabriella was not a kind of kiss, it was some sense of the timeline of my stay in Guanajuato, like give or take tell me the month when I arrived, and tell me about the months I have lived through in the meantime, and talk to me a little about the grim-faced men, and what made them grim-faced, and when had I met them. In the photos she'd taken I'd looked like I was drunk, and since I hadn't had a drop for as long as I could remember, meaning give or take the better part of two long days, why was I drinking and what got me started, or maybe the real question was what got me stopped? And what about this lump on the back of my head? While it hadn't taught me much about my own inner being, it was, after all, only a few days old, and might mark the beginning of my becoming Alvaro, a name that struck me as rather elaborately contrived; though for all I knew, I had it all backwards, and that I, Alvaro, had proved to be such a phony, such a bag of hot air and elaborate contrivance, that the grim men had struck me just to shut me up. What I needed, in short, wasn't the silence of a kiss; what I needed was a briefing on when I'd arrived here, and how I'd spent my days, and my actual location in the spacetime continuum, but sitting all alone on the starlit terrace, talking to myself and not really listening, I drifted off course on the neutron soup of time, staring at Polaris and gripping my vacant star map, doing celestial navigation with a compass and an hourglass, and headed toward the Indies in the exact wrong direction.

Instead of going directly to Gabriella in the kitchen, and posing my questions regarding the spacetime of grimness, I returned once again to the question of myself, specifically as to why I had so many theories on the history of the cosmos, and so little knowledge of my own natural history. I knew, for example, that the heavens purportedly originated nearly 14 billion years ago, and yet I didn't have a clue as to the year of my birth. I also seemed to have some theoretical convictions on the subject of Relativity and Quantum mechanics in relation to the chronology of the Big Bang scenario, and some vehement, though purely hypothetical, opinions, with regard to the originality of this *de novo* explosion, the sort of opinions that could lead to a somewhat misguided discussion after drinking too much wine at a quiet little supper party, and yet if someone had argued that I'd been born 40 hours ago, not only would I not have been able to dispute this, for all I knew, he could be telling the truth. With all due respect, sir, I'm having a few problems with your timeline of the Universe; you cosmology experts, if you'll pardon my saying so, are all alike, extrapolating backwards using the Theory of Relativity, until you reach the Planck Epoch, at 10 to the minus 43rd second, where your theory breaks down, and you refuse to admit it. This rewinding of the clock, toward the first Planck instant, and that moment just beyond it, the Big Bang itself, in an infinite density and temperature singularity, misses the whole point: how do you make it back from 10 to the minus 43$^{rd}$ to T=0, the beginning of time? Ah, an amateur cosmologist, isn't that refreshing; perhaps you'd care for some more of this perfectly lovely Riesling while I offer to set the record straight regarding the history of time. Just to keep things in perspective, we have a clean crisp theory that more than adequately accounts for the last 13.73 billion years, and yet you seem to be having problems with the first Planck instant, an interval of 10 to the minus 43 seconds? I don't know what sort of wristwatch you normally wear, perhaps some sort of Ultracold Strontium alarm clock, mounted no doubt on a railway flatcar, but I think you'll notice, if you check your watch, you won't find Half Planck Time anywhere on there; you're complaining about a time frame that's not on our clock. I'm only suggesting, sir, that your theory needs to account for this T=0 singularity problem. You're claiming that Time started at some finite point in time, that you can rewind the clock to the very beginning, and if you ask me, be careful around here, you'll never make it back there with your intellect intact; your whole theory blows up long before the Big Bang. Agnes, I must tell you, the schnitzel and spaetzle were absolutely heavenly, but where did you find this man, living in a box under a bridge abutment? He's obviously unaware of the Hartle-Hawking no-boundary condition, which rather elegantly describes the finite limits of time, with no need at all for some T=0 spacetime singularity. Really, sir, I must object, I too loved the schnitzel, and while I may well have been living under some sort of an overpass, with you celebrity cosmologists in your chauffeured black sedans passing over my head on your way to the next conference, I'm well aware of the Hartle-Hawking State, this whole notion that the Universe started as a wave function, but seriously, and again, with all due respect, do you actually expect me to dismiss your whole problem, your failure to reconcile General Relativity with Quantum mechanics, by resorting to some sort of hypothetical vector in a Hilbert Space theory of quantum gravity? Help me out here, Agnes, tell this man who I am, even if I myself haven't got the foggiest, I mean I may well be a mound of tau and muon neutrinos, living down in the weeds under a high-speed rail line, but he's trying to tell you he knows the whole past, right up to the point where spacetime got started. Gentlemen, please, have another slice of cake; I mean really, in the grand scheme of things, this makes very little difference. You seem to be bickering over virtually nothing. Let me tell you, Agnes, there's a hole in his theory; if he can't make it back to T=0, maybe his Big Bang start was really a Big Bounce instance, and instead of us living in the first incarnation of a flat Minkowski Universe, with the curvature of a Riemann tensor or two, we could just as well be living in the give or take two billionth. I'm not buying any of it, his whole history of time. First of all, just to begin with, he has to put Relativity and Quantum mechanics back together, right at the start, to fill in that hole, and to get from T Zero to the end of the first Planck instant, at right around 10 to the minus 43rd second. And how is he proposing to fill in that hole? By shoveling in gravitons? Theoretical spin-2 massless particles? Then he proposes we continue forward in time, from the end of the first Planck instant to somewhere just past 10 to the minus 35th, where cosmic inflation somehow comes to a halt, with the Universe stuck in a quark-gluon plasma, and suddenly something goes horribly awry, some inexplicable reaction like baryogenesis, which violates the conservation of baryon number, and leads to a "small excess" of quarks and leptons over anti-quarks and anti-leptons; I mean seriously, ask him to explain this, why there's a lot more matter than anti-matter than there should be. Most amusing, sir, certainly most amusing; while I'll grant you that the Standard Model has a small violation of the conservation of baryon number, which admittedly results in a global U(1) anomaly, what would you have us do, resort to some sort of holographic String Theory? That, I can assure you, is a giant hairball, and certainly not the sort of topic for polite conversation. The Sachertorte is marvelous, Agnes; this time, honestly, you've truly outdone yourself. And the port, just extraordinary. Now where were we? Well I don't know where you were, sir, but I was preparing to tell you that you're completely full of shit, that you're theory is full of holes and mysterious blank spots and empty sorts of timepoints filled with a waving of hands. If you ask me, you don't have a clue about anything in history before 10 to the minus 15th second; back me up here, Agnes, tell this windbag who I am, I must be someone, if only for the sake of argument, even if I myself feel distinctly anomalous, like I've come up a few anti-quarks short of a whole. Actually, sir, I don't think we've been introduced; as a matter of fact, I've never laid eyes on you. Just how did you get in here? Were you even invited? I must say your manners leave something to be desired. And what's that in your hair, some sort of a bird's nest?

Alvaro, are you still out there? Yes, angel, I'm still out there.

Evidently, in my head, I was not a good dinner guest. From the way my own mind worked, having arguments with itself that I too found uncivilized, one might even surmise that I'd have problems dining alone, debating some obscure point in loop quantum gravity physics, while trying to pick the peas out of a Swanson frozen dinner. Gabriella put her knife down and slipped off her kitchen gloves, leaving a half-mound of orange-red chilies on the countertop, and leaving me to wonder just what I was in for. She was wearing a plain black wraparound skirt, and a white silk blouse, with a pattern of lavender and gold in brocade, maybe butterflies and plum blossoms plucked from thin air; the blouse had a high, Mandarin Chinese-style, collar, with silk-covered buttons, like pearls, up the front. She would have looked right at home in Singapore or Hong Kong, or maybe sitting in my lap, if I'd stop doing physics problems. The furnishings of the living room also seemed to be well-travelled, not just through space but also through time; they looked like they'd been lifted from a 1930s Bang and Olufsen ad, or the course catalog from a school of industrial design, equal parts Bauhaus radical simplicity and Vkhutemas Constructivism practical absurdity; a Barcelona chair, where a man could sit comfortably, faced a tubular steel abstraction of something, apparently intended as a place for sitting down, and perhaps better thought of as a perch for a seagull. What these things were doing in a flat in Guanajuato I couldn't begin to guess, particularly given the fact that they didn't appear to be contemporary reproductions; these were Modernist antiques, the revolutionary furniture of a failed revolution. Let's see now: if you constructed a chronology of 20th-century furnishings, beginning with right now, and then proceeded to read it backwards, you might end up right here, in Gabriella's living room, with a vision of the future as it might have looked from the past, before the Nazis and Stalinists simply put an end to all of it, and called a sudden halt to any thoughts of Utopia; of course, some of this furniture was so radical in its intent that it continued pointing forward, into the revolutionary future, on a timeline that could be traced along the surface of a Möbius strip, drifting away through time until the future doubled back on itself with a Möbius half-twist, and found itself right back where the future in fact had ended, right at the beginning, on the obverse side of the 1930s. The room, in other words, while certainly orderly, was almost worse than a physics problem; all the time it was flying around, going round in my head along a Möbius time-strip, the furniture itself was perfectly still, and nothing had moved even a fraction of an inch. I could almost picture Joseph Stalin, attempting to just get comfortable in one of Vladimir Tatlin's Constructivist chairs, tracing the tubular-steel framing around like he was trying to follow a strange flock of sparrows, twisting above the wheat stubbles on an old Georgian farm, near the Bronze Age settlement of Gori where he was born, with the birds flying around in a Möbius-strip-like stationary pattern, and finding himself at last with the beginnings of a headache, deciding it might be easier if he just shut Vkhutemas down. I myself had an interesting headache, itself constructed like a Möbius strip, starting off with the knot on the back of my head, pointing off into the immediate and possibly troubling future, where my pounding head was relentlessly headed, and then suddenly doubling back on itself with a twist, and arriving at last at its inevitable conclusion, that someone was about to strike me, with a bullet perhaps, on the obverse side of the back of my head.

Perhaps a lesser man than I might have stopped right here, with the sudden realization that he would soon be dead, and gone directly to the kitchen, maybe thirty feet away, to ask Gabriella just who was trying to kill him; unfortunately for me, at this crucial juncture, it proved difficult to imagine a lesser man than I, since everyone, at a minimum, had a mind of their own, while I had a mind that appeared to have been rented, fully furnished no doubt, from an absentee landlord; for all I knew, I was renting by the hour, and would soon be on the street, begging for spare change, surrounded by my own rather meager possessions; and so off I went, on yet another tangent, possibly inspired by this strangely furnished room, in the general direction of my possessing *chirality*, those mirror-image twists to a man's own identity, drifting off into the future with my future back there waiting for me, the future of my grim-faced pick-and-shovel past, no doubt headed toward me, in the form of a bullet, along a Möbius time-strip with a chiral half-twist; if I were hoping to try to locate a lesser man than I, and call a halt to all these tangents that my mind seemed prone to, perhaps a bullet to the head would be just the thing to do it.

.

Can you hear me, Alvaro? What are you thinking? Really, Gabriella, how on earth should I know, I who don't know even which way I'm twisted?

A figure in mathematics is said to possess *chirality* if it's not identical to its mirror image; a Möbius strip is one such figure, twisted as it is either to the right or to the left. If you look in the mirror, and you yourself are right-handed, you'll notice your mirror image is precisely the reverse: a left-handed you, a man who would face some difficult identity problems; even signing for the dinner check would pose quite a challenge, with the waiter staring down at some illegible scrawl, wondering Really, sir, this signature, it's completely indecipherable, do you know who you are, on the one hand, and on the other, are you sure this is you, this appears to be written backwards. I myself had more than a few of my own chiral-image problems: my image in the mirror could be said to be identical to the famous poet, Fernando Pessoa; but Fernando Pessoa, the famous poet, could never be said to be identically me. I myself, a man in his 50s, was telling the world I was Alvaro de Campos; Alvaro de Campos, who died in his 40s, would never even have considered telling the world he was me. Pessoa, in fact, when he looked in the mirror, was far from identical to the man that he saw. Pessoa himself saw 72 others, not only a man named Fernando Pessoa, who never quite got comfortable with his own identity, but 71 other so-called heteronyms, a whole cosmos of people who lived in his image: not only Caeiro, Reis, and Campos, but Soares and Mora and the Baron of Teive; not just Pacheco and Raphael Baldaya and I. I. Crosse, the poetry critic, but also a 19-year-old hunchback consumptive, living all alone on a backstreet in Lisbon, writing desperate love letters to an unnamed steel worker, a man who no doubt was identically himself, but known only to our desperate Maria José as a man who passed daily under her window, on his way back to work in the world of the living, completely oblivious to Maria's existence, as the fictitious pen name of a middle-aged man. Pessoa himself, who lived in obscurity, and died an utterly anonymous death, was chirally related to all these lives; all of these lives were identically him, while he himself was identically no one. It occurred to me that Gabriella's Möbius-twisted furnishings would have looked right at home in the mid-1930s, right around the time of Pessoa's corporeal and signed-by-the-doctor certified death, which was also the date on the birth certificate of Fernando Pessoa, the Modernist Master and everlasting poet; Pessoa the man was a Möbius strip, with a life that twisted back on itself, and slowly travelled backwards from out of his famous future, on a time machine he hadn't bothered to invent, since his future identity had invented it for him. As for Gabriella's radical furniture, furniture that dated from around the time of his death, when he still had his whole life triumphantly ahead of him, Pessoa would have found it thoroughly depressing; it mirrored too closely his own existence, as a failed and dying poetic revolutionary, and soon-to-be Modernist classic antique.

Would you like a beer, Alvaro? No, angel, I'd like to kiss you, but I can't seem to get out of my own twisted head.

Gabriella, my exotic angel, in oriental silk brocade, with lavender flying butterflies and the twigs of permanent plum blossoms, had put her gleaming knife away, and started up singing another *fado*, while making her own peculiar way forward, by dancing backwards out of the kitchen, toward where I sat under the heavens on her starlit terrace, stationed at some still-point of my own turning world, *neither flesh nor fleshless, neither from nor towards*, not wanting to kiss her but beginning to want her kiss. And how was I supposed to know whether or not I should kiss her? I, being the sum total of whatever it was I knew, minus any knowledge as to who it was that knew this, had no real insight into what sort of man I was; I certainly hadn't done very well at my own private dinner parties. Did I have some sort of philosophy of desire in general? Was I the type of person who tended to act on his desires? Or did I hold myself back out of moral scruples? Was the desire for a kiss to be followed by a kiss? Or did I keep some sort of ironic distance between myself and my own desires, like Pessoa's heteronym Bernardo Soares, living all alone on the Rua dos Douradores: *poets are all fakers and their faking is so real that they even fake their desire, the desire that they really feel.* Unfortunately for me, wanting to kiss her was like wanting to kiss her, it was completely tautological, I had about as much rational access to my own feelings of desire as the reader of Kant has to the construct of Time, once he finally figures out that Kant has no desire at all to explain or define or clarify time, that he wants us to understand it as a fundamental intellectual structure, to which we, as humans, have no rational access.. Or maybe all of this was far too complex, maybe I was feeling some sort of biological imperative, something in my bones and genetic-cosmic-circuitry that made me want to kiss her before it was far too late, before the pork shoulder stew had passed beyond tender, and the time to eat our fragrant and tautological supper had slipped by unnoticed, and missed us altogether.

Maybe, in short, this wasn't really the time to be getting overly analytical, perhaps it was high time I simply gave her a kiss, but I couldn't help wondering if this was totally unlike me, and that really, deep down, I was not that kind of man. Not knowing who I was, my relationship with myself was strictly professional; I was an object to be studied, as a concrete abstraction, the way a man at an archeological dig studies a bowl or amphora, seeking clues to the way of life that could be inferred from such an object. Imagine the surprise of our learned archaeologist, having only recently unearthed some odd-looking eating implement, at finding that not only was he hungry himself, but that the artifact he was studying had confessed to wanting supper. I stared at her lips as she twirled around dancing, and couldn't help confessing that I wanted her kiss, that I wanted in fact to make a meal of her lips, right there and then, before I was carted off and catalogued and promptly mislabeled, and placed under glass at a local archeological exhibit. Where was this coming from, and how had it arrived here, and why did it feel like something long-ago familiar, like the ache of a memory I myself could not articulate, but which was always already beginning to arrive here, on the tip of my tongue as it moistened my lips? I looked again at Gabriella, dancing in her living room, and it was immediately apparent where the feeling was coming from, right out of the future from her humming red lips, which I couldn't help hoping were about to arrive here, on a humming red time machine she hadn't bothered to invent, since my own humming heart had invented it for her; her lips seemed to be whispering something intimate and familiar, something about a kiss, which should have gone in one ear and immediately out the other, and instead went in my ear by way of my eyes, and came out on my lips, in a strange ancient language, some *Lingua Antiga*, that I had no hope at all of ever learning the first word of, but couldn't for the life of me even begin to forget.

Gabriella tossed her shoes away and joined me on the terrace, took one long look up at ancient Arcturus, or maybe it was Polaris, why on earth should I care, and holding her hair back as she slowly leaned down, kissed me on the neck below my burning left ear, still humming a few bars of what sounded like *fado*. Let me ask you, Gabriella, why do you want to kiss me, or forget about why, that's far too complicated, let's say you want to kiss me, just how do you do it? I didn't say this out loud, apparently I wasn't a complete and everlasting idiot, I like you Alvaro, I had the feeling that a kiss was long overdue, a time comes for everything, this goes without saying, you'll notice that I'm not talking so this must be that time, and then she kissed me on the lips and I felt like Bird's Nest Tom letting go of his tree-rope and plunging with flailing arms from high up above his home-is-where-the-heart-is warm Nebraska swimming hole. We have time, Alvaro, her kiss seemed to say, before the stew will be finished and our meal will be over, and she looked me in the eyes, memorizing the moment, if only for a time, which wouldn't last forever, not nearly as long as this everlasting kiss; knowing Gabriella, she had almost already begun to forget, and then everything inside me began to turn counterclockwise, reversing the normal flow of cause and effect, as though I'd always already long ago begun to kiss her, and were working my way backwards toward the first brush of lips.

No one needs to know precisely what happened next, or how tangled the sheets were when the moaning was over, or whose touch was whose and whose was the other's, and no one on earth needs a detailed explanation as to why our two bodies could not be pried apart. And then Gabriella laughed and skipped off toward the bathroom and emerged in a terrycloth robe with her hair up and her face scrubbed shiny and looking brand-new, and returned to the red-tiled counter in her kitchen, where the stew had now passed just beyond tender, singing *fado* to herself, and not meaning a word of it, singing past and present sorrows with bitterness and sadness, and meaning what a bird means when it sings the word *lament*. By now she was probably recalling the act of putting her hair up and scrubbing her shining face and putting her terrycloth robe on, exactly these actions, but precisely in reverse. How soon the time arrives when there is nothing left to wait for, and our slowly cooling sheets have fallen backwards from life's list. While Gabriella stood at her red-tiled counter, taking out the bowls for our chile verde stew, I lay gazing up at the senseless and nameless Heavens, just killing time, still keeping myself amused with the vagaries of forever; we have no idea at all where the stuff of time got started, and no need to know how it all turns out. Four stars. Four stars in the Heavens. How does this even begin to be possible?

# 21

W hich brings us to the story of Dacha Wireless, a fascinating story, fascinating, though it's a story, as will soon
become apparent, that I, among other things, am not
at all equipped to tell, in the sense, in the unfortunate sense, that
I find myself, even now, stuck in the very middle of it, seated at a
faux-wood plastic desk, at a Radisson Hotel in Juárez, Mexico, with
half of the story behind me, the half I am able to reconstruct, and
the other half somewhere off in the future, the half that hasn't happened yet, the half I'm maybe hoping won't. This, I can tell you,
isn't exactly what I had in mind, not when I invested in Dacha
Wireless, not when I set out to complete my *Memoirs*, this *Inside
Story* I was planning to write, before the whole thing turned on me,
and started writing *inside of me*, and not when I got into the venture capital business in the first place; I was, after all, a half-decent
poet, which might have prepared me for any number of things, like
teaching English Composition at a community college in Wisconsin, but which didn't prepare me for any of this, I mean not even
*this* could have prepared me for *this*. Which reminds me, shit, it
must be after 4 am, April 16, it's the 16th of April. I'm sitting in a
standard no-frills room, in a gigantic Juárez Radisson that got lost
on its way to Cleveland, at a laminated-plastic replicant desk that
was probably made in Guangdong Province, on Avenida Tecnologico or maybe it's San Lorenzo or Panamericana or Rafael Perez
Serna, not far from the airport in any case, and not only am I up
to my neck in shit, opiate-crazed heat-seeking sado-militaristic ab-

solute shit, but I haven't had much sleep in the last few days, and I completely forgot to pay my taxes.

Not, come to think of it, that I was planning to pay my taxes. Dacha started out innocently enough; "dacha" in Russian means "something given," and the deal, at the time, looked a lot like a gift, a nice tight package wrapped with a ribbon. Most of my best deals, over the years, have come in an oversized used cardboard box, full of spare parts gathered at a bankrupt junk yard: a couple of bright and intuitive guys with an admittedly striking but somewhat sketchy idea; a Business Plan written on a mental paper towel, with the cash flow model of an aging crack whore; and "bankable" executives supposedly in the wings, twenty years removed from some fluke that made them bankable. These are the best deals; they can be fixed; by dumping the whole mess down the nearest trash shoot, and starting all over with a blank white page, and a cold bright spark of business intuition. The rest of the deals are something else again, the sort of deals best left to the professionals up on Sand Hill: four or five execs with impeccable pedigrees, wearing the latest power ties and polished personas, with a game plan adapted from the occupation of Iraq, and reeking of self-confidence and technological condescension; these are the morons that can't be helped, but I have to meet them anyway; trust me, I've tried, it can't be avoided. The morons set up in my ocean view conference room, connecting their massive laptop to my miniature projector, and start in on the PowerPoint living color boredom show, full of dramatic build slides with custom animation, projecting a casual aura of inevitable success, around an idea so dead, they won't need engineers, they'll need a team of embalmers. All-knowing but not particularly bright, absolutely certain but generally clueless, I'm tempted to suggest that they just throw away their slides, and come back with something that packs a little more punch, something along the lines of a bomb threat or a ransom note, but I usually find it easier just to let them drone on, watching as the slides build and pretending to listen, maybe treating it as a piece of avant-garde performance art, nodding now and then to make them think I understand, even closing my eyes to protect them from all the brilliance, before gradually shifting over into deep-thought inspection mode, staring out the window at the sailboats on the Bay, or watching the blonde bikini girls rollerblade the bike path, as the Ferris Wheel turns on Santa Monica Pier, now there was a guy with a hell of a big idea, George Washington Ferris, a bridge-builder from Pittsburgh and a Rensselaer Polytechnic grad, even his beta test version was over 250 feet tall, with 60-passenger cars that held well in excess of 2,000 people, although unfortunately as always technology marches on, with the Star of Nanchang, which surpassed the London Eye as the wheel world's tallest, at something I'm thinking over 500 feet, itself about to be surpassed in turn, I mean nearly dwarfed, by the Great Wheel of Beijing, it's a competitive market among the world's Giant Wheels, and given the ticket price of under 50 yuan, there's not much gross margin when you boil it all down, maybe not the sort of market you want to enter a century late, even if you were backing George Washington Ferris, and then asking the moron slideware guys "What's your gross margin?" Of course, after twenty-some years of not listening to morons, and eventually losing interest in the whole Ferris Wheel concept, you're deeply grateful when some bright guys wander in, so grateful you wouldn't care if their slides were done in crayon. I usually stop them around slide number six, and ask them to sit down, and turn off the projector. We talk about a lot of things; about life in the real world, the world where most of us used to live, before the bankers ran off to join Le Cirque Imaginaire, and left us with trillions in conceptual artworks; about what it was they really wanted to build, before their minds got warped by talking to venture capitalists; about life growing up on a small family farm, or maybe playing point guard on an undersized squad, learning to spread the ball around, and share the points with everyone; and then I offer them money more or less on the spot, and spend the next five years trying to prove I'm not stupid, which amazingly, on occasion, it turns out I'm not, which is how I've managed to remain gainfully employed, while amassing a couple of billion or so of perfectly legal profit.

The billions, unfortunately, mostly belong to my investors, pension funds, University endowments, charitable trusts for children's hospitals; don't get me wrong, while I may be a Marxist, I'm not, strictly speaking, opposed to Massive Wealth Creation, just as long as my fair share of the wealth ends up inside my pockets. And while I may be the world's only Marxist Venture Capitalist, at least outside of China, I once knew a Communist securities analyst, and an

M&A banker who used to quote Che Guevara, and an index fund manager, with over a trillion under management, who was a completely unreconstructed but obscenely wealthy old crypto-Stalinist. If you yourself have high ideals, and are just getting started in the wealth accumulation business, and find yourself worrying about the injustice inherent in the few growing wealthy while the rest grow hungry, it may be useful to know that all of these men, men of high ideals who abhorred injustice, proceeded by applying a fairness test proposed by the poet, Fernando Pessoa: I cut the orange in two, and the two parts couldn't be equal; to which was I unjust—I, who am going to eat them both? While this would appear to cover most of the moral dilemmas that you're likely to encounter in day-to-day life, even the true idealist, the sort of man who's passed his fairness test with flying colors, may find himself facing a kind of geography quiz that we all, to be honest, find grossly unfair, particularly when you're on a deadline on an asset allocation issue, and can't find your desk beneath an immense pile of orange peels: if we are not on the side of those whom society wastes in order to reproduce itself, where are we? *Where are we?* If you've seen a recent photo of Julia Kristeva, the post-structuralist psychoanalyst who memorably posed this devious little question, you'd know with some certainty that we're either in her office, just down the hill from the rotunda of the Pantheon, getting ready to teach a class on psychosemiotics, in the Linguistics Department at the University of Paris; or far more likely, given that book cover photo, we're in a small but chic hair salon on the Rue Saint-Surplice, near Boulevard Saint Germain, in the 6th arrondissement, waiting for our foil-wrapped highlights to set, before getting that beautiful new retro-'70s wedge cut. We, in short, with our high ideals and inherent sense of fairness, shouldn't have to deal with Kristeva's devious questions.

Somewhere along the way, however, as we sank ever deeper into this whole Dacha accounting mess, and started quizzing ourselves, at odd hours of the night, on all sorts of topics that were out of our domain, as though we of all people were expected to pass a test on whether we knew the difference between wakefulness and dreaming, we not only had to deal with Kristeva's devious questions, but short on sleep, and apparently overestimating our own inner resources, we must have cut some sort of deal to acquire her entire corpus, and while she'll never wind up obscenely wealthy selling books like *Powers of Horror: An Essay on Abjection*, or those *Black Sun* meditations on the poiesis of self-debasement, or *New Maladies of the Soul*, or *Time and Sense*, or *Strangers to Ourselves*, a personal nemesis, a kind of who-the-hell Hello to all the aliens breeding inside us, or even the more obviously and immediately applicable *Severed Head: Capital Visions*, she would appear to possess a rather detailed map to the terra incognita we currently inhabit, a map that, let's face it, we couldn't possibly afford. So *where are we?* I'll be damned if I know; I started out, innocently enough, making a rational-looking investment in the cell phone business, and the next thing I knew I had a one-way ticket to a massive Hotel Radisson on the *Severed Head* side of the border, so we're not so much asking ourselves where in fact we are, as we're wondering who to pay in order to get the hell out of here.

Silence is argument carried out by other means.

Which is a topic that, obviously, we'll need to come back to. Dacha Wireless, as I was saying, appeared to have been gift-wrapped, the business plan cohered, the technology looked flawless, and the market, theoretically, was potentially enormous, meaning every single cell phone terminal installed on this Earth, handling two billion cell phones and growing by the tens of millions, would use Dacha amplifiers if they knew what was good for them. The execs were like the Dream Team from the 92 Olympics; they had small-scale purchase orders already in hand, based on lab test results showing striking linearity, optimal efficiency with minimal distortion, and an order of magnitude signal-to-noise-ratio vast improvement, which normally would have translated to "it just might work," but somehow made a beeline straight through my filters, and came out a distorted "what could possibly go wrong?"; and while the deal was going to eat a tremendous pile of cash, they had two Sand Hill venture funds prepared to share in the care and feeding, and strategic investors in China itching to write a check, and a dumb-money hedge fund, Third World Partners, that was price insensitive and ready to lead on the Series B. So what's wrong with this picture? Basically, everything; the deal, among other things, made far too much sense; in my entire career, spanning 20-some years and 70 or 80 investments, I've never once made a dime on a deal that made sense; if you don't build senselessness into your deal, the Future, rest assured, will build it in for you, as the Future has a plan for your sensible-looking deal, a plan to render it utterly senseless. Unlike my usual impulse buys, I actually did my job, analyzing the market, bringing in a consultant to validate the data, doing the background checks and reference calls and building the file, vetting and re-vetting, double-checking everything for signs of cracks and leaks, some water mark on the ceiling that would lead me up to a wounded roof, some low-pressure water tap that would send me down to the mangled plumbing, and everything came back with a clean bill of health, meaning not only was it likely that I'd missed something vital, since early-stage startups are inherently unhealthy, but that I'd somehow started thinking like a real VC, and was now mixing metaphors that were so brutally simpleminded that I might not know the difference between buying a new house, and pumping blood, meaning cash, into a sentient entity. While this would appear to be a difficult error to make, losing sight of the difference between a house and a startup, if there's one thing I've learned over the course of my career, if a mistake can be made, trust me, I've made it; these deal files we build get so crammed with facts, market data, design specs, competitive analysis, and leave so little room for the human element, sapience, reasoning, cognition, self-awareness, that our deals start to look like inanimate objects, the sort of things that wouldn't move if you poked them with a stick. So if you ever find yourself in my position, building deal files so thick that you can no longer lift them, and unable to tell the difference between a house and a startup, I'll give you a hint: houses don't die of their own stupidity.

So what did I do next? The exact wrong thing. Instead of going back to see what I might have missed, I set up a conference call with the pros up on Sand Hill, and we came to a consensus around one essential fact: our new house was beautiful, with immaculate copper piping and a magnificent slate roof. Did it strike us as odd that our house came with a lawyer, Albert-something, who knew virtually nothing about the cell phone business, and virtually everything about offshore investing? Albert? Albert is wonderful. Albert has all of our initial sales locked down, and contracts in place with new-network suppliers, so new in fact that not one of us has heard of them, and a funding-deal lined up, with a dumb-money hedge fund, so dumb in fact, and so ignorant about our business, that unbeknownst to us, they already own an option to buy the entire Series B. Albert's a bit *slick*, or maybe the word we used was *sleazy*, but Albert owns the blueprints to our beautiful new house. Were we troubled by the fact that Albert had built our house, which didn't, come to think of it, come equipped with a single window, somewhere around the bottom of a Cayman Island mailbox, incorporating everything, slate roof and all, inside a box made of legal docs that none of us owned a key to? No, not really; the Caymans sound ideal; most of our revenue will come from offshore, so why pay taxes on our offshore profits? Just think of all the money we'll save on audits; those auditors in the Caymans are dirt-cheap and clueless. Besides, if we want to go public on the Hong Kong Exchange, our new Island home makes the perfect location; if we should happen to have a problem with a regulator on the Islands, we'll replace it at a store that sells underwater diving gear. Were we at all concerned that the data might be fudged, or that the consultant we'd all used to validate the product had now joined the company and owned an immense pile of stock, along with, what was it now, a $200K starting bonus? Of course not, never, what could possibly go wrong, just goes to show you how lovely our house is, our consultant moving into a 6-room suite seems perfectly normal, particularly given the fact that he's been living outdoors, eating out of cans and drawing unemployment, and hasn't had an office for at least five years. There's a saying I have, for whatever it's worth, that might be useful to know if you encounter a similar process: *reality*, as the saying goes, *is a group project*. So what was I saying about maybe I was missing something? I had a pretty firm grip on the *group reality* of it all, right down to the details of the design specifications, though there may have been some subtleties that I'd managed to overlook, like the fact that the Dacha WiMAX amplifier, the go-to-market product whose performance I'd double-checked, was designed to amplify cell phone signals from an alternate reality in a parallel Universe.

To make a long story short, to get to the point, before once again

beginning to make a long story pointless, I wrote the check, I signed
the docs, I did the inevitable deal, tilting back at last in my uncomfortable Aeron chair, in my spacious corner office with its views up
to Malibu, feeling good about myself, feeling for once like a true
professional, and then in all likelihood blowing off the remainder
of yet another lovely day, catching a movie on the Promenade, or
daydreaming at a Starbucks, not knowing, among other things, that
my mind wasn't right, that I'd just consumed a massive dose of a
psychotropic substance, not that stuff left over from the black-proj-
ect mind-control MK-ULTRA psy-ops wars, or an Ayahuasca brew
concocted by a Peruvian Shaman, from the vines of oco yage and
the leaves of the N-dimethyltryptamine varieties of chacruna, but a
far more dangerous mind-altering euphoriant, Smoke of Group Reality Root, also known on Sand Hill as *breathing your own exhaust*,
and would soon be wandering the beaches in an Angel's Trumpet
delirium daze, sifting the drifting sands for the last few grains of sanity, and mumbling under my breath about *a design flaw in reality*.

Obviously, I exaggerate. Not only is Angel's Trumpet, a highly toxic deliriant, somewhat redundant when you're shitfaced on
money, but I've spent 20-some years wandering around Sand Hill,
with a little yellow spade and a red plastic bucket, and while it's
altogether possible that I'm missing the whole point here, there's no
such thing as sand on Playa Group Reality.

So how did our launch go? Exploded on the launch pad? I'll
spare you the details; you wouldn't understand. Not only that,
but I don't actually have them, the details that is, since once the
orders start pouring in, no one gives a damn about the details in
the first place, we care about raw speed and market acceleration,
and that wind-in-the-hair going-ballistic feeling. Who cares about
details when you're headed straight up, burning through cash as
though you can't afford a fuel gauge, toward revenue outer space, at
orbital-escape pure-run-rate velocity? The Board of Directors? You
have to be kidding. That guy at the craps table, one of those larger-
than-life types, with a Three Forks Stetson on his Abilene head, a
tall platinum blonde on his off-hand shoulder, and a 5-by-3 fruit
stand, offering $1,000 lemons, stacked 30 deep on the Pass Line

in front of him, is not only getting ready to make his 12<sup>th</sup> straight
pass, but cares more about the details of this next throw of the dice
than does the entire Board of a Bank on a derivatives-fueled profit
binge: placing his sour mash rocks glass down, in the exact same
ring as the last eleven passes; watching as the Stickman twirls the
red cubes, through endless combinations that all make 7; waiting
until the dice for his come-out roll read 6 and 1 before he'll even
touch them; picking his pair up, with two fingers and a thumb,
and shaking them gently, trying not to wake them, or disturb that
6-and-1 spell that they're under; holding them out, red-lip high, so
his weekend girlfriend.can whisper a blessing, and whistle a lucky
tune for the 5-2 to dance to; and then giving them that identical,
God-is-in-the-details, long-last-look in their round white eyes, and
an Abilene kiss, and a 4-3 tap on the rock-hard table, dropping a
small load of mercury down a capillary tube from the heart of each
die to the 3-4 soles of its heavy-metal boots, meaning this next fucking dance had best be a waltz, or Three Forks will vaporize a large
pile of fruit...before flinging them away, with a foot-long could-
give-a-shit backhanded motion, like he's skipping red stones across
a green-felt lake, toward the green-felt banks at the end of the table,
under guidance from his glory-to-the-dice-loader prayers, and his
Big Red! Big Red! sing-song incantation, awaiting the inevitable
roar and the shaking of heads and the isn't-that-incredibles from the
crowd around the dance floor, while the Stickman calls the win,
and the Dealer deals the fresh lemon chips, and the Boxman folds
his chalk-striped arms, with the vacant stare of complete indifference and master-of-motion intense concentration, as the Pit Boss
turns and walks away, awaiting word from his security detail, the
Eye-in-the-Sky that never blinks. You want details? Talk to the guys
in a well-run casino; that Boxman master of every move knows each
chip, and the betting history of the guy who palmed it; some numbnuts tries to waltz wearing mercury boots, he won't dance long on
the Boxman's watch. You talk to the guy on the Board of the Bank,
he knows the square yards of his Palm Beach curtains; risk com-
pliance on their Snowballs and Floaters, how much they have bet
on Credit Default Swaps, why they are holding CMOs made of
mortgage bundles full of loans in Fresno, where some independent
contractor, without a word of English, making $14,000 a year in

the agricultural sector, borrowed every last penny he needed to buy some piece-of-shit spec-house house with a vinyl-paneled rec room, on a cul-de-sac deep in Foreclosure Glen, for $726,000 and then some, why would he know anything at all about any of this monotonous shit, details, details, don't bother me with facts, just look at these amazing piles of lemon chips. You ask the Boxman, he shakes his head; bunch of fucking morons is all he says.

So let's just say the bookings came roaring in, with up-front cash to solve our little burn problem, from Third World countries that none of us had heard of, Lesotho, Eritrea, Comoros, Guinea-Bissau, and places like Malawi and Suriname and Timor-Leste, places from a 5$^{th}$ grade geography quiz, where you're supposed to match the country to the name of a continent. Do you know the difference between Kazakhstan and Kyrgyzstan, in terms of which would be most interested in buying UFDMA packet-based downlinks? If the government of Turkmenistan ordered enough amplifiers to blanket the Black Sands Desert with solar-powered cell phone towers, would you find that a little odd? How much do you actually know about 3GPP Long-Term Evolution? If I told you it used E-UTRAN on the network core side of the Evolved Packet System, and EPC on the access side, would you be able to tell me that I had it backwards? Exactly. Me either. Have you ever heard of companies like HTNL, IGO, TOT Corp, and Enforta, as opposed to companies like HNL and Bhartos and Kordian and Whish Wireless? I'll give you a hint: some of these are real, and actually deploying WiMAX networks; and some of these are not so real, and probably deploying an elaborate smokescreen. If you're sitting in a Board meeting, and the CEO tells you that they're selling a bunch of power amplifiers through a company named Infocom, for WiMAX systems in Kampala, Uganda, you should probably start feeling pretty good about yourself; if the CEO says new orders have just come in, with payment in advance, for SC-FDMA uplink amplifiers, purchased by Velocicom for Paramaribo, Suriname, you might want to call a lawyer who speaks a little Dutch, and knows a fair amount about the bauxite industry, like how to turn bauxite into an aluminum explosive, and hide most of Suriname under a dense cloud of smoke, because you yourself will have no way of knowing whether these orders are real or not. Real? How can they not be real if somebody actually paid for them? What could be more real than Cash Up Front?

While this would turn out to be an excellent question, it not only wasn't a question that I was prepared to answer, it wasn't even a question that it occurred to me to ask, as I'd witnessed so much fraud over the course of my career, and knew so much about spotting the fraudulent, that I had no idea how ignorant I was, or how brutally simpleminded were the frauds that I'd learned to spot: round-tripping sales and booking them as revenues, almost as though real cash had changed hands; shipping empty boxes off, or boxes filled with bricks, into waterfront warehouses, in bill-and-hold schemes; stuffing the sales channel with returnable merchandise, and acting like you sold the stuff, and actually think the orders are billable; selling the customer a two-part solution, one part software that you book as revenue, and add to your balance sheet as a 30-day collectible, and one part side letter that you hide in a drawer, telling the customer that there is no need to pay you; even running your whole company like you're writing a novel, thinking up names for fictional corporations, and selling them mountains of Magical Realist products, hot off the presses of the Arcane Mysteries Lab. In all of these cases you learn to spot the fraud by keeping one eye on the cash and the other on the receivables: if one of them is rapidly sinking, and you can't pay your water bill, and the other is through the roof, and you're going to need a much taller building, you may have a problem; do us both a favor, don't tell them I warned you. So how can it be fraud if the equipment has all been paid for, and the cash, at long last, is finally piling up, and our receivables are down around let's-call-it zero? Not getting the picture? Precisely. Me either. You and I have the exact same problem, spherically everted and ontologically reversed, as the guy on the Board of Derivatives Bros., when he finds out they've squandered an absolute fortune on Synthetic CDOs, which is the real world equivalent of losing the family farm, including the kids and a thousand-head of cattle, by betting it all on Fantasy Football. What the fuck is a Synthetic CDO? One day you're telling me they're worth about a dollar, and our pockets are so full, we may need new pants, and the next day your telling me they're worth about ten cents, and we'll have to report billions in actual losses, and they may keep our pants if we all wind up in prison; can you run that by me again? How in the hell do you lose real money on the depreciation of fictional assets? Are we running a goddamn business here, or playing some kind of videogame? How on earth could an entire modern office tower get reduced to a pile of rubble by imaginary planes?

If you ever find yourself in my position, up to your neck in shit, and feeling happy about it, with your self-esteem up where the big birds fly, feeling sorry for the little guys who work for a living, and it suddenly starts to feel too good to be true, like maybe your wireless amplifier company is amplifying signals from an alternate reality, you have to ask yourself one simple question: what would the Boxman do? By now, of course, it was a little late for all that, by now we were accelerating through a $100 million run rate, projecting Forward Twelve Months at let's-call-it twice that, and had already filed on the Hong Kong exchange, with a pristine balance sheet, margins and cash flow that a pharmaceutical company would envy, and a backlog of orders from HNL and Bhartos and Kordian and Whish Wireless, companies that when cell-phoned by the IPO-sanity-checking Investment Analysts, raved about the Dacha products: not only did they love our stuff, they wouldn't exist without it. If you called the Minister of Telecom in Abuja, Nigeria, to discuss their WiMAX rollout plans for Lagos and Port Harcourt, the outlook was upbeat: the trials in Abuja, using the Alvarion BreezeMAX 3500, supplemented of course by the Dacha 1200 3.5 gigahertz amplifier product, could not have gone more smoothly had the entire deployment been a complete fabrication. If you phoned in with questions for the Velocicom managers, in charge of installations on the Dacha 1201, at their downtown headquarters in Paramaribo, Suriname, you knew with some certainty that the demand must be vast: these guys were so busy installing new product that all twelve calls produced a busy signal. When you finally got through to the Royal Palace in Tonga, and debriefed the Wireless Network Strategist on their Go Forward Plan, hoping to gain some insight into new-network requirements, and get a better understanding of their need for Dacha products, you got an answer so replete with acronymic technobabble that you thought about changing jobs, as if you actually had a skill you thought you could market. "We're planning to overlay our GSM network with WiMAX for broadband, with the goal of having full 4G, and a fully integrated IP system, via 3GPP LTE as the products become available. We've been concerned for some time about the long-term stability of gallium arsenide and silicon carbide-based substrate coupling, and thus the Dacha CMOS product was very attractive. At the moment we're watching the Do-CoMo trials, using Space-Time Trellis Codes in a 12-by-12 MIMO, and VSF-OFCDM for their spatial-domain multiplexing, and have noted with interest their ability to achieve 5 Gbps IP-packet transmission rates for mobile reception at 10 KPH. We believe that the Dacha Software-Defined Radio product will give us the flexibility needed to surpass this, using Cognitive Radios in a Spread-Spectrum Mesh, and have therefore concluded that Dacha Wireless will be uniquely suited to fit our long-term roadmap." For some strange reason you have this image of life on Tongatapu, where a man is leaving his palm-thatched hut on an oxcart piled with coconut products, an oxcart with enormous and slow-moving wheels, well within the 10 KPH DoCoMo speed limit. What is this man doing? Watching high-definition television on his mobile handset? Does a rutted track through the palm tree orchards sound like something that needs a long-term roadmap? Would a man feeding his family on $2 a day, by multiplexing cartloads of coconut packets into the bottom of a food chain that turns them into biodiesel, pay $29.95 a month for broadband access? We'd suggest you get a grip; take a look out your window; these visions you're having aren't valid due diligence. You're running with the Big Dogs, 40 stories up, with one of those breathtaking views over Victoria Harbor, and if your boss is telling you the deal is going out, then the deal's going out, no question about it. It's really not your job to be applying common sense, start wondering why some country that's never heard of indoor plumbing needs fourth generation cell phone networks or enormous bandwidth Internet connections; you keep this up, you'll wind up working in a Dai Pong Dong, and instead of buying bottles of pink champagne, on Ladies Night at the bars in Lan Kwai, the F-Stop maybe, an excellent choice, just across the street from the Hong Kong Space Museum, you'll be hunkered down in a cheap hotel in Tsim Sha Tsui, chewing on your nails and drinking beer for a living.

And so the deal went out, Dacha went public, at $800M pre,

with the IPO banker's books a good 12X oversubscribed, and a lot
of traction in the aftermarket, meaning the funds that couldn't get
in on the deal were buying like crazy and driving the price up.
When the lock-up came off, we started selling our shares, into a
rising market with a massive amount of trading volume, and came
out smelling like a fresh-cut rose, or maybe a whole vase full of Pink
Mystery lilies. It's a beautiful thing when you finally cash out, stop
worrying that the orders are about to level off, or that your supply
chain will implode, or that some guys at Datang, who've been focused on TD-SCDMA 3G products, have decided it's finally time
to rip-off your design, commoditize your market, and drive your
gross margins from 65% to something that struggles to break double
digits. The money goes out to your Limited Partners, with a 20%
cut of the profits for your troubles, and as the wire transfers clear,
and the money is in your wallet, and you're thinking about buying
that next corporate jet, move up from the Hawker 800XP to the
Citation X, or maybe the G4, with that beautiful new blonde as a
cabin attendant, it finally becomes clear that your whole life makes
sense, that every single mistake you've ever made in your life, the
whole mangled mess of poor judgment and blunders, was a rounding error compared to this, and that you're a man of deep savvy and
fungible substance. Why not buy that yacht? That 6-bedroom ski
house in Vail or Deer Valley? Why not have it all, you're a genius
with money, you've made a small fortune on a single deal alone,
after all those other fortunes and with plenty more where this one
came from, your future has the sweet aroma of a Pink Mystery lily,
and you're buying up cases of Baccarat crystal, and the stars in the
sky were arranged just for you, the invincible investor, to grant your
smallest wish, and underwrite your dreams of endless prosperity.
Even a man with his head firmly screwed on tight, who keeps things
in perspective, and is a closet Marxist, has to admit that he's one
in a hundred million, the real fucking deal, the master Alchemist,
the new Zosimos of Panoply. And while even a total idiot knows
that money can't buy happiness, self-esteem can, and you now have
quite a lot of it. Of course you know, with humility, that you'll have
to give something back, maybe set up a foundation for the underprivileged, but frankly, in relation to you, the whole fucking world
looks underprivileged, since they, after all, have to live with them-

selves, while you live with you, which is quite a fucking privilege.

And then you wake up one fine morning, with a massive self-esteem and Pink Mystery hangover, and find yourself in a Board meeting at Dacha Wireless, where you continue to serve on the Board of Directors, and the news, to be honest, is not all good. Remember the Boxman? What has happened in effect is that Abilene's waltzing, and piling up the money after twelve straight passes, has begun to get on the Boxman's nerves. He calls the Floorman and the Pit Boss over, they have a quiet chat, turns out the Eye-in-the-Sky has finally spotted something: after the 7th straight pass, when the dice bounced out and were caught by that tourist, the middle-aged low-roller in the I Heart Vegas T-shirt, who's been betting the Don't Pass line for a good fifteen minutes, she palmed the table's dice and threw back the loaded ones. The Stickman shuffles a fresh pile of dice, the loaded pair vanish, to be studied by the Floorman, and the Stickman declares New Shooter coming out, and Three Forks, his girlfriend, and the tourist in the T-shirt, are given a brief tour of the casino's impressive new Network Video Recording facilities, as the crowd around the table begins to dwindle down, and normalcy resumes with a fresh roll of Boxcars. The analogy, to be honest, is not intended to be exact, however…some short-seller running a Spot the Bullshit hedge fund, with a million shares plus in short positions, has called in the Eye in the Sky, and spotted something on Dacha Wireless. Turns out those orders, from Velocicom for Paramaribo, are not being deployed at a particularly rapid rate; after $20M in shipments, with another $10M worth sitting on the loading dock, not a single WiMAX wireless terminal is actually functional, and far from adding value to the bauxite industry, with high-bandwidth data rates and full-motion MPEG video, the Dacha Wireless amplifier products seem to be doing something else, like piling up in a warehouse in Marienburg, Suriname. Heh, what the heck, that's telecom for you, maybe there's been a delay in the WiMAX antennae-tower permitting process, which probably would explain the deployment shortfalls, if it weren't for the fact that no one in Suriname has the slightest fucking interest in WiMAX in the first place. Have you tried calling the Velocicom guys, get them to explain this, why they own $30 million worth of WiMAX amplifiers, and have most of them stacked up in a 3PL, an aluminum shack, where the reception is probably terrible? Well, here's the thing, they won't return our calls; in fact, if we had to guess, they don't own a telephone. Turns out the office was a one-man shop, and now the one man's gone, and so is the office. Jesus. How much do they owe us? Funny thing is, they don't owe us a nickel; they paid list price for everything, and everything is paid for. So what you're saying is, it's really not our problem. Yeah, well, here's another funny thing, turns out the deal with Bhartos is very similar; they seemed to be making progress on the Tonga field trials, turns out there's nothing in Tonga but, well, fields. Have you spoken to the Palace? They still moving forward with their 3GPP-LTE roadmap? We could always go direct if Bhartos has gone under. They're never going to get there with that BreezeMAX box; maybe we should talk to Alvarion, or Aperto or WiChorus, set up some kind of resale agreement. Sure, sure, we should probably talk to Alvarion; unfortunately our contact with the Royal Family, their Wireless Network Strategist, who said he reported directly to King George Tupou the Fifth, left several months ago and hasn't been heard from since, though the King, from what we've heard, thoroughly enjoyed the gentleman's company, and is apparently wondering when to expect his next check. Check? Don't tell me we've been paying him. No, no, look, we're no Siemens, running around bribing these Third World dictators; everything we've done here is completely aboveboard, it's just that, apparently, there's no such board. Tonga, as a matter of fact, is a constitutional monarchy, and King George himself has no real authority. So why the hell are we bribing him? What about Kordian? We still moving forward on the Eritrea deal? Look, let's be honest, the Eritrea deal has gotten a little complicated, they seem to be involved on several sides of the wars in Somalia, their border with Sudan is piling up with troops, even the Yemeni's are threatening to invade them, the U.S. has them down on the list of rogue states, and the press is shut down tighter than North Korea. It's hard to say where WiMAX fits on their list of priorities. So what are you telling us? This quarter may be tough? Do we need to preannounce some sort of earnings shortfall? And where the hell is Albert, he negotiated all these deals, through the guys at the hedge fund, what's their name, Third World Partners? Albert. Yes, Albert, our lawyer, you remember him. Oh, certainly we remember him, we just haven't seen him; he went back to Beijing, claiming he had to deal with a family illness, and completely disappeared; we're hoping just maybe he might have been kidnapped. Though we don't think that's his name, by the way; apparently he was in the country under an alias, illegally. Our lawyer? Illegally? Christ, what next, I mean really, what a mess, maybe you better step back and try to net this all out for us, last quarter we're cranking and headed straight up, and now, I mean Jesus, *where the hell are we?*

Where we were, as it turned out, was not on the Rue Saint-Surplice, getting highlights and a foot massage before our beautiful new wedge cut, we were somewhere altogether elsewhere instead, in the middle of some kind of pyramid scheme, inspired more by Crazy Eddie than by Charles Bianchi Ponzi, and were just about ready to take a massively ugly haircut, and shave about nine-tenths off of our market capitalization. Just to give you some idea of the brutality of the market, once it finally begins to sense that something might be amiss, who do you suppose might have Spotted the Bullshit, and bought a million-plus shares in short positions? Exactly. You got it. You catch on fast. Our own investors, Third World Partners. So let me ask you something: how much do you actually know about the money laundering business? When you got that Harvard Business School MBA, did they happen to include a Business Case Study on the revenue model of Crazy Eddie? This was back in the 1980s, long before the technology or housing bubbles, which were themselves nearly indistinguishable from pyramid schemes, although unfortunately for most of us, they both turned out to be perfectly legal; Eddie, in all likelihood, hadn't yet mastered such subtle distinctions, though neither, come to think of it, have your Harvard Professors. Crazy Eddie's was an electronics retailing chain, positioned in the market as the low-price leader, able, in other words, to beat the next guy's price, because the next guy was supposedly rational, while Eddie took the position that he was completely INS-A-A-A-ANE. Eddie, Eddie Antar was his name, started his little scam innocently enough, by stealing a pile of money from the IRS, which most of us do from time to time, and isn't, in and of itself, a true innovation. Eddie's real genius, and the apparent inspiration for the Dacha Wireless revenue model, itself an innovative-variation on traditional stock-fraud money-laundering methods, a kind of Pump-and-Dump 2.0 for the laundering business, lay in the fact that instead of simply pocketing the pile of stolen loot, he washed it through the banking system, and put it back into his business, in a scheme that came to be known as "The Panama Pump." Antar took the cash, smuggled it into Israel in the form of U.S. currency, strapped to his body in bank-wrapped bundles, or stashed in his Louis Vuitton false-bottom luggage, and stuffed it in small amounts into innocent-looking bank accounts, in the "placement" phase of the money laundering process. The "layering" phase was accomplished by wiring the money to Panama, which is just the sort of place that Eddie must have loved, since the guys doing time in Panamanian prisons aren't actually the people who evaded their taxes, but the poor misguided souls who attempted to report them; tax evasion, in Panama, is perfectly legal; reporting it, however, will land you in jail. So far, so good, although there is nothing at all original about stashing funds in Panama, or the Channels Islands or Philippines or an IBC in the Czech Republic; there are hundreds of billions of dollars' worth of pirated loot buried all over the world in offshore havens, nearly every last dime of which is perfectly safe, but regarded with suspicion by the banking authorities, who may set off alarms if you haul the funds ashore. The genius of Crazy Eddie was in the "integration" phase, where instead of trying to wire the loot to a Swiss account to the sound of sirens, he used the money for purchase orders, to pump up the revenue on Crazy Eddie's stores, prior to taking the company public, where he could reap the profits from his high-flying stock, to the tune of $75 million or so of thoroughly respectable good clean funds. The problem with Crazy Eddie was that he was, as it were, literally Crazy Eddie, not just in the sense that he was pulling a lot of lunatic shit, an enormous tangle of fraudulent scams, from inventory inflation to phony vendor charge-back schemes, but that Eddie himself was an actual human, and was not, as a human, all that hard to track down. Now suppose that instead of Eddie the Human, running around New York, screaming I'm INS-A-A-A-ANE at the slightest provocation, which even on Wall Street tends to raise a few eyebrows, you had a thoroughly unregulated hedge fund group, shrouded in secrecy in the Cayman Islands, out in the Gulf Stream where the pirates used to roam, let's say a hedge fund called

Third World Partners, who for all we knew, might in fact be pirates, burying treasure in the white sand beaches, but were, after all, our largest investors, and worthy, as such, of a certain respect. Hedge funds, SBICs, angel investors, DIP-loan lenders, venture firms, Private Equity shops, Vulture Capital bottom-feeders: when you need cold cash for Money-Shredders, Inc., you don't ask too many questions, do you, particularly if it turns out they happen to be pirates.

Which is not to say the hedge fund guys are actually pirates. No pirate in history ever sank enough ships to rival a hedge fund, when it comes to pure profits. The #1 pirate on the all-time list, Black Sam Bellamy, earned $120 million, in modern-day equivalents, over the course of his career, which sounds like quite a lot of money, now doesn't it, until you notice the hedge-masters scoffing and chuckling. You're thinking Black Sam was a real swashbuckler, a true heavy hitter, a big swinging dick; come to find out the guy was a piker. Triple his earnings, squeeze it all down to a single year, Sam doesn't even make the Hedge Fund Top 20; try $400 million to even get on the list, earn some honest respect, a little peer-recognition; if you have your heart set on being a true buccaneer, don't bother with ships, you need to sink whole industries. Even #25 on the Alpha List made more in a single year than the top three pirates in their entire lifetimes; Black Sam, Francis Drake, Thomas Tew, "The Rhode Island Pirate," may have been wallowing in Portuguese gold and Natal indigo and African ivory, but $340 million just isn't going to cut it. You take a guy like Tew, who barely topped $100M, he's sailing around the Mandab Strait, chasing a 25-ship Mughal convoy, while some derivatives expert in Greenwich outearns him on a single trade, and damned if Tew isn't hit by an actual flying cannonball, completely disembowels him, he'll never make the Alpha List, his days of swashing and buckling are over. But what, you're asking, about the Famous Pirates, someone like "Blackbeard" Edward Teach, with his big feathered tricorn, his swords, knives, and pistols, setting fire to his beard to intimidate the market; guy was a real monster, during the Golden Age of Piracy, had like 14 wives, a 300-ton British-made ship, with 40-some guns, and the latest technology, must have made a fucking killing, what about Blackbeard Teach? It's apparent from your question that you don't quite get the picture; you need to grow up,

stop living in a fantasy, maybe learn a little something about the nature of true piracy. You study the young man buying Credit Default
Swaps on his laptop computer, on the Wi-Fi network at your neighborhood Starbucks, he's not weaving hemp and matches into his
beard, he's sipping a latte and a bottle of Ethos; when the housing
bubble craters, taking out the mortgage industry, and most of the
U.S. Federal Reserve, guy makes an $800M actual killing, makes
it part way up the Alpha List, sips his Ethos, keeps on trading. You
can't always spot the men who are doing the real looting by looking
for knives and pistols, and feathered tricorn pirate hats. Blackbeard,
Harry Morgan, and "Black Bart" Bartholomew Roberts, all of these
infamous pirates combined, with hundreds of cannons and dozens
of wives, made $60 million in modern-equivalent buying power, or
about as much in their entire lives as a half-decent put-call trader
makes in a 3-month quarter, or what a real heavy hitter makes in 2
part-time weeks. The top hedge fund operator for 2007 made the
median U.S. family annual income every two minutes, or $3.7 bil-
lion, give or take a hundred million, and he isn't even famous; in
fact, I'll bet you can't name him. How did he do this? What did
he know that you and I didn't? What was the key to this wealth
creation, what fundamental insight made him almost $4 billion?
Our houses were overpriced, and about to suffer a moderate correction. If you're thinking this was some sort of one-time aberration,
a single huge killing that he couldn't possibly replicate, it might
be useful to know that the exact same man, who must have been
eating oranges at a fairly rapid clip, made right around $5 billion
for one of his that's-more-like-it years, no doubt falling just shy of
his annual target: matching the Gross Domestic Product of let's say
Nicaragua. Just to net this all out for you, then, and maybe drive a
wooden stake through your little piracy fantasy, no self-respecting
hedge fund manager would ever consider becoming a pirate; not
only would he need a whole new set of clothes, but he'd have to
take a deep and truly frightening sort of pay cut, maybe vacate one
or two of the 18 duplex rooms, full of Park Avenue Louis Quinze
and Renaissance tapestries and Monet Giverny Waterlilies, or drop
a few servants from the Southampton budget, or rent out the Cap
Ferrat mansion for a month. The house in Deer Valley? Don't even
go there; one of his exes many exes now owns it free and clear. No,

the hedge fund money-masters are not about to change. Why fire cannons when the world economic system can be looted by key-strokes on a laptop computer?

So where the hell were we? Ah yes, over here, out in the Gulf Stream, with Third World Partners, hauling treasure out of the beaches with a Panama Pump. Unfortunately for me, and my membership status in Club Group Reality, no one on the Board has ever heard of Crazy Eddie. They call in the auditors and everything is fine; the deals with Kordian and Velocicom are ironclad, the sales are irreversible, our P&L is 100% GAAP-approved, our revenue recognition policies are body-armored and bulletproof. But what about the Panama Pump? Are these customers we're dealing with actually legitimate, or are they using illegal layered funds, pumping our revenue and stock price up, and raking it off in integrated profits? Remember Crazy Eddie? The auditors smile and shake their heads. Crazy Eddie? Never heard of him. He one of our guys? Must not have made Partner. What about Third World? Who the hell are these guys, where do they get their money? For all we know, these guys could be terrorists. Do we know if they're investors in HNL and Bhartos? Well, boy, I'll tell you what, if it turns out they are, these guys are pretty stupid; you want our opinion, these companies are not in the best of health, they maybe could use some time in a good ICU, they're basically goners, like brain-dead vegetables; you should be thankful these companies have already paid you. Just humor me for a second: suppose these guys are like Crazy Eddie, pump in maybe $180 million worth of phony WiMAX amplifier orders, make like $300 million cashing out our pumped-up stock? Doesn't that sound like a pretty sweet deal, launder their money and still turn a profit? Don't you think we should maybe report this? Report what to whom? Call the Wall Street Journal or 60 Minutes, tell them your customers need a compassionate hospice? With all due respect, sir, our men in the Caymans are among the finest in the world, we're all from the respected firm of Deloitte Touche Ernst Young KPMG PricewaterhouseCooper, we don't get involved with the criminally insane, or pink sheet microcap pump-and-dump stock-fraud schemes; you've been reading too many Mafia novels. That may well be true, but how do you account for this? We're about to report record earnings for the March 31 quarter, and

Q2 looks like what? A gigantic earnings shortfall? Help me out here guys, what does Q2 look like to you? Revenue of what, like absolute zero? Too soon to tell; we've got a lot of irons in the fire, a lot of big deals that are still in the works, we may come up a little short, there's a risk of delays in the procurement process, but this is no time to panic, let us walk you through our new projections, we've still got nearly a full three months, and a hell of a pipeline, our sales guys are on it. The other Board Members are nodding their heads, no time to panic, let's see what happens, you have to admit the pipeline is huge, Timor-Leste alone could make up the shortfall. I'm telling you, guys, if it's a Crazy Eddie Panama Pump, we're all in deep shit, it's an accounting nightmare. Accounting? What's wrong with our accounting? We have audited financials, prepared by professionals, these guys are all Certified Public Accountants, our statements are clean, the accounts are all current, there's no need to start calling our accounting into question. Granted, the price of bauxite has essentially collapsed, and Velocicom's sales into Suriname are slowing, and maybe there's been a glut of coconut products, and Tonga is reducing its WiMAX deployments, and the ylang-ylang market has taken quite a dive, which will clearly have an impact on broadband in Comoros, we agree the world economy has hit a bit of a rough patch, but things will bounce back, they always do, don't tell us you think the world has an accounting problem.

As a matter of fact, I do, I think the whole world has an accounting problem.

It is not, however, time to argue about accounting, it's time for me to resign from the Board of Dacha Wireless, and hand in my membership card to Group Reality Fitness and Spa, maybe join a little dojo, learn some hand-to-hand combat. I know what you're thinking: I need to report this. You smell a stock-fraud laundry scheme, you phone the thing in to the proper authorities. I'll warn you in advance, though, since I've tried it myself, don't expect much out of law enforcement. Tell them you've spotted fifty thousand dollars in street corner drug cash, the DEA shows up in like 35 minutes, two guys in grey suits in an unmarked car, with a bag of

Egg McMuffins and Styrofoam coffee; tell them you're involved in a $300 million worldwide money-laundering stock-fraud operation, they'll have to get back to you, which pretty promptly doesn't happen. How much do you know about the DEA's Money Trail Initiative? I'll give you a hint: if the trail is made of banknotes with heavy loads of coke residue, these guys are all over it; if the trail is made out of amplifier orders, from real corporations with phony cell-tower rollout plans, don't be getting your hopes too high, start thinking these guys know fact from fiction. Out of $100 billion a year in U.S. cocaine profits alone, these guys have managed to track down like $130 million, nearly every last dime of which was in the form of coked-up cash. At the other end of the dubious-profits rainbow spectrum, the Financial Action Task Force on Money Laundering, or FATF just in case you need to call them, comprises 29 countries plus the European Commission and the Gulf Cooperation Council, and is extremely effective at putting out white papers and organizing meetings and producing the sound bite talking points for the occasional press conference; actually stopping sophisticated laundering schemes is not their real strength, which is more in the area of organizing lunch buffets; if they stop a $100 million, that's a banner year. Call the local police? Where the fuck are we? Try the SEC? Not their jurisdiction. How about the Hong Kong equivalent, the SFC, the Securities and Futures Commission? I'm sorry, sir, you'd like to report a what? Some kind of drug money laundering scheme, or maybe it's terrorists, using Afghani heroin and Saudi charities; not really sure I know how it works, may need an auditor who's fluent in Pashto. You ever hear of Eddie Antar? Course, in Eddie's case, it wasn't Saudi charities, it was money he'd stolen from the IRS, smuggled into Israel, washed through Panama. Perhaps you should consider phoning the Panamanians, or the IRS, I'm sure they'd be fascinated. No, no, I'm not talking about Crazy Eddie, I'm talking about something called the Panama Pump, using maybe it's drug profits and a Cayman Islands hedge fund. If you'd like to report a drug trafficking problem, you should call the Public Security Bureau; I can give you the number for Guangdong Province; what sort of drugs did you say these were? I have no idea, in fact I'm not totally sure it was drugs in the first place, just seemed to me like a logical choice, I mean where else do you find hundreds of millions of dollars in untraceable free cash flow; it has to be drugs or Islamic Jihadists. So let me see if I've got this straight: you can't find your drugs, your wash isn't clean, the man who does your laundry may be a Jihadist, and you believe you can trace the problem to a pump of some kind that you think was manufactured in, where was it now, Panama? I can't recommend actually calling the PSB; you sound to me like you're high on something; your drugs aren't lost, you've recently consumed them. If you want my advice, you should stay away from China if you've got some sort of drug problem; as for your difficulties with the Panamanian pumping device, don't start calling in the IRS and trying to tell them that you can't get your wash clean; get yourself a copy of the local area Yellow Pages, pick up the phone, call a good honest plumber.

Not that any of this happened, this stuff with the SFC, I don't even know their phone number to call them in the first place. What happens next? I'm coming to that; it may not be something that happened either, but trust me, I was there, or at least I seem to think I was, so really, in the long run, what the fuck's the difference? I get a phone call from nowhere in the middle of the night, guy says You're dreaming, and then hangs up the phone. What is one to do with this sort of information? Next night, same time, guy calls back, says Imagine I'm talking and this is not what you're hearing. Maybe I dreamed this; I can't be sure. Third night, same guy, gives a whole florid speech, Our revels now are ended, these our actors, as I foretold you, were all spirits and are melted into air, into thin air, I want back my profits, pretend I never called you. Shakespeare, Prospero, guy's not very subtle; even if I dreamed him, he still isn't subtle. Fourth night, I can't sleep, I'm waiting by the phone, pacing back and forth, thing doesn't ring. This, at least, actually happened, the phone didn't ring, at least I don't think so, maybe I fell asleep and dreamed that I was pacing. Fifth night, phone rings, there's a woman on the line, tells me to get the money and better make it cash and bring it to El Paso, meet her at the foot of the Stanton Street Bridge, shall we say noon, the 15th of April, gives me the name of a hotel to stay, starts to hang up, I'm like How much money? Better to bring too much, better safe than sorry, better a live rat than a dead lion, better a little which is well done than a great deal imperfectly, do you want me to read you the rest of these things, I have a whole long list, if it will help you to remember, I'd be happy to read it backwards, better a thousand times careful than once dead I think she said, better a witty fool than a foolish wit, more useless Shakespeare, I'm like What the fuck are you telling me, she hangs up the phone. I'm holding a dead phone, staring around the room, pinching myself, trying to wake the fuck up, memorizing the objects that are sitting on my nightstand, a cup full of ballpoints, a sheet of blank checks, a pair of rusty scissors that are rusted halfway open, a half-finished book that I know I'll never close, a black-and-white photo of a dog in an empty field, I'll check these in the morning, see if I was dreaming. I wake up, or I think I'm awake, double-check my nightstand, the dog in the photo is nowhere to be found, there's a photo of a field with a wide-open gate, but the dog is long gone, the grey field is now empty. What the hell? Did someone come in here in the middle of the night, change out the photo, or is all of this a dream? This, as it turns out, is only a small sample, of reality and unreality getting their accounts commingled. When you're trying to run a venture firm, you really can't allow this; you put fact and fiction in the exact same account, your investors will kill you, and they have hit squads of lawyers and armies of accountants.

If you're planning a little trip to Ciudad Juárez, you might want to consider some testing at a sleep clinic, make sure you know the difference between wakefulness and dreaming; it may seem like a needless expense, and it's exceptionally tough to sleep when you're hardwired with electrodes, but it's worth every nickel if you wind up in Juárez.

A single day in Juárez is like a year in a bad dream.

# 22

So, what, you think I'm being blackmailed? Give up my winnings on the Dacha deal, or live with the threat of being exposed to the public? Prominent VC Admits It Was All a Sham!, that sort of thing, wind up with my investors forced to face the ugly truth, pay back their gains, disgorge all their profits? I'm not sure how much sense this makes; I can appreciate your concern, since we have, in some sense, profited illegally, but trust me when I tell you that you're out of your depth; you've entered one of the grey zones of real-world investing. While *blackmail in a grey zone* isn't a logical impossibility, it doesn't sound to me like much of a threat, in fact it sounds like more of an exercise in Kripke semantics; we could always set this up in a proper modal frame, specify some truth-values for our "grey zone" scenarios, and then lay out the proof of our little threat-supposition under the truth-tree branches of a semantic tableau, although I doubt that either one of us wants to go to the police, and try to tell them I'm being blackmailed by a modal logician. Let's face facts here: we'll take it as a given that formal modal logic is not your real strength, and that it's a little late now to start learning Boolean algebra, and that temporal modal operators and doxastic modalities are as confusing to you as they are to me, so we both may be forced to use a little common sense, and common sense is useless when it comes to fraudulent profits. I know you're only trying to help, and don't doubt for a moment your concern for our welfare, but you might want to consider the distinct possibility that I don't actually give a shit that Dacha was a scam, because fraud isn't fraud unless someone can prove it, and my illegal gains are all perfectly legal, and not one of my investors will have to face an ugly truth, in fact the truth is so beautiful, so glittering and bright, and so richly endowed with our Dacha winnings, that the truth and my investors are now legally married. You'll no doubt need time, and a wealth of experience, to discover some of the nuances of professional investing, but in the meantime we'd suggest you keep your thoughts to yourself, because life isn't nearly as logical as you think, it's stuffed full of donkey-pronoun problems and counterfactual-conditional if-then puzzlers and non-monotonic inference relations that can't quite cope with these modal grey zones; life, in short, is a logical nervous wreck, and real-world fraud is best left to trained professionals.

I went back into the office, my high-rise on Ocean, which as you'll no doubt recall from my Sunday/Monday Dexies all-nighter, is 17 floors up from asphalt oblivion, on where are we now, April 14th, a lovely Tuesday morning after a half-decent sleep, and while my appearance in the hallways may have caused quite a stir, my showing up for work being admittedly unusual, everyone adjusted and tried to go about their day, as though my presence there among them could ever be thought of as in any way normal. I sat up nice and straight at my rainforest desk, staring off up the Coast, over the red-tiled rooftops of Spielberg's Palisades, and the grey-slate mansards of Eli Broad's Brentwood, toward the lush green foothills of the Santa Monica Mountains, stair-stepping down toward the beaches to the north, where the Stars all sit around, neck-deep in cash, waiting for sea level to rise fifty feet, and drown every house in the Malibu Colony; it probably goes without saying, but if these stair-stepping rock formations, in the context of money, meandering up and down on their way back to sea level, remind you of something, like your 401(k), and that nightmare you've been having, since the '08 crash, of a chart of the S&P 500 going backwards, don't look at me, my money is all in T-Bills. It's an absolutely blue, sparkling-clear morning, where I can see from snow-capped Baldy and Mt. Wilson in the east, all the way out to Santa Catalina, with only a thin brown ribbon of toxic-particulate haze to mar the lovely illusion of crystal-clear transparency. It's hard to even imagine the vast amount of wealth, in real estate alone, that lives in all this loveliness. You see that house on the Amalfi Rim, overlooking Rustic Canyon as it wanders down to the Pacific Ocean, the one with cedar Nantucket shingles, and huge Doric columns from a Mississippi cotton plantation? It's a spec house, as you might have guessed, maybe 12,000 square feet if you don't count the servants' quarters, and it recently sold for $15 million; the exact same house, maybe six blocks down, overlooking the golf course at Riviera, could have been yours for fourteen-five, but that one's in escrow, so forget we brought it up. Don't these people know they're in an earthquake zone? That if the world financial system takes one more good shock, we'll all wind up in a deep Depression? It's hard to feel depressed, one can only suppose, when you're living on Sycamore tree-lined streets, with yards full of Winchester Cathedral white roses and Giverny Waterlilies and purple bougainvillea, and you paid for everything with cold hard cash. My ex-wife, for example, lives there among them, in an 8-bedroom Cape Cod with maybe nine or ten bathrooms, and I seriously doubt that global deflation, the whole grinding machinery of massive deleveraging, is the first thing she thinks of when she wakes up each day. Only an honest mortgage broker could hate this sort of place, for making a total mockery of his opulent array of innovative finance options, No-Doc Alt-A's and Interest-Only Super Jumbos and Pick-A-Pay Balloons and Cash-Back Wraparounds and Option ARMS with 3/1 hybrids: how is he supposed to sell his 125%-LTV negative-amortization liar-loan monstrosities to people who can afford to write a $15 million check? Our only advice is don't give up hope; from what we've heard, some of the cold-hard-cash guys have recently been burned, though they don't yet know it, in a $50 billion Ponzi scheme that makes Dacha Wireless look feeble-minded, and they may need to borrow a million or two fast, to tide them over for the next few months, while they wait for their accountants to call them back. Some of these people have so much money, and so little idea where they actually put it, that you can't help feeling a little sorry for them all, maybe slip them a twenty to pay the valet parking.

So you think I'm being blackmailed on such a beautiful morning? It's certainly blue out, I'll grant you that, and we're so high up that you can gaze into Eternity, where the Bottomless Wealth Hills will forever be lined with fit blonde angels and expensive foliage, pink flowering dogwoods and lavender jacaranda and snow-white weeping cherry trees; yes, it's blue all right, and the world is lovely, it's precisely the sort of deep-focus morning that is easily confused with mental clarity, but the fact is we're somewhere that's legally grey; we are not in a world of clear-cut outcomes and deontic modalities and deterministic finite-state discrete automata, we're deep in the fog, with a lot of reference-frame loop complexity. Even supposing Dacha was a sham, an empty hollow shell of dubious legality, I was only a member of the Board of Directors, and Boards don't worry much about dubious legality, we worry much more about our financial exposure, though it's far from clear that we actually have any; while Board Members, technically, can be sued for fraud, you'd first have to assume we knew something about it, and permitted it to proceed without trying to put a stop to it, and if there's one thing we've learned about corporate fraud, after several decades of deceiving the public, the Board itself can safely be assumed to know nothing at all about anything, ever. The Directors can't be sued, much less blackmailed, for utter incompetence, and even if we could, we're fairly well insulated; in fact, some of these guys are so well-insulated, you could burn the whole building down, guy wouldn't move. If you've ever read the fine print of our annual 10-K financial statements, those fictional accounts regarding the progress of our businesses, you may have noticed that we, meaning Directors as a whole, have spent untold billions on Directors and Officers liability insurance, and while we may well have vaporized trillions of dollars in shareholder wealth, by nodding along at strategy sessions, and rubber-stamping mountains of executive compensation, and sleeping through dozens of audit committee meetings, if you have any problems with the quality of our work, you'll have to take it up with our D&O insurance company, which in this case, in all likelihood, turns out to be AIG, itself so lost in a smoking-hole crater that not one of their Directors even knows his own name, so you might want to take a number and pack a lunch and stand in line, I'm sure they'll get around to you within the next half-century. Of course, our policies don't actually cover incompetence, for the simple reason that they just don't have to; our D&O policies cover our legal liabilities, and not only is incompetence not a legal liability, it would appear, from what I've seen, to be legally mandatory. So if you should happen to find yourself, one crystal-clear morning, trying to tell a Board

Member that the sky is blue, and he continues to maintain that the sky is actually yellow, he's only trying to satisfy his competency requirements, and remain in good standing as a Member of the Board.

And just to put this whole fraud angle into proper perspective, nearly all of my friends in the venture industry have found themselves involved in a scam or two. For every case like Media Vision, with a build-and-hold scheme involving floating barges, there are 80 others, from Asyst and Brocade to RSA and Verisign, who've had some serious problems involving whimsically dated stock option grants. Nearly every last technology company on Silicon Valley's God's Green Earth has found itself deep in costly litigation over some sort of give or take shareholder fraud, for back-dating or spring-loading or bullet-dodging options anomalies: Altera, AMC, Juniper Networks, Marvell Technology, Cirrus Logic, Vitesse, Broadcom, Autodesk, MacAfee…the list goes on, maybe 200 companies, $50 million here, $300 million there, from Able Energy to Zoran Corporation. For every exec who gets sentenced to prison, the unfortunate few like Worldcom's Bernie Ebbers, or Stuart Wolff and Joseph Shew, the masterminds of Homestore's revenue round-tripping, or Peregrine's Steve Gardner, or Computer Associates' Sanjay Kumar, or Enterasys Networks' Robert Gagalis, there are hundreds of others breathing sighs of relief, there but for the grace of, etc., etc., and one thing you'll notice about every last case: not a single solitary incompetent Board member has ever been sentenced to anything, ever. And as a matter of record, I myself have already made quite a tidy little bundle off of fraudulent revenue accounting schemes, including a company named Critical Path that had a hell of a scandal; by the time the fraud had come to light, with a torchlit-mob of screaming investors, and the stock had crashed from $150 to $1.50, with $2 billion in losses along the way, I was sailing around the Dodecanese Islands on an Italian-built yacht, headed for Gocek on the Turquoise Coast of Turkey, and my profits were deep asleep inside a soundproof isolation booth. I wasn't actually on the Board for that one, I'd traded them my shares in a company called Isocor, rode the stock up maybe six or eight floors, cashed out nicely before the elevator incident, and was last seen buying some Hermès ties at a sweet little boutique on the island of Symi. If you ask the VCs who invested in Media Vision, and made quite a haul in the sound card business, sound cards floating on a barge that is, and counted as sold to jack up the stock price, How'd you make out on that whole deal? they'd say Just fine and change the subject. But wait, you're thinking, the thing was a scam, they made a small fortune off of phony accounting; didn't they have to give the fortune back? Well…no, not really. Admittedly the stock took a turn for the worse, and the mood of the public could have been better, but these things happen, we take them in stride: whether it's equipping a barge with audio products, or amplifying reality in a bauxite warehouse, while it's apparent that shareholders can't take a good joke, by the time these smoking holes have been filled in with dirt, and a few billion in wealth has magically vanished, you'll still hear the sound of a distant muffled laugh, because a cashed-out VC has a wonderful sense of humor. The key to making money on scams, as an investor, is to be long gone when the fraud comes to light, and don't, for Heaven's sake, write anything down, and if you do, for some reason, have a factual account, you'll want to put it all through a high-grade reality-shredder, long before the subpoenas and the FBI show up. I can personally recommend the Powershred DS-1, for instance, or the PS-67 with 8-sheet feed, which is just where these pages would be headed in due time, if it weren't for the fact that I'm stationed in Juárez, at a rose-pink Radisson surrounded by armored infantry, the sort of place where no one worries much about written accounts and legal technicalities, because reality itself is already a giant powershredder, and even the simple truth comes in piles of confetti.

So even supposing that Dacha was a scam, blackmail itself is not among my current worries, and I doubt that my investors will be worrying either, once they've dumped the last of their pumped-up stock. Do you think the investment banking guys who made a pitiless fortune on the Crazy Eddie Housing Bubble, selling Triple-A Junk Bonds to the barefoot pilgrims, including their own banks, whose balance sheets now look like the Black Hole of Calcutta, are planning on handing their bonus checks back? Do you think their own Boards had a sense of reality? Will anyone be sentenced to anything, ever? You're beginning to get the picture. On my desk, however, sits a FedEx package, from what appears to be a business, Fabricantes de Tonos de Marcar, or maybe it's intended as a joke at my expense, since this translates roughly to "makers of dial tones,"

in any case from somewhere in Ciudad Juárez, the Parque Industrial A. J. Bermudez, postal code 32470; this sounds like a business
with nearly infinite demand, if they could somehow adapt to the
wild growth of cell phones, but I'm trying not to picture how you'd
manufacture dial tones. I open the package, it's a bundle of El Paso
Times newspaper clippings, gruesome stuff, bodies discovered in
normal backyards, most of them headless and limbless torsos; bodies dissolved in high pH vats, reduced to a mass of unrecyclable
goo-clumps; bodies dumped off in fenced-in fields, just across the
street from the assembly plants, with piece-parts scattered in the
milkweed and paintbrush, the families left staring at swatches of
trash. The bundle has a note attached, on a six-by-nine sheet of unsigned paper, a note perhaps written with an antique fountain pen,
in a backward-slanting, analysis-defying, confidence-inverting flowing black hand: You're dreaming. Not this again; this waking-sleep-
ing dial-tones business is beginning to get on my nerves already. I
stuff the bundle in a drawer of my desk; leave the little note out as a
gesture of defiance; and head off in the direction of going about my
day. What, precisely, is my day? Deleting e-mails, failing to return
phone calls, refusing to sign checks for the most ordinary of office
expenses; there isn't nearly enough absence-of-content here to fill
in the structure of even a six-hour day. By 11:30 my Inbox box is
empty. By 11:40 it's 11:32. By 11:45 I am vaguely anxious; there
isn't even much that I can fail to accomplish, I've tried to think of
everything I can put off for a day or two, I have a whole long To
Do list that's a page full of intricate dollar-sign doodles, interesting
to look at, but impossible not to execute. By noon, I have the clippings back out on my desk, the whole gruesome bundle, spread
out to cover every last inch, to hide what's actually under there,
the blank expanse of desk. By 12:20 it hits me: I could never be
blackmailed for something I've done, and I'm not being threatened
with the revelation of something; this, in a sense, would be a relief,
my office would be the center of a whirl of activity, the command
center perhaps of my legal defense, the whiteboards filling with the
details of the case, the timelines and minutes and audited statements. It's possible I suppose that I'm being threatened with bodily
harm: give them the money or they'll stuff me in a lye vat; but this
in turn seems a little farfetched, given my ability to hire protection;

people of my means don't wind up as goo-clumps. What we have here is something far more subtle: no one is threatening direct action or revelation, because this in fact would give me something to do, like hire a good goon squad, or start polishing up on my Kripke semantics, maybe practice a few of the classic modal operators, the empty white square or L meaning *necessarily*, the blank white diamond or M meaning *possibly; blackmail in a grey zone*, just think of the possibilities, the color theory alone would get me through to the cocktail hour, which once upon a time was my favorite time of day. What I have instead is an empty field of grey, like snow on a TV screen, the electronic noise of a receiver without a signal. What I have in fact, as the FedEx pack predicted, is the mental equivalent of a telephone dial tone, a *tono de marcar*, to be followed, if I'm not careful, and fail to start dialing digits, by the permanent termination signal that occurs when the off-hook dial tone times out, producing what's known as a *howler tone* in telephony jargon, and while it may well be jargon, outmoded in fact by cell phone technology, a *howler tone* sounds like something I can definitely do without.

So now the real question is: what do I do next? Leave the clippings out and wait for the howler? Or put them away and stare at my empty desk? My *Dream Dictionary*, normally reliable in these situations, as it's an excellent guide to the somnambulatory life, contains an unusual mix of ambiguous information, not particularly useful as a basis for action, unless contradicting myself were the indicated act: my *desk* seems to signify inner exploration and self-discovery, which I can tell you for a fact just isn't true; while my *tono de marcar*, my off-hook dial tone, tells me I'm shutting myself off from myself, which may well be true, but isn't exactly a recent discovery. And my FedEx *You're dreaming* note is no help at all: like what the fuck, *where the hell are we*, you think there's any chance I didn't know that already?

I know what you're thinking: man's mind's not right; guy should be watching they don't chop off his head, here he is worrying about whatyoucallit, ambiguity, maybe being threatened by howler tones and telephony jargon, maybe being menaced by a blank expanse of desk. Let me think. No, that's not it, it's not ambiguity, I am not, strictly speaking, in an ambiguous situation, ambiguity in fact is an entirely different thing, a matter of meaning being context-dependent; ambiguity is what happens when you say the word *bank*, and don't know for sure whether it's that place where you keep your money, or that place beside the river where you toss in your fishing line. In other words, *where are we?* And what the hell are we doing here? Where I am, more properly, is in that singular state of mind of the man making a deposit at the branch office teller window, putting his money away in an FDIC-insured account, at Too Big To Fail Hedge Fund Casino, where money itself, the whole money concept, is disappearing fast, in a nuclear-accident chain-reaction what-the fuck-happened Chernobylesque plume, a power-excursion meltdown, with the U.S. Treasury and Federal Reserve, the full faith and credit of the U.S. Government, standing over the steaming and radioactive hole, pouring trillions of dollars through what looks like a garden hose. The man holds one end of his monthly check, the teller holds the other, there's a momentary struggle, and as his earnings disappear beneath the teller's grey ledge, replaced by a Too Big deposit receipt or lottery ticket, the man can't help asking himself, "What is a Bank?" This man, properly speaking, is not suffering from something that could be described as *ambiguity*; he's suffering from *vagueness*, which arises when the boundaries of meaning are nebulous, and he's feeling a little hazy about some bedrock institutions, which is a completely different condition, and one not subject to disambiguation. *What is a bank?* That man standing by the river, doing a little fishing, knows perfectly well what is meant by the word *bank*, but what is he to make of that thing floating by him, which may be a bundle of clothing fallen overboard, or may be a body headed over the roaring falls. This is no time to be running around looking for a dictionary, trying to figure out the difference between vagueness and ambiguity: either jump in the river, find out what's out there, or walk around forever feeling what's the word, *vague*. And to push this whole analogy to my usual extreme, in my case what's out there is not just floating by, it's something that I myself played a role in pushing overboard, and I don't know what it is, or how the hell it got there, headed toward the boundaries of Nebulous Falls, getting ready to turn *vagueness* into a permanent condition.

*Live Like You Mean It.*

Silence implies consent.

So I pick up the phone, start dialing digits, call my Private Banking guy at the Alex Brown unit of Deutsche Bank in Baltimore, tell
him I need, oh, say, $20 million in cash, better make it $20 million in Kuwaiti dinars, the world's most valuable currency, about
how much do you think that would weigh? He puts me on hold;
comes back on maybe two minutes later; tells me give or take 700
U.S. pounds, 11,200 avoirdupois ounces; the dinar only comes in
20-dinar notes, awful lot of currency for one man to handle. What
about dollars, in $100 bills? Right around 440; might need a fork-
lift. How about gold, I'm getting a little suspicious of Government-
issued banknotes, maybe what I need is put the whole thing in gold.
About two-thirds of a ton. A ton? You're thinking maybe you carry it
around in Fort Knox bricks, 400 troy ounces to a 6" by 3" by 2" bar,
you've been watching too many of those James Bond movies, you're
going to need maybe 50 of those 27-pound bricks, about two-thirds
of a ton by my calculation. You might be better off with 20,000
Krugerrands, or holographic kinebars from the UBS bank vault, be
like something you'd find in the treasure chest of a sunken pirate,
maybe gold escudos from the mint at Cartagena, or the Pillars and
Waves coins from Cuzco or Bogota, course you find out that most
of that pirate loot was in silver reales from the mint at Potosi, and I
don't think you want to be carrying silver around, take like 60 tons
just to make $20 million. This, while fascinating, isn't getting me
anywhere, I'm not boarding a plane with 60 tons of silver. Look,
Jeff, I need something lighter, I wasn't planning on paying a $6 mil-
lion excess-baggage surcharge. What do you suggest? Well let's see
now; $20 million in Latvian lats, that's about 70 pounds, though the
lat's a little volatile; you could try 500-euro notes, maybe 75 pounds,
but you'd still have to pay for the overweight luggage. Tell you what
you do, just sit tight, we'll get you $20 million in lavender Burck-
hardts, 1,000-Swiss-franc notes, nice stable currency, weigh a shade
under let's see here less than 50 pounds, check it right through, no
problems with your baggage. Do you mind my asking where the
hell it is you're going? If you're planning on exiting the banking
system, this doesn't make a dent in what you're actually holding;

if I were you, I'd dig a giant backyard pit, line it with concrete like you were thinking about a swimming pool, fill the thing with rhodium, cover it all with Comcore road plates, bury the plates in two feet of sand, maybe four or five inches' worth of crushed stone or pea gravel, another twelve inches' worth of sand and aged compost, maybe peat mixed with tree bark and sawdust or rice hulls, rake it all level, pack it all down, seed it with bent grass or TW72 dwarf-hybrid Bermuda, plant yourself a putting green, with a nice deep Virginia white sand bunker, take a good five strokes off your short game, trust me. Course it's a little tough to access if you need ready cash; hard to find a rhodium pit that comes with an ATM card.

Jeff, apparently, has thought this through, and isn't really counting on the future of the banking system. I gave my friend Jeff the go-ahead, ordered up round-trip airline tickets, and sat back to wait on delivery of the cash, wondering about the wisdom of storing up value in rhodium pits. Reading between the lines, with U.S. Government debt rapidly climbing past $11 trillion, with no real end to the climbing in sight, Jeff didn't seem too bullish on Treasury securities either, be like loaning a bunch of money to juvenile delinquents; that "full faith and credit" verbiage, lifted from Article IV of the U.S. Constitution, might not be something you could take to the bank, even if you found a bank you thought you could bank on. If there is one thing we've learned from the whole War on Terror, the U.S. Constitution is a remarkably flexible document; once you've deleted the Bill of Rights, and 220 years of judicial precedent, you'd only be left with a few thousand words, and 10,000 lawyers in the Justice Department, any one of whom could solve your little verbiage problem, craft a quick clean workaround for things like torture and habeas corpus. *Full faith and credit* is only four words: how long would it take to seize all the T-Bills? Can't help but wonder how big a market this opens up, turn the world's richest nation into Putting Green Survivalists.

My musings were interrupted by the arrival of my cash, in a pink Samsonite hardside that wasn't quite my style, and certainly didn't look all that what's the word, professional. On the other hand, maybe Jeff was right: someone sees me walking around with a Gehrer Sharp Viper System, with handcuffs, ripcord, and Chelsea clamps, destination-programmable security features, and a high-

speed-penetration ink-dye bag-ripper, I might attract some unwanted attention, though I'd certainly look like I knew what I was doing,
like walking around with a shitpile of cash. I packed some worn
jeans and linen shirts and toiletries, I even packed my half-finished
book, and my bank-wrapped Swiss franc notes, into an old green
duffel bag: keep it low-key and casual. I did, admittedly, leave some
shit in the duffel that I maybe should have pitched, a piece of orange plastic and a map of the L.A. harbor, but since I couldn't seem
to remember why it was that I owned them, as far as I knew, they
were probably indispensable. My transfer to the airport, in a driver-
equipped black sedan, was completely uneventful; my usual greeter
met me at Terminal 5, had my bag checked curbside, handed me
my boarding card, and whisked me through security to the Delta
Crown Club Lounge, to wait for her signal to start the boarding process. The Lounge itself was nothing out of the ordinary, mostly businessmen stationed in brown leather chairs, calling the office for the
latest sales figures, or negotiating contracts that made them sound
important, or wearing their thumbs out on miniature smartphones;
I've waited in lounges for hundreds of flights, and nothing ever happens, I mean really, why would it? That deal you're bragging about
so the whole lounge can hear? It's a complete crock of shit, and both
of us know it. So given all that, the ordinary surroundings, the complete lack of eventfulness, the brown leather loungers, and the usual
hour wait for the perfectly normal boarding process, why did I find
myself with a drink in my hand, two-thirds consumed, with more
ice left than bourbon? This wouldn't, in and of itself, be considered
an event, if it weren't for the fact that I don't drink alcohol; in fact,
I haven't touched a drop in nearly fourteen months, though I used
to be something of a consummate drunk, the Winston Churchill
of early-stage investing, the Frank Sinatra of Series A, the William
Faulkner of Audit Committee meetings. My grandfather, Big John,
ran the lumberyard in Dickinson, North Dakota, on maybe a quart
of Jack Daniels a day, like 25,000 bottles, and 75,000 packs of unfiltered Camels, right up to the age of 87 years, never lost so much as
a finger or a thumb; he had all ten, and could probably count them.
On the other hand, alcohol nearly killed Big John; one morning, at
the age of 91, he was driving to the store, inexplicably sober, when
he was T-boned at a light by a drunken driver, and had to be pulled

from the burning sheet-metal pile with a severely broken neck and mangled organs. We all marched to Dickinson to pay our last respects, Big John with a halo brace bolted to his skull, real end-of-life stuff, so sad to see, reduced to skin and bones, finished and done for; John waves me over, to say his goodbyes, says "Son, do me a favor, get me the fuck out of here," which pretty much sums up his way of standing in the world, his limited tolerance for our whole life-and-death mournful sort of attitude; six months later, he gets the fuck out, marries one of his nurses, maybe 30 years his junior, dies in his sleep at the age of ninety-nine, 3,000 bottles of Jack Daniels later. I come from a long line of high-caliber drunks and functional alcoholics, so I know what I'm doing, I'm having a drink. Alcohol is a beautiful thing, fills in all the emptiness that drinking it causes; you never run short of useful things to do, like hunting that bottle you buried in the garden, the last time the wife threw you out of the house. That story, if you've heard it, by the way, is a total distortion and a complete misrepresentation; I wasn't, in fact, laughing at her dress, I was laughing about the butcher knife she broke off in my desk top. Drinking is really the ultimate existential sport, out walking the blood-brain ethanol tightrope, high up above the Dead Drunk Falls, and the churning whitewater gorge the stuff carves out of you. Just keeping your blood alcohol reading at about .12 through a three-hour Board Meeting is itself quite a trick; I used to fill one-liter Arrowhead bottles with two-thirds water one-third vodka, titrate my way through the PowerPoint slides, the endless digressions on chip design problems, things about floorplanning and netlist placement and timing and routing and mask generation, all of which translated to a three-month delay, and 90-some bottles of vodka while I waited. I never missed a day of work in maybe ten or fifteen years of serious drinking, the sort of drinking that started when the poetry ran dry; I did the dishes after every meal, I walked the dog, I took all the trash out, so it's not like my drinking was a problem or something, though it did have a dark side, I'll grant you that, it wasn't all fun and games and high-wire walking. Imagine chugging two-thirds of a bottle of '82 Lafite at three in the morning, hoping just maybe you can get back to sleep. While it can be done, I don't recommend it, though the '82 Lafite is certainly overrated. After six or eight times through the detox treatment, sweating it out alone in my raw-nerves bedroom, huddled in the dungeon of anxiety hell, the skin-crawling wormhole of each blistered instant, I finally just stopped, and rejoined the living, which has to make you wonder what I'm doing here now, with a large empty rocks glass, tilting a bottle of good bourbon.

I put the bottle down; this is no time to start drinking. The flight to El Paso is the usual grim affair, an hour and a half of sitting on the tarmac, just for starters, then staring out the window at more or less nothing, the occasional string of lights of a one stoplight town, the clusters of wattage of maybe it's Ontario or 29 Palms, the spiral nebula galaxy of Phoenix or Tucson, a gap in mid-flight, as though the plane might have landed, though a midair landing sounds somewhat implausible, then on over Silver City or Carlsbad or Las Cruces, I'm making this up, I don't know what's down there, I'm mostly seeing myself reflected in the glass, and I'm making that up too, I don't know who's out there. Darkness below, and a vague sense of aimlessness, that sense of being interchangeable with more or less anything, a mechanical being of no earthly use, amplified by a meal of synthetic white iceberg, dotted with droplets of sticky-orange salad dressing, blast-frozen nothingness emulsified in corn starch, and chicken covered in something that might have been more useful as an industrial glue, comfort food for an alien life-form, or a sentient/insentient philosophical enigma, caged behind bars at a robot zoo. Time doesn't pass, time doesn't have to; you could sing all the choruses of Beer on the Wall, and maybe get to Palm Springs with three bottles to go. I try reading a two-month-old Delta Sky magazine, Wanda Lust's column on Valentine Romance Getaway Weekends, the Escape Romance Package at the Renaissance Resort at the World Golf Village, or the Get Hitched With George and Martha Wedding Package, at Hotel Monaco in Alexandria, Virginia, offering a vow-renewal ceremony with George and Martha Washington replica look-alikes, or the Get Out of the Doghouse You Fuck-Up Package, at the Fairmont Le Chateau Montebello in Quebec, where breakfast comes equipped with a milk chocolate bowl, full of dog-bone-shaped cookies, and a cute li'l stuffed animal, and God knows what else, maybe his and hers suicide pistols, all for $249 a night, and the rest is up to you and yours. And then on to Rio or Brussels or let's make it Seoul, where the dull drab '60s have been wiped away, and a hip sustainable 21$^{st}$ century image of something totally Other has taken its place, epitomized by the reincarnation of the Cheonggyecheon, the stream at the heart of the ancient village of Seoul, its waters flowing crystal clear, playfully even, over a concrete riverbed between banks of concrete, surrounded by gleaming office towers and soaring architecture and glittering lights, while tourists step, gingerly, across well-placed steppingstones in their shorts and T-shirts, snapping pictures of an artificial waterfall world, trying to prove that they exist, or might once have existed, as the days slide past, on their 7-day Honeymoon-in-Asia Vacation, and another week down on their march to oblivion. And then on to Guatemala, and a "Voluntouring" Tour among the Q'eqchi' Indians, a dignified quiet people, eking out a life from tiny maize plantations, while we, the Voluntourists, are eager to work hard to do our small part in solving the world's poverty problem, discovering the untold riches that come from helping our fellow man, by spending a no doubt strenuous week, with a pick and a hoe and a virtuous shovel, mixing cement, pushing wheelbarrows around, pounding on a post, living shoulder to shoulder, while the Q'eqchi' Indians, descendants of the Maya, eke another few days from their miniature lives, the lives they've been living, on their tiny maize plantations, for a good thousand years without the help of Voluntourists. Maybe it's just me, but something has gone wrong here. The First Class cabin is now mostly dark: people bent and twisted, in a shallow twilight no-man's-land wakefulness sleep-state, under refugee blankets, exiles from the land of the concrete streambed, and the artificial waterfalls of the Renaissance Resort at Happily Ever After; people wearing headphones, watching a third-run movie, not sure whether to laugh or cry, and absently doing neither; people reading novels in small pools of light, reading about vampires, Anne Rice's Lestat de Lioncourt, or Stephanie Meyer's Byronic Edward, and the everlasting graveyard-wandering undead-fanged yet bloodless life, which feels like what I'm living now, like do me a favor, Son, get me the fuck out of here. I order a watery coffee and a miniature bottle of Courvoisier, hoping to get the emptiness to talk back or reverberate, maybe feel an emotion I can linger on and savor, but whatever is left of my own inner life, that sense of myself as formerly authentic, feels watered-down and miniaturized, better watch out for the guy in seat 3A, I think he's one of those whatyoucall, look-alikes. I'm headed toward El Paso in a hollow airframe state of mind, thousands of metal parts and fly-by-wire control surfaces, with only a thin aluminum skin between me and the abyss of absolute nothingness, which might not make for a great vacation, but sounds to me like a vast improvement. To make an endless story stop, when it comes to flying, I'm not really the white-knuckle-worried type of guy; I'm more the guy who sits vacantly praying, hoping the whole thing will fall out of the fucking sky.

I stagger off the plane at last, not sure who I am, or how I ended up here, or what went wrong along the way, to leave me feeling so emptied-out and hollow; I've exited close to a thousand flights, and always end up in the exact same state, dead inside and physically shaky, like a man coming to after pulmonary surgery, or like a poorly reanimated human corpse. Fortunately for me, I've landed in El Paso, whose airport is small, and easy enough to navigate; unfortunately for me, I seem to think I'm in Atlanta, whose airport is enormous, and impossible to escape. So how much do you know about Philosophical Zombies? We should maybe give you a minute, let you look this up, because we'll never get out of this airport alive if we leave it to a P-Zed to walk us all through it. By the time I'm thirty feet from my arrival gate, standing in a blaze of lighting florescence, I'm maybe one-part human, three-parts P-Zed, though the concourse itself is so brightly lit, and my own interior so lacking in luminance, that I'm not sure I know which parts are which, and the human part, in any case, is slowly leaking qualia. One thing is certain: I need to find Baggage Claim, reclaim my luggage, and get the hell Out of this, before I've lost the ability to claim human sentience. So which way is Out? I have no idea. The assumption would be that Out could be found by descending an escalator toward the Baggage Claim area, so I turn several circles, in search of an exit, assuming there's a sign that will point me toward Down on a descending escalator, which will soon get me Out if I can just stand still, but there isn't any Down, there aren't even any escalators, the assumption now would be that Down had found an Out, after decades of descending in search of an exit, and took the escalators with it while escaping the airport. To my immediate right lies the Security Area, which even a zombie knows is not the way Out, so unless I'm sup-

posed to walk backwards through Security, and pass through the
backscatter X-Rays in reverse, it's safe to assume that I can't turn
right, because the area to my right holds a good thousand people
who are trapped in an endless zig-zagging maze, slowly inching
forward and gradually shedding clothing, attempting to remember
how they got trapped, and why in God's name they want In here in
the first place. To my left lies, what? In Deeper, I suppose. There
are dozens of signs, and numerous gates, and hundreds of people
who seem to know where they're going, but no sign at all of a way to
get Out; I'm virtually certain that at this end of the concourse lies a
cluster of gates, and not a wall of glass with red-lighted Exits, but the
concourse itself doesn't appear to end, it appears to reach a vanishing point, deep in the distance, well before reaching anything that
would constitute an End; and the traffic in the hall is equally divided between those who seem frantic to get In Deeper, and those,
much like me, who must be frantic to Get Out, and yet all of them
are moving with that stiffed-gaited stride and absence of affect of
zombies in a horror movie, so whatever sense of urgency lies beneath all this movement must be something that I've imparted, possibly from watching too many horror movies. Given no real choice,
I set off on my search, assuming that by following the numbering
on the Gates in ascending order, I'll reach some sort of Exit before
the numbering runs out, though as far as I can tell, there aren't any
Exits, perhaps Down took the Exits when it made its escape. People
rush past me, going both ways at once, wearing Dawn-of-the-Dead-
like facial expressions, maybe too much white face-paint and liquid
latex, dragging tipped-over rollerbags that might just as well be human corpses, or perhaps they've chopped the corpses into piles of
human parts, and put them through a meat grinder to make them
easier to pack; I, in any case, am rapidly leaking sentience, and
must get Out before it's too late, before this film that I'm stuck in
reaches those frames at The End, and everything has vanished in a
zombie apocalypse. As I wander through the terminal's upper levels
on Concourse B, searching the signs for the Baggage Claim area,
past symbols meaning Men's Room or Currency Exchange or Lost
and Found, which you'd think, at a minimum, I at least might have
paused at, or maybe the Bright-Red-Heart-with-a-Lightning-Bolt
symbol, the sign of an Automated External Defibrillator, which re-

ally, at this point, isn't worthy of comment, I'm not feeling like part of a zombie apocalypse, the collapse of civilization in a plague of the undead; in fact, everyone around me looks perfectly normal, which only serves to deepen my sense of estrangement, since I, deep down, am the one true zombie, while all of the others are merely undead. By now you're probably thinking: there's no way out, guy's all P-Zed, got like zero human sentience, the null hypothesis in a thought experiment, hasn't got a clue whether he's *inside* the film, getting ready to die when the zombies finally get him, or *outside* watching a bunch of stiff-gaited actors, dragging bags of phony meat to the zombie graveyard, and in either case, let's face it, guy deserves to die, for dragging us all around this airport in the first place; in fact, come to think of it, he's probably not a P-Zed, he's probably just a moron, got like zero common sense, let's poke him with a stick, or the sharp-pointed end of a golf umbrella, bet when he says *ouch*, the mother really hurts, and at least we'll get out of this dimwitted discourse.

I, in short, have a problem with airports. I find the missing escalator, right beside my arrival gate, and descend at last to the lower level, regaining some semblance of narrative drive, and a heightened sense of structural urgency: it's time to get us *out* of here; there's a reason they call these airline *terminals*. Instead of my usual limo driver, waiting with a sign at the baggage claim carousel, in an undertaker's suit, with my name in big block letters, I remember to my horror that I have to rent a car, drag my bag to the curb and wait for the shuttle, face some replicant being who could care what I am, show a credit card and driver's license, initial things everywhere, and finally drive off in an anonymous grey sedan, which is just what I do, get the hell out of there. It's an enormous relief just to be at the wheel, with the map light on, struggling to find the freeway, not knowing north and south from east and west from driving around in endless circles because I have them all completely backwards, but knowing, if I chose to, in the blink of an eye, I could drive full speed into a bridge abutment. I follow the MapQuest directions to a T, get hopelessly lost and completely turned around, drive 20 straight miles out the wrong road in the night, with shadowy mountains directly up ahead, and a wasteland of scrub brush full of MapQuest nonsense. I finally pull over to the shoulder of the road, abandon the car, and walk into the desert. The moon isn't out. The stars are above me. In the direction I'm headed there is nothing at all, while directly behind me, in the other direction, lies a large pile of light, brownish and yellowed, like a garbage-dump heap of lighting refuse. This may be El Paso, and Ciudad Juárez, for instance, or maybe I'm outside Tempe somewhere, and the way I'm feeling is, what the fuck's the difference. I go up over a gentle rise, where the air is warm, and feels like velvet, and then down into a wood-littered streambed or gulch, where the air is chilly, and smells like coolant. I crouch down to sink my fingers in the soil, sandy and still warm, vaguely re-assuring, until something I think is a broken piece of stick suddenly moves, and slithers off into the bushes. I lie back at last on the dense desert floor, with my hands under my head, staring up at the heavens, wondering a little nervously if all of this is real, existence that is, the original question, *Why is there Something rather than Nothing*, closing my eyes like a child playing dead, making it all disappear into darkness for a while, and bringing it all back, in the blink of an eye, as though the stars and the sky and the dense desert heavens would vanish forever without my presence, but then hearing something rustle in the brush to my left, and quickly standing up, knowing that my absence wouldn't make the slightest difference. Call it a dream; it does not change anything. I gather some driftwood and light a small fire and watch while it burns, the pale flames flailing, pretending that I at last am the last man on earth, or maybe the first, the one true original, with only the fire there to watch me as I work, patiently bringing Nothingness in and out of existence. This doesn't work either; maybe I'm just not trying very hard, and even my own emptiness can make do without me; if man is the being by whom Nothingness comes into the world, you couldn't prove it by me; it strikes me as fairly large, and possessed of an eerie sort of absolute self-confidence. Using the fire as a marker, I walk another hundred yards or so deeper into the desert, and scramble up the side of a pile of drifted sand, maybe twenty feet tall, from which the top few feet of a Yucca plant protrude, like a porcupine covered with sword-like quills, and with a single narrow column of whitish-green flowers growing three feet up, out of the porcupine's back, for no real reason I am able to fathom. Somehow or other, maybe twenty feet down, beneath the pile of sand, the plant has roots, sunk deep into the desert, the taproot itself drawing water from below, and feeding it upward toward the whitish-green flower column. Where on earth did we ever get the idea that man himself has anything to do with it, much less dominion over a world like this? I walk back to the fire and take a seat; maybe the world could use a disinterested spectator. I think I hear a coyote howl. I think I hear a coyote howl. It is just that kind of sound I suppose, a sound that seems to happen twice, once when you hear it, and once when you think of it as something heard. Another delusion, in other words, man's capacity for self-refection producing the illusion that creation needs us. Few things on earth are quite so full of Nothingness as the sound of a coyote, making itself heard. I count the bones on the right side of my rib cage, picturing what I'd look like if the coyotes picked me clean, a bleached-out skeleton in a dry wash arroyo, the victim of reality as a thought experiment, a pile of human sticks made of calcium and manganese, coming to rest at last in an ephemeral streambed. And then the dry pile of mesquite starts crackling and scintillating and throwing off showers of bright hard sparks, and the whole thing strikes me as slightly ridiculous, sitting in the desert, fifty yards from my car, playing ontological games, maybe set off a brush fire. I let the fire die down, sizzling and humming, bury it in dirt, dust off my hands, climb the little rise, and walk back to the car by the light of a thousand stars, smelling of real smoke from an imaginary fire, and feeling half-embalmed with mental refrigerant.

By the time I arrive at my anonymous grey sedan, and climb behind the wheel, and reinsert the ignition key, I'm having second thoughts about completing my journey; I'm not at all sure I even know who I am, much less what I'm doing here, out in the desert; this might be a good place to bring my journey to an end. There are all sorts of places, of course, for a journey to end: at a Welcome Back party surrounded by friends; in an Ensenada jail among smiling policemen; a thousand feet up, eye to eye with an angel, somewhere off a cliff in the Big Sur headlands, which very nearly put an end to the rest of my journeys. Stranded in the desert, however, in the middle of nowhere, twenty miles out the wrong road in the night, while having second thoughts about completing a journey, doesn't sound like much of a place for an ending; in fact, it sounds like more of a place for an ending to begin.

# 23

I stopped at a liquor store on my way into town, bought a fifth of Old Grand-Dad 114 Barrel Proof, with a lovely bite of butter-scotch and vanilla on the nose, and just a hint of spicy-orange on the leather-lash finish, maybe wash away the sense of having Prestone in my system, get something warm in my bloodstream fast, after nearly fourteen months spent circulating coolant. I finally found the 10, sipping little jolts of my bonded bourbon, exited at North Mesa, drove out past Las Palmas Medical Clinic, and the Providence Memorial Hospital on the campus of UTEP, wonder-ing a little if I should check myself in, see if they have a cure for terminal jaundice. My motel was up ahead under orangish-brown crime lights, a two-story dump in a U around its parking lot, with pale yellow bulbs sloshing light back and forth inside the caretaker's office, and pink-flamingo/turquoise-blue neon-tube signage, flick-ering on and off in the dark sky overhead, with the VACANCY sign burned out, more or less permanently, but with the red NO illumi-nated, somewhat paradoxically: I completely understand; couldn't have said it better myself if you tortured me. I paid cash for the night, signed a leather-bound register with a ludicrous phony name, remembering a similar book, one that I'd tried to sign truthfully, at the Reina Christina Hotel in Algeciras, Spain, where I spent the night with one of my ex-wives, before crossing on the ferry to Tangiers and Rabat and Casablanca, headed at last for Marrakesh, in the ancient spice trails burgundy desert, an amazing wine-red and oasis-green display, beneath the snow-capped Atlas Mountains, and beyond them, nothing. It's hard to remember if I was sober back then, but I *was* still writing, still full of a sense of purpose, still climbing the Absolute Mountains of my spiritual fatigue, not knowing that up ahead lay the one true Sahara. Let me think; how long ago was that? My room in Marrakesh was a startling revelation, hand-carved exotic hardwoods, luxurious white linens, quarried peach marble, for $20 a night; I'd been living in Portugal for the better part of a year, writing and reading and translating Pessoa, and life itself was a magnificent surprise, fresh crusty bread and homemade jam and tiny green melons, in the bluebird mornings; cabrito and cozido and carne de porco à alentejana, just to cover the "C's", with my artist friends at night, living like a rich man in Sintra's glorious Eden, on writing and friendship and $10 a week. Maybe it's just me, but something went wrong here. My room at the dump was about what you'd expect, thirty-year-old carpet and a broken down bed, linoleum bubbling in the moldy-smelling bathroom, and a profound sense of vacancy and utter displacement. I tore the luggage tag loose from my bag, thinking at first that I'd stay and unpack it; took a good long leak without disturbing the irony-proof sanitization strip; flushed the piss and the bag tag down the fifty-year-old toilet; and basically grabbed my bag and got the hell out, put the NO back in VACANCY, and ran for my life. Are you at all familiar with spiritual terror?

I dragged my bag and bottle back down to the car, and sat behind the wheel with the engine turned off, wondering what next, and smoking a Partagas or a Dominican Montecristo, a cigar I'd picked up at the whiskey store, wishing I'd remembered to pack some of my Cubans. A little jolt of bourbon, blow a couple of smoke rings, sitting in the parking lot of the U-Turn Motel: maybe I can't get back to Marrakesh and Portugal, but there has to be something better than bubbling linoleum, waiting for me now, in the El Paso night; now that I'm drinking, almost anything is possible. I retreated down North Mesa, toward downtown El Paso, with no sense at all as to what lay ahead, but with an absolute certainty that I now knew what I was doing. At the top of a hill, in Sunset Park, next to Providence Memorial, I stopped at a light, where I could see the whole layout of the Rio Grande valley: the skyscrapers of El Paso mostly dark this time of night, and Ciudad Juárez, like a toppled-over Christmas tree, blazing with electricity, mirror-brites and flexible rope lights and logo sculptures at the glittering neon core, lights strung up on wires and poles in the barrio-sprawling ramshackle desert, for miles in every direction, as far as the eye could see. If you've never paid a visit to downtown El Paso, let me tell you, don't even bother; the only things left there are the things that could not get out; the place is like something that died twenty years ago, and someone forgot to bury it, while Ciudad Juárez is almost monstrously alive, a Frankenstein masterpiece of human activity. I drove into a dead zone around the cold dark heart of town, the Camino Real Hotel, the Judson Williams Convention Center, the Abraham Chavez Theatre, the El Paso Museum of Art: not only were the streets all rolled-up tight and empty, but no one had left a light on for me; this didn't look too promising. The restaurant signs were dark, the Camino Real looked like a mausoleum, the last few pedestrians out wandering around the streets might just as well have been mental patients, shuffling along, holding bottles in bags, searching for signs of life in the cracked and tilted sidewalks, knowing deep down that they had nowhere to go, but maybe looking for clues, a trail of breadcrumbs or screw-top bottle caps, to lead them back to their private asylums. What about bars? There have to be bars. You have a whole substantial city center, a structural grid of human concourse, where do you go to get a drink? I parked the car, doused the lights, double-checked the trunk to make sure that it was closed, but semi-deliberately left it unlocked: there wasn't enough human energy here to generate a sense of plausible caution, much less actual criminal intent. This time of night, in Madrid or Barcelona, people would only now be sitting down to eat, or waiting for friends at a zinc-topped bar, ordering tapas and a cool glass of fino, the plazas gradually filling with students and street musicians, the restaurants spilling out over the treelined walks, the evening only now beginning to begin, and everything alive to the endless possibilities. There I am now, at a table outside a warmly lit café, drinking a tinto, waiting for someone, dreaming about Velazquez or Goya or El Greco, my whole life in front of me, art, poetry, mathematics, philosophy, time to write and read and think, time to become and even more time to be, so how the hell did I wind up here, and where did the time go, and where the hell are we? A drunk ambled past, mumbling something in Spanish, maybe trying to remember who Judson Williams was, or why El Paso felt the need for a symphony orchestra, and bouncing strangely on the balls of his feet, like a fighter still dancing when his ten-count is over, no longer cognizant of the structure of boxing, ready to go another two or three rounds. This, in some sense, must have happened to El Paso. Now playing at the Abraham Chavez Theatre? Sesame Street Live: Elmo's Green Thumb.

I followed the drunk down North Santa Fe to San Antonio Avenue to South El Paso, stopping outside the Camino Real, wondering about the wisdom of calling it a night, probably sleep safe and sound inside a 17-story, ninety-year-old, hotel/crematorium, and then giving up and getting back in the car, pointed the thing east, let's see what's out there. I was a little out of shape for high-caliber drinking, so I was taking it slow on the Barrel Proof Bonded, but this still wasn't the time for a field sobriety test, and directly ahead were maybe fifteen police cars, standard black and whites outside a concrete monstrosity, the El Paso County Downtown Jail. I veered off San Antonio onto Magoffin Avenue, driving nice and slow, and seeing absolutely nothing, housing mostly, a tire store or muffler shop, shotgun shacks and low-rise apartments, a few old classics with wraparound porches, a few blocks of things that looked like projects. At some point I must have given up on going east, drove a block north, and headed back on Myrtle Avenue, where what do I see but an actual sign of life, a dive named Sonny's with the front door open, and music playing, and real people laughing and looking happy to be alive, happy just to be there, in the juke joint lamplight. Ah, that's more like it; park the damn car; let's go have a look. Sonny's was like a time machine, taking me back to East Los Angeles, drinking with my dad in the windowless bars of El Sereno, ground zero of the Chicano gangbanger life, the drive-by-shooting, lowrider-cruising, Chevy Impala chrome-wheel capital, and random-violence-central for the Viva La Raza '70s. My dad was an atom-smasher, a particle physics engineer, the guy who ran the Synchrotron at the Rad Lab in Berkeley, an engineer admittedly turned part-time plumber and dimebag weed dealer, living in a shack up on Ferntop Road, with homebrew in the closet and no electricity. Dad was mostly a beer drunk, though you never actually saw him drunk, and he would have felt right at home at a place like Sonny's, the jukebox blasting Norteño music, corridos and rancheras that sounded like Spanish Polka, the crowd three-deep around the waterlogged bar, four cholos playing eightball for pitchers and tequila. I waded right in through the milling around the door, turned left and headed east toward a pitcher-littered bar-top, running north to south along the far eastern wall, found an empty red stool at the south end of the counter, and ordered up a shot of Silver Patron, and an ice-cold bottle of Pacifico I think it was, seem to recall the label being yellow, but then again it could have been Indio or Sol, or maybe Superior, or it might have been Modelo, the bottle was clear, or maybe it was brown, that much I remember as if it were yesterday, though I'm thinking at this point it was actually two nights ago. I couldn't find the salt, so I tossed off the tequila, bit the limon, and swallowed half a bottle of the clearly bottled beer; whatever it was, it was an enormous improvement. Sonny's was a maybe thirty-by-forty single packed room, decorated with streamers in red white and green, red and gold neon, adver-tising Carta Blanca, classic Montejo and Corona bar mirrors, and a green felt pool table that tilted to the northeast, where one leg had come to rest near a concrete concavity, at the bottom of which was a saucer-shaped drain. The crowd was two-thirds working men, in boots and jeans with wide buckle belts, and pearl snap shirts with bright embroidery; the men had hands that looked as large as my head, and the women looked tiny, with upside-down-teardrop-shaped radiant faces, and long dark hair, and gold hoop earrings, wearing halter-top dresses in aquamarine and pink, ready to polka, if you gave them enough room, ready to slap you, if you drunkenly didn't; quite a crowd for a what's this, a Tuesday, everyone talking, apparently all at once, in perfectly accented Mexican Spanish, and waving at friends as they poured into the bar, and laughing and drinking to the 2/4 jukebox.

I had another round to get acclimated, and two hard-boiled eggs to protect my stomach, and forgot about Marrakesh and Barce-lona. There is nothing like a crowded bar to make you forget your personal history; maybe you're a particle physics nuclear engineer, maybe you're a plumber selling weed to delinquents, maybe you're a VC who used to be a poet, have another beer, what the hell's the

difference? A thin bleached blonde, maybe ten years past her Sell
By date, took the seat to my right, around the corner of the bar, ordered something weird, like a Singapore Sling or an Apricot Sour,
in staccato broken Spanish, placed an unlit cigarette between her
lavender lips, and waited for a moment while I fished out my cigar
torch. Where y'all from, darlin'? I was so surprised to hear actual
person-to-person speech that I fumbled my response, before finally
coming up with something like Let's say Los Angeles. Is that really where y'all from? Or you just puttin' me on, don't wanna say?
You're not from around here, I can tell just by lookin' at you; you
look like the kind of guy who could be from all over. Me, I'm from
Kansas City, but I've been living in El Paso for thirty-some years,
followed my ex here when he was transferred to Fort Bliss, had a
nice little ranch-style place in E4 on-base housing, green lawn in
front and trees out back, two bedrooms, bath, and a whaddayacallit
breakfast nook, real central air conditioning, nice place to live if it
weren't for my ex, though I'd probably still be living with him now
if the dumb son of a bitch knew how to keep his pants zipped. My
daddy warned me about Bobby, but then Daddy was a preacher, so
that sorta goes without saying, problem wasn't really Bobby himself
so much as Bobby's drugs, got him OTH'ed, that was Bobby all
right, Other-Than-Honorable right from the get-go, transferred his
ass back to good ole Fort Living Room, so I got me a job as a cocktail waitress, back in the days when the Old Plantation was just a
regular place, not all these strippers and gays and transvestites, so
I guess you'd have to say I'm from El Paso by now, but you know
what, I really miss the place, drinking to flamenco music at Bar
Sevilla, dancing at El Padrino and Adrian's Lounge over the bridge
in Juárez, eating at El Bronquito, hiking up around Mount Cristo
Rey, looking for the old pig farm up on the mesa. Jesus. Where the
hell did everything go? Seems like El Paso just sorta moved on, and
I stayed here, if you know what I'm saying. You married or something? I lit her another cigarette while shaking my head, not altogether sure I could hold up my end of this particular conversation,
and then swiveled on around away from the bar, watching while a
guy who was built like a cinderblock scratched on the eight ball,
with the cue ball curling around and waffling a little and hesitating
briefly, before draining itself at last in the northeast pocket. Time

for maybe one more round; then go see about locating suitable
housing. Along the far western wall, in the southwest corner, sat
two mismatched Anglos, both drinking beers, one of them compact
and confident looking, dark-haired and handsome, and the other
a guy who was about twice his own size, and three times too large
for the chair he was dwarfing. Maybe it was just me, but the colors
in the room were starting to look a little bright, and the chemistry
in the room seemed I don't know, edgy, like the place was some
kind of voltaic pile, with anions and cations drifting around in an
electrolyte solution, migrating slowly toward opposite poles, and the
place filling up with a weird electricity. The confident-looking guy
said something I didn't hear, and the cinderblock pool-player must
have taken it the wrong way, because he took a few steps in the
southwest direction, holding the pool cue thick-end up; I've been
in maybe a dozen bar fights, from Hussong's in Ensenada to the Ice
House in Pasadena, and I've never really figured out exactly what
goes wrong, one moment you're laughing and ordering drinks, and
the next thing you know, there's all kinds of chemistry. Cinderblock
was standing at the Anglos' table, pointing the cue stick, butt-end
forward, and waving it a little at the dark-haired man, who didn't
seem to blink, or look up at the guy, much less acknowledging that
he maybe had him a situation. The laughter seemed to hang like
smoke in the air, the way one minute you know you're in a smoky
room, and the next you're seeing wafts and drifts, and all of a sudden it's specifically smoky; no way I'm telling you the room quieted
down, it was more like everyone suddenly noticing it's noisy, like
the laughter started to sound a little conscious of itself, which is
just what happens before the room goes quiet. Two or three pool
players were resting their cues on the concrete floor, and staring
southwest, just barely smiling. And like I was saying, the lighting
wasn't right, it was way too full of bright reds and yellows and like
adrenaline-orange surges, which might just explain how I missed
what happened next, where the handsome-looking compact guy,
by which I mean a person with a high specific gravity, is somehow
holding up two broken parts of stick, offering to hand them back to
the cinderblock pool guy, not that they'd be of much use anymore,
as far as him maintaining a pool-specific context.

    And then everyone took a gulp of whatever it was they were

drinking, and the lighting settled down, with the laughter maybe
sounding a little more natural, and I tossed off what I proposed to be
my final shot of tequila. Miss El Paso, 1979, was ordering another
drink, which turned out to be a Rosita, tequila, vermouth, Cam-
pari, Angostura, beside which the bartender placed something he's
calling a Savannah Whore, a shot of Jose Cuervo with a cinnamon-
dusted orange. I'm not making this shit up; the things some people
drink, you'd think they'd never heard of waking up with a monster
hangover. Miss El Paso was apparently well along in a speech she'd
been making, and acting like the guy beside her, Mr. Smooth, from
Let's say All Over, had the first fucking clue what the hell she was
talking about; trust me, I was there, and I really and truly didn't. You
know, Dillies, Juice, Footballs, D's. What's the problem, you hard
of hearing? You never heard of a D before? Won't do much for your
hearing loss, maybe you need to stay away from your whaddayacal-
lem ototoxics, you on chemo, sweetheart, Vincristine or Cisplatin
or they got you maybe on Nitrogen Mustard? Excuse me? Course
Erythromycin and Neomycin, same damn thing, even that stuff
they feed a horse, to keep it from having a pulmonary hemorrhage,
you planning on running the mile and an eighth out at Sunland
Park, been takin' Lasix? Speaking of horses, you ever try Ultras?
Shit's not even a controlled fucking substance, vets give it out like
it's opiated pet treats, get you 'bout as high as a red-tailed hawk. I'm
sorry. What were we just talking about? 'Bout me being a nurse, an
APN, a nurse anesthetist up at Providence Memorial, weren't you
even listening? Tell you the truth, I was watching two guys about
to have a fight, whole thing was over before it even started. Don't
worry darlin', you wanna see a fight, you've definitely come to the
right damn place, give 'em 'bout an hour, they'll all be breaking
chairs and shit. So you wanna buy some D's or what? My mortgage
is overdue, gonna wind up in foreclosure, end up with Ma's furniture all over the yard, got to pay these vultures now, or find myself
a moving van. I got eight-mig pills worth forty dollars each; I'll give
you all ten for two hundred dollars. Have to warn you though, you
goin' into Juárez, eat 'em all there, better yet you plug 'em, or you'll
wind up in a shitstorm with the CBP, they don't much like Dilau-
did coming back across the border; better off taking these Ultras,
darlin', tell 'em they're for your dog or cat, no one ever been busted

for their dog having arthritis. I'll give you the whole bag for two hundred bucks, worth four hundred, even if you bought 'em from an online pharmacy. Whaddaya say, help a girl pay the mortgage? I downed my last tequila, or the one just after my last tequila, peeled off two hundreds from a large round roll, not without realizing that I carry around too much cash, and told her to keep it and keep her pills, the last thing I needed now was opiates on top of good tequila. You want the dillies or the Ultras, sweetheart, I don't take charity from strangers, no how, I may not know how my mortgage works, or why my house is worth like half what it cost me, but you take the pills and we'll both be square, wash a couple of Ultras down with a bottle of beer, you'll see what I mean, you'll feel like you're up on the mesa somewhere, chasing the pigs around Mount Cristo Rey.

She handed me a brown paper bag with two large containers of hospital pharmaceuticals, and I sat at the bar, drinking tequila, like a man whose wife had packed him a sack lunch. Call it a dream; it does not change anything. I did like she told me, with the Ultras and beer, then bought three more of what the Anglos were drinking, and carried them over to their corner table, past the tilted green felt and the muttering Latinos. Almost certainly, greetings were exchanged, and thanks and salutations and the clinking of bottled beers, and then somehow or other three tequilas just appeared, and there's no doubt we drank them, there definitely came a moment when they were no longer there, though I distinctly remember, when it came to the next round, the twice-his-own-size guy was voicing his dissent, saying Jesus, Raymond, we have to get up early, let's head on back, get us some sack time. Which it turns out, really, would have been a good idea, because the next thing I know, we're out on the sidewalk, with four pissed-off pool players and me with my sack lunch and Cinderblock acting all aggrieved or something, and then toppling over as if he'd been punched, though I'm not all that sure that I saw someone punch him. A certain amount of discussion almost certainly ensued, not that any of it was all that memorable, other than the part where someone pulled a knife, which I think actually happened, though I can't say I'd swear to it. Adrenaline will do that, make you remember certain things that you would otherwise not, and what I think I remember is a knife being produced, and this might have been a switchblade, and I actually saw it, or it might have been a case where a weapon has been inferred, from something gleaming and metallic that I tasted in my mouth. There is something about the color of sodium-vapor lamps that makes you feel like you're part of a crime scene already, and there was, admittedly, a good deal of blood, down there where Cinderblock was face-first on the sidewalk. If I had to hazard a guess, the crime-scene sensation was a lighting problem, and the moaning I was hearing was the result of a fractured nose. Did two black and whites suddenly appear, with flashing red lights and uniformed authorities, or am I thinking about events from a whole different night, where I wound up facedown in a restaurant dumpster? Let me think. No, there were no black and whites, that definitely must have been a separate occasion, drawn pistols and handcuffs are an entirely different vibe, and it wasn't at all like that night at Hussong's, where I came to on the pavement a good mile away, with my friends pulling one arm and the Policía the other; that night I eventually woke up in a ditch, with the sun in my eyes and half of my clothes gone, after using my motel money to pay La Mordida. There are all kinds of ways for an evening to end, tucked in your bed alongside a loved one, or out in a field full of grazing livestock, or with a two-inch piece of surgical steel pin, inserted to stabilize your fragmented cheekbone; in this case, it must have just come to an end, though I can't really tell you I was there when it ended. Luckily for me, since I would have made a somewhat numinous witness, my friends must have had a house that was somewhere nearby, because when I woke up that morning, with both of them gone, and me with my car keys but no actual auto, I was able to find it in like fifteen minutes flat, right where I'd parked it, on the street in front of Sonny's. Sometimes it's better to be lucky than good, and sometimes you're lucky just to regain consciousness, though there's no way I'm saying that waking up was good. Lucky, maybe; but definitely not good.

I pulled the car around, reparked it in front of the mustard-yellow ramshackle rambler of a house, and went back inside; about the last thing you need, when you're suffering from a severe case of alcohol-induced inner-being fragmentation, is to be trying to drive a car around; you're far better off just driving the thing drunk, than trying to figure out whose hands are doing the driving. I know what you're thinking: take a few aspirin, wash the things down with like a quart of warm water, then find something to eat, maybe milk thistle and gingerroot, maybe fresh fruit and vegetable juices, replenish the nutrients that alcohol leaches out, rehydrate the battered and blood-poisoned body, but we both know that's a crock, a complete load of shit, and the only real cure for a hangover is time. Or is it? Is it really? You're lying there on a moldering sofa, nauseous, lethargic, completely dysphoric, with a hypersensitivity to light and noise, strangely erratic motor functions, suffering from acute acetaldehyde intoxication, with ethanol dehydrogenase causing a total collapse of your gluconeogenesis, meaning basically that your brain is slowly being starved to death, and someone's trying to tell you oh just give it a little time? Three minutes in a state of morbid anxiety is the moral equivalent of a week spent in solitary: not only is time not the actual cure, time is the disease you need to find a cure for, time is like a tumor that needs to be removed, and the only real way to take a scalpel to time is have a good stiff drink, or make it two and call it chemo. Of course, maybe a glass of milk wouldn't kill you now and then, but the milk in the icebox smelled rancid and noxious, so I poured a tumbler maybe one-third full from the bottle of whiskey I had left over, topped it off with water from the sulfurous-smelling tap, and drank it all down with two or three Ultras. There are very few things that are better in life than getting relief from a rampaging nihilistic deathwatch hangover, and while opiates aren't really a standard of care, and rarely show up on the medical protocols, you'll find that as the minutes once again begin to pass, and your shattered inner being slowly becomes reintegrated, some semblance of life seems to resume once again, and while it may not be your life, at least it's alive. There's a reason that when Churchill awakened with a groan, in Roosevelt's White House, after an evening of brilliance, the great mind fed by Cognac and cigars, following bottles of Bordeaux from the strategic cellars, the White House porters knew just what to do: bring him a tumbler of Scotch, pronto. Bacon and eggs and a nice glass of tomato juice? You have to be kidding; the man's a professional, show him some respect, or skip the whole show of deference routine, it's wasted on the man, but try to keep it quiet, and leave the whiskey, won't you? In short, I was fine, I had once again resensitized the N-methyl-D-aspartate system of the cerebral cortex of my starving brain, causing it to be receptive to the neurotransmitter glutamate, gradually increasing my synaptic plasticity, and bringing about a state of bodily relaxation, with my neurons now transmitting in coherent alpha waves, very similar to the state that a Yogi reaches, when he's deeply engaged in Transcendental Meditation, where thought as thought is transcended at last, and we reach the source of thought itself, the higher plateau, Transcendental Being, which all things considered is a fine place to be, though you have to be careful, the place may be trademarked. No wonder the Allies won World War II; not only was Hitler all amped-up on Pervitin, a particularly vicious form of methamphetamine, while Churchill's kicking back in a transcendental state, but Germany's pharmacologists totally failed their own troops; the drug that could have won the war, called D-IX, a mixture of cocaine and methamphetamine with Eukodol opiates, languished for years in a bureaucratic maze, and never got past their testing procedures, on tiny little sailors in the world's smallest submarines. Pervitin may be perfectly fine, to get your best Waffen men to stand up and fight, instead of lying down in the Soviet snow, and going to sleep forever in a Leningrad forest, but it leaves your nerves a jagged wreck, and does nothing at all for your self-esteem problem. Eukodol alone would have fixed all that; Hitler's men would have felt like giants, walking around on oxycodone stilts, in a massive state of Superman euphoria. I mean, Burroughs traded his typewriter in for several small boxes of Eukodol ampules, which just goes to show how good the stuff is: a little majoun to smoke and some Nazi opiates, who needs a typewriter, write it all out in your own massive head; though on second thought, there is something a little odd about *Naked Lunch*; you might not want your everyday troops going all nonlinear, wandering around in an Interzone daze, throwing violent orgies and wreaking bloody havoc and decapitating people and becoming Liquefactionists. No; you know what? Cancel that; turns out you're a Nazi, that's just what you want.

Like I said, my hangover was fine, though maybe the opiates were a whole separate topic. I still had another hour to kill, before my sleep-clinic meeting at the Stanton Street Bridge, so rather than pondering Nazi pharmaceuticals, and the nature of Transcendental Meditation as a litigable trademark, I decided to get up and maybe

find a shower and put on clean clothes, make myself look present-
able. The Ultras, to be clear, didn't feel like stilts, it was more like
walking with lifts in my shoes, so I took two more, with a few sulfurous inches of diluted bonded bourbon, and while I wasn't yet ready
to trade my typewriter in, I felt pretty good, all things considered. I
went out to the car, took a nice fresh shirt and my toiletry kit from
the lumpy green duffel bag stashed in the trunk, and locked things
back up with the remote entry key, though not without encoun-
tering a few basic reality problems; these might have been the result of my hitting the red panic button, just below the door-lock on
the keyless remote, and inadvertently setting off the high-pitched
scream of the car alarm system, a sound that struck me as somehow deeply true, and yet wildly at odds with the stillness of the
morning; or my problems might have started with the duffel bag
itself, which seemed to be stuffed full of Monopoly money; there
is something about the color lavender that does not contribute to a
sense of reality; these might be Swiss banknotes and real-world currency, or maybe I was planning to build a hotel on Park Place. In
any case, I went back in the house, and found a little bathroom off
one of the upstairs bedrooms, a bedroom that itself didn't look all
that real, covered as it was in sky-blue wallpaper, with chubby pink
children blowing tiny golden trumpets; I stood for just a moment
in the dormer-windowed room, listening while a dog barked off in
the distance, perhaps in response to some canine-intuited threat, or
perhaps hearing trumpets and howling along, and in either case the
message was abundantly clear, I needed to keep moving and get out
of this bedroom, these tiny pink children were beginning to look
ominous. I had, in other words, completely zoned out, wandering
off alone into a sky-blue-bedroom irreality continuum; call it a day-
dream, a moment, as the Spanish say, of thinking about the immortality of the crab, or call it a simple lapse of functional attention,
the problem, in either case, is basically the same. This man staring
at the wall, pondering golden trumpets, and the howling of distant
canines, and the nature of ominous pinkness in the sky-blue world
of wallpaper children, may in fact believe that only a moment or
two has passed; turns out he's been standing there for a good seven
minutes, and has lost another battle in our war against time. The
next time a man says he's "just killing time," stop for a moment and

think this over; just to be safe, use a good stopwatch, because while it may well be true that crabs are immortal, you'll find out eventually that time's killing *you*.

I entered the bathroom, which smelled like a lagoon, placed my toiletries on the tank of a slow-leaking toilet, ran cold water in the basin of a calcified sink, and set about the process of brushing my teeth. There are few things in life, after an evening of drinking, that are better for the soul than brushing your teeth; not only does it wash away that sense of oral depravity, that inkling of having butchered something, whose remains are decaying inside your mouth; but it's also a way of proving to yourself that you still have fine motor skills, the ability to coordinate small muscle movements, with enough manual dexterity to scrub and polish each grisly tooth, thereby ridding yourself of the deep conviction that your brain is full of neuro-corrosives, that it has, in effect, been completely demyelinated, each axon stripped of its myelin sheathing, perhaps by sheep dip or commercial weed killers, and that your central nervous system no longer works; as you rinse away the aftereffects with a palm-cupped sip of holy water, and spit the last of the evil out, into the swirling sink, you feel yourself regaining at last a sense of your own humanity, a sense of atonement and expiation, as you stand at the water basin and bend and spit. You are not the first to suffer, of course, from this particular form of spirito-lexico verbal confusion: expiation and expectoration are two completely unrelated words, but at least your teeth are a little cleaner, and your breath, for the moment, is vastly improved. As I stared at the result in the bathroom mirror, checking my teeth for sparkling whiteness, and filling my lungs with cool mountain air, from somewhere high up in the wintergreen forests, I made the predictable tactical blunder, so common among humans after a night of hard drinking, and yet so costly in the full light of day, of staring into my own two eyes, which were glaring back from the dusty mirror: Jesus God, what have I done, bloodshot and gory, a ghastly wreck, find the Visine or a bottle of Wite-Out, or use a brick on this reflective substance, forgive us our trespasses as we forgive others, but please don't make me look at *that*. Nothing so mars a well-maintained tan, gathered on beaches from Hawaii to Aruba, on a two-weeks-per-quarter work-study plan, as a pair of beady rat-red eyeballs, so out they go, even if I have to gouge them. Having once again passed the fine-motor-skills test, with two drops of Visine in each beady eye, I warmed up the water in the moldy stall shower, and searched the tiny bath-room for a nice fluffy towel. Let's just say this wasn't the Paris Ritz; the towel rack hung from two loose screws, and held a foul-odored washcloth, a grease-stained dishtowel, a motor-oil T-shirt, and two strips of rag that smelled of maybe cleaning solvent, like the Dunk-Kit my dad used to decarbonize his guns. Underneath the sink? Nothing but Ajax and Liquid-Plumr. Maybe find some linens in the bedroom hall closet? Nothing even vaguely resembling a basic human towel, though I did find a generous supply of something I'd have to think about later, like several large boxes of Gamebore Black Gold shotgun shells, and several more of Winchester 9mm Luger ammo, in red-lettered white boxes, with full metal jackets, 115 grains per round, 100 rounds per box. This, as they say, is this. The boys, apparently, weren't expecting guests; or if guests were expected, someone ought to warn them. No harm done, I can al-ways drip-dry, though I now had to pass the razor-handling test, and when this was passed, with a certain amount of tremor, and my body and hair had been lathered and rinsed, I exited the bathroom feeling better than ever, feeling, as they say, like a whole new man, though this is one of those expressions that sort of makes you won-der, since just who he was, I didn't have the foggiest.

I gathered up my belongings, placing my toiletries and phar-maceuticals and whiskey in a bag, and then went running back upstairs, to the sky-blue bedroom, feeling as though I'd forgotten something, which turned out to be my dirty shirt. The fact that I'd left my glasses, on the coffee table beside the living room sofa, nev-er even crossed my mind, until I walked outside in the near-noon day, and noticed that the rental car appeared to be underwater. I ran back upstairs, searched the bathroom, searched the bedroom, I even searched the ammunition closet, but I couldn't find them anywhere; each place I looked was only another place I'd looked. It's hard to imagine a full-grown man having some sort of object permanence problem, but a man who stares at a toilet tank, for the third or fourth time, without the object appearing, definitely has an object problem, something to do with his glasses maybe, where he doesn't believe his own two eyes. This man we see staring at the toilet tank is engaged in some sort of magical thinking; you'd think he's maybe nine months old, and has never heard of Piaget. It's fortunate that the man is alone in the house, as there are very few things so deeply irritating as the conversation surrounding a missing object. Honey, have you seen my glasses? I can't seem to find them, I've looked all over. Where did you have them last? Probably on my face, what the hell difference does that make? Try retracing your steps, they're probably there, right where you left them. Honestly, sweetheart, I've looked all over the entire house, I can't find them anywhere, they've disappeared. No, dear, your glasses didn't just up and disappear, they're around here somewhere; where were you standing when you took them off? How the hell should I know, probably right next to the place I put my glasses, if I find the fucking things, I'll let you know. Did you check on top of the toilet tank? That's where they were the last three times you lost them, they're probably on the toilet tank, if you've checked there already, check again. I've checked the goddamn toilet tank, I've even checked the ammo closet, I tell you the things have disappeared, they were right here somewhere a minute ago, and now they've simply vanished. Umm, dear, since when did we have an ammunition closet? Since the last time we had this fucking conversation; if I don't find my goddamn glasses soon, I'm planning on blowing somebody's brains out. There's no need to get agitated, sweetheart, you'll find your glasses, right where you left them, there in the last place you'd think to look. Stop for a moment and try to remember: where is the last place you'd think to look? I don't know. I've never really thought about it. Wherever they are, I suppose. Well there you have it. You left your glasses right where they are, so why don't you put the gun down, darling, and please stop staring at the toilet tank; you're beginning to scare the children. If you don't mind my saying, dear, your glasses would seem to be the least of our worries. Staring off into empty space, waving a German pistol around, running all over from room to room looking wild-eyed and tormented, I'm afraid you may be having another one of your little episodes; I want you to go straight to the doctor now, will you do that for me? Yes, dear, right away; I didn't mean to scare anyone; the gun's not even loaded; I just can't help feeling like I've been staring right at them, but I just can't see them, if you know what I mean. Of course, sweetheart, we

know what you mean, we're on your side, really we are, it's just that
we've been though all this dozens of times already, so please give
our regards to the doctor again, won't you, and don't forget your
glasses, whatever you do; we can't have you driving around without
them now, can we? You, my dear, are blind as a bat.

Apparently I'd suffered something of a setback; take a couple of
Ultras, and a slug of Barrel Bonded, and call me in the morning; I
don't make housecalls. I found my glasses, right where I'd left them,
when I sat back down on the living room sofa, and set the Ultras
and bourbon out. I left the house, now in something of a hurry, and
pointed the car down Myrtle Avenue, while trying to read the car-
rental map. There seemed to be some sort of conspiracy at work,
between the guys who make the car-rental maps, and the guys who
put up one-way street signs, and the guys who build the bridges of
El Paso, in places you can't get to, not without driving your car in
reverse, or maybe half-speed down a crowded sidewalk. I made a
few U-turns of dubious legality, bounced the new car over a median
strip, took lefts and rights that were more or less at random, found
Stanton Street at last right where they'd built it, in the last place
you'd think of, like right where it is, and drove on down to the end
of its beginning, and parked in a lot at the foot of the bridge. There,
that was easy; now where the hell are we, and what happens next? I
seemed to be in some sort of no-man's-land dead zone; behind me
lay El Paso, going about its normal day, and directly ahead lay the
International Border Crossing, which sounds more imposing than
it actually is, a few modest tollbooths, a short span of two-hinged
five-lane arch bridge, a longer span of deck-beam or plate-girder
bridge, everything nice and simple, from an engineering perspective, essentially just an elevated roadway from one place to another,
from point A to point B, reading north to south; such a road could
be going almost anywhere really, only this road goes from Texas
into Mexico, which it turns out, in many ways, is a whole different
story. Beneath the bridge to the east, the Bridge of the Americas,
lay a mind-boggling tangle of industrial stuff, mostly transportation
media, railway lines and flatbed trailers and long-haul truck cabs
and articulated well cars, everything chaotically modularized and
standards-based for stacking and shipping, in 40-by-8-by-8-feet ISO
containers, all of which translates to goods on the move, the Port of

El Paso in a globalization feeding frenzy, from lead-painted toys to toxic electronics; beneath the Stanton Street Bridge, on the other hand, lay empty rail lines and patches of fencing and the wetback waters of the Rio Grande, which is more like a dried-up concrete flood channel than an actual river, something any three-year-old could ride a trike across easily, as long as he avoided a few pools of water that looked more grim and stagnant than flowing and grand. Something, obviously, got lost in translation. What else? I don't know, not much of anything, though if you say the words Port of El Paso, and it brings to mind something like white-winged seagulls, drifting and circling high overhead, in the deep-blue-sky morning of some imaginary harbor, you're nowhere near where I actually was, at the foot of a bridge over drainage-ditch waters; you'll need to let go of that image of the morning, and the fresh-salt-air feeling of radiant white gulls, because what we have here is a stagnant afternoon, and a bird population that seems to have boiled down to crow. At rest on the galvanized grey-steel railings, sitting on top of the tollbooth modules, taking the sun on the phone lines above me, everywhere I look for avian imagery, there is nothing really up there that is actually flying, but jesus the place is stuffed full of crow. There is nothing on earth more supremely indifferent to human existence than a stationary crow; it's an armor-plated instance of absolute nothingness, the proof that something's missing from our knowledge of the world, like nature's final answer to a question no one's asking; if you really have to ask, you just don't want to know. You're thinking you could maybe get one to fly, hurl a fistful of rock, or a gnarly chunk of concrete, thing would be startled, probably head for the sky, on great black wings, prove to yourself that you're a force to be reckoned with, and that that thing on the bridge-rail is some kind of life-form; turns out you may need a .50 caliber sniper rifle, maybe the Barrett XM-109 Hard Target Interdiction System, chambered with five-inch armor-piercing shells, mounted on a tripod via the monopod socket, and equipped with some ultimate optical gear, say the Leupold Mark 4 front-focal riflescope, or the Nightforce Benchrest, with a BORS multi-language ballistic computer, hook the beast up to your field-hardened laptop, boot it all up, fire up your browser, Google the word "Crow," or maybe try "El Cuervo," case the bird's thinking Spanish, bound to be nothing left but an empty pile of feathers; unfortunately, what you'd find, right between the crosshairs, is basically just a thing you missed, maybe moved an inch or so. Crows don't die; crows don't have to; they're so close to nothingness, just to begin with, the thing could be stone dead, you'd never even know. What's happening to me here is that I'm staring out at a single bird, high up above on a high-tension power line. The thing's sort of taunting me. Whatever it is I'm thinking, it's not going to move. I'm in, let's face it, a weird frame of mind, two parts bourbon and hospital pharmaceuticals, one part basic-instinct existential crow. And now, on top of everything, some moron's banging away on my driver's side window, acting all officious, Can't park here, Mister, move it along, like I'm just supposed to go. If you followed that whole bit about one-way street signs, and bouncing over median strips, and rental-map bridge-locale conspiracy theories, you know as well as I do that there's no way out of here. I'm not going anywhere. I'm one-third crow.

I palm the guy a twenty, act like I think he's a tour guide, pretend I'm leaving for Juárez like almost any second now, not specifically parked here, just trying to get my bearings. You have a map? No, not really. They gave me this thing at the car rental company, but it's mostly blank as far as Juárez goes. I can see the 375 Border Highway, and Chamizal Park, and Highway 45 headed down to Chihuahua, but everything else is a big brown blank. That, my friend, is Juárez as it ought to be, but Juárez itself is a little more complicated; there's a reason they call it the Land of Encounters. Well, let's see now. You get to the other side, you ought to see an information booth at the end of the bridge, get yourself a tourist map, wherever you're trying to get to, find it on the map first, then go there directly, whatever you do don't stop. You have business in Juárez? No, not exactly, just thought I'd visit, take a look around; maybe go see the old Mission or something. Take a look around, eh? Let's see now, the old Mission, Nuestra Señora de Guadalupe, that's on Avenida Septiembre, two blocks west of Juárez Avenue, you get there alive, light yourself a candle or two. You know anything at all about Ciudad Juárez? Seem to remember visiting back in the '70s, walking across the El Paso Street Bridge, drinking margaritas at a little bar in the Mariscal; seem to remember having a wonderful time. Why, is there a problem? No, no problem at all, nothing you couldn't solve with a medium-range ballistic missile and a ten-megaton warhead, turn it into a science exhibit, tourists walking around in hazmat suits with Geiger counters, might even visit the place myself, they fix it up right, light me up a candle or two, out in the nucular desert. First thing you do, when you get across the bridge, you find the information booth, pick up one of them tourist maps, then drive nice and slow down Avenida Lerdo, soon as they stick a gun in your face, get out nice and easy, stick your hands straight up like you were catching a breath of air, stand still for a spell like you don't know you're a moron, then tell them you're a little lerdo yourself, un poco de luces, a little bit slow. Not sure what you're telling me. Like I said, you're a little bit slow. You wander around Juárez for a while, no idea what the fuck you're doing, you'll wind up even slower, like dead-stop slow. Muerto del Lerdo. So you're saying don't go down there. Not in that nice new car you're driving; get yourself a SWAT truck, or one of them Polish Dzik-3s like the Iraqi's use, or maybe hail a Battle Taxi, just don't get out of the goddamn vehicle, whatever the fuck you do. Ex-military guy, obviously; not only a likely Fascist, but prone to ad hoc spelling and metathetic colloquial pronunciation, the sort of thing you come to expect when you elect the wrong President, guy with his hands on the nucular launch codes, with a paranoid schizophrenic as a best friend and confidant, let them run the Executive Branch however the hell they want to, redact whole sections of the U.S. Constitution, just don't go showing them that target map of Pakistan or Iran. Appreciate the advice; mind if I just sit here for a while; I'm having second thoughts about going to see the Mission. No problem; take your time; you want to go into Juárez and pretend you got lost on the way to the asylum, we'll call in an airstrike, clear out one of the neighborhoods for you. Course, no need to bother if you're going to the Mariscal, looks like what's left of the Gaza Strip already, be a little redundant us trying to re-bomb it. What you want to do is to pack the car with explosives, maybe C4 or Semtex, or daisy-chain some artillery shells, hook up a blasting cap, with a detonator cord wired into your cell phone, then drive into the Pronaf, say the middle of the street on Lopez Mateos, dial 411, say where the fuck am I, next thing you know, you won't be needing any driving instructions, wherever you're trying to get to, you're already there. You beginning to get the picture, or am I going too fast for you? No, I'm with you; place isn't safe; let me ask you though, what's the Pronaf? Jesus; you really are a moron. Tell you what we do. I'll loan you my pistol, you take a good long slug off that bottle you're holding, fire one shot straight up through the back of your soft palette, you won't have to worry about driving the car at all, whole trip'll be over before you even know it. Now y'all have yourself a real fine day, but I need this space back in like ten or twelve minutes.

Sounds like a good thing I'm not headed south. So it's like 1:20 now; maybe I leave here at let's say 1:30, catch an afternoon flight back to the Land of Dwindling Plenty. Where, I'm wondering, is Ms. Shall We Say Noon, with her better-make-it-cash, better-safe-than-sorry, won't-say-how-much, cryptic sort of attitude? Ms. Aphoristic Platitudes, the admin presumably to Mr. How Much Shakespeare Can One Man Stand, with his Where-Did-My-Dog-Go approach to telephony, and here I am sitting with a trunk full of lavender, and a head full of useless car-bomb instructions. They seem to want cash, about which I could give a shit, while what I want most is a little basic knowledge, or at least information, like who the hell pulled off this phony WiMAX pyramid scheme, and how did they do it, and is this give or take what they do for a living? I know what you're thinking: just let it go, they duped you fair and square, grow up, get over it, an approach that, in retrospect, strikes me as sound; maybe, come to think of it, you could have proposed it sooner. As of right now, I'm seriously willing to trade them straight up, though I'll admit to some second thoughts regarding my negotiating posture, which is right around the time Ms. High Noon gets in the car, a drop-dead Latina with a face out of Raphael, maybe the woman holding the three-year-old in the Sistine Madonna, and without so much as a simple hello, or any of the basic introductory items on a properly structured meeting agenda, starts in on giving me driving instructions, which seems a bit abrupt, but is probably an improvement on that whole auto-rental-map conspiracy business. Go across the bridge. Okay, right off, maybe I should retract that; an improvement would be we find ourselves an El Paso café, have a couple of bottles of wine, conduct some sort of preliminary discussions. An improvement would be a sit-down, at an oval-shaped conference table, 20 floors up in a Stanton Street Board Room; black coffee, no sugar. An improvement would be a face-to-face, next to a long-abandoned bridge abutment, with a trash-can fire, and six or eight hobos, just as long as the bridge doesn't leave El Paso; pass the rot-gut, have a cigar, now teach me the basics of the laundry business. So where are we going? Juárez or something? Maybe, in retrospect, I said this in my head, or maybe she answered back, and I just didn't hear her answer; she had, after all, ducked her head down hard, like completely underneath the rental-car dashboard, and for all I know, she might have whispered something sweet, like o Darling, I love you, take me to Acapulco. I pulled out of the parking lot, onto a one-way street headed east toward Stanton, reached an ordinary intersection in maybe forty or fifty feet, and was faced with a classic sort of existential dilemma: either turn to the right, and squeeze between cars in the tollbooth bridge line, or sit there forever at a large octagonal stop sign. Back up, you say? Throw it in reverse? Just peel the fuck backwards in a toxic puff of burning tires, a thirty-foot cloud of benzene and butadiene and cadmium-laced styrene, these pedestrians are all doomed to die of manmade toxins anyway, what's wrong with right now, in a polycyclic aromatic hydrocarbon rush, in a white-hot smudge of 2,3,7,8-tetrachlorodibenzo-p-dioxin poisons, whatever you do, just get the hell out, do not go over that fucking bridge? Now you tell me. Now you tell me.

Be that as it may, I wedged my way into the line of cars, soothing my nerves with bourbon and Ultras, practicing patience, and pharmaceutical yoga, while the car line flowed of its own sweet will, which is more than I can say for some of the assholes behind me; as I pulled up to the tollbooth, a large black truck swerved crudely into line several cars behind me, and as I paid the $2.25, in change left over from last night's escapades, the guy in the truck is sort of pounding on his steering wheel, like he's practicing something hard, but it certainly isn't patience, though it may be some form of Karma Yoga. The weird thing to me, aside from the truck, which looks like a giant black bird sitting stationary, is that all at once, as if they'd been signaled, every single crow has all of a sudden gone flying, like maybe they respond to Dharma itself, or maybe they've been rattled by Ms. High Noon's Sistine silence. I tool across the bridge, wondering a little vaguely if I should stop at the information booth, but by the time I arrive, where the booth would be, the whole fucking place has gone absolutely military: maybe three hundred fifty well-armed troops, in green and black camouflage, carrying flat-out assault rifles and randomly waving them; ten or twenty Gun Trucks and Technical Vehicles, mounted with .50 caliber heavy machine guns, and LMGs and SAWs and AT4 rocket launchers, all of them manned, possibly by humans; and what looks to be a tank, with like an M4 Howitzer pointed directly at me. Fortunately for me, my first job out of college, back in the early '70s, when I still had my whole life stretched out ahead of me, was planning the basic tactical scenarios for fighting nuclear wars with the Soviet Union, which means that I got to hang out with a lot of heavy-weapons experts, the sort of guys who looked at Jane's Defense Weekly as a form of armament and weaponry hardcore pornography, so I know more or less what I'm up against here, which essentially boils down to a lot of mangled death-forms. Nice friendly place; bring your own friends; though they might want to consider how peaceful and quiet El Paso is, maybe buy themselves a bottle, and a copy of let's say Hustler, pick out any one of the many empty rooms at the U-Turn Motel, then go back where they came from. If your friends insist on getting a better picture of Juárez daily life, tell them to use Google Earth, get their picture off of the satellite; not only does life look better from 200 miles up, but most of these weapons don't reach quite that altitude. This whole time now, while I've been gallantly driving the where-am-I-going car, Ms. Noon's been huddled right next to the floorboard, meaning I'm basically flying blind through pent-up machines, and high-caliber weaponry, and like a whole armored battalion, with no idea at all where the hell I'm supposed to be going, and so I wind up just plunging into a side street in Juárez; pick any one of them, that's the one I'm on.

If you happen to be planning a visit to Juárez, I'll give you a tip, forget the information booth; it's probably there, and you could probably find it, but the problem with Juárez isn't access to information.

Juárez, like death, is packed with information; the problem, if anything, is that it's a little overwhelming, and there's far too much of it to properly absorb.

# 24

S o I know, I know, drug legalization is out of the question. There are far too many humans getting high already; what are we supposed to do, just call off the Drug War? You've got yourself a War to fight, against humans getting high, you go ahead and fight it; you don't stop to worry that this may be a spiritual, not a military, problem. Be like some guy down in the trenches at the Battle of the Somme, up to his knees in Senfgas muck, his lungs half-full of BASF chlorine, watching 70-some tons of incendiary shells raining down smoke on the German bunkers, knowing it don't mean shit, that trench-war ground, at five dead per inch, is pretty much a waste of good humanity, and so instead of hoisting his Springfield rifle, and his 60-pound pack, and assorted gear, and climbing to the top of the sandbag parapets, getting ready to join the next great wave of humans wandering off toward the general slaughter, he's suddenly having some second or third thoughts, like *I don't think this is such a good idea.* I'm not, admittedly, in the trenches at the Somme, I'm sitting in a rental car, neck-deep in traffic, my lungs half-full of vehicular exhaust, on a take-your-pick side street in Ciudad Juárez, staring at the back of a Pepsi Cola delivery truck, and while I may well be going slowly insane, I mean it's maybe moved a foot in the last ten minutes, I don't think, basically, that the War on Drugs is such a good idea. As a general rule of thumb, if you want my opinion, which may just be the bourbon and opiates talking, before you go declaring a war on something, double-check first, make sure the thing itself is essentially mortal.

Drugs don't die, drugs don't have to; they're the pharmaceutical equivalent of a stationary crow. If you were even paying attention when I tried to shoot that crow, you'd know as well as I do that weapons don't work; you could fire all the weaponry in your whole fucking arsenal, wind up with drugs that maybe moved an inch or two; and while it's altogether possible that I might have gotten the wrong impression, those LMGs and SAWs and AT4 rocket launchers, a hundred yards behind me on the Stanton Street Bridge, weren't actually designed to kill a lot of drugs, but they'd certainly do a number on a whole lot of humans. You could, I suppose, just kill all the Drug Lords, bound to put a stop to all these humans getting high, but I'm guessing that Drug Lords don't die either, they probably just replace themselves, like a shark replaces teeth; not a lot of Great Whites been rendered harmless by pulling all their teeth, and while it probably isn't sharks, this far from the water, leaving severed heads and limbs scattered all around Juárez, whatever the hell it is, it certainly isn't toothless. Something a little odd about this Drug War we're fighting; whatever you try to kill, thing doesn't die, it eventually turns up as a pile of human corpses, out in the milkweed and paintbrush debris, with families left staring at patches of garbage, and a whole lot of crows thinking they'd died and gone to Heaven.

So I know, I know, it's time to move on. I'm not only missing the point about the Drug War's purpose, but I'm apparently exhausting metaphors at an alarming rate; we need to get off of this Juárez side street, and move things along toward whatever happens next. So what happens next? Absolutely nothing: truck doesn't move; car doesn't move; we don't move, at least not onward, and so I find myself off on a drug-abuse tangent, having visions of all sorts of blissed-out humans, and the whole sordid history of humans getting high, a topic about which I know far too much to ever be considered in any way healthy; if you managed to survive the 1960s, with a few neural pathways remaining intact, you know what I'm referring to; we may know nothing whatsoever about the years themselves, but we certainly know a lot about stoned human beings. In fact, come to think of it, now that I've brought it up, I may be grossly underestimating the scope of the problem: archaeological records, showing psychotropic-plant use, go back 2 million years, long before hominids even knew that they were high, or possessed much of anything you'd think of as sapience; I'm picturing a guy like Australopithecus, knuckles dragging around, mumbling psycho-dysleptic nonsense, explaining his massive drug-use away as part of some primitive Bwiti religion, while lost in an ibogaine-fractal haze, searching for the path to spiritual enlightenment, or at least a way out of the Tanzanian trees. The path, to be sure, would appear to be long, and backed up for miles with baked homo sapiens, like a 40,000-year-old outback aborigine, making his way slowly from euphoria to catalepsy, chewing on a wad of sun-cured pituri; or one of the natives kicking back in a Timor hut, maybe 13,000 years ago, with fresh-smelling breath, a red-stained smile, and teeth that are going to need a good deal of brushing, when he's not quite so amped on areca nut and Betel leaf; or some avant-garde self-por-trait artist, 8,000 years back, painting on the walls of an Algerian cave, suffering under the delusion that those toadstools he's eaten have magically started sprouting all over his body, and turned him into the world's first Psilocybin Mushroom Man; or we're up in the clouds in the Andes somewhere, like 5,000 BC, skeeted on lines of pure-flake Peruvian; or somewhere in Ethiopia, with a cheek full of khat; or maybe Polynesia, chewing on high-grade kava root; or dec-orating our Egyptian and Sumerian tombs with carvings of opium's sacrosanct poppy. Belladonna witch flights; Xhosa Dream Roots; Datura growing straight from the chest of Shiva; Mandrake Cow's Eye, in Ugaritic cuneiform; Mandrake Love Fruit, in the Book of Genesis; Morning Glory Aztec's, hardwired to the Sun gods, per-haps seeing Oaxaca in a whole new light, perhaps having visions of immense inner-landscapes; Druids spaced-out on fly agaric, wandering the sacred groves of oak and hazel; Vikings feeding on Amanita muscaria, preparing themselves for life as it is, and battle as competent and complete Berserkers; Yekwana and Tukano aya-huasca worshippers, high on life, as nature herself has so richly pro-vided; the Tarahumare knowing with absolute certainty why Father Sun left them his best hikuli, to cure man's ills and ancient woes, and lead the herd up to the higher pastures. So what's my point? Not really sure; what were we just talking about? Ah yes, the Drug War. Seems to me the Drug War is getting pretty old, and maybe in the end it's man's existence we're fighting. It probably isn't relevant, in fact it's probably just weird, that there's evidence of a certain amount of co-evolutionary activity, between man's inner being, his deep-mammalian brain, and the psychotropic substances found in plant-life abundance, but we might want to consider, before we kill all the drugs, that man is the animal, unique to the planet, that comes fully equipped with opiate-receptor sites, and try to keep in mind that man as man might never have existed without a few decent pain relievers. Man, in all likelihood, doesn't have a drug problem; far more likely that Man *is* a drug problem, and if there's one thing that's certain, given all the evidence, Man can't be trusted to make his own decisions; though it sort of makes you wonder, from a capitalist perspective, why sociopathic criminals get to keep all the profits, buy a shitload of guns, and maybe use them against us, wind up getting chewed on by dryland sharks, and the crows out having themselves a huge fucking field day. I'll tell you what, though, right about now, having ground to a halt on a Juárez backstreet, with a lot of mangled death-forms on the bridge just behind me, I don't care at all where the profits belong, but I sure could use a hit of Brazilian Virola: take a wee small dose of deep-red resin from the bark of the holy tree, mix it with leaves of the Hummingbird bush, and a pinch of flowering Justicia to smooth out the high, then snort it through the hollow bones of a Skylark or Starling, get my mind deep-focused and my priorities realigned, like a Waika cumala shaman gearing up for psychic battle, in a state of total readiness for whatever the hell Juárez has in mind; when the gigantic Hekulas, who control the affairs of man, materialize out of nowhere waving AK-47s, I, for one, would like to be prepared to fight, and I don't think these Ultras are quite going to cut it.

What's happening to me here is that I'm trapped behind a Pepsi truck, watching its driver walk the pavement, in a Pepsi-blue work shirt, unloading cases of soft drinks for a local tienda, and maybe it's just me, or maybe it's lack-of-motion sickness, or they may have slipped something into these pills that I'm eating, or it could be High Noon, and her whole Sistine vibe, I mean she hasn't said two words in the last 20 minutes, but whatever the hell it is, it certainly isn't readiness, my mind has wandered off on an aging-stoner drug-use rant, long on substance-abuse rationalizations, but short on sources for weapons-grade Virola. I could, I suppose, just throw

it in park, walk twenty or thirty feet and buy an eight ball of cocaine, maybe snort it through the bones of a Goldfinch or Redwing,
though I doubt that the Hekulas would be all that impressed, and
I don't see a store selling hollowed-out bird bones; in fact, come to
think of it, I don't even see anyone who looks like a coke dealer,
I'm seeing all sorts of people who look like dealers, but most of the
stuff they're pushing here would appear to be food, and while I
have spotted a guy hauling weight up the sidewalk, using something
he's improvised from a red-wagon toy, I'm not going to war with
the gigantic Hekulas on a fructose high from honeydew melons.
After all of the hype from the CBP-ICE guy, with his car bomb
instructions and nuke-the-place attitude, Juárez, if anything, looks
more or less ordinary; the traffic is awful, I'll grant you that, but
I'm from LA, where gridlock is a birthright. Here I am expecting
automatic weapons fire, with civilians peering out between security
bars, and grocers in aprons trying to hide behind their push brooms,
and mothers lying down in bullet-chipped arcades, covering up
the bodies of their weeping children, and what we have instead is
people going about the basic business of their day, buying a rump
roast at a carniceria, squeezing the melons at a sidewalk fruit stand,
selecting pastries from the glass display case of a perfectly lovely
little pasteleria. There's a taco vendor, maybe forty feet ahead, grilling carne asada on a barbecue pushcart, with a foot-tall stack of
corn tortillas, and three or four bowls of various salsas, maybe pico
de gallo and green tomatillo and red salsa rojo, made from arbol
chilis simmered with garlic. I'll tell you one thing, this Pepsi truck
moves, I'm buying some tacos, load 'em up with rojo and cebolla
and cilantro, and a bowl of menudo if he's got that too, man's got to
eat if he's going to fight Hekulas. Two kids who might be brothers,
wearing identical blue and red soccer uniforms, materialize out of
nowhere waving bright-orange soda bottles, gaze across the street
as if intending to cross it, pause for a moment as though they've
encountered some sort of problem, and then start crawling from
left to right across the hood of my car, which has apparently drifted
too close to the Pepsi truck's bumper; when the soft drink delivery man returns for the next case, he shakes his head sadly at my
thoughtless proximity, but continues his unloading from the truck's
curbside entry; thoughtlessness, apparently, is accepted with resig-

nation, without so much as a word of reproach, which makes it all
the more sad that when my foot slips off the brake, and gets applied
with equal force to an entirely different pedal, possibly causing the
car to lurch forward just a bit, an entire case of Jarritos crashes to
the ground, leaving a pool of mango soda that just didn't have to
happen. I jump out of the car, fully expecting violence, waving a
substantial green banknote to pay for the damages, and this in turn
is graciously dismissed, my *lo siento mucho* met with *de nada no
importa*, which would no doubt have improved my overall mood,
if it weren't for the fact that, as I'd departed the vehicle, I'd thrown
it in reverse, with some obvious consequences, including the fact
that my rented car, now free to move about of its own volition, rolls
a good six feet backwards and strikes an ancient flatbed produce
truck, sending a crate of ripe tomatoes flying awkwardly toward the
pavement, preparing to provide, in the form of splattered fruit, yet
another fine example of the superfluous event.

I wish that I could tell you that a shotgun suddenly appeared,
and fired a single loud warning shot over the head of my ineptitude,
but the gentleman driving the truck just smiled and waved, and the
bystanders laughed, and one of the farmer's co-workers regathered
the rolling produce; it was like an epidemic of civility had broken
out in the Juárez street. The street itself was one-way and narrow,
full of Mom-and-Pop shops and the mothers and fathers whose
business it is to tend them, and while it scarcely seems possible
to feed six kids, from the proceeds accruing to a single lechería,
this didn't seem to mean that Mom was running a meth lab; she
seemed, in fact, to be running a little dairy store, and right at the
moment, she was washing the windows. Given all this, the general
air of courtesy, the going-about-their-business, taco-pushcart and
sidewalk-fruit-stand, live-and-let-live, sense of normality; the ease
with which those directly impacted had absorbed a stranger's vehicular stupidity; the elbow-grease grace with which Mom herself, putting in a personal appearance on the store's behalf, was nearing the
completion of the self-appointed task of cleaning her hard-earned
plate-glass front window, with a four-square-feet square in the lower
right corner about to be dried with a clean white towel; and the fact
that an entire line of human conveyance was sitting here patiently,
minding its business, awaiting a soft-drink-delivery subordinate's ul-

timate return, and completion of missions assigned by his superiors; given all this, this block-long display of basic human solidarity and perfectly ordinary civilian activity, with the possible exception of a rented sedan, apparently prone to operator error, one wonders what the military might quite have had in mind, as they sealed off the street with Light Strike Vehicles, black tubular-steel birdcages for prehistoric birds, bristling with belt-fed high-caliber weaponry and an ominous abundance of ammunition bandoliers, draped around androids in black tri-hole ski masks, helmeted beings from a caved-in world, wearing Blackhawk Hellstorm ballistic goggles, their lenses so dark and blatantly opaque that they might have been lifted from eyeless space aliens. Our street, which had obviously gotten a little out of hand, with all this kindness to strangers and testing of honeydew melons, was now, it was clear, under absolute command, of faceless green creatures that used weapons as eyeballs.

My immediate instinct was to back the fuck up, but it was apparent that I'd done enough damage for the moment; my second instinct was, fuck it, Run, just jump the hell out of the boxed-in car and try to make a run for the Texas border, as eight or ten of the black-masked forces made their way slowly up our one-way side street, still apparently sightless but searching for something, maybe waving M-16s like blindmen with canes, or maybe seeing everything they needed to see, through their birdcage and duckbill muzzle-flash suppressors. So how far did I run? Not very far. While I felt fairly certain that these things weren't equipped to see much of anything beyond their Hellstorm goggles, much less to hit a target from maybe 300 feet, by the time they cleared the edge of the Pepsi truck in front of me, giving me an unobstructed line-of-sight view, I was no longer calling their vision into question, I was no longer preparing to make a run for the border, in fact I wasn't even reaching for the handle of the door, I was hearing a little voice, from a few minutes back, saying *I don't think this is such a good idea*; a thirty-second burst of assault-rifle fire, with the M-16s firing off rounds at 900 per minute from drum magazines, wouldn't take much, other than 20/20 hindsight, to find a lot of targets that never knew that they were targets; these things could wear a blindfold and put a bullet between my eyes. I might have been just fine if they'd stopped right there, perhaps deciding it was time to leave well enough alone, instead of coming forward, past the 200-foot mark, dragging the whole street into the darkness along with them: one moment our little side street looked sunlit and lively, and I was picking out shades of pale pastels, the powder-blue facade of Mom's Lechería, the custard-yellow awning of a pasteleria, the rose-pink walls of a four-story building whose bottom floor was occupied by the Pepsi tienda; the next thing I know, it goes brute-force black, black on the black-masked alien faces, black on their matte-black body-armored torsos, the black-on-black of assault-rifle weaponry, black on the handguards, black on the buttstocks, black on the burst-fire barrel assemblies, all very black, and dead inside, like they were trying to prove a point about Death being blind, but able to pick you out from a crowd of billions, and while it's altogether possible that I was missing the whole point here, I certainly wasn't planning on holding up an eye chart. If you're thinking I should have realized that these were ordinary soldiers, military men in green and black camouflage, wearing dark ballistic goggles to protect their eyesight, black balaclavas to shield their identities, and no doubt attempting to make some sort of drug bust, you're nowhere near where I actually was; when they paused on the sidewalk, 100 feet off, a crack opened up in a solid wall of buildings, and as a narrow shaft of light passed through the crack, I, among other things, got a very good look at them. Mutants, possibly, a genome mistake, a cross between a human and a greenbottle blowfly; or maybe something that escaped from a detox facility, the hypnagogic visuals of an Ativan addict, five days deep in benzodiazepine withdrawal; or they might have crawled up, through cracks in his massive head, out of the caved-in world of a William Burroughs novel, like I'm now seeing the reason he traded his typewriter in, tried to fill in the cracks with good Nazi opiates, because whatever the hell they were, they were dead inside, and there's no possibility these were ordinary soldiers.

What's happening to me here is the beginnings of a panic attack, one part Ativan-detox symptoms, one part gene-splicing category error, two parts *Naked Lunch* Interzone Liquefactionists, and while this might have been a good time to learn from my mistakes, maybe rethink my policy on mixing bourbon with opiates, there was no way I was dealing with blowfly-headed humans, and armed Liquefactionists, headed toward my car, looking like something out

of a benzo psych-ward, while trying to make a change to my pharmaceutical protocol; if my meds got me into this, they can certainly
get me out. Of course, by the time I got my mind to stop revving
in neutral, tracked down my sack lunch and bourbon bottle, and
shook a few pills loose from the jar, some fairly weird shit was preparing a little test, one of those current-state-of-readiness things that
are never really fair, and I didn't exactly pass it with flying colors:
as I chewed the pile of pills and washed it all down with a good
long slug of high-proof bonded, one of the black-masked forces,
on the far side of the street, began to interrogate a group of young
humans; all three juveniles were shaking their heads at once, vigorously rejecting whatever was being asserted. These denials, apparently, simply did not ring true, and the youngest of the three,
no older than nine or ten years of age, took a backhanded blow to
the side of the head from the black composite handguard on the
M-16's barrel assembly, a blow that sent him immediately sprawling, bleeding from a head wound that he was obviously unaware
of, leaving two youths standing, wide-eyed and wondering, and appearing to shrink from the infliction of pain. The cycle of assertion
and rebuttal was repeated, this time, if anything, more vigorously,
with the wide-eyed wonderers supplementing their denials using
palm's-up arm's-extended genuine-bafflement shoulder-shrug gestures, though the gestures proved futile in meeting their objective,
which seemed to be that of making their ignorance clear; the result of their ignorance, almost sickeningly inevitable, was another
startling blow to a baffled expression, deliberately applied with an
assault rifle's buttstock. This left only the oldest of the three, dressed
in the blue and red soccer uniform of the boys who had crawled
across the hood of my car, to face the opaque and yet intelligible
creature, whose behavior, while inexplicable, was easy enough to
predict; the boy shrugged once and let his body go slack, as though
resigning himself to the world's dark opacity, and then motioned
up the street with a brief shallow wave, in the general direction of
my rented vehicle, in the general direction, in fact, of *me*. What's
happening to me now is a full-out panic attack, everything down
to the smallest detail fully consistent with the onslaught of abrupt
benzodiazepine withdrawal, from the horrible knot in the pit of my
stomach to the hypnopompic visuals of an alien invasion to the sud-

den onset of acute macropsia, that state of seeing things as greatly enlarged, as the enormous Liquefactionists worked their way slowly up the amplified street, past towering structures and tons of asada and a 40-foot stack of corn tortillas, toward where I sat parked in my massive sedan, a vehicle that would be hard, in fact, impossible, to miss, although it was apparently being driven by an odd phenomenon, a man now living in a vast Dysmetropsia as a rapidly shrinking italicized glyph.

If you've ever been through the waking nightmare of benzo-detox abrupt withdrawal, after long-term treatment for panic disorders, using Ativan or Diastat or Nobrium or Serepax, or any of 50-some other drugs, from Rovotril mixed with Alopram, to a Xanax-Librium anti-anxiety cocktail, you already know what I'm up against here, aphasia, paresthesia, postural hypotension, tachycardic heartbeats, hypnopompic visuals, derealization and depersonalization, that sense of oneself as a hollowed-out Other, a derealized self, an italicized glyph, a thing that not only cannot drive a car, it can't reach the floor to find its bourbon bottle; I, however, do not have a clue, as this, to be honest, is my first time through this; I'm like a man who's read the warnings on the package inserts that come with his bottles of benzo-based sleep-aids, say Klonopin or Restoril or Dalmadorm or Loramet, chuckled a little, said wow, that's fucked up, and then pretty promptly proceeded to ignore them. Tell you one thing, I ever get out of this, I'm going straight home, before they kill all the drugs, and take a good hard look at my medicine cabinet, because I'm not real eager to repeat this whole experience. Of course, repeating this whole experience may be the least of my worries; it probably isn't likely that a *derealized self*, given the difficulties inherent in keeping track of its own reality, would even be capable of *having* an experience, much less the sort of thing that would bear repeating. These problems, in any case, are mine and not yours; you're not the one parked on a Juárez side street, having a panic attack at the exact wrong time, in the middle of a Drug War panic disorder, as one of the hooded beings, who I thought was about to do something reasonably human, like maybe order a taco from the carne asada barbecue vendor, suddenly fired off a burst from the M-16 assault rifle, sending black-tipped steel-penetration lead-alloy bullet cores flying off over the building tops, in the general direction of the Chihuahuan desert. You're also not the one who's been dreaming of having a taco, a soft corn tortilla, warmed on a cast-iron comal, filled with grilled skirt steak, and covered with onions, cilantro, and salsa; it's not that the dream died when the invader fired his weapon, it died when he shouldered the pushcart over, sending salsas and tortillas and skirt steaks flying everywhere. I have this image in my mind, so it's altogether possible that it's derived from experience, of the pushcart man, no longer a vendor but still wearing his tidy apron, lying facedown spread-eagled on the Juárez pavement, surrounded by burnt meat and black stone molcajetes and rapidly cooling coals from his barbecue pit, with a birdcage flash suppressor, smelling of nitro and vaporized graphite, but completely devoid of avian imagery, pressed to the base of his featherless head. This image, with its dubious olfactory component, isn't the sort of thing you should take my word for, and neither is the fact that I may well have stumbled, through no fault of my own, right into the heart of the Juárez I was warned about: civilians peering out between security bars and grocers standing sideways behind long-handled push brooms and mothers brooding over their weeping children, huddled under the arches of bullet-chipped arcades, and a PepsiCo soft drink delivery individual, a model employee and perfect gentleman, lying in a spreading pool of shattered glass and mango soda, which may well exist, but just didn't have to happen, and even Mom herself, a giant of a woman, hiding her innocent but enormous plate-glass window behind an aniseikonic layer of clean white towel; while I too have doubts that I was actually seeing giants, or that Mom was the sort of woman who would try to hide a window behind ocular illusions and verbal obscurity, if one thing was certain, amid all this impending havoc, there was no way in hell I was seeing a way out of this, having started out somewhere in an El Paso no-fly zone, an admittedly stagnant but sheltered environment, and ended up locked, on a Juárez side street, in a false-sense-security detox facility, badly in need of a massive dose of Ativan.

By the time the masked-forces arrived at my car, I was one-third stationary pharmaceutical crow, two-thirds dime-bag benzo dealer. The Being with the bloody barrel-assembly handgrip motioned for me to join them in the middle of the street, by pointing the birdcage muzzle-flash suppressor directly at my face, and then waving it slowly two or three times toward the upper-left quadrant of a body-armored torso. I shoved the empty bottle and lunch sack full of pills halfway under the driver's seat, put the car in park, leaving the motor running, and then sat there for a moment in spacetime neutral, with my hands effectively welded to the telescoping steering wheel. Now what? Maybe gather up my rental agreement and photo ID, make a nice calm exit from my rented sedan, and accept their invitation to join them in the street? Let me think. No, I don't think so; I don't think, at this point, I'm quite prepared to go and join them; I have my hands welded-tight to the telescoping wheel, I have my mind turning revs in spacetime neutral, and I've got black-masked forces, 15 feet away, heavily armed with burst-fire weaponry, shielded behind body armor, Hellstorm goggles, and a brute-force aura of blatant opacity, getting ready to haul me off, up the black-on-black street, stuff me in Light Strike tubular-steel birdcage, and add me to their human-specimen collection, so I'm not only unprepared to join them in the street, I'm in no way prepared to exit the vehicle, I'm in no way prepared to reach for the door, in fact I'm not even prepared to exit spacetime neutral. Okay, so now what? I'm sitting behind the wheel, staring at my hands, by no means convinced that they're part of my body, much less connected to the ends of my arms, when my mind wanders off on one of those anticipatory inner-narratives that have nothing to do with the course of events, and while it will soon become apparent that I'm thoroughly mistaken, I think I know precisely what lies ahead: I have a complete mental meltdown, my mind goes blank, and my hands stay welded to the wheel of the car, with no possibility of prying them loose without the blunt-force application of assault-rifle buttstocks; with my mind a blank slate, and aliens to work with, I'm halfway into a detailed sketch of the blue Juárez sky turning a deep Martian red, with vast clouds of palagonite, indicative of the presence of water on Mars, blown up from the regolith of the Hellas Basin, or maybe the sky goes a sulfurous yellow, indicative of the presence of creatures from Venus, or somewhere in the Midwest where they burn shitty coal, when I start hearing the sounds of the cracking of hollow bird bones, indicative of the presence of assault-rifle buttstocks, and I'm pulled from the car, a complete mental wreak, the null hypothesis in a thought experiment. My anticipatory inner-narrative might well have concluded with a half-finished sketch of the absence of mind, interesting to stare at, if not necessarily contemplate, if it weren't for the fact that, upon closer inspection, I came to the realization that there was something I'd overlooked: these black-masked forces, now 10 feet away, were beginning to look like ordinary soldiers, military men in green and black camouflage, wearing dark ballistic goggles to protect their eyesight, black balaclavas to shield their identities, and no doubt attempting to make some sort of drug bust; this, let me tell you, was an entirely different story. So right around the time I'm thinking Jesus, relax, you're not headed off toward a tubular-steel birdcage, these morons are getting ready to search the wrong car, it occurs to me Jesus, get a fucking grip, these morons are getting ready to search the wrong car, which right at the moment, as perhaps you'll recall, contains $20 million in lavender Swiss banknotes, which really, at this point, I'd hate to have seized, as the result of what amounts to an honest mistake; while honest mistakes are hard to avoid, if mistakes must be made, I'd prefer to make them; I don't need these soldiers compounding my problems. If you're thinking that High Noon must have come to my aid, and offered her counsel, or even spiritual guidance, on how to put a stop to this compounding of problems, you have no idea how cool she remains: when I turned in her direction, with my eyes full of questions, she was sitting there posing for her Sistine portrait, staring out the windshield of my rented sedan, offering nothing at all in the way of guidance, so what I think she was trying to tell me, in her own quiet way, was You got us into this, with your erratic driving, so don't even think that I consider this problem mine. I gathered up my rental agreement and photo ID, supplemented the instruments that I had at my command with a large round roll of U.S. $100s, thinking this might contribute to reaching an understanding that wouldn't involve an errant search of my car, and exited the vehicle to join them in the street, with my mind deep-focused, my priorities realigned, but with a great many forces aligned against me, including the fact that, when it comes to speaking Spanish, I was back to drawing sketches of a complete mental blank. There is something about an eyeless face, and a rapidly spoken foreign language, that doesn't contribute at all to mutual understanding, but even with my mind a near-blank slate, I knew what they meant by *drogas* and *narcoticos,* and *dónde están los narcotraficantes;* I'll admit that for a moment I thought they meant *me,* with my sack lunch of Ultras, and my pupils like pinholes, until I thought I heard someone say something about *fútbol,* possibly a reference to the blue-and-red kids who had crawled across my hood a few minutes back, and thinking it unlikely that I'd come to Juárez in any way equipped for a game of soccer, breathed a deep sigh of premature relief.

The next thing I knew, Juárez just imploded. So I know, I know, there's no possibility that this actually happened; there's no way a city of maybe 2 million beings completely collapses in on itself; we're standing in the street with the military authorities, calmly discussing *drogas* and *narcotraficantes,* and turning Juárez into a primordial black hole, a gravitational singularity, a Hadamard disaster, is just about the last thing I'll be able to account for, which is just about the first thing I suppose I'll have to do; you're thinking there were all sorts of interesting possibilities, after my narrow escape from a currency seizure, but calculating the Schwarzschild radius of Ciudad Juárez, in order to determine if what we're looking at here is some sort of give or take naked singularity, is, almost certainly, nowhere among them. What's happening to me here, however, is a common enough occurrence, an instance of stumbling upon a spacetime boundary, and reaching what cosmologists call the *event horizon,* where everything freezes in a redshift tableau; we don't need to be wandering around the General Relativity field equations, searching for enough true degeneracy pressure to keep things from literally just totally collapsing, to be able to spot the signs of a spacetime deformity, or to know what it feels like when a place implodes; I'll tell you one thing, you ever go through this, you won't care at all that it can't be considered a literal implosion. The next time something goes horribly awry, a head-on collision with a fully loaded tractor-trailer, or your car sails off a Big Sur cliff, or you're headed face-first, through the drive-feed system, toward the carbide-edged knives of a massive Morbark whole-tree woodchipper, take a good look around, as you're nearing the edge of the event horizon, you'll see what I mean: the first thing you'll notice is that time seems to slow, and then just as you reach the edge of all your horizons, everything freezes in a redshift tableau. I saw blue-and-red juveniles that had emerged into view; best guess is they'd been hiding somewhere, like underneath my grey sedan, and had only just dropped their bright-orange sodas, which were suspended in midair, twelve inches beneath their feet; they were so close at hand, in that frozen moment, that it almost felt possible to reach out and touch them, in their royal-blue soccer shorts, white-on-black *fútbol* cleats, and with the white five-point star, of a grocery-chain logo, imprinted across the backs of their scarlet-red jerseys; this image of them standing there, just on the edge of the event horizon, with all four feet eighteen inches off the ground, like a freeze-frame photo of a Thoroughbred racehorse, as they flee at high speed up a one-way side street, is the paradigmatic image of a massive implosion. I saw camouflaged soldiers that had leveled their weapons; there is no need to guess where the soldiers had come from, or how they wound up, on a warm dry day, immersed up to their necks in a bright-yellow flash-flood of spent brass cartridge casings and parabellum debris, now frozen back to its source in the M-16 ejection ports, though given the fact that they were still on the pavement, with their boots in a streambed of spent-brass debris, apparently believing they could hide in plain sight, I couldn't help wondering about the thinking behind their black-on-green clothing in a pastel environment; if you're wearing jungle camouflage in an urban setting, it certainly isn't likely that you're concealing yourself from others, it's far more likely that they're concealing themselves from you, so maybe it's just me, and I'm missing the whole point here, but what the hell's hidden beneath all this camouflage? Best guess the answer is probably nothing; that these soldiers were camouflage clean clear through; and that those black balaclavas weren't shielding their identities, they were conferring a black-masked existence upon them. I saw six armed men, bearing automatic weaponry, and RPGs, and shoulder-mounted rocket-launchers, who had recently emerged, at the entrance to the street, from a black-on-black Escalade with chrome-spinner wheels, though since all six men were wearing true urban camouflage, it's not clear to me how I managed to spot them; I'll hazard a guess that they weren't trying to hide, and had exited the vehicle full-auto firing, as they had bright-orange streaks of AK-something muzzle-flash, frozen at the ends of their burst-fire barrels; these bright-orange streaks reminded me of something, which turned out to be, in the freeze-frame instant, a bright-

orange ball of flash-frozen flame, only recently emerged from a
flatbed propane tank; and while I won't try to tell you that I connected all three, I saw the bright-hard spark of a bullet-core ricochet, stuck to the brick of a pastel building. By now you must be
asking yourself: what's happened to Juárez? As far as I can tell, at
this point in the implosion, with the whole sprawling city of Ciudad
Juárez now hidden within the boundaries of its Schwarzschild radius, which I'm guessing in this case is about one or two angstroms,
meaning one-tenth of a nanometer, or about the width of a hydrogen atom, there *is* no Juárez, as far as the eye can see it's a primordial black hole, a gravitational singularity, a Hadamard disaster,
though since I can still see our ordinary one-way side street, that
must mean it's some sort of naked singularity, naked in the sense
that it's exposed to detection, so the way I've got it figured, using
loop quantum gravity in a spinfoam string-net, Juárez itself is a rotating black hole, and our pastel street has spun loose from the city,
and I'm either just standing there, doing some detecting, or else
maybe standing there, just *totally exposed*. I saw crows overhead on
a low-voltage power line, staring dead-level at an immense wall of
flame, possibly the result of a poorly timed rocket shell having burst
just short of a tubular-steel birdcage, and while it came as no surprise that the crows were sitting motionless, I could have sworn I
saw signs that maybe two or three feathers had been ruffled by the
thermobaric overpressure blast wave; crows don't hide, crows don't
have to, they're like the one shining example of the world's dark
opacity, but maybe, I was thinking, you could get one to fly, if you
waited around for nightfall, and a nice new moon, and took out the
better part of the Juárez power grid. I saw an entire Juárez side street
that had emptied in an instant, though since it wasn't actually empty, one wonders about this perception: how can a street be both
empty and brimming? Best guess the answer has something to do
with camouflage, which opens up a gap between seeing and perceiving: I saw three silhouettes, razor-thin mangy bare-bones pariah
dogs, hideous to look at, much less perceive, which may mean the
hideous is itself a form of camouflage, and I was now seeing dogs
that I refused to perceive; I saw two lost toddlers, recently emerged
from a chipped arcade, one of them happy, about to lick an ice
cream, one of them sad, holding only an empty waffle cone, his

tear-stained face sort of scrunched-up and melted, covered with streaks of Juárez dirt and soon-to-be-dripping French vanilla, like Holy Mary, Mother of God, pray for us sinners, which may mean that innocence and the fullness of Grace cannot coexist with the perception of incipient violence, or it may mean that the presence of innocent children, in a rotating bolt-lock, direct-impingement, speedloader stripper-clip, chambered-to-fire environment, opens up a crack, in our frozen interiors, within which we're praying the children stay hidden; I saw taco-cart vendors and dairy-store owners and produce-truck drivers and green-melon haulers, and all sorts of ordinary pastel lives, disappear into the gap between seeing and perceiving, because I'll tell you one thing, you ever go through this, to the sound of ricochet assault-rifle fire, and grenades going off, and the whistling ballistics of exothermic-flame-front anti-tank rockets, and what seriously amounts to an immense wall of sound, the thermobaric-brickwork of tone-deaf musicians, falling out of the sky, and landing right on top on you, there's no fucking way you'll be believing your own eyes, you'll be playing hide-and-seek with the ice cream children.

The next thing I knew, Juárez just exploded, and while the explosion itself was quite an event, there's no way I'm telling you I was there when it happened, much less offering a detailed account; not only are the details hard to comprehend, but the details, I'm afraid, are a little hard to come by, since no one who's passed through the event horizon has ever come back with his details intact; one moment you're standing there, frozen in time, and the next thing you know, the whole thing is over, and maybe you're saying like Jesus, What was that? or maybe you're mumbling dysleptic nonsense, something to do with the Abyss showing up, wearing an enormously satisfied shit-eating grin, taking it all in with a single glance, and spewing it back out so the world would have to deal with it.

When the smoke had cleared, smoke was ubiquitous, burnt graphite smoke, burnt aluminum smoke, burnt smoke of a moment gone up in smoke, and the black-on-black Escalade had simply vanished, along with the blue-red *fútbol* kids, and the true-urban-camouflage orange-streak attackers, who turned out to be camouflaged street magicians, six pyrophoric men who disappeared with a puff, leaving a street full of aliphatic and aromatic hydrocarbons, but

very little carnage, in the thermobaric crush. An entire Juárez side
street had burned to the ground, leaving every last brick smoked
but intact, which all things considered, was really quite a trick, and
while it didn't exactly leave us wide-eyed and wondering, it sure
as hell left us stunned and gasping. The attackers, apparently, had
somehow set fire to the oxygen supply, leaving smoke signals everywhere, but maybe too much smoke to be able to decipher them,
like they were trying to send a message under a steganographic covertext, and security through obscurity, in deeply concealed writing; or maybe the whole message was smoke clear through, and
there was no need to be dragging Johannes Trithemius into this,
like who needs a treatise on medieval cryptography, disguised as
a three-volume book on magic, when you can smoke the whole
place using shoulder-launched High Explosive Air Bursting munitions? There was white smoke creeping from holes in the ground;
there was grey smoke pouring out of the pasteleria; there was billowing black smoke from a derelict flatbed, an ancient Ford F-6,
apparently lit up by a rocket grenade, or a ricochet bullet that had
struck the propane tank; there was smokeless smoke in my eyeballs
and ears, and it smelled like my hair had autoignited. Those two
creatures down in the Juárez dust? They had blood-colored smoke
seeping out of their ski masks, though neither of the men was seriously hurt; given a couple of days, and a moment or two to reflect
on the future of their profession, they'd probably both be back on
skis, though no doubt joining the other side, which while somewhat
undermanned had thoroughly outgunned them. I mean, how in
the hell does some farmer from Sinaloa get his hands on an Integrated Airburst Weapon, maybe the XM-29, with night-vision im-
aging, direct-view optics, and its environmental sensors set to pale
pastel, firing 25-millimeter thermobaric HEAB rounds, at 15 per
minute from box magazines, capable of setting fire to most of the
local troposphere? The answer, I'm thinking, is at an El Paso gun
show. What about the condition of the razor-thin dogs? Thoroughly
smoked, though unlike the crow, pariah dogs don't die, they don't
have the strength to; one of them was digging in a shaped-charge
explosives pit, soaking up smoke, feeding, like always, on its own
exhaustion. Innocent bystanders, what happened to them? Found
guilty of smoking at the wrong location, and sentenced to a week

at home watching television, while trying not to blink their fire-balled eyelids. The ice cream children, both happy and sad, has anyone seen them? I have no idea, though this doesn't mean anything; with all this smoke, we all look like children. Smoke in the rocket holes, smoke close to the ground, smoke drifting off toward the Martian highlands; ubiquitous smoke; these Mexicans should be careful they don't inhale it; it may have wafted south, of its own volition, from an immense toxic arsenal and shitpile of weapons. The soldiers not down were running the other way, orthogonal to the stalled flow of one-way traffic, and the Light Strike Vehicles, still full of ballistics, had maybe moved forward a good twenty feet, before their tires melted flat, and they backflipped over, coming to rest upside down, pointed the wrong way, on the tubular-steel bars of their empty birdcage roll protectors. The Army, in other words, had gone off on some sort of strategic retreat, for a little off-site planning, away from the daily work distractions, leaving the residents of Juárez to fend for themselves, with a Glory Be to the Father, or a decade on the Rosary beads, while quietly making their own collateral damage assessment. The Pepsi man picked glass from a mango-stained face; the taco vendor wrote off his pushcart losses; Mom stood staring at an empty space, which moments before had been her plate-glass window; and I ran into a nearby store, La Tienda de Licor des Dos Amigos, and purchased a liter of Tequila Herradura, Añejo Reposado, in a squat gold bottle. The damage, in my case, was apparently neurological; I'm standing here now without a nick or a cut, on a sky-blue day, the 15th of April, and while I haven't lost a drop of vascular blood, I've lost a lot of chemistry, I'm stone-cold sober. This, let me tell you, I'm going to need to fix; I couldn't do much to restore our little side street, but I could certainly do a lot to restore my own chemistry.

Jesus, what a mess; it's amazing I wasn't blasted on all the smoke I was emitting. I should probably mention, before we move on, one final item on our damage assessment. When I returned to the car, Ms. Noon was still sitting there, staring out the windshield of our spotless sedan, which had passed through the battle essentially intact, with the exception of a single round nickel-sized hole that was right beside her head in the passenger-side window, surrounded by a web spun by complex crystal spiders, spiders that had obviously crawled straight into hiding, through a poly-foam gash in the left rear seat. Only later, some blocks from the scene, would she bother to explain the bag on her lap, apparently retrieved from underneath the car, where the *fútbol* boys had amateurishly dropped it: a child's red knapsack, with a White-Star-on-Blue-S commercial logo, the logo of S\*Mart, a local Juárez and Chihuahua grocery chain, containing six perfectly professional-looking plastic-wrapped bricks, maybe 6"-by-4"-by-2" each, call it maybe twelve kilos' worth, of amazingly pure black tar heroin. This, *verdad*, I'm going to wish she didn't have; I wish she would have left it right where she found it, or stuffed it in a hole, through the poly-foam gash, and left it with the complex crystal-web spiders.

Okay, so now what? Maybe use this opportunity, now that I'm sober, to do some clearheaded thinking about my current situation? Let me think. Yes, I like it; I like this idea; this sounds to me like an excellent plan. I took a long deep swallow of the Añejo Reposado, and shook a few Ultras loose from the jar, thinking it might be time to cure Man's ills, and lead the herd back to the higher pastures; about the last thing you need, at a time like this, is to sit stone-sober, staring at your hands, inhaling your own fumes on a pyro-lyzed side street. I know what you're thinking: let's turn around, go back across the bridge, have a beer in El Paso. First off, let's face it, this was theoretically possible: make a right on Tlaxcala, cross Francisco Villa, then a right on Avenida Benito Juárez, and go back across the border on the El Paso Street Bridge. There are, however, a few practical difficulties. I have, to begin with, no real idea that these streets even exist, and even if I did, there is no way I could find them; after many long hours spent wandering around Juárez, I can say with some certainty that, with one or two exceptions, there is no such thing as an actual street sign, so if you don't know where you are, and you don't know where you're going, that's a pretty good summary of your exact location. Juárez is itself both a one-way-street maze, a maze that you're lost in the moment you enter, and an enormously complex steganographic covertext; on the surface it looks like a perfectly normal Mexican city, part tourist trap, part resident commerce, and the Pronaf area, which we're about to go through, in the one-way-only pages up ahead, could have been transplanted easily from Minneapolis or Portland, if you jacked

them up on steroids and Human Growth Hormone. There are cu-
rio shops, full of jewelry, pottery, Mexican dolls, onyx, blown glass,
and cheap ceramics; there are leather-goods stores, with purses and
wallets and luggage and golf bags; and furniture stores, full of sofas
and recliners and phony antiquery; there are open-air markets, with
fruits and vegetables and cheeses and meat; you'll see glass-factory
artisans, hand-blowing vases, and razor-thin Zapotecs, handweav-
ing rugs; the Duty Free shops are stuffed with perfumes and co-
lognes, Swarovski crystal, TAG Heuer watches, Mont Blanc pens,
Bulgari diamonds, Martell Cognac, Cuban Montecristos; the Plaza
de las Americas Mall, just up ahead, near the corner of two streets
that have wandered around blindly until they managed to intersect,
has a Cineplex movie theater and an ice-skating rink; and right next
door, within walking distance, you'll find two more malls, if you
stumble upon them, the Pueblito Mexicano and the Rio Grande,
both of which look like Mexican imitations of an imitation Mexico you'd find in Elkhorn, Wisconsin; there are Burger Kings and
McDonalds' and Church's Fried Chicken; there are restaurants
and nightclubs and sportsbooks and liquor stores; and every single
corner of every single block has at least one overstocked and compassionate Farmacia, where your prescription can be filled with a
minimum of paperwork. So I hear you asking: what's wrong with
that? Sounds like a great place to go do a little shopping. What if I
told you that I've seen the ice rink, and not only is it an empty and
forlorn sort of place, but the ice looks like some kind of biohazard
dump site, maybe sodium hypochlorite mixed with staphylococcal enterotoxins, maybe tetrodotoxin and diacetoxyscirpenol mixed
with clostridium perfringens epsilon toxins, all frozen together in a
piña colada slush. Maybe it's just me, and too many pills, and what
we have here is incipient paranoia, in this case an instance of classic pareidolia, where a vague and random pattern is perceived as
significant, a perfectly normal shopping mall attraction that looks
like a zombie graveyard for ill-advised lab experiments; or maybe
I'm coming down with a case of paraphrenia, caused by hyperphos-
phorylation of my mangled tau proteins, and we can explain it all
away as the indicia of apophenia, seeing patterns that aren't there in
randomized data; or the clustering illusion, a related phenomenon;
maybe this whole fucking shopping-for-stuff thing is exactly what it

seems, and totally All American, and it's time to just get over it; or maybe what I'm seeing is the God's honest truth, the steganographic subtext in a psychorama subliminal, and underneath the surface of the retailing experience is a totally different message about skull bones and psychopaths and Paleolithic animals. So you're saying let's turn around, go back to El Paso, and I'm not disagreeing, I am really and truly not; what I am in reality is really and truly stuck, staring at the back of a PepsiCo delivery vehicle, while sipping on old tequila and headed vaguely south, where every street I'll come to on the path that lies ahead points one way only, meaning deeper into Mexico.

In the midst of all this, which may just be me, with a trunk full of banknotes, a head full of chemicals, and a tendency to get a bit ahead of myself, Ms. Gorgeous High Noon, Ms. Enigmatic Raphael Sistine Madonna, sits here beside me, radiating silence, wearing a simple sky-blue dress, with plain white pumps to match her small pearl earrings, and holding a red knapsack that she hasn't as yet explained. There is something uncanny about the way she holds still, like she's a gemstone clamped tight in a stonecutter's bench vise, being studied before cleaving into two separate facet roughs; she looks, in other words, so utterly calm that it makes me want to wince, as though the cutter himself must be somewhere nearby, gripping and regripping his burl wood mallet, while he searches the workshop for a gem-cutting chisel. So where are we going? Nowhere, apparently. There, that's better, at least I'd managed to extract an actual sample of human speech, though she hadn't added much to the depth of my understanding; we had, at a minimum, now broken the ice, and reached the next layer down, which was itself frozen solid. No, I mean where are we going when we get off of this street? I have no idea; what street did you turn on? To tell you the truth, I didn't really turn; it was more like I veered at maybe a 20-degree angle; there were far too many traffic cops waving batons, and they seemed to be pointing in a wide variety of directions, many of which were not intended to be appealing. So what street is this? If you veered onto a street, which one did you veer on? Hell if I know; I didn't see a sign. Why do you not locate our current location through the use of your map? My map. Yes, the map on the floor, just to the left of your brake pedal, an instrument whose purpose I couldn't help noticing you seem to be somewhat ignorant of. Do not tell me that you have a similar ignorance of the use to which a map is put. That must be very much a helpless feeling, attempting to navigate an unknown city without the ability to read a map. No, no, you misunderstand; I know perfectly well how to read a map. Well why don't you read it then, and tell us where we are? I'd love to, really, nothing would make me happier, but I'm afraid we will find that the map in question is not much use as a travel aid; I have a theory about this particular map, it seems to be part of a vast conspiracy, to keep me from getting to wherever it is I'm going, but let's just say that, according to the map, we're in the middle of a large brown empty sort of blank spot. Well, I don't really see how that could be true; these little shops all have numbers, right beside their doors; what good would numbers do in the middle of a blank spot? Do you think they deliver mail to Numero Veinte-Ocho Todo Desierto? Our conversation, evidently, had itself veered off in the wrong direction, and was now apparently lost, and stuck behind a Pepsi truck. Look, you can see for yourself, here's the Avenida Malecon, here's Highway 45 headed south toward Chihuahua, and we, I would say, are right about here, in the middle of this emptiness, depicted as a streetless trapezoidal void. Ah yes, I see; you have the wrong map; you should, at a minimum, have stopped at the information booth, where you would certainly have obtained a more appropriate document. This map you are holding is completely useless. How were you planning to drive around Juárez with a map such as this? This is not giving me confidence that you are knowing what you are doing; you don't seem to know how to operate a car, and now I find that the map you are using is childish and pointless. Let me ask you something. What is that you are drinking from the short brown sack? And these pills you are taking; there seem to be quite a lot of them; are you suffering from some sort of driving malady? Perhaps you should not be driving with a medical condition; it might be best for both of us if we just get out and walk.

Walk? Walk where? Just about here, as the idling truck at last lurched forward, and the traffic started to move, and there seemed to be cause for hope regarding vehicular progress, I must have lost all patience with Ms. Noon's general attitude. It had, after all, been something of a long day; I'll spare you the details, they aren't re-

ally relevant; suffice it to say that I'd encountered a few difficulties, the struggle to find my car, while seeking a cure for temporal
cancer; the chubby-pink-children trumpet-blowing time war, with
precious minutes lost in a sky-blue-bedroom irreality continuum;
my toothbrushing confrontation with oral depravity and bloodshot
eyes and axon-stripping neuro-corrosives; the ammo-closet gun-rags
and fluffy-towel shower debacle; my eyeglass object permanence
problems; the one-way street sign map conspiracy, and problematic
morbidity of a stationary crow; our metathetic launch codes Juárez
tour guide, while waiting for Let's Say Noon at maybe 1:20; my existential stall at a large octagonal stop sign; the Crossing of the Rio
Grande, and the information-excess absorption overload; the time
spent debating on the sandbag parapets; the bird-bone onslaught of
the Virola Hekulas; the outbreak of civilities on a pastel side street
and hunger for a taco of carne asada; the arrival of the black-on-
black Interzone Liquefactionists, amid a momentary shortage of
good Nazi opiates, and an absolute excess of burst-fire weaponry;
my failure to cope with hypnagogic visuals and blowfly mutants
and benzo-blackout Hellstorm goggles; the blue-red *fútbol* birdcage
interrogatories, and drifting of projectiles over the Chihuahuan
desert; the Lockdown Hour, in a detox facility, under treatment
for a False Sense of Security addiction; my blank-slate dust-storm
welded-fingers quandary and shrinking-*glyph* sigh of premature
relief; the whole struggle to calculate the Schwarzschild status
of a perfectly lovely little Juárez neighborhood, during a redshift
freeze-frame thermobaric-camouflage Ice Cream Children street
implosion; ubiquitous smoke, pariah dogs, bystanders sentenced
to watching television; the Poly-Foam Gash; the Yes Ceasefire; the
Battle of the Street Signs; the TAG Heuer watches; the Mexican
imitations of an imitation Mexico; my dogged reporting, if I do say
so myself, on the steganographic subtext retailing story behind a
biohazard ice-rink dumpsite emporium; and now this woman chas-
tising me, for a failure to prove confidence-inspiring; I was, all in
all, getting pretty tired, and some of this stuff hasn't even happened
yet, which while admittedly confusing, is all the more tiring; the
hell with this. Where the fuck are we going? It isn't necessary to
shout. These medicines you are taking are causing you agitation.
When we come to a street, I will tell you to turn. The street that

comes next will then lie ahead of us. The street after that, who can say? I will know it when I see it; that much will become apparent. And when the time comes to halt, when we've finally arrived, I will tell you to halt, and you will note our arrival. This is very much how my memory works, like singing a song, although since my last memory of driving this goes south to north, I suppose you could say that I'm singing the song backwards. As for our destination, what difference does it make? The song of our destination need only be completed. You drive the car, we will see where the song takes us; I will sing the final note when the time comes to sing it. There is no point in my singing the last note now. We would only end up stopped in a large brown blank spot.

I couldn't argue with that, even if I wanted to; in an absolute maze of one-way streets, all headed south, deeper into Mexico, there wasn't much point in arguing over route optimization. Once a man starts drinking, the signs all point one way, and the final destination is easy enough to get to. I know you're still thinking, go back, turn around, but U-turns are pointless; you can't undrink the bottle.

# 25

The time in Juárez is let's say 7:30. There are dragon-breath flames climbing the clouds in the west, maybe exhaled in relief now that the day is finally over, and the sun is setting fast; or maybe what I'm seeing is someone sending up a warning flare, now that night is coming on, and it's the beginning of the end of local civil twilight. The paved road ended a couple of hundred yards back, at the bottom of a depression, and I drove on up a curving zigzag rut-track, to the top of this hill, where I sit in my rental car, watching the sunset. I have no idea at all where the hell I am, other than to the west of downtown Juárez, and east of the setting sun, east of California. Looking over my shoulder to my immediate south, I see the craggy Juárez Mountains, a jagged and empty rockpile that is not worth the effort. Looking to the north, over my opposite shoulder, and then back behind me, in the direction of El Paso, I see two actual landmarks that are objects worthy of mention: the forty-foot statue of a limestone crucifixion, slowly turning bloody up on Mount Cristo Rey; and the hundreds-of-feet-tall Twins, you'd definitely call them hulking, the broodingly smokeless smokestacks of the deserted ASARCO smelting plant. Below me, in an amphitheatre-shaped bowl, squats a dusty ramshackle barrio sprawl of maybe thirty or forty thousand people; I'm guessing this is a colonia called something to do with Anapra. At intervals along the shoulder of the paved road that led me here, I saw several large billboards imploring Agua Para Colonia Puerto de Anapra, and several more exclaiming ¡¡Será una Realidad!!, meaning Puerto de Anapra should have Agua any day now, though how it might be possible to call this place a *port*, at least a mile from the Rio Grande, and without a drop of natural water, is anyone's guess, and I don't really have one. I also saw signs, scattered along the way, that read Rancho de Anapra, Oasis de Anapra, and Anapra La Conquista, so whether it's a port or an oasis or a ranch, or has something to do with a conquest, in the feminine singular, whose nature isn't obvious in the middle of the Chihuahuan desert, Anapra uses the naming conventions of an Inland Empire subdivision, and is laid out in a grid of uniform square blocks, like a tic-tac-toe game that got a little out of hand. At the far northwest end, near the Southern Pacific railroad tracks, the game has been called off and abruptly concluded, interrupted by a fine line of tall cyclone fencing; since the grid has been constructed to fit the contours of the land, and the layout of the fence appears to be somewhat arbitrary, running dead straight from east to west, on a land surveyor's sightline, chopping off and eliminating a diagonal corner of the subdivision's clear-eyed but shortsighted game plan, I'm guessing that what I'm looking at here is the Mexico-U.S. border, and everything to the north belongs to guess who El Norte, where X's and O's are illegal, and subject to smudge-free Pink Pearl erasure. The streets of the grid are dirt-paved and wide, with tall octagonal light poles made of let's call it concrete; the housing in each block of two-hundred-foot-long squares is randomly architected, mostly bricolage assemblages engineered by their inhabitants; and every single house on every single street, whether made up of packing crates and cardboard and tin, or constructed of cinderblock and native adobe, has a fence that surrounds it, made of bricks and wire mesh and the usual routine, or something slightly more imaginative maybe, like shipping pallets, bedsprings, hubcaps, and auto parts. In the civil-twilight gloom, down the road I'm about to descend, sits a perfect example, a house made of nothing, scrap wood and milk crates and flattened-cardboard electronics boxes, gathered at a local dump, or lifted from a high-rise jobsite, or acquired at a recent Detritus Exhibit, hosted by the Juárez Garbage Museum, all tethered to uprights made of twenty-foot lengths of three-inch sewage pipe, a structure so sturdy, with its lead-pipe uprights, and yet so close to its own nonexistence, that it must have been designed by a whole team of crows. Sí, says Julio, esta es Colonia Anapra, un lugar peligroso, tener mucho cuidado.

Julio? Who the hell is Julio? Julio, admittedly, is not someone I know; he's something of a volunteer, though I paid him twenty dollars, a kid I picked up, off a backstreet near downtown, to serve as my new tour guide, when I lost Ms. Just Keep Driving. You lost her? What do you mean you lost her? Sí, I lost her, she vanished without a trace, into the copious seating of a tinted-window black Suburban, though she left me with a lovely and appropriate souvenir, an S*Mart black tar heroin backpack, along with a cryptic word to the wise, a word of such broad, even limitless, applicability, that one has to wonder whether she'd missed her true calling, and should have been a writer of free daily horoscopes, or those mysterious strips of wisdom you find inside fortune cookies, as in *Stay far away from wherever it is you're going.* This, truly, is a difficult injunction; perhaps I'd misheard her, and she'd said *we're* and not *you're*, and had meant nothing more than that I shouldn't attempt to follow her; on the other hand, claro, looking back on the last few days, her statement as it stands seems positively visionary. We are, however, getting ahead of ourselves; in the current instance, with this wisdom as yet to be imparted, the advice I needed most for the immediate case at hand would have pointed me exactly in the opposite direction, as in *Stay far away from whatever it is that's chasing you.* At the moment that, in retrospect, I should have been studying my rearview mirror, taking note of the fact that a white Jeep Cherokee was right on my bumper and preparing to overtake me, I was staring across the road, enjoying my old tequila, comparing notes with myself on a shiny black Ram Magnum: not only was this the exact same truck that had cut in line behind me at the Stanton Street tollbooth, but it was slowly rolling north, on an entirely different side street, and might know a shortcut back to El Paso. Before I could blink, or formulate a plan, or even remove my lips from the squat gold tequila bottle, the white Jeep dove in front of me, and slammed on its brakes, and discharged three veterans from the local Policía, dressed from head to toe in municipal black, and wearing the pale-grey, six-point, Star, with accents in red, that is the logo worn with pride by a Ciudad Juárez SWAT force. This, even to me, seems a bit out of the ordinary; since no one in Juárez even slows at an intersection, you'd really have to run quite an Existential Stop

Sign to be pulled over and ticketed by a Juárez SWAT force; these guys, let me tell you, simply do not fuck around, as in *Wherever it is you're going, you'll be there in no time.*

Jesus. Now what? If you've ever had to deal with the Mexican authorities, you know that there's a moment where your life hangs in the balance: either get the math right, on the spot, in your head, and pay off your debt to society promptly; or wind up in jail, clawing equations on the walls, while floating facedown in the Mexican judicial system. You get picked up off the pavement by a two-man squad, in a simple black and white, on a drunk and disorderly, and are driven around the block who knows two or three times, to sober you up, let you come to your senses, I'd give them oh let's say a $50 tip; the ride has been lovely; now go on about your evening. You get stopped at a checkpoint with your carpet full of weed, mostly seeds and large stems that weren't worth the smoking, and this time it's the Federales, maybe fifteen men, inviting you to join them in their Airstream Flying Cloud, in this case, remember, they have overhead involved; you can try two-fifty, it did work for me, but be prepared to go as high as $500. You find yourself fireside on a Baja cliff, surrounded by Mexican Army troops, repeatedly asking *Tienes mota?*, and while you do have several kilos' worth of low-grade marijuana, and a half sheet of blotter acid, decorated with Black Condors or Wizard of Oz Ruby Slippers, or maybe it was Owsley Stanley's Grateful Dead Dancing Bears, man, weren't those the days, where the hell did the time go, you don't, unfortunately, have an awful lot of cash, like maybe $30 if you don't count the surfboards; in this case, let's face it, the sentence you're looking at is six years and a day, with no chance of parole, so let me ask you this. How high is the cliff? All of this, basically, is 3rd grade math, while what I'm faced with here is a scrawl of tensor field equations. I recognize all the symptoms of a gravitational time dilation, with time slowing down, swelling and stalling, the closer you get to something massively heavy; or I may be looking at a rotational distortion, the whole frame-dragging effect of spinward-torqued time-tics, with the clocks speeding up, and my head doing the spinning; I'm stationed behind the wheel of an improbable grey sedan, whose problematic contents have been gradually amassed, about to be approached by a Juárez SWAT force, and these guys, I'm telling you, are not just heavy, they look like something that wandered off from a Pound-Rebka test, living proof that there's a warp in the spacetime curvature, with their massive 6-point, redshift, Stars, and black-hole aura of immunity to gravity, as I sit here staring at a tiny white logo, the 5-point star on my S*Mart knapsack, and while I know for a fact that I'm wildly overreacting, I can't do the math, like am I rapidly aging or have I turned into a child? Here's my problem, see if you can solve it: I have an open container, half-full of tequila, held up to my lips, with my eyes going teary; I couldn't pass a sobriety test, with a gun to my head, which in this case, in my experience, should be taken literally; there's a lunch sack of opiates underneath the seat, and a lifetime supply of weapons-grade heroin, professionally wrapped, on the seat right beside me; I have a $3,000 roll of one hundred-dollar bills that I'm holding in one hand, almost as though I think it might mean something; and an inexplicable quantity of lavender currency, in a large green duffel bag, stashed in the trunk, enough actual cash to buy the entire Juárez police force for at least the next twelve months or so, but that may cause more problems than it actually solves, as it strikes me as both overkill for the local constabulary, and a pretty good reason to just go ahead and shoot me; if you're with me so far, good for you, because right around here, something else goes wrong, and things take a turn for the truly complicated.

Just as I'm getting the equations straightened out in my head, with three men to pay, and a good million dollars' worth of pure black tar heroin, another set of scalar functions gets added to the urban tensor field, with another three men, including the SWAT team's leader, exiting in unison from a tinted-window black Suburban that has pulled in right behind me, blocking me in. I know what you're thinking: they've come for the drugs; give them the bookbag, and get the hell out of there, which makes a lot of sense, and would certainly explain why, as their leader approached, I was holding the red knapsack right out the window. There must, however, in all the confusion, have been some sort of left-hand-not-knowing-what-the-right's-doing moment, because the man at my window, holding a Glock 17 or maybe a Browning 9mm, and pointing it straight at me, dead center in the middle of my math-garbled head, sort of scoffed at my offering and smiled and locuted. No, Señor, this is not what you call it a robo, a stickup. As our friend Señor

Gomez would so often say, all the world has indeed its great many stages, and one man in his time must play many different parts. The Señorita, unfortunately, has brought a grave disenchantment to our amigo común. She has been giving us the círculos now three long days. She will please to come with us to the lomas de poleo, in the beautiful spearmint hills, for the pennyroyal treatment, porque... somewhere in here, as I was beginning to enjoy his idiosyncratic performance, the tequila and opiates must have begun to kick in, because I didn't catch his drift, and it was followed by a blast of in-decipherable Spanglish, something more about Señor Gomez and lomas de poleo and spearmint cooking and abortive malefactions, and something that sounded distinctly to me like *dónde está el poeta maldito?* This speech, apparently, was not directed at me; it sailed off in an arc, right over my head, in the general direction of the Chi-huahuan desert. It must, however, have meant something of impor-tance to Ms. Sistine Madonna; she let out a half-muffled helpless-ness gasp, which was totally unlike her, and was wrestled from the car, and like instantly deported. I was, admittedly, somewhat slow to react, pulling in the bookbag, but otherwise frozen. I mumbled something interrogatory under my breath, like who the hell is Go-mez and what in God's name is a lomas de poleo, but I think I may have said this only to myself, as they whisked her away, toward the vast grey interior of an armor-plated black Suburban, and she uttered her words of fortune cookie wisdom in idiomatic Cryptic, *Stay far away from wherever it is you're (we're?) going.* Now I'm just sitting here with nowhere to go, sipping on tequila, pondering my horoscope, and watching them U-turn, up our one-way street, defy-ing the flow of traffic, and most of the laws of physics, with apparent indifference and utter impunity; I can't help wondering, under the exigent circumstances, if I can still drive my car, without ending up, however inadvertently, at my own destination, which while easy enough to get to, seems impossible to avoid.

Thus commenced a period of meandering uncertainty that I can't really say I'm altogether proud of, though I did find the Mis-sion, Nuestra Señora de Guadalupe, in the last place on earth you'd think they would have built it, meaning right in the heart of Ciudad Juárez. Guided by the intelligence of the one-way traffic signs, I went gliding around the Pronaf, found the biohazard ice rink and the Church's Fried Chicken and the Mexican imitation of an imitation Mexico, and while I wouldn't guarantee it, or put lives at risk, since I didn't see a sign reading Lopez Mateos, I think I found the spot that my tour guide had recommended for placing my car bomb 411 call. What I *didn't* find, in all my meanderings, as I went gliding around in spirals through the Pronaf street maze, was either a single street sign or a way to get *out*; I knew perfectly well how to find the Entrance, in fact the Entrance and I became fast friends, but as far as I could tell, in the entire Pronaf, there was no such thing as an Exit from the maze. What I also failed to find, as I searched for the Exit, presumably in the distance, at the far end of the maze, was a way to let go of the deep-seated conviction that the Entrance and Exit were two different things; I was trapped, effectively, in a maze of my own making, having failed to consider the distinct possibility that my only way *out* was the way I came *in*. The Pronaf must be built, like a unicursal labyrinth, for people who believe in achieving their goals, and arriving at their Exits, through persistent forward movement, the sort of people who tend to think that retreating is for pussies, that failing to reach the goal, and falling short of the objective, and eventually winding up right back where you started, is something that only happens to gimps and losers, and so round they go again, repeating the same steps, not understanding that going back the way you came and ending at the beginning is the only real end; I, admittedly, am one of these people; each time I found myself back where I'd started, I went around again, with a good deal of persistence, but with nothing much to show, in the way of forward movement, for my six-or-eight-loop journey through the unicursal maze; to exit the Pronaf, you don't need a map, you need the back of an old Greek coin, a homing pigeon, and a spider-thread skein about the size of a beach ball. As for the street signs, don't look at me, I'm not the one who hid them under such a vast profusion of signs that you might need a medieval cryptographer to read them, signs for nightclubs and clothing boutiques, signs for sportsbooks and cocktail lounges, signs for electronics, signs for blown glass, signs, most of all, for luxury-good items, Swarovski crystal, Mont Blanc pens, Bulgari diamonds, TAG Heuer watches, Martell Cognac, Cuban Montecristos, all of which would quickly amount to a dazzling array of neon, from pink-flamingo horses to violet martinis, if I didn't find the Exit before the sun went down. It was fortunate for me that I hadn't followed instructions, and hardwired my cell phone to heavy explosives, C4 or Semtex or daisy-chained artillery shells, because when I found myself parked in the middle of the street, directly in front of a Duty Free shop that I'd already driven past at least six times, I might well have been tempted to exit the whole maze, using the C4-smartphone-411 shortcut.

It was also fortunate, though this may sound odd, that I wasn't already loaded on performance-enhancing supplements, because I'm not real sure what's wrong with the place, it may not be drugs, it may just be money, but whatever the hell it is, something's gone wrong here, the whole place feels like it's jacked up on something. The Pronaf, as you enter it, on your first loop around, seems perfectly normal, like an excellent place to go do a little shopping, until you start seeing symptoms that are vaguely disturbing, a sense of certain features being oddly enlarged, consistent with the abuse of Human Growth Hormone: the generalized expansion of the skull at the fontanelle, with pronounced brow protrusion and ocular distention; that peculiar thickening and protruding of the lower jaw, with gapping of the teeth and enlargement of the tongue, a difficult-to-articulate anabolic symptom known as hypertrophic macroglossia; the signs of incipient pituitary gigantism, with acromegalic macrocrania and hypertrichosis and a sense that something's off and going insidiously dysmorphic; the Pronaf, in essence, looks like a typical consumer, slowly turning into a hulking Neanderthal, which may just explain, when combined with its macroglossia, why the Pronaf avoids putting names on its streets. About the last thing you'd need, at the end of a long day, where your pigeon wandered off, your car bomb fizzled, and you ignored all the warnings about performance-enhanced shopping, finding your back covered in fur and your eyeballs bulging, with a tongue you can't move due to hypertrophic enlargement, would be trying to explain, to the Juárez Police, how the missing child vanished, right before your eyes, into a dark limousine, with military plates, on Callejón Macrodolichocephalism.

I, in short, found the Pronaf somewhat daunting. The secret, by the way, to a unicursal labyrinth, is to think of the maze as a path, not a puzzle: the same route that got you into this mess will eventually lead you out, just as long as you turn around, and go back the way you came, accepting the fact that where the path really leads is back to the start, in its first-step beginnings; this, admittedly, isn't much of a secret, because a unicursal labyrinth isn't much of a puzzle, it's more of a kind of lesson in self-acceptance. If you insist, on the other hand, on getting lost in your own mazes, and prefer turning your path into one long puzzle, and refuse to turn around before the puzzle has been solved, you, I'm afraid, will learn an entirely different lesson, because the secret at the heart of a self-inflicted labyrinth is that all paths lead to the exact same conclusion: you're not solving the puzzle; the puzzle is solving you. And speaking of getting lost in self-made mazes, and turning your path into one long puzzle, this might be a good time, as long as we're here, to apologize directly to the municipal authorities, who have enough problems to deal with as it is, without my adding street names to the list, much less making a tasteless joke about the Army being involved with vanishing adolescents. Only later, after many hours of wandering the nameless Calles, would I discover that High Noon had left me with a map, a detailed *plano* of the streets of the city, with a route marked in red to guide me on my journey, hidden at the bottom of a stack of black bricks. While I've never discovered where the street signs are hidden, they are no doubt there, concealed under the covertext of such a vast profusion of signs that you might need a quantum cryptographer to read them, and perhaps a small team of sociolinguistic-topologists, with a specialty in pairwise isomorphic deformations, to help you come to terms with the semiotic anguish of the poor urban planners, as they wander the city, searching for names for the Juárez streets. If you're part of the power structure of Ciudad Juárez, believe me, I've been there, the streets of your city are no laughing matter; they are, however, enormously confusing, so permit me to apologize, but let me ask you this. Why does Juárez need like 500 streets all named Zapata, and another 600 called Calle or Callejón or Callejuela Hidalgo? And really, come to think of it, Avenida Disneyland? What the fuck is that all about?

Completely by accident, while fleeing the area, I stumbled upon a street, in the middle of nowhere, that actually had a name, Avenida Paseo Triunfu De La Republica, and believed for a moment that I knew where I was, in a city I could cope with, where the streets had names and ran in both directions and I had my pick of good clean hotels, a Fiesta Inn and Hotel Lucerna, a Holiday Inn Express and Hotel Chula Vista. The Holiday Inn looked like a nice safe choice, and all things considered, I should have checked myself in, had a burger from room service and maybe another shower, since I still smelled of pyrolytics and aromatic hydrocarbons, and then put myself to bed and gone to sleep for three days. As I was thinking this over, however, sipping on Herradura, dreaming of a burger and a good night's sleep, the Paseo slipped away and blended imperceptibly into another one-way corridor, and there was no turning back, with me gliding past the last of the hotels, and the July-something Triumph of the Mexican Republic, and continuing on down Avenida 16 de Septiembre, a street almost certainly named in honor of something, but not named in honor of my finding a place to stay, at maybe 3:30, on the 15th of April. And there, suddenly, like something you know by heart because you've seen it in a dream, stood the beautiful little Mission, a single-room chapel from the 1600s, in a pale shade of beige and whitewashed adobe, with a two-story bell tower, and a simple cross at the top; it was joined at the hip, like a dream turned abruptly into something less pleasant, to a massively ugly 20th century cathedral, a mishmash of Greek columns and Fascist concrete and stone that must have been strip-mined from the Juárez Mountains. If you don't know Juárez, and really, why should you, those mountains you see in the immediate distance, the northern-most tip of the Sierra Madre, have a message you can't read, from almost any distance, written in simple block letters, made of whitewashed stones: La Biblia es la Verdad, LEELA, meaning READ IT, and I'll leave it to you to determine what to make of this, like maybe la Verdad is beautiful and simple, a one-room chapel with a cross at the top, or maybe the truth is a little more complicated, a dysmorphic edifice, an unscrupulous pile of rock. And then horns started honking, and my foot came off the brake, and my car lurched forward, and I continued onward, not only anxious to stop blocking traffic, but apparently determined to avoid almost anything that might be mistaken for an endpoint or goal, a restaurant, for example, a lunch stand or snack bar or fast-food counter, anything that would lead to an emptied plate of food; the far side of the river, and a patch of Texas soil, were both, needless to say, completely off limits; what I must have had in mind, on the streets up ahead, was to find a great many ways not to reach El Paso, though El Paso proved particularly easy to avoid. While I was having another drink and not paying much attention, I must have slipped right past the bright-orange Mercado, which would have been a good place to stop and have lunch, and sailed straight across Juárez Avenue, the street that would have led me back to El Paso, and found myself again in yet another labyrinth, full of one-way streets that did not go anywhere, not even back to the street-maze entrance, a bombed-out Zona out of the death of Nazi Germany, or the Cast Lead remainders of the Gaza Strip, or the neuro-corrosive aftereffects of a long night of drinking, and while I did see a couple of bars that were open for business, and a gym full of boxers wearing street-gang tattoos, I didn't see anything that looked the slightest bit edible, so I kept on drinking and driving instead of eating, and drove right on toward the cocktail hour. You'd never believe it if you tried it yourself, but I somehow came out on the Avenida Rivereño, and drove three long loops along the park beside the river, with El Paso so close I could reach out and touch it, or wade there like a toddler through some drainage-ditch waters, but I couldn't for the life of me find a single bridge-like structure that would take me across the ditch in a currency-stuffed sedan. I did find one bridge that was apparently private, and required that your vehicle be PortPass-equipped; I found the bridge that had brought me what seemed like some years ago over the border, into my own personal Mexico, the Stanton Street Bridge, with the one lane going north, for commuters only, closed up and blocked off with orange plastic traffic cones; and I drifted in a dream underneath the girders of what must have been my one and only way out, the Santa Fe Street Bridge, right there above me, with canopies galore and pedestrian walkways and Lions Club signs and a large walking crowd, but I swear to you now, and you have to believe me, there is no actual entrance on to this bridge, you must need a wand and an ancient magic passcode to wish your way up there from off of the Rivereño. When my third loop failed, and I knew that I was trapped, I pulled off again on a take-your-pick side street, just past the no-way-to-get-there-from-here Bridge, where what do I find, to my pleasure and amazement, but the shiny Ram Magnum, like a long-lost friend.

The truck was parked and empty, across the street from a mod-

ern office tower, and apparently being guarded by a kid in a track-
suit and a few of his friends. I say apparently, because by the time I
got parked, they were working on the truck with a chisel and a coat
hanger, wedging the steel chisel between the door frame and roof
seal, and working the wire hook down around the lock knob. Once
the door had been opened, they emerged from the vehicle with submachine pistols that might have been Uzis or Walther MPKs, such
that if the truck were being guarded, it was reasonably safe, and everything around it was immediately endangered. My first thought,
upon spotting the Black Ram, had been to wait for the two men
who had followed me down here, and ask them to lead me back
to El Paso. On second thought, given the burst-fire sidearms, and
my previous experience with hanging around Juárez with too many
weapons and too little to do, I decided it might be better to enlist
one of the truck guards, and have him guide me back, through the
one-way-street maze, to the source of the traffic on the Santa Fe
Bridge. Julio was recruited by waving a $20 bill, though not without
a certain amount of semiotic contortion as we sought to establish
a basis for verbal communication. Julio reminded me of those kids
you meet in Tangiers, with maybe a 3rd grade education, and like
seven or eight languages; necessity might not be the mother of invention, but it's the mother of language as a means of survival. He
started out with Dutch, Waar vandaag gaat u, knor?, switched rapidly to German and then into Portuguese, before we finally settled,
for better or worse, on Julio's native tongue, the language of U.S.
Border commerce, most of it a local variant of standard Druglish.
So you looking for drogas or putas or you prefer maybe both? I
know just the place, make a left en la esquina siguiente, you want
talco or mafu or niebla or ready rock? Maybe get an a-bomb and a
couple of diablitos, find you a chiquita at my cousin's uncle's place,
he's got diesel and diamonds and r-balls and bambita, we could
get you some red caps, smoke it in a Maserati, or maybe do a little
five-way, whatchoo say, campo? My cousin's tío es a todo dar. This,
of which I don't understand a word, from a thirteen-year-old kid,
wearing a Cubs cap backwards. No, Julio; I'm trying to get back
to El Paso. Whatchoo want in El Paso, chido? I don't know, Julio;
maybe get some sleep. Let me ask you something though: what's a
lomas de poleo? You mean Lomas de Poleo, like the place out on

the mesa? That place is badass, completely fucked up, you looking for electronics, place you want to go is Puerto de Anapra, al lado de Las Lomas, just down off the mesa, they got TVs and stereos and computers and satellite dishes, steal 'em off the train, get you anything you want. They steal things off of a moving train? Shit no, pito, they whatchoo call it, descarrilese, they derail it first, hammer open the boxcars, haul the stuff off through the chinga la migra fence. You need a new big screen? Back up, Julio; Lomas de Poleo is a place? Not anymore it's not a place, the Zaragoza's obreros fenced it all up, bulldozed the houses, raped all the women, it's a fucking carcel, a how you say, concentration camp, deme algun tequila, un pequeño sorbo, eh ese? I handed him the bottle, thinking it was probably better to be drinking old tequila in a slow-moving rental car than smoking new red caps in a high-speed Maserati. So whatchoo need, hijo? You noddin or somethin? We get you some salty water and nexus and ket, smoke a little geeter or hanyak in a kabuki, stay away from mad dog and rambo and downers, you want to go dancin, we get you some scoop and some donkey and 2-CB, top it off with tachas, you be dancin all night. Not sure I want to go dancing, Julio. I'm thinking I want to go to Lomas de Poleo. Estás chalado, pendejo? You don't need drugs, you need about ten of those TEC-9 machine guns from the gringos' black truck. Lo dices en serio? Yeah, Julio, I think maybe I am. Some guys in a Suburban grabbed the lady I was traveling with; I think they maybe took her to Lomas de Poleo. Man, you must be drunk. She out on the mesa, ella ya está muerta, corte en pedazos. No fucking way you get me to go out there. Hay te wacho, cabrón. Have a nice day. Okay, so I lied, Julio's compensation went a little over budget; I gave him another $100 as he started to leave the vehicle, and convinced him to lead me as far as Anapra. For better or worse, I'd now quite possibly solved my fortune cookie ambiguity problem, with *we're* and *you're* becoming one and the same, though *stay far away from wherever it is* I didn't do; about halfway to Anapra, I had 90% arrived.

Let me explain: Julio made me do it. When he found the S*Mart heroin bookbag, full of BP Ultimate diesel fuel, his eyes lit up like a world record Ferris wheel, picture the London Eye at night, and out came the tinfoil and my Blazer cigar torch, and we pulled to the dusty shoulder of the road between barrios, and smoked a little hunk of the renegade rambo. This, at least, was our original intention, to smoke a little match-head's worth, a "bump" in the vernacular, just enough to keep us going down the road to Anapra; somewhere along the way, however, somewhere between pulling to the shoulder of the road, and actually inhaling those first bubbling vapors, we ran into all sorts of problems with our tools, and our original little hunk turned into a little monster. First of all, just to begin with, if you've ever tried to open a triple-shrink-wrapped brick, containing a good two kilos' worth of pure tar heroin, in hopes of extracting a little match-head's worth, just enough to keep you going through a moderate stretch of tedium, you know this can't be done without a knife or a pair of scissors; by the time poor Julio got the black brick to loosen, and finally pried it open by puncturing it with his thumbs, he had a half ounce missing in the carpet of my rental, and a multigram mound in the palm of his hand. Then Julio put a bump in the center of the tinfoil, handed me the toilet-paper-tube inhaler, and started applying heat via the Blazer Pocket Micro Torch, a handheld weapon, with a gem-blue flame, capable of bringing down a fully loaded aircraft, and before we knew it, or had a chance to inhale, poof, the bump was gone, leaving burnt-tar residue on the tinfoil surface, and a bump's worth of vapor swirling around the vehicle. A brief search of the glovebox, for a candle or a Zippo, anything that would burn with a soft-yellow flame, came up empty as far as low-heat implements, and while I should, in retrospect, have set fire to my rental map, we decided to solve the problem using available equipment, an approach that, in retrospect, was particularly unsound. The solution we came up with, a bit less torch and a lot more substance, might well have worked with a soft drink straw, but the inch-wide inhaler we were forced to rely on proved far too efficient, like a vacuum cleaner tube sucking down a carpet, such that by the time our mound of tar had finally stopped bubbling, and Julio and I sat back in our seats, there wasn't a lot of vapor swirling around the vehicle, there were two stoned humans, flying around on carpets, being sucked down a hole we'd punctured in reality, and gazing up the road, maybe seeing monsters, or maybe, come to think of it, just monstrously high.

So I'm sitting here now, with a head full of junk, a mouthful of something that could be tequila, and a pool of bubbling tar that my bones have fallen into, and Julio's going like Man, this is heavy. Part of me has sailed off like a bird, over the empty brush of the Chihuahuan desert, and part of me is sitting by the side of the road, watching as a donkey cart plods off into the distance. When I was living in Portugal, in a town called Colares, translating Pessoa, and writing a little of my MIA poetry, I think I saw this exact same cart, going past me down the road one evening around sunset: A donkey cart passes, on the road toward Sintra, which is only where the road goes, because it's just that kind of road, and if it were another kind, that wouldn't make it another kind, that would only make it the same road it is when it's different; to the old man going home, with his cart full at nightfall, this road could be different, but it would still go where it goes. Say what? Jesus. Maybe Julio's right; this stuff is pretty heavy; a guy jacked up on pure tar heroin can spend hours doing nothing, reciting old poetry, staring at a donkey cart, or studying the intricacies of his own left shoe. Besides which, I'm cognizant of the fact that this is not the same road; that road in Portugal, through the Colares vineyards, winds up, in the end, maybe 12 kilometers later, in Sintra's glorious Eden, the summer home of the Portuguese kings, while the road toward Anapra wanders off through the desert, and ends up in a port, without a drop of its own water, or possibly an oasis that's dying of thirst. These are not the same roads, not by a long shot, though I seriously doubt, at least from where I'm sitting, that where the road ends up going is particularly relevant; that road through the vineyards may head straight into Eden, but if you wind up in a ditch, what the hell's the difference? You think a guy driving a donkey cart, over an empty stretch of pavement, really cares where the road ends? The man I'm watching now is just trying to make it home, eat some tortillas and frijoles, call it a day; turns out the road leads to a Palace, it doesn't much matter, he's still eating beans. I met an old fisherman one time, up the coast from Colares, down in a little cove, with like ten feet of beach, more rock-strewn than sandy, and a tiny armada of rainbow-colored watercraft; he was leaning against his boat, smoking a hand-rolled cigarette, reweaving his shrimp net with a needle made of bone. I was looking for a vineyard near Azenhas do Mar, and had stopped to ask the man if I was going in the right direction. For some reason I don't remember, I was in something of a hurry. The man worked on his net,

silently, while I waited, closing a dinner-plate-sized hole, turning it
back into netting, then looked up at the hills, in the direction I was
headed, puffed on his cigarette, thought the whole thing over, and
said evenly, in Portuguese, "I know, but I don't know today." Okay,
okay, so this isn't exactly all that relevant either; it's just that this, in
essence, is the exact antithesis of my entire way of life; now where
the hell was I? No wonder my poetry went AWOL or whatever; it
seemed to be in an awfully big hurry to get wherever the hell it
thought it was going, and it got there all right, just not in one piece.
And speaking of going places, just out of curiosity, since when have
I been driving instead of sitting by the roadside, and why am I using
phrases like *high rate of speed*, when what I really mean to say is that
I'm traveling at *high speed*? So that's where I am, right about now,
and it doesn't much matter where the road is actually going, I'm
on the road toward Anapra, which is only where it goes. Whereas
Julio, on the other hand, is having some second thoughts about the
whole fucking journey. As we drive on toward Anapra, on the road
that leads directly into What the Hell's the Difference, Julio, to my
eye, just doesn't look well, in fact he looks like he's sucking up some
fairly heavy G's, like he's halfway through his seat, toward the pavement, already, and isn't looking forward to his arrival at all. He's
mumbling things about maybe getting sick, and giving me all sorts
of warnings about the water, and apparently asking me to drop him
off now, in the middle of nowhere, which is truly where we are. I'm
seeing stationary crows, and rickety white buses, and razor-thin pariah dogs, and wasted-looking children, and a multitude of humans,
I'll grant you that, but I can't really picture myself caring what's out
there, my cart's basically empty, I haven't exactly done an honest
day's work. Probably goes without saying that that's my response to
Ms. Noon's cryptic message, *stay far away from wherever it is you're
going*, like too late now, I'm past there already. Heh, Julio, wake the
fuck up, get a load of this sunset, you think you got something you
maybe want to add?

Si, says Julio, esta es Colonia Anapra, un lugar peligroso, tener mucho cuidado. Part way down the dusty winding road, at the
house made of garbage, I drop Julio off; I offer him a brick of the
crazy bookbag shit, but Julio's so stoned, he won't even look at it.
At the bottom of the hill, where the road straightens out, I pull the

car over, and stop to catch my breath, and take a good long look around Colonia Anapra, and while it certainly isn't the worst of the slums I've encountered, it is, almost certainly, the World's Worst Oasis. Maybe it's just me, or maybe it's 1-part me, and 99-parts Julio's warnings about the water, but Anapra doesn't really look all that peligroso, what it looks like is sick, like thoroughly polluted. The main street through town, in the thickening twilight gloom, is choked with powdery dust and powdery little children, and the billowing black smoke of off-white maquila buses, and young women wheezing toward a late-night shift, and tanker trucks loaded with drinking water, itself so polluted, it's a wonder the girls can walk. Every single house on both sides of the road has 50-some gallon water containers, rusted metal drums and brightly colored trash-can bins, hiding in plain sight behind improvised fencing, like a two-by-four scaffolding jazz-hands kind of piece, strung with old barbed wire, of the tetanus-shot variety, which makes it sound like the water is pretty safe, from being stolen or tampered with or consumed by the general public, until you notice that the fence has an eight-foot reality-gap, a hole large enough to drive a good-sized truck through, which may just explain how the water trucks get in, and fill your red trash bin with water so safe that even its own drivers seem reluctant to disturb it: honestly, Señora, we appreciate your kindness, but we cannot afford the luxury of thirst. All things considered, if you believe even half of what Julio told me, you'd really have to have a fluid imagination, or a grim sense of humor, to cope with the nature of Anapra water. These trucks that deliver water here are known along the border as *pipas*, meaning *pipes*, which would probably strike you as somewhat ironic, particularly given the fact that the tap-water pipes are filled with a substance that is peculiarly deadly, fresh water laced with an abundance of arsenic; turns out a *pipa* is not what you'd think, it's not the sort of thing through which running water passes, it's a conveyor of smoke, and a *pipa de agua* is far better used for smoking your weed than for feeding your children, meaning the substance of what the tanker trucks are trying to convey is that potable tap water, in Colonia Anapra, is something of a pipe dream, a *sueño imposible*, a difficult-to-swallow figment of smoke. The *pipas*, or pipe dreams, advertise their product as *Agua Pura*, although unless you consider Hepatitis A to be a

normal component of drinking water, you'd have to begin to wonder what *Pura* is meant to signify, like maybe the best translation
would be *thoroughly corrupted*, or maybe, better yet, *hideously expensive*: your typical family, living on let's call it $30 a week, would
spend every last dime on *Agua Pura*, meaning there's no need to
worry about liver damage, your family will die of hunger first; what
the *pipas* deliver, to your family of six, is a *sueño imposible*, yet another figment of pipe-dream smoke. Anapra, evidently, is not just
sick, it also has a drinking-water figment problem; if you're scoop-
ing some substance from the Señora's red trash bin, put down your
water pipe, put back the substance, and do yourself a favor, stick
to cold beer. The entire Anapra water system, from one end to the
other, if you believe even a tenth of what Julio told me, must have
been designed by rhabdomancers, the witch-hazel dowser-men and
water diviners, who would have built the whole system by setting
fire to their tools, leaving witch-hazel residue on the smoked desert surface, and water bubbling up from the deep-desert fountain-
heads, water so pure and fresh and abundant, and yet so close to its
own nonexistence, that it must have been concocted with the crows
in mind; in any case, rhabdomancers aside, I doubt you'd last long
in Colonia Anapra if you're too much of a literalist; you'd need a
fluid imagination, a grim sense of humor, and maybe a gas mask, to
deal with all the smoke. One of the billboard signs at the entrance
to town reads Agua Para Colonia Puerto de Anapra—¡¡Será Una
Realidad!!, part of an ancient political campaign, long ago success-
fully completed, having nothing to do with either water or reality,
and everything to do with political conjugations of the future tense
of the verb *to be*; the ditches where new pipe would go are there
all right, filled to the brim with sewage muck, so be thankful that
your symptoms point to dysentery, and not just outright full-blown
cholera; the future tense of the verb *to be* has nothing to do with
the water system, it's been put to work, until Reality arrives, literally in the trenches of the Anapra Sewage Treatment Program. To
make a long story short, while I'll readily admit that this is mostly
just me, filled to the brim with 99-parts my own, and 1-part Julio's,
usual bullshit, Anapra may not be the World's Worst Oasis, but it
is, without a doubt, among the World's Sickest Water Jokes, the
sort of place that maybe Wanda Lust could write a whole column

on, without ever mentioning the future tense of anything; although The Future is almost certainly headed our way, with its cart full of water pipe for Colonia Anapra, I'm thinking it must have stopped, on the hill up above me, taken one long look at this ramshackle barrio, a long deep drag on its hand-rolled cigarette, thought the whole thing over, and said evenly, to itself, really, *why bother?*

Fortunately for me, I'm not a big believer in the future tense anyway, and in the block up ahead there's a handy tienda; the tar smoke and dust are probably making me thirsty, though I'm thinking about donuts and maybe mas tequila. By now it's almost completely dark, but Main Street is jammed with maquila buses, and *pipas* trucks, and powdery little children, with women grilling carnitas over hardwood coals, and card table fruit stands selling fresh-squeezed orange juice, and vendors in the middle of the forty-foot-wide road, peddling clothing, old shoes, car parts, and entrenching tools. I get the feeling that a gringo who is just passing through, in a brand-new auto, though it is in fact a rental, is considered to be something of an incursion on reality, and subject to doubts as to the possession of his faculties; as I pull to the side by the tiny corner store, like two dozen kids encircle the vehicle, asking me what's happening, que pasa, que ondo, holding their hands out, seeking proof, perhaps, that I believe that I exist, me with my roll of one hundred-dollar bills, which even to me possess a certain irreality. Given the fact that these hundreds are all I have, I wind up buying out the tienda's entire supply of Pepsi and Yoo-hoo and Jarritos mango soda, and handing it out to the half-dressed kids, along with two cartons of months-old Hershey bars; when it becomes apparent that the store still can't make change, and I tell them to keep it, es para usted, es para usted, they decide to throw an impromptu celebration, cervezas all around for the local men, and bright-pink champagne for the local women, while Grandma builds me, from handmade tortillas, and a cast-iron frying pan of refried beans, and a large pot of stew simmering away behind the counter, two of her hereby famous chile verde burritos. I have never in my entire life had a single meal, from Paris to Marrakesh to Kuala Lumpur to Lisbon, that tasted as good as these two burritos, washed down with a quart of cold Carta Blanca. We stand in the tienda's pilfered electric light, passing an unlabeled bottle of mezcal around, while Grandma packs me two burritos for the road, wrapped up in the family's best linen napkins. I know we're all waiting for something edgy to happen, some kids from a local crack house to show up with knives, steal my roll of hundreds, wreak some sort of havoc; I have, come to think of it, like $20 million just sitting there in my trunk, enough actual cash to support the whole impoverished valley for at least the next twelve months or so, though I doubt they'd really know what to make of my green duffel bag, stuffed as it is with Monopoly money. What happens instead is that I spot a young child, sort of hiding in the corner, maybe Grandma's great-grandson, who's been left out of the celebration; he hasn't had a Hershey bar; he hasn't had a soda. Quieres algo, hijo? Helado, he replies, just above a whisper, and while the store is well-stocked, full of piles of used clothing and re-cycled household items and massive sacks of pinto beans, and even a hand-hammered ancient copper sink, I don't see anything resem-bling a freezer. Helado, Señora? Sí, Sí, helado, bueno, bueno, and out comes an ice cream sandwich from a room in the back, such that Hijo is now beaming, and Great-Grandma is now wearing one of her ancient weathered smiles, as I take a seat on one of the pinto sacks. Of course, leave it to me to spoil the whole sparkling mood; Great-Grandma hands me the burritos, and a fresh bottle of mezcal, and I'm shaking people's hands, and saying Buenas Noches', and Hasta Luegos, all around, when it occurs to me that I haven't got a clue where I'm going, and need to get directions to Lomas de Po-leo, which brings the celebration to an abrupt screeching halt, and the place comes down with a bad case of silence. The light flickers out, then back on, for the moment; floorboards creak, as one of the men shifts his weight; Great-Grandma turns away to stir the pan of frijoles; and then an old woman speaks, in an uninflected tone, for the entire silent room, La bella mujer es su esposa? By now it must be apparent that my Spanish is atrocious, but I have no doubt at all what she means by this: High Noon must have passed through town some time ago, and was now up above, on the spearmint mesa. I try my best to reassure everyone, that she isn't my wife, that she isn't my novia or amiga or even my compañera, but that I would like to find her, and then the old woman grips me by the sleeve of my shirt and leads me into the back, to a room lit by candles, and just when I'm thinking here comes something edgy, or another word to the wise regarding things to stay away from, she pulls me up close to a weird little shrine, and offers up a prayer to the world's strangest deity.

*Santa Muerte*; Lord have mercy; what the fuck is this? This, I can tell you, is nearly impossible to describe; at first I thought it was something else, like the sudden onset of HPPD, Hallucinogen Persisting Perception Disorder, which is admittedly a condition that I thoroughly deserve, with radiating colors in patterns behind the eyes, and a sense of inner time suddenly stretching and looping, and the surfaces of objects appearing to ripple and breathe, and the whole warped world, impossible to circumvent, of an LSD-hallu-cinogenic mental-case meltdown, a terror revisitation, a complete and total cerebral event. When I recover from the initial flashback shock, I'm staring at an object, the statue of Santa Muerte, and she is, let me tell you, a little hard to take in. The first thing I notice is all the flowers and jewels and multilayered clothing, a burst of rainbow colors like you'd see through an acid windowpane: bouquets of pink carnations, yellow roses, red-orange lilies; purple and gold beads, draped around a headdress, a crown of some kind, made of scraps of used tin or maybe corrugated roofing; and a robe of red silk, with a sky-blue lining, and a hood over the head, which is the second thing I notice. The head is a human skull, you'd think I would have noticed that, draped with flowing purple scarves, glittery costume jewelry, and a large gold cross, made of spray-painted gypsum plas-ter, hanging around the place where her neck would be, if, for some reason, she actually had a neck. At the base of the three-foot shrine, which is centered on a square of warped old plywood, sits an enor-mous totemic mound, a cornucopia of offerings: prayer cards, fruit, candy, full tequila bottles, *milagros* of arms and legs and various severed body parts, cigarettes and cigars and dimebags of marijuana buds, medallions, children's toys, charm bracelets, cupcake plates, and a great many burning half-melted votive candles, as if Saint Death herself might somehow be appeased by throwing her a lav-ish candlelit birthday party. Since you know me by now, with my pray-that-the-plane-falls-out-of-the-sky idiosyncratic attitude toward death and dismemberment and dying in general, you know that I'm not afraid of dying at all, but I am truly afraid of Santisima Muerte. She, I can tell you, could make almost anyone afraid of death; guy's standing up on a wobbly old chair, with a noose around his neck, and the thick rope hanging from the open-beam rafters, gets a load of something like this, has a whole change of plans, climbs down off of the chair and decides to clean the kitchen, maybe cook up a Denver omelet with a slice of buttered toast; you find him standing at the cutting board, dicing fresh bell peppers. There is something about the wide-eyed stare of a pair of empty eye sockets, like the darkness is sort of taunting you, daring you to stop whatever you think you're doing, and lean right in, and take a good look around; that void where the nose has been eaten away doesn't appear to offer a lot of empathy either, like sure, you brought fresh flowers all right, now isn't that a lovely though somewhat ironic human gesture; and teeth without lips, Jesus, let me tell you, whatever this woman is smiling at isn't at all subtle, here's hoping she's not expecting me to share her whole worldview, and find myself standing there, getting ready to smile back. The old woman's sing-songing some kind of prayer, and I'm mouthing it right along with her; I have no sense at all what it is that we're praying for, High Noon's health, love everlasting, protection from violence and human disaster, but me I'm praying to the Saint Herself, that dead or alive, come Hell or high water, I never for any reason have to greet her face-to-face. Looking back now, of course, from my current perspective, I see this whole Saint Death thing for exactly what it is, a colorful but silly sort of ignorant superstition; devil fetishes and death deities and the worship of all sorts of strange demented demons, these things are almost as old as drugs, and whether it's Nergal in Babylonia, or the death-god Omulu among West African Yorubans, or Mictlantecuhtli, the blood-spattered Aztec, or Santeria orishas, or Ghede in Vodou, it all boils down to the exact same thing, the primitive fear of our own mortality, and the childish idea that Death can be appeased by verbal supplication and human paraphernalia. I'll tell you one thing, though, if I had it to do over, I wish I'd have left her the mezcal bottle; maybe she'd have listened and heard my childish plea, and I wouldn't, after all, have had to meet her in person.

So I'm standing outside in the cool Anapra night, with the sodium streetlamps blazing away, turning the air around them a dusty sulfurish; the stars overhead look light-smudged and faint; the moon hasn't risen; the evening constellations seem unable to constellate; and while I do have my keys out, preparing to enter my car, I have to admit that I'm having some doubts, like maybe going up there, to the spearmint mesa, is not, after all, such a good idea. I am, to begin with, physically cold; with the end of civil twilight, and gradual cooling of the ancient-seabed scorched-desert earth, the temperature has dropped to somewhere in the 50s, and I'm wearing only a short-sleeved linen shirt, which may or may not account for the degree to which I'm shivering. The street vendors and carnitas grillers and orange-juice entrepreneurs have vanished from the road and gone home to their families; the tienda celebration is a thing of the past, and while I'll never forget it, the store itself has gone empty and dark; even the powdery children and the helado great-grandson and the Carta Blanca men have receded into memory, and left me alone here, on utterly foreign soil. The two real presences hovering over the town, the twin ASARCO smelting chimneys, don't augur well; they seem to be at once both ominous and comatose, with red lights blinking, maybe 500 feet up, as a warning to aircraft that may have drifted from their glide path. Given the external conditions, which do not seem propitious, I make a quick mental inventory of my own inner resources: some sulfurous bourbon from a ramshackle tap; handfuls of Ultras that I have naturally lost count of; the Añejo Reposado, which I highly recommend; a good-sized mound of black tar heroin; a quart of Carta Blanca, cold and wet, to wash down Great-Grandma's legendary burritos; mezcal bottles, both empty and full, though the full one at the moment is leaking from the top, as I drink a little toast to the memory of Santa Muerte. Alongside all this, which makes a pretty good argument for calling it a night, is the fact that I haven't got a clue how I got here, and Julio's disappeared at the Garbage House, and the map that I'm using is empty and useless. Not much to work with if I wanted to press onward, and look for High Noon on a dark expanse of mesa; no real reason to stand here for hours, shivering beside my car, awaiting some sort of signal from a smelting plant on life-support; and nothing to guide me back if I wanted to turn around, not even a damaged aircraft, with its inertial navigation system de-gyrostabilized, preparing to light the way by gliding down the river, and crashing in a ball of flame into downtown El Paso. How I ended up here is a mystery to me: the rental car roadmap information blackout; the loss of my tour guide to a Shakespeare-quoting SWAT team;

the one-way street sign intelligence briefings; the homing-pigeon flight; the spider-thread beach ball; the old-Greek-coin unicursal street-maze; the drift past the last of the good clean hotels, and the July-something Triumph of the Mexican Republic; the ancient magic-passcode levitation oversight, leaving me grounded beneath the Santa Fe crossing; the Julio-made-me-do-it black tar construction detour, on the road to Anapra, via Past There Already; even the thoughtless layout and unidirectional architecture of bourbon and tequila and unlabeled mezcal bottles, which seem to have been designed with one thing in mind, plenty of ways to enter, and not a single well-marked exit; I'm obviously having some difficulty with assigning responsibility, and while I could always blame myself for going along for the ride, I'm not exactly sure where that would get me, other than out here in the cool Anapra night, which is where I am anyway, so really, *why bother?*

In the end, of course, there is no turning back; I have, after all, a puzzle to be solved, though you should feel free to return to El Paso; get yourself a room at the U-Turn Motel; it's not half as bad as what I'm about to tell you. I make a few false starts finding the one dirt road that actually climbs the hill to the top of the mesa, and have to retreat to find the proper landmark, a small adobe house with a fence of Chevy hubcaps; the problem becomes clear on my third or fourth pass, when it turns out I'm mistaking a Cadillac logo, shaped like an acorn, for the classic gold cross, square-on-parallelogram, Heartbeat of America Chevrolet emblem; if only some of life's problems weren't so easily solved; there's a case to be made for staying permanently mistaken. When I finally reach the end of the winding rutted track, and come out on the top of a windy barebones mesa, I can't help feeling that I've come to the right location, meaning everything about the place looks absolutely wrong: Lomas de Poleo, like Julio said, looks more like a Soviet gulag or a Fascist concentration camp than what it started out to be, an ordinary Juárez lower-income subdivision; you'd rather be the barbed-wire supplier than the guy with the home-remodeling concession, like most of these small homes have been remodeled enough already, emptied of their occupants, and bulldozed into rubble piles. I park in the desert maybe 50 yards out, choke down some Ultras with a swallow of mezcal, and take a good long look around Lomas de

Poleo; let's just say, while the name sounds lovely, if you're looking for something in a planned community, the names around here can be somewhat misleading; this may not be as bad as *Oasis de Anapra*, but even by the liberal standards of modern real estate promotion, *Lomas de Poleo* is a bit of a stretch. First of all, "Lomas," meaning "hills" or "hillocks," has nothing to do with Lomas de Poleo, any more than Puerto de Anapra has something to do with ports; as far as the eye can see, there is nothing but flat-top mesa, though "Poleo," or Pennyroyal, a toxic plant in the mint family, is out here all right, in poisonous abundance, and the flat-black night is toxically fragrant; picture yourself, in the dead of night, at a Gated Community on the outskirts of Nothing, leafing through the glossy sales brochure, for something they're calling *Pennyroyal Hills*, or *Spearmint Knolls*, or maybe it's *The Dunes at Menthol Ridge*, whatever it is, it sounds delicious, though whatever you do, don't eat the lawn, and you might want to check that your brand-new home hasn't been built with an Xcavator Backhoe. The marketing claims, on the other hand, regarding Lomas de Poleo as a gated community, are, if anything, vastly understated: surrounded by miles of barbed-wire fencing, topped with coils of razor wire; a perimeter lit up by carbon-arc klieg lights, and studded with twenty-foot sniper towers; homes protected by the latest in security, the Bulldozed and Backhoed Entry-Proof House; and the main gate, if anything, over-engineered, twin-leaf blast doors of steel and concrete, with a rebar matrix welded to the frames, like whatever you do, don't push the doorbell, unless you're wearing a ballistic helmet, and have training in Explosive Ordnance Disposal; by any standard, this place looks secure, to Nazi labor camp specifications, though the laborers, apparently, are now long gone, as if an entire Juárez subdivision had been taken into protective custody, and immediately depopulated, to guard it against anything resembling a populace. The meaning of this place has gone so totally awry that even the garbled SWAT-team leader is starting to make some sense, talking about spearmint cooking and the Pennyroyal treatment and abortive malefactions and *dónde está el poeta maldito*: like here I am now, outside Lomas de Poleo, and the endless wind-blown mesa is covered with stubby poleo bushes, *Mentha pulegium*, known from the time of the ancient Greeks, at least among the impoverished, as an effective abortifacient, or maybe just the thing to start your menstrual flow, a spearmint emmenagogic, meaning you brew up a cup of penny-royal tea, and in no time at all, you'll be bleeding and unpregnant. And speaking of time, it must be time to get moving, because the wheels of my car are once again rolling forward; while I'd greatly prefer to just sit here drinking, maybe hang around waiting for the moon's inertial climb, I don't seem to have much choice in the matter, as I, evidently, am going along for the ride. As I roll up at last to the blast-door gates, wishing I'd come more appropriately equipped, with a cyanide capsule hidden under my tongue, and my lungs full of mentholated Nazi opiates, I'm half expecting the usual snickering thugs with guns, and Alsatian attack dogs, and a brass-knuckled Kommandant in a Schutzstaffel trenchcoat, lead-ing a squad of Einsatzkommandos to greet me in the klieg lights, but the doors to the camp are ajar and unmanned, so I park in the carbon-arc shadow of a wall, and go forward alone on foot, along a stretch of barbed fencing, through the open security gates, and into the empty compound. If I were you, right about here, I would definitely turn around, go back to El Paso. If you're looking for something in an empty compound, try diacetylmorphine cut with quicklime powder; this may sound like an obvious error, mixing pain relief with corpse disposal, but trust me, I've been there, and I know where we're headed; you're far better off at the U-Turn Motel, making a terrible mistake, a hideous blunder, and standing, as it were, permanently corrected.

Just inside the gate, I slip past one of the empty watchtowers, toward a group of flat-roofed bungalows, one of which is lit from within by a sterile white lamplight. The buildings here, in this flat-roofed group, are, so to speak, not from around here; they have more in common with the klieg lights and razor wire than with the improvised assemblages of Puerta de Anapra. It would be easy enough to think that I am drawn to these buildings by some sense of their difference, the sense of their having been planned and ex-ecuted, at the end of a long day that feels highly improvisational; I don't, however, seem to have much choice, since other than piles of rebar, and bulldozed chunks of native adobe, I don't see much of anything else, and simply wandering off into a vast field of rubble, in the dead of night, unaccompanied, wouldn't appear to make much sense, even to me, at this late hour. And then there's the fact, difficult to dismiss, particularly given how few facts I possess, that I've spotted a sign that I'm on the right track, meaning heading dead straight in the wrong direction: an armor-plated black Suburban, parked let's say next to Bungalow B, one building removed from Bungalow A, and all the sterile lamplight optical clarity. In case you were wondering, the hood is still warm, and there is nothing of note amid the grey leather seating, unless you're in the market for a new SUV, in which case I can tell you that this particular model comes phenomenally well-equipped, particularly with cup holders, both pop out and fixed, in this case full of soft drink conveyors from Church's Fried Chicken; I don't know about you, but when it comes to abducting women, Diet Pepsi Max is not the first thing I think of. There's a two-foot space between the black Suburban and the darkened bungalow, and since the engine is still warm, and I'm still basically shivering, I'm comfortably crouched here, I don't know, waiting. To be honest about it, I seem to be having some trouble controlling my nerves, like the light from that window, in Bungalow A, looks so peculiarly white that the effect is unnerving. I wish I could tell you that right about here, I suddenly notice an ominous watchtower, perched at the top of a rusted metal pole, and the profile of a sniper, backlit by arc lamps, slowly taking aim through his front-focal riflescope, apparently mistaking me for a stationary crow; or that when the time finally comes to cross the last thirty feet, and take a good long look in that optical window, I find myself surrounded by men in balaclavas, and am forced to make a run for it, toward the barbed-wire fencing, through a hailstorm of bullets and light weapons ordnance; what I need now is another Hadamard disaster, a Juárez street-scene firefight implosion, with ubiquitous smoke and aliphatic hydrocarbons and some thermobaric HEAB-round verbal pyrotechnics, where I immediately disappear inside my Schwarzschild radius, and wander around forever like the razor-thin dogs, searching the smoking holes for ice cream children; or let's face it, a simple death ray would do, beamed down on top of me from a hovering spacecraft, it makes very little difference how the thing actually works, just as long as it sets me semantically adrift, out of the rubble-field, into semiotic exile. If you left it up to me, right about here, something goes wrong, I suddenly hear a group of six or eight men, behind me in the klieg lights, closing up the gates, and wrapping them with a chain, and applying a milspec Miracle Padlock, locking me tight in my own mental compound, and I'm so completely engrossed in the feeling of being trapped, which I describe in some detail, that I don't notice a man who is crouched right beside me, flicking open a switchblade and holding it to my throat, ready to put an end to me if I even so much as whisper, like I can't talk now, this guy's going to kill me. Imagine a deadly silence as we struggle for the knife, rolling over together in the barrio street dust, with each man in turn seeming to gain the upper hand, pushing the gleaming blade toward a pulsing carotid artery, until, at long last, muscles exhausted, the better man wins, and I'm lying there dead, with a knife stuck deep in my opiated rib cage. I have, let's face it, any number of ideas; if worse came to worse, I could fall down a wellhole, hitting my drunken head on a large chunk of concrete, and as I finally hit bottom, and am finished off for good, I wind up facedown in a pool of my own urine. Unfortunately for me, none of this happens, and I suddenly feel ridiculous crouching here alone, and decide to just get up, and walk to the lamplit window, though I do, admittedly, stop to take a leak; I've been driving around for hours, and certainly feel I've earned it.

So what's inside the window? Virtually nothing: two men in lab coats; a corpse tied to a chair; and basically nothing else, no SWAT team, no guns, no airburst weaponry, and no High Noon at all, unless she's the cadaver tied to the chair. There's not much I can tell you about the corpse itself; other than being a woman, with a sheet or a drop cloth draped around the shoulders, it's basically featureless, for reasons we'll come to. Let me ask you this: how much do you know about surgical instrumentation? Do you happen to know the difference between a Volkman Bone Hook Retractor, and a Ribbon Retractor, in relation to their utility on a surgical incision? If a surgically opened artery suddenly began to bleed, and they left it up to you to gain control of the bleeding, would you know how to choose between the Haemostatic Mixter forceps and the Finochietto box joint forceps, or maybe the Collin's Sellors, with a Collin lock and oval jaws? Suppose I were to tell you that a #19 scalpel, for cutting skin and muscle, and for general carving and stencil making, required a #4 handle, while a #12a, a crescent-shaped blade, sharpened on the inner curvature, required a #3 or perhaps a #7, would you be able to tell me that I finally got it right? Me neither. Why do I ask? We're coming to that as well. Inside the window, under deep-cavity shadow-control sterile illumination, are two men in lab coats, and a cadaver tied to a high-backed chair. The two men are working, in disposable latex gloves, performing a dissection of the dark-haired cadaver, stripping the flesh of the face away, using black-handled scalpels and double-edged lancets; they work taking turns, selecting their instruments from a stainless steel tray, like dental hygienists choosing scalers and curettes. The man on the left, holding a triangular blade, with a flat cutting edge that extends from the handle, is filleting the muscle over the temporal bone, just next to the ear, which was apparently removed somewhat earlier in the procedure. The man to his right has already selected a long-handled chisel blade, and will soon begin tapping on the bridge of the nose, just below the nasal bone, separating the cartilage, and then shifting from the chisel to a crescent-shaped blade, using the sharpened outer edge of the curve as a scraper, beginning with the ethmoid bone, and then down into the nasal concha, ending with the volmer, and the tip of the nasal spine. The movements here are rhythmic, steady and precise, like they're working to a metronome, although nothing is hurried; they seem to shift effortlessly between scalpel-handling techniques, alternating, when appropriate, between the Palmar, or "dinner knife" grip, and the "pencil" grip used for more precision cutting, the grip being utilized for the gradual displacement of the eyebrows themselves from the underlying supraorbital bone. Once the nose has been completed, the upper lip is carved away, in a single piece of flesh, by another flat-cutting-edge triangular blade that resembles an X-Acto knife, and dropped in a white plastic bucket next to the chair, a bucket that is maybe one-sixteenth full, though the men are almost finished; the face, as it turns out, has very little flesh. While their lab coats are smeared and streaked with Congo red dye, a sodium salt derivative of benzidine and naphthionic acid, the two men are taking remarkable care to control the loss of embalming fluid, using surgical gauze and Schwartz clips and bulldog clamps and some kind of elastomeric liquid sealant. Given the fact that the dissection itself seems to be proceeding more or less at random, with little or no attention be-

ing paid to the details of the cranio-maxillofacial structure, other
than to the underlying facial bones themselves, most of which at
this point are fully exposed, this attention to the loss of preservative fluids would appear to be somewhat puzzling, if not altogether
misguided, until an artery is severed near the hairline of the frontal
bone, and has to be clamped with a tiny micro-aneurysm clip, and
it suddenly becomes apparent that while the men themselves know
precisely what they're doing, I, for one, do not have a clue.

Why would two men, streaked with Congo red dye, dissecting
the face of an upright cadaver, in a manner more consistent with the
cleaning of teeth than with that of serious students of facial anatomy,
come equipped with a tiny micro-aneurysm clip? This remarkable
instrument, smaller than a penny, now being attached to stop the
steady rhythmic pulsing of fluid from a severed artery, is certainly
not part of a standard cadaver dissection kit. So what is it doing
here? For that matter, how is it possible that a basic human corpse,
stripped of its face flesh, down to the underlying bone structure, has
emitted a low moan and is now being resilenced by the application
of a cloth likely dampened with ether? Something has gone wrong
here. What's inside the window? Under deep-cavity shadow-control
sterile illumination, there are two men in lab coats, and a living
cadaver. This, truly, is a deep semiotic problem: call it a dream, it
does not change anything. So how much do you know about human facial transplant surgery? The first successful facial transplant
was actually something of a hideous misnomer. A young woman in
India, whose hair had been caught in the blades of a wheat thresher,
was rushed to the hospital, along with her skull flesh, which was
then reattached, in a lengthy but successful surgical procedure. She
emerges from surgery, still recognizably herself, and returns to her
village, where people know her when they see her; when they call
out her name, she answers to that name. This initial proof of concept was then followed by other, more complex, procedures, replacing the face of a dog-mauling victim with the face of a brain-dead
but otherwise living human, or a similar procedure, also successful,
that restored a face, not in any way her own, to a woman shot point-
blank, by her mentally unstable husband, with number 9 birdshot
using a 12-gauge shotgun. In neither of these cases did the women
change their names, though in honor of either one of them, I'd be

willing to change my own. So how would I respond to a woman exchanging faces, not with another woman, but with her own inner bone structure, leaving her face behind her, in a white plastic bucket, but with her own two eyes remaining strangely intact? I'm guessing it would be difficult to look myself in the mirror, from any conceivable angle, while leaving my inner being in any way intact. I'm not, at the moment, however, looking in a mirror, and I'm not looking through a window into a brightly lit room; I'm outside a bungalow, in Lomas de Poleo, Mexico, taking a few deep breaths of the spearmint night air, but basically doubled over, losing my dinner, and I'd rather put my eyes out than have another look. Unfortunately for me, I now hear voices in the shadow-controlled room, and who should I see but Ms. High Noon, Ms. Sistine Madonna, and a man in a three-piece chalk-stripe suit, holding what looks to be an antique pocket watch, and telling the lab coats to please hurry up. High Noon, at least, lets out a muffled scream, and covers her face; at least she isn't watching. She's gasping and moaning and saying Gomez make it stop and Gomez is making a cryptic sort of face, in High Noon's direction, like let this be a lesson we will keep between the two of us. This, truly, I wish they would have done; I wish, for the record, I hadn't seen any part of this, though I seem to be mesmerized by the metronomic display of surgical competence, and have no sense at all that I should somehow make it stop. I am, admittedly, holding something up, which turns out to be like a thirty-pound cinderblock, as though I might have been thinking about using it as a weapon, or throwing it through the window to create a distraction, or maybe even dropping the whole block on my head, anything at all to make myself look away, as it now appears evident that I can't help myself, I'm like the local Peeping Tom, a voyeur of the hideous, I can see myself now, reflected in the window glass, a man who can't stop looking, a man who likes to watch.

Which brings us back around, somewhat circuitously, to the Radisson Hotel, on Avenida Tecnologico, or Rafael Perez Serna, or maybe I'm on the highway, Panamericana, where the sun is coming up, for better or worse. I have no clue at all how I got here from there; perhaps I blacked out and drove my car back through the desert; or maybe I called a wrecker, and had myself towed; or it could have been a case of spacecraft abduction, and quantum teleportation via Pipe Dream truck. One moment I was standing there, aware of my own presence, with the moon beginning to rise over an alien landscape, and the next thing I knew, I was nowhere to be found, so you tell me, I'm somewhat at a loss here. I wish I could tell you I had the presence of mind to book a nice clean room, have a chat with the desk clerk, and manage my own luggage like a perfectly normal tourist; one wonders, however, what sort of figure I must have cut, traipsing through the lobby with a thirty-pound cinderblock. My toiletry kit, which I absolutely need, has turned up missing, and may be on the Pipe Dream truck, though I do have rather an interesting assortment of tools and implements for the now dawning day, spread out across the desk as if I knew what to do with them: a map of the area, with a route marked in red, to a circled location labeled Casa Cronómetro; a black brick of heroin, partially smoked, from the S*Mart backpack, to keep me company; a note from High Noon, from which the route-marks were derived, telling me to meet her at the eponymous hour, which I know from experience to be closer to 1:20; a lifetime supply of 300mg Ultras, perhaps aptly named, given some of the things I've witnessed, though this may be yet another of my problematic signifiers, since the pharmaceutical label reads Time-Release Tramadol; and a bottle of mezcal, still leaking from the top, now serving as a paperweight for this enormous pile of nonsense. I told you all along to go back to El Paso, get a room at the U-Turn, a copy of Hustler. I think we can both agree, when it comes to Lomas de Poleo, the best thing for everyone is to deny the whole thing; let this be a lesson we will keep between the two of us, though you might want to burn those clothes you're wearing, take care of your little spearmint problem. If you happen to see a woman walking around with no face, do us all a favor and look the other way; the women around here have more than enough to cope with, without people constantly staring at their gradual disappearance; women, in Juárez, are always already beginning to vanish. In the meantime, I'm thinking that you should maybe leave, I mean who let you in here, go down and try the breakfast buffet; as a matter of fact, please show yourself out, and take the room mirrors with you, they're nothing but trouble, and hang that little sign on the outside of the door there, meaning stay the hell away from me, like Do Not Disturb.

# 26

Gabriella, let me ask you something. When did I arrive here, I mean here in Guanajuato? It seems like only yesterday, though as a matter of fact, it *was* only yesterday, when I awoke in my small hotel, *El Mesón de los Poetas*, and discovered that I was somehow here, awake and alive in the mountains of central Mexico, but with no sense at all of how this had come to pass, or even who had made this rather startling discovery. That first time I saw you, with your small tin can, out on the iron-railed balcony, watering your yellow and red geraniums, it seemed to me that you were going about your life, while I, in a sense, had no life to go about; I was sitting on the edge of the bed, staring out the window at the Guanajuato valley, and everything was new to me, the cobblestone streets, the pastel buildings, the church spires and clock towers and rose-colored basilica domes, even my own knowledge was news to me, though in this case the news was far from inspiring, as though I'd just moved into another man's house, and had no use at all for the man's belongings. In place of my own identity, I had an absurdly constructed facsimile of an identity, modeled after a man who did not exist, Alvaro de Campos, one of the pseudonyms of a long-dead poet. The fact that I bear a striking resemblance to the long-dead poet, Fernando Pessoa, lent my identity a somewhat improbable air, an aura of deliberate and calculated artifice, as though by equipping me for life with a dead man's face, and the identity of a man the dead man had constructed, my own existence were somehow taunting me, mocking me into being as a kind of visual pun, an elaborate joke at my own expense. On top of everything, Alvaro de Campos himself, only one of any number of Pessoa's strange creations, couldn't have cared less about who or what he actually was, or what was to become of him, even in the short run; while I, being me, and not some stroke of poetic genius, had some immediately pressing problems that weren't so easily dismissed, like whose toothbrush was I using, and who owned my clothes, and what, if anything, was I to make of myself, given the haphazard nature of my mental foundations. And then you came out with a load of wash, and a blue plastic bucket, to hang your laundry, and I no longer cared that I was something of a sham, a man whose authenticity was out of the question; I was more than willing to go forward with what I had, a sense of all existence as utterly unlikely, and nevertheless the case, however improbable, though in my case the likelihood was improbably low, since I was, in all honesty, an elaborate contrivance. Perhaps, in retrospect, I should have faced up to the truth; I might have been better off going straight to the police, and turning myself in as an obvious imposter. Why yes, of course, sir, we see what you mean, this man in the grey fedora couldn't possibly be you; what, precisely, do you propose we do next? Have you locked up for identity fraud? If you choose to walk around impersonating a long-dead poet, or even more improbably, one of the poet's own creations, this may be in somewhat questionable taste, but it hardly rises to the level of a jailable offense. Perhaps if you'd actually written something, and published it, for example, in the dead man's name, we could charge you with some sort of reverse plagiarism, though it's highly unlikely we'll find this in the penal code; we, I'm afraid, aren't really trained for this sort of thing; you might try down the street at the Modern Language Association. In the end, of course, I had no real choice; I had to go on with my life, even though, admittedly, I had no life to go on with. And then you came out for the third and final time, well past noon, to gather up your laundry, and I was dispatched, into the streets, to go about my life as a ship's engineer, from Barrow-in-Furness, which is somewhere in Cumbria, with an ATM card whose PIN I could not produce, an identity card full of deliberate disinformation, and a sense of myself as the 1,000 Peso Man, who wouldn't last long at the rate that I was going. All of this was yesterday, Friday morning, and here we are now on Saturday night, as though a lifetime had passed between then and now, and yet it seems like only moments ago, when I think of the time between now and then; from now to then goes by in a moment, while from then to now seems endless and vast. Running into you again, and meeting Gustavo; finding $20 million that wasn't mine to spend; fighting the losing battle with Ramírez Tabares, with nothing at all at stake, over the uselessness of poetry; eating gorditas in the Quixote museum, justifying craziness to get back control of reason; discovering Bird's Nest Tom, at the end of a long linguistics error, an error that certainly bore repeating, precisely in reverse, in order to return at last to the Guanajuato time war; my wine-fueled meditation, without spilling a drop, on Nezahualcoyotl's Life Giver poetry, in microscopic print on the 100-peso note, reminding us to love our Brother, Man, though only in mistranslation can we actually stand him; getting lost on the blue-lip milk-bubble streets, and finding that none of us is rich until the least of us is cared for; the history of time, a brush of your lips, the flailing among the nameless stars, the bowl of chile verde stew that almost took my head off; I feel like I've lived enough in the last two days not to care at all if I were to die tomorrow, but if yesterday were Friday, when my true life began, what was the nature of the day before that? A moment ago, my chile verde bowl was full; a moment ago, there was a bird on your rooftop; though I know, to you, I have it all backwards, and your now empty bowl would take forever to refill, spoonful by spoonful, precisely in reverse. In just a little while, the evening will be over, we will sit and watch the candle burn down toward the wick-end, and lick its pale plate for the last of the light, and maybe for just a moment we will sit here together, though I will be headed off into the darkness, going one way, and you will be headed the other way, back into the flickering light.

You seem so quiet, Alvaro. There is something that is troubling you?

It's nothing, Gabriella. This evening has been wonderful.

And yet you are brooding, melancolía. You are not feeling like yourself?

I am worried a little, worried about the past.

Ah, the past, this is nothing. You can do nothing about the past.

It is over and done with. Nothing will come of brooding upon the past.

Yesterday, Friday, I awoke in Guanajuato. What can you tell me about the day before that?

Thursday?

Thursday.

Let me check my calendar. Thursday, the 16th of April. You were not feeling well. We came to your hotel.

And before that?

Before that, we attended the party, the April 16 party with Señor Ramírez. You have seen the photos of this evening. I think you were a little drunk.

And before that?

Before that, you were also drunk, muy borracho, on the April 16 airplane flight from Chihuahua, where your money was made safe by Tío Gustavo, and just prior to that was the disassembly of the truck.

The truck?

Yes, the large black truck that we had driven across the desert, through Sacramento and El Gallego and Laguna de Patos, and before that Ranchería, and before that, El Kilo. You were driving like a crazy man, totalmente loco, un poco demente.

Where did we start from, Gabriella?

We started from your hotel, El Mesón de los Poetas. Surely you must remember this. It is just across the street from here. You were not feeling well. You were in need of a little sleep.

In that case, where does the story end? Where is the end of all this beginning?

In the April 16 house you did not belong in, not in your condition. You were not at all functioning, you were useless and dim-witted, and the yard was like a graveyard, the men had guns and quicklime sacks, you were not as yet Alvaro, the men there called you by another name.

This April 16 house was in Juárez?

Sí. This is the end of our story. There in the Gomez clock house, where Señor Ramírez had the holes all dug, and everything happened at once, there at Casa Cronómetro, what Gomez calls his Stopwatch House. This is not a house I should ever have arrived at. If men wish to fight and die over lavender money and large gold bars, this is not a life I choose for myself, this is a life that is chosen for me, for reasons I do not wish to recall. I worry for the life of Tío Gustavo, I do not worry for your life at all. I could kill you myself for involving me in any of this. You are not a good man. No wonder they call you Douchebag.

# PART III

# 27

R aymond, needless to say, did not put the gun down. Even supposing that Ramírez was correct, and it was high time for everyone to have an open and frank discussion, there was no reason at all for anyone to believe that the absence of the Mossberg would be an aid to communication. Ray was already wearing one of Ramírez' prior communiqués, a veterinary-sutured X-shaped chest-wound, delivered via knife blade at the Bar of the Wounded Tree; about the last thing he needed, under the circumstances, was another word to the wise requiring surgical intervention. He ducked back under the window casement, easing the all-black shotgun down, out of the general and catoptric sightlines, and conducted a brief review of the tactical situation. Before we all run scurrying off for the nearest dictionary of optical terminology, "catoptric" refers to the phenomena of mirrors, and the nature of reflected imagery, and the fact that Ramírez has spotted Raymond, or more properly Raymond's mirror image, in a looking glass on the far side wall, above an open quicklime sack, eliminating, for the moment, the element of surprise, and necessitating a slight, though decisive, revision, in a plan to proceed using ambuscadal tactics. Here again, we don't need a glossary, or even Wittgenstein to remind us that to imagine a language means to imagine a form of life: ambush; think ambush; which is precisely what Raymond was no longer thinking. Seven men were seated around a large square coffee table, at the center of which stood a bottle of tequila, and a glass approximately one-eighth full of a dark brown liquid known as chuchupaste, a substance whose presence Ray found puzzling. Given the fact that several of these men have come to the table with automatic firearms, why would the presence of this simple substance, also known as osha extract, be so troubling to Raymond under the circumstances? Even though a narrative lifetime has passed, vanished forever, in the very last instant, the instant when Raúl Antonio Ramírez Tabares spotted Raymond, and offered to pose a question that has plagued the philosophers, just as he'd done at El Arbolito, the Bar of the Wounded Tree, Raymond has been maintaining an impossible temporal linguistic fiction, an imaginary form of life involving the freeing of his friend Eugene, through a precipitate-onslaught moment of explosive interrogatories, directed unexpectedly at the back of a human head, posing, as it were, most of the eternally vexing questions, while at the same time setting Ramírez' mind completely and utterly at rest; what Ray would be troubled by, what he would in fact find troubling, if he had a better grasp of propositional calculus, is that the presence here of chuchupaste, positioned dead center on a large square truth-table, exposes quite a flaw in his temporal logic. Before we bring in the Fuzzy Logicians, however, and start talking about representations on the truth-space diagram, and multiple objective evolutionary algorithms for temporal linguistic rule extraction, we should probably keep in mind that Raymond is leaking, gradually losing body fluids through a poorly sutured chest-wound, and needs to form a plan, to spring Eugene, that doesn't involve advice from a bunch of logicians; if Ray waits for us to bring him up to speed on the latest advances in temporal semantics, he'll bleed to death in a Juárez side-yard. Raymond Carlisle Edmunds III, crouched in the bushes outside a pale taupe ranch house, absently fingering the missing safety button on a Mossberg 500 pistol-grip Cruiser, knows nothing at all about Fuzzy Logicians, or temporal linguistic rule extraction, or the utility of integrating the truth-space diagram with fuzzy-logic componentry in decision-support systems; what Raymond knows is Gun, and the language of absolute steel-pellet weaponry, and right about now, to Ray's way of thinking, the solution to Ramírez' whole truth-space problem is to stand up and shoot him in the back of the head. Not that Ray's got anything at all against Ludwig Wittgenstein personally, but to imagine a language, when it comes to Ramírez, means to imagine a form of shotgun death.

Raymond, in other words, was in no mood for philosophizing, and if the philosophers needed plaguing, he planned to do it himself. And yet…in the back of Ray's mind, he's still got some sort of temporal linguistics problem, something to do with chuchupaste, and the time it would take to get his truth-space established. His evolutionary-algorithm decision-support system is setting off alarms, and he's holding his fire, though the temporal modal logic here is more than a little hazy. Ramírez, seated at 6:00 o'clock, with his back to Raymond, couldn't be more than eight feet away; his men with Beretta 93Rs, at 3:00 o'clock and 9:00 o'clock in relation to Raymond's current window, would have no rejoinders at all to the Mossberg replication, and would be dead before the Gomez French Statuary chronometer, with the Graham-pallet locking-faces of a deadbeat escapement, from the Golden Age of mechanical horology, could release another pointed tooth, on a small round escape wheel, and count another moment down, on the Universal Clock; this unusual timepiece, by the way, familiar to readers of the *Discworld* novels, does not tell what *time* it is, it instead tells Time what *it* is, going around only once, as most of us could be said to do, counting each of the moments down until the end of Time itself. The Universal Clock, telling Time what *it* is, obviously speaks a language that Raymond understands, the language of the battlefield, and the firefight time-bomb tick-tock instant, meaning kill or be killed; the thing speaks perfect Gun. What Raymond has in mind, in short, isn't waiting around for the perfect moment; he's planning on seizing the moment itself, and filling it full of O-shaped holes. So what on earth is he waiting for? Positioned dead center in the middle of a large square coffee table, like the pivot point on the hands of a clock, is a glass of brownish fluid that is puzzling to Raymond, in terms of his assessment of the battlespace chronology, and the spaciotemporal logistical dynamics of imposing several O-shaped rapid-fire deaths. The presence here of chuchupaste, also known as osha extract, points, as these things tend to do, toward any number of perfectly valid suppositions: the osha, an extract from the Bear Root plant, could certainly be here for medicinal purposes, to counter an immune-deficiency problem, or enhance the mood of an injured bear, or a bear trying to awaken from a deep hibernation, any number of which might be applicable to Raymond, though due to its similarity to poison hemlock, and water hemlock, which is also deadly, Ray might want to smell it first, make sure it smells like celery stalk, before he simply drinks it down, and finds himself jumping to the wrong conclusion. While hemlock would certainly alter the battlespace, it's not quite the battle that Raymond has in mind, and would likely leave him counting down the last of the moments, until Time expired on his Universal Clock.

Ray, at the moment, however, isn't thinking about drinking hemlock; he's thinking about drinking chuchos, chuchupaste mixed with Tequila Orendain. While this might seem somewhat odd, for a man stone-loaded on an opioid analgesic, dressed in a Rockport Shadow plaid, a shirt that was previously blue and green, and is now not only not a plaid, but is an ooze-soaked shade of bloody brownish, the drink itself has meaning to Ray, as his signature drink from El Arbolito, the bar where he and Ramírez first met, and had a lengthy and one-sided Socratic elenchus, leaving Raymond not only scratching his head, but leaking from an X-shaped cryptic wound, a worthless and illegible autograph in Braille. In the land of the blind, the one-eyed man...no, no, delete that, not only is Ramírez not in any way blind, but he seems to be possessed of a considerable amount of foresight, having prepared in advance for Raymond's arrival, by setting the table with his signature drink. While Raymond's been playing tic-tac-toe, Ramírez has laid out an endgame in chess, with All Black to move but puzzled by the position. In suicide chess...but no, no, delete this as well; it's an interesting exercise, full of mandatory carnage, but the strange world of Antichess takes time to adjust to, and Raymond, at the moment, is up against the clock. With All Black to move, in an endgame of blitz chess, where several pieces are armed with Universal Timepieces, the threat of a sudden death instantaneous forfeiture looms over everyone; tick-tock; tick-tock. He places one hand on the pump-action fore-end of the Mossberg, inserts his finger into firing position on the trigger of the Cruiser's pistol grip, and readies himself mentally to make the All Black move, when a sudden whiff of celery stalk wafts out of the open window, causing Ray to come out of a deep hibernation, and lower his weapon, and withdraw his move: Raymond's had a glimpse of the crux of the position, and the endgame outcome is a stalemate at best. Before we bring in Karpov and Capablanca, and wind up with a page full of cryptic symbols, the algebraic chess notations for Zugzwang and Squeeze Plays in the endgame of chess, we need to face the fact that we've wandered into yet another discourse realm that Raymond could give a shit about, like Ray could care less about a fucking game of chess. Can we net this out in Professional Soldier? Not only does Ray lack the element of surprise, but these men around the table have been patiently awaiting him, having long ago seized the battlespace initiative, and taken the liberty of forging his signature to the terms of surrender, in chuchupaste ink. Raymond, in effect, has been thoroughly outflanked, meaning right at this moment a machine-pistol Beretta, with its foregrip unfolded and its safety unlocked, has been stationed to the right of Eugene Booker, and positioned to burst-fire the side of his head; and while nothing would have prevented Ray from first eliminating the man who is holding this Beretta to the side of Gene's head, had the battlespace not been shaped in advance, this particular line of attack has itself been eliminated, well in advance of Raymond's arrival, by situating something, like another human head, directly in the middle of Ray's line of fire; Raymond, in short, doesn't have a shot. A limited collateral damage preemptive strike, in the Ghost-Ring jargon of the Briley-choked Mossberg, spelling out the zero-hour for Ramírez and his men, has thus been rendered effectively moot, leaving Raymond at something of a loss for words, with his mouth full of metallic-tasting but hollow propositions, and his plan for Gene's freedom buried if not dead.

Ray peaked back over the window ledge, still holding his 9-shot pump-fed ultimatum, and double-checked his thinking, which turns out to be correct: if he time-stamps Ramírez with the pistol-grip Cruiser, Gene takes a burst-fire logging-event to the head. The crux of the position, prepared in advance for Raymond's perusal, is, in essence, biochronological: the proper first move, on the 3:00 o'clock Beretta, just next to Eugene, on a 2:00 pm stool, is blocked, on the diagonal, by Let's Say 4:20, seated beside Ramírez on an off-white couch. An off-white couch? Setting aside for a moment the utter absence of imagination involved in filling a death house with off-white décor, our mention of 4:20, the pawn blocking Ray on the All Black f-file, exposes quite a flaw in our narrative chronology, the crux of which is a temporal synchronization problem, involving multimedia data heterogeneity and state machine key generation and blind media watermark protection through temporal redundancy in the watermarking key space, that Raymond himself can't be expected to solve: in the four or five seconds since Ramírez last spoke, and offered to pose a question that has plagued the philosophers, we, in all likelihood, have been going about our lives, doing the family laundry, stopping off for kitty litter, trying to keep our three-year-old from coloring in crayon all over the walls, and we have, let's face it, with so much on our minds, completely forgotten, if it ever even registered, why these men are sitting here and who the hell they are. Unless we're all prepared to take a twenty-minute break, and go back to find the pages of Ray's last chapter, which for all we know, given the interval that's passed, may now be in the middle of an entirely different book, we're going to need a brief review of who's around the coffee table, waiting to see what happens when the next thing happens, and assuming, for the moment, that something happens next.

Raymond, we know; he's a former soldier, with some history in Iraq, a man of the next indicated action, who's come to Juárez, with a friend named Jennifer, in a small white Toyota, as the indicated act; Jennifer herself, a derivatives trader for a man named Gomez, the money-laundering clock-collector and Shakespeare wit for the Juárez Cartel, is off somewhere in a nearby park, maybe riding the miniature train around, waiting for Raymond to finish up work. Ray's brother in arms, Eugene, now bound and gagged atop a 2:00 o'clock stool, has been brought to the pale taupe ranch house, in a convenient Juárez subdivision, by two of Gomez' trenchcoated men, apparently under some duress, in Raymond's Black Ram Magnum. Gomez' men do not look well: not only have Ramírez' subordinates dispossessed them of their weapon, but both are wearing ligatures, and dazed and confused expressions. One of the men, known as Tinkerbell, for his wand-like waving of an AR-15, appears to be awaiting pick-up by FedEx or the parcel post, and is seated directly across from Ramírez; if Ramírez is seated at 6:00 o'clock, with his back to the window through which Raymond's been staring, then Tinkerbell would be seated right around Noon, bound up tight with shipping tape, and rendered speechless by the turn of events, during which he's not only lost his weapon, but somehow had his mouth taped shut. The other man, known as Tinkerbell's Twin, if only because he is similarly dressed, and Ray hasn't bothered to separately name him, is seated to the right of Ramírez on the couch, at Let's Say 4:20, with a garment-bag of plastic, running low on oxygen and high on carbon dioxide, expanding and contracting in the area around his head. At 3:00 and 9:00, across the table from each other, sit Ramírez' men, holding elegant handguns; Ray knows these men to be members of the Thetas, a rival cartel's designated assassins; how these men gained control of the situation, in a Gomez safe house, is anybody's guess. Raymond has a thought: someone fucked up. If Ray were asked to expand a bit, as to the layout of the room, and its current configuration, and how it's come to pass that Gene's in the hands of paramilitary enforcers for the Sinaloa Cartel, Raymond has another thought: someone fucked up big time. Gomez' men have brought Gene here, to bury him in the garden, and bid him a fond farewell, with quicklime and shovels; caught off guard by Ramírez and his men, with burst-fire Berettas and homicidal aptitudes, they've surrendered control of their wand-like weapon, along with their hopes of being treated with fondness, and would soon be bidding themselves farewell, if such a thing were possible. The wild card in the room is a man known as Douchebag, if only because his actions have made no apparent sense, who is seated in an easy chair at give or take 10:30, across from Ramírez at something of an angle, looking like a man who has recently joined a book club, and is utterly clueless, having forgotten to read the book. Raymond has a final thought: this guy is a douchebag. After chasing the man around for the last several years, years dating back to a rose-tinted dawn, and the Morning Star beginnings of some long-forgotten day, yesterday in fact, the 15th of April, just trying to catch his name before reality overtook him, Raymond has given up on learning the man's identity, and is willing to let it go, or perhaps leave his own mark on the namespace in the time domain, by blowing an O-shaped hole in the middle of his torso. There is something of a long story behind this idiosyncratic pellet-scatter, hollow in the center, like a zero or an O, caused by an arbitrary mismatch between the rifling of the Mossberg and the triple-decker shotgun shells loaded in the extension tube, and while

Ray might have preferred the Gaussian-distributed absence created by the Brenneke Gold Magnum shells, right at the moment, he couldn't care less; if the guy winds up with an alphanumeric ambiguity problem, maybe an O in the namespace and a zero in the time domain, he probably has it coming, though when it comes to ascribing blame for Eugene's situation, it certainly isn't likely that Ray blames some douchebag, it's an absolute certainty that Ray blames himself. Gene would not be sitting here, bound and gagged, with a burst-fire Beretta pointed at his head, if Ray had been willing to deliver a briefcase, containing a good million dollars' worth of bank-strapped currency, directly to Gomez, in a timely fashion; the man who would be sitting here, bound and gagged, with a burst-fire Beretta pointed at his head, would, in fact, be Raymond Edmunds. Which brings us at last to the house itself, where seven men are seated around a large square coffee table, engaged, for the moment, in making unsafe assumptions; given that Ray is a former Army man, with solid credentials in forward spotting, we might be tempted, just to prove a point, by one of the latest innovations in multiple-target detection, perhaps the CFAR threshold-adaptive target-coordinate data extractor, to call in an air strike, and obliterate the domicile. This particular house, on Calle Avanzaro, in the Cuernavaca subdivision of Ciudad Juárez, a neighborhood you looked at rather closely, in fact, but ultimately rejected, as overly theatrical, its reputation stained by the behavior of the neighbors, planting quicklimed corpses among the flowers in their gardens, is a house that we can't really wholeheartedly recommend, unless you're in the market for a mortuary site, or plan to study blowflies and human decomposition. As far as we're concerned, the whole house can go, and spare us all the details as to what happens next. What happens next, from what we've seen of Juárez, isn't always the easiest thing to detail with precision: one moment you're standing there, waiting to see what's next, beginning to get the feeling that the place is nearly still; in fact, come to think of it, now that you mention it, the place is now so still you could hear a pin drop; and the next thing you know, there go the details, the pin doesn't drop, the stillness isn't broken, and maybe something happened, or maybe in fact it didn't, but *something* must be broken, because *nothing* happens next.

What actually happened next, much to our surprise, given the time already expended on the Tinkerbell naming-convention, was that Raymond suddenly recognized the man himself, and knew him for a fact to be Arturo Beltran. Arturo Beltran, fortunately for us, is no relation at all to Arturo Beltran. This whole situation is bad enough as it is, without adding in the complexities of the Juárez drug trade. Arturo and Pedro Beltran, leaders of the Beltran-Leyva organization, had served their drug apprenticeships in the Sinaloa Cartel, headed by Joaquin "El Chapo" Guzman, and his longtime partner, Ismael Zambada, meaning that Arturo Beltran, and the whole Beltran clan, have long been enemies of the Juárez camp. If the drug war battle lines weren't constantly shifting, we'd be looking at a fairly straightforward situation: Arturo Beltran, Joaquin Guzman, and Ramírez' Thetas, on the Sinaloa side; and Raymond Edmunds, Vicente Carrillo Fuentes, and Gomez' Zetas, on the Juárez side; if this were the case, and Arturo Beltran were Arturo Beltran, you'd really have to wonder why Raúl Ramírez had Arturo Beltran tied to a chair, particularly a chair in a Gomez safe house. Fortunately for us, not only is Arturo Beltran now partners with Gomez, having recently joined forces with the Juárez Cartel, but Arturo Beltran, the man tied to the chair, is no relation at all to Arturo Beltran; fortunately for you, you've now been provided with more than enough clarity to completely forget that we ever brought this up. Unfortunately for Raymond, who is back on the clock, and trying to figure out how to get Gene out of this, the name Arturo Beltran, the signifier itself, is more than enough to send him off on a pointless tangent, drifting a little off of dead-level center, trying to get a handle on the alignment of cartels, and how it is that Ramírez, of the Sinaloa Cartel, has come to be in charge of a Gomez safe house. We'll give you a hint, Ray: don't even bother; we've tried this already, and it's far too confusing; the man you're thinking of is your old friend Bells, and not the leader of the Beltran-Leyva organization. Arturo Beltran is Arturo Beltran, and Arturo Beltran is an entirely different man.

Ray crawled through the bushes, and came to rest in a bed of yellow marigolds, blooming like a wildflower in the side-yard crawlspace, smelling of sweet basil and tarragon and mint, and reminding Ray of something, maybe a Día de los Muertos moonlight-celebration, out in a graveyard with the whole Beltran clan, meaning that Ray and Arturo were out there alone, with like six or eight plates full of ghost chicken mole, in a patch of yellow marigolds sprouting Beltran-family headstones; or maybe he was thinking of a separate occasion, when he and Arturo were drinking beers at Club Felix, with candles and yellow marigolds on the scarred wooden tables, after a few rounds of sparring at El Choque Gym. Arturo grew up in an Anapra hovel, back in the days when Anapra and Sunland Park were essentially all just one big town, and Mexican kids could go to school across the border, before they built the fence, and declared it illegal to be Mexican. His father was a headcase who worked on and off at the ASARCO plant, when he wasn't dusted on PCP, and doing crazy shit like molesting his own daughter; Arturo used to say that his dad had moved away, which Ray took to mean that he was buried out on the mesa. From what Ray could remember, he was a smartass kid, quick on his feet in a bar-room situation, like two steps ahead of whatever was coming next, leaving everyone laughing when they were dead set on brawling; when it came to the ring, however, he was a lot like Eugene, he'd take thirty punches to get one in, though Ray had to admit that that one punch was a beauty, a straight right hand that, even through the headgear, left Raymond's head ringing like he was locked inside the belfry of a cathedral bell tower. A good kid, Arturo was; could have been anything he'd have put his mind to, though Raymond had to doubt that what Arturo had in mind was ending up in Juárez as a FedEx package. Arturo, amigo, what the hell are we doing here? Not too sure, Ray. Think this guy Ramírez is probably going to kill us. Course, you want my opinion, you 'bout half dead already, cabrón. You might want to think about seeing a doctor. Probably right, Bells; maybe he'd stop the fight on account of bleeding. Let me ask you something, though. Whatever happened to Arturo Beltran? Hell if I know; story goes El Chapo dropped a dime on his brother Alfredo, and Arturo got back at him by having the Zetas kill his son. So he's on our side now? See if I've got this straight. It's us and Beltran-Leyva and the Zetas and the Gulf Cartel, against our old partners, the Sinaloa Cartel? All our old enemies are now on our side? Not real sure you got a side to be on, pendejo. Gomez said to kill you first chance I got. Jesus, Bells, this place is a fucking mess. Who's this guy Ramírez? I'm picturing ex-AFI, Trip, you know the type, cold motherfucker, talks a lot of bullshit. Think he's now head of Los Negros, call themselves the Thetas. You see those Berettas? Nice piece of gear. They jumped us when we came in here, me and my buddy, the one you've been calling Tinkerbell's Twin, before we had a chance to plant Eugene in the garden. Why the hell would you want to kill Eugene? Don't ask me, dude, quién fuckin' sabe? Seems like you the one got him into this mess. What were you thinking fucking with Gomez? I don't know, Arturo, something didn't feel right, telling me to kill some guy, won't say his name. So what the fuck's the story on this guy I'm calling Douchebag? Who the hell knows, guy's in Juárez with a shitpile of money, don't think he's smart enough to have much of a story. You sound like Eugene. Tell you what, Bells. Let's you and me and Eugene get the hell out of here, before Ramírez plants us all out in the garden with the blowflies. You got a plan, Ray? No, Bells, I don't, I most certainly do not. Maybe you better get one, amigo, or we'll wind up sprouting marigolds, and when the time comes for storytelling, you'll be the douchebag.

Raymond, like we said, had drifted just a bit off of dead-level center, and taken a seat with his back to the wall, talking things over with the tarragon marigolds. Ray drifted back a little closer to dead center, and searched around the side yard for a slightly different angle; the proper first shot, on the 3:00 o'clock Beretta, would need to be taken from an entirely different window; if he sat there at 6:00, his current window, waiting for 4:20 to go take a leak, he'd bleed to death without firing a shot. What Ray needed most, right about now, was a change of time zones, try to set the whole clock back about an hour, get Let's Say 4:20 out of his sightlines, give him two clean quick shots on the elegant Berettas, before Ramírez could get the AR-15 out of the off-white sofa cushions. The first problem he faced was about six feet ahead, where a vicious-looking yucca plant, also known as Spanish Bayonet, was blocking the side-yard's second window; the 5:00 o'clock shot, from the second window, would certainly improve his current position, but would leave him with multiple bayonet wounds to deal with. The only other window was on the front of the house, a large plate of glass, which was basically perfect, though as he thought this over, and pictured the shot, 3:00 o'clock would be sitting at about 6:00 PM, with the other Beretta up

around Midnight, meaning Raymond needed the clock set forward
not backwards, somewhere three time-zones to the east of Juárez,
like the picture-perfect spot would be a beach in Bermuda. Too bad
about Bermuda; ever since his dispute with Gomez began, and he
formed an odd bond with a genuine civilian, Ray's been having fantasies about getting out of the drug trade, maybe buy a little corner-
store mom-and-pop tienda, or a sweet-science gym where he could
teach a little boxing, and the deeper Ray sinks into blood-loss reality, the closer he gets to the turquoise waters, and pink-sand beaches, of a Bermuda escape. Ray pictured himself walking around St.
George, or going for a swim in the turquoise waters off the pink-
sand beaches of Horseshoe Bay, or heading out to Shelly Bay to bet
on the horses, watch the tic-tac bookmakers hand-signal odds, with
their clean white gloves against the blue Bermuda sky. The problem with Bermuda was any number of things: to begin with his odds
of getting out of the drug trade were like 33:1, also known in tic-tac
as a double carpet, the two hands placed flat, and crossed against
the chest, like a corpse laid out for viewing in a Juárez garden; there
was also the problem with Shelly Bay itself, like the picture Ray's
looking at is about 60 years out of date, and the race track isn't
there, it was long ago demolished; and the final little problem was
reaching Bermuda from Juárez, as in the view Ray needed from the
plate-glass window, which was out there all right, on the front of the
house, just next to the chimney and the hearth of the home, where
the Gomez French Statuary twin-horse chronometer was ticking
down time on the fireplace mantel; between Ray and Bermuda
was another tall gate, topped with concertina wire and hundreds
of gleaming razors, so this vision Ray's having of traveling to Bermuda, and using the pistol-grip slide-action Cruiser to solve all his
problems, was just about as likely as having tea in St. George, out
in a little garden, with lavender Passion Flowers and Pink-tipped
Begonias. Meaning Jennifer, of course; Ray could care less about
a bunch of fucking flowers. Ray, man, this is Bells, wake the fuck
up; you're drifting a little, you need to get centered. Why don't you
blow a hole in the base of that bayonet plant, knock the thing down,
come out firing at random? Be better than just sitting here letting
the clock run out, falling fast asleep with your back against the wall,
sniffing on mint and basil in the tarragon marigolds, wind up get-

ting your brains blown out by the 9:00 o'clock Beretta. Give you 9:4 on you getting out alive, you don't stop dreaming of walking around St. George, and firing off shots from a beach in Bermuda. Guy comes out the sliding glass, sneaks that gun around the corner, he'll shoot you from the patio before you even lift the Mossberg. I'm just thinking out loud here, Ray, but correct me if I'm wrong, 9:4 in tic-tac is exactly what you'll get, two gloves up and pointing, call it Top of the fucking Head.

Ray came to with a start, like a man coming up for air from deep in the turquoise waters, and whipped the all-black Cruiser around, and pointed it down toward the corner of the house. No sign of the Beretta. Bells was right about one thing, though: he had to get out of this sitting position, and out of the yellow marigolds, and forget about Bermuda. Not only was he well on the way toward falling fast asleep, but his vet-sutured chest-wound had now soaked through the top of his jeans, meaning that Ray was now looking at an altered battlespace, where the enemy he faced was not just time, but the blood-loss reality of his own leaking body. Ray searched the side yard for something to slow the bleeding, and seeing nothing even resembling avitene or thrombin, much less Surgicel or a Gel-foam sponge, the agents that might have helped if he had a cutman in his corner, decided to take a less conventional approach, involving a vicious-looking Yucca plant and sweet yellow marigolds; we'll spare you the details on how this worked, but the Yucca plant itself was apparently wounded, and leaking a sticky sap from several of its wounds, a sap that Ray gathered and applied to his chest, in a six-inch backslash, just above the heart where the blood loss was rapid, before covering the sticky mess with marigold blossoms, like a man applying tissue paper to a razor-cut nick, leaving Ray with several feet of sutures still exposed, and a marigold patch over the worst of the bleeding. While the doctors would probably laugh at Raymond's solution, Ray knew for a fact that the Zuni's would approve, as they not only use Yucca sap to clot an oozing wound, they use yellow marigolds as a wound antiseptic; sympathetic magic from a wound-ed plant might sound to you like a complete waste of time, but the medicine man on a Zuni reservation might wonder about your faith in Western doctors, who seem to know a lot about running up your tab, and virtually nothing about the healing-powers of plants;

Ray's plant-spirit cure may have cost him a bit of time, but your doctors, rest assured, somewhere along the line, will cost you your faith in Western medicine. Ray, in any case, buttoned up his shirt, and returned to the problem of springing Eugene, with a small yellow patch made of marigold blossoms, making a sweet basil, mint, and tarragon, case, for the use of aromatherapy in getting a tired man moving; no more tic-tac; no more Arturo; no more dips in the turquoise waters; it was high time Raymond started speaking native Gun. He crawled back to the chessboard window, peaked back over the windowsill, and double-checked the stalemate layout, which had in fact measurably improved: Arturo's twin, Let's Say 4:20, seated next to Ramírez on the off-white couch, and blocking Ray's shot on the 3:00 o'clock Beretta, had apparently grown tired of his stale self-debate, conducted in Gas, inside a garment-bag of plastic, and had simply abandoned the pro-oxygen position, and fallen face-forward off of the couch in a heap. Ray hoisted the Mossberg up to the window, centered a human head in the Ghost Ring O, and bracing himself for the Cruiser recoil, prepared a simple counterexample to a philosophical conundrum, a question borrowed from Wittgenstein, and posed by Ramírez at the Bar of the Wounded Tree: what remains when I subtract the fact that a man lies dead from the fact that I shot him with a 12-gauge shotgun? You'd probably find the answer in the coroner's report; maybe Ludwig Wittgenstein might want to sit in on the autopsy. Does there seem to be some problem regarding human intent? Perhaps you think Ray isn't *meaning* to kill him? When a man has to live with the indicated action, aiming through a Ghost Ring sight, and gradually squeezing a pistol-grip trigger, he does not have a problem with semantic arithmetic, or doing the mental math on human subtraction; he knows for a fact that, in order to survive, *he* must be the Ghost-Ring remainder; it may well be true, as Wittgenstein said, that philosophy is a battle against the bewitchment of the intelligence by means of language, but if language gets involved in intelligence-bewitchment, Raymond himself planned to do the bewitching, and Ray, rest assured, speaks pitch-perfect Ghost.

And then, all at once, Time stood still. The clock on the Mossberg reads an Instant Before Explosion, the moment before the firing pin, transferring energy from a spring-loaded hammer, impacts the primer on a triple-decker shotgun shell, igniting a small quantity of double base smokeless powder, which causes a rapid expansion of gases in the barrel chamber, which in turn forces a mass of metal to exit the weapon at breathtaking speed. It's now 12:20, by the Gomez chronometer, with its deadbeat locking-face locked on a pointed tooth, awaiting the downbeat of a pendulum swing, and its statuary horses reared-up but frozen, fully prepared to wait an eternity for time to move along in the statuary world. Seven men are seated around a large square coffee table, similarly suspended, with the Wittgenstein conundrum being held in abeyance, and Time at a standstill, holding its breath: a Blue Diamond match-flare, brazenly headed toward a small dark cigar, has halted just short of complete combustion; a greenbottle blowfly has stopped in mid-flight; a wide-eyed man, dreaming of Kansas, has been caught in the act of wishing he were elsewhere, with his eyes fixed on the moment when the thresher blade and wheat stalk meet; a garment-bag of plastic, in a heap on the floor, is not about to move, but neither is it a good example of Time standing still, unless you think eternity has its own separate time zone. The 3:00 o'clock Beretta, on a ladderback chair, a man whose own Time is an instant from expiring, is now a man trapped in a strange situation: he has no way of knowing that *he* is Ray's target; he has no way of knowing that the blowflies stopped buzzing; he has no way of knowing who or what he is; he doesn't have a self or a single idea; he has 100 trillion synapses, 85 billion neurons, 100 unique molecular structures among his array of neurotransmitter chemicals, but of the 10 thousand trillion neural network connections this rather ordinary brain would otherwise be capable of, not a single one is working, though if you gave him just an instant to gather his thoughts, this utterly amazing neural-network machinery would turn, on a dime, into the mind of a killer, the sort of mind that we in turn would have no way of knowing, particularly given the fact that, an instant from now, this mind would be full of large steel pellets. Somewhere in Bermuda, where it's now 3:20, a Ruby-throated Hummingbird, slowly flying backwards from the petals of a Scarlet Beebalm flower, has not only come to rest, but is an utter confabulation, an anachronistic artifact of an El Paso gunman's Bermuda delusion: today, in reality, is April 16, and the lovely Scarlet Beebalm plant won't begin to flower until early July. Too bad about Bermuda; with time having stopped, not only have the flights to Bermuda been delayed, but the beautiful pink-sand beaches of Horseshoe Bay are no longer pink, they're the exact same color as the turquoise waters, they're the exact same color as the lavender Passion Flowers, everything on Earth is the exact same color you'd see through the eyes of the 3:00 o'clock Beretta, in the instant that his mind went perfectly blank. So what, if anything, have we done with Raymond? Are we planning perhaps to leave him here, suspended forever, with his mind treading water, locked on a pointed tooth in a statuary world? We have no idea; it all depends upon what happens next. If the man standing behind him, with the Olive Drab, polymer-framed, recoil-operated, subcompact pistol, a striker-fired 10mm Auto cartridge Glock 29, decides to pull the trigger, unleashing a whole shitpile of ballistic-projectile kinetic energy equations, Raymond can call it a day; not only will he leave the world with the muzzle-flash equivalent of a Kodak moment, but he'll leave our current narrative trajectory suffering from all kinds of neural damage, a condition known to battlefield medics as cerebral derangement due to hydrostatic shock; the mathematical equivalent, in terms of our plot arc, would be the pathological continuity of a Weierstrass function. Sorry, Ray, but these things happen; perhaps, in hindsight, one of us should have seen this coming. Ray eased his index finger off of the Mossberg pistol trigger, and slowly put the gun down, with the Glock 29 resting gently against his head. He felt a little foolish standing up in the bushes, with his hands in the air, and his weapon around his ankles, but at least the locked locking-face on a deadbeat escapement released the loose tooth on a saw-toothed wheel, and the clock started up again, and Time itself took a long deep breath. If you've never seen a plot of a Weierstrass function, with the jagged-edged teeth of a mind gone fractal, just be thankful that the Glock did not go off; the self-similarity of a Mandelbrot set, in a world that's continuous but non-differentiable, may be interesting to look at, as a zoom sequence, but it's a hard plot to follow without a protagonist.

With eight men now seated around a large square coffee table, and the clock restarted, and everyone focused on what happens next, you'd think we'd be in a position, now that we're all here, to set things in motion inside Casa Cronómetro; we have, unfortunately, Ramírez to contend with, and he seems content to leave us all held in limbo, with time dragging around at an absolute crawl. This is clearly a man with a flair for the dramatic, but no sense of pace, and the Gomez chronometer isn't really helping, ticking off the moments as a constant reminder of the emptiness of existence as a temporal structure; it may well be true that a man who lives in the present lives in eternity, but try telling that to a constantly ticking clock. Perhaps we need a roll call: moving counterclockwise, beginning with the man in charge of the proceedings, we have Ramírez at 6:00, in the middle of the sofa, a sofa that runs the length of the room, orthogonal to the fireplace mantel, and the Bermuda picture window at the front of the house; on the floor at 4:20, Tinkerbell's Twin, slowly turning blue, orthogonal, we're guessing, to the world in general, and non-responsive when the roll is called; the 3:00 o'clock Beretta, on a ladderback chair, with his back to the fireplace and the Gomez chronometer; Eugene up at 2:00, bound and gagged, tied-up tight with shipping tape, with his heart dead-set on a Kansas home, and the spacious skies of an amber wheat field, and his body fully prepped for rapid delivery, to a nearby parcel of Juárez subsoil; Tinkerbell himself, also known to Raymond as Arturo or Bells, stationed around Noon, beneath a small mirror, with his back to the open quicklime sacks, and their caustic critique of his molecular composition; Douchebag in the flesh, our 10:30 lounger, staring at a squat tequila bottle, the pivot point of our imaginary clock; at 9:00 o'clock, the other Beretta, Model 93R, an elegant machine pistol, a weapon that somehow seems strangely out of place here, like a bespoke suit in a land without tailors; Raymond Carlisle Edmunds III, just in from outside, seated at 7:30, with his Ghost-Ring visions a thing of the past, and his eyes slowly adjusting to the room's dark interior; and at 6:45, the Glock 29, a subcompact monster, capable of stopping a full-grown boar, that has a serious design flaw, unlikely to prove important, but worthy of mention. If you've ever had to fire a Glock 29, as a backup perhaps to your Savage 110 rifle, when the bolt-throw malfunctioned in the face of a charging boar, a 200-pound mass of hurtling muscle, and razor-sharp tusks, an absolute handful, you know what we're referring to: the pistol grip itself is extraordinarily short, with room on the grip for only two fingers; you are, in essence, trying to blow away a boar, with the fingers you'd use while lifting a teacup. So what are we doing here? We have no idea; we, apparently, are just killing time, waiting for Ramírez to begin the proceedings. The room itself has the look and feel of an emergency hospital waiting room, with people staring off wearing vacant expressions, caught between thoughts, in narrative limbo; you might think they were waiting to see a physician, seeking rapid assessment and critical care, but the fact is they haven't been triaged yet, and like everyone else in Ciudad Juárez, they'll just have to wait until their wounds have been inflicted. Raymond, of course, is the obvious exception: he's beginning to look a little the worse for wear, with stucco-scraped knuckles, and razor-wired leg-flesh, and a nasty-looking X-shaped vet-sutured chest-wound, delivered as a message, in heavily encrypted longhand, by a man with a real gift for voice-less velar fricatives, using a Fairbairn-Sykes Fighting Knife as the ultimate pencil; while he's already at risk of wound dehiscence, and mediastinitis due to esophageal perforation, the last man on earth that Ray wants to see is a Juárez doctor, entering the room carrying an empty black bag, and a Malco high-tension pistol-grip hacksaw. What Raymond really needs is to get the hell out of here, maybe find some sort of clinic with a higher standard of care, where DOA isn't the usual diagnosis, and quicklime sacks aren't involved in the treatment protocol; in the meantime, the waiting room had slowed to a limbless crawl. A dark-suited man had finally finished lighting a small dark cigar; greenbottle blowflies were buzzing around everywhere; a wide-eyed dreamer was collecting his thoughts, which seemed to be suffering from straw-walker overload; Douchebag was drooling; Arturo was still speechless; the Berettas seemed content to let the silence go on forever; a garment-bag of plastic was mostly just that. Ramírez was blowing smoke rings through the middle of each other, like a man rehearsing speeches, in smoke signal Apache, full of quotes inside of quotes inside of quotes. Raymond had a thought: let's cut the shit.

"What's on your mind, Ramírez? More philosophy lessons? Or you planning on making us sit here until we all die of boredom?"

"Patience, Mr. Edmunds. As Ovid put it, everything comes gradually, and at its appointed hour. Boredom is itself a rather interesting problem; perhaps, as Schopenhauer said, boredom is direct proof that existence itself is valueless. Now you might think, after Schopenhauer, that there is little more to be said on the topic, but Heidegger, characteristically, was still capable of producing a rather dense hundred pages or so on the phenomenology of boredom, focusing in particular on its relationship to the passing of time, though one can't help wondering if Das Fuhrer der Freiburg would have tolerated boredom among his students and faculty; this seems rather out of keeping with the National Socialist spirit. The University, under Heidegger, was certainly not a refuge for the mediocre or cowardly; as he himself pointed out, whoever does not survive the battle lies where he falls, and one can only suppose that those who suffered from boredom must have ended up near the bottom of the pile. In any case, assuming Schopenhauer is correct, and boredom is nothing other than the immediate sensation of the emptiness of existence, there are few things that could better account for the insatiable demand for our products in the United States, a nation that so values the vacuous and empty that one marvels at its capacity for fighting off boredom. Rather than complaining of boredom, Mr. Edmunds, perhaps we should be celebrating; we are, shall we say, among the arms suppliers in the epic battle against boredom in America, and if there are those who do not survive the struggle, we must, as Heidegger suggests, let them lie where they fall."

"Fascinating, Ramírez, fascinating. So if I die of boredom listening to you talk, it's really not your problem. Is that what you have in mind, or am I missing something?"

"Regarding the question as to what's on my mind, grammatically speaking, I can't really comment. I can know what someone else is thinking, not what I am thinking. It is correct to say 'I know what you are thinking,' and incorrect to say 'I know what I am thinking'."

"So what am I thinking?"

"You're no doubt wondering what we're waiting for. Perhaps our friend with the duffel bag has one or two ideas."

"Probably waiting for High Noon."

"Noon? It's like 12 fucking 30."

"I believe he may be referring to a young woman who was to have met us here. She seems to be running rather unconscionably late."

"Never should have named her High Noon in the first place.

What she calls Noon is more like 1:20. Tells me to meet her at the Stanton Street Bridge, has this whole Shall We Say Noon attitude about time, leaves me in a parking lot with a ballistic computer, Googling the word Crow on a .50 caliber sniper rifle, wind up with some guy from the immigration service, you know the type, Can't park here mister, full of ad hoc spelling and metathetic colloquialisms, wants to turn Juárez into a nucular desert. Mind if I have a drink?" This, apparently, was Douchebag speaking, as he reached for the tequila bottle, and not only poured a drink into the chuchupaste glass, the glass at the crux of our stalemated chessboard, but picked the glass up, thereby disassembling our whole pivot point analogy, leaving the clock hands in place but completely unhinged. "Jesus, what's this brown shit?"

"Let me ask you something, Ramírez. What the fuck is he talking about?"

"What the fuck am I talking about? I'm talking about Ms. Aphoristic Platitudes, Ms. Better Safe Than Sorry, Ms. Better a Live Rat than a Dead Lion I think she said, and her friend Señor Prospero, gives me like a synopsis of the whole florid Tempest speech, our revels now are ended, the baseless fabric vision bit, we are such stuff as dreams are made on, says he wants his money back, leaves me wondering if I need to see a sleep clinic. What did you think I was talking about?"

Now it was Raymond who needed a drink. Having apparently forgotten the situation he was in, like a scene out of *Guns and Ammo*, or the latest issue of *Handgunner* magazine, and no doubt suffering from the somnambulatory effects of Douchebag's solipsistic interior monologue, he stood up abruptly as if to leave the room, and wandered toward a sideboard, on the far back wall, on the way to the dining room that led into the kitchen, where he picked out a glass suitable for chucho-drinking; if he's thinking that the osha extract will bring him out of a deep hibernation, so he can make sense of Douchebag, maybe formulate a plan, we wish him all the best with his future endeavors, but he's seriously fucking dreaming as far as Douchebag making sense. Finding three vigilant weapons trained on him as he turned, and his own little life about to be rounded with a sleep, he waved the men off with the chucho glass, and resumed his seat, and started in drinking.

"So this is the douchebag Gomez sent me to kill. No wonder I couldn't find him in Ciudad Juárez. Guy can't even talk straight, can't imagine his driving."

"I must object to that characterization, Mr. Edmunds. My driving was fine. The problem wasn't my driving. There seemed to be some sort of conspiracy at work, between the rental car mapmakers and the guys who put up the one-way street signs. I may have been suffering from ethanol dehydrogenase, causing a near-total collapse of my gluconeogenesis, with my axons stripped of their myelin sheathing, and my brain half-full of neuro-corrosives, but a few drinks of bourbon took care of all that, restored me to something like synaptic plasticity. I will admit to having something of an object permanence problem, regarding my eyeglasses, I couldn't find them anywhere, they'd completely vanished, I searched all over the entire house, I even searched in the ammunition closet, I kept thinking I must have left them on the toilet tank, in the bathroom just off of the cherubim bedroom, turned out they were right where I didn't think to look, like right where they were, on the coffee table beside the living room sofa, not far from where I was sitting when I took the fuckers off."

"Jesus. Cherubim bedroom? You're the guy who slept in my house? The guy from Sonny's? What the hell happened? You look like you've been living under a highway overpass."

"I had a little problem with my toiletry kit. I think I must have left it on the Pipe Dream truck."

"Gentlemen, please. Perhaps we can confine ourselves to actual events. You were to have met with Gabriella at noon, on the El Paso side of the Stanton Street Bridge. I take it that she arrived at closer to 1:20. She was to have brought you to the Holiday Inn Express, on the Avenida Republica, and stayed there with you until this morning. She was then to bring you here, and assist us with providing for the security of your currency. What in fact occurred after Gabriella arrived?"

"Gabriella you call her. To me, she looked like the Sistine Madonna. So she gets in the car, tells me to make a right and go across the bridge, and right off the bat, I've got one of these one-way street sign conspiracy problems, like I'm thinking right here I should back the fuck up, leave a puff of burning tires, a thirty-foot cloud of benzene and butadiene and cadmium-laced styrene, a polycyclic aromatic hydrocarbon rush, probably kill all the pedestrians, but get the fuck out of there. Never should have crossed the bridge in the first place. Should have been sitting pretty, maybe 20 floors up, at an El Paso conference table, drinking single malt Scotch."

"There was a woman in the car with you? That can't be right. I was two cars behind you, driving the Magnum, there was no one with you. The passenger seat was empty."

"So you're the Karma Yoga guy, made the birds go flying. You want my opinion, you need more practice, and you maybe need to learn to chill out a little, stop pounding on the steering wheel, scaring all the birds. No, you know what? I take that back, the crows don't scare, they're barely even animate, they're like too close to nothingness just to begin with, I'm thinking the Sistine silence was the thing that unnerved them. Me, I'll admit I was in a weird frame of mind, two-thirds bourbon and hospital pharmaceuticals, one-third basic-instinct existential Crow. So who's this guy Gomez who sent you to kill me?"

"Must be Señor Prospero, from the way you describe him. Guy's like two-thirds Money, one-third Thesaurus."

"Why would he want me killed? I thought he just wanted his money back."

"No idea. You steal his money?"

"Hell no. There seems to be some sort of misunderstanding here. We were in imaginary business together. Like if the government of Turkmenistan wanted to blanket the Black Sands Desert with solar-powered cell phone towers, we were your guys. Picture a farmer on Tongatapu, leaving his palm-thatched hut with a cart full of coconuts, watching high-def television on his mobile handset, getting totally turned around in the palm tree orchards, we were the guys with the LTE roadmap, like 12-by-12 MIMO using VSF-OFCDM in CMOS maybe, help some poor farmer find the right rutted track. Or maybe you're running with the Big Dogs in Abuja, trying to pacify some anarchists in the Niger delta, and you're thinking instead of sewage treatment and buildings for schools, you'll lay in some WiMAX over your GSM network, like who needs plumbing if you've got full-motion video? What can I tell you, we sold an absolute shitpile of SC-FDMA uplink amplifiers into places like

Kampala and Paramaribo, Suriname. Probably all my fault, should of learned to speak Dutch, or get a fucking clue about the bauxite industry, but it was fun while it lasted, until it all went through the reality Powershredder. Turned out these companies like Infocom and Velocicom were Señor Prospero's thin air fabrications, and right when I'm thinking I should buy a new plane, I find out I've invested in a Crazy Eddie Laundromat chain."

"So you're saying you're just plain stupid, is that what you're telling me? Must be why they call you The Poet, can't understand a fucking word you're saying. Let me ask you something, Douchebag, you make all this shit up?"

"Yeah, most of it. These technology guys all speak native Acronym. Might as well be listening to parrots talking Etruscan."

"Gentlemen, again, we seem to be drifting somewhat off of the topic. What actually happened to you and Gabriella?"

"I'm coming to that. First thing that happens, when I get across the bridge, instead of an information booth, where I could maybe get a map, I've got like M4 Howitzers and AT4 rocket launchers, like way too much information to properly absorb. Next thing I know, I don't know where I am, I'm stuck behind a Pepsi truck, with a little pushcart taco vendor grilling carne asada, and a bunch of Liquefactionists coming toward my rental car, wearing Blackhawk Hellstorm ballistic goggles, like I'm having some sort of benzo-detox hypnagogic visuals. Now I've got a case of acute macropsia, and when they're almost on top of me, looking for the soccer kids, and the S*Mart backpack full of black tar heroin, all of sudden, Juárez just implodes, and I'm right in the middle of a Hadamard disaster, headed face-first toward a Morbark woodchipper, and the whole Ciudad is wearing camouflage, and I couldn't figure out if they were hiding from themselves, or maybe they just got lost inside their Schwarzschild radius. I noticed this tinted-window black Suburban, with five or six guys carrying an XM-29 Integrated Airburst Weapon, and then the Abyss showed up wearing a shit-eating grin, and then the whole place exploded, and I'm looking all around for the pariah dogs and ice cream children. When the smoke had cleared, it was a huge fucking mess, like the HEAB-rounds must have set fire to the actual air, leaving smoke signals everywhere but no way to read them, one of those Johannes Trithemius steganographic covertext stories, made of aliphatic and aromatic pyrolyzed hydrocarbons, like I think they set fire to most of the local troposphere. You ask me, they ought to legalize drugs, and outlaw firing rockets on mom-and-pop lecherías."

At this point it became clear that Ray needed another drink, and maybe a few more pet pills, before even attempting to fully absorb this. Douchebag, it was apparent, had some sort of semipermeable osmotic barrier guarding his internal reality from the Juárez exterior, and Raymond's own buffer was wearing a little thin, with fluids leaking out, and the truth seeping in. The fundamental truth, regarding Raymond Edmunds, was that time was running short on his subject-object duality problem; once Ramírez reached the bottom of Douchebag's cryptic tale, Ray's inner life wouldn't contain much of interest, other than to blowflies and the local taphonomists, whose primary concern, as far as Raymond's insides, would be abdominal gas formation during black putrefaction. Ray winked at Gene as he poured a couple of chuchos, like now was no time for Douchebag to stop talking. He may have said "Skol!" and clinked glasses across the table, but he seemed to be searching around the Sedlec Ossuary, looking in the bone pile for the right toast in Slavic. Ray's thinking "Okrzyki!" is the Czech word for "Cheers!" which would certainly be true, if the Czechs spoke Polish, though Ray should keep in mind that this cheerful Polish toast translates to something closer to "Outcries." "Outcries!" it is, then, let's drink to Douchebag's health; in the boneyards of Juárez, such a toast would seem appropriate.

"I take it that you and Gabriella proceeded on from there? Where exactly were you in Juárez at this point?"

"Beats me. According to my map, we were in the middle of a brownish sort of empty blank spot, outside a lechería that was an empty smoking hole, Numero Veinte-Ocho Todo Desierto. Ms. Noon had apparently lost confidence in my driving, which struck me as unfair, given the length of my morning. In retrospect, I may have been the slightest bit harsh, since many of the grievances I felt at the time, like my journey through the Pronaf, and the outbreak of apophenia, and my dogged reporting on the covertext story behind a biohazard ice-rink dumpsite emporium, hadn't even happened yet. I didn't go through the Pronaf until I lost High Noon, but let me ask you something. How would you feel, finding sodium hypo-chloride mixed with staphylococcal enterotoxins, and tetrodotoxin and diacetoxyscirpenol mixed with clostridium perfingens epsilon toxins, and them calling the place an ice rink, expecting kids to skate there? Maybe it hadn't happened yet, and I was stuck behind a Pepsi truck, and I shouldn't really have been blaming her, but the morning, as you can see, had certainly been a long one. Just the struggle to find a towel, and my toothbrushing confrontation with oral depravity and bloodshot eyes and axon-stripping neuro-corrosives, were enough to wear anyone out, and I haven't even told you about the Battle of the Somme, or the bird-bone onslaught of the Virola Hekulas. Given what she's been through, however, I wish I hadn't yelled at her."

"You lost Gabriella?"

"Yeah. Didn't I already mention that?"

"What exactly has Gabriella been through?"

"Oh God, that's a really long story. The time in Juárez is let's say 7:30. There are dragon-breath flames climbing the clouds in the west, maybe exhaled in relief now that the day is finally over..."

The Poet let his voice drop, somewhere in mid-sentence, and left his words trailing away over the vast Chihuahuan Desert. Per-haps, like the crows, he had intuited something, some dharmasastric truth regarding the silence between two noises, or the blueness of the sky, or the overwhelming Qi of the Immense and Empty Mind. Perhaps. Ramírez hadn't moved. The chronometer was barely tick-ing. The greenbottle blowflies sat licking their appendages. A gap had opened up, in the surface of identity, and something odd had vanished into Ramírez' dark interior; maybe we've started seeing things, but it looked like a box of crayons. Picture the sort of man whose basic internal nature is a large vat of lye, strangely discolored, with all kinds of gooey stuff suspended along the bottom. What you see drifting down, and slowly dissolving, is whatever mental picture you just drew of Ramírez, along with your crayons, and your mental sheet of paper; just let it go, forget about dark interiors, try not to picture Ramírez at all, or you'll wind up staring at a neural map-ping of shapeless and colorless deep mental goo. When you reach the next page break, do yourself a favor: don't lick your fingers, even subliminally, without giving everything a good thorough wash.

"This won't do. Begin again. Tell me precisely what has happened to Gabriella."

"Well, in that case, let me ask you something. How much do you know about human facial transplant surgery?"

Whatever you do, don't move a muscle. Don't lick your fingers. Don't even blink. Pretend you're a piece in a speed game of chess, when your opponent says of it: That piece can't be moved. Ramírez has borrowed an Olive Drab, polymer-framed, recoil-operated, sub-compact pistol, a striker-fired 10mm Auto cartridge Glock 29, and leveled the weapon on an unwitting civilian, intent, evidently, on concluding their discussion, with one final comment on human stupidity. Ray can't be expected, at this point in his life, to have a deep understanding of Søren Kierkegaard, or to understand the role that patience might play in maintaining a sense of personal identity, given the essentially fleeting and temporal nature of the finite self in relation to its own infinitude; it's easy enough to see, as far as Ramírez is concerned, that the maintenance of his identity, as a patient task to be achieved, is completely beyond him, like he's totally fucking lost it. With all eyes focused on the Glock 29, and quoting from Kierkegaard out of the question, Ray raised his glass as though proposing a toast, maybe something along the lines of "Outcries!" in Polish, and dropped it on the coffee table, ending its quest for everlasting glasshood, and shattering the crystalline silence with its cries. When the Glock went off, the startled shot sailed high, splintering the mirror on the wall behind Douchebag, and the teacup grip of the subcompact weapon lived up to its reputation for inadequacy under recoil, with the gun ending up behind the off-white couch, where Raymond picked it up, before the Berettas could blink, and pointed it at the head of Raúl Ramírez.

Life, as Søren Kierkegaard observed, can only be understood backwards, but must be lived forwards. Ray could care less about understanding his own life, if, for example, Raymond were dead, but he certainly has an interest in life moving forwards, which perhaps makes it awkward that when Gabriella arrives, inconsiderately late, but not unexpectedly, she not only has a tendency to view her life in reverse, without much foresight, except perhaps in retrospect, but she also has an announcement to make, needlessly complicating Raymond's current plans, and subtracting precious sand from his pink Bermuda beach, while at the same time adding a breath of fresh air, to Douchebag's smooth sailing toward utter oblivion.

"Gomez and his men are right outside. He told me to tell you to send out the Poet, along with the duffel bag, the keys to the truck, and *every last dime of his fucking money*."

That being said, with Gomez at the door, and events now set in motion at Casa Cronómetro, there would seem to be little or nothing to be gained by pointing out that Ramírez left some unfinished business, having failed to deliver on a commitment he'd made, to pose some sort of question that has plagued the philosophers. While we'd hate to leave the man with unfinished business, the current situation certainly doesn't lend itself to putting words in the mouth of Raúl Ramírez: with a Glock 29 pointed at his head, and Gomez' men, members of Los Zetas, standing in the yard outside the pale taupe ranch house, Raúl Ramírez is himself nearly finished, and unlikely to feel he has anything to gain by leaving this world with a philosophical flourish. And even if we attempted a tactical intervention, by furnishing an appropriate question to pose, we'd find Ramírez situated in a target-rich environment, but one not rich in philosophical possibilities. Take the Glock, for example: the Glock appears to point toward the mind-body problem, and the questions that arise out of Cartesian dualism, but if you've ever seen the head of a Glock-shattered boar, having fully absorbed the import of a 10mm Auto cartridge, you know more or less where Ramírez would leave us, with a hell of a flourish, but without much to work with on the mind-body problem; the only real questions that would appear to arise out of craniocerebral slug penetration, and nervous cell necropathy, and neurological deficits due to massive cerebral hemorrhage under high-velocity projectile impact and intracranial bone fragmentation, are the ethical conundrums, perhaps better left to the transplant-ethicists, as to when to call the brain-dead legally dead; our mind-body problem would effectively be reduced to the legalities involved in organ harvesting, leaving Ramírez in the somewhat improbable position of carrying out a debate with his own organ harvesters, questioning their distinction between a persistent vegetative state and total necrosis of whole brain neurons. As Ramírez might have put it, this won't do; once the self is gone, subtracted in effect from the legal equation, it has very few questions, and oculocephalic reflex, papillary response, and intracranial blood flow are certainly not among them. And in any case, if you've ever seen a ranch house after Los Zetas have attacked, leaving nothing but charred bodies in rocket-grenaded rec rooms, you know that any questions regarding organ-transplant harvesting may soon be rendered completely irrelevant; Ramírez would leave us, no questions asked, with charred remains of no use to anyone. If Raúl Ramírez, to net this out, had questions to pose on the mind-body problem, or when to call a halt to the brain-death debate, or what remains when we subtract the self from the legal equation in organ harvesting, he probably should have posed them before Los Zetas arrived, because the Zetas, in effect, have all the solutions to the mind-body problem, and the brain-death conundrums, and the subtraction of the self from any and all equations, and far more answers than Ramírez has questions.

So before we hear that knock at the door, perhaps we should show the harvesters out of the room, and propose a simple question posed by Søren Kierkegaard: What is the self? Kierkegaard, for better or worse, not only posed this simple question, but also proposed a rather complex answer; let's listen in…The self is a relation that relates itself to its own self, or it is that in the relation that the relation relates itself to its own self; the self is not the relation but that the relation relates itself to its own self…and so on. Any questions? Is it time, perhaps, to bring the harvesters back in? To be fair to Kierkegaard, this actual quote, from *The Sickness Unto Death*, which certainly sounds appropriate to the current environment, may not only be poking gentle parodic fun at the complex dialectic of Georg Wilhelm Friedrich Hegel, but the Being who Thus has Spoken, as Lacan might have said, is not actually Kierkegaard, but one of his many pseudonyms known as Anti-Climacus. Anti-Climacus? As in Anti-Climax? This sounds like something that Douchebag might have come up with, in giving Gabriella the name High Noon, using the offhand conventions that led to Tinkerbell's Twin; how on earth did Kierkegaard, the Father of Existentialism, come up with a pseudonym like Anti-Climacus? Let's put it this way: if we were granted permission to ignore our own questions, this is a question we would choose to ignore. What he should have had in mind was the dialectical antithesis, the complementary opposite, of a man by the name of John Climacus; this, at a minimum, would have kept things simple. Finding himself faced with a dense Hegelian text, on the topics of despair and the descent into sin and the universality of human self-sickness, expressing the beliefs of The Ideal Christian, beliefs that Søren Kierkegaard didn't claim to possess, and would therefore need a pseudonymic *self* to express them, what he actually had in mind was something far more complex, and so thoroughly confusing that we refuse to explain it: Anti-Climacus is the antithesis of Johannes Climacus, himself another pseudonym derived from the name, and parts of the identity, of a man by the name of John Climacus, and by Anti-, of course, he hadn't meant Anti-, he'd actually meant Ante-, as in antecedent, a fact that Anti-Climacus, a dialectician, would find difficult to swallow, much less explain. Rather than explain this, let's sum it up with a single statement, and then quickly move on before it raises any questions: Kierkegaard wasn't the author of *The Sickness Unto Death*; Kierkegaard was the author of *the self* that wrote it. So who on earth is this man John Climacus? John Climacus, also known as John of the Ladder, John Scholasticus, and John Sinaites, was not, as you might suspect, some crime boss walking around with too many AKAs, but a writer himself, in fact the author of a book, *The Ladder of Divine Ascent*, which just happened to be the first ever printed in Mexico, and a roughly 6th century Roman Catholic saint. Once again, to be fair to Søren Kierkegaard, who stole the man's name, toyed with his faith, and made quite a pseudonymic mess of his identity, we should probably point out that Climacus himself was a man whose real name was almost certainly not Climacus: since "Climacus," as in "Climax," means "Of the Ladder," what we're looking at here isn't St. John's birth name, it's a name that *The Ladder of Divine Ascent* gave birth to, meaning that Climacus wasn't the author of *The Ladder of Divine Ascent*, *The Ladder of Divine Ascent* was the author of *Climacus*. By now it must be obvious where all of this is headed: perhaps so confused as to how he's been authored that he thinks he's the antithesis of the title of a book, Anti-Climacus begins writing on the nature of despair, and despite the fact that he's The Ideal Christian, rather than making John's long *Ladder* climb, continues his descent into *The Sickness Unto Death*, like a man digging himself into a deep Hegelian hole, and trying to climb out of it up an *Anti-Ladder*; all things considered, this is not an entity that should be trying to write a book; this is an entity that needs a thorough rewrite. As Saint John Climacus himself may have said, "Repentance is a contract with God for a second life," which suggests that what is needed isn't yet another rewrite, but a clean blank page to begin at the top of: if you're sickened by the Self that answers to a name, sign here and here and show a little penitence, perhaps there's a chance that God will redact it. Kierkegaard himself must have signed a pile of these things: from Victor Eremita, the editor of *Either/Or*; to A and Judge Vilhelm, who penned the book's articles; to Vigilius Haufniensis, whose name alone could give you hives, and whose book, *The Concept of Dread* or *The Concept of Anxiety*, may itself have been the cause of all of Kierkegaard's angst; to Johannes de Silentio, of *Fear and Trembling* fame; to Hilarius Bookbinder, the publisher of *Stages*; to H. H. and Inter et Inter and Constantin Constantius, to, of all people, Johannes Climacus, Kierkegaard wrote the book on *The Onomastics of Pseudonomy*. So who the hell is Kierkegaard? Is the sum of these identities Kierkegaard himself? Do the *Journals* and other works that were signed by Søren Kierkegaard contain the actual thinking of the self named Søren Kierkegaard? What is the self named *Søren Kierkegaard*? *What*, come to think of it, *is the self*? We, evidently, haven't got a clue, and even a partial answer, along Kierkegaard's lines, would leave Wittgenstein rolling around in an unmarked grave.

Permit us to pose a question then, after giving this some thought, that has plagued the philosophers, whose plaguing may be warranted: Why did the *real* Søren Kierkegaard express the beliefs of so many patently fraudulent identities, including, quite possibly, *Søren Kierkegaard*, and the obvious follow-up, Did any of these patently fraudulent identities believe there was a *real* Søren Kierkegaard?

By now you must be thinking: what's in a name? Kierkegaard is Kierkegaard, no matter what name he uses. This, however, is not precisely the case; Adorno, for example, made a similar blunder. Whatever your position on the nature of the self, don't be too sure you have all the answers; try to remember that *Gomez* is right outside the door, meaning he'll be here any second now, and he isn't bringing roses.

# 28

*B*y the time I left Gabriella's apartment, and finally reached the bottom of her staircase steps, the moon had begun to rise, and the entrance to my hotel, El Mesón de los Poetas, was surrounded by men in uniform, and musicians wearing dark sombreros. With the streetlamps lit, and more than a few of the building facades bathed in the glow of warm-yellow lanterns, the street itself looked like a jewel box, full of exotic-wood shades of gemstone crystals, teak, mahogany, pheasant-wood, myrtle; at some point, however, I would need to cross the street, and walk the forty feet or so to the hotel's entrance, and my gemstone forest jewel-box illusion, while lovely to look at, did not look safe to wander around in, filled as it was with dark-suited men, men whose presence seemed difficult to account for. What, among other things, were the musicians from the Calle Luis doing on Calle Pocitos at nearly 3:00 am? Had someone ordered a moonlight serenade? I had no doubt at all that this was the quartet that had sung "Cielito Lindo" on the steps of the Teatro, as Gabriella and I watched the crowd flow by, backtracking occasionally for *jugos* and fruit cups; not only were they wearing the same silver-studded costumes, and carrying mismatched guitars and an enormous bass fiddle, but even from where I stood, sixty feet away, on the cobblestone paving of Calle Cantaritos, leading up to my hotel, and a warm bed to sleep in, I could see that the accordion that completed the quartet, a right-hand piano model with white mother-of-pearl, was missing the same three keys from its musical keyboard, like a gap-toothed smile the loving heart finds endearing, only to discover that it looks a little gruesome, in the cold hard light of the morning-after day. *Canta y no llores*, sing and don't cry, even if your pretty-little-heaven of a bird's nest has been turned back into twigs, and your girlfriend wants to kill you, and has taken to calling you Douchebag, and oh, by the way, now that you bring it up, every last twig of your girlfriend's bird's nest belongs to a Fascist poetry critic named Raúl Ramírez; my evening with Gabriella, to make a long story short, hadn't exactly ended on a perfect note. Just as I was beginning to think that Gabriella herself had had second thoughts, and phoned in the order for street musicians, planning a late-night serenade and sincerest apologies for the names she'd called me, I noticed that one of the dark sombreros, dressed in all-black like the policeman beside him, had not come equipped for bass-fiddle playing, unless he planned to pluck it with a semi-automatic handgun. I ducked back out of the streetlight glare, and retreated several feet down Calle Cantaritos, keeping my eyes on the entrance to the Inn of the Poets, as an officer came out and joined the small crowd, saying something to the effect of The Dickhead isn't in there. My first thought was to back up, return into town, retreat down the cobbled slope and get away from this crowded intersection, where Cantaritos T-boned into Calle Pocitos, the wake-up-and-smell-the-coffee side street of my hotel, but the path back was blocked by two armed guards, standing at ease, facing the other direction, and listening to the music of a police radio squawk, through the wide-open doors of a black-on-black Suburban. Not only had my evening not ended well, but it was readily apparent that it was far from being over; while it seemed like the perfect night for a moonlight serenade, with a waning crescent moon coming up over Guanajuato, "Cielito Lindo" would have sounded better on guitar, and would never really harmonize with ricocheting bullets.

As I huddled in a doorway, across the street from Gabriella's, a group of drunken working men came weaving past the guards, singing what sounded like an old Spanish polka, and headed for the tunnel to the left of my hotel, right through the lobby of La Casa Del Quijote. The entrance to the tunnel, a semi-circular arch, like a mouth in a partial rictus from which the teeth had been extracted, was absolutely black and in no way inviting, and the tunnel itself drilled straight into the hill, meaning I had no idea at all where the passageway ended, but I joined with the workers and tried to fit in, though I was a good five inches taller than the tallest of the men, and didn't wear a hardhat, and couldn't sing Spanish polka. It would soon turn out that polka singing, and hatlessness, and my personal stature, should not have made the shortlist of paramount concerns; since the random and inscrutable Guanajuato maze of interconnected tunnels, and subterranean roadways, and paved-over sluice-channel underground rivers, were intended to carry cars, and were next to impossible to navigate without illumination, I should have been raising more salient issues, like why were the tunnels pitch-black dark, and where could I get a flashlight at 3:00 am, and the soon-to-prove pressing but unanswerable questions, like Where on earth am I, and Who turned the lights out? Eighty feet inside the tunnel, and a whole world away from the gun-toting fiddle player, I stopped in the roadway, knowing exactly where I was, and thinking it might be best to let the weaving men go on ahead, to wander off together towards their warm homes without me, a decision that at the time must have seemed perfectly sane, but with the benefit of hindsight, was a huge mental blunder. Within four or five seconds they had completely disappeared, into the sort of darkness that's like a physical substance, not the absence of light but the presence of its absence, forcing me to go forward by pushing it backwards with my hands. I had very little doubt that the tunnel went through the hill, and into another barrio where the polka men were headed, but I have to admit that when their singing had stopped, and left me groping around with no sound to guide me, I couldn't help feeling that something had gone wrong, as though the men had not only utterly vanished but had somehow managed to cease to exist. For a few hundred yards, I had the comfort of looking back, and seeing light at the tunnel entrance as a marker and beacon, but at some point the tunnel must have subtly curved away, and out went my nightlight, which didn't seem fair, as I went forward alone without it by slowly slipping backwards, into dark-bedroom childhood hob-goblin terrors. And then a few moments later, even the gremlins were gone, replaced by something more maturely appropriate, like a full-blown case of nyctophobia, where the darkness itself had invaded my interior. I had made the simple error of turning around, seeking stray rays of light to keep me oriented, and finding nothing but blackness as far as the eye could see, I tried to turn back, to continue my progress toward the tunnel exit, and found myself lost in an infinite room, where *forward* and *backward* were no longer applicable. This room, to be clear, was also infinitely small, as though the blackness that had swallowed me had in turn just been swallowed; not only did forward and backward not make sense, but there was no real difference between *exterior* and *interior*, since the darkness that I occupied was itself now my occupant. On one level I was still a rational adult, tracing nycto- and phobia back to "night fear" in Latin, and preferring scotophobia, or "dark fear," as more descriptive, but the heart-racing dizziness, and hunger for air, and sense that I was buried under a mountain of darkness, were autonomic reactions that rendered language irrelevant; I might as well have been suffering from Alvaro de Campos. Gasping for breath, pushing the darkness out of my way, I managed to move forward a few feet at a time, with both arms stretched out like a gauze-wrapped zombie, searching for the pitchforks of torch-wielding peasants; for whatever it's worth, if you're ever in a village when things have risen from the grave, and are wandering the backroads inducing terror and panic, I can tell you for a fact that there is nothing to fear, the zombies themselves are more frightened than you are, and are only hoping for someone to lead them back to their crypts, or light them on fire so they can see where they're going. In the end, I got lucky, and ran out of room, and stumbled over something that turned out to be a sidewalk, and pitched face-first into a solid block wall, opening a slick bloody gash at the hairline of my forehead. While I still had no idea whether I was headed forward or back, toward the polka-singing barrio men or the semi-auto fiddle player, I at least had the comfort of feeling my way along, using the left-hand wall of the tunnel as a guardrail. In retrospect, I probably should have foreseen what happened next, which was that the stone wall ended, I mean it simply nulled out, and I fell headlong off the sidewalk to the pavement, and rolled thirty feet down an empty concrete hill, and came to rest ultimately in an enormous swamp of darkness, with no skin at all on one side of my face, and wounds on both elbows, and holes in my pant legs. Permit me, at this point, to make one thing clear: if you're ever in Guanajuato, and don't know who you are, with $20 million in the bank, and gunmen maybe after you, don't go in the tunnels, in the dead of night, without asking someone to please turn the lights on. I had apparently stumbled upon the ramp to another road, which must have led off toward some underground elsewhere, and had no real choice but to crawl back up the ramp, slowly widening the holes in the knees of my pant legs, and then crawling to the left where the pavement leveled off, and once again rejoining the relative comfort of the sidewalk. Not only was my exterior a little the worse for wear, but I'd added a few symptoms to my scotophobic interior, including dizziness and vertigo, and hot and cold sweats, and parasthesiac tingling in all my extremities, and a slowly deepening dyspnea starving me of breath, which all sounds vaguely rational given the fact that I was drowning. Somewhere in the bowels of Guanajuato Water and Power, a sharp-eyed old bureaucrat sat chuckling over his accounting ledger, running the numbers on the electricity he'd saved, by flipping the light switch on the entire city's tunnel system, while some bent-over hunchback stumbled around, bloodied and drooling, scarcely even hominid, confirming his suspicion that, at this ungodly hour, the dark city's underground was no place for the upright. And then, in due course, everything got worse. As I felt my way forward with one hand on the wall, groping for air, my lungs filling and refilling with a sense of their own vacuity, I suddenly became convinced that I wasn't alone, that something was in here, like right there beside me, some sort of being that had the uncanny malevolence of not being real but still being present. I swung my right arm two or three times, hoping to catch it in the act of momentarily existing, but my arm must have passed right through it, whatever it was, it was not that sort of thing, it was that sort of thing's ontological opposite. I pushed myself onward maybe ten more feet, and then came to a halt, in a viscous pool of nothingness, and crouched on the ground, choking down drool, and essentially giving in to a kind of sanity-free zone of absolute total and complete utter panic, within which I thought I heard something start to breath, and felt its warm breath, on my neck, right beside me. I reached out with my hand, convinced that it would vanish, and leave me with an arm that ended in a bloody stump, and encountered the oddest thing you could possibly imagine, even if you're insane, and can imagine almost anything, a living breathing being, now licking me on the chin, and as happy to find me as I was

to find him: a dog, just like that, nature's perfect incursion on the
sense of unreality, and not just any dog, but a whole dogful of dog-
ness, being wagged by his tail and cleaning my bloody head and
humming his ancient dog-song of existential pleasure. I'll concede
that for a moment I considered the possibility that the thing was a
phantom, just another malignant instance of what the darkness can
come up with, but there's something about a dog that would seem
to rule this out, since a dog keeps our home fires burning within it,
and a dog's ontological opposite is the exact same dog, and few
things in creation are as ontologically friendly as a tail-wagging dog,
just being friendly.

I followed my guide, down the path of his clicking nails, as he
sniffed his way back to the barrio smellscape, and we exited the
tunnel in my kind of world, where the darkness is on the outside
and not in your interior. The crescent moon had risen through
one-eighth of a starry sky, leaving maybe three hours before the
sun would be coming up, and while I had no real idea where in
fact I was, I'd managed to put a mountain between myself and the
hotel gunmen. We turned to the left down a scruffy-looking commercial street, full of sleeping carnecerias, and mop-and-broom
supply stores, and a mom-and-pop lechería that wouldn't awaken
for hours, with a palette-load of *leche* cartons stacked on the front
stoop. I left my last 100-peso note in exchange for a box of milk,
found a sack of day-old tortillas in a garbage bin next door, and
was just getting ready to serve breakfast to my dog, when I noticed
that he was growling at I didn't know what, maybe some sort of
delivery vehicle, slowly coming toward us with its lights turned off.
The dog let out a bottomless all-dog sigh, maybe half black Lab-
rador and ninety pounds of Rottweiler muscle, and started off at a
trot, up the steep cobbled path of a narrow callejuela, a word that
in one sense means *side street* or *alley*, but that in this case meant
something that translates to *subterfuge*, an evasive-tactic passageway
out of why-are-their-lights-off intuited danger. We climbed straight
up the dew-slick ancient stones, with the walls so close on either
side that I could almost reach out and touch them both, apparently
headed up the exact same hill that I had already passed through in
the nyctophobic tunnel. Maybe fifty feet up, we stopped and looked
back, seeing nothing at all but hearing an engine idle, and then

the dog sighed again and continued up and on, until we reached the intersection with Calle Suspiro, which may have been a reference to catching our breath, though since my dog didn't read street signs, and was not out of breath, it was far more likely that he meant to have breakfast. I found a dusty tin bowl outside a tall iron gate, rinsed it with water from a flower-garden hose, and filled it with a carton of 100-peso milk, worth every peso from the dog's perspective; the day-old tortillas, from the all-night dumpster, might as well have been made by hand on the spot, fresh off the masa press, and served up warm from a cast-iron comal; my dog looked up once, after chewing down a particularly well-cooked example, and gave me one of those dog-looks of such thorough approbation that I'll know on my deathbed what it means to be a hero.

So where on earth are we? We are, on the one hand, maybe 200 feet up, with another 600 feet or so, and a good mile of walking, to complete our climb of the hillside back toward town, on a narrow callejuela up the ridge of the hill, with the streets falling off precipitously in either direction; we're surrounded by whitewashed walls and homes that are fast asleep, with a few twinkling lights on the valley floor below, and the silhouette of a church spire at the top of our moonlit climb; we're stopped at the corner of Subterfuge Lane and Street of Sighs, eating our breakfast of milk and tortillas, with downtown Guanajuato somewhere up ahead, and what sounds like footsteps down the alley behind us; if we've somehow lost track of where we stand in the world, it's not the world's fault, the world is there all around us, with well-marked streets and a landmark straight ahead and what sounds like a search party coming to take us back. We are, on the other hand, in an odd mental place, with problems mounting up faster than we can count them, and with no way of knowing just what they amount to: I have $20 million in the bank, an ATM PIN with a mnemonic-device malfunction, and not a peso in my pockets at maybe 4:00 am on a Sunday morning, meaning that my financial-stature worries have finally come to an end, and while I may have signed a contract, somewhere along the way, to end far too many subclauses with terminal prepositions, I'm the Zero Peso Man, which sounds like a bargain that even I can live up to; I have a credulity-straining, fact-checker-defying, personal ID, with a Fedora-wearing license photo clipped from an old book, in the name of a man, made solely of words, who never believed in his own existence, if for no other reason than that he didn't in fact exist, though his words were all real, and not even he could ever doubt them; and I would seem to be in the middle of a B-thriller plot, shot in black-and-white from an improvised script, using live ammunition and imaginary film stock, involving drug lords and gunmen and possibly stolen loot, and a femme fatale for whom the movie ran backwards, capable, in the end, of the ultimate betrayal, revealing that our hero is basically just a douchebag. So this is what we've come to, eating garbage on the Street of Sighs, listening for footsteps down the alley in the darkness, with no sense at all that our life might add up, other than to the belief that it doesn't really need to; I'm not trying to deny that there are problems to be faced, like if I don't get a move on, I might be dead in 40 seconds, but the fact is it simply feels good to be alive, and even though my life can hardly be called my own, it still feels like something worth making a run for.

And then time was up, and the black dog called Time, pricking his ears and coming to attention and swallowing a whole tortilla without taking a single bite, and sighing as he trotted up the narrow cobbled lane, headed toward the church spire silhouetted in the distance. The alley, to be honest, didn't actually exist, if you're picturing a kind of path with linear integrity; there were zigzags and ellipses and spatial incongruities, with forks in the road that seemed to lead to dead ends, and sections where I would have sworn we were pointlessly backtracking, and hills that we descended that appeared to make no sense, but that ultimately gained us altitude, and proximity to the church spire; the path was a kind of sentence, with its own tortured syntax, and misleading punctuation, and deliberately cryptic solecisms that bordered on total gibberish, the sort of thing you can't help thinking only a dog knows how to read, until you finally reach the church spire, a moonlit exclamation mark, where the sentence ends in Ah! so that's what all that meant. Standing on the hilltop, with a near-half waning crescent moon still rising in the east, downtown Guanajuato lay stretched out beneath us on the dark valley floor, still sound asleep at maybe 4:30, with lights just turning on as deliveries began at the Mercado Hidalgo, and El Pípila striking a pose, directly across from us, lit up but stoic in a

crossfire of spotlights. From our hilltop perspective, it was possible
to see that Guanajuato itself was not a single valley, but a series of
separate barrios set apart by rolling hillsides, with the downtown
churches and fountains and plazas in a valley that ran from east
to west, or left to right from where we were standing, following the
course of a river, the Río Guanajuato, whose waters once flowed at
their own sweet will in the underground channels beneath the city,
before they dammed them up, and put a stop to all the flooding,
leaving phantom-river ghosts in a dark maze of tunnels. We stood
on the edge of a small public park, which contained within its borders a patch of tilted headstones, and surrounded the church spire
with flowerbeds and greenery, and empty wooden benches, and
great weeping willow trees, admittedly admiring the twinkling view,
but listening for footsteps in the street maze behind us. Directly
below us was another tangle of narrow streets, the streets just above
Guanajuato University, and then my own hotel, and the Plaza de la
Paz, and the Basilica of Our Lady, with its soon-to-be custard walls
and dusty-rose domes, and then the HSBC bank branch and the
Calle Luis and the One Hour Photo shop one-minute stop, on the
evening side of time in the honey-smoked twilight, the stop that preceded our stooped-over entrance into the Revenge of the Gardeners trueno hedge, where Gabriella had shown me her Theta-party
portraits, and the evidence that I, whoever I was, had apparently
been present but not altogether there. Just beyond this would be
the Quixote museum, the Museo de Iconografía, where we'd eaten
gorditas and discovered ideals and learned the power of craziness,
or maybe it was genius, to take back reason, on the minute hand of
human hours, from men who have the power to make the clocks
run for cover. And next would come the climb up Pípila Hill, and
the Callejuela Subita mistranslation, and the Callejón Desvío Passageway to Nowhere, the Circuitous and Roundabout Way Not
to Get There, which had led me up to Bird's Nest Tom, and tea
served up with the word-salad wisdom of home-is-where-the-heart-
is schizophrenic normalcy. Then my Harold Bloom knight's-move
poem in reverse, back down the hill to the Guanajuato time war;
my study of Aztec poetry, in microscopic print, while preparing the
Coyote, Nezahualcoyotl, for his *nemontemi* day of chanting and
fasting; out wandering the impoverishment Life Giver streets, with

tiny blue milk-bubble cornflower lips, and Styrofoam cups out begging for pesos, while forming the yet-to-be-tested hypothesis that we're all interwoven and in this together, that no one is rich until the least of us is cared for, and This Is Our Body, and *what thou lovest well remains*; my how-is-this-possible evening beneath the stars, and the history of time in Max Planck instants, while the soup pot simmered until the sheets became tangled, before Gabriella served me her chile verde stew, and wound up taking my head off, backwards, which I, it turns out, no doubt deserved. From Friday morning vacant awakenings to predawn Sunday church-spire Ahs!, it had been quite a journey for someone like me, a beginner who had reason to doubt his own existence, but with reasons of his own for beginning to believe. *Tiempo!* barked the dog, there must be footsteps approaching; the time for nostalgia ended abruptly; and *down* the steep hill we plunged in a hurry, into a future that leads back into the past, along a chirally twisted Möbius chronology.

Our flight from the hilltop, in the *act of fleeing* sense of flight, made no sense at all, other than to the dog, and believers in the force of gravity. We chose streets at random, just as long as they went down, past shuttered-up windows and padlocked iron gates and small wooden flowerboxes whose flowers I couldn't see, not at the rapid rate that *fleeing* demanded. How close our pursuers were, I just couldn't tell: the acoustics in the alleys, in terms of the fidelity of sound, were not to be trusted, with footsteps right on top of us, or even out ahead, and then fading away into nothing as we entered a different corridor; I was tempted at times to panic, when the footsteps sounded close, maybe break into someone's living room, and hide in a dusty broom closet, until I caught a glimpse of something that didn't appear to belong here, and slowly began to wonder about the nature of our pursuers. We had just made a turn into a narrow callejuela, where the footsteps behind us seemed particularly close, and we were, if anything, picking up speed, with our pursuers right behind us, matching our pace, and even closing in as the passageway narrowed, when something caught my eye, as we fled straight down, making a headlong dash through the narrowing roadway, past shuttered-up windows and padlocked iron gates and a small wooden flowerbox whose pink, purple, red, and violet geraniums seemed trapped in a moonlit charcoal sketch, awaiting the sun, the morning locksmith, and his brilliant twin, the autonomous still-life flower painter; this flowery effect, which must have popped into my head out of nowhere as we fled, seemed so out of place in a chase scene scenario, and inappropriate to the mentality of the headlong dash, that I couldn't help wondering if my mindset had shifted, headed off in the direction of a different state of mind, namely the gathering suspicion that we weren't being chased, that we were effectively being pursued by the hill's strange acoustics. And then somewhere along the way, as the dog raced ahead, his paws nearing the point of literally flying, like 4/4 sixty-fourth notes gone utterly awry, and I tried to follow along in stuttering-duplet steps, doing an odd Balkan dance down the steep slippery cobbles, to the ghostly-ghostly-galloping of a 7/16, or something out of Stockhausen, maybe *Klavierstucke XI*, whose aleatoric structure forms a rhythm-matrix maze, or *Klavierstucke IX*, whose curious rhythmic proportions follow a Fibonacci spiral, or perhaps worst of all, as I stutter-stepped the stones, hearing a pure but irrational time notation, and echoes of Stradivari building violins in *phi*, as though my feet had somehow stumbled upon a Golden Ratio, the *Divina Proportione* mathematical constant that Phidias prefigured in the Parthenon, the matter, for me, was effectively settled: it was time to face the fact, from the evidence at hand, that the footsteps pursuing us were essentially my own. I stopped for a moment in the empty road; the world all around me was dark and quiet; my dog continued on, racing alone, but no doubt certain of his own internal rhythms, and chasing the thing that had started him barking, which turned out to be a small grey squirrel. There was a lesson to be learned here, about the mind's incessant noises, and allowing our own footsteps to constantly pursue us, but the lesson was somewhat convoluted, perhaps not worth the breath expended, and it seemed to be slowly erasing itself, as I completed my descent in manifest silence.

Having finally treed the cowering squirrel, the dog raced ahead at the bottom of the hill, toward an ornate stone fountain at the center of a small plaza, where he stopped for a drink of water, took a long look around, and then pivoting on his axis until he found the right spot, corkscrewed to the ground and came to rest with the pigeons. Not one to argue with a dog's sense of place, I took a seat right beside him on the fountain's stone ledge, washed some icy water over

my facial abrasions, and performed what started out to be a brief reconnaissance. The plaza we were centered in, a narrow rectangular
colonial plazuela, surrounded by multi-toned three-story buildings,
was in itself so radiant, and made such a dazzling first impression,
after a dark night's journey through a maze of lightless streets, that
it seemed to possess the uncanny benevolence of not being real but
still being present: with the streetlamps lit, and more than a few of
the building facades awash in a flood of halide spotlights, this narrow rectangular colonial plazuela looked like the music room in
a gemstone palace, full of songbird-shades of tourmaline crystal,
rosefinch, blue jay, yellowthroat, robin; at some point, however, as I
was dreaming up shades of tourmaline stucco, I must have come to
realize that my room lacked a ceiling, and that my birdsong palace
crystalline illusion would shatter in an instant if the sun began to
rise. While the night sky was dark and starry-eyed and moonlit, a
few low clouds along the buildings in the east had just reached the
point of beginning the process of beginning to turn a pale shade of
grey; the morning star had risen maybe an inch above the clouds,
which would soon be turning pink, unless the world stopped revolving; a dark night's journey, in short, however extensive, was nearing
the very end of the beginning of an ending, and I was fairly close to
right back where I'd started. We were somewhere to the east of the
poet hotel, with the trueno hedge ahead of us, and then the Calle
Luis, and then the steps of the Teatro and the Quixote museum; if
the handgun-musicians hadn't moved an inch, they could cover every inch of the ground between us with something on the order of a
four-block stroll; and if someone had been following us, now would
have made an excellent time to put in an ominous dramatic appearance, as the plaza, as noted, was brightly lit, had nowhere to hide,
and had very few places to enter or exit. At this point it should have
been readily apparent that my brief reconnaissance would need to
end here, with a few final notes on the room's dimensions, the limited duration of a game of hide-and-seek, and a cautionary note, as
a final entry, on the ease with which the exits could be barred; at
the time, however, I was not just exhausted, I felt like I'd spent my
night in the mines, and the semi-precious jewels of my gemstone
illusion appeared to be something I'd paid for in advance, as though
every missing watt from the nyctophobic tunnels had been spent on

lighting the pinkfinch, yellowthroat, and robin's breast walls of my semi-precious gemstone tourmaline palace, and while I knew for a fact that the thing wasn't real, now that I was here, with the jewels all paid for, I'd certainly earned the right to sit and enjoy them.

From my fountain-edge perspective, I took another look around, dispensed with all of the birdsong hues and semi-precious gemstone paraphernalia, and found myself surrounded by three-story buildings, in a narrow rectangular colonial plazuela, and in yet another room whose ceiling was missing, but whose floor was a rock-solid stone parquet; the room had been decorated with ornate but uncomfortable-looking cast-iron benches, like Louis Quinze settees in a metalworker's drawing room; the lighting was supplied by standing lanterns, evenly spaced around the edges of the room, with spotlights up in the room's four corners, beaming down on top of me and the antique fountain. The fountain itself was a little over-whelming, like a three-layer wedding cake that had lost all sense of wedding-cake proportion, growing to nearly twenty feet tall, fright-ening off both the bride and groom, and whatever remained of the wedding party. The baker had started simply enough, with a layer of edgewise Cantera paving stone; the second layer, similarly pro-portioned, was a thick solid block of the same native stone, green-hued and porous, from a local mountain quarry; and then things had gotten a little out of hand, with the baker losing track of the original assignment, adding in a top layer of allegorical complex-ity that didn't bode well as to the prospects for the marriage, and leaving the over-elaborate baker faced with the possibility that, all things considered, he'd soon have some serious explaining to do. An enormous bronze scallop shell sat balanced at the top, barely supported by a thin tapered column, beneath which were stranded two near-life-sized cast-bronze dolphins, darkening with age, and no doubt longing for the sea. What exactly is this, Pablo? It looks like some sort of bowling trophy. But don't you see, Don José? It is the tale of the Birth of Venus, the goddess of all that's lovely, arriv-ing at the seashore as a full-grown woman, with her sacred friends the dolphins, in honor of your daughter's beauty. Perhaps you've seen a photo of the Botticelli painting, worthy of a Medici; I have used the same scallop shell. So where are the bride and groom? I thought they were to be depicted at the top of the cake. Ah yes, as to the bride and groom, I have thought long and hard on this. The groom, to begin with, is completely irrelevant; your daughter could have married any number of suitable men, and I hardly think the gentleman in question is worthy of such a beauty. And in any case, if you recall Botticelli, Venus does not arise from the foam of the sea with a man in tow, beside her on her scallop shell; she is a goddess, your daughter, and while I concede that your prospective son-in-law is good with a horse, he scarcely belongs in the same room with such a woman, much less the same scallop shell. You are right, of course, Pablo; many times I have told her this; to think that such a boy should inherit my hacienda, and my vast holdings in the silver mines, and all of my agile polo ponies; but her mother insists; what is a man to do? My condolences, Don José, on the loss of such a daughter; perhaps you may be consoled by the tale of the wedding cake, with its scallop-shell reminder of Venus rising from the sea. So we will place the figurine of my daughter alone atop the cake? This is genius, my friend, genius; we will teach the boy a lesson, eh Pablito? Keep his hands to himself, and off of my beautiful polo ponies. As to that, Don José, I do not think it advisable. Venus rises from the sea, in all her wondrous glory, completely stark naked, with only her long red hair to cover her intimate delicacy; perhaps it would be best to leave your daughter's glorious beauty to the viewer's imagination, and leave the scallop shell as it is, in honor of your daughter's modesty. An empty shell, then? Yes, Don José, an empty shell, with only an intimation of the true wedding that might have been, if the women had just stayed out of things, and left the arrangements to us. Pablo, my friend, my sentiments exactly; my wife, as you know, is a Furie when crossed; I can hardly be blamed for any of this. As to the cake itself, don't you think it's a little large? The cake, of course, was not a cake, and Pablo and Don José were products of my fatigue, and a fertile but empty imagination, with the dawn just now beginning to begin, and the truth of a dark and sleepless night slowly but surely sinking in; the cake, in fact, was a hopelessly ornate Florentine fountain in the Plaza del Baratillo, a fountain that once stood at the heart of the city, in the Plaza de la Paz, back in the days when the Guanajuato River still flowed from its source under the sun-drenched streets, and the fountain was fed by underground waters, from the Presa de la Olla reservoir. How it had ended up here, in an out-of-the-way plaza, cut off from its underground sources of water, was anybody's guess, and the fountain didn't have one. As to how the marriage had worked out, I couldn't really comment; presumably the bride and groom, at the height of the endless wedding party, had run away to sea, and never again been heard from. Which reminded me a little of me, of course, with my shipwrecked tan, and my not having been heard from, though I, in truth, was not that man, and not only did I not remind me of me, I didn't remind me of anyone.

And then...as I sat on the edge of the ornate fountain, with the sun about to rise, and the streetlamps gone dark, and the fountain, apparently, full of stagnant water, recalling for a moment the musical fountain from my Mozart Starling twin-song breakfast, the fountain where the future had already happened, and time moved forward by flowing back toward its source, an odd thing occurred to me, two things in fact, having something to do with language itself slowly flowing back toward its source inside me. I was just getting ready to serve the last of the tortillas from the all-but-empty plain brown sack, and as the black dog looked up at me, with those 50,000-year-old eyes of his, eyes that speak of the bond with humans, while basically saying Where's my breakfast?, I came out with one of those singsong word-strings that humans are prone to employing with canines, who pay very little attention to the words that are spoken, but are absolute masters of the music of tone: "Good dog, good dog, you want some breakfast?", followed immediately by another string of words, with no tone at all, without inflection, the sort of statement that a dog skips over and ignores, while staring directly at a bag of tortillas. "I have a dog." I have a dog? This didn't sound at all like human speech, it sounded like something out of Wittgenstein's Brown Book, one of his language games, lying flat on the page, intended to remind us that to imagine a language means, first of all, to imagine a form of life: imagine two men who are building a doghouse, with hammers, called "dogs," and a sack of nails, called "cats"; one man says to the other, "I need a cat," while the other man, who is perfectly competent, but who has, unfortunately, run out of nails, says to the other, "I have a dog." While these words sound puzzling to an ordinary speaker, in the form of life we are asked to imagine, both of these men mean precisely what they say.

Imagine a man named Alvaro de Campos, whose identity, incidentally, while completely fictional, is every bit as meaningful as the carpenter's cat. Imagine further that Alvaro himself is sitting on a fountain, in a dimly lit plazuela, rooting around in a sack of tortillas for something to feed a large black dog. Alvaro says to himself, in an uninflected voice, "I have a dog," and apparently means precisely what he says. What form of life does Alvaro imagine when he says this to himself, all the while knowing that this life he's been living started two days ago, that Alvaro, in fact, is a bit of an imposter, and that if he tried to cash a check with his phony ID, even a bank teller with a passing acquaintance with Pessoa's poetry would spot him as a fraud? Alvaro, evidently, has a large black dog; he's even now feeding it a day-old tortilla; and while the dog doesn't care that Alvaro's an imposter, if the owner of the dog came along to reclaim him, along with the clothing that Alvaro has been wearing, Alvaro would surrender both his dog and belongings, and sit there stark naked, with an empty brown sack. So what's our next move? Our naked Alvaro, stripped of his dog and his phony identity, exposed to the world as a dog-stealing fraud, says to himself, in a voice without a tone, "I have a dog," and for reasons that Alvaro himself can't fathom, apparently still means precisely what he says. The "I" in this statement is every bit as meaningful as the carpenter's cat and Pessoa's fishy heteronyms and the hammer named dog, pounding on the doghouse, which ordinary speakers, as you might well imagine, positioned beside a hole in a brilliant green lawn, one sparkling blue day, or a day just like it, would no doubt call a *coffin*, before lowering it in the hole, covering it with dirt, and going about their lives as *ordinary speakers*. The games, unfortunately, must have ended right here, and passed me along to an ontological puzzle, a puzzle that all my laborious reading had in no way prepared me to attempt to solve. As the dark sky faded, and my dog ate his breakfast, and I waited for Pablo to finish his fancy cake, a wedding took place between me and my history, and I knew all at once that there was a language inside me that wasn't Alvaro's but some other man's. *I have a dog*, said that man who was my other, and in some form of life I couldn't begin to imagine, I, evidently, was precisely that other man.

Two things occurred to me when the gunmen appeared: first of all, in terms of reconstructing some prior identity that the gunmen seemed intent on doing away with, "I have a dog" was not a lot to go on, though by the time I got around to framing this thought, my own dog let loose with some terrifying barking and teeth-bared snarling and general animosity that caused the startled gunmen to retreat rather abruptly, and hide around the corner of a building to my west, leaving only the chrome plating of a bull-barreled Ruger exposed to the last of my gemstone illusions, reflecting a rose-fuchsia-amaranth array of deeply refracted predawn reds; and secondly, with or without anything to go on, I now had to go, and make some sort of run for it, as I was no longer the groom at a wedding with my history, I was already married to a target on my back. I took off running down the length of the plaza, and went out through the exit that maybe led to the Jardín, and The Revenge of the Gardeners, and the Calle Luis, which by my calculations, could be almost anywhere, but might just as easily be right up ahead. My dog stood there barking for another few seconds, just time enough for me to get out of range, and then lit out after me as I ran down the hedge, made a left on the Calle at the steps of the Teatro, and headed in the direction of the Quixote museum, and the narrow callejuela up Pípila's Snood Hill. We climbed straight up the staircase steps, swallowing whole stairs three and four at a time, and losing sight of the staircase entrance itself, as at some point the stairs not-so-subtly curved away, through a sequence of chicanes and lateral displacements that left us in the dark as to where in fact we were, either alone on the staircase, with the gunmen losing track of us, or with the gunmen there with us, still in pursuit, and then stopping at the midpoint, where Gabriella had lost her keys, and hearing footsteps run past us on the Calle Luis, concluded that we'd managed to make a narrow escape; my dog mulled this over, with his ears pricked up, his head slightly tilted, as though puzzled by something, and then a split-second later, righted his head, stopped solving puzzles, and started climbing stairs, pulling me along at the end of a rope that required him to pause when the rope grew too taut, looking back, now and then, to make sure that I was there, and hadn't wandered off into my own mental shrubbery, and then halting altogether when the stairsteps gave out, at the Desvío/Subita left/right fork, and unwilling to proceed without further instructions, pretended to promote me to the position of commander. With what sounded like an army now marching up stairs, and my recent promotion still subject to review, this was no time at all for Subite indecisions and inverted-iambic poetry readings and knight's move thinking about the endless varieties of Ways Not to Get There, up a no-exit cul-de-sac; at the fork in the road at the top of Calvario, I made a decisive and counterintuitive and contraindicated left onto Callejón Desvío, and headed straight up the Right/Wrong hill, toward Bird's Nest Tom's, and the NO TRESPASSING rosebush hedge, and the apophanous perception of a matte black shotgun, half-buried under dirty clothing in a bricolage shack. The verbiage-ruined houses flew by in a flash, with my flowery effects now locked up and useless, and Stockhausen rhythmics a thing of the past, and the sound of my own footsteps vaguely reassuring, since as long as I was running, I knew that I wasn't dead. What I also should have known, given my history, was that somewhere along the way, I was bound to get us lost, a story best told by means of analogy, the exact same analogy that got me lost in the first place: the cobblestone dead-ends of stairways and alleys were no more coherent than on my first trip through here, wording my way through a narrative maze, in a lost-thread, bored-to-tears, where-was-I-now, talking jag, an approach that, apparently, my dog disapproved of; as I stood there staring at a fork in the narrative, in the middle of a particularly peculiar subclause, my dog sniffed around, picked up the thread, having something to do with retracing my footsteps, headed off at a trot up the path of my scent, and then dropping the whole pretense that he considered me a leader, demoted me back to subcommander.

While I was now at the end of a canine-intuited precautionary rope, being towed up the hill by my street-savvy dog, I did have the consolation that my problem with street signs, and mistaken left turn onto Callejón Desvío, meaning Blind-Alley Detour or Passageway to Nowhere or Circuitous and Roundabout Way Not to Get There, had apparently confused the reasonable men who were far-too-literally attempting to pursue us, and who must have assumed that I knew what I was doing, and would not think of Nowhere as a good place to be. As the cobblestones ended in the mule-droppings pathway, I could hear their voices on the next hill over, following the altogether rational but misguided assumption that I knew how

to climb a hill, up Callejuela Subida, which is, after all, the Spanish word for "Climb,"and would soon be attempting another narrow escape, at the top of Snood Hill, in a Pípila-hill tram car; it
was in fact so patently obvious that my only way out of this was to
follow the road out of this, avoiding Dead-End Detours and Roads
That Don't Go There, that I doubt they thought twice at the Des-
vío/Subida fork in the road, and were now nearing the top of the
Wrong/Right hill. If they followed this line of thinking to its logical conclusion, they'd wind up taking the tram back down, end up
where they'd started, back in the city center, and finding themselves
with nothing better to do, hopefully go to church under the rosy red
Basilica dome. It was, of all things, a beautiful Sunday morning,
one of those sparkling blue days that's unlike any other, with the
altar boys, even now, donning their black cassocks, and their crisp
white surplices, and preparing the incense to burn in the swinging
thuribles, and praying they didn't fumble the cruets of Holy Water,
on this day of all days, April 19, Divine Mercy Sunday, the Sunday
after Easter, when Our Lord's Mercy grants forgiveness to even the
most hardened of sinners, and wouldn't that be a lovely sight to see,
outside the 8:00 am Mass in maybe 15 minutes: a lifetime supply
of assault-rifle weaponry and burst-fire handguns and speedloader
stripper-clips abandoned in the flowerbeds of the Plaza de la Paz,
particularly that Ruger Mini-14 rifle, with its ominous-looking bull
barrel plated in chrome.

    At the end of the dirt path, in the detour-to-nowhere dead-end
cul-de-sac, we stopped outside the padlocked gate and peered in
through the chain-link fencing and wondered a little if this was a
good idea, disturbing the Birdman on April 19, which in addition
to being the Sunday after Easter, was one of Tom's odd days, which
is a whole different story. The vacant-lot junkyard from Gulliver's
Travels, full of kitchen appliances and claw-footed bathtubs and La-
Z-Dog love seats and the Dreamline recliner, was still sound asleep
in the Wahneinfall morning, where everything seems to come to
you from out of the blue. The only things moving were the cinderblock chickens, the White Rocks and Chanteclers and Shaver Reds
and Cubalayas, which had to be the ultimate in free-range poultry,
feeding on yellow corn that Tom grew down the hillside, and free to
roam around, not just in the yard, but in the exact same yard in any

number of locations, meaning even their own surroundings could not be confined, since they existed in a wide range of reduplicative landscapes. This home-is-where-the-heart-is home that Tom had built, with the conniving-little-goofball support of his mother, and the make T*ah*m say *ah* hammer-it-in assistance of his VA doctors, and the Capgras-syndrome muscle he'd supplied, to plant his own corn, and dig his own well, and build himself a home that wasn't full of imposters, not only came equipped with a NO TRESPASS-ING sign, but had Do Not Disturb written all over it; this whole hearth-and-home that Bird's Nest Tom had achieved, after fleeing the pink house and the Chlorpromazine lobotomy, was itself so peaceful and poignantly deranged that it made my heart ache to even think that I might disturb it, and I'll freely admit that I had frozen in the roadway, and decided to just go back, and face the music without him, when all at once Tom's Shepherd, apparently asleep on the cool tin roof, crashed-out and dreaming atop the bri-colage shakery, woke up barking at the top of his lungs, and my dog now named Hammer started to bark along, and an entire junkyard chorus of mutts and mongrels and look-alike strays joined in on the polychoral barking arrangement. If I described the sudden sound as *shattering* the silence, or used some similar dead-metaphor cliché, you'll have to excuse me, I couldn't hear myself think, but trust me, I was there, and the silence got pulverized, ground down to something so powdery and fine that it autoignited and the junk-yard exploded. And then Hammer, bless his heart, found a hole that went under the iron-wire mesh, disappeared from the roadway, and reappeared in the yard, and when I vaulted up and over the rosebush hedge, I blew the landing by an inch or two, came down on the corner of a microwave oven, and lost my composure in a sprained-ankle heap. So much for poignancy and aching-heart un-willingness to disturb Tom's hard-earned slumber and peace; I was now caught in the middle of a cacophonous mixed-breed All Dog riot, with Hammer's black jaws closing down around the throat of a well-built pit bull terrier neck, and Tom's own massive and howling Shepherd getting ready to leap from the improvised rooftop, and some sort of schnauzer and cockapoodle mix trying to sink her tiny teeth into my rapidly ballooning ankle, and just as I was prepar-ing to lose a hand or two in an enormous pit-bull-Rottweiler snarl, what should break out but...complete and utter stillness. Bird's Nest Tom, a stick-figure charcoal sketch of a man, if anything even thinner than the last time I'd seen him, which was, come to think of it, maybe thirteen hours ago, had emerged from his hut yawning and stretching in the same rotting camouflage, with twigs and rose petals and kite twine in his hair, still awaiting the final landing of a bird flying backwards; he held up a hand in what might have been a wave, but that commanded total assent in the language of canine, like an orchestra conductor who had raised his baton, and without making a sound, or moving a muscle, called a halt to the polytonal sonic conflagration.

"Not-Really Alvaro, are you lost again?"

"No, Tom, I don't think I'm lost. I think some men are chasing me, and I've been trying to get away from them."

"Persecutory delusions those are called. Do you need to use the book?"

"I don't think these are delusions. I think the same men who sent the FedEx package, with the note saying they had not forgotten, have come back to find the man who maybe took their money, the man exactly like me who isn't exactly *me*."

"That's interesting, I find that interesting, that you would say that. This man exactly like you must be a replica. That's only logical, it's Capgras syndrome. That's why I went on the beach, I think it was in California, and put bleach in my hair, so the men at the VA wouldn't think I was an imposter. Is that why you erased your face?"

I had, to be honest, in the crush of events, completely forgotten about my facial disfigurement, the scalp-line bloody gash at the top of my forehead, the left-side-of-my-face Skin Bank deposit that I'd left on the off-ramp in the nyctophobic tunnels; my face, come to think of it, was something of a mess, the semio-ontological syntactical equivalent of trying to use a question mark as the subject of a sentence.

"I didn't mean to erase my face. I fell on the concrete, going through a dark tunnel. It was pitch-black in there. I couldn't see where I was going."

"I hate tunnels. Tunnels are murder. I see you have a dog, a dawg, a *dawg*, open up say *aw*, that's good for you, a seeing-eye dog for when you're stuck in a dark tunnel. What's his name?

Given Tom's various problems with Chlorpromazine nails, this wasn't a good time for a dog named Hammer, not on an odd day, which is a whole different story.

"I don't know, Tom, I just found him. I'm sure he already has a name."

"What name?"

"I mean a name I don't know, something his owner gave him, a name he would answer to when his owner called him."

"So you think he's an imposter? Comes when you call him but he's not the same dog? I had a cat like that when the tractor turned over, a white cat named Vanilla, it *melted* into the bushes. You can't drive a tractor in a Tastee Freeze. You can't put a cat in the freezer you moron what the hell is wrong with you, you can't even hold a job. So these men who are chasing not-exactly *you*, what do they look like? Do they look like men who can hold down a job?"

"I can't really say. I didn't have time to get a good look at them. When my dog started barking, they hid around the corner of a building to my west, and all I could see was the barrel of a rifle, a bull-barreled Ruger, plated in chrome."

"That can't be right. You'd have to be a moron to chrome-plate a rifle barrel. Probably not chrome-plated, probably stainless steel."

"You may be right. I never thought of that. Tom, look, I hate to bother you, but can we go inside for tea? It's cold out here, and I've been out all night. I could use a cup of tea."

"No one ever asked me that. I guess I'd have to think about it, if someone asked to go inside, go *inside*, *gohhh inside*, from out of the blue. If you ask me, I can't let just anyone in *out of the blue*. These are my surroundings. Just who do you think you are?"

He had me there. I didn't think I was anyone. Though I was, come to think of it, a man on the run, married to a shooting target, but hoping for an annulment, and fully capable, if push came to shove, of saying "I have a dog" with near-Lacanian conviction, becoming simultaneously the being who thus has spoken, and a man who could really use a change of surroundings, having hammered himself deep into Wittgenstein's doghouse.

"Look, Tom, it's me, Alvaro, or Not-Really Alvaro. I know it's one of the odd days, but can we go inside?"

"Sometimes when it's an odd day, I have to think about things, because people back away from me and shake their heads and say he's odd like I'm not even there and I don't exist, I don't *exist, I don't exist*. That's why they call it Cotard syndrome, so you can look it up in the book when you feel like you don't exist and need to know it's logical and you didn't die in Vietnam on one of the odd days and that's why people back away from you, like something smells funny, because you're *putrefying*. If you died in Vietnam, something smells funny. Odd means strange. So I guess we could have tea. Stranger things have happened."

So I guess we could have tea. We went inside the bric-à-brac lean-to, which sat in the shade of a spring-green oak tree, and was pretty much as I'd left it, thirteen-some hours ago, with a mattress down on the packed-earth floor and a crock of flat unbottled beer and a collection of black-and-white movie posters, tacked up all over the packing-crate walls, *Sunset Boulevard, Sullivan's Travels, Touch of Evil, Portrait of Jennie*. Tom's curious reference library was piled on the desk, *The American Psychiatric Glossary*, the *Book of Lists*, and a well-worn copy of the *PDR*, the first still marked in dozens of places with torn-off strips of poster paper, and the last left open for late-night study, next to a burned-down pool of wax, to the entry under Geodon, a drug he'd recommended to control my akataphasia thought-train derailments and my asyndesis habit of changing subjects in mid-sentence and my what's-my-name-again Cotard Syndrome, where you don't think you exist but they call you Alvaro, and you're an exact dead ringer for a man with bloody eyeballs. It may well be true, as the name suggests, that Geodon would help bring me back down to earth, but as for actually treating my Capgras syndrome, where my friends were all imposters who seemed to be out to get me, being brought down to earth was not going to help; even if I was suffering from Cotard's as well, where my name is Alvaro and I don't exist, this was a problem I blamed on Pessoa, and my down-to-earth friends were a symptom of something that might well respond to guns and money, but wouldn't respond at all to brand-name meds. And if this was in fact a case of me wandering around in a fugue state, a polyphonic composition in multiple voices, involving contrapuntal treatment and gradually mounting complexity, featuring unexpected travel and traumatic events and a loss of personality and personal identity, it certainly wasn't clear that the *Physician's Desk Reference* would be useful, unless it had a section under Unexpected Travel Agents, or offered some sort of drug that made the music play backwards. Tom filled the kettle from the yellow plastic bucket, and pointed the Coleman stove toward tea for two, and we returned to our positions in the moldering ancient wingbacks, on April 19, Divine Mercy Sunday, one of the truly odd days on God's synoptic calendar, when Our Lord's Mercy grants forgiveness to even the most tin-eared of the tone deaf, and those who have lost their way through His *Out-of-the-Blue Fugue.*

"So Look Tom It's Me, Alvaro, or Not-really Alvaro, which one are you? I know you're not Tom, last time I looked."

"I don't know, Tom. I know my real name is probably not Alvaro, but I can't remember anything about what my name really is."

"Probably Not Alvaro, these men who say they have not forgotten, what about *you*, what do they remember? What name do they call you when they call you *you*? *You*? *Mister You*? My name is Tom so she used to call me Leonard or get your ass in here *you*, I've got a bone to pick with *you*. You're in the doghouse *mister you* fucked up big time. What the hell *happened*, what were you *thinking, what in God's name* is *wrong with you*? Cat got your tongue? That's not God's name, *wrong with you*, so it's Eli Lilly and you gain a lot of weight. That's not *me*, that's a home with a Leonard. It's not in Australia, *Aus-tral-ia, awe's-trail-ya*, open up say *awe*, that's good for you. *Who in God's name do you think you are?*"

"From what Gabriella said, I think they called me Douchebag."

"Douchebag isn't a name, it's an apparatus. That's quite a contraption, a rat trap gadget. What were you *thinking*? *What* the hell *happened*?

"I have no idea. Gabriella's memory seems to work all backwards, from Sacramento to Gallego to Laguna de Patos, and then back to Chihuahua where the money was unloaded, and put in the bank by her uncle Gustavo, and then back to something called Casa Cronómetro, what Gomez calls the Stopwatch House, where I must have done something wrong because Gabriella said she could kill me herself, and I'm not a good man, and no wonder they call me Douchebag."

"*Now* look what you've done. You can't make a cat out of a pile of cat shit, how many times do I have to tell you stay out of the kitty litter. Vanilla's not a cat it's an ice cream flavor. Probably Not Alvaro, *you miserable douchebag.* Cat's have green eyes they can see in the dark in the freezer when it's hot out and the time work is and so it's down to the swimming hole to get cool in the water and cats don't swim they don't like water and the freezer is only logical because ice cream goes in the ice cream cooler. Don't make me come in there *you* I know what you're up to. *You,* you *froze* the fucking cat, how's *that* grab you. *That* isn't good. It's not in *awe's-trail-ya.* It's a pink house in Nebraska with a bunch of imposters. You have to put the scissors in a small wooden drawer."

This wasn't exactly getting *me* anywhere, other than off the streets, and closer to an appreciation for what Tom meant by *odd.* When the tea kettle whistled, Tom made the tea, and then served it up into two small teacups, though not without a rather startling display of movement disorders and motor-control dysfunction and neuroleptic aftereffects from all of his hammer-it-in phenothiazine treatments. As he started to tip the teapot, hypokinesia took over, and the pot wouldn't tip; once he'd finally overcome this, and movement had been initiated, tardive dyskinesia seemed to seize him by the hand, in a Parkinson's-like trembling that sprinkled tea here and there, including, of all places, the interiors of the teacups; and when the cups were finally full, he couldn't halt the tilting, other than in an agonizing freeze-frame slow-motion, an extrapyramidal symptom known as bradykinesia, and the pot continued to pour until the now brimming teacups were floating in a pool of steaming liquid, ready to sail away, or perhaps go waltzing, right off the edge of the table's surface, and crash to the floor with a bow and a

flourish, in a graceful exhibition of phase-plane transience, and entropy at work on enamelware spillage, and a live demonstration of
Newton's universal laws, as extended by Euler to porcelain motion;
and finally, at last, for no discernible reason, the tilting reversed,
the liquid settled back in the neck of the teapot, the waltz of the
teacups hit a patch of unwaxed floor, the ships ran aground on an
uncharted sandbar, the phase-plane stabilized on the surface of the
table, and I, for one, took a long deep breath. There, that was easy.
Now what? Tom bent down to pick the teacups up, and handed me
one in a brimming saucer, an act of sustained kinetic energy conservation that seemed to steady his nerves, at least for the moment,
permitting us both to sit back in our chairs, and pick up the thread
of our threadless conversation. So I guess you could say, all things
considered, that we could now have tea; I'm virtually certain that
stranger things have happened; though needless to say, given my
history, there is no possibility that you could prove it by *me*.

"So who are you really, Probably Not Alvaro? I'm *me*, I'm not
*you, you miserable Douchebag.* Are you an apparatus?"
"I don't know, Tom, maybe I am. To tell you the truth, if it
weren't for the fact that Douchebag did something wrong, maybe
stole $20 million of someone else's money, I wouldn't care at all who
I really am. Douchebag must be me in my prior life, the life that I
must have lived before waking up in Guanajuato, but Douchebag,
to me, is like an entirely different person. I don't know who he is,
or what he was up to at the Stopwatch House, Casa Cronómetro,
but even supposing he took someone's money, I was nowhere near
there when the money disappeared. Gabriella seems to think that
Douchebag is *me*, she could kill *me* herself for involving her in any
of this, but whatever *this* is, *I* didn't do it, and I don't know what
he was thinking, but they weren't *my* thoughts. That's on the one
hand. On the other hand, no one's going to believe that Douchebag
isn't me, that he's a man exactly like me, but he isn't exactly *me*.
That's what the books call an ontological problem, and I doubt the
men chasing me read these kinds of books. As far as I'm concerned,
Douchebag is dead, he died sometime on Thursday, April 16, at the
Stopwatch House, with a bag full of money, but if someone comes
to bury him, they'll bury me instead, and I doubt they'll really care

that they buried the wrong person. On the one hand, whatever he was involved in doesn't involve *me*, and if it were possible to bury him in the past where he belongs, I myself personally would shovel in the dirt. On the other hand, as far as I'm concerned, ontological thinking is not going to help me, it's far more likely to get me killed, and if I sit around thinking that I'm not involved, that whatever happened is Douchebag's problem, like don't look at *me*, I didn't do it, I might just as well be digging my own grave."

"As far as you're concerned, *you* should stay out of it. Your thinking *stinks*, it's *putrefying*, you need to take the bucket and wash *both hands*. You're making a lot of stewing noises, you're not making sense. *What in God's name are you trying to tell me?*"

"Sorry, Tom, I got a little carried away. Let me see if I can explain this better. Do you remember the man you were before you went to Vietnam?"

"Thomas Leonard Hoffman? Of course I remember him. He used to be *me*. He didn't work at a Tastee Freeze, he worked on a tractor where the time work is and the corn grows high when it's hot in the pasture and so it's down to the swimming hole to get cool in the water."

"Well Douchebag, to me, is like Thomas Leonard Hoffman. He used to be *me* in my prior life, it's just that, in my case, I can't remember him."

"Maybe Douchebag died in the Cu Chi Tunnels. It was pitch-black in there. He couldn't see where he was going. Thomas Leonard Hoffman had to go to the bathroom."

"Unfortunately, no, Douchebag isn't dead. He's still alive, I just can't remember him."

"As far as you're concerned, Douchebag is dead, you need to give him a decent burial. I buried Thomas Leonard in a hole in the garden, him and his dogtags, though sometimes when it's an odd day I'm not so sure, I have to think about things when odd means strange, because Thomas Leonard Hoffman crawls out of his hole and gets under my skin and makes my skin crawl. I'm me *Tom*, I'm not a *Thomas Leonard*, he makes my *skin crawl*, he's *putrefying*."

"Jesus, Tom, that sounds awful."

"Skin so thin it crawls right off, it's terrible, *terrible*, *tear-able*. You can't let a Leonard get under your skin, it crawls right off, it's *tearable*. As far as you're concerned, you should see your face, skin crawled off it, that's just *creepy*. Put your like a Leonard in a hole in the garden, he's *dead meat*, he's *decomposing*, and *you*, you *moron*, your hands are *filthy*, I *thought* I *told you* to *wash* your fucking hands."

"That's what I'd like to do, just dig a deep hole and bury him in the past, and then wash my hands of Douchebag altogether, but it's too late now to bury him in the past, he's already here, here in Guanajuato, and if these men who are chasing him put Douchebag in a hole, he's not going away without taking me with him. And as far as letting Douchebag get under my skin, he may be under my skin already. This morning I was at the fountain in the Plaza del Baratillo, washing the blood from my face where the tunnel had erased it, and it suddenly dawned on me that *I have a dog*."

"A dog, a *dawg*, of course you have a dog, a seeing-eye dog for when you're in a dark tunnel. I've seen him myself with my own two eyes, two *eyes*, two *eyes*, *my own two I's*. That's *me, seeing-I's*, it's nowhere near Nebraska."

"I was feeding him the last of the tortillas for breakfast, with the sky turning grey just before sunrise, and I said to myself "I have a dog," but it wasn't the dog I was seeing with my own two eyes, it was some other dog that must belong to Douchebag. And now I'm afraid that I may have Douchebag's eyes, and I'm going to start seeing things with Douchebag doing the looking, like he sees what I see, and has some sort of say in things. As far as I'm concerned, *he* should stay out of it. I've already seen the photos of how Douchebag *looks*, he was staring *straight at me* with his red-laser eyeballs, and his whole way of *looking* just gives me the creeps. I don't want to look at the world through Douchebag's eyes, and let him have a say in things, in terms of that beady-eyed world that he lives in, and have it turn out that I'm living in his world."

"You want him to keep his eyes to himself, his *I's to himself. Just who does he think he is?*"

"Exactly: *who does he think he is*, he doesn't even know me. I want him to keep his *I's* to himself. He lives in a different world, it's *nowhere near here*. I want him to stay *there*, and do his own looking. *I have a dog*, that's *his* problem, he should speak for himself, and leave me out of it, but he's not leaving me out of it, he's taking me with him, and even worse than that, I'm taking *him* with *me*."

That, you might say, was *that*, although I'm not sure at this point I could have told you the difference; perhaps under the influence of Tom's tilted shack, and his Thomas Leonard Hoffman horror story, I had started hearing voices, from an old silent film, whose stylized intertitles were slanted and oblique, something along the lines of *The Invasion of the Graphemes*, shot in black-and-white on 20 pound bond. I might point out in my own defense that one thing had become apparent from my attempts at conversation, whether arguing the politics of poetry with Ramírez, or seeking Tom's help with my Douchebag problems, or talking things backwards with Gabriella: while I was perfectly capable of expressing my thoughts, I had no sense of personal style when it came to self-expression, and borrowed my idiolect to suit the occasion from whomever I was talking to, whether schizo or Fascist. As to the internal voice by which my world was maintained, the whole world-made-of-language I both formed and was formed by, it was built like Tom's lean-to, out of packing crates and junk parts, ready-made already to collapse at the first good puff. I'd already discovered a crack in my world, at my *I have a dog* wedding with my history, and the last thing I needed was to find another crack; what if, for example, *I have a wife*? I took a shallow sip of tea, shifted in my chair, and made a mental note to think this over later, though if my own tilted shack finally gave way, I'd be thinking it over in fluent native Rubble, a language whose structure sounds inherently unstable, its lexemes held together with baling-wire and duct tape, but whose real-world equivalent, if my psychiatric lexicon was any indication, can be found on any psych-ward, with clinicians shuffling around looking glassy-eyed and dazed, mumbling things like "entgleisen" and "jargon aphasia."

   We sat for a while in schizo-affective silence, sipping our breakfast tea, shifting in our chairs, on Divine Mercy Sunday, April 19, one of the truly odd days on the *make-a-mental-note* calendar, when Our Lord's Mercy grants an audience to even the most cracked of the crackpots, living in our own tilted corners of the world, fumbling the teapots and cruets of Holy Water, and pleading for clemency, or a brief stay of judgment. Hammer had come in and was lying at

my feet, sound asleep after a long night of running, but still chasing
something in his muscle-memory dreams, and moaning and sighing, full of his own being; even in their dreams, dogs know where
they stand; if the dog does not bark, the patient is not in danger; *no
one has ever died beside a sleeping dog*. From my ancient wingback
facing the door, I could see into the yard-sale yard, where the chickens were making their rounds through the Lilliputian appliances,
and the roses were in full bloom in the out-of-the-blue morning,
and the Dreamline recliner seemed content to recline, absorbing a
sunlit-reality moment, taking it all in without blinking an eye, and
apparently daydreaming of this very moment. Just for a moment, the
world stood still, and the narrative machinery by which its meaning is sustained ground to a halt, and yet the world still stood there,
with the bricolage hut falling over but not down, and the blue sky
above still thinking itself up there, and the Alice in Wonderland
appliances in the yard maybe searching for a rabbit hole but not going anywhere. Just for the record, I couldn't help smiling, so if the
world stops revolving, I know what I'll be wearing: an improbable
smile that is simply the case because everything around it is equally
improbable. The ensemble of mongrels and mutts and strays was
scattered around everywhere, enjoying the stillness, awaiting some
signal from the orchestra conductor, a downbeat of the baton, or
a large bag of kibble. The thirty-pound cinderblocks still hadn't
moved, and really, why would they, their building days were over,
and right where they stood was as good a place as any. Tom's Easter
oak tree, in the early days of spring, with thousands of shades of
green to choose from, in the new-beginnings portion of the visible
spectrum, had chosen instead to invent a new one, and was out in
the yard, standing by its choice, altogether proud of its new-green
invention. I didn't see any signs of birds flying backwards, though
there was a single hawk, like the India-ink drawing around the eyes
of a Macaw, hunting for something in the hilltop scrub, and sketch-
ing lazy figure eights on an empty blue transparency. The patient,
meaning me, was resting more or less comfortably, with my micro-
waved-ankle propped-up on the tabletop, its phase-plane stabilized
on the surface of the table, meaning no more running for me for
the day; I'd need wings to get down from the Bird's Nest hilltop.
Tom got up to retrieve the teapot, poured more tea into two small

teacups, and then sat back down, directly across from me, with his chair standing still, but with his mind slowly receding; as I think I've pointed out, this was one of the odd days, and while it might very well have been Divine Mercy Sunday, this *particular* Sunday was a whole different story.

"These men want to put you in a hole a dark tunnel. No wonder you have persecutory delusions. I have those, you can look it up in the *Glossary* so it has to be real, but there's no such thing as Viet Cong and Cu Chi Tunnels and private get in there or I'll blow your fucking head off and please let me out of here I have to go to the bathroom. The tunnels were all in my head they told me, so I booby-trapped them all with bamboo stakes so the VA doctors wouldn't try to get *in*."

"Sorry, Tom, I was thinking about something else. What are we talking about?"

"We're talking about *Non Gratum Anus Rodentum*, not worth a rat's ass, couldn't give a shit if you have to go to the bathroom. She used to sit around the house chugging her drinks and stewing, dragging sixty pounds of gear across the Saigon River, throwing my dad out on his ass when the corn turned yellow."

"You lost me, Tom. Where are we? Nebraska or Vietnam?"

"Some people go down there in the Cu Chi Tunnels because they say they're volunteers, volunt*eers*, volunt*ears*, private get in there you're a volunt*ear* or I'll blow your fucking head off and there's no such thing as the corn is yellow and walking around for hours all hunched over. All you can see is black. I'm all *ears* you stupid schizo why did you freeze that poor little cat. Jesus motherfucker you really ripped him a new one. *That* fucking gook never knew what *hit* him. I didn't mean to hurt the cat with the little green eyes that could see in the dark, *that* just happened, *that's* in Vietnam. Are *you* in Vietnam? Is that how you got in here?"

"So this was in Vietnam. Were you some kind of tunnel rat?

"I was never a tunnel rat, those are mostly in Australian, and Vietnam's another place that's not in the same solar system and a rat is a small animal that's caught in a contraption. How in the *fuck* did you drop your *flashlight*? Black-bearded tomb bats. Bamboo vipers. Punji stakes. Stakes, snakes, rats, cats, bats in your earballs, bats are volunt*ears*, the walls crawl with Krait snakes, rat trap fire wires, private get down there I didn't ask you your opinion, *you* motherfucker just volunt*eared*. *Now* look what you've done, you shit your pants, you *shit*-for-brains, you can't even work the tractor. Long Phuoc, Cu Chi, Ho Bo Woods, the Iron Triangle. Scorpions and spiders, *spyders*, *hiders*, *cats* with *orange eyes* that *glow* in the dark. The cooler's only logical. Tunnels are *murder*. What are *you* staring at? *I'm all ears.*"

*That* can't be good. *That's* only logical. To be perfectly honest, I only caught about a third of this, and was in no position at all to ask Tom to repeat it. It's altogether possible that he said something else, in which case, I apologize; *he said something else.* I will say another thing in my own defense: whatever he said, it sounded just like this, and if I've twisted his words, they were already twisted, making shit-your-pants turns in a booby-trapped tunnel.

"Relax, Tom. You're not in Vietnam, you're in your home in Guanajuato. Remember you told me that home is where the heart is, and now we're in your home, where you can be comfortable."

"*You* make me uncomfortable, *you* erased your face, down in the *dark*, in the pitch-black tunnels. Tell me the truth: *you* brought the *dark* here *with* you, *didn't you?* Some people say I'm a goofball psycho, but I can read minds, and *you* don't *have* one, you're the *orange cat* in the black pajamas, with the Halloween eyes and scooped-out head. No wonder these men want to put you in a hole, you should see your face, you make my *skin crawl*, you're *dead meat*, you're *decomposing*, you need to go home and have your head examined. I'm *me* Tom, I'm not a Smith and Wesson. *What* are you *staring* at? Cat got your tongue?

"No look, Tom, it's me, Alvaro, or Probably-Not Alvaro. I was here yesterday. We had tea. Let's just sit here, or I can go if you want me to."

"*Go? Go? Go where? Where are you taking me? Down in the tunnels?*

Of course, this being one of the odd days, it turned out Tom was right, I *had* brought the *dark* here *with* me, hadn't I, and down we went, into the pitch-black tunnels. One minute we're sitting there, sipping our tea, with the men who were chasing me on the next hill over, and the dogs lying around in *Gulliver's Travels*; and the next thing we know, tea is a memory, the dogs are all barking, and the men are at the rosebush hedge, dressed up as a local SWAT-team force, prepared for a close-quarters combat mission, wearing body-armor vests and ballistic helmets and black-on-black camouflage, perfect for the occasion. Black-on-black camouflage? In broad day-light? This cryptic coloration form of concealment, allowing an otherwise visible object to virtually disappear, may seem like an odd choice for a bright Sunday morning, with chickens strutting around in the cinderblock yard, but it will soon become apparent that dark-ness has just descended, in cryptic black-on-black, from *out of the blue*. A fifteen-round burst from an MP5 machine gun completely obliterated the tilted-gate padlock, and the darkness fanned out to fill the reduplicative surroundings, taking up positions behind the kitchen appliances, the ranges and refrigerators and a Westing-house deep freeze, all products of Tom's Lilliputian delusions, and Tastee Freeze memories of a deeply frozen cat. While perfectly self-evident, nothing about this seemed the slightest bit real, and I found it next to impossible to initiate movement; this clearly wasn't a case of bradykinesia, Tom's freeze-frame slow-motion teapot problem, but something more along the lines of Blocq's disease or Aboulia, which rendered me a speechless and akinetic mute, a man out wandering on the dopamine pathways, searching for a nearby neural road sign, or maybe a distant mesocortical signal, to point the way back toward Motor Control Central, and the paralyzed ma-chinery of my own free will. Although frozen in my chair, unable to move a muscle, completely disconnected from the oncoming SWAT-force visceral reality, as if seated in a darkened movie theater watching a film reel unspool, I did uncover a rather startling cache of knowledge regarding automatic weaponry and burst-fire bulletry, from common submachine guns like the MP5s, with their 9x19 parabellum pistol cartridge; to the usual Rock River and Bushmas-ter and ArmaLite AR-15 small-caliber clichés, firing a derivative of the .223 Remington civilian hunting cartridge; to the true-warrior shitstorm firefight stuff, the sort of stuff that gets chambered with a 3" round, which looked a little out of place on a Bird's Nest hilltop, and must have come directly from somewhere on high, like the Mexican National Arsenal in Mexico City. Here I'd been worrying about a bull-barreled Ruger, whose ill-conceived chrome-plating had been prominent at my wedding, when it turns out the Ruger was maybe the least of my worries: to my immediate left, behind a pale-pink Maytag washer-dryer combination, stood a man holding a Fabrique Nationale SCAR-H, a Special Forces battle rifle with the closed-gas system of an M1 carbine, featuring a Picatinny rail that runs the length of the receiver, a 20-round box-magazine full of God knows what, maybe Full Metal Boat Tail hollow-point rounds, and an intangible but evident amount of acronymic ferocity, where the H stands for Heavy, in reference to its firepower, and the SCAR stands, memorably, once firing commences, for whatever the hell it wants to, so run for your life; while off to my right, fifty feet from the hut, using a vintage Kelvinator icebox for cover and gun prop, stood a soldier in darkened tactical goggles and a Kevlar Covert ballistic vest, equipped, in this case, with one of the latest innovations in mass-casualty infliction, an apparently brand-new FN Para-style FAL, with its 7.62x51mm full-power NATO cartridge, maybe four times the size of a Remington round, which was aimed through the doorway of the bricolage hut, but was better suited conceptually to firing into crowds, since the FAL is prone to spraying things in every conceivable direction, with the possible exception of whatever it was aimed at; and completing the picture, in the immediate dead center, yet another of the men, crouched in the weeds behind a broken-down range, an ancient O'Keefe and Merritt, in fire-engine Red, featuring twin stopped-clocks, a handy stovetop pancake griddle, and a side-of-bacon Grillevator that was truly unique, although its patent application must have long ago expired, and was no doubt gathering dust in the bowels of the Antique Patent Office, this man, as I was saying, before I carelessly wandered off into the Guanajuato weeds, was obviously wielding quite a geographical anomaly, a Heckler and Koch HK416, manufactured in quantity for the Norwegian Armed Forces, not the likeliest of Forces to be deployed in central Mexico.

The whole idea of this excessive show of force, in the middle of a yard sale full of harmless-looking household items, struck me as far too stagy and outlandish to be real, although it was, admittedly,

visually enthralling, combining brink-of-violence armaments with
a touch of the everyday; there must have been something about this
landscape dotted with brown and white chickens, plucking bright
yellow corn from the home-is-where-the-heart-is cinderblock dirt,
that struck some sort of chord in my virtual emotions, and left me
pinned to my seat, with disbelief suspended, indulging a genuine
moment of cinematic empathy. There, just for a moment, they almost had me, me with my tub of popcorn and extra-large Coke,
as the scene gathered momentum independent of my will, until
someone decided to top things off by training one of these high-
tech weapons on a spot just above my actual head, performing one
of those movie-history homagistic allusions, a touch better left to
Tarantino or De Palma, using a LaserMax rail-adapted green-dot
light beam to focus on the face of Charlton Heston, who if you
think back for a moment to A Touch of Evil, is not only in the process of kissing Janet Leigh, but is an American actor impersonating
a Mexican, a violent but pure-hearted drug enforcement official
named Ramon Miguel Vargas, a highly unlikely choice for a man
immortalized as Moses, but far closer to plausibility than Probably-
Not Alvaro. Now what? If these men opened fire on Tom's improvised lean-to, they'd reduce it to toothpicks, a device better suited
to Sterling Hayden in Crime Wave than to a Guanajuato hilltop
Living Technicolor scenario. What actually happened was that I
suddenly came to, penetrated by the reality of that green-dot laser beam; if you've ever seen a movie in which laser-sighting has
been employed, you know what I mean, because the laser is always
red, and only in the real world would the green dot be appropriate, since the 532nm emerald-green wavelength, visible in broad
daylight, across the open expanse of a Guanajuato yard, would be
far more useful in actually trying to kill someone than would the
670nm red of a darkened-conference-room laser pointer. With my
muscles now at last fully re-engaged, and connected to my will
by intricate neural pulleys, I could, I suppose, have pulled Tom
from his chair, but he was already crawling through the hut-tunnel
floor-dust, alerted no doubt by the barking of the dogs, headed for
his dirty-clothing pile, and a matte-black shotgun. Maybe he was
remembering the bright-orange muzzle-flash from his old Smith
and Wesson, which may have been useful on a *glowing orange* cat,

but wouldn't leave a scratch on a body-armored chest; and maybe I was thinking about an Over & Under Remington, which might have been perfect if we were out hunting pheasant, but wouldn't do much good against acronymic ferocity; but what he finally came up with, out of the bottom of the pile, was a thing of pure beauty, *The Shotgun from Hell*, which is not just a shotgun, it's a whole different story. How he'd come to possess such an ominous weapon, an Atchisson Assault AA-12 Close Quarters Battle Shotgun, I not only couldn't guess, I could barely comprehend it: it was an all-steel, zero-recoil, gas-actuated armful, firing 300 rounds per minute from a drum magazine, a cylindrical device in which munitions are stored in a spiral, in this case a drum full of FRAG-12 HEFA shells, meaning I was using the term shotgun for what was really something else, a high-speed grenade-launcher, and the things I called shells had nothing to do with buckshot, they were High Explosive Fragmenting Antipersonnel bomblets, not the sort of things you'd use hunting pheasant, although the grenades sprouted wings as they exited the barrel, and flew through the air like explosives-stuffed Falcons, a species of raptor whose name is derived from the Latin word for "sickle," for reasons best left to the Grim Reaper's imagination.

There is no other way to put it: Tom came out firing, spraying FRAG-12 HEFA shells all over the landscape, and the entire Bird's Nest hilltop went completely kinetic, with overpressure waves from munitions detonations and sheet-metal ballistics from appliance demolitions and exothermic hot gas enthalpy expansions from a Guanajuato junkyard exploding into flames. Imagine your surprise, if you're part of a well-armed SWAT-team force, extensively trained in displacement principles and cornering methods and cross-angling techniques, with a history of stacking and breaching into the hardened perimeters of fortified bunkers, with fire-rated blast doors and bulletproof aluminum windows and walls clad in Durasteel fibre-cement composites, and here you are staring at a low-life lean-to, a hut made of packing crates and Wizard of Oz roofing, at maybe 10:15 on a Sunday morning, facing some lame-ass assignment that's completely beneath you, with nothing to breach, not even a fucking door, when suddenly some guy who looks like a charcoal drawing, in rotting jungle camouflage, with twigs and rose petals and kite twine in his hair, simply steps outside firing a WHAT THE

FUCK IS *THAT*, and you don't, HOLY *SHIT*, quite know what just hit you, you, of all people, after all you've been through. The first victim of the AA-12 was a certain quiet confidence, the SWAT-force Alpha Male military swagger; the second victim, once the junkyard erupted, was any sense of conviction regarding the use of such expressions as "seeing is believing" and "I'll believe it when I see it with my own two eyes"; I spent a good forty seconds studying the scene, watching black-on-black forces, who are not prone to doubt, struggle to maintain their own fixed positions, and can say with some certainty, when it comes to the FRAG-12 HEFA shells, that not only is seeing not in any way believing, but it's a pretty good way to die for your beliefs. Blind faith, I think you'd call it, if you're standing around watching as a blazing AA-12, firing fin-stabilized 19mm high-explosive warheads, sets fire to the world around you, and you don't start having doubts regarding your standing in the world. I saw a Kevlar-vested man looking down at his zippered boots, as the Kelvinator covering him abruptly exploded. I saw a man holding a Fabrique Nationale SCAR-H, his face lit up by flames from a burning one-piece Maytag, staring straight up at the clear blue sky, maybe searching for signs of rain or a bolt of lightning. The O'Keefe and Merritt man, now facedown in the weeds, was not looking at anything, and although he had pulled the trigger on the HK416, he seemed to be firing sideways, pouring full-power NATO rounds into the tufted goose-down cushions of a sagging lavender love seat and a Berkshire Rocker Recliner; the twin stopped-clocks, the convenient stovetop pancake griddle, and the Patent Pending Grillevator, were nowhere to be found, although the sky was raining appliance shrapnel, at least some of which was Red enamel. The brown and white chickens appeared to be hovering an inch off the ground, which might have served as proof that chickens can fly, if it weren't for the fact that an apple-green cake mixer, with a 300-watt motor and planetary-action batter beater, had climbed to the same altitude, without proving anything. The black-on-black camouflage scheme, in which overwhelming firepower cryptically disappears, and takes up positions under cover of its own darkness, appeared, in this case, to be fatally flawed, as the hilltop lit up with flaming ranges and icebox explosions and HEFA washer-dryers, with their moisture-sensors melting and their dials all set on Blaze. Tom paused for a moment to reload the AA-12, from a gym bag stuffed with drum magazines, and enough FRAG-12 warheads to incinerate the junkyard; he seemed to be operating in a full-auto daze, with 20-round drums being emptied in seconds, including a magazine full of armor-piercing shells, which can only be seen as overkill against unarmed appliances. There were smoking-hole versions of ancient Norge ranges and vintage Magic Chefs and antique Tappan Deluxes with matching double broilers; a Frigidaire AP-12, with its white-on-grey porcelain beginning to bubble, and its stained-wood door-trim showing signs of wear, had been completely restored as a FRAG-12 pizza oven; a '47 Coldspot, featuring side-pull handles, a meat defrost tray, and glass-bottomed vegetable bins, could have smoked a side of beef, in a baste of molten metal. Imagine your dismay, after all your precision rifle training, with your mastery of low-light angle shots and wind and distance trajectory drift and the use of the mil dot reticle on your scope as a bullet-drop-compensation calculation mechanism, having set up properly in the battlespace, with your Expert Marksman rating badge carefully sewn to your armor vest, and your brand-new KA M110 prepped and at the ready in the prone position, a gas-operated, rotating bolt, semi-automatic sniper system, with the Leupold 10X variable sight and the Harris swivel bipod as a weapon stabilizer, and here you are faced with a complete no-brainer, a can't-miss target maybe thirty feet away, some moron wandering around with kite twine in his hair, and no apparent grasp of ballistic reality, when it suddenly occurs to you that you may have skipped a step, as you're facedown in the weeds breathing vaporized enamel, and that not only are the Appliance Wars effectively all but over, but that you, of all people, after all these years of weapons training, HAVEN'T FIRED A SHOT, and are basically just lying there, unwilling to look up, PRAYING YOU DON'T GET YOUR HEAD BLOWN OFF. By the time Bird's Nest Tom had advanced fifteen feet, and was standing in his junkyard, demolishing appliances, the SWAT-team force had started advancing in reverse, firing over their armored shoulders into the Guanajuato sky, not knowing what had hit them, not even knowing they didn't know, content with the knowledge that their feet were still attached, and that they could still find their way down the dopamine pathways. The logic behind the Birdman's rotting-camouflage scheme was readily apparent in the hilltop smoke: a charcoal sketch of a man standing still, reducing his surroundings to smoking rubble, is difficult to distinguish in a world reduced to charcoal. And by the time the black-on-blacks had reached the rose-bush hedge, with most of their NATO weapons abandoned in the weeds, the steady shrapnel rain had turned to a powdery snow, a fine white flurry of paint chips and particulates and pulverized baked-off vitreous enamel, from Wedgewood double ovens and Lady Ken-more washers and glass-lined Hotstream Instant Hot water heaters, a flurry that left the hilltop dusted and dazed, and Tom's Easter oak tree probably thinking it's almost Christmas.

When the firing finally stopped, the Bird's Nest hilltop sounded like an aviary, as though someone had built a birdcage in my head, and stuffed it full of phantom songbirds. Tinnitus, I think you'd call it, when you're suffering from acute acoustic trauma, and maybe you think the birds are singing, or it sounds like an army of lo-custs approaching, or maybe what you're hearing is a forest full of tree frogs. Whatever it was, I was utterly deaf, and the music I was hearing was subjective in nature, with my HEFA-deadened audi-tory system rapidly compensating for input loss by filling the air with cochlear creations, not one of which resembled a tree frog. I heard acoustic-nerve versions of Chopin's Canyon Wren, and a lovely tinnitus flute concerto, featuring the chirps of Vivaldi's Gold-finch, and most of the spiral-ganglion movement of Beethoven's pastoral 6th, full of Nightingales, quail calls, and cochlear cuckoos, although since my hearing-loss orchestra did not include strings, such that the "Scene at the Brook" had no flowing water, it sound-ed like my songbirds had been left to die of thirst, in the auditory equivalent of the Chihuahuan desert. And then came the dogs, as my hearing slowly returned to me, barking and wailing their intri-cate polychoral dog-song arrangements, maybe chasing away the last of the strangers, or drowning out the sound of a distant siren, or singing along with the birds I was hearing, though for all I knew, they heard their own phantom songbirds, singing Cielito Lindo to the Bird's Nest rubble. It was, after all, Divine Mercy Sunday, when our Lord's Mercy grants forgiveness to even the most hardened of assault teams, the members of which had managed to escape, through the tilted-gate fencing, past the verbiage-ruined houses, down the mesocortical pathways that can lead almost anywhere, down into the Durasteel fortified bunkers, into a café for pancakes and bacon, or even to mid-morning Mass at the Basilica, with their speedloader stripper-clips dumped in the flowerbeds, and their trigger fingers dipped in the sanctified waters, and not that I'm saying this is likely to happen, but wouldn't that be a lovely sight to see, if the world at long last simply put down its weapons, and decided it was time to forgive its own sins, for whatever remains of our slice of eternity.

I hobbled into the yard under the blue Guanajuato sky, where a lone red-tailed hawk was riding the updrafts, maybe hunting for quarry in the hilltop brush, or searching for a landing strip that hadn't been strafed and mortared, or maybe happy just to be up there in the home-is-where-the-heart-is clear-blue sky, held effortlessly aloft by the feeling of being airborne. I sat for a while in the Dreamline recliner, watching Bird's Nest Tom feeding corn to his chickens, floating around the wreckage as if nothing had happened; it was April 19, which had certainly turned out to be one of the odd days, and maybe he'd finally lost it and turned into a swallow, flying off alone in the Wahneinfall morning, equipped with the latest in delusional avionics, on autochthonous paraschemazia wings, toward the bombed-out remains of his own Capistrano; or maybe he'd finally solved his landscaping problems, and had finally seen the last of those phonies in Nebraska, now that his reduplicative-paramnesiac surroundings had been turned into a FRAG-12 twisted-metal sculpture garden, which was not, to say the least, a duplicate of anything. I had a pretty good look at the morning-after morning, and while the post-apocalyptic world may be hard on brand names, it's a beautiful thing to see once the smoke finally clears, and an ontological peace settles in over the landscape, with the ground laying down good grounds for its existence, and the stones holding nothing more stonelike inside them, and the Guanajuato hills rolling off toward the horizon, at ease with the land they both form and are formed by. Tom's Easter oak, in the dawning days of spring, basking for the moment in its own quiet limelight, as green as a green tree possibly could be, and lit up from within by its radiant new beginnings, seemed to have wandered into Being right before my eyes, and the next thing I knew, without doing a thing, it had rooted itself forever in that precise instant. Downtown Guanajuato, all church spires and basilica domes and rose-reds and custards, with just those very balconies and geranium flowerboxes, and those cobbled streets that knew exactly where they were going, and cathedral bells ringing their tribute to Time, having chosen this very moment as honored among the hours, held itself up, in the crystal clear morning, as that one shining example of itself above all others. Even the beauty of the moment wasn't lost on me, that magical sleight-of-hand by which it vanishes every instant, and shows up the next in the last place you'd think to look, like right where it is, where even the empty heart can hold it.

I wish I could tell you that my story ended here, with me sitting in a La-Z-Boy Dreamline Recliner, enjoying a final moment in the Guanajuato sun, feeling certain that I had earned it, after all I'd been through, at the end of a long war that lasted forty or fifty seconds; if you've never had a moment of existential peace, where you don't know who you are and you're Probably Not Alvaro and all you have to go on is a sentence about a canine, along with the fact that you are known to be a douchebag, let me explain something: it won't last forever, so you might as well enjoy it. I had, let's face it, basically sat out the war, in an ancient moldering wingback, staring out the doorway, with a cup of lukewarm tea in a dyskinesia puddle, and an emerald-green laser-sight focused on the face of Charlton Heston, a man whose real name, for whatever it's worth, is John Charles Carter, a man who must have struggled for most of his life, through hundreds of roles and constantly shifting identities, with the fact that he was born outside Evanston, Illinois, in a place known as No Man's Land, which has to make you wonder. And here I was now, after all I'd been through, the facial-erasure spills in the nyctophobic tunnels, the Street of Sighs pause to feed my dog with tortillas, the Stockhausen dance toward the Plaza del Baratillo, where my wedding was interrupted by a stainless-steel Ruger, which you'd have to be a moron to plate with chrome; the dash past the trueno hedge, down Calle Luis, up the narrow callejuela, toward the Dead-End Detour, pausing along the way to offer up a prayer, my prayer for the white-surpliced holy-water altar boys, on Divine Mercy Sunday, this very day; my disturbing-the-peace qualms at the tilted-gate fencing, with its hedge-roses blooming in the limelight days of spring, while preparing to play a role in the cacophonous mixed-breed All Dog riot, which was halted by a stick-figure orchestra conductor, wearing a birds-flying-backwards bird's nest in his hair, and a charcoal tuxedo, perfect for the occasion; the Tastee Freeze cat, the Black-Bearded Tomb bats, the Krait Snake rat-trap private-get-down-there's, on one of the odd days, which is a whole different story; and then darkness descending on a bricolage tea party, with its Para-style FALS and its well-armed Norwegians and its full-power NATO-cartridge acronymic ferocity, until a thing of pure beauty, *The Shotgun from Hell*, came out firing, exposing the fatal flaws in a camouflage scheme, in which a SWAT team tried to hide under cover of its own darkness, only to discover, in the full light of day, that they should have come dressed as Guanajuato weeds, or in the flaming-Red coveralls of appliance repairmen; and at the end of all this, while I'm enjoying a moment's peace, using a red-tailed hawk to teach me to stay airborne, I suddenly discover that the truce won't hold, and not only am I stranded up on Smoking Rubble Hill, with the only way down being some mode of bird-flight, but I've somehow been caught between enemy lines, out in No Man's Land, which is not in Illinois, it's in the middle of a time war between warring identities. Stay with me for a moment; I'll try to explain this. For no real reason, my tinnitus had started up again, and as I was listening to the dogs bark, with my songbirds going crazy, including a string of notes from Mozart's pet Starling, singing two songs at once, one on each vocal cord, I was suddenly aware that I'd added another word string, like *I have a dog*, to the arsenal of the Other who seemed to be pursuing me: *Dogs bark because the world is singing*. Dog's bark because the world is singing? This struck me at first as making no sense at all, a possibly dangerous misunderstanding of the behavior of canines; or it might have been the beginnings of the lines of a poem, the sort of thing you might use at the dentist's office, to distract you from the unpleasantness of an oral procedure, although I'd certainly need more than this threadbare statement to get me through a procedure of any duration; the words themselves sounded pleasant enough, until it came to me all at once that these innocuous little words were words, in fact, of my own invention, and I found myself in the middle of a dangerous procedure, in which the being thereby endangered was

Probably Not Alvaro. As I picked at this bit of thread, wondering what was attached to it, feeling certain that I deserved at least a whole piece of thread, the cloak surrounding my being, which is itself a kind of cloak, came apart at the seams and began to unravel and out came two lines that I was at the end of, which maybe should have taught me not to pull on a loose·thread: *Dogs bark because the world is singing, and dogs / Love to sing, but they don't know the words.* I gave one hard tug on this strange linguistic filament, and a whole inner life, like an enormous ball of kite twine, was dumped in my lap, along with a collection of miscellaneous items that I wasn't altogether sure I knew what to do with: an entire book of poetry in another man's name; a thirty-pound cinderblock from a Juárez demolition site; a Do Not Disturb sign from what appeared to be a Radisson; and a breezy little note in a cryptic foreign hand, saying *Hi, Alvaro, wish you were here, so get a fucking grip,* signed *Your friend, Douchebag.*

"Probably-Not Alvaro, you look like you've seen a ghost. Are you feeling like a duplicate? A replica imposter? I hate ghosts, ghosts are murder. They all have *orange eyes* that *glow* in the *dark.* You need to put your ghosts in the ice cream cooler."

"My ghost has my eyes. He needs to poke them out. I don't even want to look at them. Where do you keep the scissors that go in the small wooden drawer?"

Tom didn't have any scissors. They were somewhere in Nebraska. My name is Alvaro. My name is Douchebag. We're both in Guanajuato, and this is how we got here.

So how much do you know about human facial transplant surgery?

# 29

Not that Gomez bringing roses would be particularly appropriate; a funeral wreath possibly, something made up of conifer branches and shiny red rowan berries, with Larkspur perhaps, and Lily of the Valley; or we might suggest a casket spray, of blooming white orchids against tropical greenery, with a sympathy card written out in a fluid sloping hand, reading *Sorry for your loss, you will be missed for all eternity*; although if Gomez is truly sincere about making the appropriate gesture, having shown up unexpectedly at a crucial point in our narrative, he can certainly skip the flowers, flowers we don't need, and set aside the rowan berries, a bitter April green, which won't be ready for funeral wreaths until well into September, and forget we even mentioned the blooming orchid casket spray, there is something about myco-heterotrophs that strikes us as vaguely morbid; in fact, come to think of it, given the exigencies of the circumstances, with a house full of anxious people who are poorly equipped for life, and a driveway full of Zetas with a startling array of weaponry, Gomez should feel free to skip this whole flowery sentence, however reluctantly we depart with the larkspur and Lily of the Valley, and do the right thing by the people inside, like supply us with the names of the dead before he kills them. Ray shifted the Glock from his right hand to left, and put a finger to his lips to indicate silence. This is a suggestion with which we'd happily comply; Ramírez, unfortunately, had other ideas.

"I'd suggest you remove the weapon from my head. You're likely to need my help, and I don't do my best thinking while being
held at gunpoint."

Ray wrestled Ramírez from the seated position, and pulled him by
the neck over the back of the off-white sofa cushions, while the
couch itself, a cream-colored thing, inappropriate to any outcome
we can currently imagine, slowly tipped over and fell to the floor
and came to its penultimate resting place, back-down staring upward, with its feet pointed directly toward the quicklime sacks, and
a Glock-shattered mirror on the wall just above them; Ramírez himself, a still-sentient being, his face turning a pale shade of human
crimson, landed face-first in a chokehold on the Juárez hardwood,
with the Glock pressed directly against his occipital bone, in the
general vicinity of an oval-shaped cranial structure, where the medulla oblongata enters the base of the human skull, a region known
to anatomists as the *foramen magnum*, which is Latin for "great
hole" or "important opening" or "oversized aperture," for reasons
Señor Ramírez would probably rather we not go into, particularly
not in Glock, where from point-blank range, the precision of Latin
might be lost in translation. The clock on the mantel reads 12:52;
a dog is barking maybe three houses over; a large black bird, from
a Stanton Street Bridge rail, flies deeper into Mexico, with its luck
placed on hold. Ramírez' men, standing four feet from Ray, one at
each end of the cream-colored sofa, having likely never heard of
the medulla oblongata, held burst-fire Berettas pointed straight at
his head, no doubt certain that a split-second burst from the Berettas, directed at any portion of Raymond's upper cranium, would be
equally effective in freeing their boss, though they didn't need to
be told with anatomical precision that an oversized aperture at the
base of his skull, significantly enlarged by the Glock 29, would not
be something that the boss would welcome. These men, however,
were rather difficult to read, and other than raising their arms to
aim their weapons, they hadn't moved so much as a facial muscle
in response to Raymond's seizure of Ramírez; perhaps these were
men, accustomed to taking orders, who having wearied of Ramírez'
baffling monologues, were contemplating a change in their own
command structure; or perhaps they were trying out hypotheti-

cal explanations, as might be required for upper management in Sinaloa, as to how some unfortunate mistranslation from the Latin turned into an oversized hole in their boss' head; or perhaps the real problem was far more simple, and these men were preparing to burst-fire Raymond, without much thought, for no particular reason, leaving nothing to read behind those deadpan expressions. The clock on the mantel reads 12:52; a dog is barking maybe two houses over; these men holding Berettas seem to be animated by nothing, the stationary human equivalent of azoic crows. Ray looked up once from the Juárez hardwood, took one brief look at an inanimate expression, and was no longer certain that this standoff he'd created, in effect yet another of these stalemated endgames, had been worth all the trouble he'd gone to in creating it; while he certainly had Ramírez pinned to the floor, and was applying constant pressure, via razor-wired kneecap, to an area between the shoulder blades known as the thoracic curvature, where he was currently stationed on the seventh vertebra, or right around the midpoint of the *tt* curve, this wouldn't mean much, to either him or Ramírez, if the Berettas took control of the anatomy lessons, beginning at the top, with Ray's upper cranium. To make matters worse, Raymond himself was not in the best of health, a fact that was now manifesting itself in the form of a simple mind-body problem, where Ray found himself in charge of his body, keeping Raúl Ramírez pinned to the hardwood, but found his mind, in effect, taking charge of itself, and headed off, adrift, in search of something, in no way pinned to the Brazilian Walnut that Gomez had selected for his hardwood floors. So what on earth could be so important that Ray would drift off at a moment like this? Ray pictured himself resting up on a little knoll, with a briefcase full of cash lying by his side, watching missiles fly around in the contrailed desert; he pictured himself seated in the cabin of the Magnum, with the sky roof open, and his Mossberg at the ready, after retrieving the same briefcase from the Juárez police; he pictured himself sitting, on a backward-facing chair, at El Arbolito, the Wounded Tree bar of the Wittgenstein conundrum, playing tic-tac drinking games with Ramírez and his henchmen, while the briefcase sat stashed in the false-bottom truck bed; and he pictured himself, finally, in a yard full of dogs, with a case of Pabst Blue Ribbon in place of the briefcase, and his dad smoking a brisket over mesquite coals, when suddenly Ray caught a glimpse of something, something he'd missed in his previous pictures, as his dad dropped his tongs and reached in his pocket, pulled out a Zippo and a pack of Pall Malls, and offered Ray a cigarette to complement his beer; while Ray would have settled for the beer alone, what he really needed, right at the moment, was to reach in his pocket, pull out his Zippo and his pack of Pall Malls, and light what might prove to be his last cigarette. As far as Ray knows, that's about it, the books are closed, time to move on; something, however, would appear to be missing here, something that Raymond himself can't picture. What Ray may have missed, on his brief excursion, as he was savoring the smell of a home-smoked brisket, readying a can of cooler-chilled beer to tilt from the upright and initiate drinking, and preparing, in short, for his dad to drop his tongs, and conclude Ray's search for a much-needed smoke, was the fact that two gunmen, staring straight at him, were not unmindful of his lapse of attention; there was in fact a moment to catch him unaware, and burst-fire his cranium without the Glock being fired; for a split-second instant, one of the gunmen went tense, applying pressure to the trigger of a hammer-fired handgun, readying a mass of spring-tensioned metal to pivot on its pin and initiate firing, and preparing, in short, to simplify our narrative, with the machine-pistol equivalent of a blunt red pencil; for a split-second instant, Raymond's existence, and our whole delicate narrative, teetered on the brink; but before his brief lapse could cause real damage, Ray closed the book on his search for a cigarette, returned his attention to the immediate situation, and found himself faced with two deadpan expressions, and what might or might not be a stalemated endgame, particularly given the fact that those deadpan expressions were attached to two men whose thinking must be orderly, but not in any way governed by rules. The clock on the mantel reads 12:52; a dog is barking say one house over; the clear blue sky over the empty Chihuahuan desert is slowly filling up with azoic crows. Ray licked his trigger finger, and without moving the weapon, or engaging the trigger safety lever, shifted the self-loading locked-breech Glock to his natural right hand.

What in God's name is that funny taste in Raymond's bone-dry mouth? Why are the metallic-looking greenbottle blowflies licking their appendages, or darting around the living room, searching for rotting meat? It can't be the man who lost the oxygen debate, lying on the floor with his head sealed in plastic; he has just been pronounced, within the last ten minutes, and the body is still warm, and smells of human exertion, which while certainly distinctive, is a far different odor from what the flies find so appealing. Perhaps the flies were expecting Gomez to arrive bearing a different sort of wreath, possibly something involving pawpaw flowers and Dead Horse Arum, which smells more or less just as you'd expect, and has the uncanny ability to raise its own temperature, through a process known to botanists as thermogenesis, filling the stale air with the odor of warm carrion. While Ray knows nothing about Dead Horse Arum, or how pawpaw flowers use dead meat odors to try to draw flies as an aid to reproduction, he was beginning to think that maybe the room could use a fan, or someone to just get up, and go open another window. Ray's third move, after shifting the Glock, proved to be something of a tactical error, and uncovered a small problem with the lighting in the room, a problem whose source kept a room of its own, deep in Ray's dark and battered interior. Ray brushed a fly off the barrel of his pistol, fiddled with something on the Glock itself, and was right in the middle of attempting to lift his head, in order to reposition one of the room's current occupants, and get a better look at what the Berettas were up to, when he discovered one of the symptoms of hypovolemia, that blood-volume problem he's been hauling around inside him for a good ninety minutes: the sunlit room, on a blue-sky day, went completely dark, with the exception of a small round pinhole he could see through, a symptom known to oculists as Kalnienk vision, commonly referred to as tunnel vision; what Ray needed most, right about now, wasn't in fact a last cigarette, it was three days of bed rest and some meals rich in protein, which is just about the last thing this day holds in store; if Ray has to operate in a darkened theatre, that's just the way it is, there's nothing for it. Ray motioned Gabriella deeper into the room, which was now not just dark, but seemed to be taking on the psychic consistency of slowly congealing soup, or the colorless and tasteless collagen substance that results from boiling animal skins and bones; gelatinous, you'd probably call it, cerebrally gelatinous, like if Ray can't generate some mental kinetics, he won't be in bed, eating meals rich in protein, or spending a sunny April swimming in Horseshoe Bay, he'll wind up in a Jell-O mold, or suspended in Juárez aspic. Ray stayed crouched, in a kneeling position, gradually adapting to the darkened conditions, and steadying the barrel of a striker-fired pistol by pressing it directly to the back of a human head; two men stood still, in an upright position, persistently pointing hammer-fired handguns, and readying masses of spring-tensioned metal to pivot on their pins and burst-fire a cranium; and the greenbottle blowflies continued their movements, either cleansing their femoral sensory organs, adopting what amounts to a wait-and-see approach, or darting around the living room, searching for something, and while we haven't as yet pinpointed the object of their search, the flies seemed fairly confident that, one way or the other, something truly appalling was bound to turn up.

The flies, unfortunately, had Ray to contend with, and Raymond's a soldier; Raymond adapts to fluid situations. Ray chose to ignore his blood-volume problem, left the stalemated endgame exactly where he'd found it, and tried his best to go on about his business, though even the first order of business, the freeing of his friend Eugene, did not go well; someone must have used an entire roll of shipping tape to bind Gene at the wrists, and when Gabriella started picking at it, like she was afraid she'd crack a nail, Ray had to stir the pot just a little, rising up abruptly from the kneeling position, where he was keeping Ramírez pinned to a Glock-hardened floor, and wheeling the pistol on the man with the blunt red editing pencil, a man that we happen to know, from a previous encounter, carries a close-quarters Fairbairn-Sykes double-edged fighting knife, developed in Shanghai before World War II, but useful to this day for opening up an artery, when you're faced with a triple-wrapped shipping-tape disaster, and suddenly discover that you've had about enough. Why Ramírez' man put the Beretta down, and handed Ray the knife, we'll probably never know; it's possible that we all share a deep-seated antipathy to the sight of someone picking at an overwrapped shipping package, knowing that only a whetstone-sharpened blade will finally shred that smug little puzzler, and save us all from living in suspended animation, staring at a mystery box, in parcel post hell. There was also, admittedly, something vaguely ominous in Raymond's dark eyes, as though he personally didn't give a shit whether or not he lived; we've seen this expression on another occasion, with the crazy Chechen plumbers in the Uzi ravine, when some sloppiness with weapons caused a case of indignation, and an indifference to life and death that may be the ultimate weapon, particularly when it's backed by a full-power load. Ray's apparent indifference should not be misconstrued: he has no intention of dying in such a sordid environment, but neither does he care much for clinging to life; his allegiance, as always, is to the indicated action, which has to make you wonder, if you're the burst-fire Beretta guy, whether or not your immediate extinction may just turn out to be the indicated act. A Fairbairn-Sykes fighting knife sliced through layers of shipping tape; Ramírez' men had their weapons collected; Raymond returned to his kneeling position, one notch higher on the *tt* curve; the head sealed in plastic, with its fealty to nothing, still hadn't moved, though unlike that hideous Dead Horse lily, its contents began to cool. And the green-bottle blowflies continued their movements, licking and cleansing, dipping and dashing, but apparently growing tired and more and more frenzied; they've been darting around the living room for a good 90 seconds, searching for something like rotting meat, or a liquid meal that's rich in protein, or possibly something they can bathe their limbs in, and perhaps having wearied of the shipping-tape topic, were now eager to reveal the object of their search, and give us just a glimpse of their ultimate reward.

And then the blowfly frenzy simply stops us in our tracks; we can't think of anything relevant to say, at least not anything the flies would approve of. Words; more and more words; do we need all these words? Raymond, for example, doesn't need words; he needs a bowl of soup, which is just what this room is slowly turning into. The clock on the mantel reads 12:54; the neighborhood dog has suddenly gone silent; a large black bird, from a Stanton Street Bridge rail, has vanished completely into narrative thin air. Tick-tock; tick-tock; Gomez is waiting. The room feels stuffy, like the air is congealing; we're beginning to think that someone's pouring blood in Ray's soup. What is Gomez cooking, Ray, a giant pot of *czernina*? Duck's blood and poultry broth, with kluski noodles and rowan berries? Sounds like we may be dining at the Sedlec Ossuary, with its pelvic-girdle candleholders and bone-heap chandeliers, which while perfect for decorating dark interiors, seem odd somehow as a light source, though with Raymond's own interior growing darker by the minute, he can certainly use all the light he can find. The lighting, however, may not be the issue, not when compared to what Gomez is preparing: since the shiny-red rowan berries are a figment of narrative time, and the nearest source of duck's blood is the lake at Parque Hermanos, where Jen is waiting patiently, watching the electric train go round, sitting in her surprisingly capacious Corolla, with room to spare in her currently vacant trunk, maybe someone ought to warn her what Gomez is serving for supper, in a room full of femur floor-lamps and human-skull sconces, like cold blood soup for everyone, so wear something somber. Ray caught just a glimpse of himself in the Glock-shattered mirror, where hundreds of dark-eyed Raymonds looked back at him with apparent indifference; for Christ's sake, Ray, pull yourself together; the least you could do is get out of those dirty clothes. Flies; more and more flies; do we need all these flies? Someone has left the sliding-glass door into the garden slightly ajar, so we're going to get more flies whether or not we need them, since the flies smell death, in the same way our words do, by walking right into it, with rainbows in their eyes, and their feet covered in some sort of coagulating sticky substance. Finally, at last, the flies get their payoff, and bask in the glow of the narrative spotlight. What's that funny metallic taste in Raymond's bone-dry mouth? Turns out to be blood, unfortunately quite a lot of it, from a veterinary-sutured X-shaped chest-wound; while there are plenty of proteins in human blood, Ray's not going to live by licking it off his fingers, and he should probably keep in mind that, despite his good intentions, he's dripping all over everything, and beginning to draw flies.

And Gene, what about Eugene, how's he doing? The last time we looked, he was enjoying the sunset, a few wispy clouds blazing trails across the sky, while dreaming of his home in Grainfield, Kansas, after an honest day's work, is that too much to ask? Course then Gene went AWOL with Ray's truck and a wad of money, overshot the wheat fields and the blue Kansas sky, ended up here in a Juárez death house, with no fucking clue what the hell's coming next. Neither do we, Gene, neither do we, though with Raymond wandering around in a mental Czech Republic, eating Polish duck's blood soup and thinking he's in Sedlec, you should maybe keep an eye on his protein consumption; he's had about enough of the local soup. Gene went to crouch at the Bermuda picture window, performing a brief reconnaissance mission, searching for signs of enemy forces, with one hand shading his eyes from the reflected noonday glare, and one hand hiding a magic wand, retrieved from the cream-colored sofa cushions, a Drop-In Auto-Sear or Lightning-Link submachine gun, meaning a full-auto conversion of the civilian AR-15, firing high-velocity, moderate-recoil, steel-case hollow-point parabellum rounds, a hell of a weapon in a normal environment, but the Juárez equivalent of a full-auto BB gun, and muttering "Jesus" under his breath, which is never a good sign. What Gene was seeing simply did not look good: eight or nine men dressed in Universal Camouflage, wearing Interceptor Body Armor, with boron-carbide ceramic plates, and Wiley X Nerve tactical goggles, with matching Blackhawk StrikeForce gloves, the whole thing topped off with some interesting headgear, the U.S. Army's Advanced Combat Helmet, meaning these men had come to exfiltrate some douchebag called The Poet, along with the ignition key to a black Ram Magnum, and an olive-drab duffel bag stuffed full of currency, dressed as a Special Forces rapid-strike unit, but looking properly attired to fight a long bloody war. They had also come bearing an interesting assortment of Resistance Is Futile military hardware: Heckler and Koch G3s, with the Brugger and Thomet railed forend, chambered in three-inch NATO rounds; Barrett M82A1s, with the Leupold & Stevens telescopic sight, chambered in .50-caliber sniper projectiles; handheld, shoulder-mounted, RPG-7 rocket launchers, with their warheads painted shamrock green, with all due respect to Hezbollah's pine-green Iranian rockets, and the Shahada-green missiles of let's say Hamas; and a weapon that, frankly, Gene doesn't understand, and mistakenly believes is a local variation on the Russian-made RPG-29, firing PG-29V shaped-charge-explosive anti-tank rounds, but that turns out, in retrospect, to be an entirely different weapon, a weapon known to arms merchants as the SMAW-NE, an 83mm, man-portable, fiberglass-launch-tube, Housing Demolition System, based on the Israeli B-300, which proved so effective in the Gaza Strip, where the SMAW stands for something to do with launching a rocket, while resting the launch tube atop a human shoulder, which isn't exactly a new class of weapons, since shoulder-launched rockets date back to World War I, and the Fire Arrow Rocket Launcher, developed by the Chinese, dates back a thousand years to the Song Dynasty, which not only revolutionized military technology by employing gunpowder, the first truly weapons-grade chemical explosive, as a solid-fuel propellant in their Fire Arrow Rockets, but added to our own understanding of the planet, by discovering True North on a military compass, and where the NE stands for Novel Explosive, which is not just a whole new class of explosives, it's a doctoral exam in thermobaric science that Gene must have skipped in his weapons training. We should probably, at this point, pause to catch our breath, and let Gene catch his, if he can still draw breath. Let's just say that there's something Gene's missing here, something to do with that SMAW-NE, and not only does Eugene not get the picture, but he wouldn't understand it, even if he did. As for the rest of us, if we don't have the stomach for a thermobaric science class, we should simply turn around, go back across the border and out of Juárez, and avoid getting involved in housing demolition; if, on the other hand, despite all our warnings, you still have an interest in this particular neighborhood, the Cuernavaca subdivision just south of downtown, you might ask your realtor to show you the listings of houses For Sale in the Death House Demolition Zone, under Large Smoking Rubble Pile/Occupants Included, or Pre-Demolished/Zero Stories, or even this very structure, on Calle Avanzaro, known for its larval gardens, and its breathtaking views of Time, which may soon be on the market at a significant reduction, under Famous Architectural: The No More House.

Apparently unconcerned about the vagaries of the local housing market, Gomez stood upright in the middle of the street, leaning on the far-front sheet-metal quarter-panel of a Sonora Gold Pearl Toyota Land Cruiser, looking like a man in control of the situation, but also like a man who was weighing his options. Perhaps he was contemplating a home invasion, though in a legal sense, this wouldn't be possible, since technically speaking, this is his house; technicalities aside, he may already have discarded this particular option, as he seemed to want The Poet brought out in one piece, not the likeliest of outcomes in a living room firefight, particularly one involving shamrock grenades. Or perhaps he had

Gene in his sniper-crosshairs, and was readying his equations to solve for Eugene, though this might not be the solution to his ignition key problem; with the back end of the truck frame sitting nearly atop the axel, as though the dead space of the cargo bed was loaded down with something heavy, fresh plutonium possibly for the irradiated desert, or more likely gold bars for a Panamanian bank vault, Gomez might want to relocate the vehicle, and with Ray having installed some kill-switch machinery, to discourage the local ladróns from hotwiring the Ram, Gomez might not reach the end of the driveway, before he started crying My kingdom for a key. Or perhaps he was considering deploying his rockets, just abolish the entire structure and then pick through the rubble, in hopes of tracking down the right set of keys, though he must have been wavering on the whole demolition project, like how do you extract $20 million, contained as it is in perfectly liquid but flammable currency, from a mound of smoking rubble that used to be a house? Lachrymatory agents, was probably what he was thinking, maybe a couple of canisters of CS tear-gas, 2-chlorobenzalmalononitrile, which may be harder on the mouth than it is on the eyes, and translates loosely, in Gomez Shakespearean, to "If you have tears, prepare to shed them now, for tears are the silent language of grief." This, admittedly, is pure speculation; we have no more idea what Gomez has in mind than we would if we attributed thoughts to a blowfly; though if you're thinking maybe Gene should challenge Gomez on his Shakespeare, confront him with the fact that his teary "silent language" quote had nothing to do with the Bard, and is actually from Voltaire, try to keep in mind what the blowflies think of death, expressed so delicately, in their own silent language, by finding some guy like Gene, with a suppurating head wound, and slowly walking around in it, licking their feet for joy.

Gene, poor Eugene; how are we ever going to get him out of this shit? If it weren't for the fact that it's the 16th of April, we'd suggest sending Gene out to work in the hayfields, maybe put him to work raking the hay into windrows, permitting it to dry, under the hot Kansas sun, before baling it up, and stacking the hay bales; unfortunately for Eugene, that beautiful Kansas prairie hay won't be ready for cutting and baling until sometime in July, by which time, in Juárez, there won't be a lot of livestock, and no market at all for fresh cut hay. Remember Gene's not the one who is fluent in tic-tac racetrack signals, but he's looking out the window at the Zeta brigade, wondering about the odds of him and Ray getting out of this, without some sort of time machine, or a closed-cab rigid-platform variable-transmission combine harvester, equipped with a reciprocating knife cutter bar, set to harvest oats and dump them in the auger, along with a fresh batch of paramilitary body parts, fed into the threshing drum, via the chain-and-flight feederhouse, and separated from their weapons by a steel bar mesh; probably be easier just calling in an airstrike, or a nine-line Medevac pick-up request, with the signals for a hoist and a non-ambulatory litter, and an X on Line 6, meaning enemy troops in the area, a B on Line 9, meaning biological contamination, and the Line 7 signal, which seems all but inevitable, that the site will be marked by an enormous pyrotechnic fireworks display. Eugene, however, is not getting out of this via Medevac chopper, and he's not raking hay into Kansas windrows, or using his combine knife cutter bar to harvest the Zetas and dump them in the auger; with that SMAW-NE parked in the roadway, equipped with the latest in Novel Explosives, Eugene is still not getting the picture, and by the time he completes his weapons training, and calls it a day on his thermobaric science lessons, he may have some final Medevac requests, but he might just as well phone them in to the crows.

So what's Gene missing here? What exactly is Eugene's problem? While we're not trying to suggest that Gene's somehow engaged in a war of words with a Zeta Special Forces Unit, he may soon, in effect, have a massive hole in his own vocabulary, beginning with the definitions of terms like "thermobaric" and "dense inert metals" and "fuel-air explosives," or even, if you get right down to it, in the dense inert discourse of precision-guided war, what an enhanced-lethality munitions expert might mean by the word *Novel*; if that SMAW-NE punches a hole through the picture window, and exposes Gene's ignorance as to what might be implied by "metal augmentation" in terms of blast-wave pathogenesis, not only will Casa Cronómetro be burned to the smoking ground, but Gene won't have the language to describe what just hit him. Remember Gene's basically a farmer, and a Kansas boy at heart, the sort of kid who joined the Army to do his part in something larger, something trued-up and aligned with our nation's sense of higher purpose, putting boots on the ground, and humans inside the boots, in the war between good and evil, as if we would know the difference; unfortunately for Gene, that's not how war works, particularly when it comes to thermobaric weapons, where when a fuel-air explosive goes off overhead, setting fire to the local oxygen supply using liquefied hydrocarbons, you might want to check that impulse to look down at your boots, which may be down there on the ground all right, but full of liquefied pedestrian. This, admittedly, sounds more than a little primitive, setting fire to a massive vapor cloud of methane or ethylene oxide; in fact, it sounds like the sort of approach that even the Nazis might have abandoned, knowing that a cloud of ethylene-oxide vapors, while highly explosive, was not the proper paradigm for a novel explosion, which requires that one ignite, not a massive cloud of vapor, but a fuel-air suspension of fine-grain particulates. The Nazis, unfortunately, got the paradigm right, but went down the wrong mineshaft when it came to particulates; if you're living in an age of hydrocarbon fuels, and picturing the sorts of things the word *burn* conjures up, which likely excludes the whole class of metals, you're headed straight down the same Nazi mineshaft, in fact you're thinking itself seems more than a little primitive, and nowhere near the state-of-the-art in metal-augmentation explosive munitions; we're sorry to spoil your little *burn*-conjured picture, but the best the Nazis could manage, with their coal-dust detonation, was to knock down a few trees, and turn them into Yule logs in a snowy Bavarian forest, whereas our Massive Ordnance Air Blast, setting fire to a cloud of aluminum powder, not only crushed nine city blocks, but burned at something like 5,000 degrees. We wish we could tell you that the innovation stops here, with our metallically augmented MOAB munition, painted an alarming-looking shade of Crossing Guard Orange, perhaps as a warning to local pedestrians, and that Gene, for one, could rest assured, amid all this dense vocabulary and inert terminology, that we know what we mean, and mean what we say, when we use the word *Novel* in the present context; unfortunately for all of us, we're not even close, because not only is the MOAB painted Crossing Guard Orange, but it's maybe thirty feet too long and ten tons too heavy, and needs to be dropped from a C-130 transport plane, not fired from down near ground level by an otherwise ordinary human being. To be perfectly blunt, Gene, the MOAB isn't *Novel*; it's certainly fucking Massive, but *Novel* it's not; *nano*, Gene, think *nano*, a suffix that means "one-billionth" of something, and then stuff it inside a rocket grenade, mount it atop an ordinary human shoulder, and make a Massive Fucking Explosion out of a billionth of something, or in ontological terms, *just next to nothing.*

So what's Gene missing here? Pretty much everything. You think you can explain to a Grainfield wheat farmer, a combine guy, not a trained ontologist, how a Novel Explosive, full of *just next to nothing,* is made of the same stuff as an Azoic Crow? As far as Gene's concerned, we need to stick to Soldier; massive fucking explosions he most certainly knows. First of all, in a Novel Explosive, which, like any truly modern thermobaric explosive, is based on the fine-grain particle-cloud-suspension principle that causes a Kansas flour silo to occasionally just explode, the normal thermobaric fill, of fluorinated aluminum powder, is replaced by something so radically innovative, and meticulously refined on the ultramicroscopic scale, that it struggles to contain its blast-wave shockfront and thermal kinetics, in order to stay within the design constraints of enhanced-lethality moral equivalence, maybe sol-gel-processed nanometric tungsten powder, or carbon-based nanotubes, in a nanodimensional supporting gel, as though the flour in the Grainfield elevator silo had been bio-engineered by a lethality geneticist, and ground down toward nothingness from some mutant strain of wheat, leaving us to deal with the nanoethical implications of a nanoflour-suspension having vacuum-bombed half of Kansas. Just so you know; remind us not to tell you about the shattering detonation velocities of nanometric RDX in a porous chromium(III)-oxide matrix; that SMAW-NE is bad enough as it is, without our wandering around out on the bleeding edge of weapons science, where all that seems to remain of the mysterious human mind is a blood-soaked breeding-ground for greenbottle blowflies. What Gene is missing is an overpressure blast wave, followed by a wave of superheated gases, which is capable of producing human-head amputees, without leaving a mark on the rest of the body, and without the need for doctors, or surgical intervention. What Gene is missing is an oxygen-consuming fireball, with the flame front progressing rapidly through the house, seeking fresh oxygen, and leaving an asphyxiated wake, until out the front door comes the oddest fucking phenomenon, a desperate-for-oxygen, O-shaped, Fire Ring, exiting the building in a dragon's-breath whoosh, as though the structure just collapsed while celebrating victory, by puffing out fire rings on a weapons-grade cigar. What Gene is missing is the Medevac signal, an O on Line 0 of the Medevac request, a message that by its nature would need to be pre-recorded, meaning Don't Fucking Bother, We're *Nano*-Cremains. What Gene is missing is like the rest of his life, and a place to call home, now that there's no more Kansas, but really, aren't we all, so what the hell's the problem? The problem is that Gene is standing up in the picture window, having visions of sipping beer on his porch in Grainfield, Kansas, which from where Gene's standing, is getting harder for us to picture, and he no longer seems to care how close he is to the everafter, which while easy enough to get to, is clean out of beer. Or maybe he's thinking back to his childhood in Kansas, and thinks he's standing outdoors in one of the farm's purple sorghum fields, watching what he calls finches, which are really American sparrows, fly in the tight formation of a crazy figure-eight, like the whole flock of sparrows, which is actually called a host, is flying in whirling place, in a six-foot-wide pattern, inches above the sorghum stalks, as if they're planning to live forever, a solid body of bird cohesion, a bird made of birds whose body isn't moving, which is all Gene really wanted out of life to begin with, to be out there in the flow of things that lives on beyond us. Gene, Gene, wake the fuck up: you're not out standing in a sorghum field, part of something that will live forever; you're *this close* to dying in a whirlpool bloodbath, or its thermobaric science moral equivalent, the 5,000 Fahrenheit self-cleaning oven, so stand the hell down and step away from the window, meaning *now*, Eugene, this monodimensional *instant*, before all that remains of what you wanted out of life is the white space that lies beyond a terminated sentence. What Gene is missing is an antonym for Time, since whatever survives us, on such a militarized planet, will need to be well armed, and suitably attired, to walk the burning earth on bone-plate prosthetics; that bird Gene envisions, whirling above the sorghum fields, and equipped to outlive us, would appear to be an inanimate and fire-breathing Onto-Drone.

Jesus, what a mess; not only is Gene on the brink of extinction, but our amazingly precise narrative chronometer, accurate to within a second over 80 million years, equipped as it is with the stunning precision of a resonance-driven, auto-correcting, caesium fountain atomic oscillator, bathed in the violet light of a spectral Bermuda bay, a laser-cooled masterpiece of continuous-cold near-absolute-zero caesium atoms, launched vertically into space from the frigid depths of an optical molasses vacuum chamber, and searched in graceful ballistic flight for their resonant heart by a photon detector, seems to be running unconscionably slow, as though we may have a power plug loose in its socket, or an optical molasses wiring error, or a load-shedding brownout on the Juárez power grid; by now, for example, much as we'd all love to see Eugene headed toward home, and a Grainfield porch swing, we should at least be seeing Gene stepping back from the window, and we're not seeing Gene stepping back from the window, in fact we're not seeing Gene even shifting his weight, or blinking his eyes as he stares out the window, or moving even one of his skeletal muscles; something is wrong with the violet clock. This, certainly, is a curious phenomenon; while we seriously doubt we have a load-shedding problem, with the room's current occupants showing no signs of movement, events taking place at the rate of now and then, and the space between events now packed with explosives, we would appear to be headed, at a laser-cooled crawl, toward one Big Event in the pale taupe ranch house, with nothing whatsoever taking place in the interim, and no real need for caesium precision; this time-shredding outcome could likely be achieved using a hand-wound 30-minute kitchen timer, or by glancing now and then at the umbral edge of the gnomon-cast shadow on a garden sundial, or by watching the sands in an hourglass ampoule sift between bulbs as time runs out. If you're still not getting the clock-slowing picture, think of it this way: the last real event in the narrative domain was Gene standing up in the picture window; do you happen to recall, in the powdery past, the event that occurred just prior to this? The violet clock is hardly moving. This, truly, is a bitter pill to swallow; we managed to assemble our caesium fountain, which interrogates caesium at a death-defying clip, down to the millionth-of-a-billionth of a second, using a laser-fired femtosecond frequency comb, and yet we seem to have for-

gotten, if we ever even knew, that a narrative chronometer, as the
name suggests, isn't exactly an electrical device, it's more of a kind
of dialectical device, both powering and powered by the narrative
itself, and it has no source of power, and no real precision, unless it's
drawing power from its narrative source; something or someone in
the pale taupe house must be the source of this chronic slowdown.
If we draw back the grey-velvet curtain of words that keeps the violet
clock hidden from view, we discover that even the Gomez mantle
clock, powered as it is by Gomez himself, and the imminent threat
that his name embodies, keeps far better time than our caesium
timepiece, a device whose precision should be unsurpassed, but
can't keep pace with a ticking time bomb. That tick-tock sound
we can hear in the background is coming from the mantel clock's
deadbeat escapement, counting down raked and pointed teeth on
a small round escape wheel as time goes by, and it serves as a reminder that time is passing, while Gomez stands beside his Gold
Pearl Cruiser, perhaps still weighing his tear gas option, or solving
for Eugene in his sniper equations, or perhaps, by now, given the
time he's expended, measuring the house for a thermobaric coffin.
If a fuel-air suspension of nanometric tungsten ignites in the somewhat stale midair of the living room portion of Casa Cronómetro,
unleashing a flurry of thermodynamic events that grind Time down
to a *just-next-to-nothingness* femtosecond powder, one trillionth the
size of a grain of sand, one millionth the size of a particle of tungsten, one three-hundred-thousandth the size of a caesium atom,
then we'll all know the reason we came to the house equipped with
a femtosecond frequency comb, but we won't be using it to interrogate caesium, down to the millionth-of-a-billionth of a second,
we'll be using it instead to comb through the rubble, searching for a
power source that's feeding off the land, clocking events in geologic
stages. For everyone's sake, we'll need to stop here, halt that mantel
clock's deadbeat ticking, shut our narrative down completely, and
try to trace this power problem back to its source. Since we're all a
little tired of these rhetorical searches, and Raymond himself is in
the middle of the room, we're going to ask Ray to take a good look
around him, and try to spot something, anything at all, that might
be the source of our load-shedding slowdown.

Imagine for a moment that Ray looks up, from his head-down

position and whatever it is he's doing, and takes a good long look around the living room portion of Casa Cronómetro, the pale taupe ranch house. What exactly does Raymond see? To his immediate right, at the picture window, Ray sees his partner, Eugene Booker, who may have drifted off toward his porch in Kansas, but is so amped-up on weapons-fed adrenaline that he can't be the source of our power problem. Directly in front of him, ten feet away, Ray sees a woman in a sky-blue dress, a woman by the name of Gabriella, who not only has a tendency to run unconscionably late, but having guided both The Poet and Gomez himself to the pale taupe ranch house, is also the source of a great many problems; Gabriella, however, has only recently arrived to deliver a message, and since we ourselves are in the messaging business, we don't make a habit of blaming the messenger. Upright beside her, toward the door to her left, stands a man known to Raymond as Arturo or Bells, holding twin Beretta model 93Rs, and if Ray trusts Bells with these hammer-fired handguns, that's good enough for us to rule Bells out. At an angle from where he's kneeling, beside a cream-colored sofa, which itself has come to rest beside a large square coffee table, Ray spots a man, on the far side of the table, sleeping in a perfectly comfortable-looking chair, made all the more comfortable by the empty space inside a five-eighths-empty tequila bottle, and while this man would look suspicious in nearly any environment, we seriously doubt that our caesium chronometer is trying to draw power from an empty-headed dimwit. All around him as he looks around the sunlit room, Ray sees any number of inanimate objects, the quicklime sacks, the Glock-shattered mirror, the man on the floor with his head sealed in plastic, but if our timepiece is powered by inanimate objects, particularly that man lying dead on the floor, we have a much deeper problem than our caesium oscillator. As far as Ray can see, we've ruled out five of the room's ten inhabitants, and left him with only the four Thetas to consider: Ramírez himself, lying facedown on the floor, apparently engaged in suboptimal thinking, with a Glock 29 pressed directly against his head; the twin-Beretta men, off to Ray's left, wearing the deadpan expressions of bipedal theropods, no doubt brooding over the loss of their burst-fire handguns, but unwilling, for the moment, to share their thoughts; and just to their right, the last of these men, the original owner of the Glock 29, perhaps thinking back to his moment in the sun, when he caught Ray unaware in the side-yard garden, just after Ray'd installed his yellow marigold patch, using a wounded Bayonet plant Yucca-sap adhesive, to try to staunch the worst of the loose-suture bleeding from a nasty-looking X-shaped fighting-knife chest-wound, itself installed, with admirable precision, at El Arbolito, the Bar of the Wounded and Drifting Tree; while any of these men could have ended our narrative in a burst-fire-instant blink of an eye, having lost their weapons and positions of authority, they're in no position at all to power our chronometer, they're in a far better position to remind us all that Ray's in no condition to conduct our little search. Let's back up, in imaginary time, to the point when we asked Ray to lift his head. What exactly does Raymond see? Ray sees nothing but the darkness closing in, because with his marigold patch having lost its adhesion, his vet-sutured chest-wound coming apart at the seams, and his blood volume dropping, Raymond has some power source problems of his own, and Raymond himself is the source of our problem: our resonance-driven, auto correcting, laser-cooled clock must be plugged directly into an otherwise ordinary human life-force that is ebbing and flowing, and must, at the moment, be headed out with the tide. Imagine for a moment that, instead of his movement, we restored Ray's awareness of his immediate situation. How much of any of this is Raymond aware of? Raymond is aware of every last inch of the darkened living room operating theater; Raymond is aware of his blood volume problem; Raymond is aware that Gomez is waiting; Raymond is aware that time is running out; and Raymond is aware that, all things considered, and bearing in mind the rate at which life is leaking out of him, he would greatly prefer to be elsewhere instead, sitting up on a little knoll watching the vapor-trail sky, sipping a Pabst Blue Ribbon with Jennifer in person, or maybe running a modest little bike-rental shop on the pink-sand shores of Horseshoe Bay, which may or may not be on the island of Bermuda, in a whole different time zone, and a whole different story, surrounded by lavender Passion Flowers and Pink-tipped Begonias, staring out to sea over the turquoise waters, waiting for sunset to close up shop, and head on home, up the jasmine-scented walkway, to greet Jennifer at the door of their white-picket cottage. Which makes it somewhat ironic that when Jen shows up, in maybe three or four minutes from right around now, having slipped in through the back into the ranch house kitchen, she'll be carrying two beers and wearing a flower in her hair, as though maybe she and Ray are on the same turquoise wavelength, though Jen, to be honest, will not yet be up to speed, on either thermobaric weapons or hypovolemia; Raymond will look up, from whatever he'll be doing, and give Jen a wink, a kind of white-picket greeting, the sort of wink we should be hoping doesn't prove to be too memorable, or in any way ironic, particularly given that beautiful white jasmine blossom in her hair. With our search at an end, our power source located, and our resonance detector attuned once again to the ebbs and flows of an otherwise ordinary human heart, the time has come for us to go on about our business, find that white jasmine we planted in the garden, restart our narrative caesium fountain, and hope for the best from the violet clock.

Moving, Ray thought, we need to get fucking moving. Gene, do me a favor, will you? Step the hell back from that plate-glass window. Sure, Ray, sorry. The clock on the mantel reads 12:55; the absolute time elapsed is 196-Gomez seconds; a large dark bird, like a mnemonic device, flying circles in the sky over the empty Chihuahuan desert, is growing more than a little hazy on its reasons for being up there, but give us just a moment, as the black crow flies, there'll be more than enough for everyone to begin to forget. How many men, Gene? Looks like eight or nine, Trip, not counting Gomez, and not counting whatever the hell's stationed out back. Well-equipped? Jesus. Norwegian AG3s, IRA Barrett M82s, Iranian DIO RPG-7Vs, with those olive green hand-guards and the H&K pistol-grip, and some sort of anti-tank rocket launcher, maybe an Israeli B-300 or a Russian Vampire RPG-29, fucking things walk right through reactive armor, probably blow a good-sized hole, you run it through stucco and three-eighths-inch hardboard. I'm thinking we should go ahead and give them the poet, maybe they'll take the money and just go away. Course, they may want your truck. Thing was loaded down with something fairly heavy, like it could be product, but I'm thinking more like gold. Yeah, well, they can have the truck, just as soon as they kill me. Where's Gomez? He's just standing there, Ray, right out front, behind the hood of that gold Land Cruiser that Ramon drives him around in, wearing the same fuck-

ing suit he had on at the office. He wearing a vest? Sure, blue pin-
stripe, just like the rest of his suit, probably getting warm out there,
like whatever you're thinking of doing, we might want to do it soon.
You have a clean shot? If he's not wearing a vest, why don't we just
shoot him? I don't know, Trip, not too sure that's such a good idea.
First off, I might miss, firing at him through a plate-glass window.
And then again, even supposing I hit him, still have to deal with the
rest of these goons. No way we win a firefight against all these munitions using an AR-15 and a handful of pistols. You're forgetting the
Mossberg. Yeah, even still. Don't think maybe you're really getting
the picture. Looks like a Special Forces fireteam squad, wearing full
ARPAT digital camouflage, with those new MICH 2000 Combat
Helmets, and Interceptor body armor, with groin and neck protectors, and MOLLE ballistic panels, and side-SAPI plates. Best I can
picture is them field-dressing some leg wounds, and if one of those
anti-tank rounds goes through the front wall, they won't have far to
walk, like Ramon'll be driving that Land Cruiser right into our living room. Face it, Ray, time's about up. If Gomez wants to listen to
this douchebag's story, let's send him on out, far as I'm concerned,
they're made for each other. Probably right, Gene, but I'm thinking we should maybe try giving him Ramírez, and the rest of these
morons he brought along with him, might make a nice trophy for
Vicente and the Zetas.

"Gentlemen, please, if I could just interject. It isn't clear to me
that you have any sort of grasp of the politics involved in the current
situation."

"Politics? Place sounds like a war zone, not a nominating convention. What the hell's politics got to do with anything?"

"If you'll just let me up, perhaps I can explain. Gomez is here
under his own initiative. Señor Carrillo Fuentes is almost certainly
not aware of this, and the troops out front have nothing to do with
Los Zetas."

Ray tilted the sofa painstakingly upward, and righted it finally on its four wooden feet; shifted the self-loading locked-breech
Glock back on around to his unnatural off-hand; and firmly grasp-
ing Ramírez by his Turnbull & Asser collar, a beautiful two-fold

weave of Sea Island cotton, lifted him upright to a standing position, dragged him on around by the collar of his shirt to the front
of the upright cream-colored sofa, repositioned him slightly to permit him to land at right around the midpoint of an off-white cushion, and then finally letting go of his pristine collar, not only left
Ramírez comfortably seated, but left a bright bloody thumbprint
on a crisp field of white. Time permitting, of course, we'd suggest
immediate soaking, in a quart of warm water, with half a teaspoon
of laundry detergent, and a tablespoon of ammonia; if your primary
concern, on the other hand, is crime-scene forensics, and the presence of a dead man's thumbprint on your otherwise pristine collar,
it might be useful to know that the fire point of *Gossypium bar-
badense*, following bleaching with calcium sulphite and sodium-
oxide mercerization, is right around 410 degrees Fahrenheit, so you
could soak the bloody shirt in a gallon or so of gasoline, and set the
thing ablaze at your absolute leisure; though just to be safe, if you're
actually worried about a dead man's thumbprint, and your shirts
are made by Turnbull & Asser, you should probably keep in mind
that your $400 shirt would never have been mercerized or bleached
in calcium sulphite, and that while petrol makes a nice blaze and
all, it burns at an unfortunate 500 degrees, too close for comfort to
the maybe 490 required to set fire to that Sea Island collar, and far
below the six or six fifty needed to rid the world of that stubborn
human thumbprint; turns out your problem is not the man's blood,
which boiled off long ago in your petrol solution, it's his eccrine
secretions leaving palmar sweat, and a nice clean latent of ferric
chloride; if you're truly intent on a decent night's sleep, you'll need
to go back to "time permitting," and find where the dead man keeps
his ammonia, though why you're reading a book while cleaning
up a crime scene is something of a mystery, a mystery that we're
more than willing to address, further down the page, time permitting. Raymond, however, did not have time to find a tablespoon of
ammonia, and clean a bloody thumbprint from a pristine collar, in
fact he didn't have time, given his limited field of vision, to find his
own blood on a crisp field of white; all Ray had time for, all things
considered, and bearing in mind the rate at which life was leaking
out of him, was to look around the room for something to slow the
bleeding, open those Kalnienk pinholes he was looking through,

and try to find some light at the end of the tunnel.

Ray took a deep and suture-shredding breath of thrombocytic oxygen out of the room's stale air; took a good long look around his darkened living room operating theater, attempting to pinpoint one or two items that might prove useful with his blood-volume problem; and while still standing upright beside Ramírez, began to unbutton the top few buttons of an old plaid shirt, a Rockford Shadow Plaid, once blue and green, but now a blood-drenched shade of woozy-brownish, and taking one brief look at what was underneath the buttons, nearly keeled over, right on the spot. So what exactly was underneath the buttons? To be perfectly honest, with regard to Ray's chest wound, we refuse to even look at it, much less describe it; if Ray had been a schnauzer, under the patient loving care of a decent veterinarian, we would not have had the stomach to permit this to go on; let's just say that, underneath the buttons, it wasn't just his customary vet-sutured chest-wound, it was Raymond himself, coming apart at the seams. Part of Ray was in a Juárez living room, with a hole in his esophagus overflowing into his trachea, meaning Ray was not just eating but breathing his own blood, which instead of being expelled via violent coughing, was slowly pooling up in the tissue of his lungs, as though the knife may have severed a laryngeal nerve; his temperature was low, and dropping rapidly, headed toward something down in the range of the snow-covered Sangre de Cristo Mountains, as a result of both blood-loss hypothermia, and the evaporative cooling of opiate sweats, itself the result of the rapid ingestion of a full vial of an opioid analgesic, to suture up some leakage in his mental capacity; and we don't, finally, need an inflatable upper-arm blood-pressure cuff to tell us that Raymond should not be standing, that he was closer to the someone-better-phone-the-family, it-won't-be-long-now, blood-pressure stage, than he was to standing up without leaning on a friend. While Ray had friends, like Bells and Gene, with Jen about to join them, in his darkened living room operating theater, he had only one friend in his dark interior: the complex human body machinery of the baroreceptor reflex response, by which the sympathetic branches of the autonomic nervous system were even now attempting what amounts to a resurrection, by elevating Raymond's cardiac output, via increased contractility and arterial vasoconstriction, and this was the friend that was keeping him standing, while Ray, for the most part, was coming unglued. The remainder of Ray was in a turquoise lagoon, dreaming of a life on the island of Bermuda, maybe running a modest little bike-rental shop on the pink-sand shores of Horseshoe Bay, surrounded by lavender Passion Flowers and Pink-tipped Begonias, as if Ray might have been thinking there was a way to get them out of this, although the only real reason he was not facedown, lying at the bottom of his turquoise lagoon, was that this dream too had a friend to lean on, meaning Jennifer herself was keeping him afloat. In the end, of course, while Ray had a friend that was keeping him standing, and yet another friend who was keeping him afloat, what Ray needed most, right about now, was a center to pull the parts back together, and keep what remained, of both his body and his dreams, moving on forward toward the light of another day. Ray, let's face it, needed to dig down deep here, find the indicated action, and the strength with which to execute; beneath the shattered surface of the ordinary man, which was slowly coming apart under physical exertion, there was something still intact, meaning absolute soldier, and this was the center that was holding him together, and keeping him moving to fight another day. While the sight of a living corpse out on a combat mission, still pressing forward despite his gaping wounds, and digging ever-deeper into a ghastly-looking hole, may be painful to contemplate, there's one thing we know about Raymond Edmunds: if Ray's still standing, he's still moving forward. Do us all a favor, Ray, don't dig too deep here, like all the way down to skull and bones; we'd certainly prefer to bury you later, at the age of 92, in a one-sentence epilogue at the end of our chronicle, out back of your jasmine-scented white-picket cottage.

Ray stood still for a moment longer, perhaps to prove to all of us that he could still stand up, and took a seat beside Ramírez on the resurrected couch; had Bells bring a roll of reinforced shipping-tape, and the double-edged blade of a Fairbairn-Sykes fighting knife; and taking a good hard look at the cream-colored sofa, which would soon require a good deal more ammonia to return it to anything resembling off-white, found the indicated action, a tool with which to execute, and a path to be followed to close that gaping wound. A twelve-inch gash in the middle of a cushion exposed a thin layer of cotton batting, which Ray gathered up by the bloody handful, turning much of it a pink-shade of cotton candy, and placed on the coffee table, beside a double-edged fighting knife, a full roll of shipping tape, a five-eighths-empty litre of tequila, a four-ounce bottle of Osha extract, an ounce or so light of its maximum capacity, and completing his assembly of operative implements, a completely empty cut-glass rocks glass, as if Ray might have been planning to pour himself a chucho, which is precisely what Raymond proceeded to do. While it was easy enough to see what Ray had in mind, it was difficult to picture what Raymond was thinking, as the man had a strange sort of gleam in his eye, and some truly strange noises coming out of his mouth. What sounded like Ray maybe gargling something turned out to be Ray sort of chuckling to himself, not the easiest thing to do with blood in your trachea; what Ray found amusing, under the circumstances, would be difficult to say, particularly with blood pooling up in your lungs. Maybe Ray was thinking back, like all the way to yesterday, to the fact that he'd ingested maybe one too many chuchos, the drink his old boxing mentor, El Conejo, had taught him to drink as an aches-and-pains cure-all, when his wound was first installed at the Bar of the Wounded Tree; his aches-and-pains cure-all, for pre-fight care, might have come fairly close to getting him killed, but it might prove useful as a post-fight cure-all. Or maybe Ray found it amusing that the Fairbairn-Sykes, the same knife that wounded him, was about his only hope for coping with that shipping tape, which was not only resistant to moisture and abrasion, but thoroughly resistant to human hands, reinforced as it was with a fiber-yarn filament; there was, in fact, something a little twisted about the knife that nearly killed him being needed to save him. Of course knowing Raymond's peculiar sense of humor, this particular chuckle likely had something to do with his dad, a man whose sudden departure, when Ray was just a kid, had left him without a mom, and with something of a hole in his parentless adolescence; his dad, among other things, who knew virtually nothing about holding down a job, knew virtually everything about Native American medicinal cures, which his dad had learned directly from the medicine men, who in turn had learned the best of them from studying the animals; the Osha, for example, a liquid extract from the Bear Root plant, which bears both eat and rub on their fur when they finally come out of deep hibernation, wasn't just a reminder of his dad's weird cures, from the Zunis and Navajo and White Mountain Apaches, it was just about exactly what the doctor ordered, as it raises your temperature, improves respiration, and heals up cuts as a wound antiseptic; his dad might have left him with a hole in his past, but he'd left him equipped to close that hole in his future. Ray took a look at the mess that he'd assembled, ran a hand through his hair, and laughed out loud, a laugh that Eugene may not have found amusing, but went right ahead and laughed along with him; just as long as Ray could laugh, Eugene could still hope. What Ray had assembled, on the coffee table, lacked the sympathetic magic of his bright yellow marigold side-yard patch, whose Yucca-sap adhesive, itself a Zuni-approved wound antiseptic, had been gathered from the wounds of a Bayonet plant; setting aside the possibility that the gash in the couch might be sympathetic to Raymond's plight, what Ray had instead, and in fact, assembled, which wasn't the sort of thing that a shaman would approve of, was more along the lines of a memory patch, reminders of today and the day before today, reminders of the ways Ray wound up wounded, reminders of Ray's own memories themselves, as if a man's wounded past contained a sympathetic magic that might be gathered up to heal the wounded man. Ray knocked back his post-fight cure-all; bathed his wound in straight tequila, and whatever remained in the Osha bottle; sorted his cotton into two distinct piles, one the color of cotton candy, the other the pure white cotton shade of the pristine collar on a Sea Island shirt; and attaching the dry white cotton batting to both of his two-foot strips of tape, severed from the roll by the Fairbairn-Sykes, installed his brand-new blood-loss patch, made of reinforced shipping tape with a permanent adhesive, and a dry white cotton exudate dressing, over a wound-antiseptic that even the bears would approve of, in an X across his chest, hoping to close his gaping chest-wound, open those Kalnienk pinholes he was looking through, and maybe find that light at the end of the tunnel.

When Ray looked up, from his head-down position, and his attempt to button up the top few buttons of an old plaid shirt, he found Jen standing there, with a flower in her hair, a couple of brown bottles of cooler-chilled beer, and a bright pair of eyes whose color Ray recognized, the color of that turquoise lagoon he's been floating in, the turquoise color of the predawn sky, but whose pres-

ence in his darkened operating theater Raymond couldn't even
begin to account for, much less recognize as embedded in reality;
when Ray looked up, from the last of the buttons, and gave Jen
that white-picket wink that we promised, intended, no doubt, as
a gesture of reassurance, a point-to-point signal that all was well,
that he was fully cognizant of the immediate situation, and had the
situation under his command, the gesture fell short of being truly
reassuring; to be perfectly honest, with his eyes blinking rapidly,
attempting to account for Jennifer's presence, he didn't much look
like a man who was winking, trying to tell Jen that he was feeling
just fine, and altogether ready to go on about his business, he looked
more like a man coming out of anesthesia, trying to figure out if the
world was still there. Was the world still there? The answer to this
rather simple question, which would appear to require a rather brief
and simple answer, would be Yes, indeed, and not just there, but
slowly closing-in on the room's living occupants, and not just there,
slowly closing-in on the room's living occupants, but closing-in in
such a way that it might well be a warning, as if a warning were required, regarding the dangers involved in asking simple questions.
Gomez, in the meantime, had not gone away, and if that thermobaric weapon ignites in the living room's stale midair, setting fire to
a powdery and glittering cloud of submicronic RDX and titanium-
boron nanolaminates, the world's huge walls will close in rapidly,
and the gristmill stones of the world's vast thermodynamic machinery will lock together perfectly, one atop the other, and grind Time
down to a just-next-to-nothingness femtosecond powder; Gomez, in
short, without much more than a plate-glass warning, would leave
us on the order of 200 femtoseconds, the time required for the pigment in the eye to register the fact that the world's gone white, to
change our answer from a simple yes, to a brief and rather terrifying
*absolutely not*. And to further complicate this simple question, Raymond alone was a two-part question. While Ray had a patch, with a
permanent adhesive, holding his exterior chest-wound together, he
still had a hole in his own interior, a hole in his esophagus overflowing into his trachea, with blood pooling up in both his stomach and
his lungs; when it comes to Raymond, we don't need to worry about
the walls closing in, Ray's whole world was about the size of a closet,
where Ray might be pictured as comfortably seated, sorting himself

into two distinct parts. Part of Ray had the best of intentions, to wake the hell up and just slow down, ease up a bit on all the physical exertion, and dial-back the rate at which his pool was filling up with a garden-hose stream of his own warm blood; this part of Ray might well be positioned to catch an evening flight to the island of Bermuda, and wake up at last to see a new day dawn, with the heavily refracted predawn reds of the sun blazing away just below the horizon, lighting up the sky with the pink-cloud sands, and the crystalline waters, of an infinite predawn turquoise lagoon, meaning Ray would wake up right back where we found him, but seeing the dawn at last with his own two eyes, and Jennifer's, of course, let's not forget Jen, because Jennifer herself would be right there beside him, and Jennifer's eyes are the exact same color as that turquoise and infinite predawn sky. The remainder of Ray had no intention of ever slowing down, or easing up at all on all the physical exertion, or dialing-back the rate at which his pool was filling up with a garden-hose stream of his own warm blood; this part of Ray would be perfectly positioned to take a long slow walk in the middle of nowhere, somewhere dead center in the hourglass equivalent of the gypsum drifts out on the White Sands Desert, with no real reason to wander the earth, searching the drifts for the last grain of Time, and no way of knowing that the violet clock may have blueshifted over, and left him white-blinded by ultraviolet radiation, meaning Ray just woke up on the wrong side of Time, in which case maybe someone might like to rise from the pews, step up to the pulpit, and maybe say a few words.

# 30

C hrist, Ray, what happened to your clothes? Looks like you've been crawling around in a mud bath or something."

"Some of it may be mud. Most of it's the fact that my sutures came loose, left me with something that wasn't pretty to look at, had a hell of a time figuring out how to patch it. Speaking of which, how the hell did you get in here?"

"I walked. Why? You think I should have flown here, landed my Mooney on the roof?"

"Aren't there a bunch of troops stationed out back, guarding the exits?"

"I don't know if you'd call them troops. Looked like a couple of Juárez cops, kicking back on a sunny day in an unmarked car. If they're supposed to be guarding the exits, they'll need to back up about three or four houses, and ease up a bit on that reefer they're smoking."

"Jesus. That's just plain weird. Should be a whole damn squad out back there, or at least a full fireteam with military gear. Makes no fucking sense."

"Don't look at me, Ray, you're the expert. Maybe they got hungry, or went looking for a Starbucks. Speaking of which, looks to me like you could use a beer, and then maybe we take a drive over to Juárez General. You look about half dead, you sure you're all right?"

"Little woozy is all. Probably need a bone saw to remove this new patch. Give me a few minutes, be good as new."

"Even supposing that were true, Trip, which I seriously doubt, as I recall the mission was to get Gene out of here. Any particular reason why we can't do it now?"

"Not sure I can answer that, but then I haven't had a lot of time to think about it, and I'm still having problems digesting the fact that the exits aren't blocked. Curiosity I guess. This whole damn deal makes no fucking sense. I've been going around in circles for the last two days now. 'Bout time I had a clue what the hell I've been up to."

"If you say so, Ray, but I'd certainly feel better if we found you a doctor, and put you to bed until that knife wound has healed. Maybe it's just me, but if that guy in the bag, with his lips turning blue, and his eyes going red from petechial hemorrhage, is any indication, this place isn't exactly conducive to healing. So this must be Douchebag, seems pretty relaxed, considering the circumstances. What's happening, Gene, how you doing? You might want to think about staying away from that window. Seems a little late to warn you I saw Gomez go by, but I think I ought to warn you about his travel companions, like that man behind the tree there, aiming a rifle at your head. Don't think I've had the pleasure with the rest of your friends, but let me ask you something, Ray. How the hell did Gomez' admin get in here?"

"You mean Gabriella? I don't know. Maybe you should ask her."

"I rode here with Señor Gomez in a gold Toyota Land Cruiser, down Avenida Tecnologico, and before that, Avenida San Lorenzo, and before that, a street whose name I do not recall, and before that, we were driving on the Stanton Street Bridge, weaving through cars that were traveling too slowly, moving away from the building where our offices are kept. Before that we were driving, in the early morning hours, back the dusty dirt road out of Colonia de Anapra, and before that, let's see now, there we were, up on the mesa, in the middle of nowhere, outside the fences of Lomas de Poleo, with the moon beginning to rise and the sky full of stars. The air smelled of spearmint and the desert night was beautiful."

This little speech was followed by silence, which was followed by a moment of imaginary spearmint, which was followed by the moment when the empty-headed dimwit passed an upright tilt test, and lifted his eyelids, and took a long slow look around the sunlit room. Apparently Douchebag was not sound asleep; he had just drifted off in a pharmacological haze, and had something to add to Gabriella's inverted chronicle.

"Why don't you tell them about just before that, and how much you know about human facial transplant surgery? It's an interesting procedure, if you've never seen one done, though while the removal process itself seemed to go rather smoothly, they somehow failed to provide for a facial flesh replacement donor, and seemed to have in mind leaving the woman changing faces, not with another woman, but with her own facial bone structure, though to tell you the truth, once I got a better look at her, I wasn't really watching, I was losing my dinner."

"Let me ask you something, Gabriella. What the fuck is he talking about?" This, obviously, was Raymond speaking. He and Douchebag have an ongoing communication problem, as though the two of them are neither on the same wavelength, like Raymond and Jen, nor from the same solar system, if that's humanly possible.

"What am I talking about? I'm talking about Gomez and his dental hygienists, with their deep-cavity lighting and a corpse tied to a chair, using a Collin's Sellors forceps, and maybe a Ribbon Retractor, and a bunch of fucking scalpels, all laid out nice and neat on a stainless steel tray. Let me ask *you* something. Would you know the difference between a number 19 scalpel, for cutting skin and muscle, and for general carving and stencil making, and a number 12a, sharpened on the inner curvature? If I told you I was about to use a Volkmann Bone Hook Retractor, in advance of making a face-flesh incision, would you be able to tell me I'm completely full of shit? If a surgically opened artery suddenly began to bleed, would you pick up a Finochietto box joint forceps, or a thirty-pound cinderblock, and maybe drop it on your head?"

"This man is obviously crazy. Señor Gomez would never permit such a thing."

"Ms. Hernandez, perhaps you would do me the honor of explaining to me exactly what happened last night. As you well know, you were to bring a man, code-named The Poet, to Casa Cronómetro at noon today. I take it this man Douchebag is the so-called Poet. I rather pointedly advised you not to invite your supervisor, and in fact informed you in reasonably graphic terms exactly what would happen to your uncle, Gustavo, if you failed to adhere to my precise instructions. And yet you show up here, nearly fifty minutes late, having apparently informed Señor Gomez of our meeting. Since you have now put us all at considerable risk, perhaps you would care to comment, for my own edification, as to *what precisely* you could *possibly* have been *thinking?*" This, of course, as Ramírez well knew, was not really a question that Wittgenstein would have approved of; when you subtract the fact that Gomez has arrived from the fact that Gabriella apparently brought him, all that remains is the floral arrangements. It might be better to ask her what Gomez has in mind, standing in the roadway with that SMAW-NE, preparing to supply us with an ending for our narrative, using a shoulder-mounted weapon armed with *Novel Explosives.*

"I was thinking of a lesson that Señor Gomez had taught me. Prior to that, I was thinking about the difficulties of finding street signs in Juárez, when several vehicles pulled us over and removed me from the car. Prior to that, I was concerned about the ability of this man to drive his automobile, since he seemed unable to operate the brake pedal, and was using a childish and pointless type of map to tell us that we were parked in an empty brown blank spot. This was not giving me confidence that this man was being competent, and I also supposed, from the pills he was taking, kept in the short paper sack between his knees, that he may have been suffering from a driving malady. In my opinion, this man should not have been driving with a medical condition, and I was thinking it might be best for us to abandon the vehicle, and walk from where we were to wherever we were going next. Prior to that, I was thinking of doing everything you asked, bringing this man to the Holiday Inn Express, meeting him at the foot of the Stanton Street Bridge, at shall we say noon, on the 15th of April, calling him on the phone to tell him to make it cash, reading him the list of quotations you gave me. Just prior to this, I was there at the desk, when Señor Gomez phoned him to read from *The Tempest,* in order to help him sleep I was told, and this I was thinking of as not being necessary, since according to Gomez, the man was already dreaming. Prior to that, I was thinking about how you told me to do exactly what you said, or find Tío Gustavo decomposing in an acid vat."

"Not acid, my dear, lye. Decomposing as a result of alkaline hydrolysis, an accelerated version of ordinary human burial. Am I to infer from this that Señor Gomez may have threatened you, and caused you to reveal certain details of our plans? What exactly happened on the Lomas de Poleo mesa?"

"Hold on a second, let me get something straight. Who was the asshole tried to land me in a sleep clinic, waking me up to tell me I was asleep? Which one of you guys was Señor Prospero? And while we're at it, what the hell am I doing drinking tequila in Juárez? I brought Prospero's money back, what the hell else does he want? I should be sitting pretty, maybe 20 floors up, drinking single malt scotch in an El Paso conference room."

"It was no doubt Señor Gomez playing the part of Prospero. As to what he wants, beyond delivery of the currency, I believe he may desire that you vanish without a trace, without so much as a DNA fragment, leaving the civil authorities without a civilian to connect him to the receipt of the funds in your duffel bag. Gomez, presumably, for the moment at least, must be particularly wary of the IRS, and while I doubt that your existence or nonexistence means a great deal in the scheme of things, you're a loose thread he might prefer to tie off. As for your diversion to Casa Cronómetro, this appears to have been a rather unfortunate embellishment, a gilding of the lily, if you will, an embroidering of the embroidery, for which, rest assured, you have my deepest apologies. And as to the money itself, as I was trying to explain to Mr. Edmunds, Gomez has been building a retirement fund, a construct that his superiors would almost certainly not approve of, which in turn would explain the use of trained mercenaries, likely men currently serving in the Mexican Army, to avoid the possibility that the Juárez Cartel might inadvertently become apprised of his impending retirement."

"So you're trying to tell me you wouldn't make a good trophy. Not too sure I'm buying that. I'm thinking we trade you straight up to the Zetas, catch a plane to another time zone, maybe open up a bike shop."

"If you doubt my veracity, you need only examine the contents of your vehicle. You'll likely find a ton of the Cartel's gold bars hidden beneath the truck bed in the false-bottom space, a rather crude form of misappropriation for a man of Gomez' acumen, but with a

number of distinct advantages over wire transfer. I can assure you
that I would add little of value to Gomez' substantial retirement
fund. And while you would appear to have the option of retreating to the rear, I can also assure you that an orderly withdrawal
would be a difficult manoeuver with Gomez in pursuit. In short,
Mr. Edmunds, you're only hope of finding yourself pursuing another occupation is to send out the truck keys and the duffel bag of
currency, along with our somewhat inebriated friend. In any case,
we are wasting valuable time. Let me ask you again, Gabriella: what
precisely took place on the Lomas mesa? How much did you reveal
regarding the workings of our operation?"

"I have no idea what you are talking about. And now, retracing
my steps back to yesterday's noon, prior to all of these problems I
am having, prior to my meeting this man at the bridge, I find that
I am somehow lacking in cash, and unable to obtain it using my
ATM PIN. This street I am walking is filled with machines, differing in some of the ways they are working, but alike in refusing the
cash that I seek. I enter the number, the number that I recall, and
am told by the machine that my entry is invalid."

Tick-tock, tick-tock; Gomez is waiting. A man steps out of his
rose-pink house, several streets over, to water his small garden of
cantaloupe, watermelon, cucumber, and squash. His pear trees
and plum trees would appear to be flourishing, and his apricot
and peach trees, while not yet in season, seem in perfect health,
although a plucked fruit now, in the middle of April, would reveal,
if bitten into, a harsh and bitter flesh. The peach trees, in particular,
will require a certain amount of patience, but then the man who
remains patient, and in possession of his teeth, outside the context
of a comparison with dental records, will be amply rewarded with
a mid-July peach. Five armed men, in a forest-green pickup, drive
slowly past the rose-pink house, and park up the block, at a distance
of perhaps seventy or eighty meters. Who are these men? We have
no idea. They don't belong here; perhaps they play a role in a separate Juárez narrative; they would appear, among other things, to
be uncharacteristically patient, in the manner of blowflies taking
a wait-and-see approach. Gomez, unfortunately, is running low on
patience, and is likely unaware of Kierkegaard's thoughts on the

role played by patience in the maintenance of identity. Gomez has his men fan out, in an orderly-looking arc, perhaps a quarter of a semicircle, like the lower one-eighth of a deadbeat escape wheel, the characteristic movement of a pendulum clock, instantly recognizable by its raked and pointed teeth, or in this case an assortment of high-powered weaponry, of Norwegian, Iranian, and possibly Russian origins. Tick-tock, tick-tock; the wheels are turning. Imagine a world in which the blowflies are armed, and capable of inflicting massive human head wounds. How long do you suppose the flies would linger, contemplating the wonders of human morbidity, before chambering their weapons and firing the first shot? If you think the flies would wait for those mid-July peaches, and an ample reward for their evident patience, you've simply lost your way in the next narrative over, because here at Casa Cronómetro, on Calle Avanzaro, local Juárez savings time is Perfectly Ripe.

"No wonder you were late. You might want to try putting the number in backwards. Your memory works perfectly, but apparently in reverse. Think back from the moment you are driving on the mesa, looking up at the desert stars, with the moon beginning to rise, and the cool night air smelling distinctly of menthol, in an armor-plated black Suburban that's phenomenally well-equipped, slowly rolling backwards toward the razor-wire fencing, half-expecting a man in a Schutzstaffel trenchcoat and Einsatzkommandos to greet you in the klieg lights. You roll in reverse under the twenty-foot sniper towers, through the twin-leaf blast doors, and into the empty compound, with a cyanide capsule tucked under your tongue, and an enormous load of soft drinks in case you're too dry to swallow. You park the car backwards beside Bungalow B, and suddenly notice an unnerving white light, in the window of Bungalow A, the next building over, a sterile white lamplight whose optical clarity seems totally out of keeping with the state of the community, where most of the current models, if you happened to read the sales brochure for *The Dunes at Menthol Ridge*, come equipped with the latest in home security, the Bulldozed and Backhoed Entry-Proof House. Just when you're hoping some sniper has a bead on you, and is slowly taking aim through his front-focal riflescope, Gomez has you moonwalk into the sterile white room, where two men in white lab coats are dissecting a cadaver. Now. Let me ask you something. What the fuck are these lab coat guys up to? They both seem to know exactly what they're doing, but I'll be fucked if I do, like the guy on the left is holding an X-Acto knife the same way you would if you were cutting up dinner, only he's not cutting his dinner, he's filleting the face flesh, and it's probably not an X-Acto knife, it's some kind of scalpel, about which I know like approximately fucking zero. The guy on the right starts in chopping away below the bridge of the nose, using a hammer and a chisel, and then shifts to an object that looks like a scythe, trying to scrape out all of the connective shit that keeps your nose tied to your skull bones, only we're not in a village in India somewhere, where some woman got her hair caught in the blades of a wheat thresher, and that thing he's using is definitely not a scythe, it's a surgical instrument, sharpened on the outer curvature. What the fuck kind of dissection is this? I realize you weren't in the room at this point, but if you want my opinion, these guys know exactly what the fuck they're up to, and they don't give a shit about facial anatomy. If you're thinking this is some sort of transplant surgery, it's a good idea, but that won't work either, because that woman in India with a yanked-off face isn't about to get a new one from this particular cadaver, unless you think they're planning on piecing the whole thing back together, maybe hold it all down with facial-flesh Super Glue, and a few tubes of Sephora Smashbox foundation primer, out of the garbage piling up in the white plastic bucket. So I'm not really sure I know what to make of any of this, I'm thinking I must have dreamed it all up to begin with, I was pretty fucking wasted on black tar and Mescal, but the weird thing is, there in the dream, you show up with a guy you're calling Gomez, like Gomez make it stop is literally what you're saying, and I wouldn't know Gomez from Adam at this point, but it's the same fucking guy who's out there in the road, and you're still calling him Gomez, like maybe that's his name or something, and he and the dream guy are the exact same person. So let's say I'm still dreaming the same demented dream, and I'm not really here, I'm somewhere in Suriname, probably doing what I should have been doing in the first place, like trying to figure out why the bauxite industry needs a boatload of WiMAX for their 4G cell phones, or what the fuck, since you're not here either, pretend you're a bunch of Lacanian psychoanalysts, trying to help me get out of the mirror stage of development, but one way or the other, wherever the hell we are, I may need your help here, because I'm having some real problems with this whole demented dream, where I look in the wall mirror of a Juárez hotel room, and my face looks like something that got yanked off by a wheat thresher."

This little speech was followed by silence, which was followed by a moment of yet more silence, which was followed by the moment when the silence in the room began to make the silence feel distinctly uncomfortable.

　"Please ask him to stop. This man needs a doctor, he's obviously overmedicated. There is nothing I can do for him. He needs to be told to keep his dreams to himself."

　"No, Ms. Hernandez, I would prefer to hear him out. It is, you must admit, a rather fascinating dream, although to be more precise, since the man gives no indication of having been asleep, these images he's describing would not be called dreams, but oneirogogic visions, consistent with the mental phenomena that occur during a state of threshold consciousness, perhaps as a result of opiate inhalation. Please continue, sir. Perhaps I could ask again that you be somewhat more concise, and refrain from the use of profanity, as there are ladies present."

　"Hey Ray, if you're hearing what I'm hearing, may I make a suggestion? Let's get the fuck out of here, before this gets any weirder. This guy is beginning to give me the creeps."

　"I'm with her, Trip, two baked cops we can handle with pistols. If the civilian's the hold-up, we can bring him along, but if you were listening to Ramírez, I've got another suggestion. Man needs help with these badass dreams, let's send him on out with Gomez's money, worst that can happen is his dreams go away. Or better yet, send him and the money out with one of our pistols. Guy gets in close enough with one of those Berettas, might throw a wrench in Gomez' battle plan, save us the bother of making sense of either one of them. Both full of shit, far as I'm concerned."

　"Yeah, maybe so, can't disagree, but like Ramírez said, let's hear the man out. Don't like the sound of what Gomez has been up to."

"Okay, so here's my problem. These men I'm referring to, in what must have started out to be clean white lab coats, seem to be taking remarkable care, using surgical gauze and Schwartz clips and bulldog clamps, and what seems to be some sort of elastomeric liquid sealant, to prevent the loss of embalming fluids. Even if you discount this whole description, like say I'm making the whole thing up out of thin fucking air, if you'll pardon the expression, as I'm standing there watching them going about their work, and wouldn't know a bulldog clamp from a Schwartz clip if it bit me, I'll tell you one thing I'm totally not making up, which is that they're paying no attention at all to the cranio-maxillofacial structure, other than to the underlying facial bones themselves, and yet they seem to be obsessed with preservative leakage. Maybe you're not really getting the picture. Let me try again. Why would two men, streaked with Congo red dye, dissecting the face of an upright cadaver, in a manner more consistent with the cleaning of teeth than that of serious students of facial anatomy, come equipped with a tiny micro-aneuryism clip, with which they are even now stopping a hairline bleeder? How is it possible that a basic human corpse, stripped of its face flesh down to the underlying bone structure, has emitted a low moan and is now being resilenced by the application of a cloth likely dampened with ether? Something has gone wrong here. There in the room, under deep-cavity shadow-control sterile illumination, there are two men in lab coats, and a living cadaver. This, to me, is a big semiotic problem, like right about here, I'm losing my dinner, which is when I hear voices in the sterile white room, and peak through the window, and see Gomez and Gabriella. So let me ask you something, Ms. Sistine Madonna, Ms. Shall We Say Noon, Ms. Better Safe Than Sorry, now that we're both here and we're in this together, do you see what I see, or am I making this shit up? I've got no fucking clue what to do with any of this. I know it can't be real, but what the fuck is it? I tried calling it a dream, but it didn't change anything. What do you call it? What do you call it when a woman changes faces, not with another woman, but with her own facial bone structure? What do you call it when they turn a human being into something that looks like one of those Santa Muerte roadside shrines? What do you call it when a fourteen-year-old girl, picked up in the night on her way to a maquila, has to walk around Juárez in the cold light of day, with no face at all, like she's gradually disappearing? What do you call it when they leave her with eyes, like how in the fuck does that even begin to be possible, so she can look in the mirror one bright Sunday morning, having finally woken up from what she took to be a dream, and see looking back at her, not her own face, but her eyes set in the sockets of exposed human skull bones? What do you call that thing that we're staring at? What do you call us for just standing there staring? I can just see us now, under deep-cavity lighting and sterile illumination, watching this happen and not doing anything, like we can't stop looking, we're the local peeping Toms, that's what I'd call us, we're voyeurs of the hideous, oglers of the loathsome, we're like human face-flesh paraphiliacs, the sort of people who just can't help themselves, like don't look at us, we're not the problem, because no matter what happens, no matter how subhuman, that's just the way we are, we're people who like to watch."

Santa Muerte, indeed. This, goodness knows, we did not see coming; had we known about any of this, we might well have adopted a slightly different tone. Gabriella held still, for just a ghost of a moment, and then buried her face in her beautiful slim hands, the hands of the Madonna in the Sistine Raphael, holding up what looks to be the picture of innocence, our savior and redeemer as a golden-haired child. Is it possible that somehow there is a child in us all, a child who still believes, despite all the evidence, that there is something inside us still worthy of redemption? All things considered, a simple *no* should suffice, though if forced to elaborate, we might put it this way. The Sistine Madonna moves us to tears, we're prepared to believe that anything is possible, our redemptive child, a divinity in each of us, a path toward perfection of the human spirit, but given our record of bald-faced indifference, and our willingness to abide the most ungodly behavior, we suspect that the Madonna might have dropped her own child, and buried her face in her own slim hands, had she known where the human spirit was headed: into Juárez, with tears in our eyes, and our instruments at work on living cadavers.

"I didn't watch. I couldn't. I don't want to know."
"I know you didn't watch. Sorry I brought it up."

When the first shot was fired, a silence entered the room, a strange cotemporal subaudible silence, a silence whose entrance would be difficult to detect, concealed as it was beneath the muzzle-blast impulse wave, and the supersonic whipcrack of an explosives-hurled projectile. This proved to be something of a mystifying moment, this moment in time when a shot was fired, and a silent entrant entered the room, and a silence completed its rather mystifying entrance, made all the more mystifying by a narrative blunder: while the room at the time was sunlit and bright, with nothing to obscure the narrative sightlines, this first-shot firing caught us unaware, in the middle of a momentary lapse of attention, attending to a tale so lightless and opaque that it left us in the dark when a shot rang out, obstructing our view of the firing event, and thoroughly obscuring the narrative timeline. If you've ever been a witness at a gunshot trial, where you're asked to recount the sequence of events, and place each event in a temporal order, you may well have noticed a kind of sequencing error, a rather fundamental flaw in the temporal arrangement, right at the heart of our opening statement: when the first shot was fired, a silence hadn't entered, the silence would have to wait for the muzzle-blast to arrive, and the muzzle-blast arrived, not at the time of the first-shot firing, but at the end of a lengthy sequence of events, events leading back to a triggering event. This sequencing error requires a correction, in the form of a brief retracing of steps, headed back in the direction of the triggering event, to pinpoint the moment when a weapon was fired, and locate the first-shot's point of origin: in the instant just before the muzzle-blast arrived, and a silence entered the silent room, a gunbarrel muzzle-flash blazed orange-white, a fireball of light that was captured by the eye, with a 200-femtosecond time-lag allowance, and in the instant just before the muzzle-flash flared, a wad of triple-base smokeless powder, buried at the base of a pistol cartridge, waiting to be ignited by a firing-pin strike, exploded in a smokeless-powdery puff, a powder composed of a tongue-twisting mixture of fivonite-tetramethyl and di-ethylene glycol and picrite-nitroguanidine explosive propellants, as though the bullet had been propelled by a phoneme explosion, and in the instant just before the pin hit home, at the beginning of it all, at the point of origin, someone who was present, in the room itself, must have pulled the trigger on a striker-fired handgun, because if that gunbarrel muzzle-flash is any indication, the first shot was fired from inside the room. For those who were present, inside the room, when the trigger was pulled on a striker-fired handgun, it's doubtful that silence was the first thing they noted; the muzzle-blast alone, weighing in at on the order of 160 decibels, would be capable of causing temporary deafness, but deafness, frankly, would be a subsequent event, in no way cotemporal with the muzzle-blast itself, and while they may have missed the whipcrack of a bullet's sonic boom, what they truly missed was this silence that entered, cloaked in the sound wave of a smokeless explosion. So without getting involved in koan-like riddles, how had a silence entered the room, apparently dressed in auditory camouflage, and the bulletproof body-armor of a striker-fired blast, without being noticed by the room's own occupants? To make matters worse, and complicate the question, by the time the first shot had arrived at its target, and an ordinary hush filled most of the room, it was apparent that the silence had subdivided, and sorted itself into two distinct pools, one pool belonging to startled observers, those caught off guard when the first shot was fired, and the other belonging to a koan-like riddle, the man in the room who fired the first shot. We'll need go back to the very beginning, and conduct a brief search for this silence in question, apparently subdivided into two distinct pools, while keeping in mind that this silence in question hadn't entered the room through a door or a window, it had entered the room through the barrel of a gun.

When the first shot was fired, the pressure being applied to the trigger of a handgun, pressure supplied by a human finger, readying a mass of spring-tensioned metal, and preparing a weapon to initiate firing, had finally reached the point when the weapon was self-sufficient, when human intent had been subtracted from the act, and then the firing event went off like clockwork: once the trigger reached the point of no return, three inline-safeties were completely disengaged, mechanically eliminating the human element, a trigger-bar connector pulled the firing-pin back, and the striker moved rearward within the pistol, increasing the tension on a firing-pin spring, and positioning a mass of spring-tensioned metal to hurl itself forward as the trigger-bar released; once the trigger-bar released the firing-pin lug, the striker hurled forward toward the base of a cartridge, striking the primer on a centerfire round, and igniting a wad of triple-base powder, that powder composed of a tongue-twisting mixture of fivonite-tetramethyl and di-ethylene glycol and picrite-nitroguanidine explosive propellants, as if a bullet could be propelled by an allophone explosion; and once the explosive propellants finally ignited, unleashing that flurry of thermodynamic events that grind Time down to a femtosecond powder, they exploded in a femtosecond powdery puff, and two milliseconds later, a gunbarrel muzzle-flash blazed orange-white, registered as light by the pigment in the eye, with a 200-femtosecond time-lag allowance, and a millisecond later, the muzzle-blast arrived, a blast that hadn't sounded as if allophones exploded, it sounded as if the whole world had exploded, leaving only an echo of the human voice, and human intent, and the human element, all of which were present when our explosives were composed, but absent long before their blast wave arrived; and here, at long last, at the end of it all, at the termination point of a clockwork sequence, a silence entered the silent room, arriving arm-in-arm with the muzzle-blast itself, and dressed for the occasion in auditory camouflage, and bulletproof body-armor, and God knows what, perhaps a bright-orange rose in its muzzle-flash buttonhole, though it hadn't much mattered what the silence was wearing, as it wound up buried beneath the auditory rubble of a deafening muzzle-blast sonic explosion. Perhaps we need a moment to catch our breath; suffice it to say that when the first shot was fired, it unleashed an utter-whirlwind sequence of events, and only at the end of this whirlwind-sequence had a silence completed its rather mystifying entrance. That being said, if you don't see the point of all this gunshot minutiae, think of it this way: a man's own history, human history, the history of our place on the planet we inhabit, are narrative affairs, and our narratives begin with narrative blunders, and continue to behave as if human intent hadn't been subtracted once we'd triggered an event, and end with the entrance of a mystifying silence, made all the more mystifying by its having been created at the exact same instant when human consciousness was born.

When the first shot was fired, a clockwork sequence of events ensued, events intrinsic to a striker-fired handgun, beginning with the moment when a trigger was pulled, and a striker-fired handgun subtracted its handler, which was followed by a moment of mechanical movements, which was followed by a moment of a powder igniting, which was followed by a moment of smokeless explosion, which was followed by a moment of a bullet ejecting, which was followed by a moment of a muzzle-glow in rose, a timeless moment of a muzzle-glow in rose, whose complementary color stood just outside the door, basking in the glow of the spring-green trees, in the spring-green leaves of the Easter-blooming lilacs, in the luminous heart of spring's open offer to begin once again in the spring-green days, with a red-tailed hawk in the azure skies, riding the updrafts of an infinite ceiling, and the dogs at a trot in the mesquite scrub, chasing the scent of bobwhite and pheasant, and the streams running high in the snows above the Pecos, waiting for the fly lines of trout-fishing season, really all that human consciousness could possibly ask, in the timeless beauty of a mid-April day, which was followed by the moment when a bullet left the barrel, which was followed by the moment when a gunbarrel muzzle-flash blazed orange-white, which was followed by a second flash of white-hot-pink, which was followed by a third flash of flame-yellow light, which was followed by a final flash of bright hard sparks, the blazing-metal fragments of a pistol-bullet jacket, which was followed by the moment when the muzzle-blast arrived, which just happened to be the moment when human consciousness died, and in its momentary absence, a silence was born, born in the minds of startled observers, in the form of a momentary absence of noise. While we could, we suppose, repeat these attempts at a gunshot-history *ad infinitum*, each time correcting a minor flaw, what this final iteration ultimately exposes is a rather fundamental error in each of our histories: no one could have noticed a silence *enter*, because a silence in fact never *entered* the room, a silence in fact was *born* in the room, born in the minds of startled observers, in the form of a momentary absence of noise. That being said, if you can't quite pinpoint this noise that we're referring to, the noise found missing once the muzzle-blast arrived, and you've ever been present when a striker-fired pistol, fired without warning, went off in a quiet space, think back for a moment to the discharge chronology: in the instant just before the muzzle-blast arrived, assuming you hadn't noticed all the multi-colored lights, or drawn some connection between hand-gun-intrinsics, and the clipped dry tone of a pistol-trigger click, you were probably just sitting there, going about your inner life, maintaining your sense of self, and the continuity of identity, despite a baffling array of narrative fragments and gibbering figments and cognitive incongruities, all ricocheting aimlessly, inside your head, with nothing in common, and no inner unity, aside from the belief that all this babbling must be yours, because if you came to believe it was the babbling of others, you'd be forced to admit that you've long been hearing voices, or picking up signals from an alien space-craft, and that your entire sense of self, your unified identity, was either a sick cosmic joke or a lunatic fiction; whoever invented the interior monologue, at least the literary version, with its overlay of eloquence, which dates back as far as the Parables of Luke, and Hellenistic novels, and even Homer himself, either had no clue at all what goes on in people's heads, and made the whole thing up, out of literary vanity, or faced with the reality of all our jittery neural noise, dismissed it completely, and simply didn't want to hear it; your entire inner life, in fact most of human consciousness, is a narrative blunder, full of sequencing errors and eventless triggers and temporal disarrangements that can't be retraced, with no place to stand that keeps the sightlines clean, or keeps the inner-time-line in any way sequential; perhaps you've noticed the difficulty, in fact the utter impossibility, when asked by a so-called loved-one for a hint as to what you're thinking, of coming up with something, anything at all, which might prove simultaneously truthful and in any way cogent. When the lightless tale finished, in the moments before the blast, you could have heard a pin drop, or a crow land on a power line, if it weren't for the fact that the room itself was silent, leaving everyone present, with the possible exception of the greenbottle blowflies, and the koan-like riddle who fired the first shot, forced to listen to the sound of their own mental machinery, with all of its strange bells and whistles, grinding on itself. In the instant just before the muzzle-blast hit, with the moments of ignition and smokeless explosion and gunbarrel-muzzle-flash all long gone, and the silent observers in no way prepared for their

160-decibel muzzle-blast surprise, about to set fire to their whole
sonic universe, and reduce their sputtering mental machinery to
a smoking-hole pile of massless metal, in the instant, as we were
saying, just before the blast, even if they'd been sitting in a sound-
proof booth, with only their own thoughts to keep them company,
they'd have to admit that the noise was incredible, the cerebrum an
explosion of voltage-gated sodium ions and potassium leak-channel
neural effluxions and axon-pathway electrochemical-pulses, most
of which passes without being noted, and some of which translates
to human consciousness, through a process we're not yet prepared
to address, with its momentary absence still a full instant off. When
the muzzle-blast hit, a full instant later, human consciousness died
a rather momentary death, a death whose duration we decline to
assess, though you might want to note that a massless metal would
travel like light in a spacetime equation, and obviate the need to
experience time, and in its momentary absence, a silence was born,
born in the minds of startled observers, in the form of a momentary
absence of noise, producing a *pool of silence* so pure that it couldn't
be broken by a shattering cry, or disturbed by the ripples of a rock or
a pebble, because the pool, after all, had nothing in it. While this
perfectly pure and empty pool would certainly account for most of
the silence we set out in search of in our subdivided pool, if you've
ever been a Friend at a Quaker meeting, where a *pool of silence* is
summoned into being, you know that this pool is not an absence
of noise, which could easily be found in a rock or a pebble, it's a
pooling of the presence of silence itself, which couldn't be found in
a rock or a pebble, or inside the minds of startled observers, those
caught off guard when the first shot was fired, or even in a mystifying koan-like riddle, the recourse to which we've been hoping to
avoid, it could only be found in a stone-like presence, the man in
the room who fired the first shot.

    Once the first shot was fired, Ray sat back on an off-white
couch, still working in his darkened operating theater, darkened
by blood-loss hypovolemia, with a permanent patch on an ancient
chest-wound, but with a hole in his esophagus overflowing into his
trachea, and blood pooling up in both his stomach and his lungs.
Ray shifted the Glock from his right hand to left, and put a finger to his lips to indicate silence; licked a bit of blood from his

trigger finger, and washed away the taste with a slug of cold beer; and then completing a cycle we should all be familiar with, shifted the self-loading locked-breech Glock back on around to his natural right hand. Our gunshot-history would appear to be complete: the first shot was fired from inside the room; the first shot was fired on a striker-fired handgun, a Glock 29 self-loading pistol, with a 10mm Auto cartridge loaded in the gunbarrel's integral chamber; and the trigger on the Glock was pulled by Raymond, the man in the room who fired the first shot. And our gunshot-history would almost certainly be complete, if it weren't for the fact that we've skipped something vital: the weapon in the room that fired the first shot. While the firing event would appear to begin with the trigger being pulled on a striker-fired pistol, the firing event did not begin with the trigger being pulled on any kind of pistol; and while the firing sequence was a sequence of events, events that connect to a triggering event, the triggering event in the firing sequence had nothing to do with a pistol trigger; and while the weapon involved was a calibrated weapon, the weapon involved was not a handgun. We'll give you just a moment to properly absorb this, and then take the moment back to properly restate it: the firing event did not begin with the trigger being pulled on a striker-fired pistol, it began instead with a triggering event, and the triggering event could not be found in a Glock 29 self-loading pistol, or in a self-sufficient firearm's firing machinery, or in a clockwork-sequence of handgun-intrinsics that subtracted the handgun's handler from the act, it could only be found in human-intrinsics, and in human intent, and in the human element, when in the moments just prior to the shot being fired, a clockwork sequence of events ensued, events leading up to a triggering event, and once the triggering event had been properly absorbed, a trigger was pulled in Raymond Edmunds, the weapon in the room that fired the first shot.

When the first shot was fired, in the middle of a momentary lapse of attention, it was preceded by a moment of narrative white, that space on a page where nothing seems to happen, and it's there in that moment of narrative white that all of our gunshot-history was written; we'll need to go back to before the beginning, and darken the narrative whiteness of the page. Just prior to the shot, in the moments before the blast, Ray could still be pictured as comfortably seated, sorting himself into two distinct parts: a part of Ray that had the best of intentions, to wake the hell up and just slow down, and ease up a bit on all the physical exertion; and a part of Ray that had no intention of ever slowing down, or easing up at all on all the physical exertion. Raymond had been listening to a lightless tale, with half a mind inclined to believe not a word of it, and half a mind inclined to believe that it was true, a state of mind that didn't end when the lightless tale ended, it ended the moment Gabriella responded, by holding a moment of silence for a moment, and then burying her face in the palms of her hands. Just prior to the moment when a trigger was pulled, in that moment when pressure from a human finger was preparing to be applied to a handgun trigger, Raymond was in a peculiar state of awareness: he wasn't aware that his off-white cushion had turned from an off-white shade of cream, to a pink-like shade of cotton candy, to a blood-drenched shade of woozy-brownish, the color of Raymond, through and through; he wasn't aware that a Glock-shattered mirror, positioned on a wall above some quicklime sacks, reflected a change in his shattered state, leaving hundreds of luminous dark-eyed Raymonds staring back at their patched but fractured owner, with something other than apparent indifference; he wasn't aware of jittery neural noise, or narrative fragments, or gibbering figments, or cognitive incongruities ricocheting aimlessly inside his head; he wasn't aware of Gabriella's final words; he wasn't aware of anyone's words; in fact, Ray wasn't aware of a moment of awareness that had altered his awareness just a moment before, in the moment when Gabriella responded, by holding a moment of silence for a moment, and then burying her face in the palms of her hands, and it was there in that moment of a timeless gesture that Ray became clear-eyed and flooded with awareness as to just what had happened on the Lomas mesa, leaving Ray with no awareness of the tears in his eyes, but with an absolute rock-hard stone-cold conviction that Gomez was a predator whose time on this earth would need to be limited, through a sequence of events that would need to begin, inside the room, with a shot being fired on a striker-fired handgun; when the trigger was pulled in Raymond Edmunds, if Ray could be said to be aware of anything, it would resemble that moment of a boxer's awareness that a looping left-hook has just been launched, and before the fighter is aware of anything, he counters with a straight right hand of his own. Our gunshot-history is all but complete, and the gunshot itself is a foregone conclusion: the first shot was fired from inside the room; the first shot was fired on a striker-fired handgun, a Glock 29 self-loading pistol; but the first shot was fired when the pressure being applied to a human trigger, pressure supplied by a lightless tale, pressure supplied by a horror story, pressure supplied by a human predator, whose instruments were used on a nameless child, whose instruments were used on a living cadaver, whose instruments were used on a divinity in each of us, had finally reached the point when the weapon was self-sufficient, when human intent had been added to the act, and then a firing event in Raymond Edmunds went off like clockwork, putting a bullet through a bullet-hole in a Glock-shattered mirror, leaving hundreds of shattered but clear-eyed Raymonds scattered on Gomez' hardwood floor. If this sounds like a man just letting off steam, and firing off a shot, more or less at random, you've forgotten what you know about Raymond Edmunds: Ray's not fond of sloppiness with weapons, and Raymond's not a man of random actions; if Ray fired a shot, you can bet he had his reasons. Once the first shot was fired, Ray sat back on an off-white couch, started cycling the Glock on around between hands, and put a finger to his lips to indicate silence, but he couldn't be pictured as comfortably seated, sorting himself into two distinct parts: that part of Ray that had the best of intentions, to wake the hell up and just slow down, and ease up a bit on all the physical exertion, had vanished in a smokeless powdery puff, leaving only the Raymond that had no intention of ever slowing down, or easing up at all on all the physical exertion, or dialing-back the rate at which his pool was filling up with a garden-hose stream of his own warm blood, the Raymond in fact of the indicated action, the Ray who would never fire a shot at random, the Ray who would always have a reason for the shot. Not that Ray knew anything at all about Hegel, but as Hegel might have said, *a man's being is his act*, and while Ray's two eyes were pools of tears, Ray's whole being was a rock-hard stone-cold *pool of silence*, summoned into being in the indicated act, as though Ray's warm blood had turned to stone, which couldn't be broken with a hammer and chisel, or shattered by a deafening muzzle-blast cry, or found in the minds of startled observers, those caught off guard when the first shot was fired, or even in a mystifying koan-like riddle, which may well account for those empathetic tears, but the recourse to which we can certainly avoid, it could only be found, when all is said and done, in the stone-like presence of silence itself: that silence in the calibrated mind of Raymond, that silence in the eyes of a stone cold killer.

Gene, I'm going out. I need you in the window with the AR-15; five seconds of suppressive fire to the right of Gomez. Arturo, same thing, to the left of Gomez, out the front door, use the Berettas. Remember the Berettas are set to fire in three-round bursts, but the burst only lasts a fraction of a second, so go easy on the triggers, maybe pause between pulls, try to lay down a steady stream of fire to my left. Don't even bother trying to kill these guys, you'll never get a 9-mil through all that armor, I need them distracted while I get to Gomez. If it turns out they're mercenaries, like Ramírez says, they'll never get paid once Gomez is dead, so maybe we can pay them to just go away. Jesus, Ray, what the hell are you thinking? I'm not really thinking, I'm more like hoping, hoping they'll think I'm coming out with a body, and are maybe just a split-second slow to react. I'd try a white flag if I thought it would work, but these guys will shoot me if I stroll through the yard. I'll need a running start to get to Gomez, and can't have them firing before I'm even out the door. Ray thought this over, went back through his training, and then fired a second round through his imaginary body, leaving the Gomez Statuary Mantel Chronometer stopped at right around 1:14, Juárez Standard Ripeness Time. What the fuck, Ray, that'll never work, all you're going to do is get yourself killed. Let's go out the back way, and get the hell out of here. This might have been Gene, or even Arturo, but was in fact Jennifer, expressing doubts about Ray's plan, the sort of doubts that might arise in any civilian, while Gene and Arturo are effectively soldiers, and have very little training in questioning orders. Jen's fundamental reasoning, of course, that since Raymond's about to die in an immediate hail of gunfire, he might want to consider seeking alternate modes of egress, while certainly sound, fails to account for several peculiar features, as previously noted, in Raymond's mental landscape and moral topography; while we're naturally hesitant to speak of such things, which have no real place among logical propositions, and would seem to imply the noumenal existence of some unified sovereign self with its own terra firma, all of which, frankly, seems a bit far-fetched, particularly in a place like Ciudad Juárez, which with its slippery porous borders and shifty terrain, is exactly the sort of place that Wittgenstein had in mind when he put that final bullet through his own Tractatus, *Whereof one cannot speak, thereof one must be silent*; still we can't help feeling that Ray's the sort of man who knows who he is, ontically speaking, and knows the ins and outs of where he stands in the world. Given Raymond's blank-eyed stare into the face of his own extinction, his belief that his plan has a slim chance of working, and his apparent conviction that Gomez is a predator, if there's one thing we can say about Raymond Edmunds, in his search for the imperative Kantian action, there's no chance in hell he's going out the back way; if Ray's going out, he's going out the front. Ray handed Jen his cooler-chilled beer, took one last look at the flower in her hair, and then gave her a wink, which could have meant almost anything, but in this case meant Honey, I'll be back for that beer, just give me ten seconds, I'm going to kill that motherfucker. Ray put his off-hand on the handle of the door, pushed Arturo down beside the doorframe with his Glock hand, and opened up the entry on a blazing Juárez day, blue sky everywhere, crows up on the power lines, and a gold Toyota Land Cruiser, glittering in the sun, loaded down with empty cup holders, and all but empty cups.

If this were the sort of world that we'd all like to live in, where a blue-sky day would be cause for celebration, Ray would be getting ready to take the dogs for a run, out in the gypsum desert, in the mesquite and acacia brush, flushing a covey of bobwhite out, nice clean arc in the clear April air, and maybe Ray and Jen having a quiet conversation, or maybe it's one of those days where things speak for themselves, and the pure joy of creation is present and accounted for. We'd like to think the world could still be such a place, with Ray doing the inventory in his bike-rental shop, and staring out to sea over the turquoise waters, or hosing down the sidewalk outside his small bodega, after sweeping all of the horseshit that man brings down on himself into the fucking gutter with an Eagle Twin push broom, and then looking up at the sky where a red-tailed hawk is riding the updrafts of an infinite blue-sky infinite ceiling, on a day like today, when anything is possible. Instead of which, what we have here, with far too many weapons, and explosives innovations, looks to be something of a suicide run, Ray crouched in the doorway, and then on the front stoop, Arturo firing behind him to create a distraction, Gene opening up with a full-auto BB gun, and Ray getting ready for a forty-foot dash, fueled by adrenaline, and arterial vasoconstriction, out the automatic doors of a darkened living room operating theater, and into the recovery room of total oblivion.

# 31

*J*ust when we were thinking we'd seen the last of Raymond, that his forty-foot dash would end in six feet, in a withering cross-fire of assault-rifle weaponry, he paused for an instant, there on the stoop, like a man doing a double take: something doesn't feel quite right. Ray stayed crouched, under the shadow of the eaves, for not much more than the blink of an eye, scanning the road, to the left of Gomez, attempting to pinpoint the source of his discomfort, and in not much more than the time between blinks, or the time it would take for a man to do a double take, discovered three vaguely unsettling figures: stationed just left of the gold Toyota, in a standard upright firing position, was a man with a full-auto AG-3, chambered in three-inch rimless rounds, holding the rifle by its railed forend, but pointing the weapon straight at the ground; to his immediate left, and all the more unsettling, stood a man with a Barrett M82, chambered in five-inch armor-piercing shells, holding the Barrett by its telescopic sight, but pointing the weapon at nothing at all; and completing this somewhat puzzling picture, Ray saw a man with an RPG-7, topped off with cyclonite in a green grenade, gripping the launcher by its H&K grip, but pointing it upward, into a tree. With his vision and hearing both impaired, but his battle-field instincts fairly acute, what Ray may have sensed, in the course of an instant, would be the war-zone equivalent of *too good to be true*: while he couldn't see much down his Kalnienk tunnels, like looking at the world through a paper-towel roll, he felt fairly certain that his well-armed opponents, loaded down with assault rifles and rocket grenades, didn't have their weapons trained on him; and while he couldn't hear a thing with Bells firing away, holding burst-fire Berettas up close to his head, he felt fairly certain that the AG-3s, chambered in full-power NATO rounds, and the Barrett M82A1s, chambered in .50 caliber sniper projectiles, and the Iranian DIO RPG-7Vs, mounted with warheads painted shamrock green, hadn't fired so much as a single shot; and while Ray knew better than to trust his feelings, what Ray may have sensed, with his battlefield instincts, was that somehow or other, his plan may have worked, and as Ray would have known, from his time on the battlefield, if you ever get the feeling that your plan may have worked, something is about to go horribly wrong. Ray's plan, if you could call it that, of firing two rounds through inanimate objects, trying to buy enough time to come out of his crouch, and get a running start on his zigzag through the yard, by creating the impression he was coming out with a body, while Gene and Bells opened fire with 9-mil firearms, trying to cover up the holes in Ray's flawed scheme, and maybe get him off the porch with his head intact, by creating a distraction for his well-armed opponents, had worked, if anything, far too well, so well, in fact, that it created the impression that his plan, if anything, hadn't worked at all. Ray stayed crouched, under the shadow of the eaves, for maybe one blink more than his plan had called for, scanning the road, to the right of Gomez, attempting to verify the source of his unease, and in not much more than the time between blinks, or the time it would take to double-check a double-take, got a very bad feeling, down in his bones, that somehow or other, he was missing something. How was it possible that a fireteam squad, eight or nine men dressed in Universal Camouflage, wearing Interceptor Body Armor, with boron-carbide ceramic plates, and Wiley X Nerve tactical goggles, with matching Blackhawk StrikeForce gloves, wrapped around the Brugger and Thomet railed-forends of a shitload of NATO assault-rifle weaponry, and chambered Barrett's, and cyclonite propellers, about to shred Ray in a withering crossfire, had not, with one exception, even shouldered their weapons? And all the more unnerving, from a tactical perspective, how was it possible that not one of these men, including the man who had shouldered his weapon, was even looking at Ray, much less trying to shoot him? Every last man, without exception, was looking up above, at the blue Juárez sky, toward a point in midair, maybe twenty feet up, measured from the base of the pale taupe ranch house, where some sort of object that Ray couldn't see, crouched as he was under the shadow of the eaves, had been launched up above them, into the blue midair, and while every last man, without exception, had his head tilted upward, toward the sunlit sky, not one of these men, with the possible exception of the man with the launcher, was aware of the fact that, a moment from now, something was about to go horribly wrong. By the time Raymond Edmunds comes out of his crouch, and steps out at last from under the shadow of the eaves, into the dazzling brilliance of a blue-sky day, into the timeless beauty of a spring-green April, where Gomez stands waiting for him, staring skyward, shading his eyes against the noonday glare, not only will Gomez be running out of options, and everyone present shading their eyes, but Ray may find himself casting two shadows, because Ciudad Juárez will have grown a second sun.

And then just when we were thinking Ray's time had come, that his only real choice was to take a step forward, and cast those final shadows on the front porch stoop, Raymond discovered a little window we hadn't noticed, a window in space, a window in time, a narrow window through which he might still squeeze, and head for Bermuda on an evening flight. Ray came out of his crouched position, stood straight up in the shadow under the eaves, spotted a man, maybe thirty feet away, with what looked to be a puff of launch-tube smoke slowly drifting off from the rear of his launch tube, and then finally leaning forward toward the edge of the roof, and peeking out from under to get an unobstructed view, not only discovered his little spacetime window, but knew he couldn't stand there, double-checking double-takes: one way or the other, Ray would have to move. Strange as it may seem, so late in the day, so late, in fact, that it might as well be over, Ray, even now, at this late hour, still had time for the indicated act: that object up above, in the blue midair, filled to the brim with brilliant ideas, and man's latest thinking on enhanced-lethality thermobaric objects, was not, as we suspected, coming down, it was in fact still climbing skyward, headed toward the top of a wounded arc, maybe thirty feet up above the ranch house yard, and it was here in this upward arcing motion that Raymond caught a glimpse of his spacetime window, as an object climbing skyward, in parabolic flight, like a 9th grade pop-quiz in projectile algebra, would still need time, and still need space, to ascend, top off, finally topple over, begin its descent, at fifteen feet per second, and put a midair end to Raymond's trials and tribulations. This upward arcing skyward motion, which didn't look at all like a rocket trajectory, it looked as if a man, on the roof of the house, had somehow caught a rocket, with his own bare hands, and tried to lob it back to the man who fired it, didn't leave Ray doing high school math, solving for time in quadratic equations, but it left him alone to make a difficult decision, and very little time within which to make it. Given the limits imposed on Raymond, let's skip the math on arcing projectiles, and give you just a glimpse of what was in Ray's window: with the world's huge walls about to close in rapidly, and the gristmill stones of the world's vast thermodynamic machinery about to lock together perfectly, one atop the other, and grind Time down to a femtosecond powder, Ray's whole world was about the size of a jewel box, but the contents of the jewel box, two blinks more than one precious second, were just about the size of an extraordinary gemstone, another day of life on our living and breathing blue jewel of a planet. Dividing Raymond's time into rational proportions, using three-tenths of a second as an eye-blink equivalent, Ray had one blink to come to a decision, one more blink to initiate movement, and one precious second that could go either way: if he thought that the rocket was preparing to detonate, he would use his second to go back through the doorway, and put something solid between himself and the warhead; if he thought that the rocket was preparing to land, and bounce off the grass as unexploded ordnance, he would use his second to dash toward Gomez, and put a bullet between the Glock and Gomez' head. The truth, however, used a different decision tree, a tree that required a midair explosion, though it would still hold true that Ray's precious second could go either way: either back through the doorway, toward blast-wave shockfront hardboard insulation, and a chance to see the turquoise and crystalline waters of a new day dawning in Jennifer's eyes; or forward on the stoop, toward the blast-wave shockfront visceral horrors, without so much as ballistic goggles, and a chance to see the spring-green leaves of the lilacs stripped to a bare-metal thermobaric grey.

And then just when we were thinking that Ray'd finally...no, delete that, no one really cares what we were thinking. How in God's name did that rocket get up there? A man by the name of Juan Pablo Herrera, born in the small town of...no, no, strike that as well; much as we love rhetorical questions, whose answers we frequently know in advance, we couldn't help wondering, in advance of an answer, if this was a question that should even be asked. While this question would appear, from a narrative perspective, to be a fundamental question whose answer we would need, it would also appear, from Raymond's perspective, to be a question whose answer would be completely irrelevant: with Ray given one blink to come to a decision, one more blink to initiate movement, and one precious second to save his own life, why would Ray care how the rocket got up there? And this, all in all, would make a far better question, though perhaps we should frame it a slightly different way: why would Ray care how the rocket got up there? Raymond would care because Ray was all soldier, trained on the ranges of Fort Hood, Texas, trained on the battlefields of southern Iraq, trained on the backstreets of Ciudad Juárez, trained to react, on milliseconds instinct, to upward arcing explosive projectiles, and given one point six seconds to save his own life; Raymond would care because Ray knew projectiles, from artillery shells to rocket grenades, like the back of the hand he was now trying to save; and Raymond would care because Ray, among other things, knew almost exactly how the rocket got up there, and given what he knew about rocket grenades, knew almost exactly how its warhead would behave, and trained as he was, to react on instinct, knew almost exactly how to react, all of which he'd learned in less than an eye-blink, in something on the order of 200 milliseconds, about the time it would take for a fighter to react, on pure ring instinct, to a straight right hand that was headed toward his head. Before we even started our rocket's story, Raymond, in effect, knew the whole story, but then Ray knew something about battlefield narrative that he hadn't exactly learned in a writers' workshop: by the time he got around to forming one thought, much less something involving language, he'd be well on his way to being dead already, with a fully formed thought he could take to his grave; if Ray put a thought, or conscious thinking, between himself and his mind-body's battlefield instincts, his body would wind up six feet under, and his battlefield instincts could call it a day. While Ray might have suggested that a clean white page, uncluttered by conscious thought and human language, would paint a far better picture as to how he went about this, we still had a duty, from a narrative perspective, to put words in motion and move them down the page, particularly given the fact that, from Raymond's perspective, we'd missed something vital that Ray hadn't missed: when Ray came out of his crouched position, and stood straight up in the shadow under the eaves, he not only caught a glimpse of his spacetime window, he spotted a man, maybe thirty feet away, on a sightline just left of the Gold Toyota, with what looked to be a puff of launch-tube smoke slowly drifting off from the rear of his launch tube, and knowing what he knew about tube-launched rockets, knowing what he knew about time and distance, knowing what he knew about crush-switch ordnance, and detonation timers, and piezoelectric fuzes, and knowing what he knew without knowing that he knew it, had a windfall moment that patterned the data, and mapped a narrow path, through this wilderness of input, that might lead back to land of the living. Ray stood still, under the shadow of the eaves, for maybe one blink more than our plan had called for, while we went back to the narrative drawing board, trying to make sense, if not true meaning, out of a slowly drifting puff of launch-tube smoke.

By the time we arrived at the narrative drawing board, prepared to make sense, if not true meaning, out of a slowly drifting puff of launch-tube smoke, we found ourselves engaged in something altogether different, reexamining our rocket trajectory equations, and timeline math, and eye-blink assumptions, and beginning to suspect that the truth as we knew it was not quite the truth as Raymond knew it, because by the time we arrived at the narrative drawing board, the rocket had reached the top of a wounded arc, maybe thirty feet up from the ranch house yard, the launch-tube smoke had drifted to the west, perhaps on the order of one or two millimeters, the pigment in the eyes of the men on the ground had registered a great many chemical reactions, and might well have altered certain facial expressions, but Ray hadn't moved a skeletal muscle, Ray had done nothing to initiate movement, and while the truth as we knew it left him one precious second, Ray was still standing under the shadow of the eaves. While there might be one truth, from a narrative perspective, and yet another truth, from Ray's perspective, there was only one truth from the rocket's perspective, and with a rocket now hovering, thirty feet up, not only preparing to tip and topple over, not only preparing to begin its descent, but preparing to provide us, at a microsecond's notice, with far more truth than we could possibly absorb, we didn't have time for trajectory equations, or timeline math, or eye-blink assumptions, in fact we didn't have time, despite our preparations, to tell you what we'd learned about launch-tube smoke, we only had time for one simple question: what did Ray know without knowing that he knew it? Ray knew the two types of rocket launchers, one type that lights up the rocket motor while the rocket is still in the barrel of the launch tube, and the other that uses an initial propellant to expel the rocket from the barrel of the launch tube, and then lights up the rocket's internal motor when the rocket is off at a nice safe distance, at a distance Ray knew to be eleven meters. Ray knew the motor on the rocket in question had not been ignited in the barrel of the launch tube, as a barrel-lit motor does not leave smoke-puffs, or slowly drifting puffs of pale-grey smoke, it belches blue smoke out the rear of the launch tube. Ray knew the motor on the rocket in question had not been ignited at a nice safe distance, at a distance Ray knew to be eleven meters, as the man who launched it was thirty feet away, a bit too close to the window he was aiming at, a bit too close to the chimney that he struck. Ray knew the rocket struck the base of the chimney while traveling at a rate of 300 feet per second, and not at a rate of 1,000 feet per second, as the motor hadn't fired in the barrel of the launch tube, the motor hadn't fired at a nice safe distance, the motor on the rocket had never fired at all. Ray knew the crush-switch in the nose of the warhead, designed to initiate the detonation sequence when the rocket made contact with something solid, had not been designed to initiate anything when the rocket made contact with the base of the chimney, as despite the solidity of a red brick chimney, the rocket was traveling far too slowly to crush the crush-switch in the nose of the warhead. Ray knew the backup to the rocket's crush-switch, a backup required to avoid the possibility that unexploded ordnance *might* harm the innocent, a backup required despite the near certainty that *all* explosive ordnance *will* harm the innocent, was a detonation timer that would soon time out, but that left him on the order of one full second to begin his dash in the direction of Gomez, plus three full seconds before the warhead would detonate. Ray knew the odds of being shot in the process were something on the order of fifty to one, signaled in tic-tac by raising both arms, forming a fist at the end of each arm, and then placing the right fist on top of the left, as right around the time he arrived at Gomez, there was likely to be a rather large explosion, and during the time he was dashing through the yard, the men in question would likely be preoccupied, with a time bomb ticking in the thick green grass, and 9-mil suppressive-fire flying around their chins. Ray also knew the odds were right around even that none of the above would prove to be relevant, in fact Ray knew the odds of a midair explosion, or an explosion on impact with a single blade of grass, were right around level, signaled in tic-tac by raising both arms, extending a finger at the end of each arm, and then moving them up and down in opposite directions, as damaged ordnance was highly unstable and prone to exhibiting explosive behavior on an absolute whim, if for no other reason than that man builds ordnance specifically to exhibit explosive behavior; for all Ray knew, without knowing that he knew it, the rocket might exhibit explosive behavior while he was flipping coins in the middle of the yard, and praying to the gods of damaged ordnance to grant him time to complete his mission. And while Ray knew the timer left him one full second to begin his dash off the front porch stoop, there was no way Ray was waiting one full second to begin his dash off the front porch stoop, in fact there wasn't much chance that Ray might be waiting for the rocket to topple over, and begin its descent, as Ray had better things to do with his time than to stand around watching a rocket descend, like get close enough to Gomez to put a bullet through his head; Ray wasn't waiting one full second, Ray wasn't waiting for the rocket to topple over, Raymond was waiting for the top of its arc, and since the rocket was now at the top of its arc, Raymond must be waiting for right about now.

When the rocket tipped down, finally toppled over, and began its descent, at millimeters per second, accelerating rapidly toward thirty feet per second, and bringing its truth down with it at an accelerating rate, Ray stood still, under the shadow of the eaves, for yet another blink more than even Ray's plan had called for, as if Ray, without thinking, might have been having second thoughts, leaving Ray enough time to dive through the doorway, and us enough space to pose one last question. So without trying to sound like the absolute morons who send troops to war using narrative fictions, and tend to behave as if human intent had not been subtracted once they'd triggered an event, what did Ray *not* know without knowing he didn't know it? Ray didn't know that poor Juan Pablo, born in the small town of Guelatao, in the mountains just north and east of Oaxaca, the birthplace, by the way, of Benito Juárez, having never been a soldier in the Mexican Army, having never been trained in shoulder-mounted weapons, having only ever fired one type of launcher, a Russian-made Vampire RPG-29, a launcher that lights up the rocket motor while the rocket is still in the barrel of the launch tube, had no way of knowing that his rocket wasn't tube-lit, had no way of knowing that its motor wouldn't light, had no way of knowing that it would strike the chimney while traveling too slowly to crush the crush-switch, had no way of knowing that the top of its arc might have left him one second to run for his life, and had no way of knowing how the rocket left the launch tube, because poor Juan Pablo, as far as he knew, despite being startled when the door swung open, and a man came out to crouch on the stoop, had not pulled the trigger on the rocket launch tube, so the trigger, in conclusion, must have pulled itself. Ray didn't know that the detonation timer, the backup designed to ignite the warhead, in the event that the crush-switch failed to make contact, or failed to initiate when contact was made, was damaged on impact, and was now preparing to detonate the warhead, not in four seconds, per Raymond's timeline, but in not much more than two precious eye-blinks, point seven seconds from right around now. Ray didn't know that the warhead itself was filled to the brim with brilliant ideas, and man's latest thinking on enhanced-lethality thermobaric objects, thinking provided by our friends at Nammo Talley, an arm's manufacturer in Mesa, Arizona, who also provided us with a lovely brochure, whose title alone, *Thermobaric Urban Destruction*, might well have altered Raymond's thinking, not that Ray had time to think. Ray didn't know that the lethal blast zone, defined as the radius of a circle of death, a circle within which everyone present would find themselves flipping one-sided coins, a circle outside which everyone present could safely assume that coins have two sides, was not quite the usual six or seven meters, the radius of a warhead loaded with cyclonite or C-4 plastics or Composition B, but something enhanced by lethality experts to divide Ray's world into two distinct zones, one zone for those who were inside the house, for whom today would be a page in a book of tomorrows, and another zone for those who were outside the house, for whom the book of tomorrows would be one blank page. And Ray didn't know that that voice in his head, a voice that was telling him not to move forward, and keeping him standing under the shadow of the eaves, a voice that didn't sound like human language, a voice that sounded like pink-sand beaches, and turquoise waters, and jasmine-scented walks to a white-picket greeting, was not in his head, it was eight feet behind him, where Jennifer was standing, with a flower in her hair, saying Ray, what the fuck, *get back inside here.*

About the time we had answers to the last of our questions, and could only assume, from Ray's hesitation, that he must be headed back through an open doorway, as if Jen had gotten through with her jasmine-scented plea, as if Ray might be worried about a mid-air explosion, the suppressive fire stopped, abruptly, completely, as Gene and Bells fired the last of their parabellum rounds, and it was here in this instant of an ammunition shortfall that we knew all at once that Ray had other plans, and answers to questions we hadn't bothered to ask. Ray wasn't headed through an open doorway, Ray wasn't listening to jasmine-scented pleas, Ray wasn't hesitant, or changing his planning, and Ray wasn't worried about a midair explosion, in fact Ray's whole plan was based on the premise that he could put a bullet through a falling projectile, cause it to explode before it hit land, and send flying metal everywhere to cover his advance; Ray would take his chances with rocket shrapnel, but if the rocket came down, bounced off the grass, and wound up lying there as unexploded ordnance, without flying metal to keep men at bay, these men would throw it back through a plate-glass window, and Ray and his friends, one way or another, would serve as reminders, to battlefield planners, of the dangers involved in an ammunition shortfall. Ray stood still, in the roof-cast shadows, with a Glock 29 at the end of his arm, aiming at a point, maybe five feet up, that he hoped might optimize the shrapnel pattern, while we stepped back to a nice safe distance, staring at a point, maybe twelve feet up, that we knew would minimize Raymond's lifespan, and knowing what we knew about falling objects, knowing what we knew about damaged timers, knowing what we knew about Novel Explosives, and knowing what we knew while wishing we didn't know it, knew we had space to make one final comment, but very little time within which to make it. If this were the sort of world that we'd all like to live in, a world that didn't need lethality enhancement, a world that didn't need any thermobaric objects, a world where the human spirit wasn't headed into Juárez, with rainbows in its eyes, and its instruments at work on living cadavers, Ray would be getting ready to trade the truth as he knew it for a truth it had taken him a lifetime to find, truth in the form of a white-picket greeting, truth in the form of a pink-sand beginning, truth in the form of the crystalline waters of a new day dawning in Jennifer's eyes, but with a rocket coming down, at three feet per second, accelerating rapidly toward thirty feet per second, and Ray given one chance to save his own life, by turning back around and going back through a doorway, all we had left was the truth as Ray lived it: if Ray was still standing on the front porch stoop, if Ray was still standing under the shadow of the eaves, if Ray was still standing upright at all, there was no way in hell that Ray was headed backward; Ray had his hopes, Ray had his dreams, but Ray had one way of standing in the world, and just as long as he could stand, he was still moving forward.

And so, as they say, here goes nothing. Ray stepped out from under the shadow of the eaves, steadied the Glock in his natural right hand, tracked the rocket's arc like a man shooting skeet, and by doing little more than what he's done all his life, by simply putting one foot in front of the other, stepped out to the edge of the front porch steps, and into the haze of a pale-toned grey zone, ten milliseconds prior to the thermobaric blast. Which is not to suggest that the sky wasn't blue, or that the marigolds blooming in a front-yard border had lost even one of their marigold yellows, or that the spring-green leaves of the Easter-blooming lilacs had been stripped of their radiant springtime colors, as the world hadn't yet gone bare-metal grey; neither was this grey zone, just in advance of a four-step ignition, meant to suggest something temporal in nature, a twilight amalgam of night and day, a pale-grey blend of presence and absence, or something more semio-linguistic in nature, the grey-toned verbiage of lethality science, the grey semiosis of weaponized chemistry, both of which would be valid suggestions, both of which would need to be addressed, but both of which would appear to suggest that Ray wasn't cognizant of this grey zone he'd entered, and Ray was not just cognizant, he was staring straight at it. Ray's first greys were optical in nature, which is meant to suggest that the sky wasn't blue, and that the marigolds blooming in a front-yard border had lost every one of their marigold yellows, and that the spring-green leaves of the Easter-blooming lilacs had been stripped of their radiant springtime colors, as the pigment in the eyes of a man going blind, with the darkness closing in due to hypovolemia, register a great many chemical reactions, but may not register a single color. By the time Ray completed that last step forward, and stepped to the edge of the front porch steps, not only was the Glock not being steadied, or tracking a rocket like a pistol shooting skeet, but Ray had both arms raised to the heavens, in the shape of a gesture with which we're all familiar. Which is not to suggest that Ray had surrendered, as Ray had both arms bent at the elbow, with upturned palms at the end of each arm, but may well suggest a simple solution to the Wittgenstein conundrum that's plagued Ray's narrative: what remains when you subtract the fact that his arms went up from the fact that Raymond raised his arms? All that remained, at this late hour, at the end of what amounts to one long day, beginning with the predawn reds of a knife wound, and closing with the greys of an optical twilight, was the human intent to offer the heavens one final comment on the course of events, a comment in the form of an arms-raised open-palmed shrug of a gesture, meaning next to nothing, but signifying *Now what?*

*Now what*, indeed. Against the pale-toned greys of a temporal twilight, against the tone-deaf greys of explosives semiosis, against the bare-metal greys at the back of a grey zone, the blue-orange spark of a detonation timer sparked on a whim, perhaps on the whim of a damaged delay fuze, or perhaps nothing more than an electrostatic discharge, a triboelectric-leap of seven millijoules of static, created by the metal-on-red-brick friction when the rocket struck the base of a fireplace chimney, or perhaps to show the world that man builds ordnance specifically to exhibit explosive behavior, but in any case, be that as it may, the world being *everything* that *is* the case, against a pale-grey blend of presence and absence, the blue-orange spark of a detonation timer sparked off a pile of styphnate crystals, a bright yellow salt of styphnic acid, sparked off a pile of lead(II) azide, an off-white assortment of exothermic crystals, sparked off the core of a crystalline igniter, sparked off the crystalline core of *the detonator*, the small rear car of a four-car explosive train, train in the sense of a sequence of events, train in the semasiological sense of a black-draped funeral train packed with explosives, suggestive of a world where *nothing* is sacred, its world being *anything* that *isn't* the case, and once the rear car vanished, its shock wave propagated to the next car on, igniting a pellet of a penthrite booster, the phlegmatized cylinder of a shock-wave amplifier, and once the penthrite vanished, its shock wave propagated to the next car on, sparking off an exothermic chemical reaction, sparking off an ordinary ordnance explosive, sparking off a mass of Composition B, buried at the core of the rocket's warhead, and once the Comp B ignited, a microsecond later, the third car vanished from the core of the warhead, shattering the warhead's immaculate casing, expanding in a fireball of white-orange flame, sending flying metal everywhere to cover Ray's advance, but scattering a cloud of fine-grain particulates, a pale-grey cloud of unlit particulates, difficult to see, much less articulate, against a pale-grey background of presence and absence, as if the cloud had come equipped with semiotic camouflage, concealing its brilliance, just prior to ignition, in the grey-toned verbiage of lethality science, the grey semiosis of weaponized chemistry, perhaps nothing more than sol-gel processed nanometric tungsten powder, thermally enhanced with a nanometric metalloid, germanium or silicon or tellurium or arsenic, or perhaps something further up the periodic table, a nanometric cloud of aluminum-molybdenum, in a nanolaminate of aluminum-Teflon, barometrically enhanced with a T4 waveguide, cyclonite wrapped around carbon-walled nanotubes, in a nanodimensional silica supporting gel, or perhaps something further out the power curve of barbarism, a reminder of a reminder of the need to forget the shattering detonation velocities of nanometric RDX, itself already a shattering explosive, in a chromium(III)-oxide matrix, in a binder of thermoplastic fluorocarbon polymers, lethality-enhanced with a bare-metal blend of titanium-boron nano-dust, and as if mere death would not be sufficient, perhaps yet another reactive-wave amplifier, perhaps yet another metastable composite, perhaps yet another nano-metal metalloid, submicronic aluminum-antimony, in a nanofoil-wrapper of nickel-Viton, any and all of which would imagine an intelligent form of life whose intelligence was devoted to lethal ideas, which in turn might suggest, if it wasn't already evident, that the human mind won't rest, or find a true and lasting peace, until the last human thought has been eradicated, but in any case, be that as it may, the world being *many things* that *shouldn't be* the case, the warhead shattered, scattering a cloud of pale-grey particulates, heated by the warmth of a Comp B fireball, heated by their own intermetallic reactions, heated to the ignition point of white-hot particulates, the immense front car on the black-draped train, leaving the boots on the ground, and Gomez' Barker Black bench-made shoes, something on the order of point four milliseconds to get their final affairs in order, pack their luggage for the black train's departure, and make any last few microsecond arrangements to prepare to leave the grey zone's blue skies behind, and prepare for a sky gone Thermobaric White. When the detonation paused, as if to catch its breath, microseconds away from the birth of a second sun, microseconds away from Ray's last shadows, but close to a full half-millisecond away from the black-draped train's final departure, we were left with a good deal of explaining to do, very little time within which to do it, and a very bad feeling, deep in our narrative's narrative bones, that we might just as well be saving our breath: if Ray was still standing at the edge of the steps, if Ray was still standing in a temporal grey zone, if Ray was still standing upright at all, Ray, in all likelihood, was still leaning forward, but Ray wasn't headed into the yard, Ray was headed out of the eye-blink world, Ray was headed out of the pale-grey present, Ray was headed out of a darkened Kalnienk hypovolemic tunnel, and deep into the pure white absence of the light.

And so, as our weapons say, *Fiat umbra.* Ray stood still, at the edge of the steps, one step out from under the shadow of the eaves, for not much more than two or three microseconds, staring at a fire-

ball of white-grey flame, staring at a flying-metal pattern of shrapnel, itself about to vanish in a thermobaric puff, staring, in effect,
at a shattering explosion whose presence would have registered in
the pigment of his eyes, but not yet have registered as present to his
mind, when as if all at once, right about here, perhaps in response
to his *Now what?* comment, his arms-raised opened-palm shrug of a
gesture, Ray got the answer to a question he wasn't asking, Ray got
a *who knows?* shrug from the heavens, Ray received a message he'd
never know was even sent, and Ray got the inevitable surprise of his
life: a white-hot cloud of fine-grain particulates, consisting of a *who
knows* mix of ideas, perhaps little more than nanometric tungsten,
and titanium-boron nano-metal metalloids, in a binder of thermoplastic fluorocarbon polymers, and cyclonite wrapped around carbon-walled wave-guides, in a nanodimensional silica supporting gel,
and nano-particulates of Octanitrocubane, the world's most effective chemical explosive, in a nanofoil wrapper of God knows what,
something from the dark side of weapons science, where ideas go to
die in a complete moral vacuum, and the Almighty wanders around
in an Explosive Ordnance Disposal suit, self-ignited in a flashball of
Bright, an immense exhibition of explosive behavior, not just rich
in 5,000 Fahrenheit of thermal energy, not just rich in 400 kilobars
of barometric pressure, but supersaturated in ultraviolet radiation,
stripping all of the yellows from the marigold flowers, stripping all
of the greens from the mid-April trees, leaving everyone present,
with the exception of the men wearing Wiley X Nerve tactical goggles, with traumatized corneas and ocular conjuctiva, like snow-
blind crows, in the dead of night, hunting pure black butterflies
in the blackened snow, and much as we'd love to see a snow-blind
crow, or explain the mechanics of photokeratitis, we couldn't afford
to linger over this pure-black image, because just inside the edges
of the thermobaric blast was a man-made heaven-sent response to
Ray's comment, a thin sheet of nothingness, beginning to expand,
preparing to cross the boundaries of the visible blast, preparing to
emerge as a darkened halo, preparing to advance across the ranch
house yard, preparing to behave like the Shadow that it is, and less
than 400 microseconds from Raymond's position. The Shadow, you
say. Yes, a shadow that began with the infinite thinness of a detonation shock wave's planar wavefront, a shadow that emerged with

the finite thickness of a detonation blast wave's dark corona, a shadow only now being cast on the lawn, the shadow of a thermobaric blast-wave shockfront, doing light-blocking violence to the medium through which it passes, with the finite thickness of the blast wave's blast wind, and the nearly infinite thinness of the shock wave's shockfront, preparing to advance through the air that surrounds it, preparing to advance across the ranch house yard, preparing to behave like the Shadow that it is, doing light-blocking violence to the beings in its path, and less than 100 microseconds from Raymond's position. Not that Ray would care, or appreciate the irony, but the detonation shockfront was ordinary air, compressed to the thinness of a nanometric razor, as if Ray had circled back to El Arbolito, the Bar of the Wounded and Drifting Tree, to finish up a knife fight with a lifeless opponent, equipped to leave Ray with yet another cryptic message, inscribed inside his body using a razor made of air. When the blast-wave shockfront continued its advance, beginning to behave like the Shadow that it is, with a heart-stopping message for the bodies in its path, across the ranch house yard, across a marigold border, across a snow-blind world that Ray was headed out of, and began to make its climb up the front porch steps, microseconds away from Ray's position, microseconds away from Ray's front boot, microseconds away from Ray's last shirt, a Rockford Shadow Plaid, once blue and green, but now an ooze-soaked shade of bloodybrownish, and as if mere death would not be sufficient, continued to advance up Time's front steps, microseconds away from Ray's own skin, nanoseconds away from a penetrating razor, picoseconds away from a temporal disaster, where the gristmill stones of the world's vast thermodynamic machinery lock together perfectly, one atop the other, and grind Time down to a just-next-to-nothingness femtosecond powder, and with Time grinding down to a femtosecond powder, one trillionth the size of a grain of sand, one millionth the size of a particle of tungsten, continued to advance like the Shadow that it is, with a clock-stopping message for the being in its path, and as if death's door were its true destination, arrived at the edge of Time's last step, a femtosecond away from our clock's inner limit, a femtosecond away from a page gone White, a femtosecond away from *Raymond Edmunds*, and someone rising from the pews to maybe say a few words, we'll readily admit that words failed us, as we couldn't begin to imagine how Ray could respond with anything other than a lasting silence, but then again, who knows, Ray, even now, was still all soldier, and while Ray's whole world was about the size of a lightwave, a wavelet of violet, beginning to fade, blueshifting out of the visible spectrum, we seriously doubt that Ray would let a weapon send him a meaningless message to absorb, without at least responding with a message of his own: with the warhead itself effectively disabled, with the ranch house occupants, Gene and Jen included, reasonably safe as the shockfront advances, and with no possibility that these men on the ground could even throw a pebble through a plate-glass window, Ray's own response to what our weapons have to say might be something along the lines of *position secured*.

Which is not to suggest that Ray's time had come, as even Time's last step itself takes time, but with a blast-wave shockfront still on the move, advancing on Ray through an attosecond blizzard, and blueshifting wavelets into gamma radiation, it won't take long to crash death's door; neither is Ray's response to the weapon, his *position-secured* final communiqué, meant to suggest that the ranch house occupants, among them Ray's best friends on the planet, are *truly* safe as the shockfront advances, as a white-hot cloud of lethal ideas comes fully equipped with a truth of its own, and with an overpressure blast wave of unknown proportions, followed by a wave of superheated gases, currently advancing on the pale taupe ranch house, for all we know the house itself, including all eight of its living inhabitants, will crash death's door right along with Raymond; with Ray's last mission all but completed, and only the final outcome yet to be determined, we'll need to leave the truth to the powers that be, and turn our attention to what these weapons have to say, before the shockfront fades in the open desert, and its message is lost on the mesquite and acacia brush. The Shadow may sound like a figure of speech, but the humans who died on the streets of Gaza, or beside the Silk Road in eastern Afghanistan, or in our thorough liberation of the living of Fallujah, turning 40,000 homes into pyrolyzed rubble, certainly didn't die of a figure of speech, a great many died when a blast-wave shockfront passed right through them, in a just-next-to-nothingness razor-thin assault on the tissue-density interfaces of the human body, air-tissue interfaces, liquid-tissue interfaces, dense-tissue/loose-tissue boundary-interaction spaces, as if the body had been assaulted by a differential equation, shearing flesh from flesh, and flesh from bone, scraping away the linings from intestines and lungs, eliminating human digestive systems, rupturing any and all of the gas-containing structures, disorganizing the heart, the liver, the kidneys, through a sudden leap in entropy whose details we'll spare you, an assault so general that nearly every human organ fails simultaneously, an assault so precise that we may need a neurosurgeon to properly explain it, as it's capable of dividing, along a tissue-density interface you were no doubt unaware of, white matter from grey matter inside the human brain, producing human corpses without a mark on them, corpses whose clothing had not lost a button, corpses with shoelaces properly tied, or corpses whose spines had been crushed by the blast wave, an overpressure wave, barometrically enhanced to extend its duration, that advances just behind the thermobaric shockfront, or corpses found missing the usual extremities, lost in the blast winds that follow the blast wave, when the overpressure drops to a vacuum-like nothingness, and rips bone from bone in an overpressure-backlash, all of which amounts to a human-tissue waste, an inoperable pile of human debris, with the blowflies left licking their sensory organs, and the crows having visions of a Last Supper meal, visions cut short when the heat-front arrives, thermally enhanced to a 5,000 Fahrenheit smelting furnace, to fuse the dusty streets and carbonize the remnants. The Shadow is not a figure of speech, and what our weapons have to say is brutal and grim, a message encoded in a subhuman language, a message that reminds us of Gomez' lesson, and Gabriella's face, buried in her hands, and our golden-haired child, still searching for something redemptive in each of us, but nearly dropped by his mother when she discovered the truth: the human spirit could be soaring with the red-tailed hawks, riding the updrafts toward its own perfection, but right at this moment, somewhere in the world, the human spirit is headed into Juárez, with tears in its eyes, with rainbows in its eyes, with nothing but a blank-eyed stare in its eyes, and with its instruments at work on living cadavers. All things considered, as we await the final outcome of Ray's last mission, we might let Gomez share a final thought, something from his list of Shakespeare quotations, self-evident and apposite while signifying nothing, although with alloseconds left before the shockfront arrives, he'll certainly need to keep it brief: it's too late now for that quote from Macbeth, full of walking shadows and dusty death and blowing out brief but enormous candles; it's far too late to wash our haunted hands, and take to our beds in spotless nightgowns; and as for that last syllable of recorded time, we've already heard it, and simply moved on, to somewhere deep in the Book of Revelation, where the Almighty sits in judgment on all mankind, and throws the whole book, final syllables and all, onto the pyrolyzed heap of Man's version of Creation.

As our caesium fountain narrative chronometer traces the soon-to-prove-fatal but graceful ballistic flight of one final caesium atom past the photon detector, and up through the violet-bathed vacuum chamber, up through the space of a finite interior, up to the top of a caesium-atom arc, with the all-but-inevitable descent just ahead, the time has come to warn you, before entropy sets in, that our clock has malfunctioned, and our narrative time has run out, one caesium-photon short of completing our chronicle. This, truly, is deeply troubling: how could a narrative, so carefully planned, equipped with the precision of a caesium fountain, accurate to within a second over 80 million years, not only leave Ray in an attosecond blizzard, but fail to arrive at a timely ending? At the risk of an answer more troubling than the question, we believe we may have failed on a caesium-atom whim, perhaps on the whim of a spin-state wobble, or perhaps nothing more than a quantum effect, as though the atom may have lost its valence electron, creating a sudden absence of angular momentum, or perhaps to remind us that our clock and our narrative are dialectically intertwined, and may not arrive at any sort of ending, until the life-force that powers them fades from the page; be that as it may, however, whatever the case, with its atom having failed to complete a full cycle, the violet clock is certainly misbehaving. While the first pass through the probe beam went off without a hitch, with a caesium photon both emitted and detected, and the upward launch phase was completely uneventful, with our caesium atom rising to its full ballistic launch height, 36.5 centimeters above the laser-cooled optical trap, the atom itself is currently nowhere to be found, and must, even now, be hovering in mid-flight, lost in the drift region high atop the fountain, refusing to come down past the photon detector, and bring things to a close, in the narrative domain, where Ray's last mission is all but completed, but where the meaning of his mission is being held in abeyance, pending the results of a caesium descent; without that final descent, in essence, and that one last fatal photon emission, permitting us to complete the Ramsey interrogation, and locate the resonant heart of the temporal, we have, to put it bluntly, lost track of time, and have no way of knowing, much less describing, what might happen if time advances, answers the last of our temporal questions, and a white-hot cloud of lethal ideas delivers its truth to the pale taupe ranch house. If our current position, one photon away from a narrative ending, seems hard to imagine, imagine you're back in Ray's position, as Gene and Bells fired the last of the parabellum rounds, and then ask yourself this: we all know the risks in an ammunition shortfall, but what's the real risk in a narrative shortfall? If that caesium atom vectors downward, and locates the fountain's photon detector, a blast-wave shockfront will enter Ray's body, locate the appropriate organs to assault, and leave Ray a photon-emission away from a full-body crash through death's front door; and if that caesium atom vectors downward, and locates the last of the Ramsey answers, an overpressure blast wave of unknown proportions, followed by a wave of superheated gases, will locate the pale taupe ranch house itself, and leave Ray's mission a photon away from the distinct possibility of a human-tissue waste, with its meaning found buried in the semiotic rubble; if that atom, in short, begins its descent, and threatens to complete the Ramsey interrogation, the ranch house occupants would be well advised, as the roof begins to cave under the overpressure blast wave, and smoke begins to fill the narrative pathways, to begin to seek an exit out the rear of the domicile; Ray will take his chances with death alone, but if that caesium atom vectors downward, and Ray's best friends cannot find an exit, Ray's last mission will lose all meaning, and Ray and his mission, one way or another, will serve as reminders, to chronicle planners, of the risks involved in a narrative shortfall. That being said, and risks aside, with the violet clock still a luminous enigma, leaving nothing but its glow in the temporal domain, we'll need to try to close in the spatial domain, perhaps by means of a charcoal drawing, and space permitting, a watercolor painting, to give our reader, now our viewer, a sense of an ending, a sense of closure, a sense of words being set in motion, and at the risk of disclosing where our words are headed, a sense of arriving, at just this moment, when a timely ending failed to arrive.

The charcoal drawing, perhaps inevitably, proved difficult to execute within the spacetime constraints, like trying to make a move in an endgame layout, with time having expired, but with our pieces still at risk, an analogy that appears to be needlessly cryptic, an analogy that in fact is deliberately cryptic, designed to conceal, not the endgame layout, but the pieces still at risk in our charcoal drawing. Our first attempt, from the hallway of the house, with Ray silhouetted against a thermobaric sky, had to be discarded for technical reasons, reasons we'll return to, spacetime permitting, once we've scratched the surface of our charcoal drawing, and placed each piece in its endgame position, well below the surface and deeper down the page. Our second attempt, from up on the power lines, in hopes of giving the viewer a bird's-eye view, encountered a kind of problem with the birds themselves, and had to be abandoned long before the work began: with the crows having visions of a Last Supper meal, still hoping that the heat-front won't carbonize the remnants, the bird's-eye view was already taken, and the crows refused to move, or even share their bird-perspective, though having taken a quick look through the eyes of a crow, this may, in the end, prove something of a blessing; from where they're positioned, high atop the power grid, or flying up in the drift regions, waiting for things to die, it's apparent that the crows think His Darkness wasted a miracle, animating life-forms, filling their hearts with hope, giving the human species a sense of limitless possibility, when if you look at the world from the crows' perspective, creatures born as roadkill would have been far more efficient; if you've never taken a tour of the Juárez landfill, where children live in lean-to's made of packing crates and bed sheets, flapping in the wind over the toxic-gruel terrain, what looks like a kind of hell, and a waste of the human life-force, must look positively Edenic to the true Juárez crow. Given the birds' refusal to share, and our technical concerns, we took our vine and willow charcoal, and our Winsor & Newton Sketch Box Easel, to several other locations around Ciudad Juárez, and while we came back with some lovely things that the crows would have approved of, bodies stacked in an abandoned house in the Rivera del Bravo subdivision, corpses up to their necks in a greenside bunker on the Par 4 12th at Club Campestre, nail-spiked heads and hacksawed limbs in a meat-locker deep-freeze at a club in the Pronaf, we found nothing that might appeal to the casual viewer, though when it comes to writing a ransom note, they might make perfect postcards. Our hopes for a sketch capturing the street-level vitality, using the predawn greys of the vine charcoal, and the dark-night black of the charcoal willow, proved to be more than a little naïve, and might just as well have been executed in gunpowder: we had just finished roughing out the cobblestone side street, with a pushcart taco vendor rolling into position, a grocer stacking apples in a fruit-stand pyramid, and a woman washing her windows at the neighborhood panaderia, when a four-man mobile-force fire-team intruded, wearing urban-jungle camouflage, in a desert-tan dune buggy, feeding .50 caliber incendiary rounds into the belt-feed slide assembly of a Browning machine gun, which suddenly opened fire on an ancient flatbed propane truck, depriving our little street-scene of much of its vitality, posing quite a challenge to our rather rudimentary drawing skills when it came to the depiction of propane fireballs, and wounding one of the pariah dogs, whose grief-like howls proved impossible to capture; although our Tiziano sketchpad didn't stand a chance, and vanished from our hands in a blue-orange blaze of propane, we did manage to collect a tiny pile of ash, from the cobblestone crevices of the cartridge-strewn lane, an admittedly futile gesture we can only explain as a sentimental attempt at howl-depiction, in honor of the life-forms that have vanished from the earth, without leaving behind even a single DNA strand. We even tried the view from 600 feet up, setting up our easel on an ASARCO smelter smokestack, where the risks of stray gunfire appeared to be reasonably manageable, and the problems of Juárez all looked to be pretty small: the colorful grinding poverty of families displaced from their fields, given poetic-justice housing in hovels the height of cornstalks; the convenient pink-cross sign-posts, for the mothers of Juárez, where they can keep their morning meetings, at the end of a long night-shift, as the first rays of light signal another newborn day, and the ghosts of their daughters drift in across the sand dunes; the perfectly circular logic of the official accounts of death, where a corpse is the natural byproduct of the victim's own depravity; and the glowing sunset beauty of the burst-fire weapons haze, where innocence walks in safety, and only the sick and guilty die, since death, in Juárez, is a pre-existing condition, and the children of Juárez are certainly guilty of existing. Life may be hard in Ciudad Juárez, but it's all a matter of keeping things in proper perspective: from high atop the power structure, where the streets are filled with ants, lugging three or four times their body weight in memories of their loved ones, the problem with Juárez is a citizen infestation, soon to be solved forever, with the help of U.S. aid, using vast supplies of nothingness and weapons-grade insecticide.

In the end, we folded our sketch box easel, returned to the house on Calle Avanzaro, where Juárez General Ripeness Time was 1:14, give or take a caesium atom, and tried our best to go on about our business, setting up our easel in the ranch house doorway, laying out our vine and willow charcoal, and preparing to elaborate on the technical concerns that had caused us to abandon this position in the first place. The Gomez Mantle Clock, stopped by a bullet at 1:14, confronted us with the fact that Ray's entire mission had lasted on the order of 4.7 seconds, and yet our tour of Juárez must have lasted several hours, concluding as it did high atop a smokestack, in the glowing sunset beauty of the burst-fire weapons haze; the time had clearly come to bring things to a close. While few things could be easier than a perspective drawing of a dark silhouette against a white-hot sky, with no view at all of the horizon line, and very little left to put in perspective, we did not step up to our sketch box easel, we did not pick up the charcoal willow, we fell into a lengthy if shallow meditation on the risks concealed beneath the surface of our sketch, and did not come close to going on about our business, in fact we came fairly close to abandoning our drawing, in favor of an ending that was tied off with razor wire, and the address of a clinic where the stump could be cauterized, and then equipped with some sort of pincer-like device, in the biblioclastic equivalent of a Krukenberg procedure. The thought of depicting the ranch house interior, which briefly crossed our mind, turned quickly revolting: to be perfectly honest, the house was a mess, with Glock-shattered mirror-glass strewn across the floor, a hole the size of a hay bale blown out of the picture window, body-disposal lye-vats stacked in the kitchen, and the air so thick with Dead Horse Arum, pawpaw flowers using dead meat odors to try to draw flies as an aid to repro-duction, and the gelatinous atmospherics of coagulated thrombo-cytes, that we considered opening the sliding glass doors, and clear-ing the air with an industrial fan. Here we were, with our sketch box easel, about to invite the viewer to join us in the hall, and the house itself smelled like it was dying, and would soon need not so much a charcoal sketch artist, as a forensic pathologist, equipped with a gas mask. How had we let the place go like this? We felt a little like a hostess, with an all-important dinner guest arriving at any moment, slowly coming to the sad realization that the evening is about to prove a total disaster: while the table was set and the lighting impeccable, with chapel candles blazing in the human-skull sconces, femur-bone floor lamps adding a somber cast to a streamline-brutalist neo-ossuary interior, and a thermobaric fireball illuminating the entrance, the dining room itself was in need of a thorough cleansing, with a blood-sponge squeeze mop, a vat of al-kaline cleaning solvent, and perhaps that missing bottle of the dead man's ammonia; we had, in addition, a guest who had turned blue, and was keeping to himself inside a garment-bag of plastic, which while not at all unusual for an evening in Juárez, was bound to cast a pall over the dinner conversation; and finally, on top of everything, the meal we were planning was utterly ruined, since not only had the cold blood soup congealed, with its rowan berry garnish look-ing greenish and bitter, but the flies had eaten half of it, and were saving the rest for a greenbottle baby shower. Dinner, obviously, was out of the question; unless our viewer were on a charcoal diet, nothing in the house would look even vaguely appetizing; they'd be far better off taking a plane to Milan, and licking the tempera off of Leonardo's *Last Supper*. And beyond all this, there was something a little odd about the ranch house interior: since everything was suspended in an akinetic state, with even the air molecules frozen in time, and the humans in the room in suspended animation, how was it possible that the house had an odor, and why did the room feel warm and stuffy, instead of being down around zero Narrative Kelvin? Something, clearly, was still moving around in here, radiat-ing body heat, convecting avidity, indifferent to the workings of our narrative thermometer; perhaps inevitably, it turned out to be flies, unfortunately quite a lot of them, who seemed to be thriving on the absence of animation, darting around the room, leaving blood-prints on the page, refusing to sit still for a charcoal depiction. If you take a closer look at da Vinci's Mystical Meal, with the table full of delicacies like Christ's blood and body, you can't help noticing that even the Maestro himself found no way of dealing with this blowfly problem; even if Jesus was dining indoors, somewhere out in the Bethany suburbs, and not under the stars, in Jerusalem itself, there is no way on earth the flies wouldn't show, or could possibly resist such a sumptuous final spread, and yet there's not a single fly in the whole synoptic picture. The ineluctable reality is that the flies were there in swarms, up to their knees in transmuted blood, and this-is-my-body transubstantial foodstuffs, even stuck to the walls of the Sforzas' holy dining room, sucking the mix of milk and egg yolks out of the Maestro's flesh-toned tempera, with the Duke and Duchess looking on in awe, as blood-red mural paint seeped into their dining hall's life-sized dinner table, and Leonardo pondered, for three long years, the irrefutable evidence that the blowflies were multiplying, and would, in the end, have to be dealt with, by repudiating reality, and ruthlessly painting over them. One can't help suspecting that the actual foundation of all transcendent art is a base layer of blow-flies, going about their business, ruminating on the question of how art survives, when no.matter how vivid, and radiantly illuminating, it turns out to be something of a blowfly cover-up. For whatever it's worth, if you're already in Milan, enjoying the *Last Supper*, tran-scending the merely human, try to remember that it's only a meal depiction, and that while the hunger it's feeding is absolutely real, you won't want to lick so deep that you spoil the whole illusion.

Before we proceed to bring things to a close, we'll need to back up to an open commitment, where we left you with a bloody thumb-print to deal with, on the Sea Island cotton of a Turnbull & Asser shirt, and left you with a somewhat mystifying problem, a problem that we promised to return to in a moment, and while we're not yet prepared to solve your problem, we can, at a minimum, remind you that this problem remains to be solved: if you're still scanning a book while cleaning up a crime scene, don't bother searching for the dead man's ammonia; the crime scene itself lies dead up ahead, and you'll never get it clean with anyone's ammonia.

Which brings us to the story of our charcoal depiction, and our struggle to provide a perspective drawing, given the risks concealed beneath the surface of our page: having set up our sketch box easel just inside the door, two feet from Arturo and his empty Berettas, where do we place the viewer, if only by inference, looking outward toward Raymond, and into the abyss, through the charcoal picture window of our final-photon drawing? While this viewer-placement problem would prove to be quite a challenge, things could, in the end, have been far worse, if it weren't for the fact that our immediate surroundings had undergone a vast nanothermite simplification: of the two possible perspective problems in our graphical depiction, that of the implied horizon line, with its vanishing points in the Juárez distance, and that of inferring a viewer's eye, at a preset distance from the picture plane, thankfully only the latter remained, as our view out the doorway, toward the skyline of Juárez, had been totally obliterated by an illuminating display of man's inability to contain his own brilliance. The vanishing-point landscape problem, where the straight parallel lines of Highway 45, variously known as Rafael Perez Serna and San Lorenzo and Avenida Tecnologico and Panamericana, should converge to a single point, and vanish at the horizon line, somewhere around the river at the Texas/Mexico border, had itself vanished forever in the fireball light, leaving Raymond silhouetted against an empty white sky, wearing Black Body camouflage, perfect for the abyss, for his all-but-fatal portrait in willow charcoal. Raymond, at this point, without yet a viewer to give him real depth, had been radically reduced to a black cardboard cutout, consisting of an outline, with its arms outstretched, and a featureless interior, brilliantly backlit against a thermobaric sky; this image of Ray, as a black silhouette, while lovely to look at, would be gone in an instant if time advanced, and buried Ray's friends in the ranch house rubble, an image that in turn appeared to suggest yet another solution to the Wittgenstein conundrum: if we subtract the fact that his arms went up from the fact that Raymond apparently raised them, what remains is a kind of afterimage of the human silhouette, fading against an empty sky, but stubbornly persistent, as the infinite parallel lines of human acts and their intent converge at the horizon, and appear to vanish into pointlessness. Much as we

loved this rather elegant solution, it was difficult not to feel a little
like the crows, sitting up on the local power lines, waiting for things
to die, watching and waiting with blank-eyed indifference as Ray
went through the motions of solving our Juárez landscape problems: the Wittgenstein conundrum, which questions our sense of
self, and for which Ray offered an answer, using a proof by indirection; the vanishing point profusion, peculiar to Juárez, where things
seem to vanish in every conceivable direction, and where Ray's proposed solution, the black silhouette, against an empty white sky from
which Juárez has been obliterated, appeared to suggest that we deal
with this locale by wiping it off the map of things that need concern
us, leaving the pink-cross mothers, and their afterimage daughters,
to fend for themselves against the shadowy local predators, though
if you happen to be out walking in the mentholated desert, and
poke your shadow with a stick, don't blame Ray if the stench is
overwhelming; and the semiotic instability, the Oneiric Street Sign
problem, where the signs have a way of proving thoroughly misleading, and you can find yourself lost without even moving, and
the street-name signposts are a meaningless con, since right around
the time you think you know where you are, on Avenida Tecnologico, headed straight for the Juárez Airport, it turns out you're
really in the middle of a dream, on a strange river of asphalt called
the Pan-American Highway, somewhere south of the Arctic Circle
at Prudhoe Bay, Alaska, and north of Tierra del Fuego, 30,000 miles
away; this, frankly, wasn't a problem that Ray could solve, since
dream interpretation requires a certain amount of handwaving, and
a black cardboard cutout, backlit in white, wouldn't appear to care
about the meaning of human dreams, though right at this instant,
with his arms outstretched, he might have been trying to tell us
something, anything at all, to pinpoint the nature of this particular
crossroad. So where did this leave us? Where the hell were we? Ray
looked like one of those signposts in Juárez, where the road changes
names in the middle of nowhere, and neither arm of the signpost
is labeled with its odonym, and you're following one of those pipe-
dream trucks that seems to be hauling cleaning solvent, when all at
once the water truck veers to your right, and it suddenly occurs to
you what Ray's been trying to tell you, because Raymond Edmunds
knows precisely where he is, and he's not among the Condors at the

tip of Argentina, he's headed the wrong way up an unmarked one-way, a photon away from what remains of eternity. The streets of the Ciudad are a hideous twisted joke, a maze of nameless byways that can dead-end almost anywhere, a map of the heart so full of holes that it must have been drawn in embalming fluid, a steganographic suicide note from the city's last cartographer, so all Ray'd suggested, with his signpost-imitation, was that when the signs tell us nothing, we take them at their word.

Looking back now, with the benefit of hindsight, we should, in all likelihood, have stopped right here, with this image of Raymond fading to white, and a word to the wise on the semiotics of silence, and with no attempt at all at inferring a viewer; we had certainly improved on the razor-wire tourniquet solution, with its stump cauterization for our amputated narrative, and likely could have concluded with a short but sweet condolence note, written in human blood on one of our meat-locker postcards, along with a list of white papers on myoelectric limb prosthetics. At the time, however, we weren't looking back; we were standing at the easel, looking out the front door, and we weren't really thinking about stump cauterization, and trying to get our chronicle to limp back to El Paso on a transfemoral bone prosthesis made of packing crates and bed sheets, and something that looked like pig iron, salvaged from the municipal dump near Colonia Morelos; we were poised with our willow charcoal, one inch from the page, trying to position the viewer, in graphical perspective, in relation to the picture plane of our charcoal depiction, without running the risk, if our chronometer restarted, of our viewer undergoing a surgical intervention, perhaps a variation on our Krukenberg procedure, with his amputated forearm, now converted into a power tool, trying to leaf through the pages of a book on phantom-limb syndrome. So what were we missing here? What exactly was our problem? Picture it this way: rays of light from the object depicted, which in this case is an instance of Ray still being Ray, travel through the picture plane of our charcoal drawing, and into the viewer's eye, where the *Rays* all meet, a photon-detection instant before they too vanish, and leave us with a drawing only a blowfly could love, an empty white sky where the flies are seeing rainbows; without the viewer's eye, at a preset distance from our sketch box easel, Raymond's image would either have no depth, or he might just as well look infinitesimal, like trying to find a life-form on a dark ages galaxy. If you're still not getting this placement picture, imagine you're standing in front of a mirror, perhaps that wall mirror in Douchebag's hotel room, trying to figure out what happened to your hair, or why your face looks like something that got yanked off by a wheat thresher: the farther you stand from your hotel mirror, the smaller the image of *you* it depicts; we have the exact problem with Raymond's image, as the farther we place you from our sketchpad easel, the smaller the *Raymond* our drawing depicts. The problem with our working in charcoal, in Juárez, at least as far as including a viewer in the picture, is that there is very little margin for error in perspective: if we place our man out on the concrete stoop, for instance, where Raymond has stepped out from under the shadow of the eaves, the viewer might find himself on the wrong side of the looking glass, which is not some sort of pastoral scene out of Lewis Carroll, where we're out in the English countryside, feeling nostalgic about the future; on the other side of the mirror that art holds up to life, the future has already happened, all right, right before our eyes, and it looks just like Ciudad Juárez, or a suicide swim in the Songhua River, or a body-bag shortage in the hills of Caracas, or a heavy-metals harvest festival in the e-waste fields of Guiyu, or a teratogenic orphan home in the garbage pits of Lagos, or a tire-dump Dengue vector hemorrhaging through Calcutta, or a hoplophobic anxiety attack in a favela in São Paulo, where the human species is suffering from the aftereffects of an enormous binge, and is being kept alive on the consumer equivalent of pure diamorphine, with thorazine supplements, under general anaesthesia, and the future as such has spontaneously aborted, and the earth is coming down with a suppurating head wound, and the flies are taking a bloodbath in the hemoglobin fountains. This, clearly, just won't do; not only would our sketch be ruined, but the viewer would run the risk of joining the carbonized remnants, and be in no position to appreciate the irony involved in his bones being used while we attempt a second drawing. At the other extreme, where we place the eye back near the ranch house kitchen, like looking at Juárez through the wrong end of a telescope, we might leave the viewer feeling completely uninvolved, standing in a world with which he feels no connection, a world where the headstones mark hollow empty graves, a world where the dead get buried *in absentia*, policed with impunity, since no one really gives a shit, just as long as we get our light bulbs, and our Android devices; we couldn't really blame the viewer for pouring another drink, and then wandering off alone toward a well-stocked refrigerator, in search of something to eat, in the instant before oblivion. In the end, of course, we found the perfect position, though it poses certain challenges to the viewer's eponymous view of his selfless anonymity, and gives rise to more than a few concerns regarding the nature of phantom-viewer syndrome. Once the fireproof roof just above you self-ignites, and the structure bulges inward under the overpressure blast wave, the viewer would be well-advised to exit toward the rear, feeling his way along, with one hand on the wall, past the Glock-shattered mirror, and the celery scent of quicklime sacks, as the room fills up with a dense shade of smoke, and invisible shards of glass from the whirlwind windows; if all else fails, and you find yourself blinded by ultraviolet radiation, wandering around the house in a snowblind daze, unable to find your way to the exit through the kitchen, either take a firm hold of Jennifer's lovely hand, and permit her to guide you to the blowfly garden, and back to the duck pond at Parque Hermanos, or simply look away from the drawing itself, and stay away from sketches of Juárez altogether.

The irony, of course, is that you can't look away. What are you missing here? What exactly is your problem? How did Douchebag put it? "No matter what happens, no matter how subhuman, that's just the way we are, we're people who like to watch." We warned you all along to stay out of Juárez, where voyeurs of the hideous are always welcome; we warned you about the weather, where one minute it's lovely, all blue April skies, and a forecast for Clarity, and the next minute some sort of bomb has gone off, and as far as the eye can see, it's Nebulous and Murky; we even tried to warn you about the neighborhood itself, hoping you'd steer clear of the Cuernavaca subdivision, and the pale taupe ranch house, and the cold-blooded cooking. What were your even doing in Juárez in the first place? What's that you say? That wasn't you? You had nothing to do with any of this? We should leave you out of it? It's a little late now to be protesting your innocence. It's as if you think the world is somewhere else, somewhere far away, without you in it. Picture it this way: a five-year-old boy, wearing a yellow hand-knit sweater, sits in an open field in a town outside Shantou, in Guangdong province, near the South China Sea; he's posing for this particular photo, maybe fifty feet up, balanced atop an enormous mound of technotrash and e-waste products, power supplies, motherboards, PCI buses, graphics cards, CPUs, Bios ROM chips, memory modules, hard drive platters, SCSI controllers, computer keyboards, lithium batteries, cathode ray tubes from desktop monitors, obsoleted cell phones, outdated laptops, iPods, Game Boys, Blackberries, RAZR devices, flat screen TVs that look brand-new, printer/fax/copier combinations that should have been upgraded months ago, external hard drives and USB hubs, computer mice and laser pointers and WiMAX amplifiers and God knows what, the usual mound of useless stuff that has to be gotten rid of once the novelty wears off; fortunately for the boy, who has some weird-looking pustules all over his bare feet, he'll be forty feet away when they finally set fire to the great toxic heap, sending quite a large cloud of lead-filled smoke into the hazy necrotic air of an open field, where it will linger for years over Guangdong province, and an amazing array of interesting metals into the mutagenic waters of a charcoal streambed, cadmium, mercury, beryllium, barium, nickel, terbium, cobalt, palladium, manganese, arsenic, rhodium, silver, antimony, titanium, germanium, yttrium, bismuth, ruthenium, vanadium, tantalum, niobium, and iron and zinc and so on and so on, as though the child were being taught the periodic table by soaking his mangled feet in the e-waste groundwater. Or picture it this way: an eight-year-old girl, photographed at sunset, in an evocative amber light, wearing white shorts and T-shirt and a floppy red golf hat, is slowly making the two-hundred-foot climb up an immense pile of refuse in one of the garbage pits of Lagos, searching for rags, wood, metal, rubber, but especially anything whatsoever made of plastic, shampoo bottles, margarine tubs, cereal-box liners, laundry detergent, dustbin bags, soda bottle empties, milk, water, sports drink, and juice containers, motor oil liters, plastic pipe, peanut butter, pickle, jelly and jam conveyors, flower pots, beach buckets, cable insulation, vinyl floor tiles, microwave food trays, squeeze bottles of honey and mustard and ketchup, medical tubing, dry-cleaning covers, movie cassettes, wheelbarrow trays, battery cases, trash-can liners, plastic rakes, traffic cones, eggshell cartons, aquarium windows, auto-body quarter panels, ballbarrow wheels, plastic lumber, strawberry baskets, recycling bins, recycling bins, light-switch plates, thermal insulation, license plate frames, medicine bottles, dinnerware replicas and coffee foam cups and thousands of versions of kitchen utensils, a list so long we'll need to stop here, but we can rest assured that our girl won't stop, as a forty-pound bag of plastic shit is worth a good fifteen cents to her family of seven, and on an excellent day, she might make eight dollars, an incredible windfall to her rag-picker household, in a house made of refuse hauled from the heap, and conveniently located, for her predawn wake-up, at the absolute bottom of the garbage-pit food chain; fortunately for her, for every 100 kilos of product we produce, 3,200 kilos of waste comes with it, as though man's real purpose in equipping himself for life were to produce enough garbage for the impoverished to flourish, whether here in Lagos or in Mumbai or Manila, where eight-year-old girls with a Masters Degree in Plastics, from low- and high-density polyethylene, to polypropylene and polystyrene, to ready-for-the-grind polyethylene terephthalate, to spoil-the-whole-melt polyvinyl-chloride, are a thousandth of a cent a dozen, with the price dropping fast, so what she really needs most, to survive on her career path, is a particle-filter mask, salve for her leg wounds, and a PhD in Don't Ever Touch That. Or picture it this way: you're reading yet another sensational account, in the front-page reporting of your local paper, of yet another act of barbarism by the Mexican drug gangs, as the war moves on from Nuevo Laredo to Sonora Nogales to Piedras Negras to Matamoros to Agua Prieta to San Luis Rio to Sonoyta and Naco to Ciudad Acuna to Praxedis Guerrero to Tecate and Mexicali to Reynosa and Nuevo Progreso to Presa Falcon to Ciudad Camargo to Los Algondones to Puerto Palomas to El Berrendo to Lucio Blanco to Miguel Aleman and Altar and Ojinaga to someplace new, like El Porvenir, directly across the border from the town of Fort Hancock, where the border-crossing checkpoint, through the rusted-bar fence, has come to be known as Jurassic Park Gate, presumably a reference to prehistoric reptiles that need to be kept caged on their side of the border, where they can wander around forever in ghostly El Porvenir, killing on a whim, settling scores at random, setting fire to whole blocks of shantytown houses, gunning down anything that threatens to stay alive, and cutting open women to steal their fetal children; fortunately for all of us, this is a Mexican problem, the Mexicans, while lovely, are evidently quite a violent people, and though it has nothing at all to do with us, and the $30 billion in drug profits we lend to the cause, much of it repaid in armaments purchases, we are, let's say, concerned for their health, which is why we read these stories with such avidity, since the moment the last true Mexican dies, we'll feel totally bereft of violence pornography. No matter what happens, no matter how subhuman, that's just the way we are, we're people who like to watch; we stare through the windows, hands at our sides, while the world undergoes a complete facial transplant. What does any of this have to do with you? You'd never set foot in a place like Lagos? You're still not quite getting the picture, are you? Remember that stuff we taught you about perspective drawing, and how the Viewer is in the picture, if only by inference, at a preset distance from our sketch box easel? That, shall we say, was slightly misleading, and not quite the perspective we actually had in mind, where you're looking at the world somewhere off in the distance, a world that's far away, without you in it; that preset distance from our Tiziano sketchpad, where you could always look away if you didn't like what you were seeing, is maybe a bit closer in than you were led to believe, and this whole perspective drawing problem was something of a setup. You've been wandering around Juárez like a zombie in a thought experiment, an experiment in collective guilt, where the zombie is shown the morgue-slab photos, and responds by saying *I'm truly sorry*, and making out a check to Amnesty International, or Nuestra Hijas de Regreso a Casa, or maybe Save the Children or Habitat for Humanity, and then sealing the whole deal by forging his own signature. What's that you say? You didn't know it was forged? No wonder the authorities are beginning to get suspicious. We're sorry to be the ones to break this to you, but the violence that man is doing to his home is not some sort of thought experiment, and the last thing on earth the world needs now is yet another anonymous onlooker, trying to get the picture; our drawing isn't a drawing exactly, it's more of a kind of framing device, and you, mon frère, so slow to get the picture, are not only under suspicion, but about to be framed. We didn't exactly select you at random, and you're not precisely The Viewer in the abstract sense, and we're not about to give you a bird's eye view of anything, or a view of Juárez from high atop a smelting stack; we're about to put you back exactly where you belong, wearing Douchebag's shoes, in the middle of the picture, because while Douchebag isn't you in any literal sense, you appear to be standing in Douchebag shoes, and Douchebag, unfortunately, is now your problem.

In the charcoal drawing, of the all-but-fatal instant, you are standing in the hallway, maybe six feet from the door, sighting through the Ghost Ring O of the pistol-grip Mossberg's sight kit assembly, aiming at what you appear to think is a point just above Raymond's right shoulder, and what is in fact the soon-to-be-dead center of the middle of Raymond's Shadow Plaid back. You are, at the moment, so full of intoxicants, from tramadol hydrochloride to mescal and tequila to a partially smoked kilo of black tar heroin, that you wouldn't know the difference between a hypnagogic visual, brought on by opiates and sleep deprivation, and what appears to be a large and ominous-looking feathered creature, nearly three feet tall and with a good six feet of wingspan, that has recently come to rest next to Raymond's right ear. This, obviously, is not a good sign; its textual correlative would be asemic writing. *Crow*, you're thinking; this has to be a crow; a pile of empty feathers, silhouetted against the sky, that's so close to nothingness, just to begin with, that the thing could be stone dead, and you'd never even know. You think you've reached the bottom of the existential food-chain, like there's nothing on earth more supremely indifferent to human existence than a stationary crow; here, however, you're sadly mistaken, because this creature you're seeing, or more precisely, hallucinating, isn't actually a crow, which can eat almost anything, but an enormous black turkey buzzard, which feeds strictly on carrion. The telltale signs, next time you're having dreamlets and anthypnic sensations and seeing oneirogogic visuals in a borderland dream state, is that in contrast to the crow's oversized cranium, and corresponding intelligence, under all those black feathers, the turkey buzzard's head is not only bald, but amazingly small given the six-foot wingspan, and a blood-shade of red, and incredibly stupid. At the absolute bottom of the existential food-chain, and now setting up shop on Raymond's right shoulder, is the hypnagogic equivalent of a yard-tall turkey buzzard, with its bald red head, absence of intelligence, and revolting set of appetites, looking absolutely ravenous. This bird, to be clear, is not an emblem of death; death, in Juárez, doesn't bother much with emblems, though it does have its own rather lurid-looking deity; the problem you face, given this bird in your head, which wouldn't move an inch even if you could kill it, is getting way too clear a picture of how you feed on your fellow creatures, and lapsing into a permanent state of thorough self-revulsion. Just behind you in line, closest to the easel, stands Ray's friend Jennifer, who wouldn't know you from Adam, watching the wadding come apart, in a smokeless powder puff, as the shot cup exits the Mossberg barrel, sending a triple-decker pellet pattern hurtling through the air, looking vaguely misshapen and slightly off target; given the idiosyncratic rifling of the pistol-grip Cruiser, and the fact that the pellets are nine lead musket balls, we should not expect the scatter pattern to be in any way Gaussian, but rather, as predicted, a connect-the-dots O; given the shockfront's position, a photon-detection away, and the fact that the musket balls are still inches from penetration, the only real question, in our charcoal depiction, is which will arrive first, the triple-decker shotgun load, and the end to a tic-tac-toe game we wish we'd never started, or Jen's empty bottle of Tequila Orendain, and the end, via brain trauma, to your oneirogogic-dreamlet problem. If it's any consolation, when we all wake up tomorrow, we'll notice that the Mossberg was never in fact fired, as we've taken the precaution of installing a new safety button, knowing you'd never find it, even in your dreams. Having stepped out at last from under the shadow of the eaves, on his way toward Gomez with a polymer-framed pistol, Ray stands silhouetted against an empty white sky, with his arms outstretched, and a buzzard on his shoulder, making the universal gesture, a sort of shrug with upturned palms, of a man who's asking the Heavens something like *Now what?* It has, in point of fact, been something of a long morning, difficult to capture in vine and willow charcoal, but rather neatly summed up by Ray's open-armed shrug: the cold-sweat wake-up from a Napalm-drool dream, with dragon clocks chasing him wielding M9 flamethrowers; the 9:30 roll call, where Gene's long gone, and the vet-sutured chest-wound is torqued-up and bursting; the Jane Churchill wallpaper Cherubim problem,

somewhere deep in the dusty bone-pile of the endless Book of
Chronicles; the Tramadol wind off the Sangre de Cristos, cooling
down his hawk feathers, though he still couldn't comb them; getting lost in the Land of Quandaries and Qualms, on the Yucca flats,
in the nuclear desert, and winding up somewhere in the Wernicke
region, doing deep semantic processing in Dreamland or The Box;
the minus-five lighting irreality zone, deep underground in Gomez'
parking structure, where Gene's upstairs, returning the money, with
a FLAMEBOY PLUS searching around for his pituitary, while the
cobwebs glimmer in psychopathic reality, and in the sodium lamplight, everyone's guilty; Jen at the wheel, chasing the Black Ram
Magnum, while Ray swallows bone pills in the blue Texas April,
and his dad plays pool in the Jim Beam lamplight, and Gene sits
trapped, pretzelled atop the gearshift, apparently headed for the
glowing coyotes, in a truck loaded down with a ton of plutonium
that maybe turns out to be pure gold bars; problems with the weather, and the Homeowners Association, and mediastinitis and knife-
wound dehiscence, and the side-view wait for the grey Ford Fusion,
with Tinkerbell's wand compounding the problem; the Dreamland
Yellow Pages teleportation consult, pumping Gene full of rubidium
and Feshbach resonance, getting him out of the truck as a Bose-
Einstein condensate, but landing him somewhere in the Boomerang Nebula; the razor-wire climb, the disappearing safety button,
the Battle of Greasy Grass in the mental Dakotas; becoming a dip-
terologist in the blowfly garden, where the holes are all dug behind
the purple bougainvillea, and the celery scent of quicklime sacks,
and Osha-extract chuchupaste, brings back distant memories of
quail-pinkish dawns; and finally reaching the window casement,
and the chessboard-layout stalemate problem, and the rearing aluminum horses on the Stopwatch House chronometer, where the
long morning ended, and Ray headed past noon, which was a whole
different story, and another long problem. *Now what.* Ray stands
silhouetted against the thermobaric light, with his sutures long
gone, and his blood count useless; some douchebag lurks behind
him, hunting hypnagogic buzzards, and apparently trying to shoot
him with his very own shotgun; and now this wounded bird, somehow bouncing off the fireplace chimney, illuminating everything
with useless information, like a plane out doing skywriting by eras-

ing the whole sky; no wonder Ray's shrugging, and has a *Now what* sort of attitude. Raymond, drawn in willow charcoal, doesn't, admittedly, quite look like himself; he looks, let's face it, more like a scarecrow, crossed broomsticks perhaps, dressed in Shadow Plaid black flannel, with an enormous ball of kite twine as a mock-up of the head, and while it's easy enough to see that the crows are holding back, biding their time behind the thermobaric fireball, it's also readily apparent that Ray's scarecrow pantomime, so amusing to the crows that they might almost be said to empathize, does not work at all on these moronic-looking turkey buzzards, who couldn't care less if his head were made of kite twine. Jesus, Ray, you look like shit; thought you were going to buy us both a couple of six-packs, maybe sit in the yard and have a talk about the past, back when we still had a future to plan. I've been thinking about that, Jen; what would you say to getting out of Juárez, maybe live in a different time zone somewhere, someplace like Bermuda. Bermuda? What's in Bermuda? Well, just for instance; I've never actually been there; but I've sort of got this picture stuck in my head, where we're running a little bike-rental shop by this turquoise lagoon, and taking long walks on the pink-sand beaches, and having tea on the outdoor porch up at Hamilton House, right next to the harbor, with the fog rolling in, and boats bobbing on the water, and heading out to Shelly Bay to bet on the horses, watch the white-glove guys doing their tic-tac signals, and maybe we've got ourselves one of those white-picket cottages, and everything looks brand-new, and Juárez is ancient history. Sounds lovely, Ray, but maybe somewhat out of date; I think they tore the race track down back in the '60s, and Hamilton House is like an office complex, and you, at the moment, are headed into the abyss, where pink-sand beaches are a little hard to come by. So I'm a goner is what you're saying; seems like kind of a waste. I don't know, Ray. What were you supposed to do? Just leave Gene down here? Still not sure I follow why you went out the front door, trying to get yourself killed, instead of slipping out the back way and heading back to El Paso. Yeah, you're probably right, but the way I had it figured, my plan might have worked, or maybe I was thinking I was a goner already, and the world would be better off with one less predator. Tell you what we'll do then, Ray, when Gene and I get out of here, we'll all go back to El Paso, pick up your bird dogs, and take them for a run out in the mesquite and acacia brush, maybe rename one of them Raymond or Trip or something, teach him to roll over when we pop a can of Pabst Blue Ribbon. Christ, you're right, I almost forgot about the dogs. Maybe you can feed them for me. And the one you're calling Trip, take him for a run out in the gypsum desert, teach him how to wink when he looks up at you, and sees you smile, or hears your laughter, and I'll find that beach if it's the last thing I do, even if I have to build it one pink grain at a time, and I'll plant some jasmine in the white-picket garden, and whenever you think of me, the flowers will blossom.

We're dreaming, of course; down in the abyss, there's plenty of sand, but not enough organic matter to keep a turkey buzzard alive, much less a flower, and given the medium of the vine and willow sketch, the jasmine would have to bloom in absolute charcoal. Which brings us to our watercolor. We wish we could tell you it's all turquoise lagoons, and lavender Passion Flowers, and Pink-tipped Begonias, and that Ray's headed off to the island of Bermuda, which is just what he deserves, but not where he belongs. Raymond, at bottom, is basically still a soldier, meaning he's not out strolling some beach in bare feet, or wading ankle-deep in the turquoise waters; if Ray's still standing, he's in up to his neck, and if Raymond's going out, he's going out with his boots on. It's a little late now for pink-sand lagoons, and trying to picture Ray in some watercolor cover-up of his whole boots-on way of standing in the world, because Ray's not wading in the turquoise waters, catching a little R&R on the island of Bermuda, he's on one last deployment along the edges of oblivion, in the northeastern highlands of Kunar, Afghanistan.

If we're picturing some sort of barren moonscape, all rocky shades of grey from a black-and-white film, or somewhere in the South in the middle of a rainstorm, where all we can really picture is a mud-shade of brown, we've come to the wrong location, and Ray's nowhere near here, and we need to start over and paint in the pines, the lush mountain forests with green terraced lawns, and meadows slashed with color against a stark violent backdrop, yellow and purple wildflower blossoms and children in violet silk, with one child in particular, wearing a flowing red silk dress, making the long slow climb up a steep grassy hillside, from a village made of stone, in the valley down below us, to her home up a rock face,

in a thousand-year-old cave. So where the hell are we? And what
are we doing here? Ray's in an outcropping of rectangular quarried stone, part way down the hill from Firebase Bermuda, and that
water down below him is the Korengal River, and we, let's face it,
are in the Valley of Death, somewhere to the west of the Pakistani
border, fighting a mix of God knows what, Taliban, al-Qaida, Har-
kat-ul-Mujahideen, a fighting-force known locally as the Lashkar al
Zil, which translates roughly to The Shadow Army. Ray's little outcropping of rectangular stone is the remains of a village that's been
bombed back to rubble by an Unmanned Aerial Vehicle, the MQ-9
Reaper, piloted in Virginia by contract personnel, who go home
each evening for supper with their families, while the local Pashai, descendents perhaps of the ancient Gandhari, read a passage
on forgiveness from a well-worn Koran, and bury their dead under
small mounds of shelf-rock. The Pashai, admittedly, don't adhere to
this simple picture: they have an equally well-worn passage regarding revenge in their Koran, wherein the recompense for an evil is
an evil in kind; the violet brushstroke children, in a meadow full of
wildflower blossoms, seem a bit farfetched, as they should, strictly
speaking, be off somewhere working; and the child in flowing red,
apparently climbing toward safety, is completely impossible, and totally subjective, and must express something that's of a personal nature, as the Pashai in fact are strict Muwahhiduns, meaning red silk
dresses are expressly forbidden. That ridge across the river, known
as the Abas Ghar, is knee-deep in snow and covered with enormous
cedar trees and shrouded in mist at higher elevations, a mist that
even now is drifting up the river valley, complicating Ray's mission,
which is to act as an observer on a B-52 bomb run on the village
down below us, where The Shadow Army has taken up positions
among the populace, in houses whose roof beams are chiseled from
ancient cedar, with walls made of tons of truly ancient rock. If Ray
were here to observe an actual airstrike, on the village of Loi Kaley
perhaps, near the southern end of this six-mile-long valley, where
the houses teeter on stilts as they climb the steep hillside, and are
nearly piles of siltstone rubble already, constructed along the lines
of a rock fence in Vermont, he wouldn't be waiting on a B-52, he'd
be waiting for an Apache armed with Hellfire missiles, where a few
well-placed strikes would erase the whole hill; Raymond, however,

must be in a different part of reality, deep in the north end of the Valley of Death, with Sawtalo Sar mountain towering above him, up in the drift regions of the mystic Hindu Kush, and the Korengal River flowing south down below him, toward the end of the valley, where it empties into the Pech, because the houses up here are basically immortal, constructed along the lines of a Monument to Futility, or a mental construct, which is really what this is, as though we thought whole belief systems could be bombed back to rubble, or we could change a man's ethos by blowing out his brains. To Raymond's immediate left, where the child in flowing red is climbing toward the rock face, the hillside has been terraced and planted with spring wheat, which won't be ready to harvest until sometime in July, using hammer-peened scythes that are honed on a whetstone, in a process nearly as old as wheat cultivation, which is itself roughly as old as human civilization, which is in turn about as old as organized slaughter, in wars over wheat and agricultural surplus, created by scythes, honed on a whetstone. In a meadow to Ray's right, goats are grazing the grass and a man is herding sheep and a woman is pruning mulberry trees, where the silkworms are feeding and spinning imaginary silk, and the mulberries themselves have not yet ripened, and won't be ready for picking until sometime in June. Walnut trees; a small herd of cattle; farther down the valley, a tiny field of corn; as though man's real purpose in equipping himself for life is to produce enough to live on, with nothing gone to waste. Suddenly, out of the blue, Ray begins to shiver. A cloud passes its hand slowly across the light, and a silence races shadow-like over the flowing grass, in an obvious reference to a poem of Fernando Pessoa's, where one of his heteronyms, Alberto Caeiro, imagines his own soul to be a keeper of sheep. Ray checks his flock, in a world full of the innocent, for one child in particular, in a flowing red dress, noting with satisfaction that she has now reached the rock face, and is being hauled up to safety in a thousand-year-old cave. The surface of the river turns strangely metallic; the springtime green is stripped obliquely from the trees; the purples and violets and yellows of a watercolor evaporate completely, against an empty white sky; and Raymond Edmunds, wearing nothing but his absence, walks off across a page left open on a nightstand, a page left open, and perfectly blank.

# 32

The story of how I came to die on Playa la Ropa, a beach
enclave just south of Zihuatanejo, itself a seedy tourist trap
and sportfishing destination, known as Zihua to the locals,
and Ixtapa/Zihuatanejo to the airlines and travel industry, presents
a fascinating problem in narrative reconstruction, since while there
are now many things for which I hold myself accountable, I can
hardly be expected to narrate my own death. Among the obvious
problems of such a narrative reconstruction, in which one would be
called upon to supply some sequence of probative events, a chain
of cause and effect, if you will, that led up to one's demise, one
would, after all, be forced to admit that one chain-link is missing,
that final fatal link that all the others led up to; even a man writing
a suicide note, with its fatalistic tone and sense of the inevitable,
cannot, in the end, actually pronounce his own death. Ropes break;
pistols misfire; pills fail to prove lethal; the dive off the bridge, or
the vehicular plunge into the concrete abutment, somehow falls
short of complete self-effacement; and the suicide note, so painstakingly prepared and carefully reasoned, or dashed off abruptly in
a guilt-wracked scrawl, must now be read in a whole new light, or
tossed into the fire when the scrawl proves illegible. My own story,
admittedly, has nothing to do with suicide notes, or the high-speed
plunge into titanium waters; by the time I reached the end of my
existential tether, I most certainly had a kind of noose around my
neck, and one could easily argue that I myself had tied it, but the
story of how I came to die on Playa la Ropa will need to be viewed

in a slightly different light, because not only do I intend to narrate my final moments, but I fully intend to pronounce my own death.

I came to one morning in a threadbare motel that would later turn out to be a room above a tavern, where I'd evidently spent a considerable interval drinking myself blind on an absolute bender, one of those binges whose length is for the moment indeterminate, but whose depth is known instantly as perfectly formidable. The place smelled of garbage and decomposing kelp and sounded like the site of a seagull convention, and it was readily apparent that I had not, the night before, considered the possibility that there might be a sunrise, as not only were the rubberized curtains not drawn, but I'd failed to provide for my early-morning pick-me-up, leaving unfiltered sunlight driving an ice pick through my head, and last night's bottle standing unspeakably empty; without at least four or five ounces of straight gin, I was not prepared to move so much as a single shattered inch, much less face the fact that I had a sleeping companion. Even the attempt to reassemble some semblance of a self, as a basis for launching some sort of relief-seeking reconnaissance mission, is, at such a moment, hazardous in the extreme: not only has the self been blown to jagged shards, but the razor-sharp fragments are lodged in your neurons, and a thought like "get up, pull yourself together, get a glass of water and six or seven aspirin," leaves your neurons leaking toxins from billions of tiny cuts, and the shards, if anything, razored-in deeper. Imagine my relief when I opened the nightstand drawer and found a half pint of something that might well have been brandy, two-thirds of which would soon be gone in a single gulp, leaving me slightly queasy but with a reassuring burn in the pit of my empty stomach. As I sat up in bed, carefully unscrewing the twist-off bottle top, waiting to hear the satisfying click of the aluminum seal breaking along its perforated edge, a sound that would mean that the cap would unseal, without my having to search my sordid little room for a knife blade or nail file to saw through the metal, the oddest thing happened, in fact several things at once, and I paused for a moment to consider the following: on the nightstand table, propped up against the lamp, I found two strips of paper that I instinctively knew had been torn from the margins of a map of El Paso; the twin paper strips, like saw-toothed versions of fortune cookie notes, had messages that each seemed to be some sort of puzzle, made of enigmatic rebus symbols and hieroglyphs and pictograms, with an occasional block of illegible cursive, in a strangely familiar-looking backward-slanting hand, and despite the fact that I was in no condition to make any sort of effort toward trying to decode them, I knew what they said without even looking, as though I'd written them to myself for just this occasion, *Stay far away from wherever it is you're going*, and *U-turns are pointless, you can't undrink the bottle*; and as I gave a final twist to the perforated seal, truly looking forward to that first drink of the morning, the room, not the bottle top, came loose along the perforations, and I knew all at once that this was not my motel, and not actually me in the middle of a bender, and I woke up with a start soaked in neurotoxic sweat, in the middle of reality, in my pitch-black hotel room.

Call it a nightmare: it completely changes everything. I know what you're thinking: that was a dirty trick, recounting a dream using the discourse of reality, but try to keep in mind that the date was April 20, and that I, meaning Douchebag, had only recently gotten sober, while Alvaro de Campos, my sleeping companion, had never had a drink in his whole three-day life. And then I crossed the darkened room to the blackout curtains, and throwing them open, discovered that it was dawn, with the sun just coming up above the mountaintops behind me, casting the first light of morning on Zihuatanejo Bay, meaning that I, the total douchebag who got Alvaro into this, was now at the beginning of my fourth day of sobriety. There are few things in life more brutally real than the dreams of an alcoholic, believing he's had a relapse; to even begin to get a sense of the normal human equivalent, you'd have to be convinced, in the most vivid of dreams, that you'd just swallowed an entire bottle of Drano or Liquid-Plumr, and were now waiting to die, from the inside out, as a result of the ingestion of an alkaline corrosive, and can't even speak, or cry out for help, due to liquefactive necrosis of your entire esophagus. Imagine your relief, waking up from such a dream, at finding you're still alive, and haven't swallowed anything, and you'll feel just a sliver of how the morning felt to me, as the sun continued to climb above the mountains in the east, and the charcoal-grey waters of Zihua Bay turned a sunlit shade of praise-the-lord turquoise. I stepped out onto the terracotta-tiled terrace, surrounded by a railing of redwood flowerboxes, full of warm yellow marigolds and hot-pink begonias, and marveled a little at the hotel's construction, built into the cliffside, in a series of staggered steps, from where I stood all alone on the hillside clifftop, to the tide-pool rocks covered in sea-foam down below, like a seven-layer wedding cake, frosted with rose adobe. This, let me tell you, must have cost a small fortune, and the suite we were occupying was priced accordingly, though given the relative weakness of the peso against the dollar, the place was a bargain, if not quite a steal; a similar suite at Hotel du Cap, or La Réserve de Beaulieu, or the Grand-Hotel du Cap Ferrat, on the French Riviera, overlooking the Mediterranean, as I knew from having stayed at each and every one of them, would have cost seven times this, depending upon the season and condition of the euro. Playa la Madera, and El Centro de Zihua, which I knew from prior visits were a mile or two to the north, meaning off to my right as I stood on the terrace, were slowly waking up on a Monday morning, rolling up the security shutters on the T-shirt and trinket shops along Juan Alvarez and Nicolas Bravo; the headlands of Cerro del Almacen, with its sandy dirt roads and widely spaced villas, stood green-lit to the west, across the yacht-filled harbor, where a Carnival Cruise Ship, like 16 stories tall, was beginning the process of off-loading tourists; and Playa la Ropa's white arc of sand drifted south, to my left, toward Acapulco. I stood in bare feet on the cold tile floor, listening to the songbirds on the roof up above me, which brought back the memory of the name of my small hotel, La Casa Que Canta, The House That Sings, which reminded me in turn of Alvaro's hotel, El Mesón de los Poetas, The Inn of the Poets, and our Divine Mercy Sunday flight from Guanajuato. This, I can promise you, is not a dirty trick, and while it may not quite seem real, neither does reality.

When I finally came to on the Bird's Nest hilltop, I had a lovely view of the downtown skyline, but I seemed to be sharing headspace with a guy who was fairly clueless. Not only did he not have a peso to his name, but he'd just been attacked by like a NATO brigade, and was sitting in a La-Z-Boy Dreamline Recliner, sort of listening to the birds sing, not doing much of anything. Let's just say, in those first few moments, that Alvaro and I didn't quite see eye to eye; he seemed to be focused on that whole facial transplant thing, and thirty-pound cinderblocks, and Do Not Disturb signs, all of which, admittedly, would need to be dealt with, though with the yard full of bomb craters from Raptor grenades, and smoking appliances, and self-cleaning HEFA ovens, it didn't seem to me to be quite the right time; and from my perspective, we've got a few basic problems, like a phony Scottish driver's license in the name of a dead heteronym, with a photo of Pessoa that must be 80 years out of date, and an ATM card that doesn't have a PIN, meaning access to cash could prove to be somewhat limited, and Alvaro's wandering around without a single fucking credit card, mumbling something cryptic about being the Zero Peso Man. Alvaro, right off the bat here, strikes me as being more than a little naïve, as we do a quick run-through on what exactly he's been up to: the Guanajuato wake-up to the beauty of existence, with its rose-red basilica domes and custard-colored houses, where he discovers that *what is* will more than suffice, and that personal narratives are highly overrated; the search through the attic for what makes him tick, when being present to the moment is already self-sufficient; High Noon pulling clothespins from the blue plastic bucket, and birds disappearing, on a morning flight to *elsewhere*, and Alvaro finally learning how to let the past go, though he doesn't have a clue what sort of hellish place he sent it to; a credulity-straining photo ID, with a personal identity that's absurdly constructed, setting off in search of an ATM PIN, as a man who never believed in his existence in the first place; the case of the 1,000-peso rapidly shrinking man, apparently a double of Fernando Pessoa, who learns to respect the power of the improbable, since he's already living in the 1,000-peso city; taking up with Gabriella, the Sistine Madonna, who he seemed to think was some sort of tour guide, when it was as clear as the nose on Pessoa's own face that she was the angel you picture in a fairy tale; the '56 Armagnac smoldering-liquid toast, the lilac yuans, the lavender Swiss Burckhardts, the gold bullion bars in the world's safest bank vault, where $20 million was only part of the story; winning the lottery in another man's name, and having no luck at all trying to prove this can't be possible, since some must have money so that those who do not can continue to believe in the justice of the lottery; drinking by the streambed, with upturned palms, without asking questions about where the melting snow comes from, or inadvertently revealing his GPS coordinates; Tío Gustavo's Macaw named Palabra, with the India-ink sketch of a hawk around its eyes, who saw no apparent difference between "none" and "nothing," since whatever was in the bank account was effectively zero; the timeless moment stop at the One Hour Photo shop, where the street seemed to miss him, and sent him a lovely postcard; the Revenge of the Gardeners trueno hedge, the wealthy hacendado having a word with his jardineros, the grim-faced men in the dark-suited party photos, where I suppose I must have seemed *de pocas luces*, or maybe *borracho*, and in any case, *slow*; High Noon's recounting, despite her persistent memory problems, the history of Guanax-juato, the Land of the Hopping Frogs; the twin streams of time uniting in Friday night, where they sat on the steps for an event at the Teatro, and listened to the singing of Cielito Lindo, by the silver-studded pant-leg guys, the All-Black musicians; returning to his hotel to find the FedEx-package clipping-service, full of grim news of vacancies in empty Juárez lots, and bodies stacked like cordwood in excavated gardens, and learning that, after all, he had not been forgotten, in a backward-slanting hand that reversed the flow of thought; Mozart's pet Starling, Chopin's Canyon Wren, Vivaldi's silvery flute concerto, in the Goldfinch key of D, while Alvaro had his breakfast in the waterfountain courtyard, and time moved forward by going back the way it came; the Alonso Quixano mnemonic device, the string around your finger to remind you to tie a string, since while Quixote himself may be a fiction of a fiction, nothing could be more real than the name Don Quixote; staring at his fork, and his empty-headed dinner plate, during the Fascist Poetry power lunch with the critic Raúl Ramírez, where the Miracle of the Spirit was carefully dissected, and all of its vital organs were consumed in the process; absorbing Tensor Calculus in a Masonic sermonette, where T stands for Terror, and the phallically orthogonal, and you learn to square the circle by burying yourself alive, arriving before you've departed, with an awkward head-first slide; eating homemade gorditas at the Quixote museum, where the craziness of genius takes back control of reason, and Sancho scrambles around clearing children out of the way, since we don't need real blood in an imaginary village; the Mort Subite crossroads where the thought-train derailed, and Alvaro found himself up a linguistic blind alley, before finally arriving at the bricolage hut, where Bird's Nest Tom taught him a few basic knight's moves, and how home is where the heart is, if it turns out you're a swallow; and all of this was Friday, and a Saturday turned to dusk, and the war as far as time goes hadn't even started, as the dusk turned to dark and the evening grew chill, leaving tiny blue milk-bubble lips turning bluer, and the Life Giver chanting while his children went hungry, and while it may well be true that *What thou lovest well remains*, Alvaro, after all, had had to keep moving, to the history of time and the hot chile supper, and the backward-kiss tumble into warm Nebraska waters, and the long dark walk through the nyctophobic tunnels, in the late-night early-morning hours of a Sunday, where he was chased by something both imaginary and real, something like myself, a man that, in the end, I couldn't blame him for fleeing.

I sat in the La-Z-Boy Dreamline Recliner, watching a red-tailed hawk riding the updrafts, seeing the world through Alvaro's eyes, as though he, of all people, had something to teach me. Downtown Guanajuato, all church spires and basilica domes and rose reds and custards, with just those very balconies and geranium flowerboxes, and those cobbled streets that knew exactly where they were going, and cathedral bells ringing their tribute to Time, having chosen this very moment as honored among the hours, held itself up, in the crystal clear morning, as that one shining example of itself above all others. And the beauty of the moment wasn't lost on me either, that magical sleight-of-hand by which it vanishes every instant, and shows up the next in the last place you'd think to look, like right where it is, where even the empty heart can hold it. And yet somehow the story could not end here, in existential peace, and the beauty of the moment; Alvaro's entire way of standing in the world, present to existence as completely improbable, and nevertheless the case, as though anything were possible, alive in the moment as somehow divine, something we both bless and are thereby blessed with, couldn't possibly be reconciled with the workings of a world in which we're never more than a moment from the start of the next bloodbath. The hawk riding the updrafts will eventually plunge, and rise from the scrub brush with blood around its eyes, and some picture of innocence squealing and dying, as though nature itself gave man an excuse for absolute rapaciousness in dealing with his brothers, and it wasn't as if man needed much excuse, particularly not from nature, which seems more than a little punch drunk. I hated to be the one to break this to Alvaro, but Tom's Easter oak, in the early days of spring, enjoying a quiet moment in the lime-light inside it, won't have long to enjoy its quiet moment, because we live in the sort of times where the quiet feels infected, and the moment is coming down with quicklime disease, and the spring-time green that seems to be leaping into the leaves is probably just escaping from the latest round of torture. And even supposing we took Alvaro at his word, and found something divine in our blue jewel of a planet, something to be treasured as it hurtles through Time, and kept in our hearts as we hurtle along with it, what ex-actly are we supposed to do, maybe sit on a hilltop, treasuring the moment, while Blue Jewel Industries strip-mines the planet? How does one act if one believes what you say? How, after Auschwitz, is beauty even possible? What kind of times are they, when a talk about trees is almost a crime, because it implies silence about so many horrors, and the guileless word is folly, and the man who laughs has simply not heard the terrible news: Brecht's warning to the world, and those born later, about the rise of the Nazis in the 1930s, and we, those born later, having already been warned, why do we act as if we haven't heard the news? As I sat in the La-Z-Boy Dreamline Recliner, watching Bird's Nest Tom feeding corn to his chickens, his White Rocks and Shaver Reds and Chanteclers and Cubalayas, and thinking, God, I need a drink, the world is a fuck-ing horror story, the oddest thing happened, in fact several things at once, and I paused for a moment to consider the following: the bells of Guanajuato started ringing like crazy, for no apparent rea-son, other than that they were ringing, as though the cause-effect sequence between time and the bells had suddenly been reversed, and time had it backwards, like the bells weren't telling *what time* it was, the bells were in fact telling time what *it* was, and whatever it was that the bells told time, it must have rung true, because Time, for no reason, started ringing like crazy; and as I sat in my dream chair, feeling a little turned around, as though maybe my mind, or more properly, Alvaro's, had started playing tricks on me, and ought not to be trusted, another strange thought popped into my head, regarding my whole cynical way of making sense of the world, and something tried to tell me that I had it all backwards, saying the *world* doesn't need *you* to make sense of *it*, *you* need the *world* to make sense of *you*; and then a voice out of nowhere, that sounded suspiciously like Alvaro's, went in through my ears and came out my own mouth, saying the *world* is not your problem, *you* are your problem. This, frankly, stopped me in my tracks, and in the silence that followed, I handed these problems back to Alvaro. What possible use could Alvaro be in answering the kinds of questions posed by Brecht's Doubter? None; Alvaro was not of use in answering such questions, but then the questions don't have answers in the first place, do they, it is the asking of questions that is required of us first, like the question we have to ask, which doesn't help at all, but which has to be asked if we are to go on living, *How does mankind learn to live with itself?*

Which brings us back around to Casa Que Canta, where the sun was beginning to set behind the Cerro del Almacen headlands, and the time for my final words was rapidly approaching, though we still had some business in Guanajuato to clean up. So how did we make it out of Guanajuato alive, without a single peso, and zero proof of our identity? I telephoned my travel agent, a woman so deft at improbable extractions, she could pluck you off K-2 if the weather proved inclement. When we had arrived back at the Inn, we had a couple of messages waiting for us, both perhaps useful in planning our next steps. The first was yet another typographical error that Alvaro had made regarding the message that his street name was trying to send him: when Alvaro had first departed from El Mesón de los Poetas, he believed that he lived on Calle Positivo, meaning a positive reference point, and a good place to start; when he returned that evening, however, to the FedEx package, and the newspaper clippings full of Juárez horror stories, he found that his street read Calle Pocitos, meaning it was time for Alvaro to wake up and smell the coffee; in the end, of course, his actual street, Calle Positos, had something else in mind for Alvaro's consideration, because a "posito" is in fact a granary of sorts, full of grain to provide for widows and the impoverished, a useful word from any number of perspectives, in testing his *our body* and *what thou lovest well* hypotheses. Somewhat more relevant to our immediate situation, we found a friendly invitation, written out in a fluid-looking backward-slanting hand, and signed by our mentor, Raúl Ramírez, to kindly disappear from Guanajuato forever, like join him for lunch for maybe the Last Supper, or call in the high-altitude helicopter rescue squad, loaded down with caviar and Pepsi Max cup holders. I'm kidding of course about the helicopter rescue; a chartered private jet proved perfectly adequate. I am, admittedly, more than a little spoiled, but give me just a moment, as the seagulls glide, because I'm guessing that Alvaro knows perfectly well how to deal with spoilage when he takes out the trash.

Alvaro and I, in our singing hotel, prepared for a quiet ceremony on Playa la Ropa, where I'd decided to celebrate Alvaro's fourth birthday, complete with a little present I thought he might enjoy. We walked down two levels to the rear exit gate, and down the cobbled pathway that led to the beach, where we spread out a blanket on the slowly cooling sand, and prepared to watch the sunset, honored among the hours, as the time when the day fails, and we accept our own failures. The headlands turned purple, and the sky, streaked with red, went from pale shades of turquoise to a far deeper blue that slowly grew deeper and turned a bluish shade of black, and then the evening's dark magician, in his black velvet cape, swept a cloth across the heavens and made the stars shine like new. I took out my bottle of imaginary bleach, and bleached my own hair, as Bird's Nest Tom had advised, so that no one would mistake me for Alvaro's double, and he could look in the mirror, without seeing me, and maybe arrive, before he's departed, with a warm white towel to wrap around his sisters, and a way to begin to learn to live with himself. I laid out an imaginary map of the heavens, and presented my friend Alvaro with his birthday present, the name of a star to add to his collection, and to Arcturus and Spica and Sirius and Polaris, we added a fifth star, in the constellation Lyra, the second brightest star in the Northern night sky, a star known as Vega, from a phrase in Arabic meaning "landing vulture," although Alvaro preferred the Spanish, where it means moist and fertile plain. If man lives long enough, on our fertile blue jewel, and Earth is not just a rock, hurtling toward oblivion, in 12,000 years, with Earth's axis in precession, man will look up one evening at the constellated heavens, and see that Vega is now our northern pole star, near a whole new True North that maybe journeys will be guided by, and perhaps we'll go on, knowing *this too is our body*, and that *what thou lovest well remains* isn't just a line of poetry, and we will, after all, have learned to love each other well, and will in fact remain, for whatever remains of our whirling blue eternity.

I looked up at Vega, made one final wish, and pronounced my own death, just as I had promised you, and left the world, and our future, to my new friend Alvaro, with his home where the heart is, in the search for the heart.

Five stars, five stars in the Heavens. How does this even begin to be possible?

ZEROGRAM
PRESS

An Imprint of Green Integer
www.zerogrampress.com
www.greeninteger.com

Distributed in the United States by
Consortium Book Sales and Distribution/Perseus
www.cbsd.com
Distributed in England and throughout Europe by
Turnaround Publisher Services
www.turnaround-uk.com

\*